ASPEN

A lusty sprawling canvas of raw, real life . . .

ASPEN

A needle-sharp sense of where and what the action is Now . . .

ASPEN

A story as jet-propelled as the men and women it describes . . .

ASPEN . . . THE WILD PLACE.

**WHERE PLEASURE
IS THE FIRST RESORT.**

Aspen

Burt Hirschfeld

ASPEN

A Bantam Book / January 1976

2nd printing ... January 1976	11th printing ..... April 1976
3rd printing ... January 1976	12th printing ..... April 1976
4th printing ... January 1976	13th printing ..... April 1976
5th printing ... January 1976	14th printing ..... April 1976
6th printing .. February 1976	15th printing ...... May 1976
7th printing .. February 1976	16th printing . September 1976
8th printing .. February 1976	17th printing . December 1976
9th printing .. February 1976	18th printing .... March 1977
10th printing .... March 1976	19th printing . September 1977

20th printing ...... October 1977

21st printing

ISBN 0-553-02491-4

Published simultaneously in the United States and Canada

____ Prologue ____

Out of Stapleton Airport, Rocky Mountain Airways Flight Number 148. Airborne nine minutes late. Floating around Denver in a wide, graceful arc, across the neat grid of streets and houses cramped together in their development squares. Even at night, from a rising altitude, the city seemed dull and uninspired to Carl Osborne. Typical American heartland. Set down in precise dimensions for the convenience of the road builders and the profit of the building contractors. Dull places for dull lives to be lived out without notice.

The DeHavilland Twin Otter rose steeply. Conditioned to the reassuring purr of jet engines, the four passengers listened to the changing pitch of the motors with glimmers of apprehension.

The cabin had been designed to accommodate nineteen people. Less for comfort than for maximum income. Seats were narrow, and raised knees pressed inexorably against the back of the seat in front. Add the darkened cabin and the slight trembling of the aircraft. No door closed off the cockpit, and the instrument panel was a ghostly amalgam of lighted dials and pinpoints of red light. A pale, disembodied hand came into view manipulating the controls. The plane flew higher.

Behind the cockpit was a honeymoon couple.

Hands clutching with the desperation of fear and affection, they clung hard. They squinted down through the darkness at the foothills of the Rockies, or they gazed lovingly at each other. If they remembered Osborne seated at the rear of the plane, neither gave any sign.

The girl in the seat next to Osborne giggled. "Aren't they cute?"

He loathed cuteness. Loathed the cloying sweetness the word implied. He preferred his people forthright, open, and honest, their personalities clearly defined. Osborne liked to know what it was people were after, what they believed, what they stood for. In that way, he always understood what it would take to motivate a man, to get him to perform.

Osborne had always been good at manipulating people. His excellence in this area had been early recognized and he had moved up to the executive level nearly twenty years before, when he was just twenty-two years old. Boy Wonder was what they had called him, foretelling great achievements for him. Perhaps he had accomplished less than he might have, but he had certainly gone further than most men. Nor was the race yet over. This trip to Aspen promised even greater rewards. A long step upward. And from that lofty platform, there was no telling what great work he might do. After all, he was still a young man.

However, a new and disturbing failure of energy had taken hold of him lately. At first he'd put it down to overwork, the stress of business, the tension of knowing what opportunity at last lay within reach. He'd spent a week in Martinique, sunning himself, swimming, and water-skiing.

He'd drunk sparingly and spent his time with only one woman, conserving his strength, relaxing.

But back in New York, the old tiredness returned. A heaviness in his thighs in the afternoons and a new and alarming reluctance to get out of bed in the mornings. A complete physical examination revealed nothing organically wrong. The doctor used the word tension once or twice. Strain another time.

"The limits of the human organism," he had said, "are put to tests it was never designed for. Perhaps you might want to see somebody."

See somebody.

Osborne hated euphemisms. He thanked the doctor and left. Carl Osborne had no need for a psychiatrist; that was for flawed personalities, men unable to deal with the difficulties of life, weak men. Osborne told himself it would all pass.

His energy continued to flag. The drive that had brought him so far stuttered and misfired; he began to question himself, his mode of living, and his future.

That frightened him more than anything else. Even as a boy, he had been sure of himself, of his place in the natural order of things, of his growing superiority. He had studied harder than other boys, played with more fire, fought with demonic intensity when challenged or threatened. He read more books, went to more places, sought out more people, always perceiving inaction as a form of death Osborne had always been convinced that man's true love affair could be only with life itself, and he meant to carry on the romance until the end.

This new mood troubled him. He experienced

doubts. He faltered when decisiveness was called for. And an unnamed fear permeated his being, day and night now, a chill, wet layer that gave him no escape. What was he afraid of?

He looked down. Even in the night the rugged Rockies seem to reach up as if to claim the plane. They bounced, fell back, were buffeted severely. Osborne placed a hand against the low ceiling and braced himself.

Next to him, the girl gasped. Her hand clutched reflexively at his thigh, fingers digging into his hard flesh.

"Are we going to crash?" Her voice was shrill.

"Just some rough air," Osborne said. "We should be through it soon."

The currents punished the small plane. At once Osborne was short of breath. He sucked hard for more air. He figured they were up around sixteen thousand feet, the air rarified, the cabin not pressurized. A weakness settled into his knees and his hands. He reminded himself of the oxygen mask in the pocket of the seat in front of him, but he decided to hold out. He hated giving in to weakness; something unmanly was attached to surrender. It was the coward's way. . .

The plane leveled off and flew smoothly. The girl's grip on his thigh loosened and she began to beat a soft rhythm on his trouser leg. She laughed with relief.

"I was scared," she said, glancing at his sharp profile. "Aren't you ever afraid?"

"I'm human," he conceded.

"I've never known a man like you." Admiration dripped from the words.

She was a child, he told himself. Without depth or mystery or promise. Simple, simpleminded. At her peak already, doomed to slide steadily down-hill, drab and dull at twenty-one, washed up and without hope at twenty-five. Yet he found some pleasure in her fawning over him.

"You don't really know me," he said.

"Oh, we've been together ever since we left New York. I mean, that's hours ago. We talked a lot. I've learned a lot."

"For example?"

"You're a vice-president," she said presently.

One of three, he silently amended. One of three competing for the Old Man's place. The Heggland Group—run by T. Lyman Heggland with an iron fist. He shuffled men in and out of the company on whim, tolerating no mistakes, accepting excellence as minimum performance, convinced that any-thing less was betrayal. Osborne had been with Heggland for nearly five years, was senior man next to the Old Man. Now Heggland was going to cut back on his activities, spend his final years in semiretirement. He would become chairman of the board. And one of the three vice-presidents would move into the big corner office with the word President on the door. Osborne wanted that office, longed to sit behind that great dark mahogany desk and command the group. From that single seat, power flowed out across continents and oceans, dealing with Italian industrialists, Swiss bankers, Arab oil magnates, Russian managers. No one was beyond reach. Everyone did as he was told.

The girl spoke, leaning close, voice husky and insinuating. "Let's see each other in Aspen."

"I'm going on business."

"Everybody's got to have some fun." Her hand slid to the inside of his thigh.

He changed his position. Below were the dark mountains. Shadowed patches told him where the trees ran thick and heavy. Pale stretches spoke of the frost that blanketed the peaks even in summer. The idea of spending time in the high country was appealing. The pure, thin air, the rugged landscape, the flowered meadows. A good place to be alone, to meditate, to rethink his existence.

The idea startled him. He was a doer, and he left more contemplative activities to academics and monks and literary types. Carl Osborne was cut from the same pattern as the men who made this nation—pioneer stock, strong, determined, active, and unafraid. Or so he seemed, to everyone except his wife, Janet.

"Why can't we ever talk?" was her constant complaint. Three years his junior, his wife appeared to be a decade older than Osborne. The girlish beauty, the sprightly cuteness, had dissolved to flab. The once-creamy complexion was lined and grooved, and "the bluest eyes in the world," as Osborne had called them, were lifeless and streaked with scarlet. Her fingers plucked incessantly at each other. "Why can't we talk?" So had she spoken on the night before he left. A query, a lament, a plea for attention repeated to the point of nausea.

"We do talk," he had replied automatically.

"You never look at me anymore."

"What would you like to talk about, Janet?" It was difficult to confront that ruined persona.

"About us."

"All right. What about us?"

She had sipped champagne and tried to remember what it was she had wanted to say to him.

Nothing came. She smiled nervously. "I'm glad you're taking this holiday."

"This is a working trip."

"Yes, of course."

"It's only for a few days."

"I won't miss you," she muttered.

He thought he'd misheard her.

"I won't miss you," she repeated. "I never do. It's better when you're away. There's no anger in the apartment, I'm not so afraid when you're not here."

He opened his mouth to reply, thought better of it. It made no sense to argue with an alcoholic, even one's own wife.

"Have you ever been to Aspen before?" the girl next to him said. She leaned against him and her young breast flattened against his shoulder. What was it she was? Oh, yes—a teacher of physical education at some women's college. Her hand worked insistently at his leg. He began to respond.

"Do you know anybody in Aspen?" she murmured.

Yes, he almost answered. My son is in Aspen, my son who is younger than you are. My son who has left my home and rejected me and my life. My son who refuses to understand me, who condemns me, who hates me. My son, Jon. At nineteen, a stranger to his father.

She stroked his thigh, fingers kneading the flesh.

"Ah," she said thickly.

Osborne concentrated on the honeymoon couple. A wall of self-interest separated them from the rest of the world. And the pilots were doing their

job. The plane passed over Loveland Pass, swung
a few degrees south. It tipped and yawed, fish-
tailed crazily, rose and fell. Again Osborne was
short of breath and feeling weak. He thought he
might throw up. He removed the girl's hand.

"What's wrong?" she said plaintively.

"Crosswinds."

"You don't like me," she said accusingly.

"You're a very nice girl."

"There's this cat I know at Cornell, a full professor in the Department of Russian Studies. He
says I'm the best screw he ever had."

"A full professor would certainly know."

"Is something the matter with you?"

"Suppose we blame it on the altitude."

"You're afraid of flying?" She seemed delighted
at the discovery.

"Why not?"

She straightened up. "No need to be ashamed
of it. Everybody's afraid of something."

"That's very profound."

"Maybe we can get together in Aspen. Without
any clothes on, it's more fun, you know."

"I've heard that."

"Folks," the pilot's voice twanged over the P.A.
system, "we're going to make our run into Sardy
Field. I'd appreciate it if you make sure your seat
belts are fastened. Please observe the No Smoking
signs. Hope you enjoyed your flight with Rocky
Mountain and will fly with us again . . ."

"Anytime," the girl said.

Part One

Aspen

Half a billion years ago, an angry sea spread over the Precambrian granite in the area. The glaciers came next, staying their allotted time. When they receded, the ice hacked out the peaks, valleys, and crevices of what came to be known as the Rocky Mountains.

Centuries later, the Ute Indians made their way onto the Western Slope. As did the Mowatavi-Watsiu tribe, who spoke a language not unlike that of the Aztecs. William Gant, the first white man to come into the high valley, trapped beaver along the Roaring Fork River in the year 1859.

Seventeen years later, in 1876, Colorado became a state. And three years after that, a band of prospectors left Leadville and made their way across the continental divide. They pitched tents and lean-tos around a spring often used by the Indians. Thirteen of them spread themselves around, staked out claims on the fine land, and began to pick and scratch for silver, enclosed by the Arms of the Elk Range. They gave their tiny community a name: Ute City.

The Utes kept their eyes on the white men on the mountains and didn't like what they saw. The young warriors grew restless, angry, and resentful of the newcomers, and in the fall they killed

*eleven white men and subsequently ambushed an
army troop. Word of this trickled through to the
Roaring Fork, and most of the prospectors fled
back to Leadville for safety. Two men remained
to protect the claims.*

*Back east it was learned that silver had been
discovered in the Rockies. Men aiming to get rich,
or richer, cried out against the savages who were
keeping civilized Americans from pursuing their
destiny. Congressmen raised high the banner, demanding that "The Utes Must Go!"*

And go they did.

*Once the Indians were pacified, the miners re-
turned to work. With them came H. B. Gillespie,
a mining promoter, who went around buying up
claims. This done, he hurried off to Washington
to demand mail service be put through, as well as
a telegraph line, and a railroad. He also raised
capital to develop the mines properly. H. B. Gillespie was a man of vision, fortitude, and limitless
gall.*

*One day Clark Wheeler presented himself in
Ute City. He had traversed the hundred miles
from Leadville on snowshoes, an impressive feat.
He came, he announced, for his share of the silver
pie. He too bought up claims when he could, took
options where possible, and made other arrangements whenever necessary. Clark Wheeler was
tough, energetic, persistent. Miners infested with
scurvy, weak in body and spirit, were no match
for him. There were some uncharitable persons
who insisted that Clark Wheeler was a claim
jumper.*

*Wheeling and dealing, Clark Wheeler estab-
lished his own town. Using a compass to lay it out,
he put the town in the direction of magnetic north*

rather than true north; he was not a man troubled by details. He named the community in honor of the graceful trees that marked the area: Aspen.

The miners thrust shafts into the mountainside. They dug tunnels, hacked away, brought out the ore, and rolled it down the slope in hundred-pound balls wrapped in protective cowhide. By donkey train, the ore was shipped to Leadville and the smelters. A year later, a rough wagon trail was put through Independence Pass, Aspen's sole link to the world beyond. Six years later, a spur of the Denver and Rio Grande Railroad came through the rugged highlands. Aspen was on the map.

Silver was big business.

1

The street was commercially zoned and only Skip Blondell lived there, an illegal resident. The buildings, each two stories high, were framed by heavy timbers weathered a murky brown. There was a certain sameness to the restaurants, all with large plate-glass windows. Gold paint edged with silver, crimson, or black announced the Silver Queen; Topsy's; Satisfaction; the Aspen Leaf; or the Quick Bite.

The shops, too, appeared to have been designed by the same person. Each strove for a certain alien distinction, hawking wares from Mexico, Bolivia, Israel, Yugoslavia. There was a store that specialized in goods made by American Indians: turquoise and silver, tooled leather, rugs, blankets, drums for children, sepia prints of old Indian men, weathered and impressive. Antique watches, rings, and picture frames were on sale next door to a merchant who carried Victorian chests and dry sinks that gave off a stale odor.

The Blondell Gallery was in the basement of an old wooden building on the western corner of the block. Over the gallery was a restaurant that sold chicken gumbo, hero sandwiches, and huge mugs of weak coffee. Once the gallery had been a bookshop, but except for a wall of shelves along the back wall, no indication of its literary beginnings remained.

Skip Blondell's stamp was clearly on the place. The rough whitewashed walls ended abruptly in shadowed corners or spread into odd-shaped culs-de-sac. An alcove contained a small refrigerator, a two-burner stove, and a sink with a leaking faucet. A wall made of framed circus posters and a Mexican serape formed a back room which served as Blondell's sleeping quarters.

Skip Blondell was a man of diverse interests: different ways to turn a buck. The gallery was vital to him, something very much his own, a vehicle that would carry him to a rich and comfortable existence, would provide a place in the world, status, income, a thing of his own.

Three years had passed since he opened the gallery and only the last two shows had shown a profit. Blondell was convinced that he had turned the corner. Soon he would be able to hire an assistant, a pretty girl perhaps, someone who would free him for other pursuits.

But not yet. It was still hard work. The new show, for example. First he had to strip Henry Clayton's collages off the walls, pack them carefully, and prepare them for shipping. Only when that had been done would he be able to prepare Mary Goodhart's woodcuts for hanging.

Blondell did most of the framing himself. Simple wood moldings stained or left natural, designed to let the artist's work speak for itself. Blondell enjoyed placing a picture, judging the most effective position on the wall, and choosing the lighting. Real skill was demanded.

Goodhart's work was important. Blondell was

sure she would sell well. To this end, he had priced her reasonably, anxious to make a volume sale.

Goodhart was daring enough to make a splash. Even in Aspen, as free and easy as the town was. She did only nude boys and girls, usually in erotic poses. The bodies were lean and hairless, just starting to bud, and the more sexual for being so. They would surely find a wide audience.

A knock drew Blondell to the door. A pretty girl in jeans and an Indian-cotton blouse smiled through the glass at him.

"Hello," he said, opening the door.

"Hi." She moved past him briskly, taking in the place at a glance. She came around to face him and in the bright light he was able to see her nipples under the thin blouse. He lifted his eyes reluctantly.

"You must be Skip," she said.

He nodded.

"I'm Judy. The word is out on you."

He sucked his lower lip thoughtfully. She was pretty, with yellow hair that fell across her shoulders in smooth waves. Baby-blue eyes gazed at him without blinking, almost in challenge. Girls who looked like this one really put him away. Made him uncomfortable, itchy, and full of longing. Girls like this—remote, cool, untouchable— had always been beyond his reach when he was younger.

"What word?" he said. He locked the door and went into the back room and sat down on the thrift shop sofa that stood against the wall.

She went after him. "People in the streets."

"You don't want to believe everything you hear."

"Then it isn't so."

"That depends. What have you heard?"

"That you're a good dude to know."

He lifted his bony shoulders, let them fall. His body seemed put together with taut elastic, expanding only after an effort. There was a clenched look to him, arms folding across his abdomen protectively, long, pale hands reaching up to cup his own elbows, the way his narrow head sat on the almost feminine neck. He squeezed his eyes shut and forced them open again.

"You want to buy some pictures?" he said. His voice was throaty, the words only partly articulated, the whispery slur adding a casual factor that some people mistook for mystery. It was a trait Blondell exploited whenever possible.

Judy laughed—bright, open, very American. "You're funny. Nobody told me you'd be funny, too."

"You're new in town?"

"Arrived yesterday."

"From where?"

"Grosse Pointe, that's in Michigan."

"Rich bitch."

"My parents, not me."

"This town takes a lot of bread."

"I brought some along. I can get more. If it's worthwhile."

He pointed to one of Mary Goodhart's woodcuts. It showed a boy about to perform cunnilingus on a girl. "What do you think of it?"

She studied it. "The artist has a nice sense of composition."

Obviously she was putting him on. "That's all?"

"Pictures don't do much for me, only the real thing."

He patted the couch next to him.

"Uh-uh," she said. "Somebody's waiting for me."

"You made a connection already."

"A chick, a friend I'm traveling with. Listen, they said you might have some dope."

"Me! Who said a thing like that?"

"Come on."

"Somebody's giving you a lot of stuff."

"What's everybody so uptight about? Are the cops so rough?"

"I don't even know you."

"Well, maybe you will. Some things take a little time."

"Do your folks know you're a dope fiend?" he said after a moment.

That made her laugh. "You going to come through for me, Skip?"

"You going to come through for me, Judy?" he mimicked.

"I could come back later, if you want, if you think it would be worthwhile."

"Why don't you do that?"

"I'll bring my friend along."

He made a face.

"She's okay, you'll see."

"Suit yourself."

"Later," she said.

"Later."

When she was gone, he recaptured the look of her. She was the best-looking chick he'd ever met. He wanted to get her alone, rub his hands all over her, take the clothes off her. But she was careful, bringing her friend along. It would take some doing to separate them, but he was sure he could do it. There was plenty of dope being used in town, but only a few people dealing. That way the city fathers didn't get too upset; that way the cops stayed cool; that way nobody got burned. If Judy wanted to make a buy, he'd sell; at his own price, naturally.

2

They picked their way around clusters of young people standing on the sidewalk in front of the bars on Cooper Street. In Wagner Park, they skirted the groups, some talking quietly, others listening to a folk guitarist, others just sitting. The smell of pot hung on the air; neither of them remarked on it.

They spoke hardly at all until they arrived at the far side of the park. He glanced at her somewhat anxiously, as if to decipher her mood.

She gave no sign that she recognized his presence. Her small face was at ease, the dark eyes peering ahead as if seeking something not yet in sight. It was a cleverly constructed face, a succession of soft vertical planes leading from a smooth, wide brow across prominent cheekbones to a straight, gently turned jaw. Her nose flared slightly and her lips were petulant, giving her a sensual, continental look.

In a shirt and slacks of no particular distinction, she was all gentle curves, no single part of her designed to draw undue attention. She was,

Jon Osborne reminded himself, the most attractive girl he'd ever seen.

He said her name.

For a brief flash, he was afraid she wouldn't respond. Until her face swung his way. "Yes?"

"Come with me to my place." He was begging. Anger rose up in him and in that moment he hated her for not reacting as he wanted her to. The anger was gone swiftly and he felt deflated, too young, inadequate again.

"Ah, Jon." A suggestion of displeasure. A hint of annoyance. A touch of sadness. "You mustn't keep pushing me."

"If I don't try—"

"If you keep trying this way—I can't be rushed. I can't be coerced or seduced. I need to do things in my own good time."

"Time! You've been here since the beginning of July. Summer's nearly over."

She measured him. In the darkness, her skin took on an undertone of warm marble and the Tuscan eyes glowed, revealing nothing.

"I like you, Jon."

"Is it because I'm younger?"

"I like to be with you."

"Three years isn't so much."

"If it comes to that, you won't have to ask me, Jon."

"The trouble is, you're too damned good-looking."

Her laughter was a delicate peal, expiring quickly. Advancing to the point of freedom, pulling away under a tight rein. "You're used to getting your own way, Jon. It isn't that way in the real world."

"Don't lecture me, Kit." The anger broke out.

"Sorry."

"Let's get something to eat."

"I don't think so. I have to get back. There's a seminar tomorrow and I've got some reading to do."

"I never thought I'd flip out over a teacher."

"Snob," she said lightly.

"Artist in residence. A poet. Ugh."

"You don't like the institute, Jon. Why?"

"The Institute for Humanistic Studies. Pretty heavy name. Lots of people in Aspen think you're all a bunch of snots over there."

"That's not fair. People come to the institute to learn, to try to improve themselves."

"Is that what you do, improve them?"

She ignored the sarcasm. "Maybe they do hang together. It's inevitable. They're after maximum exposure."

"Maybe I ought to come out there, see what's going down."

"Maybe you ought."

"I never dug poetry much, all that symbolism and hidden meanings."

"Maybe one day I'll bring you some poetry to read. Something contemporary; it might turn you on."

"You turn me on. Let's go to bed."

"It's a game to you."

"Sex can be fun," he recited.

"Yes, but it's not a child's game."

"Is that what I am—a child?"

"I didn't say that, I didn't mean that. But sex has more importance than a game of Parcheesi."

"What's Parcheesi?"

Her grin was quicksilver, gone in a moment. "You see how much you have to learn?" She walked ahead of him.

He caught up. "I'll take you back."

"Not necessary. Anyway, I want to do some thinking."

"Okay," he said with a rush of relief. There was work to do this night. "I'll phone you tomorrow."

"All right."

She watched him stride back into the park, long and athletic, with the easy grace provided by a body tuned to action, resilient and strong. What would it be like to feel those powerful arms around her, she wondered lazily. To experience that young hardness inside her own flesh. A chill caused her to shiver and she hugged herself. It was then she remembered the party. It was then she decided to go.

——— **3** ———

Tom Keating advanced down the slope. A broad man with a thick body and a large head made larger by a shaggy black beard and hair to match, he gave off an impression of tremendous power and determination.

He was at one with the mountain night. Around

Engelmann spruce, past a grove of aspen, along a winding stream lined with water birch and willow. He knew the trees, the wild flowers, the brush, by look and touch and smell. Without thinking, he knew where the columbine grew alongside rocky outcrops and that the soil stirred up around new mountain roads gave birth to brown-eyed Susans, purple fringe, fireweed.

He carried a backpack without effort; he covered ground swiftly, with short, quick steps, boots finding a sure place to put down automatically, muscles flexing and reaching, holding against the pull of gravity. Keating had gone up into the high country nearly a week before, leaving and returning under the cloak of darkness as if to mask himself from observation. Like the animals, he felt secure at night, removed from danger, able to deal with the mountain and its tricks and threats.

Keating, born and bred in the city, felt a passion for the mountain he had never experienced elsewhere. He was drawn to the heights out of a deep-seated need to refresh and replenish himself. However, to have spoken about it that way would have embarrassed Keating, made him feel less than the man he longed to become.

Keating approved of sentiment, quiet and private, but he abhorred public sentimentality: the gush of feeling that so many Americans seemed to revel in; the quickness with which they dumped out their most personal thoughts, emotions, desires; the ease of revelation; the meaninglessness to which feelings were often reduced.

Keating had been raised on toughness. His father could quote the most obscure of Irish poets and, seconds later, hammer another human being into a bloody pulp. He was a man who, too drunk to remember his own name, would beat and brutalize his wife on the kitchen floor.

Keating had his father's size and strength, the same affection for music and beautiful language, the same lusty feelings toward women. Unlike him, Keating avoided a fight when he could, had refused to kill in Vietnam, had sought a way of living consonant with what he believed was right. When he discovered Aspen—the rugged range and the gentle slopes; the crisp, long, white winters; the colorful summers—he recognized it as the place where he belonged. But that certainty had been chipped at by time and change, and currently Keating was not so sure.

Whenever the foundation on which he had constructed his existence was shaken, Keating reacted instinctively; he went off alone. Like some wounded beast, he sought a place where he could become part of the landscape, close to the sky, deep in the natural order of things. Safe, out of reach of other men. Beyond foreign influences.

He discovered isolated spots on the mountain. Cliffs and caves and crevices and walls where most men would not dare to go. Cruel, lonely places that insured the stillness he hungered for at such times. He would pitch his shelter, eat sparingly, bathe himself in icy springwater, read, sleep, and consider the way the world was going.

His time up there ended, he came down. The sounds of Aspen reached out long before he arrived in town. A blur of voices, strained laughter. Too many people trying too hard. Transforming by their presence. Corrupting the beauty and purity that had brought them in the first place. Streets would be lined with cars, the stench of carbon monoxide everywhere. Every open space would be jammed with people. People who drank too much, smoked dope too much, labored too hard for the minute portion of pleasure they received. They came in boots from Abercrombie and Fitch, bush jackets from L. L. Bean, camouflage hats from Norm Thompson. They cluttered the land and deposited debris in memorial to their presence. In time, they went back to the cities, wrapped in the delusion that they had united mystically with nature, had improved themselves by the experience.

Keating saw them all as strangers—to him, to each other, and to themselves. Belonging only in the concrete valleys and dirty streets of cities, at home in crowded bars, unable to function unless hip-and-thigh with their fellows. The streets in Aspen had been unpaved into the beginning of the 1960s, and Keating suddenly understood that better streets had failed to improve the quality of life, had only brought more people.

Off the mountain, he shambled along Ute Avenue, into Spring Street. Car horns blared and someone screamed. In fear? In joy? A quartet of drunks staggered toward him. Keating shifted over into the roadway.

In Hopkins Street, the sounds faded abruptly. More shops, fewer bars. He was approached by a youth with the stance of an athlete and the face of a choirboy, a duplicate of the thousands who came through Aspen during the year. Skiers or tennis bums, living off the slopes and the courts, hustling men and women alike for their keep. Unwilling to pay their own way. The boy held out his hand and smiled a charming smile.

"Raising bus fare to California, mate. Give a guy a break."

Keating stepped around the boy. "Sorry."

"Put your money where your heart is, fella."

Keating kept going.

"Motherfucker!" the boy screamed. "Motherfucker pig!"

Keating turned back. The boy backed off quickly, aware suddenly of Keating's size, intimidated by the broad, implacable face.

"Good manners," Keating said mildly, all the more threatening for being so. "That's all that separates us from the jungle."

The boy hurried away.

"Ah, Tom," a voice said, "you are good."

Keating looked around to see Alex Budde. Carefully turned out in a white linen suit, a navy blue cotton shirt, a patchwork tie. Budde was a blond, muscular man in his middle thirties with the faded look of a former prizefighter. His skin was drawn tight over broad bones and it reflected light as if polished specially for the job. Large, pale eyes gave him the softly inquiring expression of a bullfrog.

Beyond Budde was Harry Rodano. Budde's dark side. Short, swarthy, with glowering mien and black, glinting eyes that missed nothing. Older than Budde by at least fifteen years, Rodano was his constant companion, errand boy, and bodyguard. Rumor had it that years ago Rodano had been a killer for hire in Cleveland and later in Cincinnati. No one really knew; no one asked. He held himself at some inner readiness, as if about to spring into action, surveying the passing traffic with the shadowed paranoia of one who thinks he will die unexpectedly and violently.

"Good evening, Alex," Keating said. "Hello, Harry."

"Hello, Mr. Commissioner," Rodano said. His voice was shrill, a thin squeak, a ludicrous contrast to his squat, strong frame.

"Would you have hit the boy?" Budde asked, smiling mirthlessly.

"It wasn't necessary."

"What if it became necessary, Tom. You, a man of peace, could you get yourself together for a fight?"

"I'm not a pacifist, Alex, I hope you know that."

"Big, isn't he, Harry?" Budde said to Rodano. "Think you could handle him, one to one?"

Rodano never looked at Keating. "Alex, you know me."

Budde laughed, a choked sound that died quickly. "How about it, Tom, figure you could take Harry? He's tough."

"I've got no quarrel with him."

"That's true, isn't it. No quarrel at all. At least not yet." He looked past Keating to where the mountains loomed in the darkness. "What's up there for you, Tom? Never understood why people keep climbing. You back up on the offside again?"

"It's where I go."

"All the way over to Hollander's Spring?"

"In that direction."

"Must be nice, quiet, peaceful."

"Fer sure, Alex," he drawled. "Try it for yourself sometime."

"No thanks. I'm a city boy myself. How are things at the shop, Tom?"

"Just fine when I left."

"I imagine they're still the same. By the way,

there's a party this evening. Scooter Lewis's place. You're invited."

"No thanks, Alex."

"Scooter's invitation."

"Thank him for me."

"You don't like me, Tom, and that troubles me. I'm genuinely fond of you. No reason we shouldn't be friends."

"See you around, Alex."

"We have a great deal in common, I'd say."

"Hope you're wrong about that."

Budde gave that soft laugh of his. "Ah, Tom, you misjudge me. I'm a decent guy, really."

"See you around, Alex."

Budde watched Keating advance along the street.

"A hard case," Harry Rodano muttered.

"Too hard for you, Harry?"

"You want me to find out?"

"No," Budde said thoughtfully. "Maybe sometime, but not now."

—— 4 ——

Carl Osborne finished shaving, ran his palms over his cheeks, and found them smooth to the touch. He rinsed with warm water, splashed his eyes with cold.

He dressed in blue: suit, shirt, and a knitted

tie. The reflection he saw in the mirror satisfied him, always had. The bony, almost oriental set to his features, his dark hair only beginning to reveal a suggestion of silver. Looking good had never been a problem for him. Except when he was about fifteen. He had suffered a severe case of acne, and, despite intensive medical attention, it refused to respond to treatment, lasted for nearly two years. Then, as abruptly as they had materialized, the blemishes departed. Once again he was the best-looking boy on the block.

The experience left an indelible scar—a sense of helplessness when confronted with matters over which he had no control. He vowed to carve out a place for himself in the world that was peculiarly his own, a place in which he ruled, in which others obeyed, where nothing happened without his consent.

He had yet to achieve complete mastery over his environment. But soon the world he had chosen to enter would be all his. Carl Osborne: King of the Hill.

In the living room of the hotel suite, Len Ralston rose when Osborne appeared. Ralston was plump with a pink, cheerful face. Yet there was no warmth in his almost perpetual smile and no softness in his round, dimpled body. Years before, Ralston had been accused of putting out a contract on a business competitor, but no hard evidence had been forthcoming, and he never came to trial. However, the competitor died of a bullet wound in the back of the head, and a year later his widow sold his business to Ralston for a fraction of its real worth. Ralston now served as chief advance man for the Heggland Group.

"Carl," he began, crossing the room, a glass in

each hand. "Here you are, scotch and water, the way you like it."

Osborne tasted the drink: perfect.

"You look like a million, Carl. Real good, but you're a real fine-looking man."

Osborne gave no sign that he'd heard. When the top job was his, he was going to have to do something about Len Ralston. A transfer to the Milan office or into one of those oil sultanates. Ralston was an easy man to dislike.

"McDevitt's late," Osborne complained.

"He called a little while ago. Be here any minute. Just as well. Gives me time to fill you in."

Osborne sat down. "I was told last week you had a lock on things out here, Ralston. What went wrong?"

"Wrong! I wouldn't say anything's wrong, Carl. Just a minor hitch here and there. The kind of thing a man with your experience can undo in a few days, get us back on the track."

Osborne made a sound back in his throat. "Have you located Jon for me?"

Ralston smiled sheepishly. "Afraid not, Carl. These things take time."

Irritation spread like a gray mist in Osborne. "How many people live in Aspen, Ralston?"

"The town itself? No more than six thousand, I'd say. Hard to get exact figures. Lot of semi-residents—part of the year here, part back east or in Dallas, places like that. Summer people, winter people, you know."

"How many in the surrounding area?"

"In Pitkin County? Another six thousand, maybe."

"That adds up to approximately twelve thousand, correct?"

"Yes, Carl."

"Somewhat less than live in New York City or Los Angeles. Nevertheless, you have failed to come up with one boy." There was a hard edge to his voice.

Ralston showed no fear, the pink face slightly sullen, but still. "I tried, Carl. I'm still trying. But that isn't why the Old Man sent me out here."

Restlessness surged through Osborne, a burgeoning resentment. As if some unnamed flaw had surfaced in his life, a deep and dangerous error that had never been corrected. "I know why you were sent to Aspen, Ralston. Apparently you haven't done that job either, otherwise I wouldn't have had to come. Did you check the police? The post office? Jon's a tennis player. He skis. Surely somebody must have met him."

Ralston shrugged and waited patiently.

Osborne restrained the urge to rip into the other man. He made a conscious effort to slow his breathing, to assume again the mantle of self-control he wore most of the time. The trouble between himself and Jon wasn't Ralston's fault. Problems: It seemed the higher you moved the more intense they became, the more insoluble they often appeared to be. Perhaps there were no solutions for anything. Osborne rejected the idea.

"Okay," he said in a mild, conversational tone, "bring me up to date."

"This could be your big break, Carl."

Ralston's arrogance was offensive. And with it was the undertone of challenge, as if he was daring Osborne to pick up the gauntlet. Osborne breathed in and out. "You have some great reward in store for me, Ralston?"

"Wolf Run." Ralston let it hang before he went

on. "Biggest domestic project going for the Heggland Group right now."

"Go on."

"Wolf Run is your baby."

"Executive in charge. You were to pull it together, Ralston. You seem to have failed."

"Oh, no, nothing so serious, Carl. Just a little foul-up. Nothing you can't straighten out."

"You keep saying that."

"Well, some people have erected a barricade. They're shooting at us from behind it."

"At us?"

"We both represent the group."

Osborne grew annoyed with himself for sparring with Ralston. Ralston was right; it was *his* assignment, his responsibility, his project to bring about.

"Between us," Ralston said, keeping a tight verbal link between them. "Between us, we pull it off, it does us both a great deal of good."

"How do you figure it?"

"Heggland is moving up to chairman of the board, everybody knows that. You, Harley Edmundson, and J. J. Kilpatrick are the front-runners to take over. I make it out to be either you or Harley."

More interested in Ralston's reasoning than he chose to let on, Osborne could not help asking, "Why not J. J.?"

"J. J. is family, married to Heggland's niece. But a mental lightweight. The Old Man isn't going to put his company in those weak hands."

"You take chances, Ralston."

"Not really, I've given this a lot of thought. You or Harley. I make it out to be pretty even. Two bright, gutsy guys. Both about the same age, same experience. Harley's the better administrator, but you've got the drive, the imagination. We're in a changing world, so creativity may be more important. Anyway, it's still a horse race. The Old Man gave Harley the truck and car deal in Russia, and you got Wolf Run."

"Moscow's a much bigger operation."

"Sure, and easier to pull off. The Russians need us these days."

"And Aspen doesn't?"

"To hear some people talk, you'd think we have the plague. We got some difficulties."

"That you're unable to get out of?"

"Had to leave something for you to do."

"You take chances, you really do."

"Measured risks. All odds carefully figured. All bets hedged to the nickel."

"Meaning what?"

"Meaning that I've done my homework. I'm prepared to fill you in on everything happening. But maneuvers are in order. I can suggest, but I can't command. Not from my lowly rung on the ladder. Only you can authorize financial commitments."

"Sounds like a cop-out to me."

The pudgy face froze in a warped clown's mask. "With my help, Carl, you will make a big splash out here. Make the Old Man happy. You get the presidency, not Harley . . ."

"And then?"

"And then you'll need a hotshot executive officer to back you up."

"And you know just the man for the job?"

"In all modesty, Carl. . ."

Osborne emptied his glass, extended it. "Another drink," he commanded. Ralston hurried to obey. Osborne decided that he disliked pettiness in people, especially himself. He invited Ralston to be seated, and he immediately regretted the gesture.

"If you'd like a little entertainment, Carl, I know a couple of great-looking females. . ."

"I'll make my own arrangements."

Ralston recognized his mistake. "Of course," he said quickly. "No harm meant. . ."

A knock at the door brought Ralston to his feet. "That'll be McDevitt."

"Let him in."

McDevitt resembled a stock character out of a western movie. Pared down to skin and bone, long and slightly awkward, he wore scuffed boots and faded Levi's and a plaid shirt with pearl buttons. Behind gold-rimmed glasses, blue eyes shone brightly. He offered a strong, gnarled hand to Osborne.

"Glad to meet you, Mr. Osborne." He asked for bourbon neat, located a paper package of Cinnamon Red in his hip pocket, planted a plug between lip and tooth, and chewed deliberately. "Your man here couldn't make the deal I wanted to make."

"What deal are you after, Mr. McDevitt?" Osborne said.

"I've got half a thousand acres out in the valley that fits right in with your plans."

"We don't require five hundred acres. Just the top land is what we need."

"Well, I aim to sell all of it, take the money, and retire down to my daughter's place in south Texas on the gulf. You need the acreage in the foothills. I've gotten me a copy of the topographical maps the U.S. government people put out, and it seems to me there's only one place for you to build your little town and that's on my land. There's only one place for you to terminate your number one ski run and that's on my land."

"Fifteen acres is what we're after," Ralston said. "We'll pay prime rates to get it."

"Five hundred is what I aim to sell, Mr. Osborne," McDevitt said cheerfully. "At prime rates."

"You seem to have things worked out pretty well in your mind, Mr. McDevitt."

"Never was very good at making money, you see. So I learned to be thorough."

"I've seen the maps, too; we do need your top fifteen."

"Take the five hundred."

"For how much money."

"I'm not a very good businessman, Mr. Osborne. Probably making all kinds of mistakes on the low end. What would you say to ten thousand U.S. dollars per acre?"

"Out of the question," Osborne said coldly.

McDevitt pulled at the slack skin along his jaw. "What would be in the question, would you say?"

"One thousand an acre."

"Seems to me we're not even close."

"Seems that way."

"Any way we can shimmy up to each other a little bit?"

"Well," Osborne said, "we do want the fifteen. If it means buying the full five hundred, okay. Tell you what—I'll meet your price on the fifteen, ten thousand an acre. You accept my offer on the rest."

McDevitt removed his glasses, cleaned them carefully with a red kerchief. "That comes to $635,000. Not exactly what I had in mind."

"See what I mean, Carl?" Ralston said.

Osborne ignored the advance man. "Stay and finish your drink, Mr. McDevitt. No hard feelings. We'll just let it slide."

McDevitt frowned and stood up. "If that's what you want." He went to the door, hesitated, and turned around. "I know you can't let me walk away without making some kind of a deal. Now why don't we stop haggling and get down to it?"

"Say a figure, Mr. McDevitt."

"Make an offer, Mr. Osborne."

"Very well. Five thousand an acre. It's what we're both aiming at."

"That's $2.5 million total, correct?"

"On the button."

"Paid how and when?"

"Three-month installments beginning the first of next year. Four payments."

"First payment on signing of the contract, three installments at six-month intervals. Title reverts to me or my heirs if any payment is missed."

"You drive a hard bargain, Mr. McDevitt."

"Then we've got a deal?"

"We've got a deal. After I take a look at the property. Mr. Ralston will make the arrangements. If I like what I see, papers will be drawn up. You can let your lawyers look them over, if you like."

McDevitt grinned. "Reckon I might just do that."

"Grubby son of a bitch," Ralston said, after McDevitt had left.

"He's out front about what he wants. Money, which puts us all in the same boat. Okay, that wipes out one of our problems. . ."

"There's the Horn parcel."

Osborne consulted his notes. "Oh, yes, Don

Horn. He only got ten acres—it shouldn't be difficult."

"They straddle the number two ski run, so we need them."

"Make him an offer. What's next?"

"There's Teddy Maxwell, Planning and Zoning Board. We're to meet him at the party..."

———— 5 ————

Route 82 drops down almost five thousand feet from where it slices through Independence Pass until it reaches Aspen. It maintains its downward thrust through Snowmass and Bassett until it links up with Interstate 70 at Glenwood Springs.

Jon Osborne followed Route 82 out of town, directing the jeep across the Roaring Fork River, across Hunter Creek, and up onto Red Mountain. Downshifting smoothly, he slipped the jeep into four-wheel drive and put it onto the trail heading up the incline. In the dark, the going was necessarily slow, but there was no need to rush. They'd wait for him.

Eastward into the national forest, he left Pitkin County behind. Now he was in the sheriff's jurisdiction. But it was the return trip that might bring trouble. Loaded down then, he would be vulnerable to a bust.

Climbing steadily, the jeep passed flickering

campfires, and the sound of voices raised in song and laughter drifted out of the woods. Jon had tried camping a couple of times soon after his arrival in Aspen, but he decided that he was at his best in a living room. Or a bedroom. Away from the chill night air and the flies.

Tennis was Jon's main connection with the outdoors. Tall, supple, with long legs and excellent reflexes, he had begun playing tournament tennis when he was twelve years old, beating boys bigger and stronger and older than he was. At fifteen (the Osborne's lived in Beverly Hills then, Carl was chairman of the board of the Bellstrom Survey, a think tank), Jon won the California boy's singles championship. He was touted as the next great American player. He seemed to have it all: a booming serve, a deadly ground game, the desire to win.

That didn't last long. Winning meant discipline and practice, hard work, and Jon turned away from all of them. Nevertheless, he was awarded a tennis scholarship to U.S.C. Midway through his sophomore year, over the objections of his parents, he quit school.

By then the Osbornes were living in Manhattan, Carl having joined the Heggland Group that winter. In the weeks after he left school, Jon stayed in California, loafing around Malibu. He gave tennis lessons to wealthy women, including two movie actresses. He swam in their pools. He ate their food. He made love to them. And he accepted enough money so that he could move on when the time came.

And come it did. A friend suggested a trip to Aspen for the skiing. They skied every day, drank and made love every night, and finished the winter with more money than they had had when it began.

When the snows receded up the mountains, Jon's friend departed. Jon stayed on. Tennis carried him along. Tennis, and his finely boned face, his ready smile, his strong young body. Tennis and women. He told himself that he had it made.

But that kind of money was slow to come by. Most women recognized that they were buying his attentions and were accordingly reluctant to fill his pockets. They allocated small amounts to him, enough to keep him coming back for more. It was a tiresome game, and Jon looked around for a less-complicated, better-paying activity. Inevitably, he met Alex Budde.

Budde offered twin inducements: money and excitement. Even danger. Working as a mule for Alex Budde put Jon on the outer edge of society; he became a maverick, a rebel, an outlaw. For the first time in his life he felt fully alive, all senses functioning at full charge. And he felt no fear. None. As if he existed inside some divine girdle.

But Jon was merely a messenger for Alex Budde, and Budde made him aware of it in a thousand different ways. Budde's superior attitude, his faintly masked scorn, the assured manner in which he commanded Jon to perform. Even the word troubled Jon: *mule*. Mules were dumb, plodding beasts of burden, and Jon loathed thinking of himself in that way. He was, he kept telling himself, meant for better things.

He was the most recent in a long line of other young men similarly employed by Budde. Three of them had been busted, convicted of possession, and dumped in the slam. Two had fallen while trying to make it across the border from Mexico with a load; the third had run afoul of a sheriff's deputy out in the county. Another boy, only seventeen, on his first run, had had his throat cut by a crazed dope fiend.

After a while, it became clear to Jon that if he was going to take the pay, he had to play the game. Unhappily, the game kept getting rougher. Occasionally Jon considered getting out, leaving Aspen, setting up somewhere else. But life in the mountains was easy, and the money kept coming. Perhaps one day, when he'd accumulated enough of a nest egg, he would move on. But not yet.

Past Lenado Gulch, the jeep trail twisted higher, and the jeep strained, struggling forward. At one point, twin pale stones rose up at the side of the trail like squat sentinels in the night; the terrain seemed gentled by them and it leveled off. Jon drove for exactly half a mile before parking the jeep among the trees. He switched off the lights and the motor.

He struck off on foot at right angles to the trail, making no attempt to conceal his movements. After ten minutes, he spotted a light off to his right. He went toward it, came into a small clearing where two men were seated near a campfire. They were smoking and drinking coffee.

They eyed Jon without urgency.

"All alone in the woods, kid?" the first one said.

"Mind if I warm myself at the fire?" Jon answered, making sure he said the words exactly as Alex Budde had instructed him.

"Man can get lost at night," the second camper said.

"Not if he knows the trails," Jon said. "Not if he's been around."

The short man, not much older than Jon, but somehow shrewder and much tougher, hunkered down. "You drink coffee without the fixings?"

"Sure." Jon was relieved that that part of it was over. It always made him feel silly. The passwords, the scripted greetings were like some child's game that had to be acted out to the finish. The short man gave him a tin cup filled with coffee. The hot liquid was coarse and bitter but it warmed him. "That's good."

"You got a name, kid?" the taller man said.

"Names aren't supposed to be necessary."

"A friend of ours gave us a couple of names. One for the buyer, one for the messenger boy. That's you, messenger. So let's have the name."

"Jon."

"Okay," said the tall man. "You did okay on that one. Now give us the other."

"What other?"

"The dude you work for."

"Alex."

"That's very nice," the short man said. "You're smart, kid, the way you remembered the names and what to say. Some mules just blow the whole thing and there's always hell to pay. You bring the bread?"

"You bring the stuff?"

"A smart mule," the short man said. "I told you he was smart, Leo."

Leo went into the woods and returned a moment later with a brick-shaped package covered with plastic. "Here's the goods, kid. First-class Mexican brown. Mix in a handful of tobacco or instant coffee. Maybe some procaine for an extra flash, the customers ride high. And come back for more. You can't miss."

Jon reached out.

"The money, kid."

Jon drew a brown envelope from under his leather jacket. "Nine thousand cash."

"Hand it over." The stocky man counted it out. When he was done, he nodded to his partner. "It's all there."

The tall man tossed the plastic brick to Jon.

"That was very good, kid. Tell Alex I said you did good."

"Alex wants to do some more business," Jon said.

"We'll be in touch. Got to replenish the supply."

"I'll tell him," Jon said. He hurried back to the jeep and drove back down the mountainside, faster than he'd come up. And for the first time since he'd gone to work for Alex Budde, he did feel afraid.

—— 6 ——

Done at last. The final woodcut hung on the wall. The last light skillfully placed and aimed. No offending shadows anywhere. No distortions. No way any picture could be ignored or blocked from sight. Skip Blondell circled the gallery inspecting his efforts, finding nothing to criticize, nothing to improve. He'd done a first-rate job.

"What do you think?" he said to the two girls who trailed after him on bare feet.

Judy answered. "Terrific, everything's terrific."

"Yeah," Blondell said. When the other girl added nothing, he grew morose, stared sullenly at her.

Her name was Gwen. She was slender with dark hair and a quiet manner. She had been a willing worker, but her remoteness, the way she held herself apart as if judging him and her friend, turned him off. A snot, he told himself. A drag, a party killer. Still, here she was, and Blondell tried to be nice to everybody.

"Oh," Gwen said, realizing that something was expected of her. "Oh, I think everything is simply lovely. Perfect."

Blondell turned away from her, not convinced. He threw the master switch to the off position and the gallery faded into almost total blackness. He led the way into the back room where soft crimson lamps gave off a spooky glow. He turned on the stereo, and Mick Jagger's harsh voice filled the room.

"You girls have been very helpful," Blondell said. "For that you get a little reward." He gave each of them a joint. "Fantastic grass. Mexico's best. Smoke and be happy."

They smoked in silence and Blondell looked at the girls. Even in the faint light he was able to see the shadow of Judy's nipples, the line of her heavy breasts. What would she be like in the hay?

But the other one—Gwen. A bitter dose. He had been wracking his brain all night trying to figure out a way of getting rid of her without insult, without antagonizing her friend.

"What's that door lead to?" Judy asked.

"My darkroom."

"I like to take pictures," Gwen said.

"Sometimes I think I should've been a model," Judy said.

"I'm a very creative guy, actually," Blondell said. "It's with the camera that I show my real talent."

Judy sucked the joint. "This is great grass."

"Be nice to me," Blondell said. "I'll see that you're taken care of."

"What kind of pictures do you take?" Gwen said.

"People mostly."

"Chicks, he means." Judy giggled. "Dirty pictures, I bet."

"Nudes?" Gwen said.

"What's wrong with nudity?" Blondell said. "Maybe you think the naked human body is dirty?" He challenged Judy.

She heaved herself erect, swaying slightly. "You must be kidding!" She flexed her body, breasts outthrust, hip angled sharply. "Dig this body, mister."

"Not bad," Gwen said.

"Not bad," echoed Blondell.

"Not bad!" Judy snorted. "I'll show you something really great." With one practiced motion, she drew the Indian blouse over her head, letting it fall to the floor. Her breasts, large and pale, shimmered high on her chest.

"Jesus!" Blondell said.

"Oh, Judy," Gwen said. "You shouldn't . . ."

"Well," Judy said to Blondell, "what do you think now?"

"Best I ever saw."

"You ought to see the rest."

"Show me."

"Judy, don't," Gwen said.

"Is she your keeper?" Blondell said.

Judy, laughing, stepped gracefully out of her jeans. Naked, she whirled across the floor with the flowing sureness of a ballet dancer, displaying herself from every angle.

Blondell became aware of his engorged penis extending itself behind his fly, onto his belly. What if he flashed it for them?

"Say something, man," Judy cried. "If you can't talk, just clap."

"You're beautiful, Judy. You know what I'd like to do—"

"I know."

"Take your picture."

"What are you waiting for?"

He ran for his camera. She struck a pose, pelvis thrust forward. Click. Another pose. Click. Click. He used up an entire role of film as she moved around the room, showing herself, enjoying herself.

Blondell reloaded the camera with trembling fingers.

"Gwen," Judy said, a soft command.

"No, I don't want to."

"Get undressed."

Blondell straightened up. He looked from one girl to the other.

"I won't do it," Gwen said.

Judy's voice turned hard. Her body seemed to stiffen in place, her features freezing. She took up a position in front of her friend and glared down at her.

"Don't argue with me, you know what happens."

"Let me alone!"

Judy slapped her across the face. Gwen fell back on the bed, protesting. Judy punched her in the back. Gwen rolled away, fell onto the floor. She began to sob, dry heaves. Judy bent down and hit her again. "Do what I say. . ."

"Look," Blondell said, worried suddenly, "if she doesn't want to, it's okay. We'll just smoke some more grass and I'll take some more shots of you. . ."

"Gwen, get up," Judy commanded.

The other girl moved slowly to obey. She stood with hanging head.

"Take off your clothes."

"Do I have to?"

"Yes."

Gwen unbuttoned her blouse. She removed her brassiere. Her breasts were smaller than Judy's, paler, the nipples pink and shriveled.

Blondell took her picture.

Gwen stepped out of her slacks. She wore no panties. She stood without moving. Judy went over to her, patted her cheek. "There, that wasn't so hard." She kissed the other girl on the mouth. Gwen moaned and embraced Judy, mouth fastened to hers.

Blondell took another picture.

They went to the floor together, Gwen's face buried between her friend's thighs.

Blondell snapped away. The roll ran out. He thrust the camera aside and struggled to get out of his clothes. Naked, he advanced on the two girls. Judy looked up, mouth gaping, hands stretching out imploringly. It would have been morally wrong to deprive her of what she wanted.

7

Scooter Lewis moved through life to syncopated commands heard by no one else. He rocked, he rolled, he twitched; he swayed and swung; he grew straight and stiff, intermittently catatonic. Lambent eyes perceived a world unfolding in slow motion. Or frozen into icy lifelessness. Scooter Lewis functioned on a private wavelength, fueled by a concealed energy source, on a slow journey from limbo to oblivion.

He was a lank of a man. All legs and arms, a neck stretched and skinny, supporting a long, narrow head off which came a silky fall of hair that went to his hunched shoulders. His beard curled off sunken cheeks and receding chin to a rather elegant point.

A glass of white wine in one hand, a joint in the other, a distant smile turning his red lips, drifting in a miasma of his own making, he was planted in the living room of his house, as if the weight of the structure bore down on him, an unsteady center pole with no place else to go, trying to make up his mind. About what? He drew a blank.

Around him the party ebbed and flowed. Concealed loudspeakers poured a rasping cacophony into the ears of the unsuspecting, vibrating their eardrums rapidly toward deafness. Grass was burned, acid dropped, pills swallowed, booze drunk, shit shot. People floated, high and low. They came and went, unnoticed by anyone around them, tripping weirdly.

"What a great party!" somebody said, drawing a chorus of nods.

"Yeah, baby . . ."

The house had been carefully designed and constructed. A house for partying. For getting high. For swinging. For Scooter's pals to crash in. So it was ordered, so it was done.

A portion of the lower slope just east of Slaughterhouse Gulch had been terraced and shored up with native stone. The house was a series of angles and walkways and cubes that rose up in the air, appeared from around corners, or seemed to float without visible means of support. Decks and balconies provided a commanding view of the town and of the Roaring Fork River and the Denver and Rio Grande tracks. People referred to the house as Fort Apache; Scooter liked the name.

In the distance, the airport. From behind his immense rosewood desk in his study, Scooter was able to drink ice-cold Coors and watch the planes drift down the valley as they landed. Scooter entertained a small hope that one of them would one day crash into the mountainside. He had never seen a plane crash and longed for the experience. A tape recorder was kept loaded and ready on the desk in order to capture his immediate response, before it had time to filter through his brain, to be corrupted by his thought processes.

In Scooter's fantasy, the plane would not carry

a full load of passengers. He didn't want to be the cause of a great many people being killed. Just enough to make it worth seeing.

"Hey, man."

Scooter worked his eyes, his nerves, his senses. The party blur faded into view; some irrelevant details pulled down within range, leapfrogging from confusion to uncertainty to clarity. A short muscular man in a blue-and-white printed silk shirt and tight blue trousers confronted him.

"Hey, man," Scooter said, trying to remember something.

"We have got to talk."

"Talk, yeah."

The decibel count peppered his brain and he flinched, shook his head to clear it. A silly grin lifted one corner of his ample mouth.

"You better straighten up, man," the short man said.

"You're being judgmental."

"Hell, yes. Look at you, spaced out like a loony bird. Cut down, man."

"Cut what down?"

"The dope. The booze. *Everything.*"

"Don't be a drag." He offered the short man the joint in his hand. "Suck this, baby."

"You're going to blow it all, I'm warning you."

"There you go again. You can't do that. Laying *your* moral imperatives on *me.*"

"You silly mother, it's bread I'm talking about. Big bread. Lots of green. The way you are, you are useless."

Scooter hooked his hand behind the other man's neck. "Love you like a brother, baby."

The short man freed himself.

Scooter teetered forward, leaning until they were nose-to-nose. "Pop a pill? Uppers. Downers. Snort some coke. Dis izz the plaze."

"Three days I've been here and we haven't been alone for five minutes. This is costing us both; I'm neglecting business."

"Tomorrow. We'll rap all day long."

"Time's running out. The deal won't keep forever."

"Everything in its place, a place for everything. Man, I am quoting! Ain't that a gas! I never quote. I mean, memory is not my strong point."

The short man stepped back. "You will blow it all, Scooter. Everything you worked for. Everything I worked for with you. I can afford it, man, remember that. I can write you off, take the loss, and still get by with my other clients. You have got nothing else to go on. Think on it, *baby. . .*"

The short man was furious. With Scooter and with himself for allowing matters to drift to this low point. He'd lied to Scooter, and that bothered him. Not that he lied, but that he *had* to. Had to put on the big act, claim clients and success he didn't have. He needed Scooter. Scooter was his main man, the only one of his clients who brought in important money. All the rest were scratching, and he had to scramble in order to sell any one of them.

Scooter was the rock of the agency. His name on the client list had *value.* Given enough time, with Scooter, the short man expected to build one of the most prestigious literary agencies on the West Coast. Television, movies, stage, books. He wanted it all. He'd worked hard to come this far, was on the edge of making it, and he wasn't about to let a crazy freak shaft him.

Fearful of losing his temper, he struggled to contain his anger. When out of control, he did terrible things. And loathed himself afterwards. His fists were near lethal weapons, his powerful arms and shoulders driving them with awesome force and speed. More than once he had left men broken and bloody, and he suspected he had caused two men to die of injuries he had inflicted on them. He lived with the memories, and the guilts. He liked people, wanted them to like him. But sometimes they—people—just refused to cooperate.

Out on the wide deck that overlooked the town, he sucked cool air into his lungs, felt the fever leave his cheeks. He stretched his limbs, caused his muscles to relax, exorcising the enraged tension.

At ease finally, he looked around. In the far corner of the deck a slender girl leaned on the railing, staring into the night. He went toward her, stopping far enough away so as not to startle her.

"Tell me what you see?"

For a long, anxious beat, she provided no response, and he accepted the silence as a rebuff. He began his retreat, telling himself he had no right to impose on someone who obviously preferred solitude to his company.

He had taught himself to be aggressive, forceful, to go after what he wanted. When that approach backfired, he felt again the old fears of his young manhood—when people mocked him, making jokes of his squat build, his lack of height, his harsh Polish features. Of course, no one knew he was a Pole these days. Bobby Wallace was strictly American. But Walinski was another story, less pretty, a name to make jokes about. A short, ugly Polack, that's what he'd once been.

No more, he thought silently; now he was a short, ugly American. He mocked his own bitter humor, his inability to cast off the emotional chains that bound him.

The girl turned around and he stopped his retreat.

"My eyes were closed."

A nut, he thought. One of Scooter's crazies. "I shouldn't have interrupted you."

"It's okay. I was listening to the mountain."

"Did it say anything interesting?" His nervous laugh was intended to indicate he meant no harm. Women were often drawn to him, for reasons he'd never been able to fathom. But he remained unsure in their presence.

"The night has a special life out here. Listen, you can hear it. The rustle of movement from high in the forest. Owls. Night animals on the move. The soft wind. And sometimes you can hear someone laughing from far back, and that's rather nice, I think."

He examined her openly. Old World features, no one of which was in itself perfect, but her face was much more than its parts.

"You're very beautiful," he said.

She shook her head as if to stop him.

He held up his hands. "No harm intended. Didn't even know I was going to say it."

"I was *feeling*."

"Feeling?" He grew uneasy again.

"At this altitude, the air is different on your skin. Lighter, almost a caress. Periodically, I feel the need to breathe deeply, to expand my lungs." Her smile was swift, engaging, a flash of ivory teeth. "Oxygen loss is all it really is, I guess, but I prefer a more romantic explanation."

"You're a strange lady, I think."

"You're right. But you're just trying to provoke me."

"Could be. You're one of Scooter's nutty friends?"

"I don't know Scooter."

"Then what are you doing in his house?"

"I'm out at the institute. All of us were invited. I decided to come at the last minute."

"I heard about the place. A frat house of big brains and culture nuts."

"You may have a point."

"What are you, a secretary? I bet they under-pay you. Those joints substitute status for salary every time."

She enjoyed him and it showed. "Maybe I'm one of those culture nuts."

He groaned. "What's your racket?"

"Poetry."

"Jesus, just what the world needs, another lady poet."

She laughed and he felt encouraged.

"I got you pegged; you're Edna St. Vincent Millay."

"Not nearly that well known. Do you ever read poetry?"

"Not if I can help it."

"Most people don't. Do you ever read at all?"

"Score one for your team. Sure, lots of stuff. Manuscripts, scenarios, outlines. Keeps me going."

"I don't understand."

"I'm an agent for writers. In Hollywood. Mostly TV and the flicks. Maybe you even heard of me—Bobby Wallace."

"I don't know anything about Hollywood."

"If I wanted to go out and get a book of your poems, who would I ask for?"

She suppressed a smile. "Katherine Pepe. My friends call me Kit."

"Sure," he said. "The *New Yorker* publishes you. Two, three weeks ago. A full page of your work."

She was surprised. "You said you didn't read poetry."

"Did I say that? Well, sometimes I slip. When the ads are not so good and the cartoons ain't funny, I give the poems a quick look-see."

"You're a strange man, Mr. Wallace."

"Call me Bobby. A huckster is what I am, like everybody else. I sell properties, a product. Some people like to call that product literature."

"I imagine you're a good agent."

He puffed himself up. "Second best in the world. And I'm catching up fast."

"It's important that you become number one?"

"Bet your sweet—" He caught himself, ducked his head, began again. "It's important."

"I take it you're Scooter's agent?"

"I'd be better off without him."

"He's an excellent writer."

"Come on, you don't read that freak."

"His book on the California commune was first-rate. Very perceptive, with an exquisite use of language."

"I guess so. The big thing is he sells like crazy. The kids love him. Very important in hardback, even more in paper on college campuses. The problem is he's too successful, isn't motivated to work anymore."

"All writers are sometimes blocked."

"Blocked! That freak is walled in. It's driving

me into cuckoo land. I can put together a package that would mean millions. Only it all depends on getting the freak to plant his ass on a chair in front of the typewriter." He frowned, measured her. "Maybe you'd like to help."

"How would I do that?"

"You writers, all of you think the same way, slightly off-center."

"Thanks."

"No harm meant, but true is true. Talk to him, tell him how important it is that he gets back to work. Say he owes it to his public."

"That would be presumptuous. I don't even know the man."

He took her elbow. "I'll make the introduction."

"I don't think so."

"It won't hurt. Much."

She laughed, allowing him to steer her back inside the house. "Jesus," he said when he saw her in the light, "you're only a kid."

"Past the age of consent," she said lightly.

"What is that these days? Eleven or twelve? Come on, let's find that freak. . ."

They stood close to each other, bodies angled as if each was intent on making a swift escape. Both were trim, pretty women, clad in slacks and blouses, their eyes never still behind tinted glasses. At first glance, they seemed no more than twenty-five; a closer look made them to be ten years older. Each had had a birthday in the previous month, each had turned forty.

"I'm always surprised," Joan Carolinian, the dark-haired one, said, "at how many new people find their way to Scooter's parties. Where do they come from?"

Her friend, blonde and fair skinned, thought she saw a familiar face across the room. She waved, received no response.

"Who was that?" Joan said.

"Nobody."

Joan had become aware lately that her friend had stopped introducing her to men. Not that Leila had to fear competition from Joan. She was much more attractive, vivacious, drew more than her share of masculine attention. Men of all kinds, all ages. Joan envied her.

Leila touched Joan's arm, not looking at her. "See you later, dear."

"Where—"

Leila moved toward a group of young men along the far wall. She looped her arm through the arm of a tall blond with straight features and big shoulders. Joan recognized him as the tennis pro at Charley's Aspen Courts. He was beautiful, and no more than twenty-two. He smiled at Leila, and she leaned against him, breasts flattening against his arm.

Joan wondered what it would be like to be with such a young man. All that strength and energy and desire. But she had too much pride to beg or pay for attention. She was still an attractive woman and deserved to be courted, longed for, paid attention to.

Leila and the young tennis player were leaving. An almost palpable longing welled up in Joan. She made her way to the bar. Drinking helped for a little while. Some of the time.

They located a rear bedroom on the third level of Scooter's house. Ralston closed the door and presented an encouraging expression to the other three men. "Carl," he began, "I've been telling Teddy here and Alex all about you."

Teddy Maxwell was a large, bloated man with a hearty manner and small eyes that peered out from behind swollen cheeks. "I have been wanting to meet you for a very long time, Carl."

"I appreciate you saying so," Osborne said automatically. He glanced over at the fourth man in the room, Alex Budde. Here was the power behind Maxwell, he decided. Here was the spine that kept Maxwell upright and on the right track. But, since the game demanded that certain unstated conventions be played out, Carl Osborne would do so.

"I wasn't expecting anyone but Mr. Maxwell at this meeting," Osborne said.

Budde nodded agreeably. "Consider me a concerned onlooker, Mr. Osborne."

"What is your concern, Mr. Budde?"

"Mr. Budde owns property throughout the valley," Len Ralston said hurriedly.

Osborne turned his attention to Teddy Maxwell. The big man shifted around uncomfortably, trying not to look sad.

"You," Osborne said, "are the key figure on Planning and Zoning I'm told, Mr. Maxwell."

Maxwell shuffled his feet. "My vote can be decisive in many matters, Carl."

"And you, Mr. Budde," Osborne said, "have property to sell, is that it?"

"Now, Carl," Ralston said placatingly.

Budde breathed out audibly. "I own property, Mr. Osborne. I own a restaurant, other businesses."

Osborne sat down on the edge of the bed. It occurred to him that he had spent a great deal of his life in hotel bedrooms making deals. Or in dimly lit bars. Or the sedate and proper studies of the very rich. So much business was transacted in private, concealed from public scrutiny. But then privacy was vital because so much business was not in the public interest. The less the people knew the better it was. For those conducting the business.

"Let's talk some more," Osborne said.

"Well—" Maxwell said.

"Why don't I begin?" Budde said quietly.

Osborne gave silent agreement.

Budde smiled. "Wolf Run Valley: I desire its success very much, Mr. Osborne."

"I'm pleased to hear that," Ralston put in. "Lots of people in Aspen have been treating us like an enemy."

"You are the enemy to some folks, you and Mr. Osborne here. So is every would-be land developer."

"The Heggland Group," Osborne said, choosing his words deliberately, "has a reputation for care and concern in planning and preservation. We make every effort to maintain the natural condition of the landscape, to improve it where possible. We mean only good for this valley."

Budde nodded slowly, as if considering what Osborne had said. But Carl understood that they were performing a practiced charade in which the final speeches, if not already written, were certainly roughed out, needing only to be delivered with sincerity.

"Two kinds of people live in Aspen," Budde said. "Those who desire continued growth and development and those who seek to slam shut the gates of progress."

Osborne couldn't have said it better himself;

in fact, he had said it equally as well in the past.
He smiled graciously. "There seems to be an abun-
dance of open space. . ."

"Yes, it's there. But limitations do exist. National forest lands in some instances run right
into Pitkin County. Many of our people are very
unhappy with what went on over at Snowmass. . ."

"What did go on, Mr. Budde?" Osborne said,
knowing the answer.

"Overbuilding, Mr. Osborne, overcrowding; a
failure to consider the ecology, the balance of
nature, the needs of man and animal both."

"We are committed to constructive—" Osborne
broke off, decided to alter his approach somewhat,
speed up the process. "You said you wanted Wolf
Run to succeed, Mr. Budde. It begins to sound
otherwise."

Budde's shining face glowed. "Only giving the
other side of the coin. You should be prepared
fully for what lies ahead."

"And what is that, Mr. Budde?"

"Trouble."

"You assured me—" Ralston said excitedly.
Osborne waved him into silence.

"What sort of trouble?" Osborne said simply.

"Enough trouble so that your project will never
get under way."

Ralston was unable to contain himself. "That's
impossible!" he cried. "The Heggland Group has
put up $3.5 million to launch this package. We've
closed a deal for land already totaling—"

"That's enough, Ralston," Osborne said.

"But, they don't understand."

"Mr. Budde understands everything." Osborne
said quietly.

"I know about the architects and planners you've got working for you. They're putting together feasibility plans, and that's a good thing."

"Well, then?" Osborne said.

"Let me fill you in about Aspen, Mr. Osborne." Osborne leaned back on his elbows. "I'm listening."

"Essentially we're a small town, but with a certain sophistication; lots of big-city people live here now. We have many natural advantages. The clean air, an abundant snowfall, fantastic panoramas. A long winter ski season, a variety of outdoor possibilities in summer. All within easy distance. A man can walk from one end of town to the other in a matter of minutes. Modern Aspen was planned, created, you might say. The automobile played a lesser role in life here than elsewhere. On the other hand, come summer, you can hardly find parking space in our streets. That kind of shakes people up a mite."

"Our feasibility study—" Ralston said. "The planners are allowing for that, providing central parking areas in Wolf Run. Every building must possess adequate parking facilities. And no cars allowed in the streets. Pedestrian malls are the key."

"Sounds good," Budde said. "Would you believe that not so long ago you could ski down Aspen Mountain right up to the Hotel Jerome on Main Street, drop your skis, and go into the bar for a brew. No skiing allowed in town these days."

"Nothing stays the same, Mr. Budde," Osborne said.

"Some people don't like change."

"You're not among them, Mr. Budde."

"Hardly, Mr. Osborne. I believe in Aspen, in its continued growth. But it will be a struggle. Elements in town have caused land use to be restricted, and they mean to keep it that way. Thirty years ago you could have bought up all the acreage you needed for a couple of hundred an acre. Now, an acre here in town might set you back as much as half a million."

"We have options," Ralston said.

Budde kept his gaze on Osborne. "I know. Twenty-two percent of the land you've optioned belongs to me."

"Goddamn," Ralston said.

"That doesn't include the McDevitt place, of course, or Don Horn's small ranch. Unless you've acquired both in the last few days." Budde allowed himself a small smile.

Osborne assessed the other man with growing interest. "Your name never came up before."

"I'm a silent partner in a number of enterprises in the area."

Osborne listened.

Budde went on. "People kept the winter Olympics from coming to Aspen for fear it would bring too much attention our way, too many newcomers, tourists, and the like. Open space is highly prized hereabouts; folks are willing to battle to keep it open. Everybody seems to get involved in land affairs, in politics. That can be good or bad, depending on your point of view."

"Your point of view, Mr. Budde, is for progress?"

"It is."

"And since some of your land is involved, I take it we can depend on you for assistance?"

"You can, sir."

"Good. I take it then that you own Mr. Maxwell here?" Osborne said without emphasis.

"Now wait a minute!" Maxwell said.

"Lock, stock, and barrel," Budde answered. "Teddy will vote for the project in P and Z. He'll fight for it privately and publicly. Teddy is a very excellent public speaker."

"Looks to me as if we have very little to worry about," Osborne said.

"Not at all the case," Budde said.

"I'm still listening."

"The two elements of the populace I spoke about. On the one hand, the old-timers who see a chance to get rich, who want to be rich. It's the old prospector syndrome."

"Very well put," Osborne said.

Budde continued without a break. "Across the ditch we've got the young people, educated types for the most part. This town has the highest per capita population of Ph.D's you're liable to find anywhere. Teachers, lawyers—liberals of course. They work at their trade, some of them, and others wait tables, do carpentry, whatever, to earn their keep. A strange breed. But they're here and it looks like they mean to stay on. It's in their heads that they are sitting in Tibet right here in the middle of the good old U.S. of A., and they would like to keep it all for themselves."

"Can they be defeated in this matter?"

"Perhaps."

"What is needed to turn *perhaps* into an unqualified yes, Mr. Budde?"

"Money."

"Ah," Osborne said.

Budde was properly solemn. "It's the system we live under. The profit motive. Free enterprise. We all approve of it, I'm sure."

Osborne straightened up. "All kinds of profit-making opportunities will exist in Wolf Run for right-thinking people. Two ski lifts and runs will be cut and built. Shops, restaurants, a variety of facilities. Homes, apartments, hotels. Building contracts will be let. . ."

"Sounds very exciting, Mr. Osborne."

"There are so many details, Mr. Budde. We'll have to meet again, just the two of us, to discuss those details."

"At your convenience. I enjoy doing business with a practical man."

"Ralston will make the arrangements. See you again." He started for the door. Budde's voice brought him around.

"By the way, Mr. Osborne, there's a young fellow in town named Osborne. Quite a coincidence, isn't it?"

"My son," Osborne said slowly.

"Is he?"

"I've been trying to locate him," Ralston said hurriedly.

"Well," Budde said, "he sometimes shows up at my place, my restaurant. If I see him, I'll tell him to get in touch."

"You do that," Osborne answered. "I'd consider it a favor. . ."

Alex Budde took up a position at the downstairs bar and drank Chivas Regal, sipping slowly. He never drank much, careful to maintain control. For Budde, control was everything. Control was power and power meant accomplishment, wealth, safety. He enjoyed shaping his environment, his mind and body, the people he came in contact with.

Next to him, seated on tall stools, were two young men and a girl. They might have been brothers and sister, each one bony and angular with sun-bleached hair that reached to their shoulders and suntanned cheeks.

The boy nearest to Alex brought a small silver spoon to his snub nose and then sniffed. What disgusting creatures they were, Alex thought, burning out the linings of their nasal passages, and for what? A passing thrill. Kicks, they called it. They ought to have their butts kicked, he told himself.

The cocaine spoon was passed along. The girl snuffled loudly and then passed the spoon to the boy on the far end. The spoon made its way back to the boy next to Alex.

Without warning, the girl toppled backwards off the stool, landing heavily on the floor. Her companions stared down at her inert form without comprehension, made no move in her direction. Then the boy at the far end fell over.

"Weird," the remaining boy said, sniffing at the spoon.

Budde left the bar. Across the room, Harry Rodano, a glass in his hand, but not drinking, followed a roughly parallel path, eyes scanning the party for signs of trouble.

Budde spied Joan Carolinian coming toward him and altered his course. No use, she blocked his way. He paused and greeted her.

"Ah, Alex, you've been avoiding me." She offered it as a mild rebuke, anxious not to offend him. "Don't you like me anymore, Alex?"

He made himself smile. "I called you the other night. No answer."

"Alex," she remonstrated, a teacher to a small boy caught in a forbidden act. "I've been home every night this week."

"It may have been last week. My memory doesn't always work well."

"Why did you phone?" she said coquettishly.

"I wanted you to have dinner with me."

She rested her hand on his wide chest, fingers moving in a delicate rhythm. "Ask me another time, Alex."

"I will." He made as if to move around her. She managed to remain in his path.

"Why not now, Alex?"

"I was just leaving. There are some things I have to take care of."

She came closer, voice a syrupy caress. "Take care of me, Alex, and I'll take care of you."

"I said I'd call."

Her hand closed on his jacket. "Alex, *please*. Don't cast me aside. Don't discard me. Alex, I am very fond of you, extremely fond. I mean it, Alex. Whatever you want, just say. Just *indicate* what it is you want of me. Nothing could be easier. I know I wasn't very nice to you last time. . ."

"Last time—"

She didn't let him finish. "One more chance, Alex. That's all I ask. Give me an opportunity to prove how happy I can make you. After all, Alex, I am not some virgin spinster lady. I have had experience."

He stared at her expressionlessly, wondering why he tolerated this absurd, pathetic creature. She was like some sad character in a Gothic novel —simple, helpless, buffeted by a mocking fate. He

ought to exclude her forever from his life; he was
unable to do so, as if some unidentifiable bond
linked them. In sudden anger, he spun about and
marched away.

She watched him go with sadness and relief.
So much about Alex Budde offended her: his fre-
quent roughness, the absence of good breeding.
He was not truly attractive, not graceful and
delicately joined like so many she had admired.
His character was blunt and muscular, a direct
outgrowth of his body. Perhaps it was the immense power of the man, the simmering sense of
impending violence, that drew her back to him
again and again.

She had always avoided men like Alex Budde.
Always she had sought men who were understanding, refined, intellectual. Not that it mattered
much; they hurt her always, each of them. Oh,
yes, they had been pretty, and willing to please
her in the beginning, but once she revealed her
true self to them, once she succumbed to them,
then it was she who was the beggar seeking hand-
outs.

Alex Budde was the personification of each of
them, a combination of all. He was her past packed
into one cruel body, her occasional present, her
so unpredictable and frightening future. He was
everything she loathed and feared, and everything
she desired.

He was her last chance and she dared not let
him go.

Jon Osborne entered the room and at once felt
a heavy hand fall on his arm. Powerful fingers
dug into his bicep. He was jerked around like a
helpless doll to confront Alex Budde.

"Where the hell have you been?" Budde hissed.

"It took longer than you said it would," Jon replied, freeing himself.

"Did you do the job?"

"What do you think?"

Budde squeezed his bicep, fingers digging in. Jon tried to free himself.

"Goddammit, Alex, you're hurting me."

Across the room, Harry Rodano placed his glass on a table and came up on the balls of his feet, hands flexing. He waited for Alex to summon him. The call didn't come.

"I'll break your arm next time," Budde said, releasing him. "Don't play games with me, kid."

"Okay, okay."

"Did you do the job?"

"Sure. I went to the Spot, but you weren't there."

"I've been here most of the time."

"You want delivery now?"

"Tomorrow's soon enough. By the way, Jon, somebody's been asking about you."

"Who's that?"

"Your father." Jon paled. Budde went on, enjoying it. "He's around here somewhere. He wants very much to see you. You never told me about your father, kid."

"What's he doing out here?" Jon managed to say, his voice clenched.

"Ask him," Budde said. "I'm sure he'll be glad to fill you in."

With a certain amount of satisfaction, Budde watched the youth rush off. He wondered about the relationship that existed between the Osbornes, father and son. There might be something there he could swing to his advantage. He turned to go and there was Joan Carolinian coming toward him, smiling broadly. And it surprised him to discover that he didn't want to send her away. At least not yet.

Jon plunged toward the front door as if pursued by a terrifying specter. Suddenly he was weary and frightened. He felt terribly vulnerable in the midst of strangers. He sought solitude and reassurance, and he required a safe place to conceal the brick he had fetched for Alex Budde. He didn't see Kit Pepe and Bobby Wallace until Kit said his name.

He swung around, eyes wide. "What are you doing here?" he said without preamble.

"Meet Bobby Wallace, Jon. Bobby is Scooter's agent."

Wallace offered his hand. If Jon saw it, he gave no sign.

"Christ," he muttered. "You said you were going back to do some work, you were too busy to spend any time with me."

"I changed my mind," she said softly, not intimidated.

"I suppose this pig is more your style than I am."

"Easy boy," Wallace said. "There's a misunderstanding here."

"Fuck off," Jon said, not looking at Wallace.

Kit said, "I changed my mind, Jon. You're being silly."

"Then go with me now," he said.

"I don't think so."

Jon took her wrist, pulling her along. "Come on."

"Let go, Jon." She struggled, braced against him.

Jon yanked hard and she stumbled, almost sprawled on her face.

Bobby Wallace moved with startling swiftness. His right fist described a short, tight arc, landing heavily in Jon's middle. The boy doubled over retching, gasping for air.

"You shouldn't have hit him," Kit said.

"He was muscling you around."

"I can handle it."

"I wanted to help, I'm sorry. I'm sorry, kid."

Kit reached out for Jon. "Are you all right?"

He brushed her hand away and staggered out into the night. Cry or kill, either would have been all right.

No noise anywhere. No loud voices. No screeching laughter. No glasses shattering. No angry accusations. No music. No people.

Darkness enveloped Fort Apache. The thrusts and levels of the house created ominous shadows against the mountain wall, appearing immense and inviolable, truly a defense position against whatever enemy awaited without.

Even in Scooter Lewis's bedroom, voice and action were in low key. Small candles flickered in the corners, creating yellow aureoles of soft light. Any movement in the room caused the light to waver, weird shadows elongating and retreating in a macabre dance. And in the shadows and the light, as if claiming property rights for reasons know best to themselves, people sat or reclined or kneeled as if in prayer.

On the large round water bed, Scooter Lewis lay on his back, glazed eyes directed at the ceiling. He sucked on a stick of grass and occasionally gave voice to an aggressive humming sound. He wore nothing but a T-shirt with a two-color impression of himself on a huge Harley-Davidson. Between his skinny, hairy naked legs crouched a girl he had met an hour before. She inspected his slack member with clinical concern. She lifted it and let it fall, as if trying to jolt it back to life. She received no response. She blew at it and the cool air sent a shiver along Scooter's spine. He remained dormant. On the floor, alongside the bed, the girl's boyfriend laughed.

"You've lost your touch," he jeered.

She shook her head in disbelief. "I think it's broken."

Scooter hummed louder.

On the floor, in the far corner of the bedroom, three girls made love to each other, shifting, turning, switching around. They were compulsively active, displaying quick flashes of anger whenever one was dispossessed. Twice, blows were exchanged; scant damage resulted and, since no blood was drawn, they continued about their affair.

Not far away, a man and his wife, fully clothed, drank Pepsi-Cola, smoked filter cigarettes, and studied the girls.

A bearded man plucked at a sitar.

A fat girl ate a brownie and drank some milk.

In the darker recesses, other people writhed and humped, or sat and stared, or slept uneasily. The air was thick with the heavy scent of grass and alcohol and sex.

Bobby Wallace watched for a long count, turned away, and made his way to the balcony room that had been set aside for him. A naked couple lay sleeping in each other's arms in his bed. Wallace swore without anger, located a pillow and a blanket, and went back downstairs. In Scooter's study, he curled up on the soft brown leather couch and closed his eyes.

The party was over.

8

Alone in his hotel room, Osborne shifted around in the bed. His mind kept ranging forward and backward in time. Confusion was the overriding element in life, he decided. And fear. All men were uncertain, never convinced of the rightness of their decisions, of the paths they trod. All were afraid of the unknown, that dark land that lay just beyond anticipation. So men planned and schemed and sought to narrow the future, to limit the possible ways in which disaster might strike them. They made studies, projections, fed information into computers, and huddled anxiously over the readouts. In the end, each man had to walk into the new day without prior knowledge, still afraid, relatively helpless, a mote on the wind of fate.

His victories and defeats mixed in his brain until he could no longer distinguish one from the other. He toted up his accomplishments; by any measure, he was a success. Yet should he fail here in Aspen, he would be judged a failure by those who mattered most: Heggland, and himself.

No defeat could cause more suffering than that.

He lay there looking through the open double doors that led to a narrow balcony. The mountains seemed to surround him, a mysterious succession of jagged thrusts, bathed in silver. One distant peak seemed particularly luminous, strangely animated in the moonlight. What would it feel like to be alone in those forbidding heights, with only his body strength and native cunning to sustain his life? All his education, all his accomplishments were designed for the city, for the usual practices of the business world. There he was at home, tough, persevering, wily. But up on that imposing peak—he would be the weakest, most frightened and vulnerable of beasts.

He was a product of style. Of fashion. Therefore, transient. Easily replaced should the general approach to life be altered. Nothing eternal shaped his being. No ancient moral strictures drove him. No biblical injunctions frightened him. No divine power influenced him. He simply was. He existed and one day would cease to exist. His coming and going mattered slightly less than that of a falling leaf. He served no omniscient master, had achieved nothing remarkable and unforgettable, had evoked no undying love. He was a flexible man, ready and able to bend and twist and distort body and spirit in order to make an immediate gain. A manager in a technological world. As replaceable as a transistor in one of Heggland's famous computers.

What was he truly after?

Where was he headed?

No good answers came. Work had always been primary in his life. Work pushed back emotion, forced relationships to one side. It had made time scarce, and he allocated less and less of it to his family.

Even sex had come to be a passing exercise. He thought of the girl on the plane. Already he had forgotten her name, what she looked like. He had felt only indifference, despair, disgust. Less for her than for himself. Yet how many others exactly like her had he known and been with? They numbered in the hundreds, he was sure. No sign of his virility. Rather an indication of how easily people were reduced to empty acts, to self-degradation.

How many times had he slept with women other than his wife? All had been receptacles for his—his what? Surely not passion. Not love, or even affection. Just a futile exercise. You layed more women than any other man, you made more money, you accumulated more things. You became powerful.

But weakness was what he lived with. Weakness and inadequacy.

He lived on the very chic, very fashionable, very expensive East Side of New York. He owned one of the most expensive apartments in one of the most admired buildings on one of the best streets in the most exciting city in the world. He lived there with Janet who had once been beautiful and now was chic and very carefully—and expensively —turned out. Janet, the perfect hostess, the perfect wife, the perfect mother and companion.

Janet who hated him.

And drank all through the day, but in a very ladylike fashion.

Janet who kept step, infidelity for infidelity.

Janet, whose bitterness was matched only by his indifference.

A searing loneliness and sense of despair made it difficult to sleep these days and even harder to get out of bed in the mornings. Nothing existed outside the company, nothing except work mattered. Get the job done, win another battle, acquire another honor.

Big casino this time. Presidency of the Group.

All he had to do was settle this Aspen brouhaha
and Heggland would surely hand over the reins of
power. Carl was the logical man for the job, mirror image of the Old Man, but younger. And he
wanted to be number one. Wanted it with rare
desperation, as if to fail in this was to fail ultimately in everything.

His eyes raked the spiny ridge of the Rockies.
Up there, life would be simple, even primeval. He
thought he could hear muffled voices summoning
him, enticing him to where the truth was concealed, where it lay untouched and unvarnished.
Out there, where men had once hunted after preci-
ous metal. A new hunt was now in order for
greater wealth, greater rewards. But to go into
that wilderness demanded a strength and courage
he doubted he possessed.

Suddenly chilled, he got up, closed the doors to
the balcony, and went back to bed. Sleep still refused to accommodate him.

——— 9 ———

The Spot was the heart of all Alex Budde's activities. At almost any time of day or night, he
could be found at his table in the rear corner of
the front section of the restaurant. From there,
he was able to see people as they entered, recognize passersby through the plate-glass window.
When he wished to talk to someone, they were

asked over for a drink or coffee and occasionally, but not often, something to eat.

The Spot was in a three-story building in the center of a Hopkins Street block, lower than the old opera house, as the law demanded. Alex Budde owned the building. He owned the bookstore in the basement of the building. He owned the sporting goods store next door. He owned three other buildings in the block. He owned the travel agency on the corner. He owned the Rocky Mountain Real Estate Bureau. He owned fourteen rental houses spread around the county. He owned Colony West, a complex of condominium apartments. He owned a jewelry store, two fast-food outlets, and a shop that imprinted T-shirts with the name of your choice or a picture of a naked woman. Owning things pleased Alex, gave him a sense of pride, allowed him to tick off his accomplishments, made clear the power he had over other people. Alex couldn't conceive of a time when he would own enough. Of anything.

Alex lived in an apartment situated directly over the Spot. The apartment occupied the entire floor: bedroom, living room, a small kitchen. Alex never cooked for himself. If he ate at home, rather than downstairs in the restaurant, his food was sent up.

The apartment played a vital role in Alex's existence. It allowed him a privacy he seldom achieved elsewhere, a sense of security, of well-being. Here he could let down his guard, entertain those very secret thoughts that often came to his mind, thoughts that sometimes made him afraid. Here he was able to muster his strength and his courage to go out and do what he had to do in order to be the man he wanted to be.

The apartment had been decorated carefully.

Subdued colors and large comfortable pieces for Alex to rest in. Thick carpeting covered the floors, and quiet draperies lined the windows. The apartment was always softly lighted, even the bedroom at night while Alex slept; Alex was afraid of the dark.

On the third floor was another apartment. Smaller, less opulent, less cared for. Here Harry Rodano lived, connected to his employer by an intercom system as well as by a series of buzzers that allowed Harry to be summoned whenever needed.

On the morning after Scooter Lewis's party, Alex woke up in his own bed in his usual way. Alex always made it a point to wake up in his own bed, no matter where the night before might have led him. That way he knew exactly where he was. That way he could be sure he was safe—as safe as it was possible to be in a world studded with concealed dangers and threats and traps.

Alex sat up and stared straight ahead, straining to place himself in time and space. The familiar brass bed, the walls covered with bloodred paper sprinkled with silver fleur-de-lis, the fine antique chests and chairs, all so important in his life. Reminding him of who he was, of what he'd accomplished.

No one in Aspen had done more.

Pitkin. Gillespie. Wheeler. Paepcke. All names associated with Aspen's history. Before he was finished, his name would be linked with them. Alexander Arthur Budde.

Gradually it seeped through to him that he was not alone. His head turned creakily and his eyes stepped across the room, struggling to remain in focus. Along the far wall, a single bed was set up under a red-and-blue striped canopy. A woman slept there.

Alex stared at the body that lay so still, breathing in slow, deep draughts. Hatred for that body leaked along his nerves, and the muscles in his face tightened. Alex managed to keep women at length most of the time. Existing without their interference, without a need for their oppressive, demanding flesh. Until, without warning, his self-discipline would collapse and a hot yearning would corrupt him; no matter how long he held out, he surrendered eventually to its constant pressure. What subtle chemical changes altered his resolve, caused him to become less than he wanted to be? He had no answer.

He studied her back, the careless, almost insolent drape of the sheet across her thighs. Her hip curved up in a high arc and her exposed bottom was smooth, uncorrupted by time. He averted his eyes.

What had she made him do to her?

He went into the bathroom and showered. Water as hot as possible, scrubbing vigorously, intent on wiping out any lingering evidence of the night before.

He dressed rapidly: clean underclothes, linen slacks, a black silk sport shirt. Satisfied with his appearance, he went back into the bedroom.

She lay on her back, breasts pale and flattened, pointing accusingly in his direction. Joan Carolinian. What insanity had prompted him to bring her here again! No more, he had vowed after the last experience. She was unworthy of him, more so than most of them. A harlot who, when satisfied, transformed herself into a complaining witch, nagging for attention, for compliments, for *love*.

As if any right-thinking man could love her. How he loathed the clogging stench of her sexuality. Always more, all of them wanted more, as if he were some kind of mechanical contrivance for female pleasure. And she had dared to direct her lips to him *there*, to suck him in between her teeth. He had ordered her to stop, and she had laughed. At him.

But not for long. The enraged expression on his shining face had stopped her, made her fearful, apologetic.

"I won't do it again if it bothers you."

Why did he keep subjecting himself to her? She was no different from a hundred other women in Aspen, all like her in so many ways. Fading beauties without special skills or talents. All giving off that slight scent of decay that both repelled him and drew him to them. It was almost as if Joan Carolinian represented all those women, that in her all their flaws were distilled and made sharper. It was almost as if in submitting his body to her clawing, demanding appetites, he found new strength. And accepted some undefined punishment.

Looking at her now, he could hear again her voice in the night, cooing against his cheek.

"You were marvelous for me," she had said, as if to placate him.

He had shifted away.

"What would you say," she had asked cutely, "if I were to tell you I was thinking of leaving Aspen?"

How often had she said that? How often did any of them say it? Those world-weary middle-aged women sliding purposelessly down the far side of life? What bores they were! What futile creatures.

Helpless, stranded in the high country. He kept his eyes away from her.

"It's getting so crowded here," she had gone on, as if he cared. "So many people, especially during the winter. I only came here because the skiing was so fantastic, the season so long. But it's getting expensive. Ten dollars a day for the lift. Aspen wasn't this way five years ago.

"Why can't things stay the same? The point is, it isn't fun anymore. Did I tell you about my job? They hired another girl. Mr. Clinton did. Barbara's her name. Tiny, with an upturned nose and boobs to match. Just a kid. She's sleeping with him, I'm sure. Not that I care. Oh, don't think he didn't try it with me. But why should I? I mean, I do my job, I earn my way. Bed is something for someone you really like.

"Now he's shifting all my work over to her. I sit around most of the day hardly doing anything. It isn't fair.

"This town is dying," she had said with some shrillness creeping into her voice. "Do you know that this county has the lowest death rate in the state? Old people are sent away to die, as if it's a disgrace to do it here. Young people who get sick are sent off to Denver. Nobody dies in Aspen.

"Ah, Alex, let me stay the night."

He had stiffened at that.

"I know you can't sleep with me near you. I'll be happy to use the other bed. I'll be still as a pussycat, you'll see. You'll never know I'm here.

"People in this town, they're all runaways. They couldn't make it where they came from. New York, Chicago, wherever. Competition is too tough in those cities. Big fish in a little pond, that's their speed."

That had been last night. And now she was still in the apartment, still asleep, as if she belonged here. He placed his knee in her back and pushed. She made a protesting sound and he kneed her again.

"Wake up."

"I'm sleepy."

"Wake up!"

Her eyes fluttered open.

"Get up," he said. "You'll be late for your job."

She gave him a flirtatious smile. "I'll phone in sick. We could spend the day together."

He went to the door.

"Will I hear from you soon, Alex?"

He left without speaking.

A waitress in a long skirt served breakfast to Alex at his corner table. Sourdough hot cakes, bacon cut in thick slabs, and strong, hot coffee served in a Mexican mug.

The Spot was famous for its food, and breakfast there was fast becoming a tradition in Aspen. At this hour, the front room was quiet, only a few couples lingering over a second cup of coffee.

Harry Rodano was positioned near the bar, unobtrusive, quiet, watchful.

Alex had just finished eating when Jon Osborne appeared. He went directly to Budde's corner and deposited a flight bag on the table.

"There it is," he said.

Alex stared at the bag, lifted his pale eyes to Jon. "If that is what I think it is," he said in a harsh whisper, "get it out of here at once."

Jon hesitated. "You said you wanted delivery first thing in the morning."

Rodano, sensing conflict, left his place at the
bar, advancing almost daintily across the room.
Alex lifted a hand, sent him back.

"Walk around the block," Alex said. "Go into
the back alley, the way you are supposed to do.
Wait for me there."

"I thought—"

"You did not think. Not this time. Mostly you
just barge ahead like a dumb spoiled brat. Now—
leave."

Jon felt the scarlet rage rise up—the lust to
punish, pain, kill. It faded rapidly. He turned
away, made his way around to the alley, and
waited for nearly fifteen minutes before Alex
came out, Harry Rodano at his shoulder.

"Let me have it," Alex said.

Jon gave him the bag and accepted a white
envelope in return.

"I've been thinking," Jon said. "I ought to be
getting more money."

Alex showed no surprise. "You want to quit?"

"I didn't say that."

"This town is loaded with kids looking to make
some easy cash. A mule is a replaceable part, remember that."

"I do your work. I'm good at it. I'm not an
animal."

Budde grinned. "Have you spoken to your
father yet?"

"That's none of your fucking business," Jon
snapped out.

Alex hit him, a short, heavy blow above the
heart. Jon fell back, brought up his fists. Somehow
Harry Rodano moved between them, broad and
threatening, his wide face expressionless.

"All right, Harry." Rodano stepped away. "Listen to me, kid. You have bad manners, correct them."

Jon's breathing returned to normal and he started out of the alley.

"I want you to pay your father a visit," Alex said.

"What's that to you?"

"Your father and I have mutual business interests. I want him to be happy here in Aspen. So you act like a son ought to act. And you might also tell him what a terrific fellow I am, how fond of me you are, how everyone in town respects me. That I'm trustworthy. You say all that for me, will you?"

Alex drove out on Route 82 past the trailer camp almost to Difficult Campground. He used the winterized jeep which, being like most of the other jeeps around town, would draw no particular attention. Just short of the campground he drew off the road, parked, and walked back into the woods.

He found Jim Sexton where he was supposed to be. Seated with his back to a tree, smoking, patient. He wore khakis and boots and a flat-crowned, wide-brimmed Stetson. He lifted one finger in silent greeting, watched Alex with steady eyes, making no move to rise.

Alex dropped the flight bag on the ground. "Don't get up, Sexton."

Sexton grinned. "Got to preserve my strength, Alex. You know how demanding police work can be."

"Beautiful," Alex said. "Best cop on the force."

"Have to be; else I'd be pulling slam time by now, and where would that leave you, Alex?"

"That'd be a big problem to solve. But not for long. You've got two pounds of pure stuff in that bag. Get it over to the lab as quick as possible. I want it cut and bagged and on the street in a big rush."

"Running short of funds, Alex?"

"That'll be the day. Take off, Sexton."

Sexton rose without haste, swaggered down the slope toward the highway. Alex allowed ten minutes to pass and then went back to the jeep. By the time he got back to town, he was hungry again. He went up to his apartment. The maid had come and gone and everything was clean and ordered. No remaining trace of Joan Carolinian's presence.

Alex showered and changed clothes before going downstairs for lunch. The Spot was crowded with chattering diners, but his table was set and waiting for him.

—— 10 ——

Gwen and Judy were still asleep when Skip Blondell woke up. They slept peacefully in each other's arms like two innocent children. There was a beatific expression on their faces, the glow of purity and grace.

Blondell climbed over them. At the kitchen sink he splashed water on his face, drew on his clothes. He filled a kettle with water, brought it to a boil, and made tea with yesterday's tea bag. Perched on a high stool, he clutched the cup with shaking hands, remembering the night.

A wild pair, those girls. Nothing too far out for them. Strange tastes, imaginative, able to take pleasure where they found it. Blondell had joined in for as long as his strength held out, performing beyond his normal endurance. They wore him down, drained him, left him a shivering hulk without lust or energy.

The gallery reeked of bodily emissions, of burned grass, and of a case of Pearl's beer drunk among them. Gwen was crazy. Coming up with weird pieces of business, into SM stuff, begging to be whipped and bitten, into far-out toilet numbers that Blondell had never even dreamed of before. He went along, willing to try anything once. Now, looking at them, it was hard to believe any of it had taken place.

Pain came alive in his right eye, a dull pounding. He searched around until he found some aspirin, swallowed four or five, and washed them down with tea. The pounding went on. It took a while before he realized that someone was at the door. It was Jim Sexton. He opened the door.

Sexton went past him, looked around. "You alone?"

Blondell, proud and embarrassed at the same time, said, "Some chicks are out back."

"Some?"

"Two."

Sexton grunted. "You're more a man than I figured you to be, Skipper." He tossed the flight bag in Blondell's direction. "Get on this shit right away. Our friend wants it out in the street yesterday."

"I've got a show to put on here," Blondell complained.

"Tell it to the man."

"He won't listen. He never listens."

"Do it, save yourself the grief."

"He doesn't *own* me. I have my own life to lead, he's got to understand that."

"Stop playing with yourself. He owns you. Do the job and keep your mouth shut, that's the best way. You're not the sort to face up to him."

"I suppose you are?"

Sexton lifted his brows. "Better believe it, friend. Now about those two chicks, what gives?"

"They're asleep."

"I'd say they drained your reservoir."

"It was a wild night."

"Show me." Sexton started toward the rear of the gallery.

Blondell hurried after him. "Oh, Jim, that's not right. You don't even know them."

Sexton stood over the bed. He reached down and pulled back the sheet, examining the sleeping girls. "Nice bodywork."

"I took photographs, great stuff."

Sexton indicated the flight bag. "Get rid of that before I wake the girls."

"Let them sleep, they're all shot."

"They've got more work to do."

"Ah, Sexton..."

"Go on, take off, play with your chemistry set. I'll look after the chicks."

"What if they don't want to?"

Sexton seemed surprised. "Boy, you sure do get some weird ideas. . ."

—— **11** ——

Scooter Lewis groaned. He'd been groaning on and off all morning. He lay back in a deck chair that was shaded by a large canvas umbrella, shifted around, and groaned again. He clutched his forehead, smacked his lips, scratched his belly.

"Ah," he said unhappily.

Bobby Wallace paid no attention. He drank freshly squeezed orange juice over ice, and he gazed out at the town below. Wearying of that, he lifted his eyes to the mountains. Above the tree line were meadows of yellow with patches of purple and crimson. There was something special about this place. To call it beautiful was to understate it; it required a poet's subtle way with words. He thought of Kit Pepe and made a mental note to get in touch with her.

He studied the closest peaks. Surrounded by grandeur, a man could justly feel diminished, an insignificant creature in nature's scheme. He quickly put such thoughts aside. Bobby Wallace had long ago taught himself to be pragmatic, to get things done, to achieve his goals no matter what obstructions were raised in his path.

"I'm writing you off, Scooter," he said bluntly.

"Ah, Bobby. Peace and pity. You see a dying man before you."

"Die already. You're no good to me alive."

"Cruelty doesn't become you, man." Scooter squirmed, unable to arrange his long legs in comfort. His narrow face folded up into gloomy grooves and creases. "I love you anyway, man."

"You're a dope fiend."

"A little grass. . ."

"A drunk."

"A brew or two is all."

"Your head is gone away from you, man."

"I'll turn it around, you'll see."

"When?"

"I'm making my move right this minute. Inside, the gears are beginning to mesh."

"Don't crap me."

"Always straight with you, pal."

"Yeah, straight as a snake. . ."

"Bobby, believe in me."

"Get packed and into my car, hit the road for Beverly Hills. I can believe in you a lot better back there."

"Bobby, Bobby, this is my home."

"It's a nut farm."

"Cruel. I never knew you were cruel, man."

"There's nothing here for you but oblivion."

"All my friends. . ."

"Leeches."

"Have you no soul?"

"I came to help. Maybe you're beyond help."

"For ten percent."

"Ten percent isn't enough to make me go on with this act." He stood up. "Good-bye, pal."

"Bobby, come back! Don't leave me like this. I need you."

Bobby Wallace sat down again. "That's the first smart thing you've said. You do need me."

"I'll try, I promise."

"Beginning when?"

"Now, today. Maybe tomorrow morning."

"You haven't put word to paper in nearly two years. Nobody coasts forever on yesterday's success. Your name is a laugh line around the studios. People are beginning to say, Who's he?"

"Ah, Bobby."

"Face it, Scooter."

"I'm a big name."

"A writer who doesn't write."

"A man's got to live."

"You're killing yourself."

"Hard rock Bobby Wallace."

"I'm gonna spell it out."

"Be kind, Bobby."

"Here it is. You know Hilary Anguiano? He's moved into the top spot at Western International. Tough cookie, smart, moves fast, knows where it's at. He's got this idea. It's good. It's topical. It's commercial. He knows all that. He asked me for a writer. I threw your name on the table and he made a face. I said you were ready to go to work."

"Work is the opiate of the masses."

"Stop the crap and open your head, man. Now here is the proposition: He wants to do a Chicano gang story. I reminded him that you had worked that route four years ago. He got excited. He wants you to do the script—if you can."

"Oh, man, I never finished that book."

"I know that. But the research is all done. All you have to do is put it together."

"Does Anguiano understand that there are no words on paper?"

"He understands what I gave him to under-

stand, that you have a highly commercial property
in hand."

"Oh, man, I ache all over."

"You've done this kind of thing before, Scooter.
The book about the black pimp. The one about the
cycle gang in New Mexico. The commune book.
All good, all big sellers.

"That was back in some other century. People
forget easy. Who's Scooter Lewis? People around
the studios don't smile when I mention your name.
One guy says, 'I thought he was dead.' What do
you think, Scooter—are you dead?"

"Funny man."

"Nobody's laughing."

"What do you expect me to do, produce a best
seller on demand?"

Wallace set his face, made his voice firm. "I
expect you to go to work, to do what you know
how to do, what you've got the gift to do. In short,
Scooter, put an end to horsing around, and put
your ass in gear."

Scooter clamped his eyes shut, raised his face
to the sky, and howled.

Bobby Wallace sipped orange juice and waited.
When his client was still, Wallace said, "Feel
better?"

"Look at me. Do I appear to be in condition to
do a book?"

"Maybe you'll get into condition when you hear
the terms. Anguiano will pay one hundred thousand out front for film rights. Plus another forty
in advertising money—for *the book*. Through the
company's distribution network, he'll buy up
twenty-five thousand copies in key bookstores. In
case you don't know what that means, let me spell
it out—instant best seller. Top of the *Times*'s
list, the papers in L.A., Chicago. I'll be able to

peddle paperback rights for at least a quarter million. With luck, the Literary Guild will go for it. Playboy Book Club. *Reader's Digest.*"

"And all I have to do is write it."

"Fill up four hundred pages with your inimitable prose style and everybody gets rich."

"And then?"

"Then, come back here, if you want. Get high and stay high for another couple of years."

"What if I can't do it?"

"Anguiano will pick up another boy."

"What if we found us a ghost, somebody to write it for me."

"No way."

"Ah, Bobby..."

"Think on it, pal. Time is running out fast. There's nothing staler than yesterday's literary stud gone soft. Take it from me."

Bobby Wallace heaved himself erect and trundled back into the house, puffed up by his weightlifter's muscles.

"Hey, Bobby!" Scooter called after him. "What do you want to be when you grow up?"

Without turning, the agent gave him the finger.

_____ **12** _____

He floated, racket extended, sent the ball winging back across the net. The woman retreated, re-

turned a weak lob. He moved with smoothly articulated grace to the arching ball, raised up to
greet it, smashed it to the far corner. She never
had a chance. She pulled up, shaking her head and
wiping her brow.

"You never let up, do you, Jon?"

"I play to win, if that's what you mean."

"Back in Cleveland, I can beat most of the men
at our club. None of them play the way you do,
Jon."

They were at the net, facing each other. She
was a tall, tanned woman of forty, her figure
slender and shapely, her legs long and smooth. A
good club player.

"Your game's getting better all the time, Mrs.
Stone. Your backhand particularly. Much more
authority."

"I think you're right."

"A few more lessons."

He followed her off the court thinking that there
was no way she would ever be truly a fine player.
It was too late. She had not begun to play until she
was twenty-five, older than he was now. But she
moved well and was surprisingly strong for a
woman of her years. And there seemed always to
be a purpose behind her game, as if she had some
large plan in mind.

"Tomorrow?" she said. "Same time?"

"Okay."

"I'm very serious about tennis, Jon."

"I'm not."

"You can afford not to be. It comes easy for you.
At nineteen, many things come easy. I imagine
you could be a champion, if you wanted it badly
enough."

"I was a champion. State boy's champ at fifteen."

"Perhaps it was too easy."

"Or too hard. I'm not willing to put out the way you have to in order to be competitive in tournament play."

"Don't you have any ambition?" She gazed at him expectantly.

"Have a few laughs. Play a few sets. Ski a few mountains."

"That's all?"

"Is there anything else?"

"The laughter will stop one day. The sets may not matter anymore. And all the hills will look alike."

He shrugged.

She smiled wistfully. "At nineteen, it seems like everything goes on forever. It doesn't. But you have to find it out for yourself."

"I imagine I will."

She donned a sweater. "My husband would not approve of you, Jon."

"It doesn't matter."

"My husband works hard. Plans ahead. Accumulates businesses and fortunes and people."

"Sounds just like my father."

"He's the right age." She hesitated. "I could be your mother."

"But you're not."

She wet her lips. "My husband is off in Greece right now, buying ships. Or olives. Or something like that. No, Frank would never approve of you."

"Fuck him," Jon said lightly.

"Try me instead, Jon. I'd be much better for you."

"When?" he said without hesitation.

"I have nothing at all planned for the next hour or so. . ."

She headed back toward the clubhouse, and he went after her, keeping his mind blank.

13

The shop was long and narrow, set deep in the arcade without entry to the street, situated between an optician and a children's clothing store. A neatly lettered sign on the glass door said:

LEATHER

T. Keating, Prop.

At his workbench, Keating loomed large in a black sweat shirt, working intently over a belt. He guided the cutting tool surely, his hand steady and strong, his manner comfortable, his face easy. He appeared almost too big for the shop, hulking over his work like a great bearded bear. Engrossed totally, he was oblivious to time, nearly so to the shoppers who inspected his wares and left without buying.

A woman entered. Slender, almost boyish in build, she had freckled skin and hair the color of a carrot. Blue eyes crinkled up in amusement while she watched Keating at his bench. Presently she took up a position in front of him; he gave no indication that he was aware of her. She said his name in a low voice.

Keating stayed with the work, inflicting a long, graceful S shape into the belt. He brushed away flakes of material and considered the result. Content with his efforts, he put the belt aside and raised his eyes.

"Hello, Annie."

She touched the back of his hand lightly, maintained contact. "Have you had a good morning, Tom?"

"Quiet. Some lookers, no buyers. It allowed me to do the work. Oh, yes, one woman inquired about the deerskin travel bag. She wanted to think about it."

"Do you believe she'll come back and buy it?"

"I'd say there's a good chance. She seemed to like it a lot."

"That would be nice."

"Yes, it would be." He held her hand in his and looked into the blue eyes. "Do you intend to tell me anything, Annie? Or is it to be a secret?"

"I have no secrets from you," she said.

"I know."

"I don't always know when you're teasing me."

"Did you call the doctor's office?"

"Yes. The lab report came back. Dr. Curley says that I am surely going to have a baby."

"Well. Now. Isn't that something!"

"I'm very pleased about it, Tom."

"So am I, very pleased. It's really nice."

"You mean it?"

"I mean it. Between us we'll make a very fine baby."

"I hope so."

"An improved human specimen, better than those that went before."

"You really think so?"

"No doubt about it."

"If he's half the man his father is—"

"Or half the girl her mother is. . ."

Her hand went to her mouth. "I never assumed it could be a girl. That won't bother you?"

"You should know better than that. I've always believed woman are morally superior to men anyway."

She frowned. "One thing bothers me, Tom."

He waited patiently, tuned in to her internal clock, able to keep pace with her deliberate rhythms.

"I don't want you to feel trapped," she said. "I mean it. Don't stay on because of the baby."

"Where do you want me to go?"

"Oh, I don't *want* you to go!" She seemed startled at the idea. "I want you to stay with me, for as long as you wish. Only—"

He put a broad finger across her lips. "Enough. Neither of us is going anywhere. We are together, you, me, and the baby. Would it be better for you if we got married? Legally, I mean."

"It isn't something I care about. If one of us has to split, okay. A marriage contract won't change that, or the way we feel. What matters to me, Tom, is the way we feel about each other."

"We're together." He retrieved the tool and the leather, began cutting into it. "For as long as it's good."

"I hope that will be a long time."

"I'm sure of it."

She took a place on the rough bench along the opposite wall and watched him work. It gave her a great deal of reassurance.

14

Bobby Wallace sat opposite Kit Pepe in the center booth in Johnson's Temptation, a few steps below street level. Greenery overflowed in profusion throughout the restaurant, and paintings by a local artist decorated the walls. With the midday rush ended, there was a bright peacefulness to the place, and they talked quietly, ate without haste. Wallace spooned an excellent lentil soup into his mouth and Kit cut a steak into small squares.

"You're a pretty terrific lady," Wallace said, not letting it get too heavy.

"Come on, Bobby. You barely know me."

"Okay, so how do I get to know you better?"

"That takes time, doesn't it?"

"I don't have lots of time. As soon as I can wind things up with the Scooter, I'm heading back to the coast."

She said nothing, offered no encouragement.

"Are you always so remote?" he said.

"Do you always ask so many questions?"

"One zip," he said. "Your favor." He lit a cigarette and studied her. "I gotta tell you, you are one great-looking dame."

She laughed. "With women's lib in high gear, Bobby, I suspect you are the embodiment of male piggery."

He took no offense. "Probably so. But what the hell, I dig dames and I'm not about to change my ways."

"I imagine *dames* dig you, Bobby."

"You can see that, huh? It's true. Only sometimes I'm not so sure. In my business, in Hollywood, a guy in my position might help to launch a chick into the big time. So maybe it's not me they like so much as the kind of work I'm into."

"A little of both seems likely."

He grinned quickly. "What the hell, the kind of world it is, you take what you can get." He sobered and shook his head. "Agh, your kind of dame doesn't get it together with my kind of guy."

"What kind are you, Bobby?"

"I'm a fast talker. A dealer in words, ideas, deals. I put together packages—this script with that director with that star with the other studio. I hustle, I wheel, I manipulate. Another time, another place, I'd be hawking ties off a pushcart for a living."

"You're being overly modest, I think."

"Maybe not. I mean, all my words, what do they add up to? Nothing important. They gush out of me. My mouth is a vending machine; push the right button and you get what it says on the label."

"I like your imagery."

"You're the wordsmith; you're really good."

"Poets are for classrooms and summer seminars. You get invited to a lot of faculty teas and all the correct intellectual parties. You meet the best people. It can be fun, but often little more than that. Most poets take themselves very seriously, but few of us will be read twenty years from now."

"Then why do it?"

"Because I am a poet."

"You could do other things as well."

"I teach, you know that."

He looked into the empty soup bowl, remembering something. "Why not give another form a crack. Say, writing a novel."

"I'm not a novelist."

"Look at James Dickey. There's a poet who hit it big with his first novel. Made a terrific movie. *Deliverance.* Did you see it?"

"No."

"And that other dame, Erica somebody..."

"Jong. *Fear of Flying.*"

"Yeah. Catchy title. Sold a couple of million in paperback. Just let it all hang out. You can bet she gets big bucks for every word she puts on paper now, poetry and prose. And on the lecture circuit—cleaning up. You could be taking in that kind of money."

"Teatime fame," she said.

"What?"

"That's what Marianne Moore called it."

"Okay," he said solemnly. "So you don't want to write a best seller. How about a play?"

"No thanks."

"Why not?"

"Chacun a son gout..."

"Which means?"

"Shoemaker stick to your last."

He examined her until she turned away. She was unlike other women he had known. She even looked different—the clean lines of her face without makeup. She thought and talked differently, without artifice. Such a woman could only mean trouble for a man like Bobby Wallace.

"What I've been working around to is the flicks," he offered.

"Movies?"

"You'd be something special on a scenario."

"The only movies I ever see are monster pictures." She had thought to make him laugh, change the conversation. Instead, he seemed to grow more intense.

"They're all money-makers. People really dig the monsters. For a long time I couldn't figure it. Then one day I put it together: The monsters are us, human beings, the bad side of people."

That surprised her. "That's very good, Bobby. It's the monstrous side of humanity. There's a simultaneity of good and evil in each of us, and we need to create monsters in order to exorcise our own evil aspects."

"Something like that."

She laughed. "You should read the original *Frankenstein,* by Mary Shelley, the poet's wife. She wrote it to amuse her husband. Monsters have been with us for a long time. Dracula, werewolves, weird beasts from the deep. They all reach back to *Beowulf...*"

"I don't know it."

"Maybe the first piece of English literature, written about four hundred years after Christ. It's given inspiration to a lot of writers since. Monsters —a kind of allegory on the nature of evil."

"You're a very heavy brain," he muttered. "I never met a lady like you before."

She imitated his harsh eastern accent. "Very heavy..." Her eyes traveled over his face. He amused and provoked her, took her mind away from herself, and that was good. Still, he remained a stranger, existing in another world; their meeting was an accident. He interested her and evoked responses that she had not yet had time to analyze. She warned herself not to allow any emotional connection to be formed; trouble lay behind that tough, aggressive facade, the kind of trouble she was not prepared to encounter.

"Where are you from?" she said, startled that she was asking a direct and personal question.

"Philly."

"Philadelphia," she said, to make sure she understood him. "I was born in Harrisburg, grew up on the outskirts of Pittsburgh."

He perceived no meaningful linkage in those two facts. He felt no loyalty to city or state, no hookups with his own history. Most of it was for forgetting, excess baggage not worth the price of transport. Keep going—that was the slogan by which he lived.

"When did you first decide to become a literary agent?"

"When I found out how much dough was in it."

"Be serious, Bobby."

"I mean it. I've got only one ambition—to become a multimillionaire."

"I think you mean it."

"It's what everybody is after. Only I admit it." An almost hostile note sounded in his voice. He caused himself to laugh, but his laugh lacked humor.

She spoke cautiously, feeling her way. "I do not want to have a lot of money."

"You're the only writer I know who doesn't. Money is what most writers talk about. Money and sex. Money, sex, and playing tennis or skiing or hunting the way Hemingway did. That's it with writers."

She grew uneasy, as if she had come under attack. She wanted to placate him, to help dissipate the anger that seemed to have surfaced. Before she could speak, he gave a loud, gasping sound of pleasure.

"The way things are going, I should have my first million before my thirty-fifth birthday. After that, it'll pile up in a hurry."

"You're so sure of yourself."

"Aren't you?"

"No. No, I'm not sure of anything."

"That's why you need an agent like me around, to buck you up when the going gets a little rocky. I do that better than anything else."

"Aren't you afraid of anything, Bobby?"

He searched her face for some sign of mockery, found none. "I'll tell you. Flying. Airplanes terrify me. I drove up here from L.A. and that's a long, tough drive. Those mountains are too much. Also . . ." he stopped.

"Also," she prodded.

He answered in a compressed voice, almost inaudible. "Of not being able to make it."

"Make it?"

"With a dame."

"I thought. . ." She broke off.

"You chicks got it easy. Just lay back and let it happen. A man can't fake it."

"Let's talk about something else." She regretted the words as soon as they were out. His expression hardened and his eyes squinted.

"Sure," he said. "I get it. Finish your lunch, I'll take you back to the institute."

"When I want to leave, I'll tell you."

"I thought you were ready to shake me."

"You thought wrong. Now tell me what brings you to Aspen?"

"Scooter Lewis. That freak. . ."

A shadow fell across the table and they looked up to see Jon Osborne standing there. He flashed a smile and held up his hands as if in surrender.

"Don't hit me again, mister, please," he said, obviously joking.

Bobby Wallace was on his feet. "Sorry about that, kid. . ."

"I had it coming," Jon said. "People like to pound on my belly. Makes them feel good—and after a while you build up immunities. . ."

Wallace sat down.

"Are you all right, Jon?" Kit said.

"Terrific. I saw you through the window and decided to say hello. Hello."

"A cup of coffee?" Wallace said.

"I don't think so. I'm on my way to see my father."

"Is he in Aspen?" Kit said.

"So I'm told. If I know the man, he's here to buy up the valley and the mountains, turn it all into a shopping center and a parking lot. He's got a flair for converting silk purses into sows' ears."

"How long since you seen him?" Wallace said.

"A couple of years."

"I haven't seen any of my people in over ten years. I can hold out for another ten without much trouble."

"I telephoned," Jon said. "Made an appointment with some guy he's got along. All very business-like, that's my father. A place for everything, everything in its place." He checked his watch. "I'm five minutes late now. Father won't approve of that."

"Then you should get over there," Kit said.

"I may just pass on this one."

"That won't do much good," Kit said.

"Time spent away from my father is time well spent," Jon said cheerfully.

"Go on, get it over with. Make peace, if you can. It helps the pieces fall into place."

"All poets are philosophers at heart," Jon said thinly.

"Are you afraid to confront him?" Kit persisted.

"I guess I am."

"What do you think you'll do, kid?" Wallace asked.

"Kill him."

"Or love him?" Kit added.

"That's absurd."

"Life is."

"You're no help, Kit," Jon said.

"Do you want my help?"

Jon wet his lips, eyes unsteady. "Will you come with me?"

Her eyes went over to Bobby Wallace. He nodded at once.

"If you want me to," she said softly.

15

Style was Carl Osborne's strong suit, Len Ralston decided. Style and nerve. Ralston had been studying the other man, watching and listening, weighing everything. Osborne was good. Smooth, confi-

dent, steeped in past success, and certain of future
triumphs. All that made dealing with trouble
easier, cut down on the fear quotient in the face
of disaster.

But Osborne was human, too. There was always
someone tougher, stronger, someone with a
heavier hand. T. Lyman Heggland, for example.
Ralston had met Heggland twice. Brief meetings,
with other executives present. More like papal
audiences. Ralston's role was limited to a barely
acknowledged greeting and an impersonal dismiss-
al. His advice had not been solicited; his experience was ignored; his opinions were unasked for.
Heggland was a man who boiled with energy and
certainty, making decisions seemingly without
consideration, snapping out commands, dictating
courses of action, brooking no argument once his
mind was made up, allowing the smallest possible
margin for error. Heggland frightened Ralston.

Now Ralston sat in a hard, straight chair as
if at attention and listened to Osborne talk to
Heggland over the phone. Ralston found it easy
to imagine Heggland's words, his responses and
attitudes. One thing came through loud and clear
—Heggland was displeased with his deputy in
Aspen, would accept neither explanations nor excuses. Osborne was in trouble, and Ralston reveled
in it, glad at this moment that he stood no higher
on the corporate ladder. He watched Osborne
squirm.

"There are obstacles," Osborne was saying.
"Naturally I believe that they can be overcome.
Most of them, anyway. The project is going
through, I can promise you that. Otherwise I
wouldn't have come out here. I take full responsibility for what occurs. No, I will remain on to the

end. A few days should take care of it. Yes, compromise is in order, but no sellout. We want to maintain the widest area for profit. I do understand your point of view, Mr. Heggland. It is also my point of view. I've got a meeting with the planning people as soon as we terminate this conversation, Mr. Heggland. I'll certainly goose them. When the project is a certainty, I'll notify you immediately."

He placed the phone gently down in its cradle as if to avoid sending negative impulses across the continent.

"Heggland is a rough old bird," Ralston said.

Osborne ignored the remark. "Run me down on these people I'm going to see."

"Marquard, Bender, and Skutch. Basically, they're architects. But they're pretty creative. Design furniture, do color consulting, landscape work. They're into planned communities, for about five years now. Did the Charleston Coastline Residences, which you know about."

"Very nice work."

"Yes. Also the Whittendon Town in West Virginia. Prizewinning stuff. Sucked up a very high dollar return per square foot and still satisfied the ecology cranks. They are definitely tuned in to our requirements."

"We'll see. Get them in here."

All three architects were in their middle thirties. Marquard and Skutch wore beards. Bender was clean-shaven: a large man with a huge belly and a ponderous style. He lowered himself into a chair and began to talk.

"We studied the maps of the site. . ."

"I've seen them," Osborne replied.

"Without McDevitt's upper rim we are in serious difficulty. I would suggest—"

Osborne interrupted. "I've got McDevitt, his entire ranch. Figure it in for future development."

"Expansion of the town site," Marquard said. His voice was squeaky, his face animated.

"We'll lay out the squares," Skutch added. He seemed unhappy.

Osborne held up one hand. "Let's talk about problems. What are they? How do we get rid of them? That's why I'm here."

"Money can solve an awful lot of problems, Mr. Osborne," Bender said.

Osborne laughed openly. "Well, money hasn't bought us Don Horn's little ranch. He turned down our first offer."

Ralston swore under his breath. "The dirty mother practically ordered me off his property. Said he was born there, raised there, intended to die there."

"We need that land. . ." Skutch said.

"I know," Osborne said lightly. "It straddles number two ski run. Don't worry, we'll get it. Horn is no different from the rest of us—just sweeten the pot and he'll come around. Len, you see him again, raise the ante a little."

"How much?"

"Enough to get him to sell. We're in business to make money, not give it away."

Marquard ruffled his hair. "Planning and Zoning, that's our initial obstacle. Once past them, it gets even rougher; namely, the county commissioners."

Osborne reflected on his meeting with Alex Budde and Teddy Maxwell. He had P and Z in his hip pocket. The commissioners couldn't possibly be much more difficult. "Let's move forward on the assumption that P and Z will approve," he said.

"Okay," Bender said. "But keep in mind that people in town are dead set against overdevelopment."

"Not all of them," Ralston put in.

"Not all," Skutch agreed gloomily. "Just those who have the power."

"Hold it right there," Osborne said. "We are not talking about *over*development. We intend to create a perfect environment, consonant with the landscape, with the town, with the present and future needs of the people who live here."

"Have you seen our impact study?" Marquard ventured.

"Summarize it for me, please."

"Let's begin with the transportation. From Wolf Run to Aspen to the other ski areas. Current public transport falls short of the demand we anticipate. We're also going to have a water problem. The Roaring Fork is being utilized down the valley with an inevitable reduction in the amount of water reaching this end. . ."

Osborne made a note. "What about sewage and utilities?"

"Again, an overload on existing facilities. We have also tried to project the effect Wolf Run will have on the area wildlife—we take it to be considerable. Add to this the question of natural hazards."

"Such as?"

"Rockslides, winter avalanches. In this situation, quantity is quality."

"Spare me the slogans."

"Sorry, I was just trying—"

Osborne went on without hesitation. "Wolf Run is a reality; it will happen. It is happening. That is why we are assembled here, to make it happen. Problems are why we get paid—to solve them, overcome them. Let's put our minds to the questions. One: transportation. What options are open to us?"

Bender answered, "We could institute local taxi service, of course. That way expenses—"

"Taxis can best be operated by private concerns," Osborne cut in.

"It might take some doing, but perhaps we can get legislation through for a municipal bus line."

"That lays too heavily on the taxpayer, will only create more opposition for us. What about minibuses. Diesel powered to keep air pollution at the minimum. Let's explore the costs, how much fares would have to be to make it self-sufficient, etcetera, etcetera. As for the sewage, can we use septic tanks?"

"There's a sewage system in operation. We'll have to splice into it."

"Will the system be able to handle the influx of waste matter?"

"We believe so."

"In the event it cannot, let's draw up plans for a holding plant to feed into the system at a rate acceptable to everyone."

"Utilities?" Marquard said.

"We could draw on present sources, but I have a better idea. In light of the fuel shortage, why not create our own generating plant? We might investigate the feasibility of solar heating and energy, incorporate it into the buildings themselves. That's the kind of thing that will swing popular opinion our way."

"That's good," Skutch said. "That's very good."

"About the water," Osborne said. "I understand the problem with the Roaring Fork. So let's check out other sources—springs, lakes, wells. Get it down on paper. Facts, not guesses."

"Yes, sir."

"When we go before P and Z, I want all loopholes closed up tighter than a drumhead. Let's give them no excuses, no outs. Let's insure approval."

"There's still the county commissioners," Bender reminded him.

"I'll get together with each of them individually, put our case."

Bender frowned. "Is that really a good idea, Mr. Osborne?"

"Tell me why it isn't."

"People might read it incorrectly, see it as an attempt to buy our way in."

Osborne sat back. "We're going to get approval. Let's accept that as fact. To do so, we'll utilize whatever means are at hand. Let me remind you gentlemen of one thing: The Constitution of the United States was created out of the Founding Fathers' respect for property rights. I believe in those rights, in the right of the individual citizen to buy or sell or otherwise deal his property as he sees fit. Nothing has happened in the two centuries since to alter that concept."

There was a long, uneasy silence. Marquard cleared his throat. "Tom Keating is going to fight you over that one. People versus property, that's his position."

Osborne felt a surge of exhilaration. He was moving; his brain was operating at a fine old pace; his senses were heightened because he was doing

at last what he knew he did so well. This man
Keating, he knew the type. Full of empty plati-
tudes about the rights of the people, about the
value of open land, about the chain of life in nature, about conservation. All the catchphrases that
people used these days to make themselves seem
important. And all the while, they accomplished
nothing. No parlor liberal was going to stand in
the way of Wolf Run.

The real power resided at the source of the
financing, and that meant the Heggland Group.
The group would own or control all the land ad-
joining Wolf Run; one of its subsidiaries would
subcontract the construction, another would write
the insurance. Big money was involved and big
money meant big power. Osborne knew how to
apply that power: You contributed to political
campaigns; you bought up property you didn't
need and so acquired men you did need; you provided jobs, deals, favors; you gave bribes and
called them loans; you manipulated and worked
and always kept the pressure on. Until you got
exactly what you wanted.

"Tell me about Tom Keating," he said with a
vague suggestion of a smile. No single man was
going to stop Carl Osborne.

"Keating?"

"The most radical of the commissioners," Ralston supplied. "If you want my opinion, he's an
out-and-out red commie through and through.
Wears a beard and sells leather belts to get by.
I don't trust a man who works outside the system."

"That's not exactly the case," Skutch said.
"Keating was *elected* as a county commissioner.
He's no bomb-thrower."

"Suit yourself," Ralston said.

"I'll have a talk with Mr. Keating," Osborne said.

Before he could go on, the telephone rang. Ralston answered. "It's your son," he said. "Downstairs in the lobby."

Bender pushed himself erect. "We'll come back another time."

"This afternoon," Osborne said. "At five o'clock. In your office. Tell Jon to come up," he said to Ralston, "and then get out."

——— 16 ———

They sat next to each other on the brown velour couch, careful not to touch. Jon was unable to sit still, to keep his hands or legs in place. Kit, precisely turned out in plaid slacks and a gray sweater, dark hair shining close to her head, held herself steady.

At first they made small talk, struggling to get beyond the initial discomfort that each of them felt. Osborne hadn't expected Jon to bring a girl along, and he was troubled by her presence, startled by her stillness, her deep beauty. He had welcomed her graciously, however, determined to do nothing to displease Jon, determined to make him feel at ease after so much time. Osborne called down for drinks and coffee and pastries. But no one displayed any interest in refreshments.

They settled into place, talking in swift gushes, unable to sustain conversation, eyes avoiding each other.

Osborne mustered his resolve. "You're looking well, Jon." His voice echoed loudly in his own ears, too much the corporate executive making a declaration. He smiled. "It's odd, seeing you again after all this time."

"You're looking pretty fit yourself, father," Jon said. "It has been a long time."

"Your mother told me you were out here when she learned I was coming. I never saw any of your letters." It was meant as a reproach and he regretted letting the words slip out. "That's your right, of course, to write your mother."

"I thought it would be better."

"Why is that?"

Jon shrugged. "I figured you'd hire some private eye to turn me up if you knew where to look."

Osborne considered that. Jon was right; that's exactly what he would've done. A reflex. Your son has left home—employ some tracer of lost persons to find him and bring him back. Push a button, get it done. All very businesslike.

"I see your point," Osborne said. "Why announce your whereabouts if you want to get off by yourself?"

"Something like that."

Osborne started to pursue the subject, to ask why Jon had left home, whether he was ready to return, to live a more orthodox and therefore, in Osborne's opinion, a more fruitful life. He decided against it. He turned his attention to Kit Pepe. Nothing was revealed in her tranquil expression. There was a shadowed mystery in that face, intrigue that would have been at home in Caesar's

Rome; she was a woman insightful and clever, the kind who gave only hints of how much she knew or of what she understood. Osborne produced what he meant to be a friendly smile.

"My son has excellent taste," he said. "Jon is to be congratulated on having you."

An almost carnal light came into the dark eyes, penetrating, assessing him deliberately. Or was it merely a suggestion of the dislike she felt for him? Osborne shifted in his chair, abruptly discomforted.

"Jon does not have me," she said coolly. Her full, nearly plump lips drew his attention, and he began to wonder about her. "Nobody has me," she ended.

Osborne, nettled at her tone of quiet criticism, offered a calm to match her own. "Of course," he said. "You're to be complimented, Jon, having a friend like Miss Pepe."

Jon grew uneasy. The air was charged and he didn't like it. He was reminded of the eternal sparring matches that went on between his father and his mother. Words alive with concealed meanings. Words used as rapiers. As clubs. As killing thrusts. Run, he urged himself. Flee for your life. For your sanity. Write off the past and put your faith in the great ever-present. There was surely no future. No genius could with certainty describe the shape, content, or duration of what lay ahead. Only now could foretell tomorrow, and few people understood today until it was far behind.

Jon held his hands on his thighs, determined not to look at his watch, committed to concealing his yearning to leave. This meeting had to come off smoothly. He wanted very much to impress Kit with how well he could deal with Carl.

Correction: *cope* with Carl. Coping was all any-one ever did with his father. Merely get by. Exist. Survive. The slightest attempt to do better, to improve one's position, caused Carl to rise up in fury and in limitless competence and to strike out, push back, smother, destroy.

So Jon defined life for himself and his mother. Doing better in relation to Carl was out of the question. Carl was too loaded with power, too demanding, too obsessive, a man who got everything he ever wanted, squeezing life dry. Winning was not enough for Carl; his friends and relatives had to fail.

"Kit—" Jon said, feeling very young, very small, inadequate, "Kit is a poet." It was a boast—see what talented, glamorous friends I have—and a futile attempt to close the conversational gap.

"I know," Osborne said, eyes fixed on the girl.

She wondered. Was he as sure of himself as he appeared to be? Often the strongest of men were wracked by inner turmoil, were capable of crying out for help, of weeping in the dark. Carl Osborne appeared to be all body and balls, power and sexuality. How strange that she should think of him that way. Not that she was interested. She knew that businessmen often gave off emanations of sex; frequently it was nothing more than their lust for success. Carl was used to getting what he wanted. To bulling his way ahead, accepting no limitations, no opposition. In some way, she was frightened of him.

"You know?" she said with exactly the right amount of surprise. She did not make him out to be someone with an overriding concern with modern poets.

"The *New Yorker* publishes you. And about a year ago, there was a book. *Repeat*, you called it.

I'm not sure I understood what you were getting at, but I enjoyed your work very much."

"Poetry can be taken on a number of levels."

"For example?"

"Read for what appears immediately. Sit back and enjoy the rhythms, the language. Words and ideas, that's what it's all about."

"You work with allegory. You're obviously deeply into the myths men live by."

At the edge of her vision, she saw Jon grimace: a slight show of distaste, of irritation, a sense of being left out. She reminded herself of why she had come; instead, she was allowing Carl to monopolize her attention, to stimulate her responses. She turned her attention to Jon, ready to draw him into the conversation, to let him deal with his father. It was too late.

"Your first summer in Aspen?" Carl was saying, unwilling to release her.

"It's your first time here," Jon said, unable to contain his growing frustration and resentment. "Have you figured out a way to fuck it up yet, father?"

Carl replied softly, "I apologize for my son, Miss Pepe. He has obviously forgotten the good manners he learned in our home."

"Come on, father, tell us. Growth, progress—those are the words you live by. Your creed. Your manifesto. You must have worked up some rotten scheme."

"I am working on a project," Osborne said.

"Hell, yes, my father couldn't come to a place just to enjoy it. To do what other people do. He has to improve things."

Carl kept his voice easy. "Let's not bore Miss Pepe with dull business matters, Jon."

"You won't bore me," Kit said.

"Well?" Jon challenged.

Carl spoke without emotion. "I am setting in motion forces that will develop a new community in the valley."

"You're going to build in Aspen!" Hostility made Jon's voice shrill, his expression tortured.

"Not far from town."

"That's awful."

"It will be good for most people."

"Horrible."

"We'll bring new life, new business, greater opportunities."

"You'll destroy the valley with people."

"I doubt it."

Kit said, "The land can accommodate only a limited number of human beings. Where do we call a halt to the spread?"

"Good question. The answer, unhappily, eludes some of our best thinkers."

"Why can't you leave things as they are?" Jon cried.

Carl stared coldly at his son. "Because things as they are, are seldom good enough."

"You'll ruin everything!"

"Was the valley ruined by your coming to it, Jon? Or by those who came immediately before or after you? Was it ruined by the skiers or the summer visitors? Did the institute ruin the valley? Or Ballet West? Or the writers' conferences?"

"You're not making sense!"

"I'm responding to your somewhat hysterical argument. Why is it that when a good place is discovered, those who can move in quickly do so and immediately opt for closing the gates on everyone else? Who gave you proprietary rights over Pitkin County? Over the Rocky Mountains?

I've got mine, Jack, now bug off—that's what you're saying."

Jon was on his feet now, his face pale and his eyes wide and round. "You make everything rotten, and I hate you for doing it."

"You have no idea what I'm doing."

"You spoil whatever you touch."

"Careful studies are being made. Nothing will be done until—"

"I'm ashamed to have you for my father!"

Jon stormed out of the room.

Carl went over to the bar and poured himself a drink. He stared at Kit who returned his gaze steadily.

"Are you going to tell me how wrong I am?" he said.

"No."

"But you believe it?"

"I'm not sure what I believe at the moment."

"Oh, come on, Miss Pepe, surely you think I should be more understanding of my brilliant— if somewhat unstable—son."

"If there is any apologizing to do, I'm sure you and Jon will find out how to do it."

"A pox on both our houses, is that what you mean?"

She rose, movements graceful, unhurried. "I must go."

"Stay and talk to me for a while. Tell me how wrong I am, if it pleases you." He smiled to show he was merely making a poor joke.

"Some other time," she said automatically.

"This may sound strange to you, Miss Pepe, but I love Jon very much."

"Not strange at all."

"Yet we always fight. Conversation between us

is impossible. The damn thing is, I'm never quite certain what it is we're fighting about. Why should my business be so important to Jon?"

"Because it is your business, I suppose."

"That simple. Are you sure of your conclusion?"

"I'm sure of almost nothing. Perhaps that's why I write poetry, to try to find some answers."

"Have you found any?"

"Just one."

"And that one is?"

"There are no answers..."

17

> The naked embrace beckons
> And I respond excitedly.
> To find chill emptiness and
> No return.

Kit Pepe put her pen aside and stared at the words she had written on the long yellow legal pad. Self-pity was the glue that held the lines in place, she acknowledged ruefully. Self-pity: an absence of strength. She closed her eyes and made an effort to isolate her feelings, to sort out the collection of random thoughts that fluttered through her head.

All of her emotions were drawn into a mindless stream, mixed by exotic currents, tumbled violently, muddied. She had come to Aspen—artist in residence at the institute, what a pretentious description!—hoping to put her unsettled emotions to rest, to find a way to think clearly and decide how it was she wanted to live her life. Twenty-two years had gone into making her what she was. Child-woman, poet of the middle rank, questioning teacher, lonely human being.

She longed.

Craved. Needed.

But what?

To speak of love seemed to fall so far short of what she really desired. Completeness in a man? Body and brain and spirit? Not enough there. Completeness in herself? That would come—from where? Surely from no one else, though the idea appealed in its simplicity, its abdication of responsibility to self:

> *Someday he'll come along,*
> *The man I love....*

The words of the old song were a trap, a device to suspend the present, to eliminate the need for personal striving. Wait for Prince Charming to arrive and do his thing. What if his thing failed to match hers? Up to now, all the princes charming she had known had in fact fallen short. But then, so had she.

Kit Pepe, poet, teacher, dreamer of fantastic dreams of glory, had produced very little. What did she want? To be famous? To be rich? To be bombarded with critical accolades, awards, cheers, the collective love of the literary community, and the approval of women like herself. It all sounded so delightful. Answers came and went, and she made no effort to hold onto even one. Questions were easier to deal with right now.

Going to Scooter Lewis's party had been a mistake. Going with Jon to see his father had been another mistake. Mistakes were familiar to her; she committed them with regularity—eased into them, unable to recognize the error even as she fell into its seductive arms. Men, jobs, friends; she had failed in all areas. And work, that most important endeavor. The work that told her who she was, what she was; that too failed to measure up.

Perhaps it was that she expected immediate results, as well as more lasting rewards. Perhaps life was designed by a mocking nature to be less than fulfilling and so separate the strong from the weak, the adaptable from those who could never evolve.

More questions. She wanted an answer. She told herself again that she should not have gone to the party. There. A solid conclusion. A definitive response. She hugged it to her like a child's teddy bear.

She should have realized that Jon might show up and that he would neither understand nor tolerate her presence. He presented himself to the world as a free spirit, a gay drifter, when in fact he hungered for some solid ground to base his life on. Some immutable body of laws and values and regulations that separated good from evil.

She had been evil to deceive him. Not to return immediately to her bed alone when she had announced her intention of doing so.

Her annoyance gave rise to self-righteousness. Jon wanted to appropriate her, to make her an object belonging to him alone.

He had labeled himself Good. As had Bobby Wallace: springing forward to protect her; bashing poor, not-so-innocent Jon.

Why didn't she feel better? Why wasn't she honored by the concern and solicitousness of those two men? Instead she felt used, slightly soiled, somehow lessened by their instinctive possessiveness, by their need to claim her.

Should she sleep with Jon Osborne? He would be a powerful, insistent lover, his body graceful and active, laboring overtime to please her. Well, why not? Because she had no need for a human dildo.

And Bobby Wallace? All that energy and vigor packed into his stubby frame. Tough, aggressive, selfish. He would give only in direct proportion to what he took; from such a dynamic personality the bed might be transformed into a wild and deliciously satisfying playground.

Afterwards: emptiness.

It always came back to that. The failure of the bed. The failure of the men she had known. In addition to her own failures. All lumped together, leaving her dissatisfied, resentful, distrustful.

Making love was a sham. Contrived gyrations and noxious sounds. So much had happened in her short life, so much that pained still, so many burdens that sat on her shoulders as if she had been especially selected and cursed by the gods.

Critics described her poetry as harsh and realistic. Without affection for people. Without warmth. Had she become an icy stick, aggressively protective, too afraid to change? What was it she really wanted? No answer came.

Katherine Margaret Pepe.

Beautiful. Intelligent. Talented.

Possessed by it all. Left with that terrible desire that cannot be sated. In the morning she would address two dozen business executives on the meaning of the novel in America. She would trace for them the connections to Dante's *Inferno*, draw them into Eliot's *Waste Land*, introduce them to the ambiguities of Camus. They would discuss a dozen novels over the course, a dozen writers, all rooted in hell. All doomed to fail, to exist in agony and punishment for deeds they knew not of.

Bullshit.

Human beings were afflicted with human longings. Nothing wrong there. Made mistakes? Well, okay, man, didn't everybody. What did she want?

To be loved, came the small silent voice. Someone to care for her alone. To have her failures and excesses understood and catered to, accepted. To be allowed to weep and to be weak.

Is that so much? The answer came: *It's everything!*

Part Two

Aspen

Silver mining was big business. To start, a man needed at least $5,000, often as much as $25,000. Small operators, unable to compete, soon slunk back over the mountains, broke and defeated. Fortunes dreamed of remained just that.

In Aspen, work went on. With proper backing, shafts were put down, tunnels dug, the ore removed and shipped out to the refineries. Some men made millions; others merely worked hard.

Aspen became civilized. A Sunday school, complete with organ, was opened. And a literary society. And a glee club where "the eternally smiling Julius Berg varied his daily routine of selling milk by day with singing thorough bass at night."

Aspen enlarged. New people struggled into the valley and went to work. Mining shacks gave way to pleasant gingerbread-trimmed Victorian structures with porches, steep roofs, and cupolas, painted blue and yellow and red and green. Plans were drawn up to build a smelter in town.

A telegraph line was strung across the mountains. Followed soon afterwards by a telephone line. Aspen's fame spread. New money was brought in to modernize the mines, to bring out more silver.

There was trouble, too. Four men were killed by a snowslide in Vallejo Gulch, and a number of others were injured. Others died at Conundrum Gulch, buried under tons of snow. In the spring of that same year, thirty-three days after the slide, rescuers returned to the site, hoping to retrieve the belongings of the dead men. They began to dig and were attracted by a whimpering sound. They found J. M. Thorne's pet dog, Bruiser, barely alive. They brought the animal down to Aspen where he recovered.

Aspen prospered. Before long all the hoists and the lighting and the drills of the Aspen Mining Company were run by electricity. Part of the Aspen Tramway was used by electric cable cars.

Two blocks east of the Hotel Clarendon, the town's best, was born the Row. Here were situated the most spectacular and flamboyant entertainments in the valley. Each large, elegantly decorated house in the Row was in the charge of a sleek and commanding presence—the madam. With an iron fist and will, she ruled a bevy of beauties who supplied "affection" and "attention" to the miners and other men of Aspen—for a suitable price, of course.

Smaller houses, which came to be known as "soiled doves," were given such names as Frankie, Nellie, and Dollie, painted signs over the entrances identifying them to all comers. Attempts were made by disapproving townspeople to send the girls packing, but the Row remained in operation, an integral and colorful part of the local scene.

Higher forms of culture would not be denied, however. As the century moved to its close, Jerome B. Wheeler constructed a spectacular opera house. A King's Fool *was the inaugural performance. A racetrack came next at the edge of town. And in 1889, the Hotel Jerome opened.*

At this time, more than eleven thousand people lived in Aspen. Silver ore production was put at ten million dollars. There were ten churches, three schools, a hospital, three banks, a courthouse that was the architectural delight of the high country, and six newspapers.

The boom was short-lived. Disaster descended on the valley in 1893. Congress repealed the Sherman Act. Silver was demonetized. Banks closed, businesses failed, mines were shut down. Aspen withered and shrank to a fraction of its previous size, supported almost entirely by the ranches out in the valley. A picturesque little town, Aspen went to sleep, drowsing on into the twentieth century—alone, ignored, forgotten.

The bonanza was over.

Nine people lived in the house. They functioned as a family, with familial responsibilities, each contributing as best he or she could in work and in money. Since they were all adults, they were free to come and go as they liked without explanations. Nothing was demanded beyond a sense of obligation to the family and to the house. Each member was expected to do nothing that might cause physical or psychic harm to any other member. No one member of the house had more authority than the other members, but in times of stress they tended to look to Keating for advice. At such times, he assumed command naturally, leading his friends only where they truly wanted to go.

Keating and Annie were a couple. Two of the women were with each other. The other five made their own sleeping arrangements and occasionally one of them disappeared for days at a time or invited a guest to stay with him or her.

On this particular night, it was the men's turn to prepare the evening meal. Keating made pizza, using a whole wheat dough liberally dosed with two kinds of Italian cheese, anchovies, onions, scallions, and a sprinkle of chopped sausage. Someone else baked an apple pie that was served with whipped cream. And one of the women, on impulse, made vanilla ice cream which was offered around with homemade hot fudge. Pot was smoked before they ate and again afterwards.

It was a quiet, relaxing evening, and they listened to a Beethoven symphony and later some Bach, the air thick and still, no one talking much. Keating, his mind empty of all thoughts, sat with his back against the wall, allowing the music to absorb him. Annie put her head in his lap and after a while he reached absently for her, fingers curling into her hair. At first, when the doorbell rang, no one stirred. Then, an impatient knock.

"I'll go," Annie said.

"No." Keating arranged a pillow under her head and went to the door. Two men confronted him.

"Tom Keating, please," the taller of them said.

Keating looked them over. "I'm Keating."

"My name is Carl Osborne. This is Len Ralston. Could you spare me a few minutes of your time? I would have phoned, but there was no listing for you."

"No telephone. What's this about?"

"Wolf Run Valley," Ralston said aggressively.

Keating decided to ignore him. "What's this about?" he repeated.

Osborne smiled grimly. Keating was going to present some difficulty. "I'm with the Heggland Group. It's a holding company that—"

"I know about Heggland," Keating said. "I did a story about him a few years back for the *Washington Post*."

"You were a newspaperman? No one told me."

"I don't think Mr. Heggland enjoyed my article. He would have been hard pressed to take it as a compliment."

Osborne laughed. "Mr. Heggland never reads articles about himself. Nor permits anyone to tell him about them. He isn't given to concerning himself about the opinions of others."

"I believe that."

Osborne went on, hoping to soften Keating's obvious resistance without fawning. "The Group employs a high-power P.R. agency. An ad agency. A variety of public information people. None of them has ever succeeded in getting anyone to do a piece favorable to Heggland."

"He's a fascist," Keating said without emphasis.

"What the hell does that mean?" Ralston said angrily.

Osborne lifted one hand. "Heggland is tough. A strong man. He's incredibly shrewd and successful at everything he does. Those are qualities that seldom endear one man to others. He presents too much of a threat."

"He's a pig," Keating offered.

"Does that mean you won't talk to me?" Osborne said.

Keating tugged his beard, rubbed his cheek, pulled his ear. "We can talk. But there isn't much point to it. Whyever you came, we're not likely to see eye to eye. Come on inside and have a beer."

He preceded them into the kitchen. "Pearl's okay?" He brought three cans out of the refrigerator and placed them on the round oak table, drew up a chair, "Okay," he said, "you first."

"Since you know about Heggland," Osborne began, "I assume you know what I want to discuss with you."

Keating shrugged. "Rumors float around this place from day to day. None of them mean much. You tell me, and that way I'll know for sure."

"Wolf Run. We mean to develop the area."

"Why?"

"What do you mean, *why?*" Ralston snapped back. "Progress. Growth."

"Progress," Keating muttered. "Define your terms, Mr. Osborne."

"A higher standard of life in Aspen. More jobs. More money. A better future for everyone."

Keating tilted the can of Pearl's and drank. He wiped his mouth with the back of his wrist. To Osborne watching, it seemed almost an artificial gesture, one designed to put him off, to make Keating seem gross and coarse. Osborne didn't believe it for a minute.

"You don't buy it," Osborne said.

"More people will mean more garbage, more trees cut down, more crud on the land and in the air. That's not progress."

"Does that mean you've decided against the project?"

"It means only that I don't accept what you've offered me so far. You came here trying to influence me, to tip me in your direction. I don't intend to be tipped. When you make your presentation to the county commissioners, I'll study it, vote on it."

"There's a great deal involved here, Mr. Keating. Considerable sums have been spent already—"

"Not my affair."

"Time, effort. . ."

"Some people are satisfied to leave things as they are."

Osborne wished he hadn't come. Keating's attitudes might freeze, his resistance might harden beyond any possibility of change. Osborne didn't intend for that to happen. There were always ways to reach a man; the right way had to be found. He decided to try another tack.

"I spoke to the other commissioners earlier today."

"I heard about it."

"What did you hear?"

"Aspen's a small town, Mr. Osborne. Very few secrets around here."

"I see. Joe Chalk seems to like the idea of Wolf Run. He has the foresight to recognize the advantages that will accrue to the present residents of the valley."

"Joe Chalk is up for grabs, Osborne. You want his vote, you get it for a nickel and a dime. Okay, you've got one vote."

Osborne set his jaw. "That's not the way I do business, Mr. Keating."

Keating smiled a Cheshire smile, letting it fade slowly. "Business operates by buying people. People, governments, intelligence agencies; whatever it takes. We know that now. That's how you become ITT or United Fruit or the Heggland Group. You buy, you take, you manipulate. Chalk will get his eventually. Maybe you'll buy that scrubby piece of land he owns up valley. Maybe he'll hire on as a consultant at a generous fee. Maybe you'll just pay him off."

Osborne chose not to pursue the subject. "What about Maurice Lewin?"

Keating sat back. "Now there's a rare old bird. His own man. Not many of them around."

"My informants tell me he's your man."

Keating laughed briefly. "Tell it to Maurice. He's sixty-six years old, but I guarantee he'll flatten whoever lays that on him. Maurice is extremely warlike."

"I've checked the records. The way you vote is the way Lewin votes."

"I see it the other way around. I go with Maurice much of the time. Because he's so often correct."

"The word is Tom Keating is a pillar of moral strength. Defender of the environment. Keeper of the natural way. Protector of land, animal, and man alike."

Keating got himself another beer. This time he didn't offer any to the other men. He sat down and drank. And wiped.

"Hear us out, Keating," Osborne went on. "Study the plan. Weigh the advantages against the faults you find. We can change, improve, take out what you don't like. Don't kill the chicken for the one egg."

"I don't believe in killing anything."

"Don't judge us before you really know us. I don't intend to cut down trees with abandon. I don't intend to pollute the countryside. I don't intend to spread a blight over these incredible mountains."

"You'll do it anyway."

"Why won't you believe me?"

"The profit motive, Osborne. That's what moves you. Not anything else. You buy and sell, you exist by values that depend on your ability to do so. In another time you might have been a pirate, an adventurer, taking risks to find a variety of rewards, including gold. No more. Your kind takes no risks. You're indoor men who see no gain to be obtained by placing yourselves in jeopardy. You don't do things for the joy of doing them, but only for what it will bring you. Profit is your god, and your devil. You have no other reason for being."

Minutes later, they left. Once outside, Ralston

began to sputter in fury. "That son of a bitch is going to kill us."

"Not if we submit an honest plan. Not if he can see that our intentions are for the common good. . ."

"You don't believe that, do you?"

Osborne shot him a quick, hard look. "I have to believe that, or else it's over for us."

"There must be another way."

"For example?"

"I'm going to talk to Alex Budde. He's got a lot invested here, too. He knows his way around. He'll come up with something."

Osborne started to object; then he decided to say nothing. There were times when it was best to allow events to follow their natural course. If Ralston stepped out of line, he'd take care of him—later. The only thing that mattered was success. Anything less was intolerable.

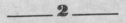

2

The Spot vibrated with sound. Tension flowed along jagged lines. Voices, clinking ice cubes, penetrating percussive sound. Strangers touched and pretended not to, waiting expectantly. Laughter screeched, died rapidly. Harsh expletives rose, dissolved, were sublimated.

Alex Budde advanced through the heaving mob without urgency. Behind him, moving step for step, pausing, altering direction, shifting back into motion, was Harry Rodano: moody, gloomily watchful, and dangerous.

Budde spoke a few words to a man, then to a woman, ordered a drink for an acquaintance, smiled, and departed, careful to make no permanent contact, no sticky arrangement.

Joan Carolinian, seated with two other women at a distant table, waved and came halfway out of her chair Budde gave no sign that he saw her, altering direction slightly, moving tangentially.

At the bar was Jon Osborne with a short plump woman Budde had never seen before. Budde didn't understand how anyone could allow himself to become involved with such a woman. A simpering, overanxious sort who almost frothed at the mouth as she babbled on. The appeared in Aspen in every season, frequently without their husbands. Rich and bored—desperate for attention, hungry for a body to share their beds. He imagined that Jon would draw a good price from such a woman; he was young, well built, good-looking. Budde walked past them without acknowledging Jon's quick searching look.

Through the kitchen and out the back door, along the alley and into the street. He went one block east, going past the county courthouse. In the light of day, the ancient red-brick structure displayed its age, along with the heavy designer's hand that had brought it into being. But night lent it an almost antique charm, a certain provincial cachet that appealed to some latent cultural pocket concealed deep inside Alex Budde. Len Ralston stood on the corner in front of the bank, smoking a cigarette. He ground it underfoot when he saw Budde.

"Let's walk," Budde said.

Ralston glanced back and spied Harry Rodano. "I don't like it, that guy shadowing us this way."

"Shadowing me," Budde corrected coldly. "He couldn't care less about you."

"Is he as dangerous as he looks?"

"Do yourself a favor, don't ever find out. Now why this meeting?"

"I thought it would be better not to get together where anybody would recognize us."

"Why'd you call?"

"Keating. The mother's going to destroy us."

"I told you he wouldn't play."

"He's dead set against Wolf Run."

"You couldn't expect it to be any other way. I warned you."

"Osborne wants to play it straight."

"Has he always been so stupid?"

"He managed to get pretty far. He's got his own rules."

"Everybody's got their own rules. That way nobody is bad—no evil people. We all justify our own actions, no matter how foul."

"There are times when you surprise me, Alex."

"Because I'm not as simple as you expected me to be? The shortcoming is yours."

Ralston was annoyed, but he set himself against feeling that way. He needed Budde, needed his ability to get things moving. He produced a pleasant voice. "There must be a way to reach Keating."

"Any suggestions?" Budde seemed distinterested.

"Money."

"You mean buy him off? Money doesn't concern him."

"I don't trust people who don't want money. It isn't natural."

Budde kept walking.

"What about blackmail?" Ralston said. "What have you got on Keating?"

Budde's mouth flapped open in a silent laugh. "He's living with a woman he's not married to."

"All *right!* That's something we can work on."

"She's knocked up," Budde said. "I found that out this afternoon."

"Great! We'll pin the sucker to the wall. We'll make him sorry he ever—"

"Don't be stupid. Who cares? Half the men in town are shacked up with chicks. And getting pregnant is no sin anymore. Where have you been, Ralston? 'The times they are a-changing,'" he crooned softly.

Ralston swore. "There must be a way. . ." His punished his brain. "Keating's a politician. His public image. . ."

"Forget it. The people who elected him, they dig his life-style, they won't be turned off by something they already know about, something they're all into."

"Chalk belongs to us. Lewin belongs to Keating. We've got to swing one of them."

In front of the Hotel Jerome, a guitarist mourned the passing of his love in an atonal plaint. Budde gave him a dollar and moved on.

"Can we scare him?" Ralston said.

"You met him. What do you think?"

Ralston jerked his thumb back to Rodano, thirty

feet behind. "Turn the goon loose on him. Give Keating a little muscle, something to think about."

Budde glanced at the other man. Alex's shining face was still and vaguely ominous in the light from a streetlamp. "You're coming close." He grinned, a flash of teeth, lips pulled tightly up. "What would your very moral Mr. Osborne say to what you're suggesting?"

Ralston swore. "I hate him. So damned superior. If we strike out, he's still okay. Vice-president in charge of making himself rich. He's not gonna get hurt. But what about Lenny Ralston? Still hanging on by his fingertips, I tell you. No place to go, no room to operate. This means a lot to me."

"In that case, I won't mention what you just said to Osborne."

Ralston stopped in place. Budde swung back, waiting patiently. "You're running a game on me, Budde. Why?"

"How far you willing to go?"

Ralston wet his lips. "That depends."

"On what?"

"On what I get out of it."

Budde examined him at length. "You're not as tough as Osborne."

"Don't kid yourself."

"I never do. Tell me what you want done with Keating. Give me the word, Ralston. Say it out loud. I want to hear it from your mouth."

Ralston shuddered, and Budde smiled mirthlessly.

"All right, do it."

"Do what, Ralston?"

"Get rid of Keating."

"How?"

"All right!" he said, fighting to keep his voice in place. "Kill him. There, I said it, kill him."

Budde began to walk again. "What if that doesn't accomplish our purpose? It will mean a new commissioner has to be appointed. The new man might be another Keating."

"I doubt it," Ralston said dryly. "I'm sure you'll find some means of preventing that, of getting our kind of man in."

"Well," Budde said, turning abruptly, "this has been a very interesting talk. See you around."

Back in his office at the Spot, Budde made a phone call. A voice came on.

"Police headquarters. Officer Brent."

"Sergeant Sexton, please."

"Not here. Want him to call back?"

Budde hung up, unlocked his desk drawer, and extracted a leather notebook. He located the page he wanted and began calling the numbers listed. No one answered the first two calls he made. On the third call, a woman listened to his question, barked out a brusque, "not here," and hung up. He made two more tries before he got lucky.

"Sexton, please?" he said.

"Who wants him?"

In the background, he could hear Sexton say grumpily, "Is that for me? Goddamn. Hand it over. How many times you have to be told, just hand it over."

"Sexton," Budde said, "I want to see you."

"When?"

"Soon as you can make it."

"Thirty minutes. The usual place?"

"That's right."

Budde let five minutes tick off on the digital

clock on his desk; then he went outside and made
the rounds of the Spot again. He noticed that Jon
Osborne was no longer at the bar, nor was the
short woman he'd been with. The kid had no taste,
no control, and no future. A lot different from his
father. What would Osborne say if he knew Jon
was a mule? That piece of information might be
worth something one day, he thought, as he
stepped out into Hopkins Street.

Harry Rodano counted slowly from one to
twenty before going after his boss.

The Blondell Gallery was locked. The pieces of
wood sculpture on pedestals throughout the long
space cast eerie shadows in the dim light that
came from the back room. Budde knocked and,
when there was no response, he rattled the doorknob. He knocked again. Skip Blondell opened the
door, his pale face displaying relief.

"Oh, Alex, it's you."

"Who were you expecting?" Budde walked inside. Blondell started to close the door behind him.
Budde placed an outstretched hand against it. Five
beats later, Harry Rodano entered. "Okay," Budde
said, "close it up."

Budde walked straight toward the soft light.

"Oh, Alex," Blondell called, hurrying after him,
"let's talk out here."

"You're not alone." It was not a question.

A sheepish grin raised the corners of Blondell's
thin mouth. "Ah, Alex, you know how it is."

A figure appeared in the rectangle of light that
led to the back room. A slender youth materialized
and quickly faded out of sight, a featureless ap-
parition.

"You make me sick," Budde said.

"Alex, Alex, it's only for laughs."

"You'd put it into a pig, if you had the chance. You're disgusting."

"You don't understand how it is with someone like me, Alex."

Budde lowered his voice. "Did you take care of that delivery?"

Blondell drew back. He'd seen Alex Budde frustrated and angry, knew how terrifying he could be. A glance reminded him of Harry Rodano standing in the shadows, all-powerful and menacing. Blondell shivered.

"It's been so busy here, Alex," he explained. "The new show and all. I've got about half cut and—"

"There's half a kilo left?"

"I'll have it for you tomorrow night for sure."

"Pack it up again, like it's going to be shipped out."

Blondell felt instant relief. "Whatever you say, Alex."

Budde stepped closer to the other man, breathing in the faint scent of his body, the stale, sweet odor of pot that clung to him, and the smell of sex. He braced himself, spoke rapidly. "I've a job I want done. . ."

Blondell's eyes rolled, his mouth worked. "Trouble, Alex? I'm no good with trouble. I've never been a fighter, you know. I'm temperamentally unsuited."

"Shut up and listen. Do it exactly the way I tell you and everything will be all right."

Blondell started to reply, thought better of it, and listened hard.

3

The cool night air helped to clear the passages in Jon's head. But the dizziness remained. He promised himself to cut down on the booze. Liquor wasn't his style; it made him cumbersome and hostile, left him weary and hung over. Pot on the other hand was exhilarating, created a happy and good feeling in him the next day.

"Your car or mine?" the little plump woman said, clinging to his hand. Her skin was moist and warm and he thought about walking away. He decided against it. Rudeness was not in order.

"I drive a jeep," he said, face tilting lopsidedly.

She drew him along the street. "We've got a Caddy. Plenty of space in the back seat."

She was right. He was able to slump down, stretching his legs across the width of the car. She launched herself at him immediately, hands stroking his chest and sides, shifting onto his flat belly.

"Ah," she said, breathing into his face. She smelled of stale tobacco. "Ah, that's nice."

He wanted to postpone it, to turn her off. "I don't even know your name?"

"It's Wassick. My husband introduced us."

"Your first name."

"Helen."

"Where you from, Helen?"

"You can't be more than eighteen," she said hopefully.

"Nineteen."

"I could be your mother." She giggled, tugging his shirt out of his trousers. "I've got a daughter your age."

"Maybe I ought to date her."

"Don't be dirty." She pressed her palms against his naked torso. "Ah—" she moaned. "Ah, how I love young flesh."

"Are you always in this much of a rush?"

"How much time do you think we've got? Jack is good for twenty minutes with that guy he met, then he'll come looking for me. He's got a terrible temper, Jack."

"Then maybe another time. . ."

"You're not frightened of Jack, are you? He's twice your age and half your size."

"I don't like violence."

"Well, Jack is violent. He beats me regularly."

"That's awful." He tried to tuck his shirt back in his pants. She pulled it loose. "Mrs. Wassick!" he protested.

She pressed her cheek against his crotch. He responded in spite of himself.

"Say," she said admiringly, "you are a terrific stud."

"Not really."

"Don't kid me." She worked the zipper down.

"I'm really a bust. A disappointment. I know a guy who'd be just right. . ."

"Listen," she said with some heat, "are you out here for conversation or action? I get all the talk I want back home."

"Well, maybe. . ."

She managed to get onto her knees on the floor of the Cadillac, pulling hard at his trousers, his undershorts. "Oh, God!" she said thickly. Her lips pressed against him, tongue flicking. "You—taste —sweet. . ."

He lay back and felt nothing.

"Tell me," she said presently.

"What?"

"Do you like what I'm doing?"

"Terrific."

"You really mean it?"

"I mean it."

"I'm so excited."

"So am I."

"You know what I'd like?" She fumbled with her panty hose, shifting, pushing, pulling. "Do me, please, do me. . ."

"That's not my thing."

"I did you."

"Nobody forced you."

"Bastard."

He sat up and began to adjust his trousers.

"Oh, what are you doing?" Alarm brought her voice to a shrill.

"It's over."

"No, no. Not yet, please not yet."

She fondled him, flung herself across the seat, head between his legs, moaning, promising to be obedient, to perform as desired, to provide rare and exotic pleasures.

He wished she would get it over with. As if in response, she drew him into her mouth, working feverishly now.

Jon felt his passion rise and he turned to allow her more convenient access. Neither of them saw

Jack Wassick come up to the Cadillac. Suddenly the door flew open.

"What's going on!" Jack Wassick shouted. He had a heavy voice for such a small man. His oval face was flushed, drool spilling over his lips. "Oh, you whore! You swore last time was the last time. Look at you, sucking off this prick you don't even know."

"Get the hell out of here, Jack!" She looked up, expression tight and fierce, protective. "Mind your own business. We made a deal."

"You're my wife."

"A deal's a deal."

"Nobody ever said it was going to be this way. In the back seat of my own car."

"You only live up to your deals when they're to your benefit. Stay and watch, if you want to."

Jon tried to pull his trousers up. She fought him, thrusting herself back down. "Ah, damn, look what you've done, Jack. It's gone all soft and little."

"Cocksucker!" he shrieked, grabbing her by the hair.

She broke loose and threw a punch at him, missing. He hit her in the mouth. Blood began to drip.

"Oh, no," Jon groaned. He crawled over her trying to make it to the door on the opposite side.

She grabbed and held on, nails biting into his thigh. "Don't go!" she shouted.

Jack hit her again, set her flat on the seat. Then he cursed Jon. "You're nothing but a cock for her to work on. One young cock or another, it makes no difference to a cocksucker." He punched Jon on the ear. A glancing blow, it stung, made his brain revolve swiftly.

Jon ducked and pushed himself across Helen Wassick's squirming form toward her husband. He grabbed the little man, yanked him into the car, shaking him. "Cut it out! No hitting. These things happen."

"Help!" Wassick cried. "Help! Police!"

"Shut up, dammit."

Jon tumbled to the street, worked his pants up around his waist, tried to run.

Wassick came after him, fists swinging wildly. "Help, police! Muggers! Rapists! Help!"

Jon struck back in swift anger. Wassick clutched his nose, fell to his knees, and began to weep. Jon started to say something, decided it was not a good time for conversation, and ran. He didn't stop until his lungs were scorched for lack of oxygen and his heart pounded wildly in his chest. He collapsed on somebody's neatly manicured lawn and fell back, looking up at the stars and laughing wildly.

Everything. . .

. . .was so. . .

. . .sad.

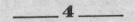

——— 4 ———

Kit Pepe and Carl Osborne were the only remaining diners in a private room in the Parlour Car Restaurant, a restored nineteenth-century railroad car. They had had an excellent meal and now lingered over coffee and brandy.

"I appreciate your having dinner with me," Osborne said. "I hesitated about calling you, imposing. . ."

"There is no imposition. You said you wanted to talk about Jon."

"I guess I've been avoiding it all evening, making small talk. Talking about myself."

"Guardedly, I'd say."

He looked into his glass, and she took the opportunity to study him. There was a definition to his face, a sense of character formed and hardened by experience; Jon lacked that. And, she suspected, always would. Carl was beyond being handsome, though his features were perfectly formed. The almost petulant set of his mouth, the slight downturn that made his nose an angry thrust, the way his eyes looked steadily out from under heavy lids. All turned it into a face not easy to forget. He was a startlingly attractive man who made her feel very feminine, and that created a deep uneasiness in her. At the same time, she was pleased that a man was able to move her emotionally. She reminded herself that he was Jon's father, old enough to be her own parent. She was amused that she had had to remind herself, and having done so, she realized that she didn't really care.

"Let's talk about Jon," she said.

"Are you sure you won't mind?"

"I'm sure."

He opened his mouth to speak, stopped, went on with a hesitancy that was not natural to him. Her presence made him uncomfortable, as if she sat in judgment and as if pleasing her was vital to his welfare. He found that reaction odd, since they hardly knew each other, might never see each other again.

"There's so much between Jon and me that's never been said."

"Perhaps it's meant to be that way between parents—unbridgeable gulfs."

"Is it like that with your father and mother?"

"They're dead."

"I'm sorry."

"Don't be. They lived out their time according to what they believed. That's about all any of us can do, I suppose."

"They must have died young."

"Yes. But their lives were full, fuller than most people."

"They were lucky then."

"Isn't your life full, Mr. Osborne?"

"Carl," he corrected. She nodded her assent, waited for him to reply. "Sometimes I think it is, other times not. Lately, well—there are periods of dissatisfaction, as if some vital element is missing."

"If you and Jon grew closer. . ."

"I wish it would happen. Time, different experiences, a variety of influences, they all work to separate people. Jon and I exist in different worlds."

"Which doesn't mean you can't make contact, exchange ideas, make an emotional connection."

"You make it sound so easy."

"Not easy, but possible."

He stared at her, eyes traveling over her face, dropping once to her breast, lifting quickly. But not so quickly that she didn't notice and grow uncomfortably warm. "You and Jon," he said, "so

damned young. The two major influences of my life
were the Great Depression and the Second World
War, far removed from you. Yet neither one involved me directly. They shaped the way my parents thought and felt about life, and all that came
down on me."

"I understand—education is the answer to all
problems. Work hard. Get ahead. Make money."

He smiled. "Somebody's been telling you my
secrets."

"I've spoken to men of your generation before.
Men and women who were caught up in the depression, who fought in the war."

"Sometimes I think I've been trapped by other
people's needs rather than my own."

"That happens."

"Not to you. Not to Jon."

"Are you so certain?"

"Well, from what I hear of this younger generation, you're different."

"You make yourself out to be an old man."

"Next to you. . ." He let it hang.

She grew thoughtful. "Age is a reality. But
being old has little to do with years. Burdens become too heavy to support. The future is in back
of you. . ."

"That's interesting. I feel that my future still
lies out front."

"That's encouraging."

"You're very young. So much time to do whatever you want to do. All of it still to come. . ."

"Being young may not be as rewarding as some
people pretend. Youth too has its problems."

"Are you all that glum?"

"Not glum, not euphoric. Do you know *The
Waste Land*?"

"T. S. Eliot?"

"Yes." She quoted: "'April is the cruellest month. . .'." Her lips moved slightly as if to smile, then pulled quickly down. "For most of us, spring is a time of rebirth, or replenishment. Eliot says it is a time that stirs dull roots. Winter kept us warm in a forgetful snow. Forgetful. Eliot was a young man when he wrote that. Some people find the forgetful winter of life much preferable to a dawning spring. . ."

"You among them?"

"In my lesser moments."

"Moral to be drawn: Stop sounding off about your troubles, Osborne."

"Did I say that?"

"You are a fascinating young woman."

She responded brightly, "At least you aren't calling me a girl."

"Let me be personal for a moment, Kit. Nuances are not natural to me. I tend to be bullish."

"Fire away."

"I would like to know about your relationship with Jon."

"What would you like to know?"

"A romance?"

"Jon would like it to be."

"And you?"

"I value his friendship."

"I see." He made an effort to picture his friends. To make a listing. The page in his mind remained empty. He knew many people. Men and women alike. Spent time with them, did business with them, argued politics and philosophy with them, went to bed with them. But no solid sentiment attached itself to any of the relationships. No closeness or warmth. No friendliness. "Tell me what you know about Jon."

"There's little I can say that you don't already know."

"He left home nearly two years ago."

"Being his own man is important to Jon."

"I don't understand him." Osborne laughed lightly. "The classic lament of a rejected parent— my child doesn't understand me. Well, there it is. No understanding on either side."

"I agree."

"Do you understand boys like Jon? Where is he going?"

"Maybe he doesn't want to go anywhere. Maybe he just wants to be."

"Be what?"

"Himself, nothing more."

"Who stops him?"

"You, me, the world. Himself. He's very angry."

"Why?"

"It's classic, isn't it?"

Osborne rocked his head from side to side. "Anything I were to say about us, about our family, would be an American cliché, I'm afraid."

She waited for him to continue.

"You don't give much, Kit."

"I may not have as much to give as you think."

"I believe otherwise. In my business—well, you get to knew people, read them pretty quickly if you intend to survive, or to prevail."

"And you think you read me?"

"You're bright, perceptive, and pretty damned deep."

"That's a superficial judgment."

"Maybe only superficially superficial."

Her smile came without warning, electric and charming, making him want to smile back at her. "Score one for your side," she said.

"The truth is," he went on, "you cause me to feel young, to make me think you have lived and experienced more—"

"We're both exactly the right ages for ourselves."

He grunted, choosing not to pursue it further. "Maybe no one can help me with Jon. Maybe it's too late for us to be close, to be father and son in any meaningful way. But I don't want to accept that. I must keep trying."

"His anger is very deep."

"What is he so angry about? We loved him. Raised him as decently as we knew how. Mistakes? Hell, yes. Mistakes are part of living. Which of us doesn't blow it now and then? I love my son, want him to come home, go back to school, make his way in some productive profession. . ."

"Do what you've done?"

"What's wrong with that?"

"Is that what Jon wants, to emulate you?"

"I don't know what he wants."

She spoke in a distant voice. "Why not try to find out."

She chose to cut the evening short before Osborne was ready. He made tentative efforts to prolong it, but she held to her course.

"Is my company so oppressive?" he said.

They were slowly, yet steadily, walking toward the institute. She glanced over at him. "Self-pity doesn't sit well on you."

"Okay. I was trying to manipulate you. Why not a nightcap?"

"Because I have to be up and out early in the morning."

"A lecture to a company of paunchy business-men?"

"Hang gliding," she answered. She was amused at the puzzled expression on his face. "Self-launched free flight, if you prefer a more technical term." She giggled and at once was almost girlish and incredibly appealing. "There, you see, that's my pretentious side. Imagine a glider, a sort of oversized kite, with a flyer hanging below. Hang gliding. . ."

"It sounds dangerous."

"To some degree."

"Aren't you afraid?"

"Of an accident?"

"Of being killed."

"I don't let myself go on about that. Part of the joy in gliding lies in how close to disaster you function. That's where the accomplishment is."

"It sounds like my attitude about my work."

They continued on their way. "Would it be all right if I went along in the morning?" he said.

"Why?"

"For the fun of it. That should be reason enough. And an excuse to spend some more time with you."

She lifted her shoulders, let them fall. "I'm leaving quite early."

"When?"

"I'll come around to your hotel at five o'clock."

He produced a mock groan, smiling all the time.

5

A mattress on the floor served them as a bed. Next to it, a high-intensity lamp and an ashtray, a can partly filled with warm beer. Keating lay on his back, head propped on a pillow, staring at the ceiling. Annie slept cradled in his arm. When he reached for the beer, she stirred.

"Something the matter, luv?" Her voice was a slow caress in the dark. She put her face against his chest, pursed her lips, but she was too sleepy to complete the kiss.

"Nothing's wrong," he said. He drank some beer, put the can aside.

"You're beautiful, Tom."

"Try to sleep, you need the rest."

"So good for me. Making it with you always is, like never before for me."

"You talk too much," he said gently.

"Is it good for you, Tom?"

"Every time. Better than good."

"Even now?"

"Especially now."

"Some men are turned off by pregnant women, can't stand to be near them."

"How would you know that?"

"I've heard stories."

154

"There are stories about everything."

"You really don't mind?"

"I don't mind."

"Maybe later you will, when I'm big and lumpy."

"No chance."

"How can you be sure? Have you ever done it with a pregnant lady? Somebody seven months along?"

"No."

"So you can't be sure."

"I'm sure."

"What makes you think so?"

"You turn me on."

"I do?"

He laughed softly.

"Stop laughing at me," she demanded without force.

"You amuse me."

"You always laugh at me when I get romantic."

"I always laugh when you say things like that."

"What things?"

"I love you," he said.

"You do?"

"Yes."

"Honestly?"

He laughed again. "When I say anything complimentary—how I feel about you, or how beautiful you are, or how it is for me when we're together— you question it. Honest? You do? Do you really mean it? Happens all the time."

"I guess I'm not as secure as I might be."

"You're pretty fantastic."

"Really?"

She pressed her neatly trimmed fingernails into his side. But not too hard. "Beast," she murmured.

He held her and they laughed and squirmed against each other for a while. Presently, they quieted and she fell asleep.

He finished the beer and craved another but was afraid he'd wake her if he got up. He closed his eyes and willed sleep to come; it wouldn't. Suddenly, a small sound outside the house trickled into his consciousness. His eyes rolled open and his senses grew sharp. Another sound. A shuffling noise, perhaps a footfall. He carefully separated himself from Annie, got up, and went over to the window.

Beyond the woodpile, where the cars were parked, he saw a pale figure backing out of the Volkswagon. Without a sound, the door was eased shut. This done, the figure floated off into the night, disappearing in the direction of the downhill trail.

Keating put on his trousers, a wool shirt, and some Indian moccasins and went outside, carrying a flashlight. He examined the VW. It perched in place like the harmless beige lump it was. Five years old, with more than sixty thousand miles put in, it displayed the scars of time and distance. It protested whenever he tried to start it, but it started. It had long ago lost whatever pickup it once possessed, it trembled and rocked in the slightest breeze, it threatened to collapse under any pressure, but it continued to get Keating around. Why would anyone sneak around the bug at this hour. Surely not to steal the old wreck.

On hands and knees, he examined the underside of the car. Nothing showed. He looked in the trunk. A few old tools, a worn spare tire. He aimed the flashlight inside the car. The usual clutter met his eye. Papers, empty beer cans, road maps.

Something was different. A subtle change that disturbed his sense of order in the disorder. He looked again. The rear seat, by nature loose in its place, a subject of repeated complaints from Annie, was situated securely in its proper position. The night visitor had been extremely neat.

The car contained nothing of value. Why had he come? It occurred to Keating that he might be thinking the wrong way. What if the prowler had come not to take something but to leave something?

But what?

And why?

He worked his way inside the VW, into the rear compartment. He eased the seat up. The battery sat in its normal place, everything in proper arrangement. He moved the light beam around and was about to give up when something caught his eye. He lifted out a precisely wrapped rectangle and considered it for a time, putting a series of questions to himself. When he had answers to every one, he replaced the seat, climbed out of the car, package in hand, and went back to bed. Very quickly he was asleep.

6

Brenner's Ledge hung off an unnamed peak back in the Elk Range, turned south-southwest, and peered into an open valley some four or five thousand feet below. It was as if the mountain simply ceased to exist, terminating abruptly in a sharply drawn edge that might have been cut with a rule.

From the ledge, the valley took on the appearance of a soft green trough, broken only once by a winding logger's trail, long since left unused. Across the valley, a thin ribbon of road edged by a line of high-tension wires made its way back toward Aspen. Beyond the road was a golden meadow and beyond that, Haskell Lake, which in fact was slightly larger than a small pond.

Standing a dozen or so feet back from the razor-like edge of Brenner's Ledge were Osborne, Kit Pepe, and Bill Heller, the flight instructor. A short, tightly knit man with clear eyes and large, strong hands, Heller seemed to be measuring the unseen wind.

"You're not actually going off here," Osborne said, alarm in his voice.

Kit only nodded. The clutch of fear in her throat was kept in check solely by her determination. "I'm going," she managed to say.

"Conditions will never be any better," Heller pointed out. "But if you have any doubts, Kit. . ."

"Either I go now, or I may never do it."

"It's your choice."

"I'm going."

Osborne wanted to protest, to tell her that she was insane, courting death in such a manner. But up here in the thin, cool air, the sun splashing its white morning rays on the peaks, one got the feeling that all things were possible. That man was indeed meant for loftier enterprises than hugging safely to the ground. Nevertheless, he was afraid for Kit, and he told her so.

"It's not so different from some of my other flights," she reassured him. "Only the numbers are different. The launching point is higher, the drop more pronounced, the flight longer."

"It's new to you, Mr. Osborne," Heller said, "but hang gliding in one form or another is as old as time. The Greeks made myths about self-propelled flights. Da Vinci explored the possibilities. Almost all the early flight pioneers were hang pilots. Even the Wright brothers."

"What if something goes wrong with the glider?" Osborne persisted.

Heller smiled. "The aircraft is in perfect shape. I assembled it myself. Inspected the joints, tested the connections, the struts, the harness. Nothing will go wrong. If I tell you a little about gliders, it may ease your fears. This is a fixed-wing type. There is also the Rogallo, which looks like a sail or a kite."

"What's the difference?"

"Fixed wing has a glide ratio of ten to one, and it provides a much better performance. The L/D ratio permits you a longer flight."

"L/D?"

"Lift and drag. In order for the craft to fly, lift has to exceed drag. The more it does, the better the flight. Mix in maneuverability and stability."

"You're confusing him, Bill," Kit said.

"Right. Let's leave it at this—the Rogallo is excellent to learn on; fixed wing is for the more experienced flyer."

"Wouldn't a ski run be a good place for this?" Osborne said.

"Yes. A lot of hang gliding goes on in winter. Or in summer on flat land behind a car on a towline. Or on water, behind a powerboat."

"And here?"

"Here you just take her over the side."

Osborne made a face. "One mistake. . ."

"Mistakes happen," Heller said. "We try to eliminate them by practice, by instruction, by gradually working up to a flight of this proportion. The glider is ready. Kit is ready. By temperament, she isn't a person to panic. She has excellent control of her body and her mind. If something does go wrong, she knows how to correct it, to compensate, to adjust."

"Conditions are good, too," Kit put in.

Osborne glanced down at the valley far below. "Both of you seem certain of that," he said, voice slightly sardonic. "I'm not convinced that what you're doing will ever be good."

Heller made a gesture toward the drop. "You could take off here without any wind at all, Mr. Osborne, drift right down into the landing zone. No sweat. . ."

"What about those power lines?" Osborne said.

"Good point," Heller conceded. "They crisscross the countryside. However, we allowed for them in our calculations."

"And the wind?"

"Running about eight miles per hour," Heller said. "That means Kit has to maintain an airspeed no greater than seven miles an hour to stay aloft."

Osborne turned it over in his mind. "Are you saying it takes a minimum flying speed of fifteen miles an hour to stay up?"

"Exactly."

"And if the wind diminishes?"

"Adjustments can be made by shifting weight forward or backward. Move up front and airspeed increases, and vice versa."

"What about sudden gusts?" Osborne recalled his flight into Aspen, the way the plane was tossed about over the mountains. "Mountain air is not famous for stability."

"Kit's going to encounter some turbulence. It should remain mild."

"Okay," Osborne said resignedly. "You go off the ledge, begin your descent. . ."

"Not exactly," Kit said.

"I don't understand."

Heller answered. "Kit is going to try soaring this morning--riding the air currents. I soared off a desert mountain about a year ago and it was an unbelievable experience. The heat buildup created thermals, which are bubbles of hot air rising through the cooler air. In the desert, you have the time and range to locate the thermals, to fly like an eagle—soaring, swooping, rising to heights, and doing it all over again."

"I still don't like it."

"Altitude works as a safety cushion," Kit said. "In case something does go wrong, you have time to correct even the worst possible mistakes."

"This *is* a risk activity," Heller pointed out.

"Too risky for me," Osborne said.

"The important thing is to strike a balance between uncertainty and control. Okay, to glide is to accept a challenge."

"I encounter challenge in my work every day," Osborne said. "Personal risk, too."

"But not bodily risk," Kit said in a low voice.

Osborne glanced over at her, trying to determine if he'd detected some criticism in her tone. "All right, I've stopped having a love affair with danger. That's behind me. But there are all kinds of combat to engage in without killing yourself."

"Death is the supreme adversary," Heller said soberly. "Adventure is out of style in our world—but not completely..."

"You believe we've become too domesticated," Osborne said.

"I believe in entertaining certain risks," Kit said.

"We're back to the challenge," Osborne said.

"Yes," Heller answered. "Some people are goaded by a grotesque idea of what bravery is all about. *They* make terminal mistakes. *They* pay the heaviest price. At the core of most injuries, or even death, is pilot error. Bad judgment. Flying when the wind is too fierce or unpredictable, for example. Launching from a point that allows too small a margin for error. Training, experience, judgment; these produce safe and satisfying flights." Heller squinted out into the void. "We've talked long enough. It's time for Kit to get off. Are you ready?"

She nodded solemnly. "Let's go."

—— 7 ——

Keating sized the belt to the customer's waist, cut it down, ground the tongue to shape on the power wheel, and darkened the exposed raw edge with a rich brown stain. Finally, he punched five holes in the leather. The customer put it on, expressed his satisfaction, paid for it, and left.

Keating dropped the money in the cash drawer and entered the transaction in his record book. He turned his attention to a billfold he had been working on earlier. Five minutes later, Jim Sexton entered the shop, trim and muscular in uniform. There was an aggressive cockiness to Sexton—in the way his clothes fit him, the way he wore his hat, the way the pistol rode on his belt.

"Morning, Tom."

"Good morning, Sexton." Keating began lacing the outer edge of the billfold.

"You do nice work, Tom."

"Appreciate your saying so."

Sexton displayed his large white teeth in a cheerless grin. His dark eyes glowed with an almost vengeful triumph.

"Guess you're wondering why I'm here, Mr. Commissioner."

Keating raised his great head, scratched at his chin through the black beard. "Never wondered at all, Sexton. We're not friends, and I can't think of any reason to expect an official visit from the law."

"You're cool, really cool. I can appreciate that."

"You here to consult me in my official capacity as county commissioner, Sexton? You interested in some leatherwork? Or did you just drop in to rap a little?"

Sexton's face hardened. "Mind if I look around, Tom?"

"You mean, search my shop?"

"Just a friendly look, Tom."

"You have a warrant?"

"I could get one fast enough."

"By then I'd've dumped whatever it is you be-lieve I have. No, you can't take the time for a war-rant, Sexton. You meant to creep up on me, a quiet stalk."

"Do you cooperate or not?"

Keating smiled. "Go ahead. Look around. If you see anything you'd like to buy, let me know."

Sexton looked into corners, supply drawers, and cabinets, searched behind the machinery. Swift, sure, superficial. He came back to Keating.

"That your car out front, Tom?"

"The Volks, Sexton? Yes, it's mine. But you knew that already."

"Mind if I check it out?"

"Help yourself. Never do lock it."

Sexton, disturbed by the other man's easy man-ner, hesitated before going out into the street. He went directly into the car, lifted out the rear seat, examined the well. After a few minutes, he re-entered the shop.

"Someday you'll outsmart yourself, Keating," he said grimly.

"Wouldn't surprise me."

"How'd you know?" Sexton said.

Keating lifted his brows, made no reply.

"You were *expecting* me," Sexton said.

"The word is you are on somebody's payroll. Anything to that, Sexton?"

Sexton's face jammed up, his eyes glittering in frustration and anger. "Don't push too hard, mister. It'd be a mistake to underestimate me."

"I wouldn't make that mistake, Sexton. You're a threat, a danger, a menace to law and order. The town can't afford men like you."

Sexton acted startled. "You threatening me?"

"Time is running out for you and your friends."

Sexton squeezed the tension out of his body. He stepped back. "I'm civil service, Mr. Commissioner. Protected by all the rights of the municipal statutes." In the doorway, he looked back. "You have had it, Tom, you really have."

Keating sat behind the counter for a long time. Then he walked to the door, locked it, and hung the Closed sign. He needed solitude. Time to consider what was happening. And why. Time to make a plan. To shape his next move. There was going to be trouble and he wanted to be prepared.

----- 8 -----

Skip Blondell squatted back in the woods, concealed from idle eyes, but in position to watch the fly-fishermen as they went after trout in the Roaring Fork River. There was a lazy grace to the way they snapped their lines, flicking flies to the water, tantalizing the fish below.

But the results made Blondell angry. The fish were entitled to remain in their native environment, to swim, to feed, to reproduce. The fishermen dragged them, squirming and struggling, into the world of human beings, doomed to die. Live and let live. Why couldn't it be that way? Hunters, fishermen, soldiers. All killing was wrong.

A huge black fly buzzed insistently around Blondell's head, landed on his cheek. He flicked it away.

It returned. He slapped at it. The fly persisted. Finally, Blondell moved to another position. The fly went after him. He cursed the fly, wishing it dead. In its own good time, the fly flew away.

Footsteps coming in his direction startled him, and for a hysterical moment he was unable to remember where he was or why he had come. When he saw Sexton, it all came back. The phone call that had summoned him, brought him to this place for this meeting. He wished it weren't Sexton. Sexton was a man who enjoyed carrying a gun and was fully capable of using it. How many people had Sexton shot, maimed, killed? Blondell shuddered and acknowledged his fear of the law officer. He calmed himself with the thought that most people frightened him.

Blondell stood up and greeted Sexton with a determined smile. "Hi, Jim, what's happening, man?"

Sexton came on silently, the bony face grimly set. Without a word of warning, he drove his fist into Blondell's soft belly. The little art dealer went down, making strange strangulated sounds. Sexton dragged him erect, shook him, slapped his face a couple of times, and cast him aside. Blondell lay on the ground moaning and weeping.

Sexton hunkered down nearby waiting for Blondell to revive, occasionally tossing small stones at his head.

"You shouldn't hit me," Blondell complained. He worked himself up into a sitting position.

"I ought to waste you, shithead." Sexton's voice was flat, low, full of threat.

"You almost did." Pain radiated from Blondell's navel through to his spine. He thought he might throw up; if so, he intended to puke all over Sexton's shiny boots.

Sexton took out his service revolver. He jabbed the muzzle against Blondell's ear. "I'd blow your brains out, if you had any brains."

"What did I do?"

Sexton holstered the weapon. "Keating," he said.

"I planted the stuff."

Sexton raised his fist, and Blondell flinched.

"Don't lie to me." Sexton said.

"I did it, honest."

"Where?"

"In the car. Under the back seat, like you told me to do. Next to the battery."

"It wasn't there."

Blondell put his face in his hands and waited for another blow.

"He must of found it," Sexton said.

Blondell saw a ray of hope. "Maybe the battery went dead on him and he had to get it charged. That way he saw the package. It could've been that way."

"No," Sexton said. "You were spotted."

"No! I was quiet, very quiet."

"Keating spotted you. After you split, he got the stuff out."

Guilt and fear enveloped Blondell and he wanted to cry, fearful of future punishment. "Don't tell Alex, Jim. Please."

"If it was me, I'd burn you. You're as useless as tits on a boar."

"Ah, Jim, you don't really mean it. . ." But he did; and both of them knew it.

Back in his gallery, Blondell made tea. It soothed his tingling nervous system. All his life, it seemed, he had been forced to deal with men like Sexton. Mean, violent men; animals who enjoyed inflicting pain; men quick to anger and willing to use any weapon to reduce an enemy to a slimy pulp. Sexton was the worst of them. He made Blondell feel helpless and weak, sharpening the pervading sense of inadequacy that so often gripped him. There had to be some way to avoid all dealings with Sexton. Of course! He would talk to Alex Budde, ask him to keep them apart. It was a small request, and certainly Budde would react reasonably to it. He would ask him. Soon.

He lit a joint and wished somebody would come to visit him, to assuage the loneliness he felt. A new chick—one with a really swinging ass and terrific boobs. He would convince her to model for him, get her to strip down. Take pictures of her in crazy poses. Shoot right up the old alley...

The image pleased him and he let it linger, dwelled on the possibilities. When the door opened, he told himself that his wish was about to come true. Someone beautiful coming to please and soothe him. To gentle him down, get rid of the tension. When he recognized Scooter Lewis, he groaned.

"Hey, man!" Scooter began.

"You look awful," Blondell said. It was true. Scooter's elongated face seemed longer than ever, bloated, rutted, depressed, eyes rolling freely. His long fingers played a silent tune on the air.

"Skipper, you are hard to reach. I telephoned."

"I was out. Big deal going down."

"I need some stuff."

Something about Scooter Lewis's apparent helplessness, his pleading, served to increase Blondell's disdain. As if in the presence of a greater weakness, Blondell grew vengeful and charged with rage. "I got nothing for you," he lied.

"I've got the dough. Look here." Scooter dragged paper money from his pockets. "I can get more."

"The cupboard is bare, Scooter."

"Name your price."

"I told you how it is." The warm bath of power caused a new headiness in Blondell. He pressed his advantage. "Look at you, a famous writer. You disgust me."

Scooter shuffled forward. "I'm all messed up."

"Go away, freak."

"You've got the stuff, I know you have." Scooter's eyes darted around. "Where do you keep it?"

"Get off my back, man."

"I have to have a fix."

"Fuck off."

Scooter lifted a pillow on the bed, tossed it aside. He looked under the mattress. Blondell giggled. "Keep going, for all the good it's going to do you."

"Where?"

"Keep looking, freak."

Scooter swept the bookcase clean of books.

"Knock it off!" Blondell yelled.

Scooter explored the record player, top and bottom, sent it crashing to the floor.

"You ruined it!" Blondell screeched. He climbed on the bed, jumped up and down. "Get out of here, you crazy freak! Get out of my place."

Blondell leaped to the floor, advancing on the writer with all the stiff-legged aggressiveness of a horny hound. He waved his fists wildly, clutched his head in despair, pounded the air in furious futility.

Scooter ignored him. He cast about for a likely hiding place. In the bathroom, he scattered toothpaste and hair oil and after-shave lotion to the tile floor. A cloying mixture of scents wafted into the gallery.

"Stop it!" Blondell shrilled, trailing after Scooter.

Scooter crashed back, went to the nearest door.

"My darkroom!" cried Blondell. "Stay away! Stay away!"

Scooter plunged inside.

"You'll spoil my prints!"

In the soft, distorting crimson glow of the darkroom, the two men came together, flailing organisms of shifting shape. They lurched against each other, fell away, pulled and tripped, crashing against the walls. Pans filled with developer spilled over. Strips of drying film were flung about. An enlarger was knocked over.

Blondell wailed.

"Where have you hidden it?" Scooter bellowed. "You. . .freak!"

They grabbed at each other, the one seeking to break free, to continue his search; the other holding on for survival's sake. They wavered, pushed, pulled, stumbled, and finally fell. Rising too swiftly, Scooter's head collided forcefully with the underside of the sink. He fell back groaning, holding his brow.

Blondell struck him with the developing pan.

Scooter protested and raised his arms protectively.

"Don't hit me!" A horrible scream issued from

Blondell's gaping mouth, pain anathema to his entire being. He crawled rapidly out of the darkroom.

Scooter went after him, arms swinging erratically. An elbow caught Blondell behind the ear, flattening him.

"You hit me!" he yelled.

"Where is it?"

"Madman!"

"I'll wipe you out!" Scooter threatened.

Encouraged by his physical success, Scooter leaped on the prostrate man. The breath whooshed out of Blondell. His head banged loudly on the floor. Instantly, he grew dizzy. He moaned, "You're killing me. . ."

It seemed like a splended idea to Scooter. He wrapped his bony fingers around Blondell's scrawny neck, held on for safety's sake, and shook like hell. Blondell's head beat a tattoo on the hard wood.

"Let—go. . ."

Cackling cheerfully, Scooter continued the assault. A vagrant idea entered his fuzzy mind and he paused to inspect it. *What was he doing?* Should he destroy Blondell, no matter how appealing the prospect, his primary source of supply would be obliterated. He needed the little man. He picked him up, brushed him off, and deposited him on the bed.

"There," he said with satisfaction. "You're all right now."

Blondell grew wary, even more frightened by this unexpected display of human consideration. He eyed Scooter suspiciously.

"I was only fooling with you, Skipper."

"You hurt me."

"Ah, no, just some funning. I like you, Skipper. But I got to have some stuff."

It seemed to Blondell that a crazy undertone had seeped into Scooter's voice. A definite threat. Unlike with Sexton, there was no reasoning with this madman. He felt himself being set up for the kill. At any moment he expected a weapon to appear in the other's hand. A shiver wracked his emaciated body, and he began to cry.

"Don't do that," Scooter said, touched by the show of emotion.

Blondell heard a threat in those words. "I'm afraid," he howled.

"Nothing here's going to hurt you. Just you and old Scooter is all."

That was it, just the two of them. No restraining influence. No one to report the manner of his demise. Blondell's fear increased in geometric leaps.

"I'm expecting company," he said, a pathetic effort to turn aside the inevitable.

Scooter brushed him off, and Blondell drew back, awaiting the deathblow. "Let me have a little something, Skipper," Scooter pleaded.

Blondell was not fooled by the softness of tone. He had pushed the insane author to the very brink; his only hope lay in complete surrender.

"All right," he said.

"All right?"

"You can have it."

"Ah, Skipper. . ."

"Look in the fridge, in the freezer compartment. It doesn't work."

"What doesn't?"

"The freezer compartment."

Scooter drew out a butter carton. Inside were glassine envelopes filled with white powder. He tore open one envelope, tasted the powder. "Fine goods," he crowed in victory, hands shaking. "I'll take it all."

Blondell remembered that there were only half a dozen bags left. He'd demand payment in some calmer future moment.

——— 9 ———

Alex Budde sat behind his desk looking up at Sexton. In a clear demonstration of his authority, Budde deliberately hadn't invited the policeman to sit down. Neither had ever questioned Budde's superior role, neither was likely to. To one side was Harry Rodano, eyes fixed on Sexton, face blank, hands hanging loosely at his sides.

"Keating is lucky," Budde said. "Sometimes, lucky is better than being good."

Sexton swore. "Let me take him out."

"You're too direct, Sexton. You'd gun him down at high noon on the mall. That wouldn't be good for business."

"Give me a little more credit than that."

"He spotted Blondell, Keating did. Does that mean he made him?"

"Maybe not."

"Maybe yes. If yes, why is he keeping quiet? He

must have a plan. He's become more than merely a nuisance."

"Keating has to go."

"I agree. He's up to something, some way of connecting Blondell with you—and you with me. Yes, he's got to go. The question is how."

"An accident," Sexton suggested.

"Yes, an accident. He's out a great deal at night."

"I could get him with a car, run him down."

"Too many people abroad at night to see that. This town jumps all the time. Something else."

Budde began to think. After a while, a look of discovery lighted his face. "I've got the answer, a way to rid ourselves of Keating and Blondell at the same time."

"What do you want me to do?" Sexton said.

"Nothing yet. But stay in touch. When I do need you, I'll need you fast."

To Skip Blondell, Alex Budde seemed bigger and stronger than ever: as deeply rooted and unassailable as the mountains all around Aspen. And adding to the danger, there was Harry Rodano, always within reach, silent, terrifying.

"I don't want to do it!" Blondell protested.

"You can do it, Skip. I believe in you."

"I hate the mountain. Heights disagree with me, make me dizzy. Doctors call it acrophobia."

"I understand," Budde soothed. "Sexton said you would refuse me this favor."

"Sexton! What's he got to do with it? Let Sexton take care of it. He's good at that kind of thing."

"I'm depending on you."

"I've never been a physical person. Violence offends me."

"Consider this an impersonal act. It isn't as if you have to come in close contact with Keating."

"Suppose he were to see me?"

"It won't matter, once it's done."

"I don't know. I'm afraid."

"Of course you are. Any sensible man would be. But you have the skills required for this job."

Blondell chewed his lip. "How am I supposed to know when he goes?"

"I've put a watch on Keating, day and night. When he makes his move, you'll be notified."

"He'll have a head start. . ."

"He goes by foot, you'll drive."

"How will you know where he's going? How will I know?"

Budde patted Blondell's shoulder. He smiled—a controlled, encouraging smile. "Keating always goes to the same place, Hollander's Spring, on the offside. No one else goes there. Therefore—no witnesses, no interference, no one within miles. I know it up there, steep and unsteady underfoot. Lots of open area, smooth rock angling down. A perfect spot to make your move. You will have plenty of cover. Trees, brush. No sweat, Skipper, you can pull this off."

"I don't know." He glanced at Rodano. "Let him do it. He can do it."

"I need Harry down here. This is important to me, Skipper. You do it for me."

"And if I do?"

"The rewards will multiply overnight. Lots of money, Skipper, lots of stuff, lots of young girls. You'll be my main man, I'll never forget you."

Blondell shuddered. "I'll do it," he said. "I know

I can. I'm sure I can." He lifted his lips in what he meant to be a smile. It developed into an anguished twist.

The wind caressed Kit Pepe's cheek and she braced herself against the gyrations of the glider as it sought to break free. In front of her was nothing but emptiness, extending out to where Aspen Mountain and Smuggler Mountain seemed to stand in rank, blending into one rugged profile. The valley below waited in green patience; the cloudless sky was a seductive blue. A perfect day for the perfect flight.

She made one final check. Harness snugly in place, flying wires and landing wires taut, responsive, the fittings secure, the control bar okay. Everything was right.

The small blue streamer tied to the nose of the glider was blowing slightly to the right. She shifted her feet, compensating in the other direction, confronting the wind head on. She lifted the kite to neutral position. Sunlight spread in shimmering golden waves through the translucent wings. She filled her lungs with air, pulling hard on the harness, and began her approach. Two strides put her into a run, and she began to pick up speed.

Without hesitating, she stepped off into space. For what seemed like an extended fragment of time the craft sagged as if about to plummet downward. She elevated the control bar, and the soft breeze brought her up. She was flying.

The green blanket of spruce and pine fell away as she soared higher, only the soft whirring of the wind in her ears. Nothing existed except her sentient flesh and a spreading exhilaration. The world below drifted in slow motion.

She adjusted the angle of flight, taking a bigger bite of the air, rising again, floating onward, dipping back toward earth before riding an updraft.

Suddenly the right wing lifted sharply and the nose took three small steps to the right. Zing. Zing. Zing. She set herself against the unexpected alteration, finally gave in to it, allowing the elements to carry her.

She flew at an angle to Brenner's Ledge, far out in space, losing some altitude, crabbing her way across the valley. Sudden turbulence shot her upwards with breathtaking speed and dropped her just as swiftly.

She worked the control bar, harness straps gripping tightly at her body, arms straining. Time fell away, a meaningless measure. Only the ecstasy of flight existed, of being at one with the airborne creatures, the sky within arm's length above. Surely she had crossed over into the nether regions of heaven.

Descending finally; zooming, and bumping back up again; prolonging the flight with great, looping dives; generating speed enough to climb almost up to her starting point. Every action designed to delay the inevitable end. Treetops rushed past, reaching out for her legs. Speed became a conscious factor again. And the whistle of the wind. Straight for the golden meadow she went, adjusting the angle of approach, working toward achieving landing speed, losing altitude rapidly.

Strong currents buffeted her about. The wings trembled and rocked. She maintained command. At fifty feet, she eased the nose down, sliding toward the ground at a good, hot speed, still with firm control. She swung right a degree or two, straightened out, pushed up, leveled off. Feet reaching, knees flexed to absorb the impact. She hit the ground running, kept her balance, slowed to a walk.

All the way back to the institute, Kit talked with uncharacteristic rapidity and intensity. She led the way to one of the houses set down in a descending arc overlooking Castle Creek.

From the living room Osborne could see straight across the patio to where the green mountains thrust themselves into the blue underbelly of the Colorado sky. Unable to cease chattering, Kit made drinks and sat next to Osborne on the couch. Her face glowed as she recalled the long flight down from the ledge.

"Nothing existed up there," she went on. "My body was weightless, elevated to a finer state, a more ephemeral condition. Just me and the wind. The glider was an extension of my flesh, responding reflexively. I *flew*. I actually flew, like some immense prehistoric bird-beast. Incredible! I tingle all over. I existed at the apex of life—the beginning of time, and the end. A creature in solitary, free to move and explore all of creation. Swooping through a silent universe. All motion was fluid, endless, going from one peak emotion to another. No valleys, no depressions, no sadness. Twice I stalled and began to plummet. I felt no fear. Only exhilaration. Death would have been simply another experience, an extension of life, the final act. But I lived and flew some more."

Watching her—her fine, glowing face, her eyes burning with the pure pleasure of existence— Osborne grew resentful. The excitement in her stirred him and made him want what she had had. He understood that in that lonely, infinite sky she had discovered some wordless mystery that only a fellow flier could ever know.

That exclusivity increased his envy. He had been left behind: earthbound, doomed to plod heavily through ordinary life.

Even more galling was the knowledge that were he to duplicate her flight in every detail, his reaction would not be the same. Life had programmed him into pragmatism, into cool efficiency, his emotions controlled and calm under pressure, not free to allow the raw animal joy to break loose. Any unexpected reaction that seemed capable of controlling him made Osborne suspicious. He was a manager of his life, of other lives, of business and business machines, of workers and great gobs of money.

Like all managers everywhere—communist, capitalist, socialist—he was interchangeable with his fellow managers. They all had the same skills, the same ability to judge, to consider, to perform. They were a breed common to the New World and the Old World. They possessed language in common. Goals in common. They solved problems in a common way.

The latter-day princes at court, Osborne had once described his kind of man. The king's messengers and captains and overseers. Most managers were satisfied to serve at their well-paid high level. Not Osborne. He sought the real glory. The highest reward. He wanted to be king himself.

As if to return her to earth, as if to exercise control, Osborne touched Kit Pepe's flushed cheek. She rose quickly and stood looking out through the glass doors.

He came up behind her. "You're beautiful. The most attractive woman I've ever known."

"The mountains were formed by glaciers, you know. In another age. . ."

"The mountains lull people into a stupor."

"They're a link with the past, a certain connection with the future."

"Is that what it was for you up there? A sense of immortality?"

"*Mortality*," she answered sharply. "A keener awareness of my own humanity. Knowing how fully I was alive. Flesh and spirit, joined as never before. The perfect marriage in our time—person, machine, elements. All unified. All striving for a single purpose."

He placed his hands on her waist. Slender, strong, flaring out to her fine full hips. "What purpose?" He placed his mouth against the nape of her neck.

She shivered. "To survive. To enjoy. To leave a trace of yourself behind."

"Immortality," he muttered against her warm skin.

"Life is a cycle—birth, life, death, rebirth."

"You believe in resurrection?"

"Nothing ever dies. Nothing is ever wasted. No matter how obscure to human beings with their limited perceptions, there is always a purpose. To everything."

"A greater plan?"

"Yes."

"A divine plan?"

"Perhaps."

"I believe in the present. In this place, in this time." He pressed himself against her; he could feel his blood pounding and he immediately began to swell and grow.

She stiffened but did not move away.

His arms circled her, hands coming to rest on her breasts. She began to tremble, turned within the circle of his grasp.

He lifted her effortlessly and climbed the steps to her bedroom. With gentle fingers, without haste, he undressed her until she stood naked in the sunlight that filtered through pale draperies. She resembled a white marble statue of a young girl that he had seen in a Roman garden years before. He remembered that the sculptor was Bernini. Then he stripped off his clothes.

He kissed her hair, her eyes, her mouth. She made small whimpering sounds in her throat and was unable to stop trembling.

"I want to love you," he said.

"Please," she managed to say. "Don't talk, not now."

In some way Osborne never understood, all of her shyness, all of her uncertainty, all of her fear drained away. The carnal mouth was a damp, inviting orifice. The eyes no longer were soft; transformed, they were luminous, voracious. Her hands played his torso like a musical instrument and his skin responded. She caressed and explored and demanded, went here and there without hesitation or shame or permission, delighting in his hard brown flesh as in her own.

All hands and mouth. All hanging breasts and

sweetly curved bottom. Mysterious shadows and crevices opened in silent invitation and delicious pink eyes winked in wicked amusement.

He went at her fiercely. Limbs bent, pushed, tightened, hugged. Bodies adjusted, humped, pounded without mercy. Flesh scraped and incited, hot and rough. Warm tongues stirred dormant fires. Filled with him, she screamed softly. Buried in her, he exulted thickly.

They swung around. Changed positions. Tried it one way and another. All was good, all was natural, harmonious—moist, warm, smooth. Forgotten rhythms went on with limitless authority. They swooped, as she had off the mountain, they soared and fell and rose again to strange, wild heights.

Somehow she worked her way astride him and galloped feverishly on the long uphill trail to glory. Until steed and rider could take no more, ending in a rough, stunning climax. They lurched together, as if to fall was to sink into the most terrible of the narrowing circles of hell.

___ **11** ___

Nothing was right for Jon. Nothing functioned properly. All systems were cumbersome and promised distress. The world he existed in seemed to be squeezing him, as if it were about to cut off his ability to work and to play—to live.

His body performed badly, was stiff and unwieldy. His mind broke out in fits and starts, grinding slowly like a car engine on a winter morning.

Pressure began to increase. At night, he could almost hear the echoing beat of his heart. His extremities were sensitive, alive with tenderness. His thighs seemed to thicken, become weary. Suddenly age bore down on him, and he was afraid.

His father arriving without warning in Aspen had precipitated it all. Intruding on his existence, causing him to doubt, to rethink everything. Detached from his family, life had been simple. No sweat, no big deal. Just doing his own thing. Now, suddenly there were questions.

Nor was he pleased by the answers he came up with. His confidence was shattered. No longer did he advance through each day without fear. Old childhood weaknesses returned. He had criticized Carl for harvesting money, for sniffing after the ancient bitch goddess. Was he any different from his father?

He worked for Alex Budde, hustler extraordinary. Wheeler and dealer in all things for profit. Budde paid him big bread to travel around the countryside, making pickups, making deliveries, a mule: slick and sleek and smart. Always coming through. He tried never to think of what he transported. He tried never to think that as much as any of them—Alex Budde, or that pleasant little man from the west coast of Mexico, or that charming Frenchman from Marseilles, or that exotic son of a sheikh from a Middle Eastern desert—he too put the needle into the arm of some hapless kid every day. Those poor, stupid, hooked kids.

Pot, okay. Hash, dig it, man. Even coke didn't trouble Jon. But the big H was something else. The big blast to oblivion. Still, he made the scene. Shipment after shipment delivered on time without a problem. He did it before, he'd do it again.

For a long time he had blamed his parents for whatever was wrong with his life. Carl and Janet, symbols of a screwed-up world. A screwed-up life. They had deprived him of the solid base of love and care everyone is entitled to. The rift in their relationship was too heavy for him to bear. They had shortchanged him.

No longer could he blame them. For nearly two years he had been physically divorced from the life they led. He was his own man, free of all claims by his parents or by their life-style.

If he were really free, why did he react so strongly to Carl's presence? Why couldn't he accept his father calmly and without emotion? It was impossible. Carl stood for everything Jon loathed.

And Alex Budde?

A matched pair—buyers and sellers. Of land. People. Things. Make a deal, turn a profit, get yours no matter who gets hurt. A bigger slice of the pie.

Jon felt under siege. Everyone plucked at him, seeking to extract some vital portion of his soul. His father, Alex Budde, the bored and beautiful older women he serviced on—and off—the tennis courts. Always getting a generous reward, of course. How then was he different from Carl and Alex? Despising the answer he knew must come, he repressed the question.

Jon wanted out. Kit had turned away from him; she was more attracted to a hustler like Bobby Wallace. Or to Carl. . .

Jon wanted to be free.

To sever the bonds that restrained him. To find a new life. New friends.

How?

One idea after another was sifted through his fine intelligence and found to fall short. He rolled a joint to lessen the anguish and sucked it persistently. In that sweetly pungent smoke, another way manifested itself—misty at first, blurred, its terminal closed off. Gradually the mist lifted and before his eyes in crystal clarity floated the ultimate answer to all his problems, all his nightmares, all his dreams. He had seen the future and it would work. It required only a little bit of patience, a little bit of planning and effort, and some luck. A whole lot of luck.

<hr/> 12 <hr/>

It was night; the streets were flowing with people. All ages, all sizes, all stations in life. They flocked to the restaurants and bars, crowded into the shops that were open and happy to accept their money. They gathered in groups in the parks and in the mall and on the sidewalks. Strollers found it best to walk in the street.

In front of Mill Street Station, two guitar players plucked away and sang folk songs in nasal voices, staring past their listeners. People listened with pleasure and deposited coins in the musicians' wide-brimmed leather hats that lay upturned on the sidewalk.

Carl Osborne listened through three songs and on impulse dropped a five-dollar bill into one of the hats. His gesture went unacknowledged. He moved along. The gentle yet insistent surge of life in Aspen at night reminded him of Aegean tides washing up on the beach on the island of Skiathos: steady, powerful in their cumulative being, but without violence. That was the playful, clearly apparent aspect of the town. He knew there were also dark undertones that promised conflict and trouble—the shadow side of life.

He made his way to Tom Keating's shop as if he had done it a hundred times before, at ease in Aspen and its ways. He cautioned himself not to grow too confident; he was still a stranger, made welcome by certain persons only because of the rewards he promised to deliver.

Keating was a different case. Stubborn, set in his beliefs, sure of where he was and where he was headed. In some ways, very much like Osborne. Yet Carl was increasingly questioning himself—what he was up to, how he had spent the past decades of his existence. Things were no longer clear-cut. Nothing was easy. The pieces of the puzzle no longer dropped smoothly into place.

He entered the arcade and stopped outside Keating's door. The big bearded man labored over a strip of soft brown leather with fierce, affectionate concentration, his huge hands manipulating the tool without effort, turning the leather easily.

A master craftsman, Osborne decided. Born out of his time; nevertheless, able to make his way. Osborne felt diminished, not by Keating's size or obvious strength, but by his contentment. He wished he could get to know this man, understand what drove him, become his friend. He went inside the shop.

Keating kept working. "Good evening, Mr. Osborne."

"Good evening, Mr. Keating."

"Are you in need of a good belt? Or a wallet, maybe?" He grinned to show he meant no harm.

Osborne returned the smile. "I'd like to talk to you."

"If you like."

"Have you given any additional thought to the things that were said the last time?"

"Not really. I'm still against mindless exploitation of the country. It has to stop somewhere."

"I believe I can show you that what we want to do won't be mindless. On the contrary, it's all being very carefully thought out. Utilities, shops, water, recreation; all planned to the smallest detail. You have questions; if I can't supply the answers now, I'll get them for you. Doubts; I'll try to eliminate them. Standards; I'll meet them."

Keating put his tool to one side. He gazed intently at Osborne. "We're into something fundamental, something irreconcilable."

"Try me."

"Okay. How many people will Wolf Run bring into the area?"

"To live? Fifteen thousand, give or take a few."

"That exceeds the total present population of the entire county." The bearish head rocked sadly. "You see, there's no room for compromise. The sort of quantitative change you suggest will inevitably mean a qualitative change. And it will be of such size and nature that it can't help but cause irrevocable harm to the valley and its people. We don't need neon signs; we don't need motels, burger joints. We don't want Las Vegas up here."

Osborne decided to try a different approach. "What are you after, Keating?"

Keating grinned. "You're going to try to bribe me, Osborne. Don't do it."

Osborne laughed. "I know better than that. Come on, what are you after?"

"Very little. Everything. My work, my woman, the baby we're going to have."

"Nothing else?"

"Nothing *more.*"

"I find that hard to believe."

"*More* is the curse. *More* is the carrot in front of the donkey. More means less on a finite planet. More people, less space. More cars, less breathable air. More houses, less pure water. More spells ultimate disaster for us all."

"I'm surprised, Keating; you're a pessimist."

"You're a businessman, Osborne. You view life like a business graph. You anticipate an upward slant always, the numbers getting bigger, profits climbing. Like all businessmen, you confuse bigger and better. They don't mean the same thing. We're in trouble, Osborne. The world, the country. Millions of people are starving, millions will die of disease, millions more are out of work. Men like you—businessmen, politicians, economists—you talk about acceptable levels of unemployment. Are there also acceptable levels of disease and starvation? Not for me, Osborne."

"Okay, have it your way. Men like me, as you put it, suppose we pull out. Stop working for profit. What then? Have the socialist countries put an end to poverty, to starvation, to disease? China, Russia, they come to us for wheat, for technical aid, for all sorts of things."

"You're discussing systems. All systems ultimately fail."

"Then what do you suggest? Out of anarchy a system would surely evolve. People require social and political and economic institutions. It's the way things get done."

"Right now, dramatic changes are in order."

"Like carving leather?"

Keating's laugh was booming, full of pleasure. "Does it bug you that I do this little task in order to feed myself? Does it bug you that one man refuses to be a part of your corporate bullshit game? Man, I do not choose to play."

"You're a county commissioner."

"A holding action. I anticipate no monumental successes. Merely a thumb in the dike."

Osborne clucked in admiration. "You're quite a guy, Keating. I'd like to have you on my team."

Keating slapped his thigh in delight. "There it is! You *are* trying to bribe me."

"No, just offer you a job. The Heggland Group has fourteen newspapers around the country. A dozen radio stations, ten TV stations. Some magazines. Wouldn't you like to get back into journalism? What part of the country would you like to live in? A good job at good pay with an excellent future."

"Ah, Osborne," Keating said sadly, "that's a straight-out bribe."

"An offer, a job offer," Osborne insisted.

"An offer that would get me out of the county commissioners' office if I accept it. That would let you get your own man in to replace me."

"I'm more subtle than that."

"Much more subtle. Too subtle, too devious to do anything but hit me with the pitch head on. But no matter how you cut it, it comes out bribe. I'm all that stands between this town and Wolf Run. A dozen Wolf Runs. No thanks, Osborne, I am not buying."

"You'd have nothing to worry about for the rest of your life."

"If I accepted, I would indeed have a great deal to worry about. My immortal soul."

"Well, I'm sorry you're not buying. At the same time, I'm glad. I don't often meet a man who can't be reached."

"Did you expect me to go for it?"

"Not really."

"Is that why you tried to set me up?"

Osborne frowned. "Set you up! I don't get it."

"Come on, Osborne, you knew about the plant, you had to know."

Osborne waited without moving.

"Okay," Keating said at last. "Play it your way. Last night someone was prowling around outside my house. I spotted some dude at my car—putting something in my car."

"Did you recognize the man?"

"I can't be sure."

"What did he put in the car?" An icy finger stepped down Osborne's spine. Was he losing his touch? Were things going on that were beyond his control? Things he hadn't even suspected?

"A brick of heroin."

"Heroin!"

"Very good stuff."

"What did you do with it?"

"Flushed it into oblivion. Couldn't have it on me when the fuzz came."

"You mean the cops came looking for the heroin? How could they know—" He broke off in wonderment and dismay.

"Is it seeping through, Osborne? I told you it was a plant, a setup. I was supposed to be a patsy. This morning Jim Sexton came to see me. Sergeant Jim hassled me a little. Checked the shop out and dived right into my VW. Knew right where to look, he did."

"Let me get this straight. You're suggesting you were set up, that the police were informed you had drugs on you."

"Fer sure," he drawled exaggeratedly; then— "I am saying that one man arranged the plant and ordered his hired lawman to go after it and take me in."

"Someone wanted you out of the way."

"Someone wanted me out of the way, yes. And also completely discredited. County commissioner, a drug peddler. That's the way it would have seemed."

"Who gave the orders?"

"Either you know already, or you don't want to know."

"Who?"

"Alex Budde."

Osborne shook his head in disbelief. "If you're right, I had nothing to do with it. I don't operate this way."

"Ask Alex. Not that he'll tell you the truth. But you might be able to read between the lines."

"If you're right, I'll put a stop to it today."

"Don't waste your energy. You can't tell Budde what to do. He has his own plans. He wants Wolf Run in and he isn't going to let one obstreperous county commissioner stand in his way. He's tried to buy me off; he's tried to frame me; next time he'll go the whole route."

"What do you mean?"

"He's going to try to kill me."

"That's crazy. This is just a business deal."

"You're mistaken if you believe that. For Alex Budde, it's a war. All life is. The kind of war the old miners used to fight for claims and for land and for the valley itself. They used to mine silver here; now they hack away for tourist money. Alex Budde intends to own the valley."

"There isn't going to be any killing."

Keating smiled wistfully.

"I mean it."

"I believe you do. But I'll look to my own welfare meanwhile."

"What are you going to do?"

"I'll go off into the mountains and think it all through. I do my best thinking up there. Maybe I'll decide to go for Wolf Run. Maybe I'll quit being commissioner. Maybe I'll show my tail feathers to all this crap. Or maybe I'll fight you mothers down the line."

"I had no idea. . ."

"Maybe not. But you failed to recognize the elements that come into play in an operation of this kind. A man with your experience—you had to know that the Alex Buddes of the world are not deterred by a small item like murder. You're no innocent, Osborne."

"I'm beginning to think that I am."

"You'll be seeing Alex Budde. . ." Keating said.

"At once. I've got a lot to say to him. But I won't tell him that you're heading into the mountains."

"I want you to. Mention it in passing. Let it drop. Let him know I intend to take off at daybreak, or an hour before."

"Why? If he means to kill you, then up there you'd be alone, vulnerable, helpless. . ."

"Let's find out which of us is right about Budde. Anyway, there is no point in postponing the inevitable."

A strange uncertainty took hold of Osborne. He, himself, felt helpless, vulnerable, alone. "What are you going to do?" he said.

"Climb higher."

—— **13** ——

"What the hell are you doing!" Osborne said, letting his anger support the words, making his face hard.

Budde, seated behind his office desk, let nothing show on his shining fighter's face. "Is something bothering you, Mr. Osborne?"

"This is a business deal, not some shady underworld operation."

"I don't understand."

"You planted dope on Tom Keating. Set him up for arrest."

"Mr. Osborne, I don't know what you're talking about."

"Somebody put heroin in Keating's car."

"And you think I did it?"

"I think you ordered it done."

Budde selected his words carefully. "Mr. Osborne, Keating set you up to think this way. Keating is using you. The man is paranoid."

"Paranoid? He doesn't strike me that way."

"He persists in believing that I am attacking him, trying to ruin him. If that isn't paranoid, I don't know what is."

"Do you deny it?"

"I don't know anything about this." Budde produced an amused laugh. "Tom Keating is not that important to me. Like yourself, I'm an ordinary businessman. Not as important as you, Mr. Osborne, but still I try."

"I don't want Keating hurt. I don't want anyone hurt."

"Neither do I. I want what you want—Wolf Run to be built and in operation. Making money for everybody. Legally. Trouble is the last thing I desire."

Osborne wanted to believe him.

"Keating is a maverick," Budde continued. "Look at the way he lives. Addicts, the lot of them. Maybe that's what got him onto talking about dope. He lives with a bunch of people just like himself. Unwashed, unwed, men and women both. One of the women is pregnant, I understand. I doubt if she even knows who the father is, the way they switch around. Keating and his friends are no problem to me."

"He is a county commissioner."

"Yes. But didn't anybody tell you, Mr. Osborne, about the election this fall. Maybe Keating will be out of office and in that case everything is turned around."

"I can't wait till fall," Osborne complained, thinking of T. Lyman Heggland, of the presidency of the group, of his hunger for the job. "I need a decision about the project in the next couple of days."

"A tide is forming, Mr. Osborne," Budde said cheerfully. "Folks want progress, development, new money coming into town. The country's in a bad way—recession, depression, whatever you call it. Folks are afraid of inflation, of being out of work, of high fuel prices. They aren't going to stand still when somebody tries to hold back the future. That's what Keating's up to, holding back the future."

Osborne breathed deeply. "He's a very interesting man, an attractive human being."

"Exactly. And there's the trap. He seems simple, direct, disarming. He isn't. He can be shrewd and tricky. Spends a lot of time up in the mountains by himself. Sort of a hermit at times. It is not natural for a man to be alone that much."

Osborne felt an uncertainty, almost a helplessness, as if essential control over his own destiny had been removed from his hands. He was here, it seemed, to serve Alex Budde, and to do Tom Keating's bidding. He fought against the impulse to speak, fought not to act as a puppet, and lost the struggle.

"Keating said something about the mountains, about how much it means to him to go up there." Don't be too direct, he warned himself, or too obvious. The role of courier was a new one for him, a strange and disturbing one. Who, he wondered, was the enemy in this campaign? Who was his ally?

"Oh?" Budde said casually.

He's good, Osborne noted. Very good at whatever game he plays. "I don't understand a man like Keating," he went on with assumed cheerfulness. "Climbing mountains at daybreak. That's when I do my best sleeping."

Budde laughed. "And me, sir. I leave the mountain to those who want it. Give me a comfortable chair in a comfortable room every time."

Osborne, proud, somehow, and at the same time dismayed by his reluctant role in this charade, edged toward the door. "I've got to be going. . ."

"Heavy date?"

"Something like that." Osborne couldn't wait to be away from this office, this man, the bad feelings this exchange had engendered. He wanted to go back to Tom Keating, to warn him. . . against what? It was Keating who was framing his own future, Keating who imagined all sorts of melodramatic events, Keating who lived with his own fantasies, his own lunatic inventions. Out in the air, Osborne moved slowly along, oblivious to everything except his own mixed emotions. . .

At his desk, Alex Budde dialed a number and listened to the phone ring. A voice came on and Budde spoke without identifying himself. "Keating's going up at dawn. That's right, tomorrow. So you take off tonight. Get out in front and don't argue. You know where he's headed; get there first and set yourself up. I don't want any mistakes this time. You do it right." He hung up without waiting for a response.

He sat back and grew thoughtful. The phone interrupted. He picked it up and said his name. A rough voice began to speak. Budde listened for a while. "No chance of any change in plan?"

"No way," the voice said.

"And the timing?"

"Just like I said, all laid out for you."

"Okay; you did okay. You'll be hearing from me." He deposited the phone in its cradle, then touched the call button in the well of his desk. Seconds later, Harry Rodano appeared. Budde gestured, and Rodano stepped inside and closed the door behind him.

"I've got a job for you, Harry," Budde said carefully. "A big job. The kid will go with you. . ."

"Jon?"

"Yes. I'll give you instructions, and I expect them to be followed to the letter. Call Jon. The job is big. . ."

_____ 14 _____

It was a tentative knock, almost a caress, and Kit Pepe hurried to answer. Jon stood there looking boyish, sheepish, terribly appealing.

Without thinking, she said, "I wasn't expecting you."

He frowned. "But you are expecting someone?"

"Do you want to come in?" She stood aside.
"For a little while."

Once inside, his eyes swept around as if searching for clues. "I have to talk to you."

"That's what friends are for."

He turned to face her. "Friendship isn't exactly what I had in mind for us, Kit." He put his arms around her waist.

She disentangled herself. "Settle down, Jon."

"I always figured we had something special going down."

"Jon, we haven't known each other very long."

"Longer than you know Carl."

"Leave your father out of this. The point is, there was never anything romantic between us."

"That's not my fault. You were with him last night."

She decided to sit down.

"I saw you with him, in the Spot."

"We had a drink together."

"What else?"

"Don't be nasty, Jon."

"Are you making it with him?"

"Is it any business of yours? Jon, my life is my own. Nobody owns me—not you, not your father. Please, Jon, don't spoil our friendship."

"It's not me who spoils things. Oh, I don't even blame you. My father is an attractive man—so strong, personable, successful. People used to ask me all the time, Aren't you proud of your father, Jon? I hated him for being so goddamn perfect. He never allowed me to feel grown up."

"He's not perfect, Jon. Nobody is."

"When I was very young, he'd take me into his bath. I loved to splash around and sit on him. He'd lift me above his head and I'd stretch out my legs and pretend I was flying. I loved to watch him shave or go to the toilet. He was a giant, beyond any of my dreams of what I could be. He looked so powerful. His penis was so big and mine was so small. Nothing seems to have changed very much."

"Don't be foolish."

"Being around him makes me feel like a child. Very young and inadequate." His face settled into an aggressive mask. "Is it big enough for you, Kit—my father's penis?"

She stood up. "It's time you left, Jon." There was more regret than anger in her manner. More sadness than hurt.

"Why?" Jon cried. "Anybody else but him would've been all right. I'd have understood."

"What I expect from a friend is friendship, acceptance, even when I displease you. Now go before I say something that will make both of us sorry."

"I came to ask you to go away with me."

"When did you decide to leave Aspen?"

His voice grew softer, more intimate. "Kit, I am going to score big. Soon. I'll be rich, richer than my old man."

"What are you talking about?"

"Bread, lots of it, all coming down on me. Heavy money. Millions. More than Carl will ever make. We could go anywhere in the world, have a ball."

She assessed him at length, spoke thoughtfully. "Where is all that money coming from?"

"It's on its way. From out there—" He waved a long arm. "—Into my pocket."

"I hope you're not planning to do something stupid."

"Change your mind. Come with me."

"I can't, Jon."

"That's it, then." He went to the door. "Think it over, Kit; there's still time."

"Whatever you're up to, it can't be good. It can only mean trouble."

His eyes turned away. "Just words. You don't care one way or another. You don't want in and that's that." He reached for the doorknob. "I love you, Kit."

"Oh, Jon. I'm a novelty to you, different from the girls you've known. That's not love."

He started to speak, thought better of it, and yanked the door open. His father stood there. They looked into each other's eyes for an extended moment. "You bastard!" Jon gritted out. "Fucking my girl!"

_____ **15** _____

It was still dark when the alarm went off. Grumbling sleepily, Skip Blondell forced himself out of bed. He made instant coffee, double strength, and brought the mug into the bathroom while he brushed his teeth.

He climbed into khakis, a medium-weight hunting shirt, and soft leather rubber-cleated boots. He filled a small backpack with fruit, a chunk of Wisconsin cheddar, some French bread, and a large bottle of Coke. Into an empty Winston box went a dozen joints he had prepared the night before. He slipped into a lined corduroy jacket, put a rain hat on his head, and left the gallery.

He climbed into the Cherokee—red with a white roof and contrasting trim—and allowed the engine to warm up. He used the Cherokee for transporting paintings, and he had come to love the vehicle more than any other car he'd ever owned. Driving it, perched up high, the powerful engine thrumming majestically, he felt in command. A force to be reckoned with.

He got the Cherokee into gear and rolled through the quiet blackness of Aspen, his head still thick, resentful that he had been forced into this early-morning activity, not thinking much beyond getting where he had to go.

He began to climb, following the jeep trails as far as they would take him, grinding his way along the old logging road that wound past Riley's Shaft, one of the abandoned silver mines.

Gray morning sifted through the trees as he turned east toward South Hook Glade. On his left, a flash of water appeared and then disappeared. Glacier River, a trembling creek of sparkling mountain water, running wild in summer and winter alike. Sweet to drink and icy, the water drained off into the side of the mountain long before it could reach the townspeople below.

He drove over the ridgeline and backed the Cherokee into a stand of spruce, facing the way he had come. Once the dirty job was over, he had

no intention of hanging around. He put on the
backpack, took a small pick and shovel from the
truck, and started the long hike over the hump
toward Hollander's Spring.

Snow still clung to the heights, but where
Blondell walked there was scrub brush sprouting
out of the loose, rocky soil, and boulders of all
sizes teetered precariously in place.

Below, the land seemed to fall away with
startling swiftness. A steep drop caused Blondell
to grow dizzy when he looked down. He closed his
eyes and clutched at a jagged outcropping until
he felt ready to continue his walk.

Twenty minutes later, he spotted Hollander's
Spring: a tiny gush sprouting like a fountain out
of a low rock wall. Not much, but important to
anyone making this climb. The only water above
Glacier River. Below the spring, a slick rock face
pitched at an unnerving angle downward to the
timberline. There, a stride or so back in the
woods, was where Keating would make camp.
That was where Blondell intended to kill him.

Part Three

Aspen

Shielded by the high range, Aspen dozed at the edge of the Roaring Fork while America made its sluggish move through the first third of the twentieth century.

The future was being formed. Tastes were undergoing radical changes—in sports, in art, in music. Jazz, symphony, opera—all attracted more and more listeners.

In Switzerland, in Italy, the mountains were crisscrossed with skiers, including Americans who had discovered the sport.

Elsewhere, artists and writers and intellectuals gathered at festivals and conferences to exchange ideas, to compare techniques, to get to know colleagues from afar.

Aspen ignored it all, slumbering on with its silver memories, a few hundred people content in their isolation. The Great Depression gripped the land, but Aspen recognized no alteration in the scheme of things. The streets remained unpaved and, for the most part, unused. The Victorian houses weathered and went unrepaired. The mines remained closed, the slopes of the mountain undisturbed. Time went by with no urgency in the valley.

But forces were at work that would alter the face of the Rockies forever. Tom Flynn, once a resident of Aspen, boasted of the incomparable mountains to international sportsman William Fiske. He spoke of the high, lush meadows, of the fine winter snowfall, of the unrivaled summers.

One July, Flynn brought Fiske to see his youthful home. By way of the Midnight mine tunnel and the Little Annie Shaft, they made their way to the top of Richmond Hill. Fiske saw the surrounding peaks still painted with virgin snow. He measured the slopes with a practiced eye, and he liked what he saw.

They surveyed the possibilities for skiing and other outdoor activities. They made plans and began to put those plans into operation. First, a lodge was put down where Conundrum Creek meets Castle Creek. This done, they went out to enlist the help of friends and associates all over the country.

Work got under way. The WPA constructed a boat tow to the top of Midway on Aspen Mountain, and a ski run was cut. Skiers could hit the slopes. The word went out and in 1930 the first ski train arrived from New York City. Winter sportsmen everywhere began to hear of the glories of Aspen. Optimism for the future of the town rose and there was talk of a revival. People began to make plans to accommodate the skiers who were sure to come—to house and feed them, to

*provide clothing and fulfill their other needs. Hope
ran high.*

*Until December 1941. The Japanese attacked
Pearl Harbor; World War II exploded in full fury;
and Aspen slid back into oblivion, buried under
alternating blankets of winter snow and golden
leaves of summer.*

1

Keating was packed and ready to go when first light broke over the valley. Annie made hot cakes and sausage for breakfast and he washed it down with two large cups of black coffee. She put food enough for two days into his pack.

"How about some beer?"

"No. I want to keep it light. There's water up there."

"Some grass?"

"I don't think so."

She watched him eat, her face unlined, but worried nevertheless.

"Change your mind, Tom," she said in an expressionless voice. "Take me along."

"You'd slow me down."

"No, no. The baby is just beginning. I'll be okay."

"I have to be free to do it my way, whatever that is."

"I'm scared."

He touched her cheek. "The nesting instinct. You've got a child to protect now."

"I've got a man I don't want to lose."

"I know what I'm doing; I'll be okay."

"You don't even know who's coming after you."

She was right; he couldn't be sure. Except that

it wasn't likely to be Alex Budde himself. Alex was too careful a man to embark on a dangerous journey when he didn't have to. Alex would take chances only as a last resort.

Sexton was a good man for the job. He would kill without conscience. Efficient, experienced, familiar with the mountains, Sexton was right for the job. But Sexton was unable to excuse himself from police work for an extended period.

Harry Rodano. A good choice. He was tough and mean, a man born and bred for dirty work. Budde could spare his bodyguard for a couple of days surely. Long enough to eliminate an irritation named Keating.

So it would be Rodano. He would probably come with a pistol or a rifle. Or perhaps a knife.

Rodano would provide him with a clear edge. He wanted it to be Rodano. The ways of the city still clung to Rodano. His instincts had been honed on concrete, his abilities trained there. On the trails, among the unsteady rocks and barely visible handholds, on the heights where the thin air made a man's heart pound wildly and caused his lungs to ache, Keating would be at home. In a strange environment, Rodano would hesitate, have to think before acting. Keating meant to take advantage of that need to hesitate.

His breakfast finished, Keating checked his equipment for the last time and swung the pack onto his back. Arm in arm, he and Annie went to the door.

"I hate this, Tom."

"I don't have much choice."

"We could leave here."

"You don't mean that. Once we began to run, we'd always have to run. We'd never be able to stand up for anything. Not our beliefs, not ourselves. No, we're not the running sort."

"Maybe you're imagining it, that Alex wants you dead."

"He's got to get rid of me—we went all over it last night."

"I keep wishing. . ."

He kissed her cheek. "I'll be back in a couple of days at most."

"Yes," she said, not as confident as he was. "Rodano is a professional killer," she said.

"He won't have an easy target."

"Shouldn't you get a gun for yourself?"

"It's going to work out, you'll see."

"Promise?"

"I promise."

She touched his hand. "You've always kept your promises to me, Tom. Keep this one, please."

"Depend on it."

But as he walked off into the morning mist, he wasn't convinced. A variety of factors were involved and any one of them might shift the balance away from him. Rodano, he assured himself as he began to climb, Rodano himself was the best chance he had for survival.

_____ 2 _____

The helicopter lifted, seemed to hang for a second or two before diving straight ahead as if intent on ramming into the mountain. Tilted forward in the doorless bubble, Osborne felt he was without support, cushioned by air, waiting to be pulled to earth. Gradually he grew accustomed to the sensation and began to enjoy the flight. On his right was Pete McDevitt, and on the far side of the rancher was Len Ralston. The advance man was pale with fright. Osborne took pleasure in that and disliked himself for being petty.

The pilot took them down the valley as the town dropped rapidly away. Past the Highlands, past Buttermilk, lingering over Snowmass with its seemingly unchecked growth, buildings dotting the landscape, stepping up the slope.

"That's what we must avoid," Osborne shouted over the roar of the rotors. "People are afraid of overdevelopment, overcrowding."

McDevitt, if he heard, if he cared, gave no sign.

Ralston leaned across the rancher. "Too much open space brings a short return on investment."

"So I understand," Osborne retorted.

"Heggland always says it—maximize profits, minimize waste."

"Mr. Heggland will be happy to learn how well you've learned the lesson, Ralston."

"He's the man we both work for," Ralston shot back.

The helicopter swung around, banking steeply, and Osborne fought for breath, staring down into space. They gained altitude, hovering while the pilot sought out landmarks; then they plunged downward.

"Wolf Run," McDevitt said, pointing.

The valley rushed up to meet them. Green slopes alternately steep and gentle, marked by yellow and purple, reaching back between two craggy humps into the range. Osborne was unable to make

out the end of the private lands, but he knew
that off to the west the federal forest reserves began, protected for all time from additional en-
croachment. Someday, he assured himself dryly,
some big operator would arrange for legislation
to be passed in Congress, and those lands would
be open for development, too. It was inevitable.
The people would demand it. . .

"That creek," McDevitt said, showing him
where to look, "squiggling along the near slope.
My property commences just beyond that point.
No doubt about it, Mr. Osborne, you are getting
a bargain out of me."

"It seems okay," Ralston said.

Osborne surveyed the land. "Swing us around,"
he commanded abruptly to the pilot. The helicopter described a tight arc, leveled off. Osborne
pointed. "This side of the creek, those buildings,
that must be the Horn place?"

McDevitt shrugged. "Right. Don Horn, an old-
timer like me. But he's only got a few acres, ten
to be exact. Raises his own vegetables, some chick-
ens, a few milk cows. Not worth bothering with."

"The creek cuts across his land," Osborne said,
"and his property blocks access to what will be
our number two ski run. We must have that land,
too. Let's pay the man another visit, Ralston. His
property also straddles the creek. Without it. . ."

"I own water rights," McDevitt said quickly,
"in perpetuity, and full access to the county
road. . ."

"Surely that covers us," Ralston said anxiously.

"There's still the slope. Mr. Heggland wouldn't
like it if some small rancher could close us out.
We'll buy him out."

When they were back on the ground, Osborne

offered McDevitt the option agreement. He signed it quickly and accepted the Heggland Group check.

"I like the way you do business," McDevitt said by way of thanks.

"We go before Planning and Zoning tomorrow," Osborne said. "Wish me luck."

McDevitt showed his teeth in a wolfish grin. He waved the check. "Don't matter much to me anymore, but still—good luck."

—— **3** ——

A gnawing anguish filled the center of Joan Carolinian's being, drifting along the network of nerves into her extremities, throbbing painfully. Her eyes watered and she fought back tears.

How ridiculous! Why should she want to cry? She was a woman who lived exactly the life she had chosen in the place she wanted most to live it. She had an excellent job that paid her an excellent salary. She owned her own car, her own apartment; her closets were filled with chic and flattering clothes. She had *everything*.

Halfway to her office, she stopped and turned away. She would not go to work today. *She would not.* She was entitled to a day off. To some *relief*. After a dozen unsteady steps, she paused again.

Where was she going instead? What would she do with her day? *Her* day.

She needed some verbal reassurance, a small show of affection, some human interest or concern —a casual reminder that she did not exist alone in a great void. A hint of a promise that held some hope.

For what?

No answer came.

She turned off Garmish Street into Hopkins, walking faster. Don't go, she warned herself. A rigid body of rules governed his behavior and he expected those people he allowed into his orbit to be governed by them as well. She was unable to halt her advance.

The Spot was crowded with breakfasters when she appeared. Her eyes went directly to the table in the corner. As usual, he sat there alone chewing carefully on a piece of toast, focused on some point in space, able to perceive that which others were blind to. The shining face was an effective mask. This man was unlike any she had ever known. Or was he no different from all the others? She had never been certain. On the periphery of her vision was Harry Rodano, immaculate in a white linen suit, a brown shirt, and a yellow tie.

She shivered. Nearing the corner table, she arranged what she hoped was a pleasant smile on her face—her pretty face—a face that still drew admiring glances from men of all ages. A good face and a good figure. She had been blessed by nature, and she had worked hard to maintain herself accordingly. Others appreciated her even if Alex Budde failed to. Perhaps it was time to let him know it, to let him worry about her.

"Good morning, Alex," she said brightly.

"What are you doing here?" His voice was dull, flat, a disinterested mumble.

"I just wanted to say hello."

"I never talk to people during breakfast."

"I know; I thought—"

"You'll be late for your job."

She wet her lips. Her thighs began to tremble. "Ah, Alex, I wanted you to know. The other night was so beautiful for me, so very beautiful."

"Not now," he said.

She made herself laugh, a gay, girlish sound, she hoped. "You might invite a lady to have a cup of coffee with you. Oh, Alex, your mother neglected your manners a bit, I'm afraid."

His eyes met hers. They were glossy marbles devoid of memory: hard cobalt orbs.

"Just one cup," she pleaded.

"You don't want to lose your job. Jobs are not easy to come by in this town."

"I hate it," she ripped out. "I hate that job."

He nibbled some toast.

She leaned forward, hands flat on the edge of the table. "Alex, when am I going to see you again? Oh, I'm not asking for a date, nothing that binding. All you have to do is phone and I'd come right over. Or wait around here until you are free. Day or night, Alex, you know that. I could be even better for you, Alex, an animal, if you wanted me to be."

Revulsion was what he felt, a sick hollowness in his guts. Visions of her naked and spread out before him caused him to squeeze his eyes shut, to wipe away that dirty image. He looked away. "You'll hear from me."

"Soon, please."

"Go away."

She took his hand, clung to it. "Alex, please don't throw me away." Her voice was louder, and diners swung around to watch. "I must belong to somebody, if only now and then. Everyone needs to belong to somebody."

He extracted his hand, motioned quickly for Harry Rodano to stay away. "Get out," he hissed.

She backed off, horrified by what she had done. "Alex, I don't know what came over me. Perhaps I am not well today. Please, forgive me."

He stood up. "I—cannot—abide—hysterical—women."

"You're right. You're right. I have been hysterical. I'm now in control. You can see that, Alex. It's the loneliness, but I'm over it now. It will never happen again. You can depend on that, Alex. I am a woman you can depend on. For everything."

He disappeared into the back room, Rodano bringing up the rear.

A great silent sob wrenched her body and she hurried into the street. Without thinking, she went to her office. There, in the privacy of a booth in the ladies' room, she cried. After a while she stopped crying and splashed cold water on her face, held her wrists under the faucet. The face that stared back at her from the mirror—lined, pouched, devoid of hope—was a distortion of what she had once been. What had gone wrong?

Looking back, she could see that she never had a chance. The deck was stacked against her. When Joan was ten years old, her father had left her mother. Simply disappeared without a word. Joan had blamed herself for his leaving, and so had her mother.

Soon after, the fits had started. Her mother had

complained of moments of weakness, of faintness, of heart flutterings. She grew weepy and called on her daughter for more and more assistance. Joan took over all housekeeping duties—cooking, cleaning, shopping. All done before or after school.

School was her only respite. She was an excellent student. She had a number of scholarship possibilities after high school, but she was forced to go to a small school close to home with scant academic standing. When she was graduated, she longed to take a master's degree.

"It's time for serious work," her mother had insisted, and Joan agreed.

She found a job as a secretary. Her shorthand and typing were adequate, her filing competent. She was dependable, eager, cooperative. After a year, she asked for a raise. The request was refused. She displayed no anger, no bitterness, maintaining always a high performance level.

Marriage became her goal in life. One day a man would come along. Not too good-looking, not too flashy. A modest, reliable sort. They would have a subdued courtship, getting to know and care for each other. They would open a joint savings account, make plans for the future. When they could afford it, they would marry. Naturally, there would be children. And a house in a quiet suburb. It was a pleasant dream, something to think about, to wait for.

Instead, there were a variety of men. Men who treated her casually, sometimes with open disdain; men she wanted to please, anyway they liked. She seldom saw a man more than two or three times. Not that she didn't want to, but they always drifted out of her life after a few dates. Not that it mattered. When you were young and pretty and reasonably agreeable, you kept meeting new men everywhere you went.

There were parties. And considerable drinking, not that she ever got really drunk. And pot in ample supply, not that she allowed herself ever to get too high. It was all fun, preparatory to finding the right man, to settling down. So there were many men and many beds and many acts she came to be good at. Some mornings she woke full of shame and a lingering guilt. But she learned how to put all that behind her, convinced that it was only a temporary way of life. After all, what was the point in being young and pretty if you didn't have some fun.

When Joan was thirty-one, her mother died after a stroke and a partial paralysis. It was a lingering death and had taken almost a year. Painful, frustrating, disgusting, expensive.

Joan had stopped going out. She had spent all her spare time with her mother—reading to her, watching television with her, talking to that awful, insatiable creature who stared up at her with dull, hateful eyes and a gaping mouth. Joan drank a great deal during that year and spoke to almost no one. One night her mother died, and at last Joan was free.

First, travel. To all the places she'd imagined, built heavy fantasies around. To Europe for a complete summer, skipping from country to country, tasting, sipping, soaking it all in. To the Caribbean, to Costa Rica, and to the Laurentians, where she learned to ski. Gradually, skiing began to occupy her winter weekends. Skiing, and the men she met on the slopes. *Après ski.* It was such a pleasant time, so jolly, with everybody loose and free.

In the summers, there was swimming, boating, camping out. And always men—anxious to take her to bed, to please her. As long as she pleased them. It was no hardship. No strain.

Until that party. It took place in a large house in East Hampton. People everywhere. The imagery came drifting back from time to time like a not so very good movie seen long ago. So much booze, so much grass, so little pain.

It began, the bad time, with the short blond man. Husky, aggressive, forceful, crowding into the bathroom after her, insisting that he could be of great assistance to her. How amusing in the beginning. They laughed and made bad jokes until he began to maul her. He had been so strong, forcing her to sit on the edge of the tub, exposing himself. She had protested, tried to get out of there. He stopped her easily, squeezed her face between his immensely powerful hands, and pressured her mouth open.

When he left, she remained sitting on the edge of the tub, crying and shaking. Until another man appeared and insisted that she do it to him, too. She remembered what he said: "One more cock can't hurt, baby. . ."

There seemed no end to them. Faceless, nameless, bodies without pretext of kindness or affection, demanding and taking. How many she never knew.

Nor did she know exactly what happened after that. Somehow she left the party, got back to New York, staggered aimlessly around the streets, and collapsed somewhere. Waking up in Bellevue. Two weeks later, she was pronounced fit and checked out.

She sold the furniture in the apartment, packed one bag, sent the remainder of her clothes and belongings to the Goodwill, and went looking. For what, she wasn't sure. Fourteen months later, she arrived in Aspen and had been there ever since. Aspen, she told herself over and over, was the answer to her quest. It provided everything she wanted.

She knew better. All life was a lie. A catalog of deceptions, large and small, that were meant to provoke one into going on, trying again. Designed to cause you to proceed without complaint until you were completely used up. Then, useless and helpless, you were cast aside. In time, you drifted out of sight, a forgotten intrusion, no more important in a place like Aspen than another snowflake up on the peak. . .

—— **4** ——

Washed up. Kaput. Bobby Wallace had a bellyful of Scooter Lewis. Writers, all of them were weird but none so loony as this crazy: a genuine freak, high as a kite and aiming to get higher, lost in never-never land.

Wallace had given it his best shot, his last shot. All morning on the horn with his Hollywood office setting the deal. Too good to believe. Newman and McQueen were willing to do the flick with a good chance of Christie and Liv Ullman for the girls' side. You couldn't beat that! And Coppola willing to direct. A smash was guaranteed; the bread would roll in in superlarge packages.

Only one thing was wrong. Scooter was wrong. The principals weren't going to stand around waiting forever. They were crying for a script. Okay, at least a treatment. Give us something! Twenty pages of outline would be good enough. Let them see the direction; let them read the words in some order; assure them that Scooter Lewis could still put together a simple declarative sentence.

Once done, the screenplay. The novel after that. All that had to be done was to fill in the empty places. Transitions, descriptions, a little stream of consciousness for those faggoty New York critics. No sweat.

Except that Scooter was in no shape to pull it off. Not this year, anyway. But a man didn't get to be the second-best agent in the world without having brains. He'd figured a way. The writer's approval was all that was needed and he expected to get that without trouble. On paper. In writing. Signed and delivered.

He rang the bell at Scooter's front door. He rang it again, longer and louder. No answer. He went round to the side and looked into the bedroom. No Scooter. He circled back to where the deck widened and saw that the tall glass doors that led into the living room were open. He stepped inside.

On the couch was Scooter Lewis. Out cold. On the floor next to the couch was a naked girl. She snored, Wallace noticed with some distaste. Across the room, on the white bear rug, were another girl and a boy. Both of them were naked.

Wallace swore and shook Scooter. "Wake up, fella. There is business to talk about."

The writer showed no signs of life.

Wallace shook him again. Still no response. Wallace put his hand to Scooter's face. It was damp and cold. He tried to locate the pulse in the writer's throat and felt no answering beat.

"Oh, sweet Jesus."

He prodded the girl on the floor with his shoe. She rolled away. He kicked her in the ass. Her eyes fluttered open.

"Hey! That hurts."

"Scooter," Wallace said. "What's he on?"

"Let me sleep."

"He may be dead."

The girl sat up. Her young face was puffy, lined with fright. Her eyes darted to Scooter, and away. "He can't be."

"There's no pulse. So what's he been using? You have to know."

She made a concerted effort to think. "Everything. Grass. . ."

"Grass didn't do this."

"You're right."

"Pills," he supplied.

"Yes, pills. There was this dude outside Tom's Market. He was dealing. Scooter bought his full bag."

"What else?"

"Shit."

"Heroin?"

"He said it was good stuff."

"Christ," Wallace said, trying to think straight.

He picked up the phone and dialed. A voice answered: "Aspen Institute for Humanistic Studies. . ."

"Katherine Pepe, please." He glanced back at the girl. She was rapidly lapsing back into a stupor. "How much did he take?"

"What? Oh, I don't know."

Kit's voice came on the phone.

"It's Bobby Wallace," he said. "I got trouble. It's the Scooter. Looks like he's dead or nearly dead of an O.D. Do you know a doctor, someone I can depend on?"

"Okay, Bobby, I'll do what I can. Meanwhile, start Scooter walking. Keep him on his feet. Slap him around if you have to, but keep him from sinking lower."

"Will do."

"Are you at Scooter's place?"

"Right."

"I'll get somebody."

"Thanks, Kit, I really appreciate—" The line was dead.

The doctor was a tall man with rugged Lincolnesque features: shoulders broad, arms uncommonly long. His manner was sober without being self-important, efficient without pretentiousness. He had been an all-league forward at Dartmouth as an undergraduate; he was a tournament-level tennis player; and he was the author of three medical volumes about drug abuse. He came out of Scooter Lewis's bedroom and held his forefingers about an inch apart.

"Your friend is lucky," he said to Bobby Wallace.

The agent was on his feet. "He'll be okay?"

"Yes. This time. I stimulated him and that brought him back quickly. It's clear that his system absorbed a limited amount of whatever crap he shot up. Heroin, I assume. Does he go this way often?"

Wallace made an unhappy face. "I don't know. I'm not this close to him usually. He's a user, of just about everything. But he lays off H most of the time, I think."

"You're probably right. Comparatively few needle tracks in his arm."

"He sure looked like he'd bought it when I got here," Wallace said.

"No after effects, doctor?" Kit asked.

His glance swung her way. "Heroin doesn't damage cell matter, Kit, so there's no danger in that direction. He'll snap back quickly. But he should be turned around."

"Well, that's up to him, isn't it, doc?" Wallace said. Then, in a more conciliatory tone, "What do I owe you, doc?"

"Nothing. I'm out at the institute to stimulate minds that have become too concerned with medical detail, too parochial. I guess doctors are like cops. Cops always wear their weapons; we always carry our black bags. Glad I could help, Mr. Wallace."

Wallace hesitated. "There isn't going to be any kind of a report, is there? I mean, some medical routine—or to the cops?"

The doctor surveyed Wallace balefully from his great height. "Next time, sir, get your man to a hospital as quickly as you can. I won't be available again."

"Sure, doc, I understand," Bobby said, anxious to move the physician out of there.

"Keep him warm and quiet," the doctor said before departing. "I'll check back this evening." His eyes went to the three young people huddled together across the room, all fully clothed now. "I assume you kids were into this party. Real swingers, the lot of you. This should teach you a lesson, but it probably won't. Stay lucky and one or two of you may live long enough to vote."

After the doctor was gone, Wallace turned to the young people, pointing dramatically toward the front door. "Take off," he commanded.

"Scooter won't like this," one of them protested.

Wallace took a single step forward. In unison, they flinched and hurried out of the house. The agent knuckled his eyes and deposited himself on the couch. "That was close."

"Scooter's a lucky man."

"Scooter's a freak; I figured he was gone."

"You'd better talk to him, Bobby. He can't keep living this way forever."

"Thanks for the medic, Kit. I didn't know where else to look. Funny, him not wanting me to know his name."

"Just protecting himself."

"He's entitled," Wallace said, his mind leapfrogging. Even if Scooter snapped back the next day, he would still be in no condition to do any concentrated writing. His head was somewhere else, pickled in some exotic chemical solution. He considered Kit at length.

"What now," she said conversationally. "Will you be going back to Hollywood?"

"I don't know. Scooter has really loused things

up. There's this deal—oh, hell, there is very big money involved. Publication of the material as a novel is all set. The movie deal is practically guaranteed. Big names, box-office draws. A can't-miss proposition. But the subject matter cries out for Scooter. It's the kind of thing he's specialized in, knows in his blood. With him, it's a winner. Without, we draw a blank."

"His style is that distinctive, you mean?"

He studied her frankly. She was everything he appreciated in a woman. Beautiful, with a sedate, controlled manner; slightly foreign, exotic, with the promise of a deep passion waiting to be unloosed. As a rule, Wallace did well with women. Despite his chunky build and his coarse face, women were drawn to him, turned on by his barely restrained energy, as if they recognized that in eruption he would be a force for excitement and pleasure. In Hollywood, his reputation was unrivaled as a lover of beautiful women; and no woman who accepted him into her bed had ever turned him away. Always it was Bobby Wallace who terminated the relationship, Bobby Wallace who sought other companionship. But Kit Pepe showed no signs of interest and that troubled him, made her seem even more desirable. Looking at her now, he felt the excitement rise in him almost to flood tide.

"I mean his *name*," he said slowly. "Scooter Lewis—people are turned on to him. Counterculture scribe. Historian of the hippies, the drug crowd, the communes, the bike gangs. The guy has the rep now, and the time is right to capitalize on it."

"Too bad he isn't more reliable."

"A million dollars ride on him, maybe more."

"Get a ghost," she suggested gaily. "Someone to do the work while Scooter recuperates. When he's ready, he can put the final touches on it. Language, style, his particular insights."

"That's what Scooter said," Wallace offered, "but I'd need somebody good to pull it off."

"There are any number of good writers around."

"Sure, but they aren't available when you need them. And I need somebody today. Yesterday."

She stood up to go. "Can't win 'em all, Bobby."

"Why not?" he asked deliberately, watching her closely, his mind turning over.

"Bobby. . ." she warned softly, anticipating him.

"Help me save his career."

She backed off, hands raised in defense. "No way, Bobby."

He inserted a helpless plea into his voice, selling hard but without force. "He wasn't always like this, you know. Not always on drugs. He got turned on in the hospital, you know."

"I didn't know."

"Scooter was a hero. In Vietnam, didn't I tell you? He was wounded, shot up pretty bad trying to save some buddies in his platoon. He's got all kinds of medals."

"They gave him drugs to kill the pain."

"Poor guy," Wallace said. "It must've been pretty awful. They started him out on morphine. Then, when he got discharged, the pain was still there. He needed something. Somebody put him on to heroin and it worked. The pain was gone. But then it was too late. He was hooked."

"Bobby," Kit said dubiously, "it sounds almost too pat, too much like a Hollywood movie."

"I swear it. The point is, Scooter could've been one of the all-time great writers. He had what it takes, the gift, the magic talent, the desire. The dope took it all away."

"I wish I could help—"

"You can, Kit, you can. I'm a great believer in intuition, and I'm getting tremendous vibes about you. You'd pull it off with no strain, and you'd love every minute of it."

She retreated further. "Don't you know how to take no for an answer, Bobby?"

"You didn't say absolutely."

"*Ab-so-lute-ly.*"

"Two careers will be salvaged, mine and Scooter's. And you'll open up a whole new field for yourself. With me representing you, you'll make a fortune. Become famous. Win an Oscar."

"I don't want an Oscar. I'm a poet, not a script-writer."

"You can do it."

"No."

"I'm in trouble, Kit. Scooter's in trouble. Either you come through for us, or it all goes down the drain. Flushed."

"That's not my fault."

"We saved his life. Aren't we responsible for what happens to him now?"

"I see right through you, Bobby."

"Think about what I've said."

"There's nothing to think about."

"Work it over in your head for a while. Study it from every angle—the artistic rewards, the material gain, the money. Kit, become a famous screenwriter and the world will break down doors to read your poetry."

"Don't you ever stop selling, Bobby?"

He sensed a lessening of her resolve and gave her his best smile. "That's an agent's job."

"And you're a pretty damned good agent."

"Second best in the whole world. . ."

——— **5** ———

Skip Blondell huddled miserably behind a large boulder, rocking back and forth, eyes closed, trying not to think, not to feel. His teeth chattered, his legs cramped, his skin leaped and twitched.

Where was Keating?

The early-morning hours had been the worst. Stumbling around in the dark on that great slanting rock face; slipping and sliding as his footing gave way; struggling to make it safely to a strategically suitable height and a secure area of cover. At first there had been only the discomfort coupled with a rising excitement, the thrill of the hunt. He saw himself as setting up a superblind where he would hide and wait for his quarry. He saw himself as a hunter beyond comparison out after the ultimate prey—man. Until fear was introduced into the equation. Fear that he might fail and have to subject himself to Alex Budde's wrath; that he might succeed and carry around the burden of being a murderer; that Alex Budde might use that information as a weapon against him. And the worst fear of all, that Keating would find him out, turn the game around, transform killer into victim, send Skip Blondell on a quick, painful path out of this world.

What if he didn't come?

Initially, he was grateful when the morning light appeared. It spread over the mountain disposing of threatening shadows and lumpish ghosts and revealing hidden falls and crevices. But that quick release from terror was short-lived.

Soon the demands of his flesh made him know exactly how badly he was being used. Budde should never have dispatched him on this mission of destruction. He was the wrong choice. Let Sexton do the killing, or Rodano. They were cut out for the job by natural inclination. They had the genes; he didn't.

Keating was twice his size, a monstrously powerful man, skilled in the ways of the mountain. A man capable of snapping Blondell's scrawny spine between his bare hands. Despite the warming rays of the sun, Blondell began to shiver again. He had to pee something awful.

Budde was wrong to lay this on him.

Roughing it was not Blondell's style. His slender limbs, his pale skin, his thin blood, all made him suited to indoor living. To an easy, stressless environment. Warmth and comfort were fundamental to his well-being.

Why hadn't he thought to bring a blanket?

He eased himself erect, peered around the boulder. No signs of life anywhere. With clumsy fingers he unzipped, searched inside, and brought out a shriveled pimple, barely long enough to make its exit through the fly. His stream was weak and pallid, and it took a very long time for him to empty his bladder.

Ah, better...

He sank back into position behind the boulder and remembered the food he had brought. He nibbled at some cheese, finding it particularly unsatisfying. Time passed slowly and he became impatient. He willed Keating to appear, to play his role in this performance. Blondell wanted to get it over with. The question of failure kept returning and with it the fear. A sinking sensation turned his stomach and he thought he might be sick.

He longed to be strong and handsome and brave.

Keating had it all. Looks, courage, size. Women were drawn to him, men respected him. He could do whatever he wanted with his life. Go in one direction until it no longer satisfied him, then move off in another. Not Blondell: All his life he had existed off crumbs, taking the leavings, scratching and scrambling for everything he wanted. It wasn't fair; it simply wasn't fair.

He longed for a girl.

Still no sign of Keating. What if he'd come to the wrong place! Budde had pointed out on the Department of the Interior Geological Survey map exactly where he was to go. Hollander's Spring. Precise directions had been provided, and he had followed them in every detail.

But after all, he was human; people sometimes goofed. Budde would *kill* him. He went over it all in his head. This had to be the place. Keating was late, that was all.

He worked his way up the slope to where the shale was looser: Small rocks broke free every couple of minutes, giving birth to rockslides of minor proportions. He lay down in a shallow dry creek bed, placed his equipment along-side, rested his head on his backpack, and closed his eyes. The rising sun warmed him.

Her name was Trish.

She had visited his gallery twice and both times had lingered to talk to him about the pictures on the walls. Each time, he had tried to get her to stay with him, to have dinner or go to a movie or listen to the rock group over at the place on Galena. No go.

Beneath the thin blouses she wore, her nipples were darkly appealing.

Warm, sentient memories flooded over him. He imagined her naked. He would take one of her breasts into his mouth, fill himself with her, bite down. She would love it. And his face between her legs. She would drive against him, pound crazily. He touched himself and was hard.

Chicks were fantastic. A never-ending feast, never fulfilling him, as if a libidinous tapeworm gnawed steadily at his innards.

She would smell great.

Not too clean. Sex and piss mixed, filling the cavities of his head. Making him crazy. Visions of Trish spun across the screen of his mind. He moaned and thrashed about, rolled and heaved, punished his flesh.

He fought to crawl into her, to deposit himself deep within those shadowed portions of her body. To become her.

"Trish!" he cried aloud.

And his skinny frame leaped in spasm. Panting, throat dry, heart pounding, he waited for tranquillity to arrive.

He sat up and fixed his trousers. A furtive glance assured him that his activities had gone unnoticed. Women made him act this way. Forced

him to lose control, to be sinful. He hated them for
forcing evil onto him. Someday he would extract
a suitable revenge.

He looked down the slope, examining the terrain. A shadow moved just below the tree line.
Or had it? He grew tense and anxious and wondered if his eyes were faking him out. He
squeezed them shut, looked again.

Something was moving down there. An animal?
A deer or a bear, even. My God! What if it were
a bear? Ferocious beasts, they had been known
to attack people. Why hadn't he brought a gun?

The shadow appeared again, detached itself
from the protective shield of the forest. Keating...
Blondell sighed with relief and for a long moment
was able to tell himself that the worst was over.
But he knew that wasn't true.

Keating moved without haste across the bare
rock face. He seemed comfortable on the slope,
unafraid, looking neither up nor down. When he
was almost directly below Blondell's hiding place,
he stopped, shook off his backpack. His eyes swept
the heights and Blondell wondered if Keating had
spotted him. If so, he gave no sign.

Keating retrieved his pack and moved into the
trees. There, still clearly in view, he strung up a
canvas lean-to between two young pine trees.
Using a hand ax, he collected pine boughs and
spread them under the lean-to. Over them, a plaid
blanket.

He built a small fire and made his way up to the
spring, filling a coffeepot with water. He hung
the pot over the fire, placed his back to a tree and
removed his boots, took some food out of his pack,
and began to eat.

Blondell watched, almost forgetting to breathe.

He cried out in silent exultation; he was going to do it! The heaviest act of his life. He was going to kill Tom Keating.

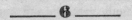

She felt as if she were under attack—as if icy, impersonal emotional pellets were bombarding her incessantly. Confusion was not a normal state for her. She had always understood that to live well, to do the things that mattered to her, extraneous concerns had to be cleared out of her life. Intrusions were to be shed the way a snake sheds its skin, so that she was constantly refurbishing her spirit.

Her life was organized accordingly around activities that were meaningful, that produced stimulation, intellectual expansion, sensual pleasure. Each in its place, each to her own benefit.

First, her poetry, and then the teaching. After that—well, she sorted things out as they came. A harsh selection method according to inner dictates that permitted no exploitation of her essential humanness.

Things seemed to have gotten out of hand. Confusion had taken over. People plucked at her, demanding attention, seeking affection, craving more than she was equipped to give or desirous of giving. They sucked strength out of her, left her empty and concerned.

Bobby Wallace for Scooter Lewis and for himself. Jon. Carl Osborne. Let them take care of themselves.

She berated herself: This was not the way she truly felt. Each person was part of the whole. *"No man is an Island, entire of it self. . . ."* They were all small but vital gears in a monstrous mechanistic construct that must inevitably grind to a screeching halt should too many of its parts become inoperable. Or function badly. Man helping man, that was the way life should be lived. An activity greased by the bodies and souls of mankind.

She mocked herself. The poet in her kept cropping up with prettified concepts that she wanted to believe. Fantasies. In fact, life was a crass, cruel, bloody enterprise that provided most of its practitioners with pain and deprivation, agony and death.

Take the money and run.

How often had she listened to someone expound that theory? Were they entirely wrong? Not likely. Not in a world that cherished property above men, power over progress, ideology over ideals.

Get it while you can, baby.

She considered the seminars at the institute. And her classes back at Antioch. What effect did her work have on the people she addressed? Almost none, she was convinced. Students came and went, heard her out, gave lip service to her ideas, to poetry, to a higher form of existence, only to drift back into a world that demanded action instead of ideas, that applauded results not philosophy. Cuckold your friend. Screw your neighbor. Make a buck.

And laugh your way to the bank.

Bobby Wallace offered the chance of a lifetime. Ghost for Scooter Lewis. With Bobby's help, she could quickly learn the tricks of the trade, establish her credentials as a professional. Television, films—they were open to someone like her. She was young, attractive, more intelligent and gifted than many people. She thought of others who had crossed over, recent residents of the Emerald City —Dickey, Didion, Jong, Hochman, Gould—so many others.

Was this her time? Just reach out and grab success. Take it.

Her concentration faltered. A fuzzy image of Jon Osborne floated to mind. Anger and resentment twisted the boyish face. The damage that only betrayal can bring. For him there had been simply another rejection, losing once again to his father.

Kit hadn't intended to hurt him. He had considered her a peer, similar in years, unaware of the gulf that separated them: a broad division of interest and experience, of attitude and desire, of passion. Jon was a child and she felt an almost maternal affection for him. No lust, no love, no yearning to present her body to his.

With Carl it was different. The bed had drawn them from the first. She wanted him as much as he wanted her. Perhaps more, and that troubled her.

All restraint was left behind. Naked, Carl was an attacking primitive, working over her flesh with virtuoso skill, with the touch and delicacy of an artist, manipulating her like a symphonic conductor.

She found enormous pleasure in him. His passion washed over her until she was weak with frenzy and continuing desire. He roused her to levels she had never before known, maintained her there before sending her crashing back to reality. He made her weak, sated, and wanting more. Words and ideas were put aside when they made love. She existed inside her skin. All feeling, hot, impatient.

She became coarse and blatant, desperate to receive more, to give more pleasure. She wished her breasts were bigger, as if in size he would find greater joy. She wanted her ass to swell and become gross in order that he might squeeze and pinch and bang away in brute violence. She imagined her cunt expansive enough to admit all of him, to absorb and to swallow him and make him part of her being.

He was a machine. A fucking machine. All parts meshing smoothly. Operating tirelessly. His lean body was strong. His cock was perfection: size, shape, texture; the way it *fit*. Everywhere. And that was what she wanted, to put him everywhere.

His climax was a thing of beauty. Thrusts and spasms that went on forever. The full extension of him riding in and out, never missing, pounding her into the bed. His hands dug into the soft flesh of her bottom and pulled her up to reach him. He moved her, turned her, raised her, spread her. He moaned. He cried out.

No whimpering seepage. No little death. This was how it was meant to be. Come flooded her belly, filled her womb, clogged her tubes. A come meant to create strong, healthy children.

Like Jon?

No one had ever given her this much. Was this then the normal way, the way it was supposed to be? Or was Carl some weird and wonderful freak created by a perverse nature to tantalize and taunt the women whose beds he graced?

After him, could she go back to the men she had known? Men who patted her tenderly and recommended books that she should read to improve herself. Men unable to do it much of the time.

Carl invited her to grow, to demand, to swell to bursting with joy, and ultimately to explode. The more female she was, the more male he became.

So it was.

———— **7** ————

Blondell was enraged. He stormed silently at Keating's duplicity, his refusal to abide by the rules, his bad performance. Blondell swore. He begged. He prayed. None of it did any good. Keating did his own thing.

The day went slowly past and Keating had not made a move. Oh, twice he had gone off to refill his coffeepot, and once he had stripped to the waist and washed his upper body and arms and face in the icy water of the spring. But that was all. He always returned to his campsite to doze, or read, or sit staring into space.

While Blondell remained uncomfortable in that narrow trench that concealed him. His legs cramped periodically and he had to urinate again, but he didn't dare, and he wondered if, when the opportunity arrived, he'd be able to perform efficiently. At last, unable to tolerate his anguish any longer, he shifted around. A handful of small rocks and pebbles immediately went skittering down the rock face. Blondell held his breath.

Keating seemed oblivious. Nothing that transpired on the mountain seemed to affect him in the least. He continued to read. Safe and smug in his bearish body.

Blondell grew angrier with Keating for not being concerned, for being so sure of himself, for being able to climb to these heights by himself and sit around unprotected, fearing nothing, as if some invisible and impenetrable wall shielded him from harm.

Blondell envied big men their size and strength, their ability to deal with whatever life handed out. Not so Skipper. He had always been scrawny and weak, a born victim. Fate had never treated him kindly, had never smiled on his attempts to improve his situation. Everything came easy to a man like Keating. While Blondell had to scheme and plot, take terrifying chances.

He decided that he hated Keating. Always had. With a fierce red rage. Hated him enough to kill him, and be glad to have done so. What if he unloosed a slide at this moment, directing it toward that small campsite. Would it do the job?

Without realizing that danger threatened, Keat-

ing had set up his camp in a protected position.
The trees would break the momentum of the slide,
fragment it, provide safe areas for Keating to
hide in. Blondell wanted to get it right. So he
waited.

Dusk fell and the air turned cold. Blondell began
to tremble. His fingers curled, his skin stretching
tightly over his knuckles.

Down below, Keating warmed himself at the
fire. He fed it some wood and it flared up as if in
gratitude.

Blondell had never been able to build a satis-
factory fire. He longed to go down there, tell Keating that he had been out hiking, that he had gotten
lost. He could warm himself by the fire. Surely
Keating would not turn him away. They might
spend a very pleasant night together, rapping,
eating, smoking a joint or two. He kept to his
place.

Night cloaked the mountain and Blondell
hugged himself in a vain attempt to keep warm.
He willed himself to sleep, commanded the night
to pass more rapidly. He heard a sound behind
him. He whirled around and the movement sent
stones skipping downward. Blondell felt the
ground shift under him and he began to slide. He
clawed for a handhold, hung on, worked himself
back into a safe place.

He was breathing hard. Afraid and cold and
very weary. It had been a mistake, accepting this
insane assignment. He was not cut out for rough
work. And while he suffered in the cold, Alex
Budde dined on gourmet food, drinking French
wine, choosing one of the best-looking chicks in
town for himself. It wasn't fair.

Blondell felt separated from everything and everyone he cared about. Deserted, disconnected. Back in school—it seemed a century ago—he had acted in a play. The title came to him after a moment—*High Tor*, by Maxwell Anderson. In it, two men had been lost on a mountain. They were venal characters; pathetic, frightened men. People laughed at their fright and their antics.

Blondell set his unsteady jaw. Nobody was ever going to laugh at him again. Not after this. He wouldn't tolerate it. By this time tomorrow, it would all be over.

Keating's fire flickered blue and yellow in the dark. By now the bearded leathersmith was probably asleep. Sleep well, Keating, thought Blondell. This will be your last sleep.

Alex drove carefully, without excess speed, eyes fastened on the road ahead. He controlled an automobile the way he did most other aspects of his life, with strength and purpose, keeping risk at a minimum.

"You go tonight," he said.

"Tonight!" Jon said. "That doesn't give me time to get ready."

"You are ready," Budde said. "Right now."

"Okay, Alex."

"I've got the plan all worked out. The timing, everything. The idea is to lift the stuff and get it back here without anybody connecting us to the job."

"How many men on truck?" Jon said.

"Two. The driver and a dude riding shotgun."

Jon made no attempt to conceal his dismay. "That means shooting."

"Harry will take care of that department."

"I didn't bargain for any shooting. That's not my style."

"Don't worry kid," Rodano said in that squeaky voice of his. "Any trouble, I deal with it. You got nothing to worry about."

They drove without speaking for a while. "Who does the shipment belong to?" Jon asked.

Budde shook his head. "Don't be nosy, kid. I want you to know something, I'll tell you."

"Syndicate?" Jon persisted.

"That's enough," Budde said.

"Okay," Jon said. "Answer this one—when do I get my share?"

"When the stuff is stashed away safely. When it's cool."

"How much this time?"

"I'll take care of you, kid. Don't worry."

"You said the shipment was worth maybe a quarter of a million, a little over."

"That's on the street, after processing. Not all of it comes to me."

"I want fifty thousand dollars."

Budde glanced sidelong at him. "Don't be a pig, kid. Nobody likes a pig. Ten grand this shot.

"Then I don't go along."

Budde thought about it. "Okay, you got your fifty." He grinned cheerfully. "That make you feel better?"

Jon gave no answer, his brain reeling under the onslaught of a barrage of unanswered questions.

Moments later, Budde pulled off to the side of the road. "Back in the woods," he said. "A blue and white Winnebago. Large enough for a couple of cats to take a holiday in. It's fully stocked, so it looks legitimate in case anybody gets curious. The keys are under the driver's seat."

"You mean we take off right now?" Jon said.

"You got it, kid."

Jon exhaled. "Okay, Alex, for fifty grand I guess my good-byes can wait."

"Do this job right, boys. The payoff is there for everybody."

They watched him drive away.

Ten minutes later, the Winnebago was on the road.

——— 9 ———

They tried Jon's apartment first. He wasn't there.

"What now?" Carl said. A deep foreboding spread along his nerves, seemed to be etched in his lean and manly face. There was a futility in all of this, he told himself; he had a sense of déjà vu. In the past, he'd tried everything to make contact with Jon, to be a true father and transform him into a true son. Nothing had worked. There was no cause to believe it would work now.

"There are a few bars Jon prefers," Kit offered.

"You know them?"

"Yes."

"Let's go."

An hour later they entered the Spot. Alex Budde, alone at his corner table, saw them at once and stood, lifting a beckoning hand.

"I'm looking for Jon," Carl started without preamble as they approached the table.

"He hasn't been in here all night," Budde said. "What will you drink?"

"No, thanks," Carl said. "We have to keep looking."

"Some kind of a problem?"

"Something Jon said," Carl replied automatically, his brain working hard to figure out where his son might be. "Something about making a big score, about getting rich in a hurry."

"Good luck to him," Budde said lightly.

"Then you have no idea what he might have meant?" Kit asked.

Budde shook his head.

"Or where we might find him?" Carl put in.

"Try the Red Onion."

"He wasn't there."

"Sometimes he eats at the Souper."

"Nobody there has seen him all day."

"Well," Budde said, "if he comes around, I'll tell him to get in touch." Budde arranged a mild expression on his bright face. "All set for the P and Z, Carl?"

"We'll give them our best shot."

"I'm sure they'll approve. Trouble will come later, with the commissioners."

"Maybe not. Maybe Lewin will come over to our side. Or even Tom Keating."

"Not Keating," Budde said. "There's no way he'll come over."

"Time will tell."

"We'll be in touch."

Budde lowered himself into his chair. He ordered some hot tea, sipped slowly, his mind working over everything Osborne and Kit had said. Jon had shot his mouth off, that much was clear. To the girl, most likely, since he and Osborne didn't get on well. How much had he told her? How much could he tell her? Sure, this was the biggest job he'd been on so far. He was going to get more money than ever before. But essentially it was another pickup, no different from those that had come before.

He could've been boasting in order to impress her, anxious to soften her up. Possible—but not probable. Jon was cool and competent, kept his work to himself. That's why Budde had been using him for so long. Most kids flitted in, grabbed what they could, and were on their way out before you knew it. Take it and run, there'd always be another score. Jon was different. A loner, a dependable mule, shrewder than most, with a tight lip.

". . . a big score," Carl had reported his son as saying. Something about getting rich quick. Budde shifted around nervously, skin wrinkling. An idea surfaced and his stomach muscles ridged, his fists clenched. He commanded himself to relax. Nothing

was worth getting excited about, turning those
intermittent stomach cramps into an ulcer proper.
Besides, there was plenty of time to correct whatever was wrong. Time—and opportunity.

——— **10** ———

Keating was in action. It all happened so suddenly, the big man apparently launching himself
from sleep immediately into the job of striking
camp. Not rushing, not frantic, yet putting things
together with accomplished ease.

Some inner signal had caused Blondell to stir.
He woke unhappily, reluctant to give up the dark
comfort of sleep. He sat up and stretched, for a
long interval not aware of where he was or why
he was there.

Until reality came crashing down on him. His
clothes were damp and he shivered against the
morning chill. He whimpered and wished himself
back in the gallery, back among familiar and safe
surroundings, in a world that he controlled, in
a world of his own choosing and making. What a
fool he'd been to allow Alex to talk him into this
foolhardy expedition. A man should always stick
to his own thing, to what he did best. His hands
folded into fists and he longed to hit out at the
elements that tormented him.

Keating, hairy and bearlike, ominous in his proportions, was on the move. Backpack in place, squinting into the high gloom as if searching for something specific. Or *someone.*

Oh, my God!

Keating climbed up the rock face, closing in on Blondell's hiding place. For an extended, breathless period, the gallery owner could not move. His eyes grew large. His genitals were sucked up into his belly. His sphincter tightened in despair. Here it was: all the plotting and scheming, the tracking, the waiting, the being afraid, all converging on a single vulnerable point in space.

Keating was coming after *him.*

It had turned around. Their roles were reversed. Just as he had feared. The hunter was the hunted. He, George Marvin Blondell, was the victim-to-be. A choked cry filled his throat and he hid his face in his hands. He was at heart a simple and gentle spirit, given to similar pursuits. He ordered himself to flee, to run as far and as fast as he could, to put Keating, Alex Budde, and all the others behind him. To put his back to Aspen once and for all.

He held his position. A steady inner voice commanded him not to panic. To consider his options in the way that a general would assess conditions prior to a battle. After all, he could always run; that was something he had always been able to do very well.

Keating continued on his way. In the gray dawn, he loomed larger and larger. A Bunyanesque figure, eyes looking upward, face expressionless behind the great black beard.

Coincidence, that's all it was. His coming in this

direction. Coincidence played a vital role in life. Accidents did happen. Keating could not possibly find him. Instead, the big man would climb past and Blondell would be safe.

And if he were wrong? With tentative moves, Blondell located the pick and the shovel.

Below, Keating picked his way. Bent over to compensate for the angle of climb, one hand reaching but never quite touching the ground, planting each large-booted foot solidly. He was in no position to defend himself from attack; he could not charge Blondell's redoubt; he could not retreat effectively.

Courage inflated the little man's chest. A new confidence saturated his being. Gripping the shovel in one hand, he stepped out in the open, waiting for Keating to recognize his presence, to greet him affably, to stand still. Keating kept on climbing.

Resentment unloosened a fresh supply of adrenaline in Blondell. His heart pumped and his eyes teared. He blinked and began to dislike Keating more than ever. What right had the big man to ignore him so? To treat him as unworthy of notice. Was Keating so beyond the normal dangers that most men were subject to that he could afford such arrogance? Blondell put it all down to growth patterns. Big men often displayed their natural superiority to smaller people. Blessed with size and strength, they scorned little men as weaklings, incapable of superior performance.

What about Napoleon?

Caesar?

Mussolini?

Blondell took two or three forward steps in thoughtless rage, and his feet went out from under him as the loose rock and shale shifted free. He fell heavily. A small slide commenced and, to his horror, Blondell discovered that he was part of it. He scrambled to end his descent, struggling onto his feet, breathing hard.

As if nothing had occurred, Keating kept coming.

Blondell spotted some large rocks. Nearly eighteen inches across. Dislodge one or two, and he would trigger a rockslide of massive proportions. Half the mountain would be dumped on Keating. He thrust his shovel behind one impressive boulder and applied pressure. The rock shifted forward. Satisfied, certain he was now in complete control, Blondell allowed the boulder to settle back into its resting-place; he maintained tension on the shovel. He drew air into his lungs.

"Keating!" he shouted. His voice cracked.

Keating didn't stop.

"Keating!" he screamed.

If Keating heard, he gave no indication. Suddenly, he was no more than ten yards away, a decided threat.

"Dammit, Keating!" Blondell cried desperately. "Look at me!"

The big man stopped, assuming a comfortable position on the slope, face upturned, an impassive hairy mask. When he spoke, it was in a moderate voice. "I'm surprised that it's you, Skip."

"What do you mean? You weren't expecting anybody."

"I expected Sexton, or Harry Rodano."

Blondell suspected that Keating was trying to put him off guard. He braced himself, physically and mentally. "Don't kid me, Keating. You thought you were up here alone."

"You should've brought warmer clothes, Skip.

You must've known you weren't going to get a chance at me right away. Didn't Alex tell you how difficult I would make it for you?"

"I don't know what you're talking about."

"That night at my car, that was you, wasn't it, Skip?"

"How'd you know?" Blondell's pride was damaged. He wanted to believe he'd been completely silent, invisible to the world.

"You're not cut out for this kind of business, Skip. You don't do it well at all."

Blondell felt the anger return. "I'm going to waste you, Keating."

"Why?"

The question confused the other man. "Because I want to, that's why!" he almost yelled. "Because it will make me feel good."

"I know you deal for Alex. I didn't know you killed for him. It's not your style."

"With you gone, things will go pretty good for all of us."

"Don't be a fool. Alex will own you after this."

"Nobody owns the Skipper."

"You can't do it, Skip."

The thin face was mottled, eyes unsteady. "The hell I can't! Maybe I'm smaller than you, but I've got a lot of heart."

Keating held his ground.

"It'll look like an accident, Keating. Everybody knows you're a mountain nut. You take chances, everybody knows that. Only this time the mountain did a number on you."

"You'll never get away with it, Skip."

"Good-bye, Keating."

Blondell leaned hard on the shovel. For a split second he was afraid the rock would not respond.

Then it broke loose, went bounding downward, carrying thousands of its brothers and sisters along. A full-scale rockslide.

"Go to hell, Keating!" he yelled over the roar.

Keating wasn't there to hear. Blondell searched the land below, swung right, then left.

"Keating! Come back! Be killed. . ." He galloped like an enraged animal, in a race with the descending slide, straining to make it beyond the perimeter of rock. Keating was gone.

Blondell sank to the ground. Failure burned sourly behind his navel. It scorched the lining of his stomach, wormed its way into his guts. Why couldn't he get anything right?

Alex would be upset. He would rave and threaten, punish him in some painful and cruel way. It was to be expected. Still, he had tried his best. Somehow, as it usually did, success had eluded him.

Keating was right. Alex should have told him how difficult it would be. He should have been instructed to bring along suitable clothes, blankets, a protective tent. Two nights and a day alone on the mountain—if Alex thought it was so easy, let him do it himself next time. A man did his best; you couldn't expect more. Alex would simply have to understand.

There was also Keating to consider now. He would be very angry with Alex. That would be a confrontation worth seeing. Let them beat each other to a pulp. Kill each other, if it went that way. He'd sit back and enjoy the spectacle. And when it was over, it wouldn't matter who won; Skip Blondell would still have his gallery, would go on as before; and he would never again get into this kind of a bind.

Keating. What would Keating do to him? The big man was out there. He had a right to be angry with Blondell. Keating would track him down, beat him, do him real and lasting harm. Blondell was not prepared to suffer pain.

He looked around, saw nothing, heard nothing. Get back to Aspen, that was the first thing. Off this rugged and awful mountain. Away from the cold and the damp; away from Keating. Alex would protect him, surely. After all, none of it would have happened if not for him.

Still carrying the shovel, Blondell went up the incline, moving as fast as he dared. The loose footing caused him to stumble and fall more than once, but he persisted, desperate to put a great distance between himself and the edge of the rock face. To tumble off that cliff meant sure death on the rocks in the valley below. He went faster.

The terrain leveled off and Blondell broke into a trot. He tried to make no noise, to attract no attention. A turn in the trail looked vaguely familiar, and he assured himself that the Cherokee waited close by. Soon he was descending again.

Ahead of him was the timberline. A rising green wall that promised concealment and cover. Hidden among the trees he would be safe from pursuit. A few minutes more to the Cherokee and he'd be on his way.

He plunged into the forest. Twenty yards along, he stopped. In the silent morning, there was only the rasping of his own breathing. Where was Keating? Had the big man decided not to pursue him, not to try to hurt him? After all, Keating had a reputation as a kindly sort, a forgiving man. Yes, that was what had happened. Keating was showing mercy; he *was* a decent fellow.

Blondell couldn't accept it. He hurried on. Three times he paused to listen and heard nothing. He went nearly half a mile before he saw the red and white of the Cherokee standing out through the green wall. He very nearly laughed aloud and broke into a run.

He clambered up behind the wheel and cranked up. Nothing happened. He hit it again. No sign of life. He couldn't understand what was wrong; the battery was brand new. He lifted the hood. The battery cables had been disconnected.

"Dammit!" he cried, head swiveling. As if the scene had been rehearsed, Keating appeared from behind a tree.

"I didn't want you to leave without me, Skip."

Blondell's features screwed up, making him look like an aging gnome. He located the shovel on the ground where he had let it fall, brandishing it threateningly. "Keep away from me."

"You're coming with me, Skip."

"No."

"We're going to see Alex Budde together."

"You're crazy. He'll kill us both."

"Nobody's going to get killed."

"You don't know anything about it."

"The police. . ."

"Oh, my God! Twenty-four hours in the slam, that's all I'd last. Alex can reach right through those bars. They make it look like suicide. You can't do that to me."

"We'll get rid of Sexton."

"It makes no difference. If not Sexton, then somebody else. Guys like Alex have connections everywhere."

Keating went toward the Cherokee. "I'll hook up the battery, Skip, and we'll go." Keating went past him without hesitation. And as he did, Blondell took a single long stride forward and brought the shovel down across Keating's back with all the force he could muster.

Keating pitched forward and rolled. Blondell went after him, shovel swinging. An upraised arm deflected the blow. Keating rolled again, coming up to his knees in time to defend himself. He grabbed, and one hand closed around the shaft of the shovel. He yanked hard and the shovel came free in his hand.

Keating stood up, trying to clear his head. Pain radiated across his shoulders and along his spine. And his arm ached where he had taken the second blow. "You silly little asshole, I'm going to shake you until your teeth come loose."

Blondell retreated. As he did, he reached into his pocket and brought out a gravity knife. A flip of his wrist and the blade clicked into place.

"Come near me and I'll cut you."

"I'm going to take you, Skip."

"No way."

In one motion, Keating picked up a handful of dirt and cast it toward Blondell, charging as he did. They came together, scrambling for position. Blondell swung his knife hand and found only air. Keating tried to immobilize the knife arm, but he moved too quickly. Blood appeared in an arc along Keating's left arm and wrist.

"Dammit, Skip, you cut me." Keating pulled away, reached for a handkerchief.

Blondell ran. Keating went after him.

Blondell flitted among the trees, soon out of sight. The sound of his retreat drifted back to Keating. Once beyond the tree line, the gallery owner moved over a natural trail that wound along the lower edge of the rock face. He fell twice, but he managed to regain his footing, and he kept going.

The trail led higher. Anticipating the other man, Keating cut up at a steeper angle, made it first to the upper rim of the slope. He went from west to east, able to see the gallery owner clearly, but behind him and so unseen by him.

At a point directly above Blondell, he stopped, setting himself securely. "Skip!"

Blondell stopped and raised his eyes. "Go away!" he cried.

"You can't get away," Keating called.

"Let me alone!"

The words echoed off the almost vertical walls above them.

"If this keeps up, one of us is bound to get hurt."

"Don't come near me."

"You have nothing to be afraid of, Skip. I promise you."

"Stay back."

"I'm coming down, Skip."

"No, you're trying to trick me."

Keating started down.

Blondell made a swift move, a sharp turn back toward the way he'd come. His feet went out from under him. On his back, he slid, gathering speed, unable to twist around, unable to slow his fall, carried along on a swiftly moving bed of small stones.

"Help me!" he screamed.

"Get your feet down. Plant your feet."

If he heard, Blondell gave no response. His haphazard struggles accelerated the fall; his body control was gone. The facing took a sudden downward turn, a precipitous drop, and Blondell, as if pulled by a heavy weight, went over the side. His scream was soon lost in the thin air.

Keating sat down and stayed where he was for a long time. Then he made his way to where the Cherokee was parked. He connected the cables, and the engine kicked over at once. He followed the trail down slowly, in no hurry to get anywhere.

——— 11 ———

At five minutes before noon, the Planning and Zoning Board reached its decision. A motion to adjourn was immediately made and seconded, and a voice vote sent the members on their way in plenty of time for the midday meal.

Teddy Maxwell hurried to a telephone and called Alex Budde. "All done, Alex," he reported happily.

"No hitches?"

"Nary a one. Some small talk, but no real trouble. A unanimous vote, signed and sealed."

"Thanks for letting me know, Teddy. You'll be getting an envelope sometime in the next few days."

"I appreciate that, Alex."

"Good work deserves a little something extra. Be in touch, Teddy."

Budde called Carl Osborne's hotel. Len Ralston answered.

"P and Z approved," Budde said.

"Terrific."

"Let me talk to Carl."

"He isn't here. Went after his lady friend."

"The poet?"

"Seems like our V.P. is stricken."

"Married man ought to be more circumspect in his private life, I'd think. What would your T. L. Heggland say if he knew?"

"The Old Man is pretty moralistic in some areas."

"Makes a man think."

"Are you suggesting that I let Heggland know. . .?"

"I wouldn't do a thing like that," Budde said. "At least, not yet. A man has to be sure of where he's going before he begins to make his move. Just nice to know a little more than people think you know, in case you have to act."

"You're giving me all sorts of ideas, Alex."

"An ambitious man should have ideas, and I assume you are ambitious."

"Like they say, the most, man."

"An admirable quality. Meanwhile, why don't you contact Osborne and have him join me for lunch. With his lady, if he likes. We'll have a little celebration. You come too, Len."

"Aren't celebrations a little premature? There's still the county commissioners to worry about."

"Let me worry about them."

It was a few minutes after one when they settled down around Alex Budde's corner table—Osborne and Kit, Ralston and Budde.

They ordered drinks, toasted their success, drank to its continuance, and studied the menu. All except Budde. He addressed himself to Kit.

"You don't seem as pleased by Mr. Osborne's good fortune as the rest of us, Miss Pepe."

She pursed her full lips before answering. "I'm not convinced that Wolf Run is the best thing for Aspen."

"Be assured it is," Budde replied graciously. "It will mean more jobs, more income for the townspeople. Everyone stands to profit. In times like these, that can not be underrated."

"The old argument," she said. "More is better."

"The nation was built on men of vision getting things done. Clearing the wilderness. Creating farms, ranches, factories, homes. What's going on here is no different from that. We are very much like those men."

Kit made a negative sound. "It sounds good, but it won't wash, Alex. Once there was a wilderness, a frontier. Even then, in order to advance our concept of what life should be like, we had to destroy another race, another way of life.

"Oh, come on," Ralston said disparagingly. "Don't introduce the Indians into this."

"These mountains used to belong to them," Kit said. "You won't see any Utes camping on the slopes."

"They were savages," Ralston bit off. "Stone Age men, contributing nothing to anybody."

"They were human beings, entitled to live their own lives in their own way. As for contributing, there are a number of ways of measuring that."

"Peace," Budde said. "Right or wrong, the Indians are no longer a power in the country. Anyway, it's all in the past. We are not dislodging anyone. Maybe a few squirrels, a raccoon or two, some deer. Nothing else." He laughed cheerfully.

"I'd've thought you'd be on our side," Ralston said to Kit.

Carl held up a hand. "Stop right there, Ralston. Kit's opinions are her own, and I'm not so sure that in the long run she isn't right."

Ralston stared at Osborne without flinching. "You figure that's what the Old Man thinks?"

Osborne chose not to reply.

"I understand your sentiments," Budde said to Kit. "You're a creative person, an artist, and you function in a pretty rarefied atmosphere for the rest of us."

Kit waited for a long beat before replying. "What you mean is, artists are impractical—we lack the hard intelligence of you more pragmatic types. I don't agree, Alex. Practical people have been running things since time began, and the present state of the world doesn't speak well of their efforts."

Osborne laughed and applauded lightly. "Bravo. You can't argue with that, Alex."

Before Budde could reply, Tom Keating materialized at the table. He fixed his gaze on Alex Budde, but he said nothing.

"Mr. Keating," Osborne said, suddenly glad to see the leatherworker, surprised at the good feelings the other man evoked in him. "Won't you sit with us?"

Keating gave no indication that he'd heard.

Alex Budde manufactured a controlled smile. "Do that, Tom. Have a drink. We're about to order lunch. Join us."

Keating spoke softly, "You're good, Alex. Very good. But you can't carry it off."

Budde raised his brows in a slight show of surprise, nothing else.

"Skip Blondell is dead," Keating said.

"Oh, no," Kit said.

"Who?" Ralston wanted to know, without much interest.

"Skip Blondell," Kit answered sadly. "He owned an art gallery here in town. A sad little man— lost, I always believed. Never in touch with who he was or what he was. He gave the impression of being in charge of things, but he was as afraid of life as any creature I've ever met."

"What did he die of?" Ralston said matter-of-factly.

Keating addressed Alex Budde. "Shouldn't you be asking that?"

"All right," Budde said, "what did he die of?"

"He died of mendaciousness and venality. Of a disregard for human life. He died because he allowed himself to be turned into an instrument of somebody else's greed."

"I don't understand," Osborne said.

"Budde does."

"You keep coming back to me, Tom," Budde said. "I don't know why."

"Skip was your tool, your weapon."

"Tom, you are not making any sense."

"You sent that pathetic little sucker after me, Alex."

"I don't know what you're talking about."

"He was supposed to kill me."

Osborne shifted in his seat uneasily. "Why would anyone want to kill you, Mr. Keating?"

Keating's eyes moved slowly, mechanically, to meet Osborne's. "Figure it out for yourself, Osborne. With me out of the way, Wolf Run goes through. That would put Budde here into the big time. How much land does he own up there? How much have you already bought? How much acreage has he got squirreled away under dummy corporate names or in the names of dead relatives? Get Wolf Run going and it will be Alex Budde who pushes all the buttons. He'll be in charge of construction; he'll own restaurants, hotels, the ski corporation, even the taxi company. There won't be anything he doesn't hold in his hand. Isn't that right, Alex?"

"A slight exaggeration, Tom."

"Not a bit. If anything, I'm understating it. Only one man stands between Budde and all he covets: me. He tried to eliminate that minor obstacle. Skip was supposed to start a slide and wipe me right off the mountain. It didn't work that way..."

"Have you been drinking, Tom?" Budde said quietly.

Ralston filled the breach. "You can't go around accusing a man of murder without proof..."

"Do you have proof?" Osborne asked.

"No, no proof. Only my personal experience. First, Alex attempted to set me up for a bust with a brick of heroin. When it didn't come off, he sent Skip to kill me."

"I've heard enough, Tom," Budde said. "You disappoint me, coming in here with a wild story like that. I always thought better of you. You'd better leave now."

"Who will you send next?" Keating said.

"Rodano? Sexton? I'm sure you own some people I don't know about."

The shining face closed up, the pale eyes glittering darkly. "Get out, Tom."

"This isn't over, Alex," Keating said.

Ralston spoke aggressively, "All this garbage about murder and dope, it's got nothing to do with Wolf Run. The Heggland Group is a legitimate operation, Mr. Keating, and nobody condones—"

Osborne felt suddenly ashamed, as if he should have delivered that defense himself.

Keating didn't even look at Ralston as he interrupted. "Anyone who believes that is a fool, and I don't think there are any fools at this table. See you around, Alex."

They watched him stride out of the Spot. It was Osborne who broke the silence. "I don't like this sort of thing. Is there anything to what he says, Alex?"

"Keating has gone off the deep end. Too much pot, I guess, and too much time alone on the mountain."

"But if Blondell did try to kill him. . ."

"Why would he do that? Skip was a quiet, peaceful sort; never violent."

"Was Blondell working for you?" Kit said.

Budde looked at her squarely, face devoid of guile. "I liked Skipper. A lost soul but inoffensive. No, he didn't work for me. I'm in real estate, I'm in construction, in the restaurant business. Art galleries are not my line."

"And dope?" Osborne said.

Budde smiled wistfully. "Never touched the stuff in my life."

——— 12 ———

They strolled along the edge of the Roaring Fork, looking into the river occasionally, following its turns, hardly speaking. They sat on the bank, close to each other, but not touching.

"Roaring Fork," Osborne said. "With that name, it should be an angry rush of white water, alive with danger and excitement."

"The water's being siphoned off. Too many people, not enough water. It's that simple."

"Another reason for abandoning Wolf Run?"

She gave her answer with some consideration. "I'm only passing through Aspen, Carl. I may never come back again. But it still retains a considerable amount of its natural beauty. What's been spoiled can be reclaimed, if people are willing to make the effort. I think it's worth saving, Carl."

"If only I'll let it alone, you mean."

"There aren't many places left worth saving."

His instinct was to fight her, to take issue with her words, but the fire for conflict soon cooled. "It isn't my choice. Heggland makes the decisions. The rest of us, no matter how important we are, simply carry them out. If I were to withdraw, Heggland would put another man in my place to carry on. The difference would be negligible."

That made sense to her and she said so and went on, "How do you feel about this business personally?"

Osborne watched the river, wishing that the water could reveal some all-purpose answer to the thousand and one questions that zipped around his brain. Nothing came.

"All my life I wanted to be successful," he said. "Achievement was the only thing that mattered. To succeed was everything; to fail was unacceptable. Failure came too easily to millions of people. I didn't want to be like them. I wanted to be different, to be better, to be a winner."

"And now?"

"Now? Nothing has changed. I believe in the same things. There's always room to move ahead, to progress. Bigger and better projects to work on. I'm a man who knows how to get things done. And there's always more to get done."

"Your private expanding universe."

"Something like that."

"What if the universe isn't really expanding? It may be finite, with clearly defined borders and resources. Or maybe it expanded only once—the big bang, and that was it."

"All right, I'll go along with that. Still, the universe, our world, limited though they may be, are infinitely more complicated than they used to be. It takes men of vision and ability to understand the complications and to do something about them."

"Men like Heggland?"

"And Carl Osborne."

"Sounds as if you are acting out the American Dream."

"What's wrong with that?"

"The dream has to be reconciled with today's reality."

"Whose reality?"

"Carl, no matter what you or anyone else believes, every man can not become president. All men are not created equal. Our natural resources will run out, Carl, and some people do go hungry in the United States. Justice isn't applied with an even hand. That's a reality a lot of people are acquainted with."

"You're beginning to sound like some kind of a radical."

"That's the remark of a man who won't confront what he finds difficult. Carl—" she said pleadingly, "I sound like a concerned person, a person like so many others who will no longer be taken in by politicians, by big business."

"I see. Watergate, ITT, the CIA..."

"Yes, and artificially rigged oil prices and avaricious landlords and food that gives no nourishment and ripoffs of poor people and the old ... oh, Carl, there's no end to it."

"You make it out to be so simple—good guys and bad guys."

"I'm sure you're a good guy, Carl, or at least you mean to be."

"There seems to be some doubt." His smile was grim.

"Is there any doubt about Alex Budde?"

"You mean you believe Tom Keating's story!"

"Don't you?"

"I don't know. Keating, Budde, they're both strangers to me. Maybe Keating is on the level, maybe not. Until I know for sure, Budde is entitled to the benefit of the doubt."

"I see."

"Murder, drugs—business isn't run that way."

"You mean girls and booze and grass are not used to entertain clients in the business world? Bribes aren't offered and accepted? Why not murder, if the profits are big enough."

"I don't work that way," he said stiffly. "I never have."

"Have you ever worked with Alex Budde before? What if Blondell *was* sent to kill Keating?"

"I can't believe that."

"I can. Alex is rough and aggressive."

"So am I, but I don't kill people."

"You operate out of a set of established principles—rights and wrongs. They don't include murder. For Alex, there may be nothing that is wrong, except failure."

"This thing is getting out of hand."

"Maybe you ought to have a talk with Tom Keating. He's a straight shooter, Carl."

"If I do, I'd like you to come along. I trust your judgment."

"No. See him by yourself. Trust your own judgment; it's worked for you so far."

He stood up, drew her to her feet. "It hasn't been very long for us, but you've become important to me."

She kissed him quickly on the mouth. "Call me later." She ran off in the direction of the institute. He went back toward town, trying desperately to make sense out of his confusion. Never had he felt so helpless, never so unsure of himself, so afraid.

—— 13 ——

Scooter's eyes fluttered, clenched, and refused to open. For a long beat he panicked, as if his eyelids were cemented in place, permanent blinds drawn between him and the world. With unsteady fingers, he located his eyes and pried them open.

Ahh.

Everything moved, flipping like a deck of magic cards. He fought the urge to blink, afraid of the darkness again. Gradually the action slowed, ground to a halt.

He sat up and almost fell back at once. He swayed and groaned and swallowed the bile that rose up in his throat, and he decided that he was going to live. He put his feet to the floor, tried to stand. Weakness unlocked his knees and he sat back down, waited for the feeling to pass. Eventually it did.

Careful to make no sound, he went to the door, eased it open. Seated in the living room, engrossed in reading a manuscript, was Bobby Wallace.

A grin lifted one side of Scooter's mobile mouth. Agents were fools. They spent ninety percent of their time reading shit, hunting for the well-shaped turd, the turd that could bring in the big buck. Wallace was a turd salesman of rare excellence.

Scooter closed the door quietly and dressed himself. Out the window and onto the deck he went. Lowered himself over the back railing and dropped to the ground. The effort made him breathe hard and he rested until his strength returned, then headed jauntily for town, swinging along Original Street, reveling in the joy and sweet satisfaction that lay ahead.

The Head Bookshop was located between an Italian delicatessen and a drugstore. Two customers were there when Scooter arrived. He pretended to inspect the paperback racks, pleased to find one of his own books. But it was out of sight, almost at floor level. Convinced he wasn't observed, he relocated the book at eye level. Pleased with himself, he moved on.

When the customers left, Scooter hurried over to the proprietor who was seated behind the register. A round man with a Prince Valiant haircut and round eyes.

"Hello, Scooter," he said without enthusiasm.

"Luke, I got to get a little something. Fix me up."

"Blondell's your dealer."

"The mother turned me down."

"Things are tight all over."

"I got to get hold of some stuff."

"The word in the street is a big shipment is on the way."

"No way I can wait."

"You want an ounce of pretty fair grass?"

"Are you kidding? I'm coming down from a ride on smack. I need something to soften the landing."

"Sorry, no can do."

Without warning, Scooter grabbed the fat man by the shirt, yanking him across the counter. "Don't fool around with me, man. I am a desperate character. You're trying to jack up the price. Okay, how much?"

"Let...me...go." He wrenched free. "The larder is empty. Has been for nearly two days. No shit, no coke, no pills. Unless you intend to buy a book, man, move your ass. I got nothing for you."

Scooter raised a threatening fist.

The little fat man brought a toy baseball bat from under the counter. He held it aloft and it took on substantial proportions.

"Prick," Scooter said, edging toward the door.

"Freak."

"Scumbag."

"Shit eater."

Back in the street, Scooter strode single-mindedly toward the mall, ignoring greetings from people he knew, charging heedlessly into other pedestrians, giving them the finger when they objected, never slowing down. A string quartet played Bach and a man with a Ph.D. in psychology from Columbia made his way around with a cup in one hand, a Seeing Eye dog on a leash in the other, and a sign reading I Am Blind draped around his neck. From behind dark glasses, he searched out newcomers to the scene who hadn't earlier contributed to his way of life.

Scooter found what he was looking for at the north edge of the mall: a pretty red-haired girl seated with three young men.

"Got to have words with you," the writer began.

"It's your nickel, as they say."

"Alone."

"These are my mates."

"I want to make a buy."

The girl grinned. Two of her front teeth were missing. "Join the club, friend. The town is dry. I can let you have some grass."

"You're holding out on me!" Scooter's voice grew louder.

One of the young men leaned forward. "Mute your pipes, man. The whole world is tuned in to you."

"Nobody's holding out," the girl said. "The stuff isn't around. But it's on the way, they tell me."

"When?"

"Tomorrow. Maybe."

"I can't wait."

"Tough titty."

Scooter ran. Wild images and strange ideas skittered through his head. It was all Skip Blondell's doing. The gallery owner had pulled away from him just when Scooter needed him most. He would have to make another connection, somebody reliable, somebody with an inexhaustible supply. But first he had to get straight.

He went stumbling down the steps that led to the Blondell Gallery. He pounded on the door and called for Skip to open. He kicked the wooden panel of the door and the glass panes shimmered and made tinkling noises.

"Open up, motherfucker! Let me in!"

He kicked harder and the glass sang out in protest.

"Rotten filthy mother. I'm going to squash your skull. Kick in your faggoty balls. Mash your ugly face." No response was forthcoming. "Ah, come on, Skipper. Open the door. I'm in a bad way. . ."

Fury raged over him and he kicked with all the

force he could muster. Again. One glass panel shattered, large shards hitting the ground. Scooter pulled back, examined his leg for blood. Reassured, he reached through the gap, turned the lock, and pushed the door open.

Inside the gallery, he called Skip's name. No answer. He passed cautiously between the rows of pictures staring down at him. Ugly, accusing pictures.

"Fuck off," he told them.

In the back room, he began his search for Skip's supply. He ripped the bed apart, shredding the mattress with a pair of shears, scattering the white stuffing all over the floor. He toppled the bookcases, found nothing hidden behind them. He emptied the kitchen cabinets, dumped coffee into the sink, drained milk cartons. The medicine chest supplied nothing he needed. He explored the water tank behind the toilet. In the darkroom, he scattered trays and equipment, ripped contact prints in frustration. Enraged at his continuing failure, he pulled paintings from the walls, stamped on them, and beat his fists in the air, crying out, "Why are you doing this to me!"

He sank to his knees, trembling, hid his face in his hands, tried mightily to think straight, to make a plan, to solve his problem. He didn't hear the policeman coming down the outside steps, picking his way over the broken glass.

"On your feet, buddy."

Scooter moaned.

"You hear me!"

Scooter sneaked a look through spread fingers. The cop was young, too young for the job. He held his pistol at the end of a stiff arm, pointed vaguely in Scooter's direction. He seemed more frightened than frightening. Scooter climbed to his feet and faced the cop.

"Up against the wall, legs spread, hands spread."

Scooter moved to obey. The cop, all youthful innocence and trust, stepped close behind the writer. Scooter pivoted swiftly, left hand chopping hard. The pistol went clattering to the floor, Scooter diving after it. Before the young cop was able to react, Scooter was aiming his own gun at him, a manic grin angling across the Mephistophelian face.

"Hey, pig, how'd you like to have your fucking ugly head blasted away?"

The cop decided not to answer.

"Cat got your tongue?" Scooter cackled happily. The gun was heavy, solid, soothing in his fist. He supported his pistol wrist with his left hand, the way he'd seen McCloud do it on the box. "I'm splitting, pig. Come after me and I'll blast your balls." He hit the street running, gun in hand, giving off shrill cries of delight.

A middle-aged couple coming his way froze at the sight of him. Scooter brandished the pistol and they shrank back against the building line. He whooped and hollered and galloped on.

He turned a corner and slowed to a walk. His nerve ends twitched and he scratched vigorously at his chest, his cheek, his scrotum. Where to make a connection? Who was left?

A dim memory surfaced, faded, returned to his disordered brain. A sketch of a faintly familiar face. *Come on, man, give us your name!* He swore and howled at the sky, stamped his feet, and threatened vengeance on an unsuspecting world.

His body tensed and his arms were weary. He spotted the pistol in his hand and reacted with alarm. Where had that come from? Remembering the cop, he hooted derisively and broke into a run, limbs flapping uncontrollably.

An empty driveway drew his attention and he edged his way along a narrow space between two houses. He heard a police siren. *They must be closing in.* He spotted an open window and went through it in a long graceful dive. His head came abruptly to rest against the thick carved wooden leg of a table. Cursing his bad luck, he waited for the pain to subside, for his eyes to stop watering.

He stood up and examined his surroundings. A living room filled with ponderous Victorian pieces and lace doilies and curtains. He grimaced in distaste and tiptoed out into the hallway. From the floor above, he heard a voice lifted in song. A female voice. He went up carpeted stairs, through a bedroom, drawn by the voice. A partially closed door led to a bathroom.

Scooter extended the pistol and walked through the door. In the tub sat a well-soaped woman with flabby arms and breasts to match. Her eyes went round at the sight of Scooter, and a small sound seeped out of her.

"No, please. Please, no."

"Where is it?" he said aggressively.

The expression she wore was all the answer he seemed likely to get.

"The stuff," he muttered.

She dipped herself deeper into the water as if for protection.

"Don't con me, lady. I know you deal."

He took dead aim at a shriveled nipple that was

barely breaking water. She gasped and covered up.

"You got a genuine killer here, lady. Wyatt Earp and Bat Masterson in one deadly package. Gonna come across or not?"

"What—do you want?"

"The stuff," he said again.

"There's some money in my purse, in the bedroom, on the chest."

He thrust the pistol into the water, directed the muzzle against her vagina, and gave her a jiggle or two.

"You hiding it in there?" he leered.

"Oh!" she squeaked. "Oh, oh."

"There's nothing a user wouldn't do to keep the shit to himself."

"Please, please go away! I'm so frightened."

"I can tell you're a dope fiend. What're you on?"

"A dope fiend!" She grew indignant. "Look here, young man, I don't even take aspirins." She climbed to her feet, sagging and dripping. "You had better get out of here before I call the police."

Scooter made a face and averted his eyes. Ugliness offended him. He gave her the finger before he left; the gesture was without enthusiasm.

Scooter cast about for his next move. No doubt about it, he was hot on the trail. About to make the Big Score. This was not the time for abject surrender. One question loomed large: which way to go?

That earlier memory, fuzzy and brief, faded in and out and in again. He worked hard to freeze the frame, and he finally did it. "Eureka!" he cried in exuberant recognition, starting off across town, the police special tucked obtrusively under his shirt.

On the trail, sniffing the scent, he selected his approach with the care of an experienced hunter. Back way's the best way. Out of sight, out of trouble. He looped and circled, checked to see that he wasn't followed. Safe at last, he moved in, past the garbage cans, up a flight of wooden stairs. On a small balcony, he shoved his face up against the tall, narrow window that opened into Alex Budde's apartment. The frosted glass was, he told himself, an offense to all decent truth-seeking peeping toms.

He glanced over each shoulder and determined that he was safe from observation by agents from the FBI, CIA, DIA, KGB, CIO, or even officials of the Author's League. He smashed the glass with the gun butt and snaked his way inside.

He was in Alex Budde's bathroom. An overwhelming desire to urinate came over him and he unzipped and drew out his penis. He measured it against the gun barrel; despite some stretching and tugging, the barrel won.

He peed in the bathroom sink after closing the drain, leaving a memento of his visit. Impatient to get on with his search, he cut off his water and, penis in one hand, pistol in the other, went into the bedroom. So much orderliness, so much cleanliness, it was sickening. He padded over to the carved wooden door, eased it open, and looked out.

In the long living room sat Alex Budde, his broad back exposed. Scooter took dead aim and advanced in a crouch.

"Get 'em up!" he cried.

Budde came around, no alarm on the shining face.

"Put that thing away, you idiot."

Scooter gestured with the gun. "I'm in charge here."

"And put your cock back in your pants."

Grinning sheepishly, Scooter obeyed. When he was all zipped up, he pointed the gun at Budde again. "You know why I'm here, Alex."

"Why?"

"To make a buy."

"A buy?"

"You're the main man, Alex. Skip told me once. As you can plainly see, I'm a very desperate person. I might do anything at all."

"Is that pistol loaded?"

The thought was unsettling. Scooter examined the cylinder, was reassured to see the blunt lead tips of bullets peeking into view. "Of course it is. It belonged to a—"

Budde kicked the gun out of his hand. It went flying across the room. Scooter rubbed his bruised wrist.

"Jesus, Alex," he complained, "that *hurt*."

Budde went after the pistol. He unloaded it, dropped the bullets into his pocket, and put the pistol on a table.

"Where'd you get this gun?"

Scooter shrewdly gave no answer.

"It's a police special."

"I got friends."

"You're crazy, walking around with a cop's gun. You'll get busted for sure."

"Ah, Alex, no sweat."

"Take off, Scooter, and don't ever come back."

"Alex, let me have a little."

"A little what?"

"Shit, man. Heroin. Gimme a blast."

"I don't know what you're talking about."

"Skip said you were numero uno. Come across, or I'll spread the word."

Budde slapped him heavily across the face. Down he went in a heap, giggling softly. "Hey, man, you are doing me bodily harm."

"I ought to crack your silly skull."

"I am not physically strong, Alex, you understand that. Any permanent damage will have to be accounted for in law, medicine, and before other pertinent authorities."

"Get out."

Scooter unfolded in sections, stood there swaying gently. "Let me have the gun, Alex."

"On your way."

"One fix, Alex. . . Blondell told me. . ."

"Blondell is dead. He fell off the mountain."

Scooter's face melted with self-pity. He wept. "My prime connection."

"Out." Budde put a hand at the writer's back, directed him through the bedroom and through the back door. "And don't come back."

Scooter grew increasingly depressed. All roads closed, all sources dried up. He went back up the hill, shimmied up to the deck of his house, and went into his bedroom. He stripped off his clothes and walked into the living room, naked and sad. Bobby Wallace lifted his eyes from the manuscript he was reading.

"I figured you died," he said.

"You're all heart, Bobby."

"You look awful."

"Bobby, I need a fix, enough to get me turned around."

"All my connections are in Beverly Hills."

"Try Alex Budde."

"Why Budde?"

"He deals man, in big numbers. Get me straight, Bobby, and I'll go back to work. I give you my word."

"Don't hustle me, Scooter."

"Honest Injun."

"If I thought—"

"Bobby, you can trust me."

"I wouldn't trust my mother, if she was on the stuff." He assessed the other man. "Okay, I'll give it a whack. But this is the caboose, baby; the last train is passing by. Better get on or forget all about getting home."

"Don't worry, buddyboy, I'm a writing fool when I get going."

Wallace left the house. Scooter sank to the floor, hoping he wouldn't shake apart before the agent returned.

14

They sat on the back deck of Keating's house and waited for the sun to drop behind the western range. Deep blue shadows reached out, but the golden light still reflected from the high peaks.

"Beautiful, isn't it?" Keating said.

Osborne grunted softly. "Aspen can get a lot more out of those mountains than it has, Keating."

"You've got it backwards. The mountains are what we want, just as they are."

"You stop building, turn to a no-growth policy, and this town will go into a decline. To simply say no to everything is a kind of self-defeating madness."

Keating raised his big shoulders, let them fall. "True progress will find us interested, concerned, and willing to cooperate."

Osborne decided that no response was in order. "Kit Pepe is convinced you're a straight guy," he said. He drank some beer out of the can.

Keating sucked on a joint. "Not always."

"Nobody is always."

Keating nodded thoughtfully, said nothing.

The silence made Osborne uneasy. "I find it hard to believe that Alex is as bad as you make him out to be."

"Is that why you came, so I can convince you?"

Osborne grinned briefly. "I think so."

"Blondell tried to kill me."

"If that's so, does it follow that Alex put him up to it?"

"Alex did."

"You're so damned sure."

"Skip belonged to Alex, and Alex sent him to knock me into the valley."

"How can you be sure?"

"Skip told me so. . ."

"I see."

Keating laughed softly. "My word against Budde's, you mean. And you're not convinced mine is better."

"I didn't say that." He changed his approach. "Is it your opinion that Budde is into drugs—dealing, I mean?"

"Biggest operator in town. He is *the* distributor in Aspen. Every ounce of stuff passes through his hands. Check that. All the important shipments. Some of the grass comes down with kids after a quick score. But the coke and all the heavy stuff, that's Alex's."

"You make it sound like a monopoly."

"About eighteen months back, a cat named Arthur, a small-time grass peddler, made a move to improve his status. The way I heard it, Arthur brought in about three kilos of junk. Forty-eight hours later, a couple of sheriff's deputies got into a shoot-out with Arthur out in the county. Goodbye Arthur."

"You figure Budde was behind it?"

"Arthur had never been known to own a gun, but they discovered a Magnum .357 on him with a couple of rounds fired. Not that he hit anybody."

"You're not the only one with this information."

"You might say it's an open secret."

"But nothing is done about it."

"Alex swings a lot of weight."

"The police?"

"Don't be naïve. He owns part of the force, and none of us knows which part or how large it is."

The sun was gone suddenly. Cool air bathed Osborne's cheeks. "Budde came well recommended as a legitimate businessman."

"So be it."

"Assuming you're right, what am I supposed to do?"

"You asked the question, Mr. Osborne; you answer it."

"Don't you care?"

"I care a lot, but it's your life. I'll live my own."

Osborne finished the beer. A premonition came over him that he was dealing with shadows; that he had moved into a crazy-quilt world that was out of synchronization, a world in which nothing meant what it was supposed to mean and nothing was what it seemed to be.

"You know my son, Jon?" he said.

"I've met him. This is a small town, after all."

"Until a few days ago, I hadn't seen him for nearly two years."

"Aspen is full of runaways of all ages."

"It doesn't bother you?"

"That they run away? No. That they come out of situations that force them to run? Yes."

"You made your point. But what do they expect to find out in this great big wonderful world?"

"Nirvana."

"Bliss forever."

"Freedom from pain and care. It's what we all want, isn't it?"

"A lovely dream. But problems are what life is all about."

"I hope you're wrong."

"I'll amend that—the solving of problems, the relief of pain."

"That's a peculiarly American point of view, I think."

"That's what I am, Keating, an American. So are you."

Osborne was troubled by Keating's ability to absorb any emotional impact and to maintain his equilibrium in the face of attack or argument. The bearded man took on a stability that Osborne had seldom encountered, as if he operated in the tranquil eye of the storm. Osborne decided to bring the conversation back to Wolf Run.

"I came out here to do a job, nothing more."

"Follow orders is what you mean."

"Someone is always around to give orders."

"A debatable point."

"Perhaps. But I'm one step removed from the top of my company. If Wolf Run goes off smoothly, there's a good chance I'll get that job."

"And you want it?"

"Wouldn't you in my place?"

"I'm not in your place."

"You find my ambition less than admirable. You think it's wrong."

"For me it would be. For you, obviously not."

"Usually I read people pretty accurately, Keating. Not you. There's more to you than you reveal. You can't be as simple as you pretend."

Keating smiled, weighing his answer. "Try this —what you read is exactly what I am. No more, no less. I exist in a pretty narrow environment. I do my work, I love my old lady, I climb a little, ski a little, get high now and then. That's about it."

"Is that enough for a man like you?"

"It could be, but events keep pinching me."

"You're not as uninvolved as you make out. You did get elected county commissioner."

"Somebody had to fight the bad guys."

"Why you?"

"Because I've got the stuff to make the fight."

"You could set up shop somewhere else."

"I think about that a lot these days. But why should I allow myself to be pushed out? Anyway, Osborne, wherever I go, men like Alex Budde, like yourself, will be only one step behind."

"Progress—" Osborne started to say, but he broke off.

Keating couldn't conceal his amusement. "So it goes."

"I intend to get the job done, Keating."

"Not if I can stop you. And I believe I can."

"Lewin and you, two votes to one."

"That's it."

"If only you would listen to reason..."

"Your reasons don't add up. Alex Budde comes off being your reason. So does Skip Blondell. There are more, and you know them all. Let's face it, Osborne, you are the bad guy."

Osborne stood up. "Take care of yourself, Keating."

"Same to you."

—— 15 ——

Budde planned the evening carefully, working out a schedule of appearances and time checks. At approximately the same moment that Jon Osborne and Rodano were stopping a white panel truck with a red star on the side, Budde joined Lou Sinicola, a local lawyer, and his wife. He bought them a drink, asked Sinicola for the time so that he might set his own watch, and moved on.

He kept making the rounds of the Spot, making sure he was highly visible, taking care to establish his presence. He greeted customers he seldom spoke to; bought drinks for strangers and invited them back; told the cigarette girl, whom he despised, that he was pleased with her work. When a waitress dropped a tray heavy with dishes, he berated her in a loud voice. An hour later he apologized to her within earshot of the bartender, making sure the man saw him pat the girl's bottom. Both the waitress and the bartender were impressed; Budde had never been known to show the slightest sexual interest in any of the girls who worked for him. The bartender made a mental note to tell his wife; the waitress wondered if she might exploit the incident to her own advantage.

Fifteen minutes before closing time, Budde reminded himself that he needed someone to vouch for his whereabouts through the night and into the morning. He considered the waitress, certain it would be no problem getting her into bed. But he knew he could not bring himself to make love to a strange female, to tolerate her idiosyncrasies, to allow her to touch him. In addition, she was an unknown factor and therefore unreliable. His mind made up, he telephoned Joan Carolinian.

"Sorry to disturb you," he started.

Only half-awake, she was surprised by even that mild apology, and she leaped to take advantage of it. "That's all right, Alex. Is there something the matter? Do you need my help?"

"It's almost three in the morning. I should never have called."

"It doesn't matter," she said hurriedly, fearful he would break off contact. "What is it, Alex? You sound worried. Are you in trouble?"

"No trouble at all." He kept his voice low. "I was lonely and thinking about you."

"Oh, Alex," she cooed. "You don't know how that makes me feel. Why don't you come over here, right now."

He clamped his eyes shut as if in pain. The thought of sleeping in *her* bed made him queasy, and he knew he could not go that far. "I can't leave just yet," he said. "Could you come over to my place? By the time you arrive, I'll be finished with work."

"I'll go around the back," she said.

No, he cried silently. That wasn't the way he needed her. "Meet me in the Spot," he said, anxious now to hang up. "We'll have a drink together..."

"In twenty minutes, Alex."

He went over to the corner of the bar—near the telephone—to wait. Five minutes later, right on schedule, it rang. He answered it before the bartender could make a move.

"We're on our way home," Rodano said.

"Sounds okay."

"No hitch anywhere. Any change of plan at your end?"

"No."

"Okay. I'll take care of it, then. See you tomorrow."

Budde went over to his table and sat down. Everything was working out perfectly. He asked for some warm milk to be brought to him.

"What time do you have?" Budde asked the waitress, when she came back.

"Five minutes to three."

He laughed and fiddled with his watch. "Can't keep this thing running right," he said. "Been off all night..."

He sipped the milk and sat back to wait for Joan Carolinian.

—— 16 ——

They began making love as soon as he entered the room. They groped and grabbed at each other, frantically stroking and rubbing. They struggled to undress each other, gave it up as an impossible assignment, and worked on their own clothes. Naked, they lurched together, tumbling to the floor in front of the cold fireplace, straining and writhing in an effort to find release. Then, a thrashing explosion: They clung desperately to each other, both afraid of falling into what seemed like a dark, bottomless pit.

Later, they smoked and sipped brandy and listened to Goldberg's Variations. They held hands tentatively, as if this touching involved an intimacy greater than anything that had preceded it.

"You'll be leaving soon," she said.

"My work here is almost over."

"We didn't have much time together," she said.

He had been thinking about that, projecting himself into a future without her. It offered no good possibilities.

"Come with me," he said.

She sat up, leaned forward, cupping her chin with one hand. In profile, she presented a series of neat body projections and depressions, slender curves fading one into the next; her breasts two prideful globes, her belly a single lean crease, the arc of her bottom a smooth, unbroken line.

"I have a few more weeks at the institute," she said, not looking at him.

"That's no answer."

"After that, the new year at Antioch."

"Don't go back."

"I contracted for another year. . ."

"They'd let you out, if you asked."

"I like to teach."

"I've got contacts in the East. At Columbia, Yale, at N.Y.U. Come to New York with me."

There was no levity in her voice when she spoke. "I've never been so desired in my life. Everyone is making me an offer."

Jealousy stabbed at his middle; he felt like a schoolboy with his first girl friend. "What other offers have you had?" He was ready to fight for her.

"Bobby Wallace wants me to go to Hollywood."

"You wouldn't, he's a disgusting man."

She allowed her eyes to meet his for a moment. "He's no worse than most. A businessman, like you. A hustler, a man who knows how to get things done. He puts deals together—producers, actors, writers."

"Are you telling me that you're considering him—?"

She laughed without humor. "Are you jealous, Carl? Good, that pleases me. But you needn't be. Bobby wants me for strictly business reasons. He made me a good offer—do some writing for Scooter Lewis—a ghost."

"You're better than that."

"I'm not so sure. Poets are very little in demand. Afterwards, there'd be movie and television assignments. Bobby says he'll make me rich and famous."

"You're a poet, not some cheap hack."

"It offends you, Carl, that I might choose to go after money. Tell me why. Why shouldn't a writer be paid as well for what he does as a banker or a broker or a crooked politician or a vice-president for the Heggland Group?"

"I've got no good answer, except that if you take Wallace's way I'd be disappointed."

"But would I be disappointed? That's the only question that counts."

"I still want you to come to New York with me."

"To do what, Carl? Sit in some glossy East Side apartment and wait for you to come around? How often will I get to see you, Carl?"

"Every day."

"What about your wife? You have some old obligations, it seems."

"I'll leave her. The marriage is empty, a futile exercise in putting up a front. She drinks too much, sleeps with young men. . ." He broke off.

"While you sleep with lady poets?"

He grinned and spoke warmly. "You're my first poet."

"And you're my first vice-president."

He sobered quickly.

"Does that offend you, Carl? Since we're listing lovers by category. . ." She shrugged.

"Let's start again," he said. "You're very dear to me, Kit. I refuse to consider losing you."

"I don't want to become an appendage to someone else's existence."

"It wouldn't be that way."

"I think it would. There's something else to consider."

"What?"

"Jon."

"Jon has no part in this. I lead my own life—"

"Yes, I know, Carl," she said softly, "but it's Jon I'm concerned about right now."

"You still think he's going to do something dangerous?"

"Jon is heading for trouble. He—"

"There's nothing I can do to stop him. He left home a long time ago. He's on his own. Besides, that 'big score' business is just talk."

"According to Alex Budde, you mean?"

"That's right. And even if something was going on, what could I do about it? Jon won't listen to me."

"Carl, drugs of all kinds are usually easy to get in Aspen. Lately, the heroin sources have dried up, or so I hear. And there's talk of a big shipment due in town any day now."

"What's this got to do with Jon?"

"Simply this: Jon wants to make a killing and split, get away from his very successful, very threatening father for good—"

"Thanks a lot."

She went on. "Jon invites me to go with him. He promises a big score, immediate wealth. Where else could he get it except from drugs?"

"That's crazy."

"Not really. Jon is into the drug scene; all young people are. The word is that Jon sometimes works as a mule for Budde."

"We're back to that—that Alex is Aspen's number one dealer."

"That's the word on him."

"You sound like Tom Keating now."

"You don't want to believe it, I understand that. But at least consider what I'm saying."

Carl shook his head angrily. "Even if what you say about Budde is true, how does it affect Jon? I mean, how is he suddenly going to get rich?"

"If there is a shipment due, Jon could know about it."

"No."

"If he is as involved as I hear, he'd be privy to that kind of information."

"Even so, he couldn't pull it off."

"Don't underestimate your son."

His mind turned rapidly and, from the swirl of emotion that blurred his thinking, he sorted out what seemed reasonable. "Suppose such a shipment did exist and Jon got hold of it. Where would he get the money for it? To peddle it in the streets he'd need a laboratory to break it down, prepare it, bag it. People to sell it."

"That would take too much time," she agreed.

"Well?"

"If he rips Alex off, Jon must have a buyer lined up. A quick exchange so he could get out of here before Alex finds out."

"What if Alex does find out?"

She lifted her finely turned shoulders helplessly. "In that case, Jon is as good as dead."

_____ 17 _____

Daylight leaked into the room and Joan Carolinian's eyes snapped open. She was instantly awake and feeling used and miserable. It was always this way after being with a man: harsh, recriminatory feelings; no sense of being loved or desired by another human being; always put aside, separate and distant, no longer worthy.

She sat up and looked over at Alex Budde. He slept on his side, knees drawn up, hugging himself, an almost pained expression on the shining face. She loathed him at once and needed him and longed for some indication of affection, some affirmation of their earlier contact, of her own humanity. He recognized none of that. She went over to him, crouched on the floor, and looked at that cold mask. She said his name. He stirred.

"Alex. . ."

He moaned a protest.

"Please, Alex, wake up." She touched his shoulder, shook him. Harder.

"What!" He sat up, blinking, trying to locate himself. "What the hell are you doing?" His anger surfaced quickly.

"Alex, I'm so afraid."

"Go back to bed."

"I need to talk to someone."

The clock next to the bed told him it was six in the morning; he was clear, all of it was done. He needed her no longer. "You disgust me." He slapped her face.

She almost enjoyed the sting, longed for a more sustained, more punishing attack.

"Be nice to me," she said.

He hit her again. "Don't ever come near me when I'm sleeping."

She straightened up. What right had he to treat her so badly? There was nothing she wouldn't do for him, nothing she hadn't done. And she was always left empty and soiled, without satisfaction, without warmth, without humanity.

"Bastard," she said.

He swung his feet to the floor. She pulled back, afraid suddenly. Defeat crept back under her skin, surfeited her spirit. Nothing she did was right, not ever.

"Get out."

"Don't send me away, Alex."

"Out." He was coming toward her.

She ran into the bathroom and locked the door. He rattled the knob, ordered her to come out. She made no reply, huddling on the tile, beginning to shiver.

"I'm going to break the door down," he threatened.

Time slowed to a crawl. Alternately chilled and sweating, she deposited herself in the tub, lying on towels and covering herself with the bath mat. She closed her eyes and heard nothing from without, listened only to the sound of her own faint memories.

She never fully realized that someone was working at the lock of the door until Jim Sexton walked into the bathroom, Budde at his back. Her eyes came open and she saw two fuzzy, vaguely threatening figures looming over her. Her eyes closed again and she tried to roll over.

Sexton spotted the empty sleeping-pill bottle. "Was this full?" he asked Alex.

"No. Maybe eight or ten, that's all."

"All right," Sexton said. "Help me get her on her feet. She'll be all right." They took her into the bedroom, ignoring her protests. They dressed her, then maneuvered her down the back staircase and into Sexton's car.

"What should I do with her?" Sexton said.

"Anything you like. Just keep the dumb bitch away from me."

Sexton brought her back to her condominium, undressed her, and led her into the bathroom. He bent her over the toilet and shoved his finger down her throat. She heaved. He held her securely until she was finished, washed her off, and gave her some water to drink. He put her to bed.

"A pretty lady like you," he said, taking off his trousers, "you shouldn't act this way."

She watched him as if through a shifting scrim. "What are you doing?"

"You don't need Alex anymore. I'll take care of you. Give you everything you need."

She made it into a sitting position. "Go away. What do you think you're doing? Leave me alone."

He shoved her down on her back, forced himself between her thighs.

"Don't!" she cried.

She tried to bring her legs together, but it was no use. She set herself against him.

"Put it in," he bit off.

She shook her head.

He hit her. Three times, rocking her head. She began to weep and all strength drained away. "Put it in," he said again.

She hesitated. But only briefly.

Part Four

Aspen

During the Second World War, the U.S. Army placed in training at Camp Hale, Colorado, the Tenth Division Mountain Infantry. Ski troops.

Many of these troopers were accomplished skiers who had worked the slopes of Italy, France, and Switzerland. They soon discovered Aspen and spent their leave time on the slopes. They composed enthusiastic paeans to their new find for the ski journals; they wrote to friends in other parts of the country and the world; they made plans to return to Aspen when the war was over. And some, like Friedl Pfeifer, did return. He opened a ski school.

Others came, too. For one, Walter Paepcke, a successful businessman. The beauty of the setting enthralled him, and he began to conjure up ambitious images—Paepcke hoped to recreate the earlier economic and cultural life of the town. He envisioned nothing less than a sporting, intellectual, and cultural life that would attract people from all over the world.

A man of action, he collaborated with Friedl Pfeifer to form the Aspen Co. and the Aspen Skiing Corporation. He leased the Hotel Jerome and modernized her. He bought up rights-of-way

*and replaced the old boat tow on the mountain
with an up-to-date chair lift.*

Aspen stirred out of her deep sleep.

*Paepcke's enthusiasm was contagious. Old-
timers saw what was happening and decided to
take similar steps. All over town, homeowners
began to restore and repaint their houses. Decora-
tors were brought in to make sure that alterations
were in keeping with the finest Victorian taste,
and it was the hope of many people to bring Aspen
back, at least architecturally, to its glory days of
the late nineteenth century. This created conflict.
Some people began putting up new houses, ignoring the area's colorful past; Swiss chalets were
erected and so were sleek modern structures.*

*Land speculators soon made their appearance.
Prices shot skyward. No longer could a parcel of
land be obtained by paying back taxes. Real estate
operators asked for and received inflated prices
for their property. Aspen was rapidly changing.*

*In 1947, the Wheeler Opera House was re-
opened; Burl Ives gave the first performance.
Every summer since, the opera house has been in
use: concerts, panel discussions, study groups, lec-
tures, theatrical performances, chamber music,
operettas, soloists. Albert Schweitzer came to
Aspen to speak, as did José Ortega y Gasset, the
Spanish philosopher. The Minneapolis Symphony
played under Dimitri Mitropoulos, and the cellist
Gregor Piatigorsky performed, as well as Artur
Rubinstein, Milstein, Traubel, Melchior, and the
like.*

*The World Ski Championships were held in
Aspen in 1950. A Design Conference became an
annual event. The Institute for Humanistic Studies*

came into being—a center for physicists, the artists-in-residence program, a film conference, community theater, and the Music Associates. People flocked into the Roaring Fork Valley to play, to be entertained, to be enlightened, to be educated, and to live well. Some stayed on and built houses. Others returned frequently. Once again, Aspen struck it rich.

Bonanza!

Theoretically, everything the architects had put
on paper made sense. There was an internal logic
to every projection. Details had been reviewed
with technical virtuosity; everything was minutely
considered and worked out. Wolf Run would be a
development in which a minimum amount of land
was used to obtain a maximum amount of pleasure
and comfort for its inhabitants.

The plans called for two ski runs, each angling
down off the heights in locations where the fewest
trees blocked the way; thus, only minimal damage
would be done to the terrain. Other outdoor activities were similarly planned. No one would be
allowed to build on the slopes. Except for the ski
runs, the mountains would be left unscarred.

Each house, each block of condominium apartments, each hotel, would be situated in such a way
that it would have an unobstructed view. Construction would be limited to two stories, and no
building would be allowed to block off the view
from any other building.

Malls, parks, and wild lands were to be maintained in their natural state, for use by everyone.
Parking areas would be restricted to the outskirts
of the community, and only service vehicles would
be allowed within the town limits. Deliveries of

essential goods were to be made only at night. Strict zoning for living and business, carefully kept.

"Oh, man," Ralston complained. "This is going to send costs skyrocketing."

"To what degree?" Osborne asked the architects. He had committed the Heggland Group to accepting this kind of treatment as the only way to get the project in operation.

"Obviously, initial costs are higher," answered Skutch, "but with a minimum impact on the ecology, property values will increase rapidly. Sales prospects are excellent for this type of development."

"I think we're worrying too much about the environmentalists," Ralston said. "To hell with them, I say. This is a free country, a free enterprise system. The dollar-land ratio must be expanded, profits must be increased, otherwise we are going to hear it from the Old Man."

Osborne waved a silencing hand. "Mr. Heggland is my concern. Yours is to execute my orders."

"Yes, sir," Ralston said with a hint of irony.

Osborne ignored it. He had stopped listening. No matter what was decided in this room at this time, the project was in difficulty. He was up to his ears in trouble. Heggland would agree wholeheartedly with Ralston's viewpoint. The Old Man was interested in only two things—results and money. The bottom line, as he liked to put it. He tolerated no excuses. Failure didn't exist for him. Let a man fail to produce, and Heggland quickly divested himself of that man's services.

There was the continuing difficulty with the land that belonged to Don Horn. As McDevitt had prophesied, the rancher had refused to sell. Osborne and Ralston had paid him another visit that morning, but no amount of persuasion, or money, seemed to sway the old-timer. A flinty man in his late seventies, Horn made it clear by attitude and words that he felt himself to be a part of the land, at one with the hills and mountains and high meadows.

"What does it mean?" Ralston had wanted to know.

"It means we can write off the number two slope, and that just won't do," said Osborne.

"Let's offer the old bastard another ten grand."

Osborne was convinced it would do no good, but he allowed Ralston to go back and make the attempt. Ralston returned with a tale of being run off the property by an angry Don Horn with a squirrel rifle cocked and ready.

With all the rest of the land bought and paid for, this was just another setback. The job should have been much further along than it was by now with building on the service areas already contracted for. Construction schedules should have been worked out, contracts let, men hired. A land office had to be established, advertising ordered, brochures written and mailing lists obtained, a sales force lined up. These things all took time, and time was what they were wasting while they were struggling to obtain approval.

Ralston was right; the Old Man was going to sound off. Osborne wondered if he should have killed the entire project as soon as he learned of Tom Keating's intractable opposition. They would have saved money and energy and been able to apply themselves elsewhere until conditions in Aspen changed. Instead, he had forced the issue, taken options on more land, ordered new studies, and committed immense sums of money to what now seemed to be a lost cause.

Why had he done it? The answer came at once: because he wanted to run up a score, build an unassailable record, convince Old Man Heggland that Carl Osborne was the only suitable man to take over for him. Ambition could dull a man's good sense, blind him to realities, make him commit stupid mistakes.

Osborne stood up, and the others did likewise. He noticed that Ralston no longer leaped erect when he did, but rose reluctantly, almost insolent in his movements. He made a mental note; as soon as he took over the presidency, he would fire Ralston.

"Gentlemen," he said cheerfully to the architects, "you've done a fine piece of work. Thank you for the presentation. If it doesn't do the job, it won't be your fault. Now it's up to me to carry the ball."

Bender shook his head. "I must level with you. This business with the Horn property—it complicates matters. It isn't simply a question of building around Mr. Horn's ranch. I have spoken with each of the county commissioners in the last two days. Even Joe Chalk admits that without the Horn land we come up empty. My impression is that he would vote against approval unless the parcel is filled out properly."

"But why?" Ralston wanted to know.

"Because the presence of such a development as this would place Horn in a totally unviable position. His land would become worthless as cattle range or farmland because of the dramatically increased population in the immediate area. The general feeling is that Horn could take us into court and stop the development at any time."

"No one mentioned this legal complication before," Osborne said, not concealing his anger.

"I'm sorry, Mr. Osborne," Bender said. "I assumed—"

Carl waved him into silence. "I haven't given up yet. I won't give up. Somehow, we must convince Horn to sell." He shook hands with each of the architects and directed them to the door.

When they were gone, Ralston spoke. "I don't like it."

"No one enjoys problems, Len."

"Horn is a problem that can be solved."

"Oh?"

"Give me the word."

"I'm not sure I know what you mean."

"I mean, I can dispose of him."

"Dispose. Not convince, not sway. Dispose."

Ralston shrugged. "He's in the way."

"Leave Horn to me."

"Alex Budde would know what to do."

Osborne's face went cold. He thought about Skip Blondell, dead up on the mountain. He remembered Keating's accusations. "Budde is not running this show, I am. Remember that, Len. Remember that you're working for me. I give the orders here." He forced the anger away, along with the sudden fear. "You review the environmental impact study. Make sure it's all in order. I'll try Horn one more time."

"It won't work, Carl."

"Perhaps not," Osborne said before he left. "We'll just have to wait and see."

When he was alone, Ralston picked up the telephone. An operator came on the line. He cleared his throat. "Get me New York City, operator, person-to-person. I want to talk to Mr. T. Lyman Heggland. The number is. . ."

Budde woke in a cold sweat, struggling to remember his name and where he was. The old running-falling dream, the awful sense of loneliness. His shoulders twisted in despair.

He recognized his surroundings and gradually the palpitations slowed and ceased. His eyes came to rest on the single bed against the far wall and he remembered how it had been with Joan Carolinian. He felt sorry for submitting himself to such filth. The way she drooled over him, making sick love sounds while using his flesh, *his* flesh, for her own perverted needs.

He hated her. Hated all women. The way they tasted and smelled and looked. The way they demanded and wheedled, seducing a man until they extracted exactly what they wanted. Courage, strength, directness—these were manly attributes, qualities to be respected and striven for.

He was glad she was gone. Perhaps she had died. In which case he'd be rid of her, once and for all. He went into the bathroom and was almost sickened by the lingering sweet scent of her. He shaved and showered rapidly, put on freshly laundered clothes, and went downstairs. He settled into his usual chair and a waitress brought him coffee. He ordered breakfast and sat back to wait for Harry Rodano to arrive with the good news.

Keating was about to lock the door to his shop when Osborne appeared.

"I'd like to talk to you, Keating."

The bearded man nodded. "Walk along with me." They moved out of the arcade into the street. "You never give up, do you?"

"There must be some way we can reconcile our differences."

"Not necessarily. We're striving for different goals, and we want to attain them by different methods. We're natural enemies, Osborne."

"I'd hate to think that. Can't you withhold judgment until after you've seen our presentation?"

"Let's say I do. Then what? You intend to double our population. I'm against that."

"What a stubborn bastard you are, Keating."

"Persistent is a word I'd prefer. You're in it

to make a buck, Osborne, nothing else. I'm concerned with other things."

"The wealth — the rewards — gets spread around."

Keating made a growling noise in his throat. "Ah, Osborne, what's the use? I'm on my way now to make funeral arrangements for Skip Blondell. The Mountain Patrol brought the body out this morning. No one else cared enough to make even a gesture."

"You mean Budde?"

"Yes, Budde."

"I can't believe what you told me about him."

"Suit yourself. It doesn't matter." He looked up at the mountain. "If I die up there, they can leave me where I drop. That's a pretty good place to spend eternity."

"That goddamned mountain. What's so special about it?"

"You've seen it. If you don't know now, you'll never find out."

"I won't contest your feelings, but a fair argument can be made for the proposition that it doesn't belong exclusively to the few people who happen to live here at the moment. It's public property."

"Exactly. So leave it alone, Osborne."

"I am not easily stopped."

"Neither of us is."

"I'll find a way to work around you."

They stopped in front of the mortuary. "If Blondell had managed to knock me into the valley, you'd have profited from it, Osborne. You'd never have wondered how I got to be dead, or who ordered it."

"That's not fair."

"I know what Alex Budde will do in a given situation. But you, Osborne, you frighten me. In a pinch, nobody knows what you stand for. I'm afraid to put my back to you..."

Len Ralston looked like a hen atop an egg. He had placed himself in a straight-backed chair, his legs gathered under him, resting gingerly. There was a deceptive softness to him, the roundness of his face and body concealing an inner resolve that most people never perceived. He seemed like the perfect advance man, an easy dude with a buck, cheerful, full of funny stories and blue jokes. A man for all occasions.

But a driving ambition simmered under that fleshy facade, an ambition that now gripped him with terrifying force. Doom on one hand, possibility on the other; he was sandwiched between, made afraid, unsure of which direction to travel. He had done everything correctly, embarked only on well-thought-out moves, designing a strategy that would bring him to exactly this place at this time. And now it was out of his control. Carl Osborne had the ball. Or, more accurately, T. Lyman Heggland.

Nothing would ever be the same for him after this. Aspen was his turning point. His Waterloo. The big question remained: Was he Napoleon or Nelson?

He sniffed the air for some hint of an answer. At the telephone at the far end of the couch was Carl Osborne. So much depended on him, on what he did and said and felt at this moment. How Osborne came across to the Old Man. Ralston shivered and wished away this flood of helplessness. It held fast.

Nothing showed in Osborne's eyes. There was no revealing twitch in his jaw. Just another moment in his existence. A winner expecting to win. Victories came easily for winners. The phone rang and Ralston almost fell out of his chair. Osborne allowed it to ring four times before answering.

"Yes."

It was Kit Pepe.

"Carl, I left Jon a few minutes ago."

"Is he all right?"

"There's something going on, Carl—something strange—dangerous, I think."

"Don't let your imagination run away with you, Kit."

"That's what I've been telling myself. But I'm convinced that Jon is into something very wrong. It has to do with Alex."

Carl was unable to control his anger. "Why Alex? Why must it always be Alex? This town has a fixation on the man, as if he's the root cause of all problems. It's unhealthy."

"Jon said he was going to see Alex. I think you ought to get over there, Carl."

"I'm waiting for a call."

"This is important, Carl. Your son needs you."

"What I'm doing is important," he rasped. "Jon's a big boy, he'll have to take care of himself."

The sudden cutting edge to his voice made her shudder. "Yes, of course," she said. "I shouldn't have bothered you." She hung up quietly.

He swore to himself and replaced the phone in its cradle. What he didn't need at this particular moment were outside distractions. For two years Jon had existed quite well without his father's help; he could get on for another hour. Carl allowed himself a sidelong glance at Ralston: The chubby man sat without moving, a watchful buddha, an imminent disaster waiting to happen. Ralston would go when the time was right.

The phone rang again. In some mystical manner, the clanging was harsher, more insistent, the demand of a caller who was unaccustomed to waiting.

"Osborne here."

Heggland always placed his own calls. His voice was rough, stippled with impatience, a caustic lilt to every phrase. "Dammit, Osborne, what is going on out there? A simple job—can't you get it done? I'll send someone who can."

"Some problems, sir." Carl was offended by the obsequiousness that seeped into his own voice. It was a new element and it disturbed him. He set himself against the fear. "That's why I came; we expected some trouble."

"Problems are to be solved," Heggland drawled. "When I pay a man one hundred thousand good American dollars a year, plus bonuses and commissions, I expect him to solve problems. I expect him to get rid of trouble. I'm an old man, ready to retire, tired, why do you bother me with these details?"

"Yes, sir. Except it isn't quite that easy. I received approval from P and Z, but now we appear to be blocked."

"Blocked! Blocked by what? Blocked by whom?"

"The county commissioners. Specifically, a man named Tom Keating. He controls the vote there."

"Are you telling me one man is going to kill my project?"

"Not exactly."

"I suppose you are referring now to the Horn ranch? I expect acquisition to be completed within the next forty-eight hours, Osborne."

Carl glanced over to where Ralston sat, tense and anticipatory, on the edge of his chair. For the first time, Osborne sensed a vague toughness in Ralston, a heretofore unperceived drive and determination. Ralston was a threat at his back, secretly in contact with Heggland, and making God knew what kind of arrangements. "Horn won't sell," he said into the phone. "I've tried him twice."

"Make him sell."

"Have you any suggestions, sir?"

The irony was not lost on Heggland. "When I must make such decisions myself, I won't send an employee to do the job. Get the land. Now, about this man Keating—I will not accept failure; you know me that well, I believe."

"Keating, sir. He won't be swayed."

"He's been pressured in every way, I assume," Heggland said in a flat voice that left no doubt about his meaning.

"He won't be bought, Mr. Heggland."

"Osborne, you disappoint me. There isn't a man alive who can't be reached. You've overlooked something."

"I don't think so, sir."

"What have you got on this Keating? There must be something. Does he like women?"

"He lives with a woman; she's pregnant."

"Are you implying they are not legally wed? Well, there you are, Osborne, your lever. Use it."

"It won't work here. Keating is not affected by such social niceties."

"What is he, some kind of damned hippie?"

"I guess you could call him that."

"You're not going soft on me, Osborne, I hope. In the past, you handled this kind of thing quite effectively."

"There is considerable local opposition to Wolf Run."

"Well, of course there is. Opposition always crops up. You are paid to defeat opposition. To circumvent it. Wipe it out. I've taught you how to function, now get the job done."

Osborne reacted sluggishly. The old crisp style was dulled, his thoughts no longer clicking competently into place. He no longer enjoyed this exchange with Heggland, no longer enjoyed the Old Man's harsh and unbending ways. Suddenly, he longed for a simpler, less competitive existence, and that upset him. What the hell was happening?

"It would be a mistake to go on," he heard his voice saying. "There are too many obstacles. Rising costs. Diminished profits. Not worth the effort."

"I don't like this, Osborne."

"It's sucking up money. Millions already—and there is no reason to—"

"There is no reason for it not to come off," Heggland gritted out in a thin voice. "Make it happen."

Osborne hesitated. "Yes, sir," he said finally.

Heggland hawked his throat clear. "Very well." He sounded unconvinced. "There is a great deal at stake here, Osborne, for the group, for you personally..."

"Yes, sir," Carl said, aware of the implications of what Heggland was saying. All that he'd worked for, dreamed about; his boyhood fantasies, his adult ambitions; it was all on the line, but the odds were growing longer every minute. "I'll do my best," he said without conviction.

"Good. Now I'll talk to Ralston. Put him on the line."

Osborne offered the instrument to the advance man. Ralston said his name and listened attentively, almost obsequiously. Twice he said "Yes, sir," and it seemed to Osborne that he stood taller, appeared more confident. After an authoritative "I'll take care of it, sir," he hung up. Without changing his expression, he glanced at Osborne and spoke with a fresh sturdiness. "Some details; nothing important."

"Like the Horn ranch, Len?"

"Mr. Heggland wants the land, Carl."

"And you'll get it for him?"

"Mr. Heggland doesn't tolerate failure."

"So I've heard."

Osborne turned away. Already his mind was drifting. What was it Kit had told him: Something's going on, something strange—dangerous.

At once the connecting links to Jon seemed to tighten and grow stronger. He had to help his son. A memory came drifting to his mind from back

when Jon was no more than three years old. They
had been roughhousing, Osborne tossing the boy
in the air, catching him on the way down. For
Jon, a sense of nearby danger was cushioned by
the strength and certainty of his father's hands
and arms. He shrieked and giggled, gasped and
cried out, until Osborne let himself fall to the
floor, the boy on his chest. Jon had hugged him
with all the tightness those chubby arms could
muster, full of affection for this father of his.
"You're the best papa in the whole world. You're
my best papa."

"There are some questions I'd like answered,"
Ralston said.

If he heard, Osborne gave no sign as he left the
room.

——— 5 ———

He was used to life bending to his will. People
obeyed him, carried out his orders with dispatch
and efficiency. Money bought that kind of assistance and dependability. Money—and fear. He
had managed to compartmentalize his life. Publicly, he was seen as a genial host and man-about-
Aspen; privately, he was a tough overlord who
ran his kingdom with ruthless attention to detail.
In this area, jobs went off with clockwork pre-
cision, without chanciness. The penalties for slop-

piness or a breakdown in competence were severe and swift.

But now, uncertainty rippled through him and he grew afraid. Afraid of the unknown failure. The event that he might be unable to anticipate and thus prevent. The deadly blow that might be delivered from out of the dark by an unknown assailant. Sweat broke out across his shoulders, rolled into the hollow of his back.

That shipment of junk to Denver. Learning about it had been luck, a dice roll that came up a winner. The kid had been a freak chewing mushrooms and burning grass in Oaxaca. There'd been a bust: A handful of Yankee heads had put together an orgy with some Mexican chicks, and the local fuzz found out about it. The fuzz had taken a dim view of gringos corrupting the local talent, and they had broken a few heads, dumped them all in the slam.

Napoleon Ramirez had broken the freak out, paying the *mordita*—"the bite"—to the right people. The freak went north on a job for Napoleon; he picked up a load of coke in Nuevo Laredo and put it across the border.

The freak was no dummy; he shaved his beard, cut his hair, and hooked up with a square-looking schoolteacher from El Paso driving a pretty new Ford wagon. The customs inspector, a John Wayne facsimile, dug her drawl and his crew cut and passed them through without trouble.

By the time the freak reached Aspen, he'd dumped the schoolteacher and got his beard going again. Alex took the coke off his hands for a price, fixed him up with a handful of pills, and listened to the mule blow his horn. That was the problem with using freaks. They had no judgment. Not one of them was dependable and, under the least pressure, a freak always opened up.

The freak talked about a big shipment. The biggest Napoleon had ever put together. Pure Mexican brown. Shipped by truck to Zihuatanejo, it would be put aboard a light plane, flown north across the Rio Grande at night. On a small landing strip on a ranch outside of San Diego, the stuff would go aboard a white panel truck with a red star. It would be tucked away amidst a load of fruit and shipped out for Denver.

Napoleon figured it to be a locked route. Nobody knew about it except himself and the various mules, but in a moment of weakness he had boasted of his plans to the freak. And the freak spilled to Alex Budde.

The freak was the weak link in Napoleon's chain, and Budde now saw him as a similar threat to himself. With the assistance of Harry Rodano, Budde had taken the freak up onto Smuggler Mountain. Rodano hit the freak over the head with a heavy rock, and together they dropped the still-breathing man into Haller Shaft. Three hundred feet straight down into the deserted mine.

After that, the operation became a question of working out the details. Time everything down to the second and put it in the experienced and capable hands of a professional; Harry Rodano. It looked like a snap; nothing could go wrong. Except that it had. Rodano should have checked in nearly six hours ago. Rodano was a dependable man who always carried out Budde's instructions according to plan.

Budde labored over the possible errors. Every step of the operation had been carefully worked out, every variation checked and considered. Every move anticipated. A quiet investigation had revealed the route by which the truckers would go, the stop-off points for food, sleep, piss breaks. There were seven checkpoints at which the driver phoned his contacts ahead, giving them his exact position. One of those contacts had been on Alex Budde's payroll for nearly three years: Alex even knew the name of the driver and where he lived; and the shotgun, the kind of weapon he preferred. Nothing could have gone wrong.

Budde considered the possibility of a double cross. By Rodano? Not Harry; his loyalty was unimpeachable, as long as he was paid well and promptly. The contact? Always possible, but not likely. He was not a man of courage or daring, not good at hiding; to betray Budde would mean his death, and he wouldn't have taken the chance.

That dumped it all on Jon Osborne. The kid was too smart for his own good. Always pushing, always trying to get his finger into the pie. He'd shot his mouth off about it, too, to Kit Pepe, and the word had gone from her to Osborne. Jon was an arrogant bastard, spoiled, and not nearly as clever as he thought he was.

It was hard to believe that the kid had gotten the best of Rodano. Especially when Harry had been primed to waste him on the way back to Aspen. Everything had been cool when he had gotten that final phone call from Rodano. Whatever happened had taken place since then.

Budde tried to put himself in Jon's place. All that smack—where would the kid go with it? On to Denver, to try to sell it back to the dealer there? The kid didn't know the buyer, but he might be able to make another contact. Or to Chicago, or Detroit, or New York? The possibilities were endless.

That didn't sit well. The kid was a mule, not a

dealer. Carrying a load that size would make him nervous, afraid he'd be ripped off. He'd be anxious to make a quick sale, get the money, and split. Who would have that kind of cash readily available? The answer came in slow, steady steps. A grim look settled on Budde's face and he called police headquarters, asked for Jim Sexton.

"Sexton here."

"A problem has come up," Budde began.

"Anything I can do..."

"On the road to Denver..."

"The interstate?"

"Route 24 is more likely."

"Yes?"

"Why don't you nose around, see if anything out of the ordinary has happened."

"Get back to you soon."

Twenty-one minutes later, Sexton called back. "Funny thing," he said. "A couple of dead guys were found this morning. One in the back of a fruit truck, the other nearby. Both shot."

"Only two?"

"You expect the numbers to get bigger?"

"What I'm expecting is a call, or a visit. I'd like to know you're handy when I need you."

"Should I come over there?"

"Just let me know where you can be reached."

"This number."

"Good deal." Budde hung up and stared at the telephone. It became the stand-in for his enemy and he focused his hatred and rage on it, vowing vengeance. When the phone began to ring, he arranged his emotions into placid order and cleared his head before answering.

"Yes," he said.

"It's Jon, Alex."

Budde produced a flat voice that would tell his caller nothing. "I was beginning to get a little uptight. Rodano was supposed to contact me long before this."

"Rodano couldn't make it, Alex."

"Why is that, kid?"

"He's dead."

"You're not hurt?"

"Oh, not me."

"Glad to hear it. And the shipment?"

"Safe and sound."

Relief made Budde feel weak, but only for a moment. Somehow the kid had turned it around, taken Rodano out, claimed the shipment for himself. He had acted exactly as Budde had figured, coming back to the source for his money. He wanted to make a deal.

"Well, kid, I'm pleased that you're okay. Come on in, we'll talk."

"Just what I had in mind, Alex."

"My place in ten minutes."

"No good."

"Why not my place, kid?"

"Let's make it someplace public, someplace you don't own. And just you, Alex. I know your people. I spot any one of them and I won't make the meet."

"Kid, I don't understand the way you're acting."

"Alex, there isn't anything you don't understand. The bar at the Hotel Jerome, Alex."

"When?"

"Right now."

The phone went dead. Budde called Jim Sexton. "Jon Osborne is in the bar at the Jerome. I'm meeting him there. Find out where he goes when he leaves."

"Anything else?"
"I want information, that's all."
"You got it."

At about the same time that Alex Budde was
heading for the Hotel Jerome, Len Ralston drove
out toward Wolf Run Valley. He parked his rented
car in the shadow of a rocky overhang, less than
forty feet from the winding dirt road but completely concealed from a casual passerby.

He made his way up the valley, angling across
the south edge of the McDevitt land, picking his
way up the steepening incline. It was slow going,
made slower by the orange-colored plastic containers he carried in each hand. He fell twice and
tore his trousers and scraped his knee, but he
went on.

He paused to rest finally at a stand of poplars
that stretched like a green wall across the landscape, shielding him from view. He surveyed the
terrain. There was no sign of life anywhere, nor
had he expected there to be. At least, not yet. A
glance at his watch confirmed the efficiency of his
plan. He sat hunched over, waiting for his breathing to become more regular, for his heart to stop
pounding, for the weakness to leave his legs. He

could not recall when he had walked this much, climbed so many rocks, carried such a heavy load.

The orange containers had made the going more difficult. The kerosine sloshed about in them and made his burden more oppressive. But the results would be worth the effort.

Out front, across nearly a hundred yards of open field, he could identify each of the buildings that belonged to Don Horn: the main house, actually a small structure with fewer than six rooms; a horse barn, now used to store ancient farming equipment; and a cow barn, also empty—the cows could be seen down the valley grazing peacefully. Ralston was glad of that; he had a great fondness for animals. Beyond the barns was a long, low building that had been used to house hired hands in days when the ranch required additional help; it too would be empty. Ralston wondered if he'd brought enough kerosine.

Nearly twenty minutes went by before Don Horn came out of the main house. He was a small, thin-shouldered man with a slow, easy way of moving. In a Stetson and faded jeans, he looked like what he was—a farmer, a rancher. He climbed into a battered Ford pickup and drove off. Ralston smiled with satisfaction; it was going precisely the way he had known it would. It hadn't been much trouble to discover that Horn went to his friend Charley Singleton's house in Aspen for lunch every Wednesday. He would remain there for about two hours: plenty of time for Ralston to do his job and make his getaway unseen.

Ralston sat in the shadows of the poplars for another fifteen minutes, long enough for Don Horn to be well on his way toward Aspen, long enough to make certain he would not make an unexpected return. Then he rose, an orange container in each hand, and began his trek.

He worked without haste, splashing the kerosine over the floor of the main house, careful to allow none of the liquid to land on his clothing. He carried the containers outside, then went back, struck a match, and dropped it on the floor. A blue flame ignited in a whooshing explosion, and ran swiftly across the room, licking hungrily at the dry wood walls.

Ralston hurried outside, retrieved the kerosine, and repeated the process at each of the other buildings. He looked back only once on his drive to Aspen, and he saw four columns of smoke climbing above the ridgeline. He had done a very good job.

----- 7 -----

Jon sat at a large round Victorian oak dining table in the Jerome bar. He had placed his back to the wall, so that he had a clear view of the entire room and through the big front window out to Main Street. Periodically he glanced into the huge mirror behind the bar, scanning the back room and the doors that led to the hotel lobby.

A strange exhilaration gripped him, as if he

were high. All his perception was sharpened; his fingers tingled with anticipation. No fear touched him, although he recognized the enormity of his acts and the extreme reaction they would evoke in Alex Budde. He wished his father were witness to this confrontation so that he could see how competently Jon handled things under pressure. Carl would be proud, would envy him his youth, his daring, his future. He swore at himself for thinking in alien terms, for reacting the way his father would react. To hell with Carl! This had nothing to do with the son of a bitch. This was Jon's blow for freedom, for personal independence, his entry fee into manhood.

A waitress brought a hamburger and fried potatoes and a bottle of Heineken's. It was almost impossible for him to swallow the hamburger. He drank some beer, and soon Alex Budde appeared by way of the lobby entrance. Jon arranged a pleased smile on his boyish face and invited the other man to sit down.

"No, not next to me, Alex. Across the table with your back to the bar. So I can keep an unobstructed view of who comes and who goes."

"Don't you trust me, kid?"

Jon laughed. "Never did, never would; surely not now."

The shining face stiffened, the skin shifting tightly over the wide bones. "All right, let's have it."

Jon took a bite of the hamburger. He chewed vigorously. "Alex, your burgers cost twice as much and are half as good. Take lessons, man."

"I'm getting unhappier by the minute, kid."

"I feel pretty good myself."

"Tell me about Harry."

Jon drank some beer. "He's dead."

"The shotgun did it?"

"I thought you'd know the answer to that by now, Alex. Rodano was very good about the shotgun and the driver, wasted them both without trouble. It was me, I shot Rodano."

"How'd you get Rodano's gun away from him? He was very good about things like that."

"It was the shotgun's gun I used. Lifted it when Harry wasn't looking. The only mistake Harry made."

"A bad one."

"Fatal."

"Now what, kid?"

"We talk business, you and me."

"You're good, kid, better'n I thought."

"Well, I take that as a compliment, I really do. But it wasn't hard to figure, Alex."

"Figure?"

"That you intended to have Rodano put a bullet into me."

"You got it wrong. If Rodano tried that, it was his doing, not mine. I like you, always have."

"Don't crap me, Alex. Rodano wouldn't do a thing without your okay."

"Why would I want you dead?"

"To cut me out, keep me quiet, just to get rid of me. Sooner or later, you'd have to do the same thing to Rodano, if he lasted."

"That's just talk."

Jon pushed the hamburger away. Food disgusted him, made him slightly sick to his stomach. "Okay, Alex, let's get down to business."

Alex's eyes glazed over. "The only business we have to discuss is the whereabouts of my goods."

Jon met his gaze without flinching. "*My* goods. I earned it. I own it. I know where it is."

"This is getting pretty tricky."

"You ready to talk about money?"

"How much money?"

Jon laughed nervously, reached for the beer. "One half a million dollars."

"Oh, kid, you're really stepping out of your class."

"You tried to con me, Alex. Told me the load was worth a quarter of a million, more or less. I did a little figuring. Cut and bagged, all that junk would bring in maybe two and a half, three million dollars on the street."

"Stop playing with yourself. Tell you what I'll do; from now on, double your share on everything."

Jon finished the beer and called for another. The waitress brought it.

"I want the half million in cash. Not new money, either."

"Even if I agreed, where would I get that kind of bread?"

"You fly up to Denver today, Alex. Talk to your contacts. You're a man who buys and sells, who borrows and lends—a dealer. Make a deal, Alex, you can do it. In the morning, you turn the cash over to me, I give you the smack and bingo! Everybody's happy."

"People have been known to die for this kind of action."

"It could happen to anybody at any time. Rodano was a cinch for me, you'd be a joke, Alex."

"What if I turn down your offer?"

"I'll peddle the stuff somewhere else."

"If you could, you'd be on your way now."

"I don't have solid connections, you're right about that. But it shouldn't be too hard. I go to San Francisco, say. I spread a little bit of pure powder around, somebody asks can I get more of the stuff, and soon I've got a solid connection. The connection puts me in touch with Mr. Big who owns a factory. First thing you know, we're in business together. The stuff is in the streets, the money comes rolling in."

"Talk is cheap."

"A half million is little enough, Alex. You'll never miss it, and it'll get me where I want to go. The bread sends me on my way for all time."

"I might be able to come up with a hundred thousand by morning, that's all."

"Decide now. A half million or you're shut out."

Budde allowed his eyes to close. "Okay. You get it in the morning."

"No tricks, Alex."

"No tricks, kid."

Jon, all charm and friendliness, said, "Way to go, man. Win some, lose some. As it is, we both get what we want."

A thin smile lifted the corners of Budde's mouth. "Exactly what I was thinking. After all, business is business. . ."

— 8 —

When Don Horn arrived unannounced and unexpected at the hotel suite, Osborne could not conceal his shock. It was as if the rancher had been transformed overnight from a robust and energetic outdoorsman into a trembling hulk, bent, drained, his skin hanging in pale folds, his eyes watery. When he spoke, his once-firm voice was shaky, and a trickle of drool bubbled at the corner of his mouth. His eyes moved nervously around as if seeking a safe point of focus.

"Mr. Horn," Osborne began with some concern, "are you all right?"

If Horn heard, he gave no sign. He made a gesture, as if to eliminate all extraneous conversation. The skin on his hand was translucent; a network of swollen blue veins was suddenly visible. "All right," he muttered.

"Would you like to sit down?" Osborne said. "Can I get you something to drink?"

"You win," the old man said, avoiding Osborne's eyes. "I should've known you'd win."

"Win? I don't understand."

"You can have my land. . ."

Elation rose swiftly in Osborne. He had put the entire package together; the parcel was complete. Only a single barrier remained to cement his victory, to satisfy T. Lyman Heggland, to elevate him to the presidency of the group. Only the county commissioners stood in his way now, and he knew, *knew*, he would find some way to solve that problem.

He offered Horn his hand. "I'm glad you changed your mind, sir. You won't be sorry." He grinned in Len Ralston's direction. The advance man remained seated in his chair, round, soft to the eye, but slumped in on himself as if plotting his next move in a strategic race. He said nothing.

The old rancher backed away, as if Osborne's extended hand was contaminated. His long, thin head rocked reproachfully, and anger flashed into his eyes for a split second. Then it was gone and he was once again a tired, defeated old man.

"You didn't leave me a thing, mister," he grumbled with uncharacteristic petulance. "Nothing left up there but the naked land. All gone."

"I don't understand." Osborne glanced at Ralston who shrugged and looked away.

"My daddy worked the land and left it to me. Ninety years of living, of work and sweat, went into those buildings. All gone now—up in smoke."

"What are you talking about, Mr. Horn?"

"Didn't think you'd do it. Figured you was a tough businessman, but not a mean man. Just never figured you'd do it."

"Do what? Please explain what you're talking about."

"Burned me to the ground, you did. Didn't leave a stick."

"Burned—!" Osborne swung back to Ralston. The pale, pudgy face was unyielding, silent. "You mean your ranch burned down, Mr. Horn?"

"Smell the kerosine a hundred yards away, you can."

Osborne spoke firmly. "I had nothing to do with it."

Horn's weary eyes rolled into focus. He almost smiled. "It may not hold up in court, Mr. Osborne, but my daddy used to say if it looks like a skunk, smells like a skunk, and hangs out with skunks, then by God it's a skunk. Still makes good sense. . ."

"You think I'm responsible?"

"Ain't nobody else would do it. Ain't nobody else wanted the old place. Even McDevitt gave up trying to buy me out twenty-five years ago.

Wasn't much good to anybody else, the way it was situated and all. Except to you and your new town. . ." He staggered backward, and Osborne, thinking he was going to fall, went after him. The old man raised a hand in a commanding gesture, righted himself, stood straight and proud. "Just give me your price, Mr. Osborne. Make out a piece of paper and the land is yours. That fire burned away all my belly for a fight. Ain't enough spunk left inside me to scare a rabbit. You finished me, fer sure. . ."

"I'm glad you decided to sell," Osborne heard himself saying. "In the long run, you won't be sorry. But we don't do business that way. We don't commit arson. . ."

Horn's expression hardened and his eyes steadied briefly. "Ain't going to be any long run for me. I've made my race. Just want the money now to settle my owings and send a little on to my grandchild. . ."

Ralston came forward, an option form in hand. He read off the price of the land.

"Where do I sign?"

"Wait a minute," Osborne said. "If you feel that's not a fair price. . .?"

"Do you reckon it's fair?" Horn said without expression.

Heggland had said it often to Osborne: "Buy cheap, sell dear. Maximize your profits." Osborne nodded once. "I believe it's fair, Mr. Horn."

"Then I'll sign the paper."

When the old rancher had gone, Osborne pivoted to confront Ralston. The advance man was laughing silently. "We *did* it!" he cried.

"You rotten bastard," Osborne gritted out. "You set fire to that poor guy's ranch."

Ralston sobered rapidly. "Don't let your imagination get the best of you, Carl." There was no longer any obsequiousness in his voice.

"If I had my way, Ralston, I'd can you right now."

"The Old Man wouldn't like that, I think. You haven't exactly covered yourself with glory in this operation. He might overrule you."

"Get out," Osborne husked. "Get out, Ralston, before I lose my temper. . ."

Ralston tucked the option into his jacket pocket and left without a word. His shoulders were straight and there was a satisfied grin on his face.

Nearly an hour later, Alex Budde appeared at the hotel suite. Osborne admitted him without enthusiasm.

"Well," Osborne said, "the parcel is complete. Horn sold out to us."

"Yes, I know. Ralston told me."

"Len is a busy boy these days."

"He seems to get things done."

"In ways you approve of?"

Budde considered the question. "I appreciate competence in a man." He frowned thoughtfully. "But I didn't come to discuss Wolf Run." He let the words out slowly.

"What then?"

"It's about your son."

"Jon—what about Jon?"

Budde lowered himself into a deep chair, crossed his legs, folded his hands. There was a threatening calmness in his eyes. "He's in serious trouble."

"What kind of trouble?"

"He murdered Harry Rodano."

Weakness unlocked Osborne's joints. He sat down quickly. "I don't believe you."

"There's more. He's stolen something of value to me."

"No," Osborne said. "No."

"Heroin, Osborne. Lots of it. The little bastard is trying to rip me off for half a million bucks for my own stuff."

"That's absurd."

"I'm going up to Denver to raise the cash. Things like this have a way of never working out according to plan. Especially with an amateur."

"You mean to kill Jon?"

"Your son has dealt himself a hand in a heavy game, and he doesn't know the rules. Returning my goods, that would be smart. That way nobody gets hurt. He can just walk away from it. Trouble is, he is pretty cocky. It's all been downhill for him up to now. But I'm a pro, and in my business I always win. A man like you, Osborne, you can understand that."

Osborne tried to think clearly. "If it's all so cut-and-dried, why come to me?"

"I have no particular need to see Jon dead. I only want back what's mine. I figured you might talk to him."

"The police—"

"Don't be stupider than you have to be." Budde's voice was a low rasp. "The police aren't going to do a thing, unless I give the word."

Osborne was inundated with fear for Jon, and for himself. "I'll try to talk to him."

"Good. Room 223 at the Henderson Motel and Lodge. Convince him to smarten up. Otherwise. . ."

He broke off, the silence more menacing than his words.

As soon as he was alone, Osborne called Kit Pepe, as if seeking support for what had to be done, corroboration for what he felt and believed. He told her everything Budde had said.

"I was afraid of this," she said.

"Will Jon listen to me?"

"You've got to make him listen."

"Help me, Kit. Come along."

"I can't do that, Carl. It's your job. I would be in the way, another reminder of what he's lost to his father."

Osborne decided to ignore that aspect of the situation. "I'll phone you later," he said.

"Do that," she answered before hanging up.

He stared at the dead instrument in his hand. Never before had he felt so completely abandoned, a solitary figure in a monstrous and threatening universe. He would have cried, if he'd had the time.

—— 9 ——

Bobby Wallace could not tear his eyes away from Scooter Lewis. With hypnotic fascination, he watched the writer as he huddled over himself on the floor, rocking gently, chanting mantras in a chesty voice. From time to time, Scooter broke off, his frail body wracked by violent shudders. One coughing fit lasted for nearly ten minutes.

Human garbage, Bobby told himself.

"Ummmm."

No man could screw himself up so thoroughly without years of practice and preparation. Here he was, the world's second-best literary agent, watching one of the country's top writing talents moaning away like some freaked-out crazy in the park.

"Ummmm."

Waste. All that ability going down the drain; all that money going to some other agent.

"Ummmm."

He made up his mind; Scooter Lewis had had it. He was finished, out, dumped like yesterday's garbage.

"Ummmm."

Word of this was bound to get out. Scooter Lewis has gone ape. A writer who can't write. A useless lump. Nobody, but nobody, was going to hire him.

"Ummmm."

No way to get him straight.

"Ummmm."

No way to turn him around.

"Ummmm."

Not even the best agent in the world could do it.

"Ummmm."

All that bread lost forever.

"Ummmm."

Pack it in, Bobby instructed himself.

"Ummmm."

A sound drew his attention to the front of the

house. Someone was knocking. He went to the door, admitted Kit Pepe, and led her into the living room.

"Look at that—a whacked-out dope fiend gone off the deep end."

"Shouldn't he see the doctor?"

"He'll live. Only his brain has gone mushy from all those chemicals. The man never did understand the principles of good health."

"It's sad."

"Come out on the deck where we can talk." They sat facing each other. "You made up your mind. You're coming back with me."

"I don't think so, Bobby."

Disgust showed on his face. "You're as messed up as that monkey in there. Do you realize what you're passing up?"

"I've given it a great deal of thought."

"Poets go nowhere," he said.

She smiled wistfully. "Maybe I don't want to go anywhere."

"Don't make a hasty decision. Let me tell you what is in it for you. You know about Terry Donahue, also a poet. She wrote three screenplays, and for her newest—an original—I got her three hundred grand. That's not play money. Don't turn your pretty back on that kind of loot."

"It's not for me."

He was genuinely distressed and confused, and he told her so. "Why?" he kept asking.

"I'd never be comfortable in Hollywood."

"Try it, you might like it."

"Exactly. What if I were seduced by the money, the excitement, the glamour? That isn't what I need or want."

"Poetry," he snarled.

"And the time to compose it, Bobby. Images leap into a poet's head. One leads to another."

"Movies are images—lots of images."

"Bobby, try to understand. Poetry is a poet's life. I want to be able to follow the images to their inevitable end—which is actually the beginning—of a poem. The process is vital to me. The germination, the execution, every step along the way."

"Okay, write poems for half a year, films for the other half."

"It wouldn't work."

"The money—you wouldn't have to teach."

"I want to teach."

His lips fluttered, giving sound to his disgust, his disbelief, his acceptance. "Antioch," he muttered. "A bunch of smart-ass kids go there, I guess."

"That's one way to put it."

"Agh, well, maybe you'll change your mind. Truth is, I kept hoping that you and me might get together. But you'd never turn on to a character like me. . ."

"Ah, Bobby, I like you a lot."

"That's the kiss of death." He lit a cigarette. "Osborne's more your style. He's got class, and plenty of important bucks."

She lowered the barrier of restraint behind which she normally functioned. "Carl asked me to go back to New York with him."

"He's married, isn't he?"

She almost smiled. "Why, Bobby, how very old-fashioned you are. Nobody pays attention to small details like family anymore."

He made a face.

Kit sobered. "Carl's problems are larger than

that. There's Jon. He's into the same tub as Scooter."

"Freaked out, you mean?"

She shook her head and told him everything she knew. Bobby chewed reflectively on his thumbnail. When she finished, he said, "Bad trouble. Bad. Bad. All that junk—Budde isn't about to be ripped off by a dumb-ass kid."

"Carl's trying to talk some sense into him right now."

"The kid won't listen. They never listen."

"I hope you're wrong."

"I'm never wrong," Bobby said, grinning to show he was making a joke. "Well, hardly ever." They went back into the house. Scooter perched in place, swaying, eyes closed.

"*Ummmm.*"

"What about him?" Kit said.

"I'll take care of him. What about you?"

"I'll take care of me."

"I hope so. You're in some heavy traffic."

They went to the front door and he kissed her on one cheek, then on the other. "You ever get out to the coast, look me up."

"I'll do that, Bobby. You're a sweet man."

"Right on."

He went back inside and found the living room empty. He searched the rest of the house. No Scooter. He went down to the garage. Scooter's wheels, a sea-green Porsche, were missing. By now, the writer was miles away, speeding down the yellow-brick road. He was bound to total himself and the car. Bobby filled a glass with a small amount of ice and a great deal of bourbon and sat down to get drunk. What else could a sane man do?

10

Kit admitted Carl Osborne, took one look at his face, and directed him to the couch. She poured some scotch into a glass and when he swallowed it in one long gulp she poured him some more.

"Do you want to talk about it?" she said.

"The world is crumbling. I no longer understand the way things work."

"Tell me about Jon."

"I went to the room at the lodge. I told him I wanted to talk to him. He wouldn't open the door. I insisted that it was important. I guess I lost control. I shouted and beat at the door and tried to break it down. Someone sent the hotel security officer along. He opened the door, but Jon wasn't there."

"What do you mean?"

"He went out the window. An easy drop for a boy in good shape. He's gone, and I have no idea how to find him."

She sat next to him.

"Why wouldn't he at least talk to me? Listen to what I have to say?"

"For the same reason he won't contact me. Both of us have failed him."

"I don't agree. I—"

"It's true, Carl. From Jon's position, everyone

he ever trusted has failed to come through for him."

"I'm frightened, Kit. My whole life is being called into question. I believed that I was a reasonable man leading a reasonable existence—a good father, a good husband. Somewhere along the line, it all went wrong."

"Don't exaggerate."

"I've even failed in my reason for coming here. Five days ago I was on the verge of my greatest achievement, my greatest success. Even that has fallen apart."

"That may not be the worst thing that's happened to you."

He looked at her dumbly.

"Failure sometimes causes a person to recheck his goals," she said quietly. "Reexamine his values."

"The damn thing is I truly believed I was a good man, a nice man, that I wouldn't ever hurt another human being."

"I've met much worse."

"And much better. Look at the damage I've done to my son."

"Jon has to start taking responsibility for himself. His life hasn't exactly been exemplary. Narcotics, now murder and robbery, extortion."

"I feel it's all my fault."

"Self-pity doesn't become you, Carl."

"I want to save my son."

She filled her lungs with air, exhaled slowly. "It seems to be out of your hands now."

"I have to do something," he said. "I have to. I have to," he repeated, looking to her for some answer. When she said nothing, he sat without

moving, not thinking, trying not to feel anything.
Waiting for it all to be over.

_____ **11** _____

Caution was his guiding principle. His eyes
roamed ahead, searching the shadows; his ears
were tuned in for the slightest suspicious sound.
He stayed behind the houses, climbing over fences,
picking his way through backyards, past vege-
table gardens, around dog runs. He avoided the
streets where possible, and the mall, advancing
without haste toward Hector's Ranch in the east
end, now a riding stable.

Past the show-ring, past the jumping area, past
the water trough, and around back of the main
barn. At the far corner, he dropped to his knees
and began to scrape the soft dirt away with his
hands. It took only thirty seconds to find what he
was after. A package wrapped in newspaper. He
undid the paper and took out a Baggie that had
been sealed with magic tape. He undid it, withdrew the pistol he had used to kill Rodano, and
jammed it under his belt.

Off again, increasing the tempo of his movements, he went up the slope, slowing only when he
was well into the woods, safe from observation.
Twice he paused to listen, to make sure no one

was following. He heard nothing and went on, confident that Carl had not been able to pick up his trail.

He made it up to a grassy bowl where water seeped out of a rock wall. He drank his fill and sat down with his back to the wall.

Safe from pursuit or accidental discovery, he relaxed. This was not a place to which people often came; it was too close to town to be considered part of the mountain and too difficult to reach to be worthwhile.

In the morning, he would retrieve the goods and deposit them in another hiding place, even more remote than the first. Only then would he make contact with Alex. Only when the money was in his hands would he turn over the stuff.

He closed his eyes and before long he was asleep. He stirred once or twice during the next hour, but he didn't wake. Somewhere above him a dislodged stone clattered down the hillside, but he failed to hear it. Close at hand, there was a sharp intake of breath, the whispered shuffle of shoe leather on the grassy floor of the slope. He never stirred.

Without warning, a great weight came crashing down on Jon, and he went tumbling to the side, stunned, trying to collect his senses. Before he could straighten up, a heavy blow landed above his left ear, and the night world tilted and spun crazily, pain swinging deep into his brain. He opened his mouth to scream, but no sound came out. A deeper darkness flowed over him. And there was no more fear. No more pain.

The world shifted. The sky went from black to gray to bright blue, the light searing his eyeballs.

He kept his lids clamped shut and rolled his head in protest. A chilling splash hit his face and he cried out in alarm, raising his arms protectively. A voice full of impatience and gloat issued commands.

"Wake up, wake up! It's time. Get up."

Behind his hands, he forced his lids apart, blinking and squinting. A blurred image swayed and shifted, blocking his view.

"What happened?"

The figure leaned back and cackled triumphantly, slapping his thighs, "Never expected me, did you?"

Jon made an effort to identify the speaker, but he failed to dissipate the blur.

"Thought you were home free, I know, I know."

"Who—?"

"You know me, you know me. You've been at my house—parties, lots of parties. We swung together."

Jon lifted himself as if to rise.

"Hold it right there, man. Don't make a false move."

"Who is it?" he said faintly.

"Scooter Lewis, man, who else? Tracker first-class, ambusher without comparison, killer on the loose."

Jon saw the writer as if through the wrong end of a telescope. The long, pale features melted, congealed; then the process reversed in a mad kaleidoscopic flow. It was Scooter.

Jon rubbed his head. Jets of pain spat hotly against the inside of his skull, into the crevices of his brain. Surely there was tissue damage.

"You hit me?"

Scooter did a jig of joy. He stamped his feet,

clapped his hand, lifted his voice in a shrill cry of victory. "I did it, I did it. With my own little rock."

"You could have killed me." Jon's head began to clear, his brain began to function once again. He wondered where the pistol was.

"Agh, not a chance. You're young, tough. You're no good to me dead. No good at all."

"I don't get it, Scooter. I never did you wrong." Jon needed time to figure it out, to plot his next move, to understand what this was all about.

"I waited for you, man, outside the lodge, waited for you to come out. I saw your daddy go in and figured you might split out the back way. When you jumped, I was there."

"You followed me?"

"Never knew it, did you? Did you? Never spotted me. I tell you, I got Indian blood in me, pure Indian. Move like a cat, strike like a snake. *Hissss.* Just that fast, I had you. Believe it or not, used to be an eagle scout. A bundle of merit badges. Read the stars like it was the newspaper delivered to my door. Always good at night tracking. Had you all the way, had you cold." He made a gesture upwards. "When you settled down, I worked my way up above. It was easy. You petered out in a hurry. Then I jumped you, bashed your head with the rock. Zap! That was all there was to it."

"Why?" Jon said. Flashes of pain leaped across the top of his head. He wanted to sleep. He also wanted to bring this madman down, to beat him unconscious, and to cry for a little while.

"Don't bullshit me, man."

Jon made an attempt to get up.

"Hold on, cowboy!" Jon knew at once where

the pistol had gone. It was pointed at his navel,
clutched by Scooter's unsteady hand. At such close
range, however, a miss was impossible. Jon fell
back. "Get smart," Scooter chanted, "and you get
dead."

"Put that thing away."

"Took it from you, easy as pie. Took it right
away. Easy as falling out of bed. You ever fall out
of bed? Done it plenty of times. Drunk and high,
and sober too. Mostly, you never even know when
you hit the floor. Made it with this elephantine
chick one time, huge she was with an ass like
watermelons and tits that wouldn't quit. She
heaved and tossed like the ocean in a hurricane,
flipped me around until I nearly got seasick.
Figured my rod would keep me securely fastened
down. Forget it. Off I went, onto the floor, sprained
my lower back, and spent nearly three weeks in
traction. Oh, that wild lady!" He waved the pistol
in the air. "Here is the power and the glory. One
false move and I'll make your belly look like a
sieve."

"Why are you doing this, Scooter?"

A wily mask settled over the writer's angular
face. He cocked his head. "Don't shit me, man."

There could be only one reason for Scooter's
sudden and alarming interest, but Jon was unable
to figure out how the writer had learned of his
haul. He spread his hands. The gesture brought
the pistol to bear on his middle. He smiled what
he hoped was a reassuring smile.

"Scooter, you gotta believe me. . ."

"I want the junk."

"I'm clean, friend. Maybe I can put you on to
a guy. . ."

"Save it." Scotter's manner became sober and

menacing. "You snatched a load of heroin. I want it."

Jon raved madly to himself. To have come this far, done what he had done, exposed himself, put his life on the line, only to fall to this freaked-out wild man. Fury rose like a black cloud in him. "Somebody's conning you."

Scooter, on his knees, propelled himself forward in herky-jerky leaps, looking to Jon like a demented dwarf. He brandished the pistol. "Lies! I know lies when I hear them! I have heard the truth and I believe it. You ripped off Alex Budde. The stuff isn't really yours. So don't get p.o.'d because you're being ripped off yourself. Tit for tat." He cackled happily. "All I need is enough for a fix. A few days' supply is all. On to the cache, man, and everything will come out all right in the end. Let's go. Now."

"Scooter—"

Scooter's long, broad thumb worked back the hammer of the pistol. Click. Click. Click. He steadied the weapon with his left hand. "Oh boy, oh boy, oh boy. Don't make me do it, don't make me. Lead me to your load, you hear! Lead me to the promised land."

Jon nodded. His chance would come later.

"On your feet. But slow, man. No tricks."

Jon stood up.

"Move out."

"It's too far to walk."

"I got wheels, green Heinie wheels, the best. Back toward town. On a nice, quiet street. You first; me third; this little outblaster second. One wrong move and you get a hole in your back. Off we go."

Jon started out.
"*Ummmm.*"

Jon settled behind the wheel of the Porsche. Scooter sat next to him, the pistol in his lap. "Drive, man."
"You're making a mistake."
"Drive."
The Porsche eased forward.
"Faster," Scooter urged.
Jon shifted and the gears ground. Scooter cried out as if in pain. "Easy, man, I love these wheels."
"Maybe you better drive."
Scooter made a forward motion with the pistol. The Porsche picked up speed. Had either of them looked back, he would have seen the dark blue Datsun B210 coming after them. Behind the wheel, cool and concentrating, was Jim Sexton.

_____ **12** _____

With the first light, she woke, but she had no sense of being rested or having slept at all. Yet her last recollection was of the night, the infinite darkness. Without turning her head, she located the glass on that night table. She tilted it to her mouth; it was empty. The bottle of scotch was on the floor. She drank from it.

All night she'd been drinking. Lying alone in her bed, shivering. The liquor warmed her temporarily but did nothing to soften the pain that had claimed her body and soul. Serrated memories drifted into the present, lingered despite her efforts to wipe them away.

Nothing had ever been good for her. Nothing was pleasing, rewarding, satisfying. Nothing warmed her and made her want to smile. There was only harshness, the persistent and excessive cruelty of living. The meanness of people. The neglect, the anguish, the hollowness of each day.

She read the hands on the clock. They told her to commence her morning routine. Start the coffee maker. Go to the bathroom. Begin to dress. In panties and bra, go after the coffee. Always rich, aromatic, always perfect. The machine did that and she loathed the machine, loathed the world that made such a machine possible. For years she had tried to make good coffee: percolator, drip, pressure. Nothing had ever worked for her. Except the goddamn machine.

Time to do her face. Assume grotesque attitudes in front of the glass. Base, powder, eyeliner, shadow, mascara, lip rouge. A strange mask stared back at her each morning, only faintly like her own face. She hated them both.

Young girls today were luckier. The world accepted them as they came. They didn't care what people thought about them. Or so they said. But for Joan Carolinian, it did matter, she did care. She cared what they said when she wasn't around to inhibit their words. She wanted to make a good impression on everybody. She wanted everybody to like her.

They never did.

They never would.

Dressed, made up, stomach lined with perfect coffee, she would strike out for the office. Visions of the place floated to mind, made her sad. Her job had been a source of pride and fulfillment until *he* had turned away from her, hired that pretty young girl with the hard, perfect body. Until *he* had rejected Joan's flesh for the new girl. Not that he had ever said anything; oh, no, he was too cunning for that. But she had known. From the first time it happened. From the expression on the girl's face the next day. Smug, gloating, superior.

It wasn't right. She would have done anything for him. Anything. There was no need for him to bring another girl into the office, to diminish Joan's authority, to take work away from her. It wasn't the personal, private matter that troubled her so much. But to make her professional worth less, and less, and less. . .

And Alex. What made him act that way? Insulting her, hitting her. She was a human being, too, with a right to express herself freely. With a certain amount of dignity. He had gone out of his way to call her in the middle of the night, to invite her to come to the Spot. He had been so sweet, so attractive and appealing. And he had asked her to come back to his apartment. He had insisted that they make love, had craved her with a high order of passion. He had told her so.

What had turned him around? What caused him to treat her like some lower form of life? Hurting her. Turning her over to a man like Sexton.

She remembered Sexton naked, using himself like a weapon. He had an innate cruelty, a frightening malevolence, violence just below his taut skin. It wasn't fair...

Getting out of bed was difficult; her body was reluctant to respond to her will. Finally, she made it into a sitting position. She stood and her knees gave way, sending her to the floor. She cried out in fear, trying to comprehend what was happening. Surely she was ill, a lingering malady not yet identified by medical science. Incurable. She would suffer, of course, waste gradually away. But *they* would suffer even more, those who had so wronged her over the years. How empty their lives would be when she was no longer among them. Only then—too late—would they realize her true value.

How ironic life was. She, who had so much love to give, had been allowed to give so little. Had received so little. She had always been a special person. Prettier than most girls her age. With a very good, unobtrusive figure. A very good mind, too. She had worked hard in school to achieve good grades and all her teachers had approved of her. Her future loomed brightly then.

Starting tomorrow, she assured herself, her eyes closing slowly. Starting tomorrow she would take command of her existence once more, make meaningful alterations, deal only with people she enjoyed and respected. Those who were good to her. Tomorrow it would all be different.

But she had to rest now, to discover some peace, some extended relief from the constant punishment she had endured. She remembered what had occurred in Alex Budde's bathroom. The pills had failed her as everything else and everyone else in her life had failed her.

Unable to stand, she inched across the bedroom floor on her belly. At last the cool tile bathroom floor was under her cheek and she felt safe. At home, and able now to make things right. This time she would not fail. . .

_____ **13** _____

Keating brought Annie up to Maroon Lake, a place they both loved. A place where he could replenish his energies and consider his alternatives.

They spread their sleeping bags in among a stand of spruce, no more than twenty feet from the water's edge. Above them, on the far side of a meadow splashed with red and yellow wild flowers, were the Maroon Bells. The rugged peaks, striated with white amidst the blue-gray, rose up in lordly majesty, the high hollows still flecked with snow.

Before they went to sleep, they made love. Annie mocked his elaborate tenderness, reminding him that the baby was not due for nearly seven months. So in the morning, at sunup, he took her more roughly, and afterwards they dozed for a while. They bathed in the lake before breakfasting on corn bread and honey and strong coffee. They lingered until the sun had warmed the heights before starting back down, going easily, in no particular hurry.

"I've made up my mind," Keating told her.

She didn't want to hear his decision, convinced that whatever it was it would disrupt their existence, cause an upheaval she had no desire to deal with.

"We'll leave," he said.

She avoided his eyes. "You love it here. Both of us do."

"We came to live in peace with good friends, surrounded by love. That's not possible anymore."

"It would be wrong to run away. That's not like you, Tom. I want the baby to be born here, to grow up in these mountains."

"There are other mountains."

"No," she said with surprising force.

"Men like Alex Budde, Osborne, they've corrupted this valley."

"They exist everywhere, those men."

"Not everywhere. We'll find a new place. . ."

"And in a few years, they'll hear of it, find it, come to change it."

"What do you suggest?"

"That we stay."

He wished he believed in a god—any god would do—to relieve him of all mortal burdens. Someone on whom he might heap his insoluble difficulties. He looked up and wondered if there were in fact other races out there, other beings, wiser and kinder and stronger than earthlings. Please come to us, he implored silently, teach us to live correctly, with tolerance and love, hope and peace. But the sky remained still and deep and gave no response. No one was out there, no beings to hear, no god to acknowledge. Only infinite space in a never-ending rush to get nowhere. Just like men.

"And if we stay?" he said to Annie.

"Stay and fight," she answered simply.

"This kind of fight is dangerous. Now there are you and the baby to be concerned about."

"If you care about us, the fight becomes more necessary."

"You're some kind of lady, Annie." He touched her bottom affectionately. "Aren't you afraid?"

"Oh, yes, I'm afraid of lots of things. I remember you said a long time ago that we have to go on in spite of fear. The alternative is unthinkable."

"Alex tried to kill me. He'll try again. He has to."

"You've never been a pacifist, Tom, just a peaceful man. You know how to fight."

"County commissioners aren't peace officers."

She waited.

"If I do fight, I might as well be equipped properly for it. There's no point in standing for reelection."

"What will you do?"

He helped her scramble down a shallow rocky ravine. At the bottom, he led her along a twisting trail. "I have to think about it some more. Come on, we'll go across Sweet Georgia Basin and down from there. It's not so difficult. . ."

"Whatever you say, Tom."

Exactly one hour later, Keating and Annie were hunkered down beneath the low hanging branches of the trees. They studied the men on the ledge a hundred feet below. Only when Jon and Scooter had resumed their climb, had disappeared to the east, did either of them move or speak.

"What is that all about?" Annie said.

"They're on their way to Elmer's Number Two," Keating said.

"Scooter had a gun." She shuddered. "I hate guns."

"I don't like this." Keating started to get up, fell back quickly. He pointed down in a simple, graceful gesture. Out of the forest came Jim Sexton, moving up to the ledge. He, too, carried a pistol. Without hesitation, he went after the other two.

"What is going on?" Annie said.

"I don't know." He tried to assemble the various bits and pieces of information he had stored away about these three men. He wasn't sure that any of the answers he came up with made sense. "I'm going after them," he said softly.

"I'll go with you."

"No. You'll count to a hundred and start back to town. Notify Chief Parker, he's an honest man. Get to him personally. Tell him what we saw and ask for some reliable help."

"Come with me, Tom."

"You were just telling me to stay and fight."

"But this—"

"This may be part of it. Do what I ask, Annie. There's not much time."

_____ 14 _____

Jon went past Elmer's Number Two and continued up to Knickerbocker Tunnel. He stopped, indicating the tunnel entrance.

"It's in there."

Scooter eyed the mine dubiously. "You left it in there without anyone to take care of it?"

"Nobody else knew where it was."

"Okay. Get it."

"I'll need help."

"No tricks." He waved the gun.

"You can trust me, Scooter."

Jon put aside the corrugated tin sheet that blocked the entrance, and he ducked inside. Scooter followed, spooked by the almost complete darkness. He saw Jon bend over and pick something up, and he shouted a warning.

"Just a flashlight. . ." Jon snapped it on. "Let's go."

They moved along the narrow tunnel to the turnoff, swung left until they came to the roomlike space. The green plastic garbage bag was where Jon had left it.

Scooter began to giggle. He reached into the bag and brought out a forefinger covered with brown powder. He tasted it. "Oh, beautiful, man. It's gonna make me feel nice. Come on, let's get out of here."

Jon could almost see the writer's mind working. It was, he warned himself, time to make his move. He announced his willingness to comply and, at that same moment, switched off the flashlight and dived to the ground. A shot echoed in the network of shafts and tunnels. Jon located some rocks, heaved them toward the place he had last seen Scooter. He got lucky. Scooter grunted and swore and quickly retreated up the tunnel.

Jon went after him. Once back in the main shaft, he saw the writer silhouetted against the mine opening. Jon went faster. He was almost at

the entrance when he heard a shot. He looked out
and saw Scooter galloping into the woods, screaming wildly.

On the ground, ten yards away, was his pistol.
Jon broke out of the mine, anxious to get the gun
back in his hand. He took three strides when a
bullet plowed into his chest, puncturing his heart.
He was dead before he hit the ground.

—— **15** ——

The second shot caused Keating to stop. He listened, heard only the sounds of morning in the
forest. Some birds, a scurrying squirrel, the cry
of a hawk in the distance.

Keating started out again. When he reached
Knickerbocker Tunnel, he stopped at the edge of
the clearing and surveyed the open ground. He
saw Jon Osborne spread on the ground, face down.
Nearby, a pistol. A sound reached him from inside
the tunnel, announcing the whereabouts of the
man who had killed young Osborne. Keating moved
swiftly across the clearing, picked up the pistol,
and pulled back into the woods.

He lay flat on the ground and aimed the pistol
at the tunnel opening. Presently, Sexton appeared,
carrying a large plastic garbage bag. Keating
pointed the pistol at the cop's belly.

"Put your hands up, Sexton, I've got a gun on you."

If Sexton was surprised or alarmed, he gave no sign. He straightened up. "What is this mister? Who are you? What are you after?"

"Tom Keating, Sexton. Make a move and I'll shoot."

"This is police business, Keating."

"This is county land, the sheriff's jurisdiction. Get your hands up."

From a standing start, Sexton dropped the plastic bag and was in full stride, dashing toward the nearest edge of the clearing. Keating fired and missed and Sexton disappeared into the woods.

Keating went after him. A shot whizzed overhead, branches snapped, and Keating dived for the ground. He took up a firing position behind a tree, saw nothing. He thought he heard movement to his left, fired without looking. He checked the pistol. It was empty.

He swore and moved to another position. Another shot whined past. He circled around, hoping to come up behind Sexton. It was a futile effort.

Another shot, digging into the trunk of a tree. Keating charged forward and suddenly Sexton appeared a dozen yards ahead. The cop brought his gun around just as Keating launched himself in a long, low dive. The two men collided heavily, and the pistol went spinning to one side.

They rolled around, struggling to land punches. Sexton's elbow caught Keating in the mouth. Keating tasted blood. He landed a punch on the officer's shoulder.

Sexton broke free. Keating started after him and met Sexton's heavily booted foot swinging forward. He went over backwards and Sexton leaped to finish the job. Keating grabbed at the boot and twisted. Sexton spun to one side, came up in a ready stance.

They circled warily. Sexton charged, landing a blow on Keating's temple. Keating struck back and Sexton went down. Keating spotted the gun and went after it. He stood up, pistol in hand, to find Sexton gone.

He followed. No effort now to be quiet. Just a clumsy footrace through the woods, heading down the mountainside. Keating tripped once, struggled up, his cheeks scratched and bleeding; one knee began to ache.

He kept going. Abruptly, there was silence. He pulled up to listen. From behind him, Sexton stepped out swinging a heavy branch. Keating took it squarely across the shoulders and pain stabbed into his chest and along his spine. He went down, Sexton after him, the branch swinging high, coming down toward his head. Keating lifted the pistol and squeezed the trigger reflexively.

An expression of pained surprise moved across Sexton's tough face. He fell to his knees and toppled forward. Keating turned him onto his back and Sexton cried out.

Keating stepped back. "I'll go for a doctor."

"You killed me. . ." Sexton said, and he died.

Keating sat down on the ground and stared sightlessly at the green wall around him for a long time. Very tired suddenly, he longed to be with Annie, to put his head in her lap. To listen to her soft voice saying everything was going to be all right.

—— 16 ——

He sat in his usual place in the Spot and drank coffee and waited for the good word to reach him. He had no doubt that it would all work out, that Sexton would put things right for him. Sexton was very good at this sort of business. With Rodano dead, he'd have to depend more and more on the cop.

A jeep drew up outside and for a suspended moment he thought it might be Sexton. But of course Sexton hadn't been driving a jeep. Instead it was Keating who strode up to Budde's table, dirty and disheveled, his face caked with blood, his trousers torn. A pistol was jammed in his belt and he carried a green plastic garbage bag. As if it were weightless, he swung it onto the table, knocking over the cup, spilling the coffee. Budde didn't allow himself to respond.

"There it is," Keating said, voice heavy with anger. "You murdering son of a bitch!"

Budde gazed at him with no change of expression. "What's on your mind, Keating?"

"Heroin! Pure heroin. It's what you were after."

All over the restaurant, people fell silent. All eyes were on the two men.

Budde leaned back, tranquil and innocent. "I

357

don't know what you're talking about, commissioner."

"Sexton shot Jon Osborne for this bag of junk."

"You mean Sergeant Sexton?"

"He was your man."

"You're talking in riddles."

"And so was Jon. You owned them all."

"The more you say, Keating, the more confused I get."

"Take it, Budde." He shoved the bag forward. "There's millions in there."

Budde restrained himself. Every impulse, every yearning, every desire in him was to destroy Keating, to wipe him out forever, to claim that green bag and its contents. Instead, he replied in a rather rueful voice. "You've made a mistake, Keating. If that's heroin, it isn't mine. I don't know anything about drugs of any kind. If young Osborne was dealing, it was Sergeant Sexton's duty to apprehend him. If Osborne resisted. . ."

"Not in the county it wasn't Sexton's duty. It was an execution. The kid never had a chance. After he got Osborne, Sexton tried to waste Scooter Lewis. . ."

Budde checked his reactions. "Was Scooter involved too?"

"Scooter's still alive to bear witness, Budde."

Budde allowed himself a thin smile. "I'm sure Sergeant Sexton can account for whatever he's had to do."

"Sexton is dead."

Fear fluttered alive in Budde, and relief. Men like Rodano and Sexton could be replaced. Dead, they couldn't talk, couldn't incriminate him. He stopped being afraid. "I'm sorry to hear that."

"I killed him."

"I see. The police should be interested in that."

"They'll hear all about it. Also about this junk. It's going over, Budde, you'll never make a buck out of any of it."

Budde kept silent.

"And one more thing, Budde. You'll be pleased to learn that I won't run again in November."

"The voters will be the losers, Keating."

"I'm putting myself up for sheriff. You'll be much better off if I'm not elected."

Budde cleared his throat. "I'll be glad to make a contribution to your campaign fund, Tom. . ."

"Shove it," Keating said.

17

A haunted expression marred Carl Osborne's aristocratic features. The eyes were pulled back deep into their sockets, cupped by shadowed hollows. The flesh along his jaw was slack, the mouth drawn down. His movements were sluggish, like a man toting an irreconcilable burden. An attaché case dangled from his right hand, properly scuffed and scarred, an expensive status symbol, once a cherished trophy—courtesy of T. Lyman Heggland.

On the sidewalk in front of the county courthouse were Len Ralston and the team of architects in a furtive huddle. At Osborne's approach, they moved silently apart, watching him. The architects were suitably solemn and mournful; Ralston, anxious to get matters under way, shifted from foot to foot in a nervous little two-step reminiscent of a toddler not quite toilet trained.

"We've pulled a hell of a crowd," he announced with the forced enthusiasm of a carnival barker.

The architects avoided Osborne's eyes.

"Your wife get off okay?" Bender was uncomfortable in the asking.

"On the morning plane," Osborne said.

"Tough," Ralston said without emotion. "Her only kid?"

Resentment made Osborne's limbs stiff and his eyes came briefly back to life. "My son is dead and buried. There's no reason for us to talk about it. Let's get inside and do what has to be done."

Skutch, who seemed often to speak for his partners, hurried to keep up. "These public meetings of the county commissioners, they're often just formalities."

"I'll make my best case."

"Decisions are sometimes made in advance."

"I have to assume otherwise."

"Work on Lewin," Skutch said. "Maurice is our only hope."

"Keating," Bender put in. "Too tough to crack."

"Well," Ralston said, almost happily, "we've got Chalk in our hip pocket."

Osborne kept himself from looking at Ralston. Distaste gathered and pushed at his gut, made him want to punish Ralston, to beat him bloody, to inflict considerable pain on that rotund body.

Osborne breathed in and out, commanded himself to remain calm, to do the job he knew so well.

In the corridor outside the meeting room, nearly a hundred people were waiting to get inside. Uniformed guards blocked the entrance.

"All filled up, folks. No more seats inside."

Osborne identified himself and his companions. As they marched down the center aisle between benches jammed tight, he felt waves of hostility. He had few friends in this room.

"Hey, Osborne!" a male voice cried out. "Why don't you split and leave us alone?"

"Shit," Ralston muttered. "It's the French Revolution all over again."

"Shut up," Osborne bit off, not looking back. "Don't say another word."

He took his place at the table, flanked by his associates. He opened the attaché case and shuffled some papers, struggling to compose himself.

He had not quite accomplished that task when the commissioners appeared, Maurice Lewin leading the way. He was a short man with wide shoulders, a fringe of white hair, and lively blue eyes. His hands were large and strong and his thick body seemed powerful and responsive. He surveyed the crowd and his personal authority brought the room to an attentive stillness.

"Okay," he said, in a rasping, confident voice, "the session is called, the stenographer will begin keeping the official record. There will be quiet and order. Remember, this is no rock concert—" That drew an appreciative laugh. "Or love-in." Another, smaller response. "We are here to do the county's business, and I aim to see that it's accomplished in a fair and open way. Okay." He studied the top sheet of the presentation set in front of him. "The Heggland Group proposes the development of Wolf Run Valley for a variety of year-round recreational activities. It is to include appropriate living space—both rental and condominiums—plus various businesses.

"The proposal, which the commissioners have studied, includes plans for utilities, transportation, schooling, postal services, police and fire departments, etcetera, etcetera. It's a good proposal, I don't mind telling you, a very professional and complete job, Mr. Osborne."

"Thank you, Mr. Commissioner."

Lewin went on. "The proposal has the approval of Planning and Zoning and includes a number of notarized statements from citizens both for and against. All have been read and given suitable weight.

"For some time, it has been the attitude of this board—generally by a two-to-one vote—that the burden of proof for new building of any kind in the county lies with those who petition to make such projects. We operate on the premise that Aspen and the county are fast approaching peak development. In order to gain commission approval, a powerful case for the common and public good must be presented. . ." A loud cheer went up.

Lewin waited for it to subside. He scowled. "Okay, this is no Roman circus, so let's knock off the sound effects. We'll handle the proposition on its merits. It won't take much for me to clear the room."

"We've got a problem," Skutch whispered to

Osborne, who made no reply, eyes fixed on Maurice Lewin, trying to assess the little man.

"Okay," Lewin said. "We will now hear arguments from Mr. Carl Osborne, representing the builders..."

Osborne rose and a few people began to hiss. Lewin came out of his chair. "Okay, knock it off. Let's have it, Mr. Osborne."

Osborne felt vaguely reassured, seeing in Lewin's response a willingness to listen to his side of the argument, almost convinced that Lewin had not yet made up his mind. He began to speak, in a voice neither loud nor soft, about improvement of the earth, of additional income for present inhabitants of the county, of the rights of all citizens to enjoy the recreational and living advantages of the mountains. As he spoke, his eyes traveled from the encouraging mien of Joe Chalk to the solemn, intense Maurice Lewin to Tom Keating.

Keating's face was implacable, like a monument carved out of the solid rock of the mountains he so loved. Rugged and unyielding, a challenge to all who viewed them; like the mountains, full of promise and threat—and unconquerable.

Osborne realized, for perhaps the first time, that all of this was for nothing. A staged tableau designed to act out a script carefully plotted and shaped beforehand. For whose benefit did he now perform? For whom did he speak?

For Skip Blondell? A pathetic little man sent out to kill when he was equipped only to perish; a man able to squeeze only small amounts of pleasure out of life.

For Jon? Dead too young in pursuit of goals he

had never truly defined. Dead of an immortal
disease—loathing for his father and too much
love for him. Dead striving to outperform his
father, certain he could never be the man Carl
was, and fearful he had already become even
worse.

Or was it for Don Horn? A lifetime scorched
away. Generations spent cultivating and loving
the earth and sent up in flames in the name of
mindless progress and profit.

Nor was that the end of it. Let the development
get built. Let Wolf Run spring up with its ski
runs and artificial campsites, its lodges and A-
frames, its fake log cabins, its imitation chalets
and prefabs, its shops and peddlers and hustlers;
thousands of other lives would be altered—but
not for the better. Values would be cheapened.
Characters subverted. Relationships mocked and
ruined.

Families would be ripped apart, even as Osborne's family had been. Fathers separated forever from their children, and husbands and wives
turning away from each other. Nothing would be
the same. All to satisfy the greed of T. Lyman
Heggland and Alex Budde and a hundred others
whose names were unknown to Osborne. And, he
asked himself bitterly, how did he differ from
them?

His mind jarred itself back to the present and
he listened in awe and growing fright to the convincing words flowing so readily out of his mouth.
Meaningless words made sweet and seductive, designed to deceive, divert, disarm. There was new
interest on Maurice Lewin's fine face, the interest
of a man who had begun to doubt his own convic-

tions, a man prepared to be convinced, to change his mind, to go over to the other side.

Osborne confronted success. And was abruptly afraid. Disgusted. Ashamed that he had at last become the man he always wanted to be. All his ability—and he was truly gifted, truly a leader of man, a shaper of events—all of that went into achieving ends that produced little that was worthwhile.

He was a creature indigenous to the American Nightmare. For profit's sake, he spread the lie of progress. He was a front man for the monopolies and cartels; the seducers and corrupters; the buyers of presidents and kings, parliaments and congresses. He was one of the shadow men who ruled and eventually ruined everything they touched.

Bile flowed into a great burning glob beneath his ribs. Pain stabbed across his chest and he wondered if he was about to succumb to a heart attack? How ironic, he told himself, if he should die while delivering this hollow peroration, this hymn to man's lust for gold. What a hero that would make him in certain quarters, a martyr to empty tradition. Once American heroes died with their boots on; these days they went out with balance sheet flying high.

His mouth clamped shut. His eyes held firmly on Tom Keating's. Did he read some message of understanding there? Some secret encouragement? Some mystical exchange acknowledging a mutuality of concern and purpose? Not likely. His admiration for Keating increased sharply; he was an enemy worth having.

The brief silence was broken by laughter. Osborne's rich, mocking burst of laughter. The caw of a man suddenly satisfied with himself. A cry of self-discovery in wasteland.

It was an alarming eruption that caused all eyes to view him with renewed suspicion. It sent a chill slithering down Len Ralston's bent spine. It caused the architects to doodle cornices and arches and Roman capitals in nervous response. The audience, as one, edged forward for a better look at the proceedings. The show was clearly getting better.

"This," Osborne said, speaking now to Tom Keating, "is a large amount of horse dung. You're stepping down to run for sheriff, to be Wyatt Earp and beat the bad guys at their own game. What if this commission does turn down the presentation? Wolf Run will rise again in the bright glare of a new commission. The Heggland group will ultimately get the commissioner it wants to replace you, Keating. Heggland will get rid of Lewin when the time comes. It is merely a question of time. Aspen will turn into a mountainous Las Vegas. Cigarettes will be hawked on the face of the mountain, and the hiking trails will be lined with billboards. Your water will turn sour and your air poisonous. Well, count me out. I won't be a part of it. Not anymore. I've had my bellyful." He swung away from the table, hesitated, glaring down at Ralston. He shoved the battered attaché case at the advance man. "There. It's what you've always wanted. The magic container full of glory and power. Now it's yours. Do your worst for T. Lyman Heggland, it won't matter... you can't win either..."

No one spoke until a long time after he was gone.

18

Methadone kept Scooter straight enough to testify at the inquest. He insisted that he had been out for a hike when, by accident, he met Jon Osborne. He insisted he knew nothing about any shooting. He insisted that he had seen no guns, handled none, fired none. He insisted that he knew absolutely nothing about a large supply of heroin.

A physician—Luke Williams—with impeccable medical, social, and political credentials was brought in from Beverly Hills to testify. He said that Scooter suffered from a rare nervous disorder and would have to be hospitalized—in the doctor's private institution—for proper treatment.

Hilary Anguiano, the well-known movie producer, testified that the production schedule of his new film was being readjusted in order that Mr. Lewis might find the time, and positive frame of mind, to write the script.

A New York publisher testified that Scooter Lewis was in the midst of composing a novel that his company was going to publish at great effort, expense, and expectation. By coincidence, the novel had already been sold to a movie company— Hilary Anguiano's company.

Bobby Wallace testified that, like most writers,

Scooter Lewis was high-strung, sensitive, given to
extended solitary excursions. He needed to refurb-
ish his depleted emotional resources in a natural
setting, there to contemplate the muse, to meditate
on important philosophical questions, and to consider any work in progress.

The police chief testified that Sgt. James Sexton
had not been on an official assignment when the
shoot-out occurred. He pointed out, however, that
police officers frequently pursued criminal cases
on their own time, being men devoted to their jobs,
the public good, and the pursuit of justice. The
chief went on to say that he was unable to quarrel
with Tom Keating's version of events, since Keating was the only living witness.

The court offered Keating its congratulations
for destroying a major dope-smuggling ring, un-
doubtedly run from out of state. Keating was
termed a hero, acting far beyond his duty as
county commissioner; a credit to the community,
the nation, and his people.

In the gush of compliments and the swift
windup of the inquiry, no one questioned the dis-
crepancy between Keating's testimony and that
given by Scooter Lewis. No mention was made of
perjury, or of a continuing investigation. There
was a certain amount of relief when the proceedings came to a close.

That afternoon, Bobby Wallace and Scooter
Lewis boarded an executive jet that had been es-
pecially chartered for the occasion, and they flew
to Los Angeles. Wallace swallowed a great deal of
Valium. When they arrived, Scooter was placed in
Pacifica House, Dr. Williams's private sanatorium.
In a padded, soundproofed room, under constant

supervision, Scooter kicked cold turkey. Three weeks later, pale, emaciated, but clear of eye and reasonably steady of hand, Scooter returned to his typewriter under the watchful eye of a sometime bouncer and stunt man named Leo. Leo made sure that Scooter worked four hours every day, that he ate a balanced meal three times a day, that he drank no booze and shot no dope. He also kept Scooter away from women, which was no hardship for Leo, but was a strain on Scooter.

When the script was completed, Bobby Wallace turned one copy over to an unknown young writer who for a flat fee of four thousand dollars, agreed to provide a novelization of the work. A year later the book was published and chosen by the Book-of-the-Month Club, the Literary Guild, and the Playboy Book Club; selections were excerpted in the *Reader's Digest* and *Harper's;* and for twenty-three weeks, it was number one on the *Times*'s best-seller list. Eventually, the movie version would gross nearly forty million dollars. Scooter's share would come to almost three million, of which ten percent went to Bobby Wallace. Plus certain out-of-pocket expenses, of course.

____ Epilogue ____

Red Butte Cemetery, between Route 82 and the Roaring Fork River, adjoined the golf course. An unobtrusive gray marble marker called little attention to the grave.

Jonathan David Osborne
1956–1975

"It isn't much, is it?" Carl said.

Next to him, Kit Pepe kept her eyes averted. "Jon wasn't much given to flash."

"So young. I keep blaming myself."

She moved to face him, all grace absent. Each shift of foot and joint was awkward, as if recently learned. "What do you blame yourself for, Carl?"

His self-pity was an irritant, a plea for forgiveness. She had neither pity nor forgiveness to offer.

"For not being a better father."

A suggestion of anger tinged her voice. "If you expect me to disprove it, think again. You weren't a good father."

"I guess I wanted you to argue with me, tell me how terrific I am. No, it wouldn't be true. These

weeks away from here, I've had a chance for a
great deal of soul-searching."

"And?"

"And I've concluded that though I did fail Jon,
many times, he ultimately failed himself."

"That's the American way, isn't it?"

He sought some hint of irony in her words,
found none. A childlike fantasy had brought him
back to Aspen, a hope that somehow he would be
able to turn his life around, find in Kit his even-
tual salvation. However, salvation was not hers to
give.

"Still," Carl persisted, "he might have been better if he had the opportunity."

"That's utopian." Her voice was unnaturally
harsh, aggressive.

"Does that offend you—that I might dream
about the perfectability of man?"

"I don't believe in the perfectability of man. At
best, he may be able to improve himself. Anyway,
there are no magic cities in this world."

"I suppose you're right," he said sadly. "The
grave is all there is; it's the end for each of us."
He walked slowly away. She followed, a few steps
behind. He turned and inspected her face as if
seeing her for the first time. "Can I convince you
to change your mind, Kit?"

"No."

"I love you."

"It wouldn't work for us, Carl. I will never be
able to exist in your world."

"That world is shot to hell. I submitted my
resignation to Heggland the day after the county
commissioners turned down the project."

"What did Heggland say?"

"He said I failed him, that he didn't tolerate failure. I knew that, too. But a part of me hoped he'd be more understanding. . ."

"Forgiving, you mean?"

"I guess so. But not that tough old buzzard. Didn't even wish me luck. Grunted once and said he was putting Len Ralston in my place. So much for expectations."

"What if you hadn't resigned?"

"He'd have eased me out somehow. Or fired me point-blank. T. Lyman Heggland is a man who gets his own way all the time."

"And now?"

"I'll wrestle with my conscience for a while, assess my needs, look into the future, and do whatever I have to do."

"As do we all."

"It's over between Janet and me, Kit," he added with a soft plea. "My marriage is finished."

She shook her head. "That's between Janet and you. I'm going back to Antioch tomorrow, do what I want to do, what I do well."

"It sounds nice." He gazed back at the grave, his expression tinged with regret. Then he looked into her face at length, kissed her, and hurried to the waiting taxi.

When he was gone, she set off for town, moving slowly, allowing the mountain air to cool her cheeks. Images formed in her mind, stringing themselves in visual chains. Anxious to reach her desk, to confront blank pages, she increased her pace. Her fingers closed around an imaginary pencil, and words began to arrange themslves in suitable order:

The youth sleeps in his private hole
The restless fever burned out.
Glad music drifts from on high.
Echoes of a dark ceremony.
Here the journey ends,
Here the trip begins.

ABOUT THE AUTHOR

BURT HIRSCHFELD is best known for his best-selling novel, *Fire Island*. A native New Yorker, Mr. Hirschfeld was born in Manhattan and raised in the Bronx. He left school at the age of seventeen and took a series of menial jobs. Immediately after Pearl Harbor he enlisted, and spent three of his four years in service overseas. After the war, he attended a southern college for several years. For the next fifteen years he worked on and off for movie companies and also did some radio and acting work. Burt Hirschfeld did not write his first novel until he was in his early thirties. He worked on it for three years and, when it only earned $1,500, he abandoned writing for several years. At thirty-seven, he decided to find out for once and all whether he had the makings of a successful writer and began to freelance. He wrote everything—from comic books to movie reviews. He also wrote numerous paperback novels under various pseudonyms and eleven nonfiction books for teen-agers which were very well received. *Fire Island* was his first major success. *Aspen* is the twelfth novel he has written under his own name, and he is currently writing the screenplay of *Aspen*. Burt Hirschfeld lives in Westport, Connecticut, with his wife and two sons.

RELAX!
SIT DOWN
and Catch Up On Your Reading!

With the ferocity of a cornered dog, she grabbed his throat and curled her fingernails into his neck.

☆

She did not run to the corner, where the snowbound traffic honked along Columbus Avenue. Instead, she licked the corners of her bleeding mouth and tasted the blood with pleasure. He grabbed the front bumper of the parked car and pulled himself up. She hit him hard into the back of the neck with the heel of her right hand, swinging at him as if she were chopping a block of wood. His big body slumped forward, skidding off the car's metal grill, and dropped into the gutter.

She couldn't let him go. She wouldn't. She grabbed him by his hair and with foot jammed against the shoulder blades, jerked back his head until she heard his neck snap.

Jennifer stayed on her knees beside the body for a moment, gasping for air. She cupped a handful of snow into her palm and, using it like soap, wiped her face clean of blood. Calmer, she moved close and saw that the predator was dead. She had killed him. She smiled . . .

☆

Also by John Coyne

THE HUNTING SEASON

Published by

WARNER BOOKS

FURY

JOHN COYNE

WARNER BOOKS

A Warner Communications Company

WARNER BOOKS EDITION

Cover design by Jackie Merri Meyer
Cover photo by Franco Accanero

Warner Books, Inc.
666 Fifth Avenue
New York, N.Y. 10103

 A Warner Communications Company

Printed in the United States of America

This book was originally published in hardcover by Warner Books.
First Printed in Paperback: August, 1990

10 9 8 7 6 5 4 3 2 1

For Nansey Neiman,
who asked, "What if . . . ?"

BOOK ONE

I wasn't unhappy or disturbed by what I was learning. Not in the least. As a matter of fact, it was a kind of liberation of understanding to realize that my life today was a result of the lives that had preceded it, that I was the product of many lives and would be again. It made sense. There was a harmony to that—a purpose—a kind of cosmic justice which served to explain everything in life—both positive and negative.

—Shirley MacLaine

I became aware that I was losing contact with myself. At each step of the descent a new person was disclosed within me of whose name I was no longer sure and who no longer obeyed me. And when I had to stop my exploration because the path faded beneath my steps, I found a bottomless abyss at my feet, and out of it comes—arising I know not from where—the current which I dare to call my life.

—Pierre Teilhard de Chardin

1

"MS. WINTERS," THE HOTEL receptionist said, "I believe we have a message for you." The small black man moved down the counter to the computer terminal and typed in a command, then waited for the response on the screen.

Jennifer glanced around the lobby of the Washington, D.C., hotel and spotted a printed sign that read:

MEET KATHY DART, CHANNELER OF HABASHA.
JOIN THE NEW AGE!
CHANGE YOUR PERSPECTIVE ON
LIFE, WORK, RELATIONSHIPS.

That's what she needed, Jennifer thought wryly, a change, especially in her love life.

"Yes, here it is," the reception clerk said. " 'Room twenty-three fourteen. Jenny, I have a two o'clock appointment. See you at four.' And it's signed, 'T.' " The reception clerk looked up. "Would you like a copy?"

"No, thank you. Room twenty-three fourteen, yes?"

"That's right. I'll delete this message?"

"Yes, please." She bent down and picked up her briefcase.

"And I'll have your luggage sent up," the clerk added, handing her a computer card. "Your room won't be ready for another twenty minutes, at two o'clock."

Jennifer took a deep breath. It was Tom who had also made sure his Justice Department meetings were scheduled for this Thursday so that they could spend the night together in the Washington hotel. She had not seen Tom in three days; they had not made love in a week. She wanted to make love to him so much now, she could taste it. Sometimes it seemed to her that all they had in common was good sex. They certainly did know how to make that work.

Turning away from the reception counter, she caught her reflection in the lobby mirrors and was pleased and surprised to see how thin she looked in her new Calvin Klein suit. The French blue color was right, she saw. It favored her fair complexion and her honey blond hair. But she wasn't happy with her lip gloss. The shade was too orange and exaggerated her lips. Her mouth was big enough as it was.

"Jenny! Jennifer Winters!" A woman's high, sharp voice stopped her. Jennifer glanced around and spotted Eileen Gorman waving to her from deep in the lounge. "Jennifer, is that really you!" the woman said, rushing toward her.

Jennifer grinned and went to her. "Eileen, I can't believe it's you!" She wrapped her arms around the smaller woman and briefly hugged her. "It's so good to see you! What a surprise!"

"Are you here for the conference?" Eileen asked.

"Yes, the foundation conference. Who are you with, Eileen?"

"Foundation, no. I'm here for Kathy Dart. She's going to channel Habasha."

"Who? What?" Jennifer let go of Eileen's hand and set down her briefcase.

"You don't know who Kathy Dart is?" Eileen asked, her green eyes widening.

She still looks like a cheerleader, Jennifer thought, smiling at her old friend. "Eileen, you look wonderful! Do you live here in Washington?"

"No, I'm still living on Long Island." She took a deep breath and sighed, then, still grinning, said, "What a wonderful surprise! It's so good to see you, Jenny." She reached over and again embraced Jennifer. "You look beautiful. Now, what do you do? Where do you live?" she asked.

"In the city. New York. Brooklyn Heights, really. I've been there since law school."

"I had heard you moved to California. Anita told me. You remember Anita?"

"Yes, of course. Yes, I did move to L.A., but . . ."

"Some guy?"

Jennifer nodded, then turned her thumb down.

Eileen laughed and asked, glancing at Jennifer's left hand, "Married?"

"No, just . . . well, involved." She shrugged her shoulders. "You know how it is."

"Tell me!" Eileen sighed, still smiling at Jennifer. Then she said, "It's so good to see you, Jennifer. What is it that you do exactly?"

"I'm a lawyer with the James Thompson Foundation. We give money to good causes—civil rights outfits, that sort of liberal thing. I came down for a meeting. Now, who is this Kathy Dart?"

"Oh, you must see Kathy. She's just wonderful!" Eileen's voice rose, and she beamed at Jennifer. "She's a channeler. A wonderful channeler!"

"What?" Jennifer asked, laughing.

"You know what a channeler is, don't you?"

Jennifer shook her head, suddenly feeling foolish. "I'm sorry, but I—"

"Channeling was written up in *People* magazine. There was a story about Kathy's psychic powers. Kathy receives information from this prehistoric human called Habasha who has returned to help us with our lives today."

"Are you into that stuff?" Jennifer asked.

"This is one of her few East Coast appearances this winter," Eileen went on.

"Appearance? Does she do seances?" Jennifer kept smiling at Eileen, amused by her overwhelming enthusiasm.

"No! She's a channeler." Eileen opened a pink folder. "It's a special session called 'A Weekend with Habasha'!"

"Who?" Jennifer laughed out loud, and then touched Eileen's arm and said, "I'm sorry to be so flippant."

"That's all right," Eileen answered. "I can't blame you. I was the same way until I heard him."

"Him?"

"Habasha. I know it's confusing, but Kathy Dart is only the channel, you see. Habasha uses her body to speak to us. It's sort of like possession, but isn't. She 'channels' him. He speaks to us through her body. What she does—Kathy that is—is to allow herself to set aside her waking consciousness to allow knowledge— Habasha's knowledge—that lies beyond conscious awareness to flow into her mind and through her ability to speak."

"A medium, you mean?"

"Yes, that, but more, Jennifer. You'll see."

"I'll see?"

"Yes, come with me to hear Kathy. She's about to have an introductory session. It's for, you know, spouses, friends. C'mon with me, Jenny, and then we can have a cup of coffee and talk, or maybe dinner. Are you busy tonight?"

"Eileen, I can't. . . ."

"Do you have plans?"

"No, but the foundation meeting opens tomorrow."

"It's just a half hour," she said enthusiastically.

"Okay, why not?" It might be fun, Jennifer thought, and also she'd have time to talk more with Eileen. "Are you sure it will only take thirty minutes?"

"It will take your whole life, once you hear him," Eileen answered, linking her arm through Jennifer's. "It's so good to see you. How long has it been? Graduation, right?"

Jennifer nodded. "I think so. It seems like an age. I mean, so much has happened in my life."

"You're telling me?"

They reached a bank of elevators, and Eileen pressed the down button. "It's set to start in five minutes," she said. "Kathy and Habasha are . . . is . . . never late."

"Who is she, he, . . . or it?" Jennifer asked, really confused now.

"He's prehistoric. A Cro-Magnon man."

"What!" Jennifer exclaimed, backing off.

Eileen laughed. "I know, I know. It all sounds silly and strange, but really it isn't. Just wait! Keep an open mind. I was the same way until I heard Kathy Dart speak. You'll see."

When the elevator door opened, they stepped out into the lower lobby of the hotel. Through a set of open doors, Jennifer saw a crowd of people already gathered on at least a hundred metal folding chairs. It looked like any other hotel conference session she had ever attended.

But at the far end of the room was a winged green satin armchair placed upon a small platform. The chair was surrounded with flowers, bouquets of bright spring blossoms, and Jennifer was struck by how incongruous it all seemed. Directly behind the armchair, a beautiful crystal pyramid was suspended from the ceiling, though it seemed to hang in midair like a halo. Of course, she thought, remembering now some of the things she had read about the New Age movement. Quartz crystals were considered a source of psychic energy.

"They're all women," Jennifer said, scanning the crowd.

"Well, yes, mostly. I really hadn't noticed," Eileen answered as they stepped into an aisle and sat down in two of the folding chairs.

Jennifer saw that the majority of women were like her. They were mostly in their late twenties, well dressed, and many were wearing business suits and carrying briefcases, as if they had just come from the office. The few men in the audience were similarly well dressed and well groomed. This was not, she realized, a way-out group of people.

"One reason I feel comfortable going to one of these conferences," Eileen whispered to Jennifer, "everyone looks like me. See, we can't all be crazy." She smiled at Jennifer. "Oh, I'm so glad I ran into you. It's so exciting." Before Jennifer could respond, Eileen said quickly, "There she is."

Jennifer turned toward the door. Kathy Dart had appeared at the entrance, and the roomful of people immediately fell silent. Jennifer looked away for a moment and suppressed a smile. It would be impolite to laugh, she knew, but the flowers, the small throne, and all the pomp and circumstance were embarrassing. And now around her, Jennifer saw, people were smiling, and some had tears in their eyes as Kathy Dart entered the room.

The channeler came up the center aisle and smiled down at her audience. The palms of her hands were turned up, and as she moved toward the stage, she reached out to caress the cheek of one woman, to touch another's hand, to make physical contact with her followers.

She was beautiful, Jennifer saw. Beautiful in a delicate and fragile way. Very tall and thin, with sloping shoulders that concealed her height. She wore no makeup, and her very long and straight black hair set off her pure white skin. She looked like a woman who needed to be protected, who was too fragile for the world. Yet when she stepped into the room, she immediately overwhelmed it with her presence.

As Kathy Dart passed their chairs, her eyes swept down the row and then caught Jennifer's face, and she stopped walking. For a moment, her eyes were riveted on Jennifer, and the sweet smile slipped from her angelic face. Kathy Dart looked startled, as if she had been found out in some way. And Jennifer, at that moment, felt a surge of heat and pain sweep through her body, leaving her flesh aflame.

Kathy Dart broke off her gaze and turned abruptly away to find another face. She smiled warmly at the next person, as if she were trying to quickly reestablish herself with the crowd. Jennifer fell back into her chair, trembling from the silent exchange.

"She's almost thirty-three," Eileen whispered. "Don't you think that's interesting? You know, the same age as Jesus Christ?"

Jennifer could not catch her breath. The eye contact with Kathy Dart had surprised her, and seeing the disturbed look on the woman's face had frightened her. She turned to ask Eileen if she had seen the way Kathy Dart looked at her, but

at that moment there emerged from the assemblage a soft
humming. It swept across the crowded room, as if dozens of
mothers were gently humming their infants to sleep.

Kathy Dart had reached the flower-decked platform, and
the humming increased to a rushing crescendo. Kathy Dart
faced the audience with uplifted arms. She was dressed in a
long white gown trimmed in light blue. Around her neck she
wore a gold chain that held a small quartz crystal.

The room lights dimmed and a small spotlight focused on
Kathy Dart. She lifted her right hand, and as she slowly
lowered it, the humming faded away.

"Thank you," she whispered, "for giving us some of your
present time, for welcoming us into your life." She spoke
slowly, smiling constantly at the audience, her bright blue
eyes flashing in the spotlight.

It's going to be one of those talks, Jennifer realized at
once. She was always uneasy around people who gushed with
deeply felt emotions. Jennifer glanced at her watch. It was
now 2:20. She had hoped to be through with her afternoon
jog before Tom returned to the hotel. She would give this
another twenty minutes, she decided, and then she'd leave.

"I'm sure you all know something—a little something
perhaps— of channeling, of who I am, and of how this new
man came into my life," Kathy Dart began, and the audience
laughed.

She certainly had a nice easy delivery, Jennifer noted,
coolly appraising her.

"My Old Man, I call him. God knows he's old enough,"
she said quickly, raising her voice in mock seriousness. "He's
at least twenty-three million years old, give or take a few
hundred years. Of course, I think he might be telling a few
white lies about that age of his," she added, raising her
eyebrows. Then she threw up both hands. "But who's count-
ing!" The audience broke into quick applause.

Beside her, Eileen beamed up at Kathy Dart.

"Many of you, however, don't know about Habasha, and
that is why I have these little talks early in the weekend, to
give you and your friends a chance to meet my lover, my
mentor, my best friend. I am sure some of you know that

Habasha was once my warrior lover; in another time we were both pirates off the Barbary Coast, and in yet another time and another place he was my son. That is the wonderful nature of reincarnation. The wonderful nature of our spirits, ourselves, our souls. With the help of Habasha, I have regressed to my distant past, have tracked all my previous lives."

She paused and looked around the room, taking in the audience. Her large, shiny, saucer blue eyes caught and held everyone's attention.

"Reincarnation is such a wonderful, strange, and also beautiful aspect of our existence. It is a basic tenet of many religions. We are reincarnated! I know. And you know in your heart of hearts, too, that somehow, someway, you have lived before, have been another person, suffered perhaps and died, and then lived again.

"We know this from the religions of our childhood. I myself was raised a Roman Catholic, and within the teachings of my very first catechism, I learned how the saints of the early Christian faith came back from death to tell us about heaven as well as hell. I learned that all of us someday will join our Maker in eternity."

She had softened her voice, Jennifer realized, to draw people closer, to force them to be more attentive. Even she was leaning forward and paying more attention to Kathy Dart.

"I mention reincarnation because some people are made nervous by the idea that they are somehow born again in another person, in another time." Kathy laughed. "I guess if I thought I'd be reborn again with these big feet of mine, I'd be upset, too, but I have hope and faith that it won't happen the next time."

The audience broke into laughter. Jennifer leaned over to Eileen and whispered, "She does have a nice way about her, doesn't she?"

"She's wonderful," Eileen answered, her eyes moist with tears.

"But how do we know that we lived before?" Kathy Dart went on. "That we might have been—as I was—a Barbary Coast pirate? Or as Shirley MacLaine has said she was once, a hardworking woman of the night.

"We know," Kathy Dart whispered. "We know." She paused and swept her blue eyes across the room as she gently tapped her heart with her small closed hand. "We know in our hearts, don't we? We know we have lived before," she whispered, nodding to the crowd. Then her voice grew stronger and more confident. "We know because we have had that wonderful experience of turning the corner in some foreign country or looking at a photograph in a mossy old book and realizing, yes, we were there; we walked through those ancient streets, lived in those times. We, too, might have been a mistress of King George, a Christian tossed to the lions in the Colosseum, or perhaps a Cherokee princess, or an American housewife living the hard life on our western frontier. I mention those people in particular because they were some of my many former lives. I have lived and passed on. Lived and passed on again and again and again. We never die. Our spirits don't die. We all know that, regardless of our religious faith. Our spirits, ourselves, our egos, you might call it, have always been, will always be."

She paused and took in the audience. She had clasped her hands together as if in prayer.

"We know all this ourselves," she went on slowly. "It is a secret that has been locked away in our subconscious, but how do we know? That's the question."

"Exactly," Jennifer said out loud.

"Shhhh." Eileen nudged her. Eileen was sitting on the edge of her metal chair. Everyone was leaning forward, Jennifer saw; they were all on the edges of their chairs, straining to hear every word.

"Let me tell you how I know," Kathy offered. Her voice brightened and the audience stirred. They were going to hear a secret, Kathy's secret. Jennifer recognized the anticipation. Despite her cynicism, she, too, wanted to hear the secret of Kathy Dart's past lives.

Kathy Dart turned to the green satin chair and sat down. Even seated, she seemed to pull the audience close to her. She took her time straightening her long white cotton skirt, letting the audience adjust to her new position on the platform.

Jennifer glanced at her watch. She had been there for nearly twenty minutes. She should leave now, she thought, while there was a lull in the room, but the thought of standing up, of having everyone stare at her, kept her in her seat. It had been a mistake to let Eileen Gorman talk her into coming to this silliness. Jennifer glanced over and saw that Eileen was wearing a ring, and remembered that Eileen had married right after high school and hadn't gone on to college. It had surprised everyone at the time. There had been some talk, back then, that Eileen Gorman had to get married.

"I was, I guess, like any one of you," Kathy Dart began again, "just going along with my life, living it day by day, trying to get by, to be happy, to find someone to love.

"I'm sure you have heard something about the power of quartz crystals. It certainly has been in the newspapers. Shirley MacLaine, in her wonderful books, talks about crystals and pyramids and how they have been important to her in reestablishing her past lives.

"I didn't know it at the time of my first encounter with Habasha, but throughout history mediums have used crystals to align themselves with spirits, to capture the energy of past lives." She paused.

"I was a freshman at the time—this was in 1974—studying English at the College of St. Catherine in St. Paul, Minnesota, and my older sister, Mary Sue, who was in Ethiopia with the Peace Corps, had sent me a piece of quartz crystal. She had found it along the Hadar River, a tributary of the Awash River in southern Ethiopia.

"Some of you may remember that in 1974 Don Johanson, a paleoanthropologist working in East Africa with the famous Leakey family, found an early hominid and named her Lucy after the Beatles' song 'Lucy in the Sky with Diamonds.'

"Lucy stood three and a half feet tall, lived at the edge of the shallow lake, and died sometime in her early twenties.

"This all happened some 3.3 million years ago. But Lucy is very important in our lives—in my life especially—because she and her friends, all who camped and lived together on the banks of that Ethiopian river, proved that men and women had begun to bond, to share, to work together, to experience what we call human feelings.

"I didn't know any of this, of course. I was just eighteen years old; I had a paper due on Jane Austen the next morning and was secretly praying that the gorgeous boy I had met at Sunday afternoon's mixer would call and ask me out. You know how it is!" She said, shaking her head ruefully. The women laughed delightedly.

Jennifer smiled, too, remembering her own adolescence.

"Anyway, I was trying to work on my Jane Austen paper and in the mail came this small quartz crystal from my sister," Kathy Dart went on, fingering the clear quartz that hung around her neck. "I held it in my fingers, rubbing it slightly—out of nervousness, I guess—while I sat at my dorm desk.

"It was a typical fall day in St. Paul. My window was open and I could hear kids on the lawn outside, and I was feeling sad that I was inside working on my paper when everyone else was having a good time—and then I heard a whooshing sound in the hallway. I glanced up and saw a brilliant blue-white light in the open doorway.

"I raised my hand to shield my eyes, and it was then, in the midst of this beautiful white light, that I heard Habasha speak to me."

She paused and looked down at her hands and the small quartz crystal. The room was silent. Jennifer realized she was holding her breath, waiting for Kathy Dart to continue.

"He spoke to me then," Kathy said softly, her head still down. "I can't say whether it was really words that he spoke, or if he just telepathically let himself be understood. But I did understand him. He said simply, 'Are you ready to receive me?'

"I remember shaking my head. I was too frightened to speak. And he went on, 'I'll come again when you are ready.' That was all. Gradually the blue-white faded. Again I heard the voices of students on the campus lawn. Habasha was gone. I didn't know his name, of course. I didn't know why he had chosen me, but I knew something wonderful had happened to me."

She paused to look searchingly at her audience. "I didn't see him again for ten years. He was waiting. Waiting for me to grow up and prepare myself to be his host in this world. He was waiting for me to agree to be his channel.

"I once asked Habasha why he had waited, instead of choosing someone else, and he explained that I had been ordained as his earthly host. Habasha and I are like runners in an endless race—passing each other and then stopping off somewhere, as it were, to spend a lifetime—and then in death flowing again in the endless cycles of the universe.

"And that is how Kathy Dart, of Rush Creek, Minnesota, the daughter of a dairy farmer, the youngest of eight children, came to be the channel for Habasha, who was first on earth at the dawn of civilization, living on the banks of the Hadar River, in southern Ethiopia.

"Habasha was killed on a sunny afternoon when a man rose up in anger and felled him with a blow of his club. His physical body died in a land we now know as Ethiopia, where my sister found a small piece of quartz crystal and sent it home to me. This piece of Africa that had once been part of Habasha's world, that was linked to his spirit, his time as a man, was now connected to me.

"When I touched the crystal that day at my dormitory, I pulled his spirit back to me through time. But I wasn't ready then. I wasn't open enough to receive him.

"In 1984 I was married, living in Glendora, California, and the mother of a darling little girl, Aurora. I woke one summer morning and realized that I no longer loved my husband, that I hated my life, and that I had to do something to save myself.

"I got out of bed before dawn and walked into the living room and over to the picture windows that looked out on our quiet suburban street. It was getting light outside. I could see the long line of palm trees that marked our cul-de-sac, and when I sat down in the window seat, I noticed my African crystal. Aurora had taken it out of my jewelry box to play with, and I picked it up and began to gently rub my fingers across its smooth clear surface. I was crying. I remember seeing my tears splash against my skin, and when I looked up again through the picture window, I saw him. He walked down the empty street, coming to me, and this time I knew

I was ready, knew that I had suffered enough to be worthy of him. I knew then that I was going to be his channel.

"I live now with my daughter and a few close friends on my family's old farm in eastern Minnesota. It is there that we produce the tapes and books that reveal the wisdom of Habasha. It is from there that I travel to conduct these weekend sessions with Habasha.

"Now for all of you who wish to hear Habasha speak, we will have a trance-channel session this evening, and I hope you will join us. I know it will change your life. And now I must go, but to use the words of Habasha, 'I leave only for the joy of returning.' "

She stepped off the platform, taking the hand of a tall, thin, beautiful twelve-year-old girl who looked just like her, and walked out of the meeting room by the side exit. The audience rose and started to applaud. At the door, Kathy Dart paused, waved good-bye, and then dramatically disappeared.

"Oh, Jennifer, isn't she wonderful?" Eileen said quickly, as the applause faded.

Jennifer hesitated. She had to admit that Kathy Dart had affected her, but she wasn't ready to say how. "Well, it certainly was different!" She took a deep breath.

"She's just marvelous!" Eileen declared, standing.

"Yes. Well. I think . . ." Jennifer stood. The woman's presentation had dazed her. "I guess I don't know what to think." She turned to leave; she wanted fresh air.

"Are you coming tonight? To the channeling session?"

"I don't think so. I mean, I have to prepare for my meeting. What does the word *Habasha* mean, anyway?" she asked, to change the subject. They had reached the lobby of the hotel.

"*Habasha?* That's his name. Kathy told us it meant 'burnt face,' which is the name for Ethiopians. He took it himself, because when he was reincarnated as the female Lucy, speech hadn't yet been developed in the hominids."

"But Kathy Dart said he's at least twenty-three million years old. I don't understand. Lucy is only four million years old."

"Yes, I know." Eileen nodded. "What Kathy said was

that Habasha's spirit appeared on earth 'in human form' four million years ago, at the dawn of man itself. Then, later, he has had other lives, other reincarnations. Just like us. But his spirit, or soul, is older than that.''

Jennifer shook her head. The spell was broken. She no longer felt unnerved by Kathy Dart. She had been briefly swept away, but now she was all right. Jennifer was not like Eileen Gorman. She was not so overwhelmed that she had lost sight of what was reality.

''Well, I don't know who I once was, but I know for sure that I've never been a hominid, protohominid, or whatever they were called.''

''But you don't know, Jenny. You don't know what you once were. And that's what's makes it all so exciting.''

''Makes what so exciting?''

''Channeling! Habasha will tell you who you once were.''

Jennifer was shaking her head before Eileen stopped talking.

''Not me. I've got enough bad memories just in this life. I don't need to learn about more lives.''

''Oh, Jenny, come on, give it a try. Come see Kathy Dart channel Habasha, and you'll learn who you were in past lives.''

Jennifer remembered the look on Kathy Dart's face when the channeler spotted her, remembered how her body had flamed up with pain and passion.

''No,'' she said firmly. ''I don't want to know.'' And she meant it. She did not want to know, nor did she want to encounter Kathy Dart again.

''Excuse me,'' a young man said, approaching them.

Jennifer and Eileen both stopped talking and glanced up at him.

The young man smiled. He looked like a college student, Jennifer thought at once. A graduate student, perhaps. She noticed his eyes immediately. They were gray and almond shaped, like her brother's.

''My name is Kirk Callahan,'' he went on quickly, as if he were afraid they would bolt away. ''I'm doing an article on Kathy Dart for *Hippocrates* magazine. And I was wondering if I might have a few minutes to talk with you about her, you know, and your experiences with channeling?'' He kept smiling and had now focused his full attention on Jennifer, who was shaking her head before he finished talking.

''Not me!'' she said defensively, and then laughed. ''Perhaps my friend will talk to you. I don't know anything about any of this stuff.'' She glanced at Eileen and said quickly as the elevator arrived, ''I'll call you later. 'Bye!'' And then she stepped into the elevator before the doors closed, happy to be away from all these New Age people.

2

JENNIFER LEFT THE HOTEL by the side door, jogged down the sloping lawn to the bottom of Rock Creek Park, and picked up the bicycle path that she knew was good for running. She turned right and followed the level path under Massachusetts Avenue, heading for Georgetown and the C & O Canal. There was some snow on the ground, but the path was clear and dry.

The hour with Kathy Dart had made her uneasy, and she knew that being outside running would make her feel immensely better. It always did.

There were only a few joggers on the path, and Jennifer easily picked up speed. She hadn't run in several days, and she was surprised that her muscles were this loose. She unzipped the front of her blue Gore-Tex jacket and lengthened her stride.

The C & O Canal was the best place to run in Washington. There was always room for both runners and bikers, and as she moved easily past other joggers, she held close to the narrow gauge of muddy water on her left. The path she was on was once the towpath used to help barges up and down the river as far away as West Virginia, but now it went only thirteen miles into Maryland.

Jennifer knew she couldn't run that far. She had never run farther than three miles in her life. She had first taken up the sport because it was important to Tom, and it gave her another way to be with him. Now she ran because she loved the feeling it gave her, of being in shape and in control of her life.

She sped past a biker bent low over his front wheel. He was dressed in a tight black biking suit, with gloves and a black crash helmet. She caught his look of surprise as she swept past him, her feet now barely touching the hard-packed earth. He was breathing hard, gasping, and as she floated by, he rose up off the seat and pumped hard. She smiled and picked up her speed. For a few yards, she could hear him behind her, breathing deeply, and the slick sound of wheels on the hard earth, but gradually the sounds faded, and when she glanced back, she saw that the biker was disappearing from sight.

As she ran, she tried to establish a smooth easy stride, as Tom had taught her. "Run within yourself," he always urged. Jennifer had never been strong enough to run with his ease and speed. But Kathy Dart had upset her, and she wanted to burn off her anxiety.

She kept up the pace. She was well beyond Georgetown, running alongside the Parkway, and had outrun the other joggers on the path and even several dozen bikers.

She should go back to the hotel, she finally decided; it was getting dark, and she wasn't familiar with the canal this far beyond Georgetown. She slowed her pace and gradually eased to a walk on the running path. Now she felt the pain, and when she saw the marker beside the running path, she leaned over to read it:

13 MILES

Jennifer glanced at her watch. It was after five. She had been running for an hour and a half.

* * *

"What did you do then?" Tom asked. He turned on his side in the bed to look at Jennifer.

"Well, I tried to run back, but I couldn't, I was in too much pain. I came up out of the canal—there was a tollgate there—and I went onto the Parkway and hitched a ride from some woman. She took me here to the hotel. She was terrific. I mean, not like a New Yorker." With a groan, Jennifer moved to face Tom.

"I can't believe you jogged that far," Tom said. He had pulled himself up on his elbows. "You've never run more than three miles, right?"

Jennifer nodded. "I just felt like running, I guess, and also I was so tensed up by that channel woman."

"What?"

"You don't want to hear about her." Jennifer moved again with great effort, favoring her sore right leg, and stretched out on her stomach. "I thought making love was supposed to relax you."

"It does. But you've got to do it repeatedly." He nuzzled down next to her.

"Easy," she said.

"It's your legs that are sore, darling."

"Everything's sore." She cuddled close, wanting to be held.

He had been waiting for her when she came back from the long run, and they had taken a shower together and then made love standing under the spray, their bodies lathered with soap. She had wanted to wait until they were in bed, but he couldn't wait, wouldn't wait, and she let him have his way.

He came at once, before she was ready for him, and then he picked her up, and she slipped her arms around his neck and her legs around his waist. He carried her back to the wide bed, where they soaked the sheets and blankets with their wet bodies and made love again, and this time she did come, a long rolling orgasm that drained all the strength from her limbs. The intensity made her cry, and when he came, she had a second climax just as violent and wrenching as the first, and she wouldn't let him slip out of her. She held him tight, as if he were a secret prize she wanted to keep hidden forever inside her.

They had fallen asleep then, still wrapped in each other's arms, and when she woke, Jennifer felt the pain in her legs and thighs and told Tom what had happened.

"What do you want to do?" he asked, whispering in her ear.

"I don't want to do anything. I just want to lie in your arms for the rest of my life." And she meant it. She didn't ever want to move. She felt happy when she was in Tom's arms, when he was holding her and she had nowhere to go and nothing to do. But she sensed the reason for his question. Tom never asked anything directly; he was always trying to position her so that he could do what he wanted.

"I've got a dinner meeting," he told her.

"Damnit!" She moved to look at him directly. His dark eyes, intense even in the dim light of the room, had always affected Jennifer strongly. She could not see his face. "Now tell me again," she said.

"Honey, I didn't know myself until forty minutes ago. I had a message waiting when I got back to the hotel. The DA wants me to interview a new person down here who they're thinking of hiring. Look, it's only dinner. I'll be free by nine, and we can come back and do some more of this." He moved against her so she could feel his erection.

"Don't," she asked, but she knew there was no authority in her objection, and she knew that he wouldn't stop. She, too, wanted to make love. She couldn't get enough of him this afternoon, and her desire pleased her. In New York they were always in a hurry, rushing to make love in the brief moments that they could spare from their work.

"Turn over," he told her, and when she heard the edge in his voice, her nipples grew hard. "This way," he said, instructing her, and she let him pull her up by the waist. He was already kneeling on the bed.

"No, honey, that hurts."

Tom didn't answer her. His hands had seized her waist, and when she tried to pull away, he wouldn't let her. Jennifer never liked it when he entered from behind so she couldn't see his face, and it was only because he was so demanding that she let him.

"Honey," she whispered, but he didn't answer. She knew he wouldn't; he never spoke when they made love. She wondered then if all men were the same. Did they all have sex like animals, silent and purposeful, without words of endearment? Or was it her? Did she somehow make men behave in a certain way?

She gasped. He was inside her, and she fell forward onto the wet sheets of the hotel bed. Her face was pressed against the hard mattress, and she grabbed its edges as he came, driving her down. It was not the way she wanted, but as he seized her by the shoulders, drove deep into her, she felt her own orgasm in a dizzying rush. It grew and grew, took her breath away, and she gasped with pain as her body shook and quaked, and then she came again and again, in wave after wave of sweet pleasure.

She awoke in the silence of the big house and heard the rooms speak to her, whispering. Her teddy bear and Raggedy Ann listened, too, and kept her safe. She pulled them both close to her and slipped farther down beneath the warm blankets. Through the window she could see the moon, and the moon's shadow, as ghostly as her dreams, seeping across the rug.

She loved her room. It was safe and cozy, and full of her toys, and she spent hour after hour in it, playing with Barbara Ann, and Sally, and all her dolls. She would make tea and sandwiches and have parties, just herself and her doll friends. And she'd have parties for Sam when he came home from boarding school. They would lock the door, and she would sit on his lap and pretend that there was no war in Europe, pretend that they were all alone in the big house, with Mommy and Daddy far, far away.

But at night, after everyone went to bed, she was afraid to be alone. Afraid of the ghosts and goblins, bats and little lizards that lived in the corners of her room. They waited for her beneath the stairs, too, and in the rafters of the attic and behind the sofa in the living room, and they darted from sight whenever anyone entered, and they came out at night to hunt down all the humans. Sam told her as much, whispering in her ear, and she didn't want to believe it, but she knew it was true, and she wanted to be held by Sam in his arms, protected by his embrace.

Sam had first told her about the flying lizards and the ghosts when they spent a warm summer afternoon up in the attic, lying together in piles of their mother's old clothes. Sam was looking for his football pads. That was the summer he turned fourteen, and he wanted to take them with him to prep school. They had rummaged together through the trunks, and Sam had told her to take off her white skirt and summer shorts and try on Mommy's clothes. Okay, she had grinned. She liked the idea of taking off her clothes. It was hot in the attic, with the sun pouring through the small windows, and Sam had seen her without clothes before, wrapped up in a towel after her bath. But it was different now. She had breasts, tiny little breasts, and her mommy had already told her she'd need a brassiere before school started.

So she had taken off her skirt and shorts and tried on clothes for a while, posing for Sam, preening in the mirror propped against the attic wall. He searched for and found the farmyard set, then assembled it in a box to carry downstairs. But they didn't want to leave the attic, and she got bored with trying on old clothes, so she lay down in the soft pile of discarded dresses. It was warm, and she liked the way her brother looked at her, so she didn't put on her clothes again. As she lay there, in the pile of velvety dresses, she fell asleep, and when she moved again, Sam was lying next to her, holding her, touching her. He told her that he missed her, that he missed not being home with her all year, that he hated going to boarding school. Then he began to cry, and she kissed his soft cheek and held him and told him she would write him every day. Then he started to kiss her on the mouth like they did in the movies. She told him to stop, that they would both get in trouble, but he said it was okay, that he wouldn't tell. And he asked her if she would, and she shook her head, too frightened and excited even to speak. Something was happening between them, and she didn't know what or why, but she knew she couldn't stop, nor did she want to stop, and she waited and watched for her brother to do whatever he was going to do.

He took off her panties then and tossed them away,

He stopped then, and they lay together, smiling, staring at each other. Then she asked, "Do you have a girlfriend or something at school?"

"No, dopey, you're my only girlfriend." He hugged her, and she kissed his neck.

"Can I come up to school and see you sometime? I mean, I asked Mom and she said it was okay."

"I don't know. Where would you stay?"

"Couldn't I just stay with you in your room?"

"No, you can't stay with me, for chrissake." He turned away from her and stared up at the ceiling.

"What's the matter, Sam?" She curled closer to him, and wrapped one leg over his.

"Nothing's the matter." He pulled loose from her and sat up again on the edge of the bed.

"Where are you going?"

"Hey, look, Nora, we can't do this anymore."

"Sam, I didn't tell Mom."

"Jesus, you're just a kid. You don't know what you're talking about. It's not right, you know." He stood up and walked to the window, and his face was silhouetted in the pale moonlight.

"But I love you, Sam. Besides, it makes me feel good." She got out of bed then and scampered across to the window to wrap her arms around him. He had grown since he went back to school.

He slipped his arm around her thin shoulders and hugged her. She turned her face into his chest and kissed the cotton top of his pajamas. She loved the way he smelled. After he had left for school, she went through his dresser drawers, took one of his summer shirts, and slept in it all fall. When her mother discovered it in her room, she only smiled and shook her head, then kissed her daughter on the forehead. She had been pleased that the two of them were such good friends.

"But don't you like me, Sam?" she asked, looking up.

He shrugged. "You're only thirteen. You know I could get put in jail or something."

"They can't put you in jail, Sam. You're sixteen. They

don't put sixteen-year-old kids in jail. And I'll be thirteen years old next month. I read in a book that girls in Europe because of the war are getting married when they're thirteen."

"Not to their brothers, they aren't." He pulled himself from her arms and stretched out again on the bed.

She followed him onto the bed. "And I'm not your real sister, anyway. I'm only your half sister. We could get married, I bet. I have to ask Mom if we could."

"Don't you say anything!" Sam grabbed her arm.

"I wouldn't. Sam, let me go. That hurts!" Her eyes filled with tears and she pulled loose from him. "I didn't say anything to Mom, you jerk!"

"Shhhh," Sam whispered, putting his hand over her mouth.

Both of them listened hard.

"I don't hear anything," she whispered, slipping down into bed and tucking her teddy bear and doll into their corners by the pillow.

Sam listened for a few more minutes, turning his head so he could catch any noise from the hallway, and then he relaxed and lay down beside her with a sigh. "I'm tired. I want to go to sleep."

"With me, please," she begged, edging closer to him, but he didn't say anything, just lay beside her with his eyes closed. "We could just sleep together in my bed," she said. "We don't have to do anything. Please?"

He didn't answer. He just pulled the blanket down, slipped his long legs underneath it, and then pulled it up over them both. Pleased, she turned on her side and snuggled down close to him, then took his arm and wrapped it around her body.

He touched her then, and she opened her eyes and stared across the room at the moonlight coming through the window. She did not move. She let him find his own way. He had begun to breathe harder, deeper, and then she began to match his ragged breath. He had put his hand beneath her long woolen nightgown and slipped it up to touch her breasts. His hand was cold for a moment on her flesh.

He was struggling now to get closer to her, to slip his other arm between her legs, and he was breathing hard, as if he had run a long way to reach her. She told him to wait, jumped out of bed, and quickly reached down to pull the nightgown over her head.

She felt a sudden draft of cold air between her legs, then the lights flipped on. With her nightgown caught in her arms, high above her head, and her brother lying there beneath the blankets, she turned to see her mother standing in the doorway.

3

WHEN JENNIFER AWOKE, TOM was gone and the room was dark. She had been conscious for only a few minutes when the phone rang. Clearing her throat, she said "hello" out loud a few times before answering so that her voice wouldn't betray that she had been asleep so early in the evening.

"Jennifer? It's me. Eileen. Did I wake you?"

"Of course not. I was reviewing some reports. They always make me sound sleepy." Jennifer sat up. "Thanks for telephoning. I needed a break." She tried to sound alert and businesslike.

"Well, I don't want to bother you. I know you're here on business. . . ."

Jennifer smiled. She was suddenly glad that Eileen had called.

"I thought if you weren't busy . . . I mean, if you didn't have a meeting, we might have dinner together."

"I'd like that, but don't you have a meeting yourself with Kathy Dart and her friends?"

"Not till nine-thirty. Jennifer, if you're busy, or whatever, I mean, I understand."

"Eileen, I'd like to. What time is it, anyway?" She reached for her watch.

"Seven-twenty."

"That's all? My body feels like it must be eleven. I went jogging this afternoon."

"Jennifer, you jog? That's a new you!"

"Yes, well, I guess there's a lot new about both of us." Fully awake, she realized she was hungry. "Eileen, I've got to change clothes. Can you give me twenty minutes?"

"Of course. Why don't we meet downstairs at eight?"

"Sure."

"See you in the lounge, then," Eileen said, and quickly added, "Oh, if you have the time, maybe you'd like to come to this evening's session with Kathy Dart and Habasha. I have an extra ticket."

Jennifer laughed. "Thanks, but no thanks. One session with your guru. But I do have some questions about her. See you at eight. 'Bye."

Eileen Gorman, of all people, she thought, hanging up the telephone receiver. Slowly she got out of bed and walked naked to the shower, still bruised from the long run and from Tom's fierce lovemaking.

"I first heard Kathy eight months ago," Eileen said. They were both looking over the restaurant menu as they talked about the meeting earlier that day. Jennifer asked how Eileen had first heard about the channeler.

"As soon as I saw Kathy trance-channeling Habasha, I knew that was what I was looking for in my life."

"What do you mean, looking for?"

Eileen set down the large menu and sighed. She sat directly across from Jennifer, but she looked off across the room and into space. "I was lost. I mean, I had my marriage, but Todd has his work, you know, and what did I have? Bridge? A tennis game? Shopping? I mean, I was living out there on Long Island. I had—I have—everything that I could possibly want. I'm lucky, I admit, and I had no reason to feel at a loss for anything, but I did. I did feel lost. Lonely. I'd go to the malls and just wander around, do endless, useless shop-

ping, and it didn't bring me any satisfaction. I don't wear
most of the stuff I have jammed into our closets. I started to
have affairs, you know, just to do something, to bring some
sort of meaning into my life, or whatever."

"Eileen, I thought—"

"Listen, Jennifer, I'm not the only one. Half the women
on Long Island are like me. I mean, you're lucky. You have
this wonderful career. You have a life of your own, interesting
friends."

"Eileen, so could you! You're attractive, you're intelligent. You were our valedictorian!"

Eileen was shaking her head, cutting off Jennifer's reply.

"You know I got married right after school. The truth was,
we had to get married. There was this guy, Tim Murphy—
I met him at Jones Beach. We were both lifeguards. Well, I
got pregnant." She shrugged her shoulders, looked over at
Jennifer, and grimaced, as if to say that was it, her life was
over, a fait accompli. But her eyes were glistening. Then she
leaned forward and smiled. "But it doesn't matter. I was
meant to have that sort of life. It was my karma."

Jennifer frowned. "Eileen, we make our own lives. We're
in control. Why do you think women fought so hard for equal
status? What do you think the ERA is all about?"

"This is not a woman's thing, Jennifer. It's beyond the
here and now, beyond all these daily problems."

"Eileen, the feminist movement wasn't—isn't—a little
daily problem."

"Jennifer, you're not listening to me. You're not hearing
what I'm trying to say."

"I'm sorry, but—"

Eileen cut her off. "Kathy Dart is the most remarkable
woman I have ever met. Maybe the most remarkable woman
alive today."

"Eileen, please." Jennifer looked down at her menu.

"I mean it! You don't know. You haven't been exposed."
Her voice had picked up, and there was anger in her tone.

"I'm sorry," Jennifer soothed. "You're right. I asked
about Kathy Dart, and I haven't given you a chance to explain.
Here's the waitress. Let's order and then I'll be quiet. Prom-

ise.'' She smiled at Eileen and for a moment tried to concentrate on her oversized menu but found she was too anxious.
When the waitress arrived, she asked for the special of the
evening.

"I saw her on television, the first time," Eileen began.
"It was the 'This Morning' show, and they had three or four
people, mediums, psychics. I had never thought about any
of that stuff in my life. But I had the TV on, and I was sitting
at the counter in the kitchen watching . . . killing time, you
know, and trying to decide what to cook for dinner. It was
September seventh, I remember, and it was rainy and cold,
and I couldn't play tennis, but I was thinking maybe I should
go to the club anyway. Then Kathy came on and I sort of
started to listen, and it was as if she were talking just to me.
She was telling me her life story, and what had happened to
her as a child, and I found myself crying as I listened. I mean,
she was talking about me, the mess I'd made of life, my
feelings of being out of it, left behind, in the wrong crowd.''

"But, Eileen, you weren't! You were the smartest person
in our class. Brighter than Mark Simon, even! And you were
captain of the basketball team.''

Eileen started to laugh, "Jennifer, I can't believe you still
remember all that stuff.''

"I was jealous of you, that's why.''

"Oh, don't be silly. You were going out with Andy
Porterfield, and everyone on Long Island wanted to marry
him.''

"Well, thank God I didn't. He's on his second wife, I'm
told.''

"His third. We see him all the time at the club. But what
I'm trying to say is that in high school you were having a
good time. I wasn't, and the only reason I even played basketball was because Mr. Donaldson put me on the team after
I tried to commit suicide.''

"Suicide?'' Jennifer whispered, remembering now the
long-ago rumors about Eileen.

"I'm sorry. Of course, you didn't know." She reached
over and touched Jennifer's arm. "I was jealous of you,
Jennifer. You were the great social one. You had all the

friends. My teenage years were a tormented time in my life, and Kathy Dart, or really, Habasha, has explained to me why I was so unhappy, why my body was out of sync with my spirit life. So I went to her. There was a conference like this being held in San Francisco, and I flew out for it."

"Flew all the way to California just to see her?"

Eileen nodded. "I had to know," she said thoughtfully, pausing and looking off across the room.

Jennifer stopped eating and watched Eileen. How rested the woman looked, how satisfied, as if all her responsibilities had been lifted off her shoulders.

"I've never been a religious person. I mean, I was raised a Unitarian, which isn't much of a religion, but when Kathy began to speak as Habasha . . ."

"He's not Kathy Dart."

Eileen nodded. "They are connected, as Kathy said. He was once her warrior lover. And they were pirates together. Kathy also told me that she once had his child in another lifetime. They are soul mates, from the same oversoul. And he speaks through her."

"So he doesn't sleep with her; he uses her body, instead."

"Okay, be a smart ass," Eileen replied with an indulgent smile. "If you'd only give Habasha a chance, you'd see."

"See what?"

"See that he can help you," Eileen said softly, not looking up from her plate.

"I didn't realize I needed help," Jennifer answered, annoyed.

"We all need help, Jennifer," Eileen replied without raising her voice. "And I think if you gave Kathy Dart and Habasha a chance, they might explain to you why you two had such a strong attraction to each other at the session this afternoon."

"What are you talking about? What do you mean?" Jennifer sat back and stared at Eileen.

"Kathy Dart asked about you," she explained.

"Yes? What do you mean, asked about me?" Her voice rose and she felt her hands begin to tremble.

"She spoke to me after this afternoon's session. She said

she had a profound reaction from seeing you." Eileen was watching Jennifer as she spoke.

Jennifer nodded.

"What did it mean?" she asked.

"Kathy asked me to tell you that she senses that she knows you, from a past life, of course, and that she thinks you should speak directly to Habasha."

"Don't be silly," Jennifer answered at once.

"Kathy said to tell you that you are capable of a great deal in this life, and to tell you also that you are involved in a romantic situation that is not spiritually good for you."

"What!" Jennifer was outraged, and also frightened of what Eileen might know.

Eileen shook her head. "I'm only telling you what Kathy said. She wanted me to invite you specially to her session this evening." Eileen paused. "And she said to tell you that Danny is fine. That he has another life now, a happy life, and that he didn't suffer."

Jennifer threw down her napkin. She couldn't eat. "I don't want to hear any more of this silliness. I'm not interested in your seances and spirit entities." She was furious at Eileen for mentioning her dead brother. They had been in junior high school when Danny was killed in Vietnam.

Her sudden rage made her dizzy. She tried to find the waitress to pay the check but couldn't. As she glanced around the room, a glowing ball of brilliant light caught her eye. It was outside the windows; she leaned closer to the cold glass and squinted into the darkness.

Someone—something—was walking round the swimming pool. It was a man—a small, short-limbed man, moving clumsily, like a Cro-Magnon.

"Look!" Jennifer blurted out. "What's that?"

"What's what?" Eileen asked.

Jennifer looked back and nothing was there. The light must have been playing tricks on her.

Jennifer stood, dropping her napkin into her chair. "Excuse me, I can't take any more of this metaphysical crap." She glanced back out the window. The glowing light was gone from the terrace.

"Don't be afraid," Eileen said softly. "It will all work out. Kathy said it would." She smiled up at Jennifer, looking conspiratorial.

"I'm not afraid," Jennifer answered back. She opened her purse and withdrew a twenty-dollar bill. "The waitress can keep the change," she said, throwing it down.

"Jennifer, you're getting yourself upset over nothing. I'm sorry I frightened you."

"You haven't upset me, Eileen. I'm just sorry you've gotten yourself all tied up with these people. I always thought you were too smart for such . . . bullshit." She spun about and strode from the restaurant.

She walked through the lobby and stopped at the desk for her messages. Tom would have called, she knew, to let her know when he would be back at the hotel.

" 'Having drinks after dinner with Yale buddies. Back late. T.,' " the clerk read, then looked up at Jennifer. "Would you like a copy?"

"No. No thank you," Jennifer told him, and turning away from the counter, she went up to her hotel room alone.

4

JENNIFER LIFTED THE *New York Times* off the mat and stepped back inside her apartment. It was Saturday morning, the day after she returned from Washington. Closing the door, she flipped the paper open to the second section and scanned the page as she walked down the hall and into the kitchen.

It was not yet eight o'clock, and the building was silent. Tom was still asleep. She had just spread the newspaper on the kitchen counter when she spotted a headline:

SPIRITUAL GUIDE FOR YUPPIES

Jennifer stopped to read the first couple of paragraphs.

Channeling, a metaphysical quest for truth and wisdom that sprang to life in California, has found its way east. Ms. Phoebe Fisher, who holds a doctorate from the Metaphysics University of San Jose, is currently dispensing metaphysical truths from her West Side apartment.

According to Ms. Fisher, the "truth giver" is a spirit

named Dance, who is a "sixth-density entity from Dor-
ran, the seventh star of the seventh sister within the
Pleiades system. He lives eight hundred years in our
own future," according to the blond and beautiful Ms.
Fisher.

Jennifer perched on the counter stool and pulled her robe
closer. It was cold in the kitchen, and she wanted her morning
coffee, but first she had to read this article.

Recently, a poll by the University of Chicago's National
Opinion Research Council indicated that 67 percent of
Americans believe they have had a psychic experience.
Many of these people are calling on the spirit world for
solace and advice, using mediums, or channelers, who
have established contact with "entities" from the past.
Sometimes these "entities" beam down from outer
space, such as Ms. Fisher's "sixth-density entity,"
Dance.

"I was walking through the Sheep Meadow in Central
Park on a hot Sunday afternoon last August," recalls
Ms. Fisher. "When I looked up into the western sky, I
saw this tall, elegant figure wrapped in a glow of brilliant
light. I stopped in my tracks, right in the middle of the
Sheep Meadow, with people sunbathing all around me,
and I said out loud, 'Yes.' Yes, for I knew he was
coming for me.

"And he said to me from across the meadow,
'Phoebe, you are beautiful. You are a beautiful person.'
I felt this enormous rush of cold air push against me. I
was nearly knocked over, but I managed to nod. I
couldn't speak. But I knew he or she—they don't have
gender in the Pleiades system—wanted to use my body.
He wanted me to bring the message of peace and love
to our world, and I agreed to lend him my human form.
We didn't have to speak. I knew telepathically. And
then I felt another rush of air, but this time it was blazing
hot. Later, I realized he had settled himself into my
home, my physical body."

Jennifer shook her head, smiling to herself. She'd clip the article and send it to Eileen Gorman, she decided. Since storming out of the restaurant on Thursday night, Jennifer had been feeling guilty. This would make a nice peace offering, she decided, and a way of getting back in touch with her old friend. She slipped off the stool and went to the stove to boil water for coffee. She heard Tom then in the other room, padding across the floor to the bathroom. She glanced at the clock. It was only eight o'clock. Why was he up so early on a Saturday? He seldom told her his plans, and in the first days of their relationship had tried to make a joke of his secrecy, saying he would let her know "on a need-to-know basis." She had thought that funny then. But not anymore.

She put the kettle on the stove and then scooped several spoonfuls of fresh coffee beans into the grinder. The little machine roared in the silent kitchen, and it was only after she had dumped the finely ground beans into the coffee filter that she realized Tom had entered the room. He was standing at the counter, glancing through the paper. When he didn't look up or acknowledge her, she said coolly, "And good morning to you."

"Good morning," he answered. "Sorry. I was just checking to see if Giuliani made any statements. There was a rumor in the building yesterday that he was going to announce for the Senate." He smiled across at her, trying to make amends.

"Well, it would be nice if you just said hello, that's all." She poured boiling water onto the filter.

"You know I never have much to say in the morning."

"I wouldn't think a simple 'good morning' is too much for a big assistant attorney general like yourself." She added more water.

"Did you see this piece about the new yuppie fad?" Tom asked, as if to change the subject.

"Be careful what you say about yuppies. They're us." She glanced over at him. He was wearing only the bottoms of his pajamas and was standing at the counter scratching the thick dark hair on his chest.

"You may be, but I'm not." He looked up from the newspaper. "Any coffee?"

"In a moment, sire."

"Just asking, Jennifer. Just asking." He grabbed the sports section of the *Times* and went over to the breakfast table, sitting down in the soft wash of pale winter sun to concentrate on the basketball scores.

Jennifer finished making coffee, poured Tom a cup, and added a splash of half-and-half. She carried his cup to the table and placed it down next to him.

"Thanks," he said.

Jennifer slid down across from him at the table, satisfied for the moment with the taste of coffee and the slight warmth of the winter sun. She studied Tom while he read. She could see only his right profile—his better side, as he liked to say, because when he was still in prep school, his nose had been broken in a lacrosse game and badly reset. This morning his better side was shadowed with an overnight growth of beard. His long black hair tumbled over his forehead and into his eyes; it curled around his ear lobes. He looked like an unmade bed, she thought fondly.

She sipped her coffee and looked out the window at the snowbound Brooklyn Heights street where a few early risers were trudging through the snow. She wondered if this was the right time to tell Tom she wanted either to get married or break off the relationship. Her friend, Margit, had warned her about men like Tom who were afraid of commitment. She knew she couldn't keep on living half a life with him. And besides, she knew she wanted to have children before it was too late.

"Are you okay?" he asked, glancing up. His cool gray eyes stared at her with the same compassion he might give the train schedule.

"I have no idea," she answered truthfully, staring at the snow that covered the street like the hard frosting of a day-old wedding cake.

"Your job?" he asked.

Jennifer shook her head. "My life."

"Your life, huh?" He nodded to the *Times* column. "Maybe you could use some spiritual guidance, one of these whatever-they-are."

"Please, Tom, I'm being serious." She looked straight at him. She was never any good at fooling people.

"You mean, us?"

"Yes, and more."

"What do you mean, 'more'?" There was an edge to his voice. At least she had his full attention, which gave her some satisfaction.

"I mean us, my stupid job at the foundation, and this!" She waved at the frozen street. All of it. The neighborhood, Brooklyn Heights, New York City. It hadn't struck her until that very moment that she was sick of New York, sick of her daily life.

Tom pushed the paper away from him. It was a gesture he always made when he was upset, as if he was clearing his deck for a new problem.

She was afraid now. She was always afraid when she got Tom angry. That was one of the underlying problems in their relationship. She wasn't honest enough with Tom, for in her heart of hearts she was afraid of losing him, of being without anyone at all.

"Well, what brought this on, this disgust about your life?"

"You know what."

"For chrissake, Jennifer, I slept with that woman once, and I was a goddamn stupid fool to tell you."

"You weren't telling me, Tom, you were bragging. You were showing off, you were being a jerk, and just so you could appear as a stud in front of your stupid friends," she answered back.

"Don't go back over that bullshit," he said softly, turning to his coffee.

"Bullshit yourself!" Jennifer looked away again, out the window at the cold day. She was surprised that she wasn't crying. She had gotten tougher in the last few years, she realized.

At the Justice Department Christmas party, Tom had gotten drunk and boasted to the other males that he had slept with Helen Taubman, the television anchorwoman, that fall, just when Jennifer had begun dating him seriously.

Jennifer had become dizzy, trying to reach the ladies' room

in the crowded restaurant before she became sick. She had blamed it on the champagne, on the excitement and the warm restaurant, but of course all his friends knew she was lying. Tom's admission had shocked them all.

"You want to talk about this, Jennifer?" Tom asked. He was focusing his full attention on her, but then she saw him glance at the kitchen clock.

"Are you in a hurry?" she asked, trying to pin him down. "Are you going into the office? What is it? Why the glances at the clock?"

"Jesus, remind me not to cross you again early in the morning." He spun around and stood up.

"Tom! Listen to me!" He set his coffee cup on the counter and kept walking. She waited until he had reached the doorway before she called after him. "I think we should take a break from each other for a while."

That got his attention. She saw the way his shoulder muscles tensed, and he halted in the doorway. She watched him make a slow and dramatic turn. He was stalling for time, giving himself a chance to think of a response. She knew all his gestures and habits as if they were her own.

"Are you sleeping with someone else?" he asked.

Jennifer recognized the tactic. He was putting her on the defensive. She stared back at him, refusing to rise to the bait. When he came slowly back into the kitchen, holding her eyes with his, she began to tense. Her fingers tightened around the warm coffee cup.

"Right? Is this what all this oblique talk is about?" He had reached the table, but he didn't sit down. She knew he liked to hover over people.

"Our relationship isn't going anywhere," she told him.

"Don't give me that shit! Who is it? One of those assholes from the foundation? Handingham, right?"

"David?" She looked up at Tom, startled by his guess. "You think I'd be interested in David?" Now she was offended.

"He's your boss, isn't he? He's got the power around that place."

"Oh, for God's sake. You think I'd have an affair with David Handingham just because he's the president of the board?"

"You wouldn't be the first woman to fuck her way up the ladder."

"Tom, that's disgusting! I can't believe you'd think that. Sometimes I don't think you know me at all."

"Sometimes I think you're right." He sat down across from her.

She realized he was upset, and that pleased her. She looked away again, back through the kitchen window. It was suddenly much brighter. The sun had reached the street and was shining off the frozen snow, and Jennifer stared hard at the gleaming surface until her eyes hurt.

"Okay, let's talk about this later." He glanced at the clock, then over at Jennifer. "I'll call you later, okay?"

She wanted to say no, but that would be unfair to Tom, and unfair to herself. She had already invested over six months in their relationship.

"I'll be here," she told him.

Tom nodded, then sighed. "Okay," he said, tapping the table and pulling himself up. "I'll call before four. We're having dinner, right?" When she nodded yes, he said quickly, "I'll make the reservations."

Jennifer knew this was an effort to appease her. She was always the one who made their dinner reservations, who wrote the thank-you notes, who did all the little housewifely chores.

Tom walked into the bedroom to dress. She got more coffee and sat by the windows and watched the winter sun grow brighter.

When Tom came back into the kitchen, he was dressed in the clothes he had left in her closet—the blue cords, his thick walking shoes, the beautiful red sweater she had given him for his thirtieth birthday. He was wearing his parka and carried a briefcase full of files. When he kissed her cheek, she could smell his aftershave lotion, his hair shampoo, and she wanted to make love to him there on the kitchen floor but didn't have the courage to tell him so.

She didn't move. She sat perfectly still at the kitchen table and watched the sun and the snow. She didn't have the strength to get up and get dressed.

She would go back to bed, she thought. She would curl down deep into the blankets and sleep. She would stay there safe and warm in the dark shadows until she discovered what was going wrong in her life.

5

JENNIFER LOOKED AT THE elephants, the herd of mammoths that dominated the museum's African Hill, as she waited for Tom. It was Tom who insisted that they meet for a drink in such an out of the way place. These days his job consisted mostly of prosecuting drug dealers, and shortly before they began to date, someone had tried to kill him. Now he carried a gun and didn't like being seen with her. It was silly of him to worry, she thought. If drug dealers wanted to blow him or her away, they would. They controlled the city as far as she could see.

Jennifer stopped at the Gemsbok display and studied the pattern-faced Kalahari Desert animals. In the Museum of Natural History's magnificent diorama, they looked almost real. Then she thought: they were real once, roaming the great savannahs. She almost felt as if she could step behind the thick glass and walk through the long grass and acacia trees into the heat and heart of Africa. She wished she were in Africa. She wished she were anywhere but in New York City on a cold, snowy Friday afternoon waiting for her tardy lover.

She stepped up to another diorama, this one a cluster of hippopotamuses, sitatunga, and waterbucks, and saw that the sign said the animals were all gathered at the edge of one of the small rivers that formed the network of the Nile. The animals were standing in the thick grass and umbrella sedge. Jennifer stared at the posed figures; although she'd never studied anything about Africa, she felt something was wrong with the scene. Then she caught a glimpse of her own reflection in the bubbled glass. She had come directly from work and was wearing her corporate uniform: a tailored, heavy gray suit with a white silk blouse and the string of pearls Tom had given her for Christmas, their first Christmas together. She raised her hand to touch the pearls and felt a warm tear on her cheek. This was wrong. Why was she crying? She quickly brushed it away, thinking, I can't look like this. I can't be crying when he arrives.

Turning from the Nile River diorama to go find the women's room, she found herself in Tom's arms.

"Hi, sweetheart, sorry I'm late. It's snowing. The whole damn city is gridlocked." He stood shaking wet snow off his shoulders and from his thick black hair.

"That's all right," she said, relieved that he didn't seem to notice her tears. "I just arrived myself."

"Well, you look great!" He turned his full attention on her, stepping closer to kiss her on her cheek. "Look, it's freezing outside. Is there someplace here where we can get a drink? Or at least some coffee?"

"Yes, there's a bar under the great blue whale on the first floor. But come with me first; let's look around. I haven't been in this museum in ages."

"Where do you want to go?"

"Oh, let's just wander. We'll take the elevator to the third floor, then walk down." Directing their tour gave her the sense of being in control. That was her problem with Tom. When she was with him, she always felt manipulated. Now she just wanted to make him do what she said, to prove to herself that she could control him when she needed to.

On the top floor, they stepped off the elevator and saw a sign for a new exhibition.

" 'Bright Dreams, Bright Vision,' " Tom read. "What's that?"

"I have no idea," Jennifer answered. They pushed through the glass gallery door and stepped into the dark interior.

"Oh, great," he said, reading the first exhibit sign. " 'Prehistoric Man.' Just what I thought when I woke up this morning: 'I wish I knew a lot more about prehistoric man.' "

"I want to see this exhibition, Tom!" Her voice rose sharply.

"Okay," he whispered, "okay." He touched her arm. "Easy."

Jennifer turned away, embarrassed by her outburst, but the gallery was nearly deserted. She noticed an older woman with a cane, a few mothers with babies in strollers, and two female guards in blue uniforms standing together at the entrance.

"Hey, look!" Tom pointed at the display in the center of the room.

The focus of the diorama was the model of a prehistoric hut, built of mammoth bone, tusks, and leather. The jawbones of the mammoths were turned upside down and fitted into each other like a puzzle to form a twelve-foot circle. The arching roof was made with dozens of huge, curving tusks, over which animal skins were tied to form a cover.

"It's a model of one of their huts," Tom said, reading from the printed information plaque, "from the Ukraine."

"It's wrong," she stated in a whisper, staring at the diorama.

"What, sweetheart?" Tom asked, moving around the model to peer inside.

"It's wrong. It's all wrong! That's Nari's hut. I know it is!" Her voice rose, startling everyone.

"Honey, what the hell are you talking about?"

"I don't know."

Tom started to laugh, then stopped, startled by the look in her eyes. "Jennifer?"

She was trembling. He put his hand on her arm, but she slapped his fingers away.

"Damnit, Jennifer. That hurt!" He shook his hand.

Jennifer caught sight of a guard. She was moving around the diorama and coming toward her.

"Let's get out of here," she said. Only when she was in

the brightly lit reptile gallery again did she take a deep breath and slow herself down.

"Jennifer, what in hell is wrong with you?"

She shook her head and kept walking. Her heels snapped on the marble floor.

"What was that bullshit about the hut?" He lengthened his stride. They reached the hallway and started down the stairs.

"I don't know."

"You hurt my hand."

"Please, Tom, enough! I'm upset, that's all. I'm upset about us." They reached the first floor and kept walking, past the Theodore Roosevelt Memorial and into the Invertebrates Gallery.

"Well, do something about it, damnit!"

"I intend to."

"What?" His voice hardened. "You're going to do what?"

"I'm going to have a drink." She walked into the Ocean Life Room, where a massive blue whale hung from the ceiling and dominated the two floors of the gallery. "Here's the bar."

Jennifer walked into the lower floor, where a few white-clothed tables were set up to create a small cocktail lounge. The room was dimly lit to suggest the ocean floor, and the huge, plastic blue whale hovered above them, swamping the room with its size. It was not a place where people went for a drink on Friday night after work. Anyone here would be from out of town, a tourist.

She let Tom order at the bar while she picked a table away from the others. When he came back, he sat down close to her, but she shifted her body to keep some distance.

"Are you feeling better?"

"I'll tell you in a minute." She took a quick sip of the scotch and water, then sat back and nodded.

"What was that all about?" He took off his topcoat and settled into the chair.

Jennifer shook her head. She was still trembling. "I don't know," she whispered. "I just had this weird feeling that I had once been there inside that diorama. All of it was vividly real to me." She took a quick gulp of her drink.

"You were saying something, mumbling." Tom shook his

head. "Maybe you saw the model in a book or something."
He glanced around then, checking out the room.

"Yes, maybe," Jennifer whispered.

"It was like you were having a temper tantrum or something." He stirred his scotch.

"I was having something." She shrugged, feeling chilled.
How she had behaved in the exhibition frightened her. "I
don't want to talk about it," she announced.

"Okay, what do you want to talk about?"

"Don't be so prosecutorial."

He started at her. "Is it going to be one of those nights?"

She took another sip to bolster herself. Tom hadn't asked
her what drink she wanted, but had gone ahead and ordered
a scotch and soda. It was like being married, she thought.

"Tom, I can't keep doing this. I can't keep seeing you. I
mean, we're not getting anywhere, are we?"

He looked away. "I'm still married, Jennifer."

"Then do something about it. You've been separated for
three years. You told me when we met that you were getting a
divorce." Her voice grew stronger as she spoke. "You shoudn't
have started up with me if you still were in love with your wife."

"I'm not in love with Carol." He was angry now.

"Then get a divorce! You don't have children. What's
stopping you? Tom, I deserve some answers and I deserve
some respect."

He glanced away again, and she began to cry, as quietly
as possible, afraid of attracting attention. She bent forward
and sobbed into her hands, using the fur of her winter coat
to muffle the tears.

When she had calmed down, Tom leaned across the small
table and whispered, "Jennifer, I love you. I want to take
care of you. I want to marry you. I want to be in your life
forever. Okay? Just give me some time. This case has dragged
on longer than I thought. I don't want to risk anything—any
danger to you—by going public and having these greaseballs
know you exist. You understand that, don't you?"

"Do you love me, Tom?" she asked. The tears were gone.

"Yes, I love you. Of course I do." He looked at her, and
this time his gray eyes did show his feelings.

Jennifer shrugged. "I'm not afraid. I want to be part of your life, Tom. I want to take the risks you're taking."

He was shaking his head before she finished.

"I won't let you."

"I have something to say about that, too, you know."

"Honey, you don't know. These are crazy Colombians. They kill each other. They kill cops. They kill each other's families. You read about it in the papers. A mother and child found shot in the face while their car is parked at a stoplight." He shook his head as he spoke. "I won't do it. I won't expose you to that violence. Honey, we're almost done. We'll have the rest of that scum in jail by the end of the winter."

"Bullshit! By the end of the winter there'll be another case. If they want to kill me, they will. Don't give me that crap, Tom. It's nonsense."

For a moment they both were silent. Jennifer blew her nose and wiped away her tears. Several of the tourists were staring at them, and Jennifer moved her chair to block their view.

"I'm sorry," she said quietly. "I guess I've caused a scene."

"Fuck 'em," Tom answered. He was leaning back, balancing himself on the two rear legs of the metal chair.

When he got mad, he acted tough. She had always found that exciting. She liked the way he brought her close to the edge of his anger, but she was afraid that someday things might get out of hand. Still, she couldn't deny her attraction to his toughness, especially in bed.

"Okay, what do you want to do?" he asked, as if summing up a business meeting.

"I'm going to go to Margit and David's for dinner," she said, not looking up from her drink.

"Fine! You go ahead and do that!" He shoved the chair back and stood. He didn't even try to lower his voice.

They were like characters in a cheap drama, she thought, listening to his retreating footsteps on the marble floor. She was afraid to look up, afraid that the tourists were again staring at her. She felt exposed and defenseless. Then, slowly, the voices of the other patrons grew louder. She waited a few minutes more, until she was sure Tom had left, and then she fled the museum.

* * *

Outside on Seventy-seventh Street, the snow had deepened, and Jennifer, walking west, knew she'd have trouble getting a taxi. Putting her head down against the sharp wind, she headed for West End Avenue, her feet plowing through the wet snow. She began to cry, but this time she let the tears flow, let herself sob out her heartache.

She crossed Columbus Avenue, stopped outside the Museum Café, and looked up Seventy-seventh Street. Already the street was blocked with snow, and both sidewalks were deserted. Jennifer had lived on the Upper West Side when she was going to Columbia Law School, and she prided herself on knowing how to be careful in the city. She had even taken self-defense classes at the YWCA to boost her confidence, but once she left school and moved to Brooklyn Heights, she had become increasingly paranoid about being alone on the West Side. It was foolish, she realized, especially now that the neighborhood was so fashionable. Still, she couldn't keep herself from being wary.

She stood a moment longer on Columbus and looked for an available yellow taxi, but the few cabs moving slowly downtown were either filled or on call.

"Damn!" she said, feeling sorry for herself. Everything, it seemed, was going wrong in her life. Defiantly she pushed forward up the deserted side street, thinking guiltily that she should have asked Tom to walk with her as far as Broadway. That was the trouble with her. She fought so hard to be independent, but whenever she felt afraid, she wanted a man around. That realization made her furious. She looked up and purposely exposed her face to the cold, as if trying to freeze the pain she felt in her heart.

Then she felt the hand on her shoulder and was stopped in her tracks.

Tom must have come after her. She twisted away and turned to him. But it wasn't Tom.

This man was taller, bigger. He seemed to block the entire street. She could barely see his face, hidden in the dark cave of a jacket hood, but she knew he was dangerous.

"Get away!" she shouted. She tried to step back and run,

but her boots didn't grip in the slippery snow and she stumbled just as the man swung at her.

"You bitch," he swore, then lunging at her, knocked them both into the gutter between parked cars.

He was on top of her, pushing through her coat and grabbing at her body. His hands were on her breasts, his thick lips on her face. He kept swearing, calling her filthy names, and then he jabbed his blunt, wet tongue into her mouth.

It was when he ripped away the front of her white silk blouse that she went for him. Reaching up with both hands, she raked her nails down his cheeks. She wanted to hurt him, and hearing him cry out gave her courage. She hadn't hit anyone since she was a little girl in the playground, and the pleasure it gave her to strike back was gratifying.

With the ferocity of a cornered dog, she grabbed his throat and curled her fingernails into his neck. She felt the skin pop as her nails broke his flesh and his warm blood ran down her fingers.

He swung at her blindly, and she ducked the blow. Then, moving like an animal, she attacked, catching him in the groin with her knee. He stumbled forward, groping for his testicles, and fell face-forward into the deep snow.

She did not run to the corner, where the snowbound traffic honked along Columbus Avenue. Instead, she licked the corners of her bleeding mouth and tasted the blood with pleasure. He grabbed the front bumper of the parked car and pulled himself up. She hit him hard in the back of the neck with the heel of her right hand, swinging at him as if she were chopping a block of wood. His big body slumped forward, skidding off the car's metal grill, and dropped into the gutter.

She couldn't let him go. She wouldn't. She grabbed him by his hair and, with her foot jammed against the shoulder blades, jerked back his head until she heard his neck snap.

Jennifer stayed on her knees beside the body for a moment, gasping for air. She cupped a handful of snow into her palm and, using it like soap, wiped her face clean of blood. Calmer, she moved close and saw that the predator was dead. She had killed him. She smiled.

Her name was Shih Hsui-mei. She was Chinese, the wife of Cheng-k'uan, and he was a young man then, living in the town of Silver Hill. It was during the boom years of mining, and he had come west with his father from St. Louis to settle claims for the government.

He delivered goods to Cheng-k'uan from his uncle's store and would see Shih Hsui-mei sitting on the porch facing the Yellowjacket Mountains, combing her hair. She was his age—sixteen, perhaps seventeen—and had come from China to be old Cheng-k'uan's bride.

She had long black hair, very long, very black, and she would comb it slowly, time after time, until it fanned across one side of her perfect round face like a blackbird's wing.

She would then take a paste made of rhubarb and comb it through the hair until it lay straight and still, like a fan, and then she would tie it out of sight.

She never wore Western clothing but dressed always in silk trousers and tight, beautifully embroidered jackets and small silver slippers. She had such tiny feet. When she walked across the boards of Cheng-k'uan's mountain shack, she never made a sound. He would see her one moment, then she would be gone, like a tropical bird.

He could never see enough of her. He went again and again to Chinatown just to catch a glimpse of the young Shih Hsui-mei, for she never came across the creek to the white side of town.

In the opium dives, he saw her tend to the men, bring

them fresh pipes of opium. The men stayed for days, lost to the world, hidden away in their private hells.

The boy's hell was Shih Hsui-mei. He wanted her. Her old husband used to laugh at him as he sat watching her comb her hair in the bright morning sun. The old man made fun of the boy and spoke rapidly in Chinese to Shih Hsui-mei, asking her if she wanted to feel the white man's prick.

The boy went to the opium dives and paid to smoke in the cells. He went because she would come to him then and give him a pipe full of the sweet-smelling drug. She would look at him with her wet black eyes and her round, perfect face, and he would stare wordlessly at her.

Then she would pass away into the den, and he would smoke the sweet opium and cough into the filthy blankets. In time he would forget her, forget his pain, and in the dimness of his consciousness, she would appear again, and he would not know if she were alive or simply in his dreams.

He had her then as he always wanted her—in a place where they could be alone together, away from the world. Even if it was only a dream, she was with him, and he would smile and see her smiling, beckoning him farther and farther into the world of opium and dreams.

When he woke, into the fierce pain of daylight and consciousness, he did not want to live. He wanted only more opium, more dreams of her passing him in the den, hearing her silk trousers, seeing her lovely small body. But he would have to leave the den, stumbling down the snowy path, crossing the cold river on the narrow log bridge. Sometimes he'd be sick there, falling off the bridge, tumbling into the rocky creek, puking the night's anguish of opium onto the slippery river rocks.

His father threw him out of his shack. He was no good to him, no good at work. The opium had destroyed his mind. He could not write down a simple claim in a government ledger or help his uncle. He wanted only Shih Hsui-mei. And now he had no money to buy opium, to spend the night watching her slip through the dense fog in her silk trousers, tending to the worthless lot of Chinese miners, or himself, a hopeless pale-faced white boy.

He stole his father's long-barreled pistol, the one he had been issued in the war, and went to get Shih Hsui-mei. He had a plan. A crazy plan. He would take her away from old Cheng-k'uan. The old man had no rights. He was a miserable Chink. The Chinese were killed by the dozens in the mines of Idaho. He would steal a horse and take Shih Hsui-mei with him across the Salmon River and into Oregon, where he had family, cousins of his mother.

When he went to Cheng-k'uan and told him what he intended, the old man laughed and spit in his face.

He shot the Chinaman in the head. The bullet made a small, neat black hole in the yellow man's forehead and splashed blood and bone and brain on the white-washed wall. The old man turned in a tight circle, dancing on his thin legs like a chicken when it's axed.

He ran into the side wall before he stopped moving and slid down, smearing the whitewash with his blood. The boy had to step over him to get at Shih Hsui-mei. She was screaming. He had never before heard a Chinese woman scream.

He couldn't get her to be silent. His hands tore her lovely embroidered silk jacket. He kept telling her to hush, talking to her as if she were a baby, but she wouldn't stop screaming. He tore her silk blouse, and her breasts were so small and lovely he was suddenly dazed by the sight of them.

There were Chinese coming from the mines, running up through the mud of late spring, through the snow still frozen under shack porches. He had never seen so many Chinese.

He grabbed Shih Hsui-mei, this time with his arm around her waist. He would carry her all the way to the Snake River, he thought. But they made it only to the little creek below Cheng-k'uan's shack. He ran through the cold water, slipping on the smooth stones, thinking that if he crossed the creek into the white part of town, he would be safe. No white man would harm him for killing a Chink.

Her people caught him at the river. There were too many of them. They pulled little Shih Hsui-mei from his arms, and one slit his throat as he might draw a blade across a squealing pig.

His gushing blood turned the cold creek water purple. He stumbled on the smooth rock and fell forward, grabbing his throat, and died faster than Cheng-k'uan.

The whites came running down from town. They found him cold and stiff and bloodless. There was not a mark on his body, except for the fine, thin slice across the length of his throat. His blue eyes held a steady, unflinching gaze, as if here in death, he had finally found the answer to his young life.

6

"OH MY GOD," MARGIT exclaimed, seeing Jennifer. "What on earth has happened?" She reached out and pulled Jennifer into an embrace.

"I was mugged," Jennifer stated, and in the comfort and safety of Margit Engle's arms, she began to cry.

"David!" Margit shouted over Jennifer's shoulder. "David, come quick! Jennifer's been mugged."

Jennifer pulled herself from her friend's arms and wiped the tears from her eyes. She felt her bruised cheekbone.

"Jennifer, are you all right?" David asked. He handed his wife his drink as he approached Jennifer. "What happened?"

"She was mugged, David!" Margit's voice betrayed her anxiety. "We have to call the police."

"No. Don't call anyone!" Jennifer blurted out. She caught sight of herself in the living room mirror and began to cry again, but this time she let the tears flow. David guided her to the sofa and arranged a pillow behind her head.

"I'll get my bag and we'll take care of these bruises. You're okay, Jennifer, don't be afraid."

Jennifer nodded, but moving her head drove a piercing wedge of pain between her eyes, and she reached up with her hand to feel the raw flesh on her forehead. It would be days, she guessed, before the bruises would be gone, and that made her start crying again.

"I still think we should call the police," Margit declared. She was standing in the middle of the living room, nervously twisting her fingers.

"No!" Jennifer said. She tried to sit up but couldn't gather her strength.

"Jennifer is right," David said, returning. "Jennifer has had enough trouble. And what are the police going to find anyway? Whoever did this is already long gone." He knelt beside the sofa. "Get me towels and warm water," he told his wife. "I want to clean up these bruises."

"Thank you, David," Jennifer whispered, but her lips had swollen and she was having difficulty forming words.

"Shhhhh," David whispered, smiling down at her. "No need to say anything, just rest. Close your eyes. You're all right."

Jennifer did close her eyes, thankful that she had made it to West End Avenue and that Margit and David were taking care of her. She did fall asleep, knowing she was safe from everyone out on those city streets. But still she was frightened of herself, of what she had done.

When she awoke she could hear their muffled voices from the other room. She turned her head carefully on the pillow, trying to avoid the wedges of pain every time she moved, and saw through bruised eyelids that they had closed the door to the dining room. The lights were off in the living room, where she still lay, now covered with a heavy quilt. Her shoes had been removed and her skirt loosened.

She wondered if she should get up to tell them that she was all right, but even as she wondered, she knew she didn't have the strength. How could she tell them what had really happened, how she had killed the man? She couldn't tell anyone the truth, ever, and when she closed her eyes again, she wished that she wouldn't wake up, that she would never have to face the nightmare of what she had done.

She woke crying, struggling to free herself from the hand on her shoulders. It was a moment before she realized she was being held by David. "You're having a nightmare, Jen-nifer. That's all," he was whispering.

One lamp was lit, and she saw David above her and Margit at the foot of the sofa, both looking pained and upset. Jennifer relaxed and slipped down into the soft pillows.

"I'm sorry," she mumbled.

"Don't be sorry. You just had a nightmare."

"I'm sorry I'm causing you all this trouble. I really should go home." Jennifer started to rise, but David placed his hand on her shoulder.

"You're going nowhere. Stay with us tonight, and I'll take you home tomorrow, if you're up to it. Otherwise, you'll be our guest for a few days."

"Thank you, but I can't. I have to go to Boston for a meeting."

"Well, we can talk about that tomorrow. You listen to me; I'm the doc here." He kept smiling, comforting her with his gentle manner.

"Thank you, David," Jennifer whispered. She was re-lieved by his insistence. The thought of being by herself was frightening.

"What about something to eat? A clear soup?" Margit asked.

Jennifer tried to smile and said, "That would be wonderful, Margit. I'm famished."

When Margit left the room, David asked, "Jennifer, noth-ing else happened to you besides being struck, am I correct?"

"What do you mean?"

"You weren't raped, were you?"

"Oh, no." Jennifer sighed, terrified that David might guess the truth. "I managed to get away."

"Would you like to talk about it?" he asked.

Jennifer shook her head. "I'm sorry," she said. "I feel so stupid, getting mugged. I mean, I should know better." She had her eyes closed and her head back. In her mind's eye, she saw the man again, saw him lunge at her, saw rage and hunger on his face, and then she hit him, attacked him like an animal, with her bare hands.

"You'll feel better tomorrow," David said reassuringly.

Jennifer nodded, but she knew that in the morning she would feel worse, not because of her bruises, but for what she had done.

"Here we are," Margit announced, coming back into the living room with a bowl of soup, a place mat and cloth napkin tucked under her arm.

Jennifer tried to sit up and again felt the wedge of pain between her eyes.

"Easy," David cautioned. He had taken hold of her elbow.

"Maybe we shouldn't try this," Margit suggested.

"No, I think getting something warm into Jennifer will do wonders. You can sit up, right? Otherwise, Margit will just feed you."

"No, I want to sit up, please." Jennifer forced herself to swing her legs off the deep sofa. She marveled to herself that she did suddenly have the strength to overcome the stabbing pain between her eyes. Something had happened to her. She was different, somehow. She was another kind of person. She had never been able to stand pain.

Margit stood hovering over Jennifer, her hands clasped together. "Would you like some Italian bread to go into the broth?" she asked.

"Let's give Jennifer room to breathe," David suggested, moving away from the sofa and sitting down across from the coffee table. Margit stayed on the sofa next to Jennifer.

"I'm not sure I'm going to be able to do this. I can't feel my lips."

"You look as if you just did a couple of rounds with Tyson."

"And I feel it." Jennifer picked up the soup spoon and realized she was no longer trembling. She smiled weakly at Margit and David.

"Well, that's better," Margit said, sighing, and she reached out to touch Jennifer's leg. "Would you like to talk about what happened?" she said softly.

"Margit, leave Jenny alone." He stood and went to the liquor cabinet.

"I just think it's better if Jennifer has the opportunity to talk it out, that's all," she answered back.

"I know what you want," David said, lowering his voice as he bent to retrieve the scotch bottle from the bottom of the breakfront. "You want all the gruesome details. And I think Jenny deserves to have her privacy."

They kept talking past her, as if she were a child.

"There are no gruesome details," Jennifer spoke up, "and I don't mind talking about it." She turned to Margit and tried to force her bruised face into a smile. "I didn't lose my purse. He didn't really hurt me. I mean, except for the obvious. I ran away, that's all."

"Well, where did it happen? Right here on West End Avenue?" Margit leaned closer, her eyes widening.

"No, it wasn't here. It was over by—" Jennifer caught herself before she said Columbus Avenue. "It was over on Broadway."

"Broadway? But it's so busy. There are always people on Broadway. Didn't anyone come to help you out? My God, this city!" She glared at her husband as if he were in some way responsible.

"There's no one out tonight, Margit," Jennifer said, returning to her soup. Eating made her feel better.

"That's right. It's been snowing all evening," agreed David.

"I still think we should call the police," Margit said again.

"Why? You heard Jenny. She wasn't robbed. She got banged up a couple times, sure, but in this city, that's not even considered a misdemeanor."

"We can't just let him get away with it." Margit glanced back and forth, upset with Jennifer as well as her husband. "A woman isn't safe."

"Margit was attacked herself last week, Jenny," David volunteered, "and she's still edgy."

"I'm not edgy, and I wasn't attacked. Someone—a little black kid—tried to take my purse at Food City, that's all. The guard grabbed him. But everywhere you turn, it seems, the great unwashed, all the homeless, the poor, are coming out of their holes, or wherever they sleep at night, and attacking us. It's the mayor's fault, him and all these liberals."

"You were once one yourself, dear," David remarked coolly. "And the mayor certainly isn't one anymore, either."

Margit stood and began to pace the long living room.

"Margit, why don't you go to bed?" David suggested, speaking softly. "Jenny would probably like to get some sleep, too."

"I'm not going to sleep. I'm too upset." Margit kept pacing.

"Darling, it was Jenny who was mugged, not you."

"I know that," she replied, biting off the words, "but it could have been me. I'm on Broadway all the time."

"Oh, if you're going to start talking like that, then you might as well move out of the city."

"I'm not moving alone," Margit snapped.

David glanced at Jennifer and smiled apologetically. "We're sorry about all this, but you caught us in the middle of a long argument. Margit has had it with the city, wants to leave, move up the Hudson somewhere—"

"Or New Jersey."

"—and I don't. I'm not going to start commuting, not at my age." He drained his scotch.

"I don't blame you, Margit. Getting attacked like this is terrifying." Jennifer finished the soup and tried to wipe her mouth, but when she touched her face with the cloth napkin, she winced. "I'm going to feel terrible tomorrow," she moaned. "And I have to go to Boston."

"Well, thank God nothing serious happened." David stood up. "Margit, have you finished pacing? Ready to turn in?" He smiled over Jennifer's head at his wife. He was a big, sloppy, overweight man, but when he smiled, he looked like a giant, lovable panda.

He had been Jennifer's doctor since she was in law school, and then she had met and become good friends with Margit. Jennifer always felt that Margit treated her like the daughter she never had.

Margit seemed calmer. "Jennifer, I've made up Derek's room. You can sleep there tonight. The boys are away at school."

"Oh, Margit, thanks. I'm really sorry I'm causing so much

trouble." She limped out from behind the coffee table, knowing that she couldn't walk to their son's room by herself.

"If you wish, Jennifer, I'll give you a sedative. It might help you sleep."

"Thanks, David. I think I do need something. My whole body hurts."

"Go with Margit. I'll get you the pill."

When he left, Margit whispered to Jennifer, "I'm sorry we carried on so. We're going through a bad patch, David and I."

"Margit, it's okay, I understand." She tried again to smile.

"No, I'm not sure you do," Margit answered back. "It's not what you think. We're not fighting over where to live. David . . . well, David has found himself someone else, someone younger, and . . ." Margit began to cry. She was holding on to Jennifer as they walked to the bedroom.

"Oh, Margit, I'm so . . . I didn't . . ."

"Of course. Of course. Why would you? He just told me." Margit straightened up to turn on the light in Derek's room. It was still littered with his teenage belongings, and a huge poster of Madonna posing half naked was pinned to the wall.

"Do you think you can sleep with her staring at you?" Margit asked, trying to laugh.

"I'll keep the lights off." Jennifer eased herself down on the narrow bed.

"Here you are, Jenny," David said, returning with the pill and a glass of water. "You can take it when you want. It will give you at least six good hours." He leaned over and kissed the top of her head. "Good night. In the morning I'll have another look at those bruises."

"Thank you, David. Thank you for everything." She smiled up at him.

When he left them alone again, Margit said, "I shouldn't bother you with my concerns. You've had enough for one night. How's Tom? Do you want me to telephone him?"

Jennifer shook her head. She looked up at Margit, her eyes filled with tears. "I don't know. It's not, you know, working out."

Margit nodded. "It hardly ever does, does it?" She sighed.

"Margit, you're going to be okay. . . . We both are."

"I had the best husband in the world for twenty-three years, and now he tells me he's in love with a thirty-six-year-old woman—one of his patients, I might add—who's an investment banker on Wall Street and makes more money than he does. She's madly in love with him, he says. Now, how do you think that makes me feel?" She shook her head. "No wonder I hate this city. You know, Jennifer, I wish it had been me and not you that got mugged. I would have let that man kill me."

"Margit, I won't let you talk like that! I won't let you believe—"

"Believe it, Jennifer. It might happen to you. Once you're over forty, they put you out to pasture." The small woman's voice rose with anger. "Well, if he leaves me, I'll make him pay."

"Margit, I'm going to cry. Please."

"I'm sorry. Please go to sleep. Don't worry about tomorrow. I'll take you back to Brooklyn Heights. David said he has to go into the office, or at least that's the excuse he's giving me." She stood up and forced herself to smile. "Sleep tight, dear," she said, and pulled the door closed, leaving Jennifer alone.

Jennifer sat very still, holding the glass of water in one hand and the sleeping pill in the other. She forgot about her own problems for a moment and thought of Margit and David: a lifetime together, two children, a long and happy life, and now David had found another woman. She hated him at that moment, even though David was her doctor.

She felt her hatred pump through her body. It began in her fingers and raged like a forest fire in hot wind. Her breath came quick and hard, and in an effort to try to control herself, she took the pill, washing it down with a gulp of water. Yet still she raged. She stood up, forgetting her pain. She wanted him. She wanted to hurt David.

She opened the door and stepped into the hallway. The lights were out and the apartment was quiet. With her feet silent on the thick carpet, she moved toward the light that seeped out from under their bedroom door.

Jennifer realized they were sleeping separately when she saw the light under Matthew's bedroom door. That he had left Margit alone in their bed enraged Jennifer more. At that moment she felt a draft of cold air and shivered. A surge of blood pumped through her veins.

With a violent push, Jennifer swung the bedroom door open. David was in the bathroom. He was wearing just his pajama bottoms, and his heavy white flesh sagged over the drawstring. He was brushing his teeth and his eyes bulged when he saw her. He looked old and useless.

"Jenny," he mumbled, his mouth foamed with the white toothpaste.

"You!" She came at him with her hands extended, fingers reaching to clutch his throat. She knew how she would kill him—with her fingernails ripping into the flesh of his neck. But suddenly her vision swam; she felt lightheaded and stumbled forward. He caught her before she fell to the floor.

"It's all right, Jenny. You're all right." He lowered her to the carpet and called for his wife.

"What happened?" Margit asked, rushing from the other bedroom.

"She passed out from the medicine. It was too large a dose, I'm afraid. I forgot to ask her if she'd had something to drink earlier. She'll be all right, though. Give me a hand."

"She's not hurt?" Margit asked.

"No, but she's going to have a hell of a headache in the morning."

"Damnit, David, why weren't you more careful?"

"I was careful. She shouldn't have had this serious a reaction. Something must be wrong with her metabolism."

They had her in the hallway, carrying her between them like a sack of potatoes.

"What was she doing in there, anyway?" Margit asked as she struggled with Jennifer's legs.

"I don't know. I looked up and saw her in the mirror. She was coming straight for me," David said, puzzled. "I was brushing my teeth. I didn't have my glasses on. She looked wild, as if she were out of her head. I couldn't tell whether she was just wandering, or whether she had—I don't know —come to get me."

"Get you?" Margit looked over at her husband. "What do you mean?"

"She looked like she wanted to kill me," David replied, setting Jennifer gently on the bed.

7

JENNIFER STOPPED WALKING AND let the other Wednesday morning commuters rush by her. She stood staring at the bold headline of the *New York Post*:

APE KILLER MAKES MANHATTAN JUNGLE

Several people bumped against her in the crowded corridor, and she moved out of the steady stream of pedestrians, then closer to the newsstand to read the smaller print:

MAN FOUND WITH BONES CRUSHED.
DOC SAYS, "ANIMAL DID IT."

Jennifer walked over to the newsstand and stealthily purchased the newspaper, as if she thought she might be watched. She took it to a relatively quiet corner and flipped through the pages for the story. There was a photograph of the street and an arrow indicating where the body had been found, wedged between the parked cars.

As she rode from Brooklyn to Manhattan, she scanned the story for details that might link her to the death. No one

had seen the murder. A neighbor had found the victim on
Monday while walking his dog. It had snowed hard all
weekend, and by then the body had been buried beneath
twelve inches of snow, but the dog had sniffed out the
blood. One foot of the murder victim had been sticking out,
like a raised flag, the neighbor explained. And so he had
called the cops. There was a close-up photo of the man's
battered old shoe.

"Inhuman," the neighbor with the dog was quoted as
telling the *Post*. "The killer must have been some kind of
King Kong. What's this city coming to?"

There was a description of how the man's neck was broken,
and the article speculated on the size of the assailant. "Two
hundred and fifty plus pounds," estimated Detective Coles
Phinizy, "and maybe six feet six or seven. We're looking
for a man the size of a defensive back, someone who'd give
Hulk Hogan a match." The victim's identity was being withheld until his nearest relatives were located, but anyone with
information about the murder was asked to call the Twentieth
Precinct.

She glanced around carefully and then tore out the article
and tossed away the newspaper. Her fear had returned—not
that it had really left her, but she had been able to suppress
it.

She had taken Tuesday off from work and, with the help
of another sleeping pill, had slept most of the night. When
she did wake, she remembered the attack but had begun to
believe that she had simply overreacted. It hadn't been as
brutal as she remembered. She hadn't killed anyone, she
finally convinced herself.

Taking a shower that morning, she had studied herself in
the mirror, searching for some telltale signs, a new growth
of hair, a change in the size of her muscles, but there were
no marks on her body, no signs that her body had changed
on her.

Now her fear flooded her body. It wasn't fear of being
arrested for murder. The police would not be looking for a
blond white woman, five foot seven and 126 pounds.

Her fear was much more terrifying and secret. She had

killed someone with the strength of her own hands, and she had no idea where it had come from.

She rushed through Penn Station, up to the street, and out into the cold New York morning. She was on her way to a meeting with the members of a nearby Catholic church that wanted funds for a homeless shelter. But as she hurried to the street, Jennifer knew she couldn't sit through any meeting. Instead of going to the church, she'd take a taxi to her office and have Joan telephone and reschedule.

The snow had been cleared from the streets and pushed into the gutter to form a high ridge, already blackened with soot and broken down at places where pedestrians had beaten an icy path into the street. A taxi stopped ahead of her and a man with a suitcase jumped out, over the ridge of snow, and went toward Penn Station. Jennifer bolted immediately for the cab. Out of the corner of her eye she saw that another man had spotted the taxi and begun to run. Jennifer picked up her pace, found an opening in the ridge of snow, and ran into the street. She came at the taxi from behind, from the blind side.

She had it, she told herself, breathing hard as she raced through the slush. She had forgotten about her situation, the murdered man, forgotten her own fear. She needed that cab.

The other man, sprinting down the street, had reached the front of the cab. When he saw her, he began to shout. "Hey, lady, this is mine!"

Jennifer opened the back door, slid inside, and slammed the door.

"Broadway and Fifty-eighth," she told the driver, leaning forward so she'd be heard through the glass. She heard the man shouting at her through the side window. She reached out and locked the door, then sank back into the seat with relief as the taxi pulled into traffic. She never looked at the man as he slammed his fist on the side of the departing taxi.

The driver swore, glancing around.

"Don't stop!" Jennifer asked. She was trembling.

"Animals!" the driver shouted. "Goddamn animals!" He accelerated his taxi, still swearing, complaining now about the traffic.

Jennifer glanced at the name and picture on his hack license. It was unpronounceable, full of consonants. Now she stared out the side window, as if by looking away she could avoid any more confrontations.

"Animals!" the driver exclaimed again.

"Yes," Jennifer whispered. "I think I am."

"Oh my God, what happened to you?" Joan exclaimed, seeing Jennifer's bruised face.

"I'm okay. I'm okay," Jennifer assured her secretary. "Joan, follow me. I need you to cancel an appointment." Jennifer walked through the foundation's outer rooms and into her own small office that looked north. The sun reflected brilliantly on the hard-packed frozen snow.

"Would you like a cup of coffee?" Joan asked, as she followed after her.

"Yes!" Jennifer called back, shedding her wool coat and dropping it on her office sofa. "And get Dale Forster on the phone. I'm going to have to break our squash date." Jennifer slid into her chair. She didn't look up, but she knew her secretary had followed her into the room with coffee. "I want you to call Father Merrill and tell him I'm sorry, but I can't make this morning's meeting. Also, I want you to clear my schedule for this afternoon." She pulled her calendar across the wide desk and glanced down at Wednesday. "What do we have?"

"You have the eleven o'clock meeting with David Meyer on his film project. That's set up in the conference room. He wants to show you his film on Sun Valley. And he's already here. Then you have lunch with Evan Konechy upstairs in the dining room. Unless you want to have me make reservations elsewhere. This afternoon, there's a slide presentation for the St. Louis project, remember?" The secretary carefully set down the coffee cup, then perched on the edge of a chair at the corner of the desk. She had her pad out, ready to take notes.

"Damnit! I forgot about St. Louis." Jennifer fell back into her high-backed leather chair, the one David and Margit had bought for her when she started to work for the foundation.

"Jennifer, are you all right?" Joan asked. "Tell me what happened."

"Yes, I'm all right now." When she'd called in sick the day before, she'd said nothing about the assault. Now she was trying to make light of the incident. "I got mugged outside my apartment, that's all."

"Oh, you poor thing! You didn't tell me! Are you okay? Did you have to go to the hospital?"

"No, I just have to go see the . . . police," she lied, avoiding Joan's eyes.

"And look at mug shots?" Joan asked. "Janet Chan— you know, the one who just took over the Woman's World Foundation—was robbed last fall, and she had to look at mugshots. That was in Scarsdale."

"Well, I don't know about mugshots. I never saw the man." Jennifer reached for the cup of coffee, thankful that her hands had stopped trembling.

"Was he a black person?" Joan whispered, still leaning across the desk.

"I don't know. I told you, I never saw him." Jennifer opened her leather briefcase and took out her files in an attempt to stave off other questions. "Any calls?"

"Yes, several. . . . Tom called . . . twice." Joan did not look up as she glanced through the yellow phone messages. "And the president's office phoned. Dr. Handingham wants to speak with you about the talk he's to give at the Silbersack luncheon on Monday."

Jennifer suddenly felt overwhelmed by her work. On her desk were several bulky files, projects that needed attention. And there were all her meetings today. But she couldn't concentrate. She couldn't take her mind off what had happened.

"Jennifer, are you all right?" Joan asked again.

"Yes, I'm just tired, that's all." She gestured at the stack of files. "I've got to get some work done. Can you keep everyone away from me for a little while?" She smiled across at Joan, blinking away tears.

"Don't worry about a thing, dear." Joan Corboy stood.

"Drink your coffee, and I'll close the door and let you have some peace and quiet."

"Thank you, Joan, for taking care of me." She smiled after her secretary, and when her office door closed, Jennifer reached for the telephone and dialed Tom at work.

"Is Tom Oliver available?" she asked his secretary.

"May I ask who is calling?"

"Ms. Winters." Jennifer fingered the telephone cord as she waited, and spun her leather chair around to look out the window. She could see a long thin slice of the park from her windows and up Central Park West as far north as the museum. She focused on the massive Romanesque museum as she waited for Tom to come to the phone. She could not see Columbus Avenue, where she had killed the man.

It hadn't happened, she told herself. It couldn't have happened. But she knew now that was not true. She had gone over the murder a thousand times. In her mind, she had killed him a thousand times.

"Jennifer!"

"Tom, yes," she whispered into the phone.

"Where have you been?"

"I need to see you."

"I need to see you, darling." He sighed into the phone. "God, I've been calling you. But your machine—"

"Tom," she interrupted, "I have to talk to you." She had cupped her hand over the mouthpiece of the phone.

"What? Honey, I can't hear you."

"I need to talk to you!"

"Okay! Okay! When? Where?"

"Can you meet me for lunch?"

"Sweetheart, I can't. I've got to be downtown."

"All right!" She spun around and studied her calendar. "Are you free later, after four?"

"I will be. Where do you want to meet?"

"Come to Brooklyn, please."

There was silence for a moment, as he decided. "Okay, but don't be late. I don't want to have to hang around on the street."

"You have a key."

"Not with me."

"I'll be home early. Tom, I need your help. Something has happened." She was crying, and she reached over to pluck a tissue from the box on her desk.

"What are you talking about?"

"It's not what you think. I'm okay." She knew he was constantly worried that she'd get pregnant. "Don't say anything. I mean, don't tell anyone in the office you're meeting me."

"I never do, honey, you know that."

"I'm serious, Tom, this is important!"

"So's my case."

"What I need to talk to you about involves just me. Me alone."

"Honey, I just don't get you."

"Did you see the *Post* this morning?"

"Of course not!"

"Take a look at the headline."

"Come on, what gives? I've got a hearing in fifteen minutes."

"The headline says, 'Ape Killer Makes Manhattan Jungle.' "

"Yeah . . . so?"

"I need to talk to you about this 'ape killer.' I know who it is!" Then, unable to say more, she slammed down the phone. What had happened to her? She stood and came around the desk as her office door opened. Joan was holding a bright red file.

"It's for your eleven o'clock with Meyer," she said, handing the thick file to Jennifer.

"Call this number for me, please," Jennifer said as she strode from the office. "Eileen Gorman. See if she can have lunch with me today in the city. Tell her it's very important. And call Evan Konechy and tell her I have to cancel."

Joan followed Jennifer out of the suite of offices and stood with her in front of the bank of elevators. "Jennifer, are you sure you're all right?" She peered over her glasses at her boss.

Jennifer stared at her reflection in the polished bronze doors of the elevators. In the contours of the metal, she looked gross and deformed, and she turned away from the image.

"I'm not sure," she whispered. And then the doors opened and she stepped into an empty elevator. Turning, she pressed the button for the conference room floor, then glanced at Joan, who was still watching her, her face knit with concern.

"You can tell me," Joan offered.

Jennifer managed to fake a smile. "I wish to God I could," she whispered to herself as the doors slid smoothly closed, locking her briefly in the safety of the descending car.

8

JENNIFER COULD NOT EAT lunch. Instead, she sat across from Eileen Gorman and listened to the woman talk. Jennifer had wanted to see Eileen as soon as possible, once she realized that everything about her had started to go wrong after she met Eileen in Washington. She and Kathy Dart had exchanged a strange look, and then she had run thirteen miles. All of it, she guessed, was somehow connected to Eileen Gorman.

She had also wanted to tell Eileen what she had done, how she had killed the man who attacked her, but now she couldn't tell her high school friend. In her heart, Jennifer still believed that she wasn't capable of doing such a horrendous act.

So she spent lunch listening to Eileen tell her about the New Age philosophy, channeling, psychic auras, all of the metaphysical beliefs that Eileen followed. Something told Jennifer that she had to learn more about this new form of spiritualism if she was going to find out what was wrong with her body.

"I didn't believe in meditation or est, or anything having to do with pyramids and quartz crystals, either," Eileen went on, "not at first, certainly. But then I began to notice how my life—what was happening in my life—had a pattern. I started to read, to investigate everything, you know, the unexplained. And that is what finally led me to the teachings of Kathy Dart and Habasha.''

Jennifer waited for her to go on, to explain what she meant.

''I just decided I had been reincarnated.'' Eileen shrugged. ''I mean, reincarnation was the only thing that made sense about my life. Anyone's life.'' She waved her hand in the air. ''None of our lives make any sense, unless there is some reason.''

''There is a reason,'' said Jennifer. ''Some people call it heaven and hell. Others call it evolution.'' She could not yet accept what Eileen was telling her, but could she dismiss Eileen's reasoning, either?

''Look, I don't have your law degree,'' Eileen said, leaning forward, ''and I didn't graduate from the University of Chicago like you did. I really haven't studied at all, not since high school. But I've learned a lot on my own just from reading the New Age material. It's incredible, really, once you see the connections, the links between lives. The plan of what we are doing here on earth.''

Jennifer raised her eyebrows.

''Listen, there's something about me I never told you. You know I married that lifeguard, Tim Murphy. Well, we had a baby. A little premie. A girl. We called her Adara, and she lived just a week.''

''Eileen, I didn't know.''

''Of course not. You were away at college.'' Eileen continued, ''It was a forceps delivery, and the poor little thing had these deep gashes on her forehead.''

''Oh, no,'' Jennifer whispered.

''No, that didn't kill her. She was just too young. Her lungs hadn't developed. Perhaps today with all the advancements in medicine . . . but she didn't live. And because of that, plus a lot of other things, naturally, Timmy and I just drifted apart. I mean, we really had nothing in common except Jones Beach.

''I went a little wild after we split up,'' she said with a grimace. ''I got kind of heavy into drugs and playing around. Some mornings I woke up and didn't know where I was, who

I was with. It was that awful. I was trying to kill myself, I guess." Eileen shrugged. "And I would have if I hadn't met Todd. He was just getting over this terrible divorce, and we sort of found each other—saved each other.

"Here he was, this big, successful New York City insurance executive, with this great house in Old Westbury. I mean, I couldn't believe how lucky I was. And he loved me, too. I actually knelt down one night by the side of my bed and said my prayers, as if I was a little kid again, and thanked God for sending Todd into my life. But it wasn't God who had given me Todd. I was simply fulfilling my karma.

"Anyway, we were married on the fourteenth of September, and our son, Michael, was born the same day, two years later. It was exactly five years before that day that I had lost my little Adara.

"Michael had a perfectly fine delivery, no forceps. Yet when I saw him, when the doctor laid him on my chest, he had two marks on each side of his forehead, just like Adara. And I knew. I knew."

"Eileen, please."

Eileen nodded. "Yes, I'm certain of it, Jennifer. Michael and Adara are the same soul. That's not so strange, either. There's a psychiatrist in Boston, Dr. Susan Zawalich, who has been collecting information on just such occurrences.

"And I read about one case. It happened in Ireland. Two boys, eleven and six, were killed in an IRA bombing. Right after that, their mother got pregnant, but this time with twins. Two girls were born, and they had marks on their bodies that were exactly like the marks their older, dead brothers had had. The same kinds of marks, in the same places, the same color eyes, the same expressions, everything."

"Eileen, you're letting your imagination run away with you."

"You mean my guilt?" Eileen suggested.

"Well, maybe," Jennifer answered, caught short by Eileen's self-awareness.

"I thought about that—that I might just be projecting onto Michael what Adara had looked like. So I did some checking. I went back into the drawer where we kept all her papers, all the hospital papers, and found that little first footprint they do of all newborns. I took Adara's and I got Michael's, and I gave them to a friend of Todd's who is deputy sheriff over in Garden City, and asked him to compare the prints." She paused dramatically. "They're the same, Jennifer. My two children have identical footprints. They are the same soul."

Jennifer looked away. She didn't believe it, but perhaps Eileen needed to believe something like that. It would give her a way to justify what had happened to her firstborn.

"The unexplained, Jennifer, is just that. It is beyond our so-called rational thinking. We were brought up, taught, to have rational explanations for all actions. Well, the truth is that there are some phenomena that just don't allow themselves to be easily explained. There is always a reason, but it is sometimes beyond our comprehension. And some people, like Kathy Dart and other channelers, they have a gift—a gift from God. There's nothing satanic about any of this. Their gift is to show us that there's a logic in the randomness of events, but it's the logic of a superior power."

"You sound like a TV evangelist," Jennifer replied.

"I'm not religious, I told you that. We don't attend church, Todd or I. But I believe in God, and I believe that we're all part of a plan, a system of life. Here, let me give you one example." She leaned on the table excitedly, ticking off the references on her fingers as she talked.

"Two of our presidents who were assassinated knew they were going to be killed. Lincoln had a dream where he saw himself wrapped in funeral vestments. This was only a day or two before he was killed. And Kennedy told Jackie that if someone wanted to shoot him from a window with a rifle, then no one could stop him. But there is more than just that. Both of them died on Friday. They were both shot in the back of the head while sitting next to their wives. Both of the killers had three-part names—John Wilkes Booth and Lee Harvey Oswald. The two killers were born exactly one hundred years apart, and both were murdered before they came to trial.

"Booth shot Lincoln in a theater and fled into a warehouse.

Oswald shot Kennedy from a warehouse and ran into a theater. Kennedy had a secretary called Lincoln. Lincoln had one
called Kennedy. Lincoln was in Ford's Theater when he was
shot. Kennedy was riding in a Lincoln, made by Ford. And
both presidents were succeeded by southerners named Johnson." Eileen sat back. "This isn't just chance, Jennifer.
There's a plan. A divine plan. And I'm not alone in thinking
that Lincoln and Kennedy were the same soul, reincarnated."

For a moment they were both silent, tired from the long
afternoon of talking. Jennifer could hear muffled traffic from
the street, and the rattle of dishes and pans deep in the restaurant. It was past time to go back to the office. She glanced
at her watch.

"I don't believe in reincarnation," Jennifer announced.

"I don't see why not. All religions do, in one way or
another. What's life after death but reincarnation? All of
nature is cyclical. The raindrop that falls from the sky into
the ocean, first came from the ocean. It's the same raindrop.
It's the same soul. We only come into existence once and
are reborn throughout time. Our soul is the home of our good,
our unselfish and noble aspirations. When we seek to aid the
homeless, to stop suffering, to go to the aid of our neighbor,
that is our soul at work."

Jennifer thought of the man she had beaten to death. To
stop herself from being overwhelmed with the image, she
asked, "Well, where does this karma of yours come into it?"

"Karma is the law of consequences—of merit and demerit,
as the Buddhists say. It is a sort of justice that is measured
out to us—so much good, so much bad—in our next life in
accordance with what we did in this lifetime. In a sense we're
condemned to pay for what we did in our past lives, to keep
reliving our lives until all our bad karma has been replaced
by good karma."

"What happens then?"

"Then we gain what our souls came into life for in the
first place: eternal peace and happiness. At least that's what
Kathy, or really, Habasha, tells us."

Jennifer nodded. She knew just enough about occult teach-

ing and the paranormal to follow Eileen's argument, but what
had suddenly happened to her behind the museum? Why
there? Why then?

"I have to get back to the office," she announced, too
weary to continue.

"All right, but, Jennifer, I'm at home, you know, whenever you need to talk." She smiled, and Jennifer marveled
again at the peacefulness of Eileen's face. Jennifer saw none
of the tension that stared back at her each morning from her
own bathroom mirror. Perhaps she should buy the whole bag
of nonsense just for that look of contentment. It would be
worth it, she thought fervently, to get a good night's sleep.

"It's snowing," Eileen said with surprise when they
stepped outside the restaurant. Jennifer walked with Eileen
to where she had parked her car.

"I'm sorry you drove into town, Eileen. The expressway
home will be a nightmare."

"I never worry about things like that, not anymore," Eileen answered. "Before I got connected with Kathy and Habasha, little things like driving in snow, making dinner for
guests, meeting new people, why I'd go half out of my mind
with worrying. Not now!" She shook her head, smiling con-
fidently.

"How? How do you stop worrying, driving yourself
crazy?" Jennifer stopped walking and turned to Eileen. "I
want to know," Jennifer insisted. She was tired of all the
general talk of love, of getting in touch with one's feelings,
of meditating and using a quartz crystal for guidance and
wisdom. She wanted answers and results. "Tell me how to
live in this city without losing your humanity, and then I'll
believe in your African man."

"It's not that simple, Jennifer. I mean, you have to be
receptive."

"I'm receptive. Believe me, I'm receptive."

"Try, Jennifer. Try. Open yourself up." Eileen smiled
and her eyes glistened from the cold. "Here!" she said,
pulling a quartz crystal from her pocket. "Take this, carry it
with you. The crystal will take care of you until you've had
a chance to talk to Kathy or some other channeler. Just think

about it, about having it in your pocket." She leaned forward and kissed Jennifer lightly on the cheek. "Be caring," she whispered, and then added, *"Tiru no."*

"What?" Jennifer pulled away, frowning.

"It's Habasha's saying, meaning, 'It is good.' You are good. We are good." She waved good-bye and went into the entrance of the parking lot to pick up her car.

Jennifer kept walking east toward her office. It was snowing harder, and ahead of her the traffic stalled as cars tried to negotiate the wet city streets. Eileen would never get home, she thought guiltily.

She crossed the street, making her way between gridlocked cars, and reached into the pocket of her fur coat to feel the quartz. It was warm in her pocket, like a small heater, and having it with her did, for some odd reason, make her feel better. She wondered why.

Once in the building, Jennifer took the elevator to her floor, and went toward the ladies' room. Out of the corner of her eye, she spotted a woman waiting at the elevator, and when she unlocked the bathroom door, the woman turned abruptly and followed after her. Jennifer stopped at the entrance, suddenly apprehensive. It was a small thin white woman that she had never seen in the building, but then she realized she could take care of herself and continued into the bathroom.

There was a black maintenance woman cleaning the toilets. Jennifer stepped to the sinks, set her purse on the ledge below the mirror, and began to apply fresh makeup. She only glanced at the heavyset woman when she came out of the stall. She moved slowly, with the roll of a big ship anchored in a harbor.

"Snowing out there, ma'am?" she asked.

"Yes, it is, I'm afraid," Jennifer answered, as she applied her lipstick.

"Oh, I hates the snow. Nothing but trouble, winter." She stuck her mop in the bucket of soapy water and came toward Jennifer. Her bulk, Jennifer realized at once, had blocked her in the corner.

"Okay, honey," the black woman said softly, almost as

if she were whispering to a child, "why don't you just dump that purse out on the counter?" Her melodic voice sang sweetly in the silent room.

Jennifer stepped away from the mirror and backed up against the tile wall. Now she realized what was happening and was unable to speak, to even think of what she might do to escape. When the door of the first stall opened, she thought at once, Thank God, it was the other woman who had followed her from the elevator, but then Jennifer saw the thin woman's eyes fix on her leather bag.

"No!" Jennifer moved as the thin woman grabbed at the bag. "Please, don't," she begged.

"Get back, you white bitch!" The heavyset woman hit Jennifer on the shoulder, tossed her off balance, then seized the purse and dumped the contents into the wash basin. Her chubby short fingers sifted through the contents.

Jennifer saw herself react. She saw herself push off the gray tile wall and jump the big woman. She seized her by the throat. She held up the woman with one hand for a moment, as if she were a lioness in Africa showing off her prize. Then she banged open the metal stall door and, still with one hand, shoved the black woman's face in the toilet bowl. The water splashed from the bowl as the heavy woman thrashed under her hands, but Jennifer leaned over, pressed her full weight on the woman's shoulder, and flushed the toilet with her foot. She kept flushing until the woman stopped struggling. Then Jennifer wedged the woman's bulky body against the back wall of the stall and left her facedown in the blue toilet water.

Jennifer backed off, calming herself with deep breaths, turned to the counter and picked up the contents of her purse, slipping them into her large leather bag. She looked up into the mirror and caught a glimpse of her flushed face and blazing eyes, but then she saw the other woman, the thin white woman, had not run. She had stayed and now was coming at Jennifer with a club in her hand.

Without pausing, without a rational thought, Jennifer lunged forward and hit the woman. She caught her squarely on the bridge of the nose. Jennifer felt the bone crumble beneath her hand and saw a flash of pain in the woman's dull eyes before her blood spurted out of both nostrils in thick red jets. Jennifer tapped her on the forehead, and the dead woman slid silently to the wet tile of the bathroom floor.

Jennifer stepped over her, straightened her suit skirt, and walked out of the bathroom. She turned away from the conference room toward the bank of elevators and hit the down button. Fright swept through her, leaving her trembling. She leaned against the wall, praying for the elevator to come, praying that no one would discover that she had killed again.

She dug her hands deep into the pockets of her fur coat and felt Eileen's crystal. Slipping her fingers around the quartz, she felt its strange warmth and at once felt better. Jennifer closed her eyes and concentrated on the quartz crystal, letting its strange calming vibrations smooth her troubled soul.

$100 REWARD

RAN AWAY from my plantation, in Calhoun County, Alabama, a Negro woman named Sarah, aged 17 years, 5 feet 3 or 4 inches high, copper colored, and very straight; her teeth are good and stand a little open; thin through the shoulders, good figure, tiny features. The girl has some scars on her back that show above her shoulder blades, caused by the whip; smart for a Negro, with a pleasing smile. She was pursued into Williamsburg County, South Carolina, and there fled. I will give the above reward for her confinement by a soul driver.

Charles B. Smythe
Norfolk Times
October 6, 1851

He stood away from the dusty dock, away from the crowds, and watched the slave speculators loading the runaways. He stood out of the wind, on the wooden porch of a riverside bar, and watched for women, but there were few of them being shipped south, and those that he saw, he did not want. They were old and beaten down by age and hard labor. Still, he waited. He only wanted one; two would be more than a surprise. It would be a blessing, he thought, and smiled to himself.

On the cold December day, the few slave women he saw wore thin dresses, little underwear or petticoats, and all were barefooted. Small ice balls hung from the hems of their clothes.

He took out a se-gar, struck a match against a post, and lit the corona while he kept scanning the busy river dock.

The slaves were already being led onto the steamer, so as to be safely in the holds before passengers like himself boarded. He watched a chain line of seventy Negroes, men, women, and children, each carrying a small bundle of their belongings, being whipped up the plank, the shouts of the soul drivers carrying clearly on the frosty morning. These slaves were runaways, being taken south to be sold at auction or returned for reward money.

The Negroes walked with their heads bent, making no protests as the whip cracked across their backs. Although he did notice in passing that several of the little ones were silently weeping, he guessed that was more from fatigue than fear. These little pickaninnies had no fear, he realized, because they did not know what waited for them in the Old South. Farther away, other slaves loading goods on the ferryboat began to sing, and their strong voices rose above the snap of whips and the shouts of the soul-drivers.

Poor Ros-y, poor gal,
Poor Ros-y, poor gal;
Ros-y broke my poor heart,
Heaven shall-a be my home.

He smiled, enjoying the spiritual. He had heard it before, sung by the slaves on Sea Island. There were no finer voices in the whole world, he guessed, than the simple voices of black people. God gives each of his creatures some meager gifts, he thought, even his blacks.

Then he saw the woman and he forgot about the spirituals. Standing up, he followed her progress as she approached the docked steamer. He had seen her once before, when he had spent a night at the major's plantation, and then she had been no more than seventeen.

But it was her, he knew at once, and his heart quickened. She was in chains, and it appeared she was the sole possession of a slave driver. It was Sarah. She was headed for Calhoun County and Charles B. Smythe. But not, he told himself, if he could stop it.

The soul driver who had Sarah was a pinelander, he saw, poor white trash from Georgia. He was a small man with a yellow-mud complexion, straight features, and the simple dumb look of one baffled by his life. He appeared as if his head had been kicked by a mule. The pinelander would be no trouble, he thought with satisfaction, already feeling the flesh of the beautiful black woman naked in his arms. He moved off the porch and made his way across the crowded wharf to where the pinelander stood with his private bounty.

He'd buy her off the man for the stated reward money and save the man the trip to Calhoun County. If the pinelander questioned him, he'd simply say he was headed south to visit the major. But the soul driver wouldn't protest, he knew. Not with a hundred green-backs in his pocket.

He'd have the soul driver deliver the woman to his cabin and chain her there to the furnishings. No one would be the wiser, nor would he be seen with the girl. His mouth watered, thinking of having her, and he picked up his gait, suddenly in a rush to buy his prize.

He waited until the steamer was underway before going down to his cabin, and then when he opened the door to his rooms, he did not see her. His heart quickened, thinking the pinelander might have tricked him, gone off with his money and the slave, but then he saw that she was chained to the bedpost and was sitting in the dark corner of the small room.

The candlelight from the passageway caught only the gleam of her brown eyes. He closed the door behind him and locked them both in the darkness of the cabin.

"Hello, Sarah," he said to calm her. "You are all right, girl. I won't beat you." He did not soften his words. He never treated slaves with kindness, for he had learned they always misunderstood intentions and later thought they had some claim on his affections. He treated all slaves the same, whether he had slept with them or not. "I will unshackle you from the bed, Sarah, and I want you to strip out of those filthy rags of yours, then use the bowl and water on the counter and wash yourself, especially your privates."

He spoke calmly, not allowing her to notice his excitement. It was best with slave women that they not understand the desire he had for them.

The girl was trembling, but he did not try to soothe her fear. She knew well enough what he wanted, and it did not matter to him how she felt.

In the darkness of the tiny cabin, he lit another corona and watched the girl. She went to the washbasin and splashed the cold water onto her face, washed her hands.

"Take off those rags," he ordered when she didn't rush to do so.

She pulled the thin cotton dress over her shoulders, doing it so as not to look at him.

"All of it," he added when she did not immediately slip out of her thin petticoat.

As she pushed off her petticoat, she began to cry.

"Stop it!" he told her, and in one quick motion, he sprang off the bunk bed and slapped her face.

Sarah slid to the floor, clutching his leg, still crying. He kicked out, but her arms were clutched around his leg, and he stumbled against the wall of the cabin.

Now he swore and, reaching down, seized her shoulders and lifted her to his face.

She weighed nothing. His massive hands held her easily off the floor. Her face was inches from his. He could smell her frightened breath, smell her flesh. Her kinky hair smelled of smoke, her body of the river musk, of her own animal sweat. He loved the smell of black women, even more than he loved their flesh.

He kissed her, forcing his mouth over hers, digging

his tongue into her gasping mouth. She tried to struggle, and he quickly slipped his arms about her, pinning her naked body to him.

She cried out, but her small voice was muffled by the heavy beating of the paddleboat, the noise of the river.

"Scream," he told her, laughing, enjoying her helplessness. No one would hear her. Then he pushed Sarah away and studied her face.

She was almost as beautiful as a white woman, he thought, with the same thin features, the small mouth of an English woman, and wide, bright, chocolate brown eyes. Her skin was copper colored and smooth. There was white blood in this bitch, he thought next, and he felt her small breasts.

She gasped, and he laughed again, clinching the tiny corona in his teeth.

"You like that, huh?" he asked. "And this?" He grabbed her sex with his right hand and hoisted her up.

She screamed and went to hit him, but he struck first, knocking her across the small cabin.

"Get up, bitch!" he ordered, "and over here."

He turned to the small bed and took off his coat, then sat down and told her, "Pull these boots off, girl." He reached down and pulled his small pistol from the top of his right boot and tossed it on the soft bed covers. "Hurry, you!"

Wordless, she crept over to him, still crying from the beating, took hold of his right boot, and jerked it off.

"There," he said, "that's better."

He raised his left leg, and she pulled off the boot. She was still on the wood floor of the steamer cabin, and she carefully placed the boots together at the foot of the small bunk bed, then slowly, still in pain, she pulled herself up. She was so small and thin that her whole body did not take up any space in the tight room. He towered in it. He crowded her.

"Forget about your Major Smythe, Sarah. I have no plans to put you back in those cotton fields. I have better plans for you. Plans of my own, girl, if you have the right temperament. How would you like to visit New Orleans?"

He was pulling off his ruffled shirt, placing the pearl buttons on a tray, and then she suddenly reached, like a hungry child seizing food, and he saw she had grabbed the derringer.

"Bitch!" he shouted, reaching for her arm.

She fired at once, not looking, screaming and terrified. The single shot would have been wild, but he stumbled forward and was hit in his left eye. The bullet smashed the socket and drove up into his brain, and the blood splattered her naked body, and then the walls and ceiling of the tiny cabin as he turned and stumbled to his death, crashing against the washstand, spilling the water and breaking the large porcelain pitcher.

No one heard the shot. No one heard her cry out in fright, and she wasn't sure whether she was really crying or whether the rage and horror were only in her head. She sat for a while, trembling in the corner, watching him across the cabin. He no longer moved, and the blood spread like sewage around his body and across the floor, seeping into the wood.

Toward morning, the first song of the slaves rose from deep in the river steamer, and she awoke. The voices called to her, came to her through the vastness of the boat. It was a funeral song. Some slave had died in the hold of the steamer.

Oh, graveyard, oh, graveyard,
I'm walking through the graveyard,
Lay this body down.
Your soul and my soul
Will meet on that day,
Lay this body down.

Sarah stood and, moving so that she wouldn't see or come too close to the sprawling dead man, she retrieved her dress and petticoat and then dressed with her back

to the man she had killed. She only looked at him once
to be positive in her own mind that she didn't know him,
and then she opened the cabin door, slipped out into
the empty passageway.

On the deck she went at once to the back of the
steamer, knowing that at any moment she would be
seen, shouted at by the white men. But it was still early
and quiet on the river. Sarah could see the green shores
and the calm river. It would be a lovely day, she thought,
reaching the paddlewheel.

Someone shouted, and she glanced around and saw
a black man, one that had helped load the cargo of
slaves. He was waving, motioning her away from the
spinning wheel, and getting up off the deck to come to
her. Sarah smiled, thinking that she was a free woman
now, and that she loved her God in heaven, and that
she was glad she had killed the white man before he
violated her. Then she jumped—as any young girl might,
full of life and energy—into the twisting of the giant paddlewheel and disappeared down into the foamy white
and deadly-churning paddlewheel water.

9

"I THINK I KILLED them," Jennifer told Tom, holding the teacup in both trembling hands. The cup was warm and comforting. She sipped the tea slowly, letting it warm her whole body. She was in Tom's apartment, sitting in the corner of his leather couch. She had telephoned him to meet her at once at his place.

Tom was in a chair on the other side of a glass coffee table. He listened patiently as she described what had happened in the foundation bathroom. He kept interrupting with questions, and he scribbled notes on a legal pad while she talked, as if she were his client instead of his lover.

"Don't," she told him.

"Don't what?" He kept writing, using the gold Cross pen she had given him.

"Don't take notes. It makes me feel like a criminal."

"You're not a criminal unless you're convicted." He finished a note, then sat back in the soft, light brown leather chair and watched her for a moment. She knew what was coming. He was framing his statement, trying to make it sound less threatening, but before he could speak, she stood and walked to the windows of the apartment, staring out across the Hudson River at the bleak industrial shores of New Jersey. The day had cleared. It had stopped snowing, and a hard-edged blue sky had reappeared. "We're going to have to talk to the police," he said behind her, trying to sound casual.

"No!" She felt a wedge of panic and reached out to touch the windowpane with the palm of her hand, as if to let the cold glass calm her. "No," she whispered.

"We're looking at justifiable homicide," he went on, speaking in the same soft, measured tones.

She had first met him on a grand jury trial, and she remembered how she had been captivated by the way he cross-examined witnesses. He was like a bird of prey, a dark handsome falcon hovering, circling, closing in. Slowly, softly, without raising his voice or seeming to intrude, he had backed each poor witness into a corner, and then stripped him bare, exposing the lies.

"No!" Jennifer shouted, turning. "I won't."

"Honey. Jennifer, please," Tom said. "You just told me. There are two, maybe three people dead. We've got to get on top of this situation. What happened to you has got to be drug related—the Colombians are on to you. If it isn't, if we've got a simple mugging, you're still okay. I mean, you'll be viewed as a female Bernhard Goetz. No one is going to send you to jail. Look. We go to the police. We start a public relations campaign. No jury—"

"But I'm not Goetz!"

"Jennifer, you've admitted to me that you killed a person. And you may have just killed two others." He nodded toward uptown. "I'm an officer of the court, for God's sake. I can't—"

"Please! Please!" She went toward where she had dropped her coat on the chair. "I'm sorry I came to you. I'm sorry I compromised your goddamn position." She was crying as she grabbed for her coat.

Tom leapt to his feet, swearing, and seized her arm.

"You're going to sit down here, Jennifer, and we're going to prepare a defense. You're a wanted woman. I'm not going

to let you damage your life and career." He pulled her away
from the door, but she jerked loose from him.

"Leave me alone, Tom. I'll work this out myself."

"Jennifer, sweetie, you're not being rational." He moved
toward her with his arms out, as if to embrace her.

She backed away. "Don't touch me."

The tone of her voice stopped him. She saw the sudden
fear and apprehension in his eyes, and that pleased her.

"Please, Jennifer, you need help," he offered, but kept
his distance.

Jennifer realized she was no longer in control of her own
body. Her heart was pounding, and she felt a surge of strength
in her limbs. My God, she thought. I am a monster.

She looked up, into the mirror behind Tom's couch, and
stared at herself. Her own brown eyes looked frightened, not
enraged. Her face was ashen, and what makeup she had put
on that morning had worn off. Her hair needed to be combed.
It frightened her to see how unkempt she looked, but her face
wasn't disfigured. She didn't look like a monster. She took
a deep breath.

"Jennifer, are you okay?" Tom whispered, alarmed at the
expression on her face.

"I don't know," she confessed.

"What happened just then?"

"I don't know. I get angry, enraged, and then . . ." She
started to cry, deep sobs, but this time Tom came over and
wrapped his arms around her. She collapsed in his embrace
and let herself be comforted.

"I've got to get you to bed," he finally said, after her sobs
had abated. He leaned over and easily picked her up. After
settling her into his bed, he pulled a heavy quilt up over her.
"Are you warm enough?" he asked, arranging the quilt over
her shoulders.

Jennifer nodded and pulled her legs up. She cuddled against
his pillow and seized his hand in her fingers. "Don't leave
me," she pleaded.

"I won't," he whispered, sitting on the edge of the bed.
She kissed his fingers, then laid her cheek against the

warmth of his palm and fell asleep still holding on to her lover's hand.

When Jennifer woke, the room was dark and silent. She came awake slowly as if she were swimming to the surface of her life. Then she recognized her surroundings, realized she was in Tom's apartment, and immediately grew apprehensive. She sat up and swung her feet over the side of the bed.

She heard voices. Or at least one voice. Without her shoes, she moved quickly and quietly to the closed bedroom door and pressed her head against it to listen. Silence. Carefully, she opened the door. The empty living room was glowing like a Vermeer, with the clean yellow light of the winter sunset.

She noticed that Tom was in his office beyond the living room. She saw his shadow as he paced in the small room. He was probably on the phone. He always paced while talking on the telephone. She crossed the room, her feet silent on the hardwood parquet floor. At the office door, she paused and looked inside.

He was standing at his desk, looking out the window at the Hudson River. The sunset froze him in profile, softened the edges of his dark features. He was listening to someone, then whispering his replies. When he turned to pace back across the office, she stepped to one side of the door and stood in shadow. Her heart was in her throat.

He came to the threshold and stood looking across the long, darkening room to the doorway of his bedroom.

"No," he said to someone, "she is still asleep. Yes, I understand. Yes, I'm letting her rest." He stepped away from the open doorway. She heard the leather of his chair stretch as he sat down, and when she chanced a glimpse inside, she saw that he had swung his legs up over the edge of his desk and was leaning back in the chair, running his fingers through his hair. It was one nervous habit that always annoyed her. It left his hair standing up.

She moved stealthily from the dark corner to the other side of the living room, forcing herself to be calm. After picking

up her fur coat and purse from the chair, she grabbed her
boots from where she had left them by the front door. She
moved quickly across the living room, through the swinging
door, and into the dark kitchen.

She knew there was a service door off the kitchen, and
behind it the back stairs and an elevator. She had used the
exit before to do laundry in the basement.

Jennifer slipped off the chain lock and stepped into the
lighted back stairwell. Her heart was racing. With trembling
hands, she slowly pulled the door closed behind her. She
kept imagining she heard Tom running after her, grabbing
her before she could escape. She pressed the elevator button
and then, too frightened to stand and wait for it, took off
down the back stairs, her stockinged feet slipping on the
concrete steps.

She reached the lobby level and stopped in the stairwell
to slip on her coat and shoes. Then she opened the heavy
steel door and looked out at the empty lobby. She saw the
doorman outside under the entrance awning, helping a woman
out of a taxi. Jennifer stepped far enough into the lobby to
see that the front elevators were closed. Tom had not yet
discovered that she was gone. Running to the entrance, she
grabbed the now empty taxi and, brushing past the old woman
and the doorman, slid into the backseat and slammed the
door. "Uptown!" she shouted.

"Where, lady?" He picked up his clipboard to note the
address.

"Uptown. Hurry, please." She glanced at the entrance of
the building, half expecting Tom to come barreling out after
her.

"West Side or East, lady?" the driver asked, still waiting
and watching her in the mirror.

"Uptown! The East Side." Jennifer was trembling.
"Hurry!" She glanced around again. The doorman and the
old woman were moving slowly toward the glass door. She
didn't see Tom.

The taxi finally moved. The driver steered with one hand
as he put aside the clipboard.

"You got to tell me, lady. The East Side is a big place."

He laughed, trying to make a joke of her indecision. The car bounced out of the apartment building's cul-de-sac and turned onto the side street.

Jennifer sank into the seat, exhausted by her fear. She was thankful that she had gotten away from Tom, but she didn't know what to tell the taxi driver. Where in New York City would "a wanted woman" be safe?

She opened her purse to take out a tissue and wipe her eyes, and there, stuffed into the cluttered purse, she saw the newspaper clipping she had meant to give Eileen, the one about Phoebe Fisher, the channeler. She pulled it from her purse and scanned it, looking for an address, then leaned forward and spoke to the driver.

"I've changed my mind. Take me up to the West Side." Now she knew where to go and who might help her.

10

AT SEVENTY-NINTH AND Broadway Jennifer got out of
the cab and called information for Dr. Fisher's telephone
number. Then, standing at the pay phone, with the wind from
the river blowing across the avenue, she called her. As the
wind sliced into her, cutting between muscle and bone, she
stamped her feet on the packed snow, trying to keep them
warm.

It was only six o'clock, and the sidewalks were crowded,
but still, Jennifer felt vulnerable. When a police car halted
at the traffic light, she turned her face into the booth, but she
was convinced they had spotted her, that the composite photo
was already out and the cops were searching for a blond white
woman, five foot seven, wearing a full-length fur coat, wool
jacket and skirt, and a wool turtleneck. She pulled the collar
of her coat up around her face and listened to the phone ring.

"Please, dear God, please let her be home," she said out
loud. When a woman did say hello after a half-dozen rings,
Jennifer spoke rapidly. She explained about reading the article, about having the strange reaction to the Ice Age display.
She told her about seeing Kathy Dart, and about the thirteen-
mile run out along the C & O Canal. She stopped herself

before she mentioned her attack on the mugger near the museum, and the women at the foundation.

When she stopped talking, she was out of breath, and crying. She couldn't stop her tears, couldn't keep herself from sobbing into the phone.

"Come see me at once," the woman said, giving Jennifer her address.

"Thank you," Jennifer whispered, wiping the tears from her face. "I'm coming." When she finally hung up the phone, the traffic light had changed, and the police car was gone. Jennifer ran out into the street, and turned north toward Eighty-second Street and the home of Phoebe Fisher.

"Welcome," a small woman said, pushing open the iron gate that guarded the basement apartment. "You were very close to me when you telephoned. I could feel your presence. I am Dr. Fisher." She stepped back, and Jennifer saw that Phoebe Fisher was lame, that she used a thin, silver cane to support herself.

"I ran," Jennifer replied, still gasping for breath as she followed the woman into the warm apartment.

Phoebe Fisher was dressed like a teenager in a tight black leotard and a wrap-around black skirt, with a bright red scarf knotted around her long thin neck. She was very small and very beautiful, with coarse black hair already streaked with gray. Her pure, white skin was the color of bisque pottery. Jennifer felt large and ungainly beside her in the low-ceilinged apartment.

"You have a fireplace!" she exclaimed as she entered the living room. The blazing fire made her feel immensely better.

"Yes, and I'll make you a cup of tea, and we'll talk." Phoebe Fisher smiled at Jennifer. Her sculpted lips were neatly sketched into her tiny face. And when she smiled, her mouth widened and made her seem even younger. Jennifer liked her at once. She felt safe here. Maybe Phoebe Fisher would be able to help her. The fear that had been building and spreading through her body all afternoon eased away, leaving her suddenly lightheaded and very tired.

"Here," Phoebe directed, touching the deeply cushioned

chair close to the fireplace, "come sit down and get comfortable. We can get to know each other a bit while I make us a fresh pot of tea. Would herbal be all right? I'm afraid I don't have anything else."

"Thank you. Anything. I'm just fine, thankful to be here." Her declarations surprised her. She was never this open with strangers, but now she felt the need to share her emotions, to tell this woman everything.

"Now, Jennifer, how did you meet Kathy Dart?" Phoebe asked, standing behind the kitchen counter that divided the rooms as she made the pot of tea. "And what were your feelings about her?"

Jennifer told the whole story as Phoebe made tea, then came back to sit beside her in front of the fire. Jennifer told her about Eileen Gorman and their chance meeting, about her jog along the C & O Canal and what had happened to her in the museum. She explained that she had known, really known, when that hut in the Ukraine had been built.

"What is wrong with me?" Jennifer asked, crying.

"There is nothing wrong with you, Jennifer. Nothing. You are a very fortunate person. A gifted person. It's your electromagnetic frequency, that's all." Phoebe was smiling. "We share it, my dear. We are both gifted that way." She reached out and touched Jennifer's knee.

"I don't understand," Jennifer whispered.

"Of course you don't. I didn't either when it first happened. None of us know, really, but we learn. You are experiencing the first flashes of mediumship. To put it in academic terms, you have already gone through what is termed the first stage, conceptualization, and now you are in stage two. Preparation." Phoebe paused for a moment, staring thoughtfully up at Jennifer. "Welcome to the gang." Her soft brown eyes widened and glowed.

"Well, what is this gang? I feel like my body has been taken over or something."

"You're right. It has," Phoebe said, "but you're joining people like Emperor Wu, from the Han dynasty in China, and the Greek Dionysian cults of the sixth century B.C., the Celtic bards in the British Isles, not to mention Jesus Christ and his disciples. You're in good company, Jennifer." When she saw the uncomprehending look on Jennifer's face, she asked, "Would you like me to try and explain how it all comes about? Why this is suddenly happening to you now, here in New York City in 1987?"

Jennifer nodded emphatically.

"Most of what we call mediumship, or channeling, is the product of an arrangement that is made between two bodiless entities—the person who is going to be the channel and the entity or consciousness that is going to be channeled. After that, one entity is incarnated in a body and begins life without even remembering the agreement. Life continues normally until the person gets to a place where he or she does remember. It's called an encounter, and it's different for everyone."

"But I didn't go through any encounter," Jennifer protested. "I was just going on with my life, and then, wham, this!"

"I don't know yet what happened, Jennifer. I don't know enough about you yet, but later perhaps, if you are comfortable, I might try to channel to see what we can learn. I'm sure you were experiencing, or suffering, something. . . . And then your frequency connected somehow."

"How did it happen to you? What was your encounter?" She slipped out of her chair and sat down beside Phoebe on the small rug. "This is a Dessie rug, isn't it?" she heard herself saying.

"Yes, it is. But how did you know about them? They're from Ethiopia and very rare." Phoebe laughed. "But of course you know. That is the wonder of being a medium."

"No, I don't know." Jennifer was shaking her head, afraid again. "I mean, I know this is a Dessie rug, but I don't know why I know it."

Phoebe shrugged. "That's it. You've always known. You learned it in another life, and you have carried that bit of information tucked away in your subconsciousness, from one age to the next."

"Oh God, I can't believe this." Jennifer dropped her head into her open palms, held herself for a moment, then threw back her head, rubbing away her tears with her hands. It was

very warm near the fire, but she didn't want to move. For
some reason she didn't want to be away from Phoebe Fisher,
who was silently watching her, smiling sweetly as if she had
all the time in the world.

"Okay, how?" Jennifer asked. "Tell me what happened
with you. That might help me understand what's going on
with me."

"Well, about three years ago, at two different times within
a two-month span, I had very close physical sightings of
Dance's spaceship here over New York City. What I didn't
understand then was that that was his way of signaling me,
sort of tapping my subconscious memory. But it wasn't until
my experience in Central Park—the one that was written
about in the *Times*—that I really began to investigate. I did
all sorts of research into metaphysical theories, and eventually
I came across ideas on mediumship.

"Then I met several mediums, and one of the entities who
came to those meetings offered to teach anyone who was
interested how to channel. Even then I didn't think I would
devote my life to channeling. I was working as an editor at
Redbook magazine. I had a career. I had a boyfriend who I
was living with, and who I thought I loved. I was happy. Or
thought I was.

"But it was in that class, in a receptive state, under the
guidance of the other entity, that Dance made the telepathic
connection. And as soon as he did, the memory of that previous agreement came back to me: who he was, who I was,
what the ship sightings and the experience in Central Park
had meant. All of this that had been blocked out of my
consciousness came back to me."

She smiled over at Jennifer. Now it was dark in the room,
and the firelight cast their shadows against the far wall of the
apartment.

"When I saw you in the doorway, I knew," Phoebe went
on softly. "I knew that you had had a similar experience.
The only difference is that the entity you're channeling is
from the past, and Dance is from the future."

"You mean he tells you what's going to happen a hundred
years from now?"

Phoebe shook her head. "Dance isn't of this planet—he's an extraterrestrial, which makes him different. Most channels—like Kathy Dart—allow discarded consciousnesses, which have been alive and no longer are, to come into their bodies. Those consciousnesses have no physical entity, but Dance does—it's just not like ours. His is an extraterrestrial consciousness, and he and I are linked telepathically."

"Why is he here? Why is he doing this to you?"

Phoebe shrugged. "I'm not sure, really. I think he is coming through now to assist us in learning that we have the answers we need, to live the lives we want to live.

"He does not appear physically, because he wants us to focus on the message rather than the messenger, which is where we'd focus, of course, if we saw this little green man walking around." She laughed. "Dance is channeling through me so the message will stand on its own. And we can decide whether the message works for us or not.

"What he has to share in no way implies that he thinks his world is better than ours, just that he—they!—are different from us. They recognize that we are learning a lot, that we are beginning to explore things that are relatively new to our society.

"Is his name really Dance?"

"No, they don't have names in their society because they are telepathic. I call him Dance because that was what he seemed to be doing when I first saw him hovering over Central Park. He seemed to be dancing before my eyes."

"But I'm not like you. No one is trying to speak through me. I just have these feelings, these weird, frightening experiences, and suddenly—"

"Because, Jennifer," Phoebe continued, "you have been trapped inside your own logical, organized, institutional world, and your so-called 'logic' has kept you from the great wealth of knowledge within what we call the spiritual world.

"There's nothing strange about psychic ability. It's simply survival. It's how our minds work to keep us functioning in the world. The reason we can see is so that we don't fall off a cliff. The reason we can taste is so that we don't ingest poison. All of our senses are keyed to survival, including the psychic sense.

"However, we know our physical senses. The mystical is what we do not know. We have to surrender to this experience and enter into it."

"I guess that's my problem. I'm afraid to surrender to the mystical world," Jennifer admitted.

Phoebe nodded. "You know, Einstein used to get up every morning and say that he didn't know anything. He believed that everything he knew could be disproven at any time. He wanted to treat his mind like a piece of blank paper. Let me experience! Let me learn all over again! That's what the New Age philosophy is all about."

Phoebe sat up straight. One leg was pulled up underneath herself, the other sticking straight out. Using her long, thin fingers to tick off the names, she listed the great mediums from history.

"Joan of Arc heard voices telling her to go to the king of France. She was then thirteen years old. Joseph Karo, a fifteenth-century Talmudic scholar, channeled a source called 'maggid.' Saint Teresa of Avila and Saint John of the Cross, both Christian mystics, were channelers. Joseph Smith channeled an angel named Moroni and, based on what the angel said, took his people to the promised land and founded the Mormon church. The list is endless."

"But I can't—"

"And didn't you just tell me you were suddenly able to run thirteen miles after you saw Kathy Dart?"

"Oh, I don't know." Jennifer shook her head and stared into the blazing fire. "I don't know anything," she whispered.

"Yes, you do. You know everything, and now you're getting a glimpse of what the world as a whole has to offer. It's frightening to realize your true potential. No one can blame you for not going forward, for saying: That's enough. I'm comfortable. I'm happy. But are you really happy with the limits of rational thought? Jennifer, give yourself a chance at least to experience life."

"How do I know it's true? How do I know you're to be trusted?"

"Begin with yourself. Trust yourself first. Ask yourself why you are feeling these emotions."

"I don't want to do this!" Jennifer interrupted. "Don't you understand? I don't want to be a channel! I don't want anyone, or anything, to take me over, to use my body. I want it to stop!" Again Jennifer kept herself from saying more, from telling Phoebe how she killed, once she was seized with the brutal power.

Phoebe kept silent. She picked up one of the fire irons and poked at the burning logs till the dry wood sparked and hissed into a burst of sudden flame.

"What is it?" Jennifer asked, realizing the woman had more to say.

"I'm not sure there is anything you can do," Phoebe said softly, then looked up at Jennifer. The sweet smile was gone from her face. "This entity wants to be heard. He, or she, wants to be channeled through your body, and I'm afraid there's nothing you can do to stop it. Just as I could not stop Dance from coming to this world to teach, you cannot stop your entity. The spirit's time has come, Jennifer, and you have been selected to serve its needs in this lifetime."

Jennifer looked away and stared at the fire. Okay, she thought, but Phoebe's Dance had come to teach. Her entity, Jennifer now realized, had come to kill.

11

JENNIFER FLUNG HER ARM out and hit the bedside lamp, knocking it to the floor. The phone was ringing. As she reached for it, she knocked the receiver off the hook. The illuminated dial of her digital clock read 5:24 A.M.

She picked the phone up from the floor and said angrily into the receiver, "This better be good." But the line went dead.

"Shit!" She slammed down the receiver. Fully awake now, she sat on the edge of the bed and rubbed her eyes. The heat was coming on in the building, and the steam pipes clanged. She knew she wouldn't be able to get back to sleep. Telephone calls in the middle of the night always made her think someone was watching from an apartment across the street or from a darkened phone booth at the corner.

She pulled on soft slippers and shuffled across the dark room. As she passed the mirror on the back of the closet door, she glanced at herself. As a child, she had been afraid of the dark, and the only way she could calm herself was to rush to a mirror. Her shrink had later told her that she'd had a low self-image. No, she had answered back, she was just afraid of the dark.

She went into the kitchen, turning on lights as she walked. Well, she told herself, if she was up, she was up. As she filled the kettle with cold water for coffee, she reached over and turned on the small Sony on the kitchen counter. Maybe she would make pancakes, she told herself, and cook sausages. She'd have a big breakfast and forget about running and staying in shape for one morning in her life.

She had opened the refrigerator and was pulling out butter and milk and eggs, only half listening to the all-night cable channel she was tuned into when she realized she was hearing Kathy Dart's voice.

Jennifer stood up and turned toward the set. Kathy Dart was sitting cross-legged, facing the camera. She was not channeling, but talking to the group of people who also sat cross-legged, in a tight circle.

"It seems to me," she was saying, sweeping her gaze around the circle of people, "that there are two generally accepted views of why we are all on earth.

"One view I'll call the religious. It tells us that we are creations of God, and damaged creations at that; that we are born into the world with sin and must spend our lives proving our value to God so that at death we can be accepted into heaven.

"The second notion about life is the modern view. It explains that we are here today because of a series of chance occurrences in space. The big bang. The small bang. The survival of the fittest. Whatever you want to call it! Every few years we are given a new explanation.

"The trouble with these two views of life is that they exclude a lot. They cheat us out of all the possibilities of our wonderful minds."

Kathy Dart paused and looked around the circle. Watching her, Jennifer noticed again how beautiful she was. It wasn't really her looks, but the calmness of her face. No wonder Eileen responded to her, Jennifer thought. Kathy Dart had such a trusting face.

"We must remember that the mind and the brain are not the same thing," Kathy Dart said next. "The brain is a physical organ, while the mind is simply energy that flows through this organ. As human beings, as bodies, we cannot be everywhere. But the mind can travel, relocate, be somewhere else, as when we have an out-of-body experience. For example, we all know how it is possible for the body to be on the operating table while the mind is up on the ceiling, looking down, watching the surgeon operate.''

"Yes,'' Jennifer said aloud. She stopped breaking eggs into a plastic bowl and turned her full attention to the screen. "Yes,'' she said again.

"We do have other levels of reality. We daydream, hallucinate, sleep, dream, and all have some sort of mystical, or psychic, communication with others.'' She leaned forward. "I will tell you a true story. It has happened to each of you. You are in a restaurant, you are on the street, you think of someone, perhaps a friend, someone you once knew in another place and at another time. His name pops suddenly into your mind, and then within moments, you see him. He suddenly appears, as if out of nowhere!''

She leaned back and smiled knowingly, and then the camera panned the small circle of people, and they, too, were smiling, in recognition of what Kathy Dart was saying.

Jennifer set the eggs aside and pulled the small kitchen stool up close to the television set. Opening up the pad she used to jot down her shopping list, she waited for the woman to continue.

"Perhaps the best way to understand what is happening to us,'' Kathy Dart went on, "is to think of our psyches, our minds, as houses with many rooms. In our everyday lives, we use only one or two of those rooms, but we do not inhabit the attic or basement, we do not know what is happening at night down the long dark hallways.''

She motioned to the group, gesturing back and forth with one hand. "We speak to each other on one level, but that is a limitation. It forces us to see our world as having only one level, one reality.

"When I go into a trance, it is as if I am moving to another room in my psychic house. There it is possible for me to have a different state of consciousness, a different persona, different knowledge. It is possible for me to speak directly to Habasha, and to have him communicate directly with you. We came naked into this world, but our psyches, our spirits, came with the collected wisdom and knowledge of all time. Plato said that the soul has been 'born again many times, and having seen all things that exist, whether in this world or in the world below, has knowledge of them all.' "

Then, as the camera closed in on her face, Kathy Dart grimaced and added wryly, "So why, you might ask, aren't we rich?"

Her audience laughed.

"We're not rich," Kathy said, "because we have in our present life only a certain amount of all the knowledge we possess, knowledge that Plato says we are remembering. Nothing is new under the sun, as the saying goes. We are only remembering what we already know but have forgotten.

"Artists tells us that they create by intuition, by bursts of creativity. What is creativity?" She paused to study the circle of students. "The act of creation is drawing from within, from our heart of hearts, from the knowledge we already know. We create what we have already created."

The kitchen telephone rang, startling Jennifer. She looked at it for a moment, puzzled by its ringing. It was not yet six-thirty.

"Jenny?" The man's voice was soft and far away.

"David? Is that you? What is it? What's wrong?" She suddenly felt cold and shivered in her wool nightgown. A window had opened, she thought. Or a door.

"Oh, Jenny," David whispered. He began to cry.

"What is it, David? Has something happened?" Even as she spoke, Jennifer knew.

"She's gone, Jenny. She's gone. I found her a few minutes ago. I had gotten up to go to the bathroom . . . there was a light under her bedroom door." He was crying, stumbling over his words. "She had taken an overdose of Valium. It was my prescription. She had said she was having trouble sleeping. I had no idea." He kept explaining, telling Jennifer the suicide was all his fault.

"It's not your fault, David," Jennifer said, raising her

voice so he would hear her through his tears. "Stop blaming yourself! I understand! Have you called the police?"

"Yes, yes, I've done all that." He was suddenly angry. "They're here. I have a cop in my goddamn living room. They won't remove the body until the coroner comes and signs the death certificate."

"What can I do? I don't want you to be alone."

"You can't take the subway at this hour."

"I'll call a car service. Don't worry."

He started to cry again. "Why, Jenny, why in God's name would she do this?"

"We'll talk about it when I get there. Hang up so I can get dressed and call a car. 'Bye, David. Oh God, I'm so sorry."

"Thank you, Jenny. Thank God for you," David whispered. He sounded like a little boy.

When Jennifer hung up the receiver, her hand was trembling. She felt the cold again, a swift rush of wind, and from the dark hallway of the apartment, she could see across the living room, through the front windows and into the street. Dawn was breaking, and the very pale light of early morning was filling the dark corners.

Then she saw Margit in the room. She was standing by the door to the kitchen, smiling, motioning that everything was all right, that she was all right. She looked a dozen years younger, and beautiful in a way that Jennifer had never seen her. She moved through the dark apartment, her body a silver envelope of light. She was wearing a white dress, a long white dress that flowed around her and spread across the floor and furniture.

"Margit?" Jennifer asked, terrified by the sight of her friend.

"Hello, Jennifer," Margit said, but she did not speak. Yet Jennifer knew just what she was saying, knew what she wanted.

"Let me hold you, please," Jennifer asked, stepping toward her.

Margit shook her head. "I'm sorry, Jenny, but you can't, not now."

"Margit, what happened?"

"David . . . David poisoned me."

"Oh no. Oh God, no!"

"It's all right, Jennifer. It's all right." She kept smiling.

"But why? Because of that woman?"

"It was more than that. I had money. My family's money, and he wanted it. Jenny, he's a very unhappy man."

"Margit, this isn't possible. I'm not seeing you. I can't be." She tried to turn away but was frightened now to look away from the misty figure of Margit Engle.

"I've seen your brother Danny, Jenny. We've talked, and he wants you to know he loves you very much and that you can't blame yourself for what happened to him. He is very happy."

"You saw Danny?" Jennifer exclaimed. She began to smile. "Let me talk to him, please. Let me come close to you, Margit."

"It's not time, not yet. But I've come to warn you. . . ."

"Warn me?"

"Be careful, Jenny. Someone wants to hurt you."

"Who?"

"A woman. She was once your friend, Jenny. In another time, she was once your friend."

"Who, Margit?" Jennifer whispered.

Margit shook her head, whispered that she couldn't, and then her image began to fade from sight. Jennifer did not cry out to hold her on earth. She watched the image dissolve and then disappear. And then Jennifer realized it was daylight, and she was standing in the bright sun. Margit was gone.

She turned from the window and walked back into her bedroom. The sun filled that room, too, spreading light across the unmade bed. Jennifer glanced at the digital clock. It read 11:47. She had been talking to Margit for over five hours.

BOOK TWO

BOOK TWO

Each of us is responsible for everything to everyone else.
                                    —*Fyodor Dostoevski*

". . . It is absolutely necessary that the soul should be healed and purified, and if this does not take place during its life on earth, it must be accomplished in future lives."
                                    —*Saint Gregory I*

12

TOM GRABBED JENNIFER WHEN she came up out of the subway at Columbus Circle.

"We've got to talk," he told her, seizing her wrist.

"You've heard?" she asked.

"About Margit? Yes. David phoned me yesterday. Where were you? I've been calling."

"At home."

"You didn't pick up. I went to Brooklyn; you didn't answer."

"I didn't want to talk to you."

"Jesus Christ, Jenny, what's happening? Why did you sneak out of my place?"

They were standing at the top of the subway escalator and morning-rush-hour commuters were pushing past, glancing at the obviously angry couple but keeping their distance.

"You were calling the police when you thought I was asleep."

"I was not," he said outraged. "I was calling your office. Talking to What's-his-name . . . Handingham."

"Come on," Jennifer said, taking his hand. "Let's get a cup of coffee."

* * *

"Margit and I talked for over five hours," Jennifer explained to Tom, "and when I called David back, it was almost noon. The police were still there. Margit's body was on the floor of her bedroom, where she told me she had died, and everyone was waiting for the coroner to come. Tom, I'm telling you: David killed her!"

Tom put down his pastry and stared at her.

"Jennifer, she died of an overdose. The coroner found evidence in her body. David told me. Besides, she died at approximately five o'clock yesterday morning. How could you have seen her? What are you talking about anyway?"

"She had traces of Valium in her stomach. Of course! David got that for her, but he wasn't stupid enough to poison her with it. He's a doctor; he's smarter than that."

"Well then, how did he kill her? How did Margit say she died?" He was treating her as if she were a child who needed to be humored. She kept her voice slow and steady. "He killed Margit with lidocaine. It's used in emergency situations to slow down the heartbeat where there's been a coronary seizure."

"I know what lidocaine is. But how do you know?"

"I don't. I don't know any of this. But Margit does—or did. She was a nurse before she married David. That's how they met. She told me about the lidocaine." Jennifer leaned over the restaurant table and continued in a whisper: "It comes in a disposable syringe called a Flex-O-Jet. There's one gram of lidocaine in twenty-five cc's of fluid. When a person has a seizure in a hospital, they inject it directly into a bag of sugar and water that the patient is getting intravenously. You never inject lidocaine directly into the vein in a concentrated form. But that's what David did. She had fallen asleep in bed, and David came into the bedroom, injected the lidocaine, and then pulled her onto the floor, so it would look as if she was trying to reach the door."

"And Margit told you all this?"

Jennifer nodded. "When we talked, she was in her afterlife—that's a nonphysical reality we all enter following death. All souls or spirits go there between incarnations."

The waiter returned to refill their coffee cups, and they both fell silent until he stepped away. Then Tom spoke without looking up. "I think maybe you should talk to someone, Jennifer."

"I agree." Jennifer sighed, feeling relieved. "Do you know the detective on the case? What precinct is it, anyway?"

"Jen, I'm not talking about cops. I'm talking about a doctor. A shrink."

Jennifer stared at him. "Tom, we're talking about a murderer."

"Sure—who was also her husband, and your doctor, and a physician on the staff of New York Hospital. Honey, you've been under a lot of stress. And I haven't helped matters with my behavior about getting married. I was thinking that maybe we should fly down to the Caribbean for a few days and let all this blow over. My case against the dealers will go down soon. I'll have time off. And you can get a long rest." He spoke as if he had decided to take over her life.

Jennifer stopped listening. Tom didn't believe her, but how could he? She had been on an immense journey in the last few days, and she had left him far behind. She could barely believe it all herself—but when she doubted, she remembered Margit and the envelope of light around her, and she believed again.

Tom was watching her. "Jenny, you're not well," he said softly. "You have to understand that. It's not a sign of weakness. I know you. I know how you never want to be caught with your guard down, but all of us have some bad patches. You're going to be okay."

"I'm okay!"

"No, Jenny, you're not," he answered patiently. "You're going through something, I don't know what. I wish to God I did, but, honey, I love you, and I'm going to take care of you, regardless of what you say. Okay?" He smiled, trying to dull the hard edge of his pronouncement.

Jennifer nodded. She had learned in the last few weeks that it was never any good to argue with Tom; it was better to go around him.

"So you'll come to the Caribbean with me?"

She nodded. "But I have to go back to my office. You go downtown; I'll come and meet you as soon as I make my arrangements with Handingham."

"I've already talked to him about it," Tom said.

"You did?" She pulled away, looking surprised.

"Yes, that's what I called him about the day you thought I was on the phone to the police. I said you'd been under some stress, and he agreed you could have some medical leave. It's no big deal, honey, your job will be there when you return."

"Well," she said, controlling her anger, "then you can also call the coroner and ask him to go over the autopsy results again."

He shook his head. "Darling, I love you. I think you're wonderful, but there's no case there. I can't do anything. You can't do anything. I know you're upset, but I'm telling you, your mind is playing tricks on you. Lidocaine stays in the blood, in the skin tissues. If it was there, they would have picked up traces in the autopsy."

"Sure, if they were like the doctors on TV. But they're not. Why is the mayor always firing coroners if they're so good?"

Tom was being rational, but she no longer trusted his cool logic, his faith in the system, in the rational world. She thought of what Phoebe Fisher had told her, how people were trapped inside their logical world and couldn't accept the mystical. But she wasn't. Not any longer. She had seen Margit in her living room, and she realized there was only one person now in New York City who would listen to her story and believe what she had to say.

ECCLESIASTICAL INVESTIGATION
RELATING TO THE VISIONS AND
MIRACULOUS CLAIMS OF VERONICA
BORROMEO
MISCELLANEA MEDICEA 413
THE YEAR 1621
STATE ARCHIVE OF FLORENCE

Account of the visions, miraculous claims, and sins of the flesh as related by the Abbess Veronica Borromeo to the Papal Nuncio, Giuseppe Bonomo, Bishop of Siena, on the thirteenth day of September, 1621.

On the First Friday of Lent of the year 1620, while in bed between the fourth and sixth hours of the night, I contemplated the sufferings of Our Lord the Most Holy Jesus Christ, and our Master appeared to me in the flesh, holding in His bleeding hands His most Holy Cross. Our Saviour was alive, and he asked me if I would suffer His own crucifixion and death.

I made the sign of the Cross, thinking that the Devil had come upon me, but our Lord said to me that He was God and he wished me to suffer His death. He instructed me to get out of my cot and lay upon the stones in the form of the cross, as He wished to implant the wounds of the crucifixion upon my body.

When I followed as He had told me, I felt great pains in my limbs and breast and saw that blood was oozing from my flesh, but afterward, I felt only peace and contentment.

During the following week, from day to day, each

121

morning, I studied my limbs and saw nothing, no marks or signs, but on the Friday next, from twelve until three, the hours that our Lord hung upon the cross, I, too, bled from my hands and feet, and from the right side of my breast, and the nuns of the convent came and ministered to me, and I begged them, beseeched them in our Lord's name not to tell the laity of what had occurred to me here within our monastery walls.

Each Friday I joyfully suffered as our Lord had suffered, and then on Easter Sunday, after our Saviour had risen and ascended into Heaven, I was praying in the cloister garden when suddenly there appeared to me an angel dressed in a blue garment. He had long white and gilded wings, and he said to me, "Our Lord is well pleased by your sufferings, and He wishes you to surrender your body to him again, living on in this world the life of a saint, and suffering, as the saints have, for the greater glory of God."

Afraid that I was being sorely tempted by the Devil himself, I fell upon my knees and begged for God's guidance. The white angel took me to our church, to our humble priest, Father Giovannetto, who told me on behalf of Jesus Christ that I was not being deceived by the Devil, and I knelt before him and received the Holy Eucharist. The angel revealed himself to me again and said that his name was Gabriel, the archangel Gabriel, who brought great joy to the Blessed Virgin Mary, and that he would stay with me now in my hours and days of great need.

From that day forth I suffered many travails, as I had wished. I was visited by the Devil in the form of a handsome young man who sought to corrupt my body and soul. In my vigils in our chapel, the stones beneath my bare feet were set ablaze by the Devil and his minions, but still I kept the name of Jesus on my lips and prayed incessantly for the strength to keep my faith.

And then our Lord came upon me another time, and said I was to be His bride.

I opened my arms to him, then, and Jesus raised his golden sword and cut away my simple heart and took it to his own, and said to me, "Lovely lady, I give you my heart, as any bridegroom must," and slipped his heart into my breast, where it lodged, too large and glorious for my body, and then he took my left hand in his and slipped upon my finger a wedding ring, and in all my life I have never felt such great contentment.

Account of the visions, miraculous claims, and sins of the flesh of the Abbess Veronica Borromeo as related by Sister Maria Sinistrari to the Papal Nuncio, Giuseppe Bonomo, Bishop of Siena, on the second day of October, 1621.

I saw her open her arms and then kiss the fourth finger of her right hand and mumble her thanks to God, saying over and over again, "I am not worthy, O Lord. I am not worthy, O Lord." Then I heard her say, "I want to have her sit on that first chair and to explain her life," and she quickly went to where our Lord sat. And she told me the candles she had lit symbolized the thirty-three years that Jesus lived in this world, and the three largest ones were the three years closest to his death.

Next she spoke of how Christ had taken her heart and given her the wounds of His crucifixion. Then she said many things which I cannot remember, and I knew she was not herself. Her voice did not sound like her own. Then she prayed for several hours. We knelt together on the cold stones and prayed together.

When she was finished, we shut out the lights and left the choir and retired to our cells. She was in great pain, and I would go to her cell at night and sit beside her. She kept telling me that a dagger was striking her body, bleeding her heart, and she would take my hand and press it against her breast so I might feel her great pain.

She would tell me, "Hold me," and as soon as I touched her heart, it would quiet her. I asked her what was causing the great pain, and she said it was Jesus testing her virtue.

And then she began to call me often to her bed. It was always after my disrobing, and when I came to her, she would force me down into her bed and kiss me, as if she were a man, and then she would stir on top of me, like a man, so that we were both corrupted.

She would do this in the most solemn of hours. She would pretend that she had a need, a great pain, and call me to her cell and then take me by force to sin with her.

And to gain greater sinful pleasure, she would put her face between my breasts and kiss them. And she would put her finger in my genitals and hold it there as she corrupted herself. And she would kiss me by force and then put my finger into her genitals, and I would corrupt her.

She would always seem in a trance when she did such corruption, and call herself the angel Michael, and speak like a man. She would wear a white robe with gold-embroidered sleeves and a gold chain around her neck. She let her hair loose, and it curled at her thin neck, and she crowned her own head with a wreath of flowers taken from the convent's garden.

And as the angel Michael, she told me not to confess what we did together, for it was no sin in God's eyes. And when we were corrupted together, she would make the sign of the cross over my naked body and tell me to give myself to her with my whole heart and soul and then let her do as she wished. "If you do this," she said, speaking in a man's voice, "I will give you as much pleasure as you would ever want."

DIARY OF SISTER ANGELA MELLINI

April 4, 1622: Veronica Borromeo was purified at age eighteen. She was brought before the Grand Inquisitor and High Priest and her sins were read out to her, and then she was burned, as was the young sister, Maria Sinistrari, until dead. Once dead, the Abbess Veronica Borromeo and Sister Maria Sinistrari were brought into the chapel as is the custom of our sisters. The bodies were then buried beyond the convent walls, in a secret place, and at night, so that the laity might not defame the remains and take the bodies of the dead women and cast them out to the wolves of the forest.

13

JOAN WAS NOT AT her desk when Jennifer arrived at the foundation. She wanted to give her secretary work to do before she went to see Phoebe Fisher. Jennifer took a stack of telephone messages off Joan's desk and walked into her office, closing the door behind her. She flipped through the pink memo slips. There were a half-dozen calls concerning foundation matters, and the others were personal. Janet Chan had phoned to cancel their lunch on Thursday. Her dentist, Dr. Weiss, had called to remind her about her appointment. David Engle had called. He wanted her to phone him at home as soon as possible. And there was a long-distance call from Kathy Dart in Minnesota.

Jennifer stared at the slips, her hands trembling. She was too frightened to call David. She didn't know what to say to him, not now. On impulse, she dialed Kathy Dart in Minnesota.

"Hello, *Tenayistilligan*," a man's voice answered.

"Hello?" Jennifer said.

"*Tenayistilligan*," the man said again, "this is the Habasha Commune. Simon speaking."

"Oh, hello." Jennifer remembered now. Eileen had explained that Kathy Dart's believers used Amharic expressions and gave themselves Ethiopian names in honor of Habasha. "My name is Jennifer Winters. Kathy Dart telephoned me earlier. I'm returning her call."

"Just a moment."

Jennifer waited for a moment. Soon she heard Kathy Dart's clear and crisp midwestern voice. "Oh, Jennifer, I am so pleased that you've called. I telephoned Eileen Gorman earlier to get your phone number. Are you all right?"

"Why, yes, I think so," Jennifer answered.

"Well, I spoke to Eileen a few days ago and she told me you have been experiencing some difficult feelings. . . ."

"Yes?" Jennifer tensed up.

"This morning when I woke, Habasha was waiting for me, waiting for me to awaken, and he mentioned your name. He said you were in trouble."

Jennifer took a deep breath.

"Yes. Well, I'm in trouble, that's for sure." She laughed, but now she was frightened. How could Kathy Dart know?

"This happens," Kathy Dart said softly, anticipating Jennifer's anxiety. "The spirit knows. We have all had premonitions. Habasha, of course, is attuned not only to my life, but to others as well. It is obvious now to me that you and I are somehow related in the same group."

"I'm not sure what you mean, what sort of group. A spiritual grouping?"

"Spiritual is the right term. You and I—and Habasha, of course—and others are all part of what is called the oversoul. I thought so when I first saw you sitting with Eileen at my introductory seminar in Washington. We have shared some previous life experience, which, naturally, isn't that unusual, as we are all part of the Mind of God."

"What did Habasha say? I mean, what's going to happen to me?"

"You have had some terrifying experiences."

"Did Habasha tell you?"

"No, but I have experienced several troubled nights, and when I spoke with Eileen, she told me that you were troubled and were also inquiring about New Age beliefs."

"Yes, I did ask her." Jennifer grew cold suddenly, and she glanced up to see if her office door had opened. She didn't want anyone to hear what she was saying to Kathy Dart. "I do have a lot of questions now about all this . . . stuff. I am trying to understand . . . you know, channeling and everything." She was talking very rapidly, realized she was perspiring.

"The channeling experience is normally a cooperative experience," Kathy Dart went on calmly. "I have accepted Habasha. I had no questions or qualms about acting as his channel, his connection with this life."

"I remember your talk. I remember how he came to you out of a California morning. But I think something else is happening to me. I have had—" She caught herself then. She could not tell this stranger about the killings. Instead, she said quickly, "I was at the Museum of Natural History the other day, and I had this weird sensation."

She told Kathy Dart about the Ice Age exhibition and her reactions to the model, how she knew she had been there once herself, had walked down the path, had slept under the bones and tusks and dried skins of the Ice Age mammoth. She knew it all, but of course it was not possible for her to have such knowledge.

"But it does make sense, Jennifer," Kathy insisted. "This place, these people were once part of your life—in another time, of course, in this prehistoric period."

"Kathy, excuse me, but I have to say something." Jennifer walked to the windows and stood there, staring out at the cold day as she went on. "I am having a difficult time, you know, accepting all of this. I have a friend, and he's—"

"That's Tom, isn't it?"

"Yes, you know . . . ?"

"Well, no, but Eileen mentioned you were seeing someone. I have asked Habasha about Tom. I have asked him to see if Tom is the right person for you."

"And what has Habasha said?"

"Oh, he takes his own sweet time about such requests. Basically he finds them annoyances. He'll tell me one of these times when I am channeling. But please go on. I've interrupted you."

"Well, none of this makes sense to him, either. Rational sense, do you understand?"

"Of course I understand," Kathy Dart replied calmly. "I had many of the same questions and apprehensions I know you are experiencing. For all of us it is an uncharted journey, a leap of faith, but also, and this was true for me, we realize that there is something missing—something out of whack, let's say—with our lives. For me, Habasha has been able to put this life into perspective.

"Look, Jennifer, this isn't terribly new or strange or weird, all this reincarnation talk. We were raised on a belief in an afterlife, in heaven and hell, but at the same time we are caught in a cultural reality that says there can't be any such thing as reincarnation, or premonitions, or ghosts! But nevertheless, man has throughout history known about our connection with the other side, with the voices from beyond."

"But that still doesn't explain why I—"

"Why you were selected? Chosen?"

"Yes! Why me?"

"Because, Jennifer, you are ready. It is as simple as that. I wasn't ready when I was a seventeen-year-old in college, but when I had children of my own, after many life experiences, I was finally prepared to handle the responsibility of channeling Habasha. Someone, some person, is preparing you to channel his or her entity. Why else would you have such sudden strength to run that far in Washington? Jennifer, I know you are being prepared for channeling some spirit."

"Oh God," Jennifer whispered, her legs weakening. She leaned forward and pressed her forehead against the cold glass. Across Fifty-ninth Street, dozens of floors below her, was the entrance of the park, where a half-dozen men stood loitering, standing out in the cold day. They were selling drugs, she knew, calling out to people as they passed by on their way to the subway.

Kathy Dart broke into her thoughts. "I think it would be good if we could talk in person," she said.

Jennifer nodded. She was crying again, and finally she

managed to say "I would love to talk to you." She turned away from the window and went to her desk to pull out a handful of tissues. Kathy Dart was still speaking, telling her how difficult it was to have this special gift, to be open to such communication, to be sensitive to altered lives.

"But I'm not that kind of person, Kathy," Jennifer finally protested. "I never played with an Ouija board or did automatic writing."

"What kind of person, Jennifer?" Kathy Dart said quietly. "Do you believe in God?"

"Yes, of course. I guess so. I mean, I did once."

"And angels? And the devil? And miracles? Of course you do. Or did. And you believed in life after death, too. It's a tenet of Western culture. We were all raised to believe in a God or some Supreme Being that established order in our universe. Even the Big Bang theory is a stab at trying to explain ourselves, why we are here on earth, the meaning of our lives." Kathy Dart sighed. They had been talking for over twenty minutes and both were getting tired. "Listen, after all of this, I still haven't told you why I really called, or what upset Habasha this morning."

Jennifer waited. She had returned to her leather chair and was sitting behind her wide desk. The telephone console was flashing, and she was sure that Joan had returned to her desk and was in the outer office taking her calls.

"Habasha was disturbed about you. He is painfully vague about much of his information but said you were in danger."

Jennifer did not answer. She thought of the *New York Post* headlines and realized again that the police were still searching for her.

"There is a man . . . I have only a name . . . a first name." Kathy Dart was speaking slowly, as if she were still trying to decide how much to tell her.

"Yes?" Jennifer asked quickly, raising her voice.

"David. Do you know a man named David?"

"Of course I do," Jennifer whispered. She suddenly lost all her strength. "David Engle. He's the husband of my friend Margit. She just committed suicide."

"Be careful, Jennifer. I am sorry to have so little to tell

you. Usually I do not like to do this—give people bits and pieces of information—but I am taking a chance with you. I feel you are someone special. Special to me, to all of us.''

"Thank you," Jennifer whispered gratefully. "I'm not afraid," she added, surprising even herself.

"Good! Remember, you are not alone. You have your guides with you always. Your guardian angels, as we used to call them in Catholic school. And you have me. Please call me. We must keep in touch. I feel—I know—we are important in each other's lives.''

When Jennifer finally hung up the phone, she sat very still at her desk and watched the lights of her phone flash. Then, impulsively, she pushed down one of the buttons and reached out to pick up the receiver.

"Hello?"

"Jenny?"

Jennifer recognized the voice at once. "Yes?"

"Is that you, Jenny? I'm so used to getting that secretary who guards your palace door."

."Yes, David, it's me." Jennifer knew her voice sounded stiff and distant, but she couldn't bring any warmth to her words.

"I'm calling to ask if you can come by later today for a drink. I have some things I need to talk to you about."

"I'm sorry, David. I have to meet Tom right after work," Jennifer said. The last person she wanted to see was David Engle.

"Jenny, please. I really need someone to talk to."

"I understand, David, but I can't. I—" Jennifer suddenly stopped talking.

"Jenny? Are you there?"

"Yes, David. All right, I'll come about four." Now Jennifer was smiling. There, in the far corner of her office, in front of the wall of bookshelves, Margit Engle sat on the leather sofa and nodded to Jennifer, encouraging her to accept the invitation from her husband.

14

JENNIFER LISTENED TO DAVID Engle lie to her. He was telling her about Margit's death—how she had said good night, gone to her bedroom, closed the door, and swallowed a dozen Valium. And how he had found her later, on the floor at the foot of the bed. He started to cry as he spoke. Jennifer guessed that he had been drinking most of the day.

Jennifer sat on the sofa and sipped her white wine, watching him. Now he was talking about their sons. They were both home from school and handling the funeral details.

"I couldn't face it," he confessed to Jennifer, coming back to where she was sitting on the sofa.

Jennifer realized how worn down he was. He couldn't be more than fifty, but he had aged since she had spent the night at the apartment. His whole body sagged, his face was gray. Gray from beard bristles. Gray from the long winter without sun. He looked like a corpse.

"Margit was a much better parent than I was," David said. He told her how when the boys had pneumonia, she had slept for a week on the floor in their bedroom. "And I was the goddamn doctor," he swore, sobbing again.

Jennifer didn't go to him. She was crying, too, but her tears were for Margit, the mother of his children, his wife for twenty-three years, the woman whom he had murdered in her sleep.

"I made friends with people easily," he said next, pulling himself together, "but it was Margit whom they came to love." He leaned forward in the chair, gesturing with one hand and spilling his drink. "Like you! Like you! You were my friend, too, but Margit took you away from me."

"David, please!"

He waved off her protest. "Don't you tell me about Margit. I knew her. I knew what she was like." He was crying, and he kept rambling on, claiming that Margit had stolen all his friends, turned them against him.

Jennifer set her drink down on the coffee table.

"David, I'm going to have to go," she said softly, reaching for her coat.

David did not respond. He was still leaning forward, staring at the rug.

"Go?" he said finally, looking up, blinking into the light. Jennifer was now standing.

"I'll telephone the boys later to find out about the service. I would like to say something, if you don't mind. I'll speak to Derek about it." She walked past him but did not bend over to kiss him on the cheek as once she would have. He would turn on her next, she knew. His self-pity was engulfing everyone he knew.

"You were my friend first, Jennifer, or have you forgotten?" The ringing phone startled him, and he stood staring at it. After a moment, Jennifer stepped around him and picked up the receiver. "Hello, the Engle residence," she said calmly.

"Hello, is . . . Jenny, is that you?"

"Yes, Tom. Hello."

"What in God's name are you doing there? Is David with you?"

Jennifer sighed and closed her eyes. She was tired of men shouting at her.

"Yes. What is it?" She glanced over at David. He was

standing in the middle of the foyer, staring at her. His eyes were glassy.

"Get out of there," Tom whispered, "get out of that apartment and away from him. What in the world possessed you to go see him? Jenny, the son of a bitch is a killer. You were right! I called the coroner's office when I got back downtown. I was doing it just as a favor, you know, so at least if you asked again, I'd have the facts, and the tests on Margit's skin had come back. There was lidocaine in the tissue. He did it, Jenny. Like you said."

Jennifer looked into the small foyer mirror and saw her own startled eyes. Behind her, still standing at the entrance, David clutched his empty glass and watched her. She was right. She wasn't some crazy person, having dreams and seeing ghosts. It was all true. Margit had come to her after her death.

"Is that Tom?" David asked.

Jennifer nodded into the mirror. She was listening to Tom explain that a warrant had been issued for David's arrest. "Now get the hell out of there, Jennifer. I don't want you involved. I don't want David to get an idea of what's gone down."

"There's no need to worry, Tom," Jennifer answered coolly. She was angry with him for not believing her at first, and now angry again that he was telling her what to do. "I can take care of myself."

"Jesus, Jenny, let's not try and prove anything, okay? I was wrong. I admit it. Now get out of there."

"I'm going home, Tom. To Brooklyn. Come over later and we'll have dinner. I have more to tell you. Kathy Dart called me at the office."

She hung up the receiver and turned around to David, who had stepped closer to her, but only so that he could lean against the wall to steady himself.

"That was Tom," Jennifer said quietly, pulling on her leather gloves. "He told me that he spoke to the coroner and that the tests came back on Margit's skin tissue. They found evidence of the lidocaine, David. I guess the police have a warrant for your arrest." She spoke without raising her voice.

"You knew?" David asked weakly.

"Yes, I knew."

"How, goddamnit?"

Jennifer went to the apartment door and paused there with her hand on the knob.

"Margit told me on the morning after her death. We talked."

"She couldn't!" David protested, stumbling forward.

"She loved you, David. She loved you all her life. She kept your home and raised your sons. She never wanted anything but your love and respect, and what did you do in return? You turned her out for another woman, a younger woman who was—what did you tell Margit—'more interesting'? And then you just didn't settle for a divorce. No, you had to kill her for her money."

He threw his glass at her. With the speed and deftness she was only beginning to realize she possessed, Jennifer grabbed the glass out of the air before it hit her, and set it down on the small hallway table. She managed to smile curtly at him, and then she went for him. It suddenly seemed so natural and so right. She would use her powers to settle the score. He had taken her dear friend's life, and now she would take his.

Jennifer grabbed David by the throat and jerked him off the floor. Holding him at arm's length, she smiled at him while he gasped for breath and tried to break her grip. Then with one motion, as if she were flicking off a fly, she tossed him away. He flew across the living room and hit the wall, then crashed to the rug.

She moved closer, knowing she had to finish him off, that she couldn't let him live, when she heard the doorbell. The sharp ring snapped her concentration, broke her desire to kill, and she turned away from him, leaving him choking up blood. She walked toward the front door, and in desperation he lunged at her, tried to grab her leg. Jennifer kicked him in the face, knocking him away, and opened the apartment door.

"You're looking for David Engle?" she asked the two men at once.

They nodded, startled by her question, and then by the

sight of David behind her on the living room floor. He was trying to pull himself up onto his knees.

Jennifer gestured toward David, who had recovered enough to begin to cry. "Well, you've found him."

Then she moved quickly to the elevator doors and caught them before they closed. She looked back and saw the two men reach down to help David Engle off the floor. They were already reading him his rights.

15

JENNIFER COULDN'T FOCUS ON her surroundings. She was thinking of Margit, of David, and of herself. She was thinking how she had gone after David and would have killed him if the police hadn't come. She was trembling, frightened again, as she realized they could have arrested her, too, there in David's apartment. She was mad, she thought, trying to kill David. She was losing her mind. In her confusion, she found herself walking along Riverside Park.

Plowing through the snow tired her, and she decided to turn left at the next corner, cross over to Broadway, and catch the subway home. Two men were ahead of her. They had come out of a park entrance, turned and walked off. Jennifer felt her heart race. She glanced around to see another man trailing her by fifty yards, and she knew instantly what they were planning. She should have crossed the street in the middle of the block and walked into one of the co-op buildings as if she lived there. The doorman there would call her a cab. Then she spotted another man on the other side of the street, tramping through the snow with his head down, his hands deep in his pockets. She should cross, she knew. Cross immediately, right there in the middle of the block. But she didn't.

She kept plowing ahead, with her own head down, as if she were consumed with her own thoughts. What was she doing? she asked herself. Why was she behaving this way?

The two men had hesitated at the corner, as if waiting for the light to change, but she knew they were waiting for her. She knew, too, that they would come back toward her as the third man approached, and then they'd surround her and pull her off into the park. A dozen yards and she'd be completely out of sight in the winter afternoon darkness. There were no joggers in this weather, no one walking dogs. She was the perfect prey. They knew it. She knew it. And the thought made her smile. She felt her blood pumping, as her body warmed to the encounter.

The men were turning toward her, and from far behind, she heard the third man pick up his pace and start to run. She watched the men approach. They had spread out on the sidewalk, as if to give her room to pass. Both had long wool scarves wrapped about their necks, and stocking hats pulled down over their eyes.

They were close enough now for her to see that they were Hispanic, teenagers who weren't more than kids, really. As they passed her, they said something in Spanish and lunged at her, grabbing her between them, lifting her slight body easily, and pulling her off the sidewalk.

Jennifer looked up to see the third one waiting. He had raised his fist and was holding a club in his hand, a short piece of pipe wrapped in electrical tape.

She waited for the surge of strength, her wild power, to consume her, and at that moment, as the small one raised the clumsy club, she thought, It won't happen, I'm defenseless. Then it hit—the rising rage of her primitive self.

She felt the sudden shudder of cold through her body, felt her heart pump, as if it had a life of its own, then her blood surged through her limbs and, using the two men who held her as posts, she suddenly lifted her body up and swung her legs. The heel of her right cowboy boot caught the short man in the mouth, driving his teeth up into the soft roof of his mouth. He couldn't even scream when she kicked him away.

The two others swore, furious, and one of them freed his left arm and swung at her head. She ducked the blow, slipping down onto the snowy path and pulling both of the men with her as she fell. She seized their thin necks with both her hands and heard them gasp and gargle for breath as she squeezed the life from them. She realized, holding them both aloft, that she was smiling at her own strength, at her own revenge.

She smelled their breath, the odor of their bodies. She smelled the beer they had drunk that day, the tacos they had eaten somewhere in Spanish Harlem, the women they had slept with. She slapped her hands together, banging their skulls.

The force of the blow, the smashing of flesh and bone and brain, sounded hollow, like pumpkins squashed by a car. There were no other sounds, no cries of pain. Their bodies sagged in her arms. She flipped them away then, into the bushes beyond the footpath, where they fell together in a lump of legs and arms, all bent out of shape.

She went for the third one next, knowing, as no animal would, that she couldn't let him escape to tell the police. The small man had recovered enough to stumble away from her and was spitting out blood and bits of teeth while he tried to run deeper into the park.

She loped down the hillside as he dashed frantically for the bushes that framed a children's playground. She grabbed him in full gallop by the scuff of his neck and, without losing speed, threw him like a human javelin into the high iron-mesh fence that surrounded the children's park.

The force of the impact bent the thick iron webbing. And when his body slipped down, the jagged points caught his clothes so he hung there on the wire like a wet, dirty rag blown up against the fence.

Jennifer stopped to pull her racing heart under control. She could smell herself, her own sweat, and the musky scent pleased her. When she looked up again at the dead man, at what she had done to him, she marveled once more at her speed and strength.

Jennifer took the subway home. She had only stopped at the park fountain to wash their blood off her hands and face. She knew her wild look would keep anyone from sitting beside her.

At home, she started a log fire and burned all her clothes, even her underwear. She got rid of her brown boots, stuffing them in a trash bag to go out with the garbage. Then she took a long hot shower and shampooed her hair, and finally she filled the tub with steaming hot water and scented bath bubbles, opened a bottle of white wine, and took glasses and an ice bucket back to the bathroom. Stretched out in the tub, she listened to WQXR playing Mozart and waited for Tom to arrive.

Tom had his own keys, and though she was drowsy from the hot water and the wine, she heard him closing the front door, dropping his attaché case, and calling for her.

She listened to his voice grow louder and nearer. She smiled and moved her arm slowly in the hot water. The bath had made her weak, and she was tired, too, from what she had done. She thought back on the murders as if they were something she'd just seen in a movie or in a late-night news clip. None of it had any connection to her life, to who she really was.

"Jenny, there you are," he said softly, appearing in the doorway. "Why didn't you call out, tell me where you were?" He came into the bathroom and sat down on the toilet seat. He had already shed his suit coat and tie, and now he carefully rolled up the sleeves of his blue Oxford shirt.

His body always excited her, and she was absurdly pleased by her own arousal. It was such a simple emotion, and so gratifying. Slowly, gracefully, she stroked her breast with the sudsy water.

"David confessed," he said. "I spoke to the detective uptown." He sighed and slumped down on the seat. "Well, why are you smiling?"

She shrugged, and when she did, her pink, flushed nipples broke the surface of the hot water. She watched him focus on her breasts, watched him catch his breath.

"Do you want me?" she asked.

He nodded. His eyes were canvassing the length of her, and she obliged him, arching her back so that the wet web of her sex, foamy with bubbles, surfaced like a pale buoy. Then she settled back in the scented, soapy water.

As Tom shed his clothes, she moved in the tub to make room for him. The water whooshed, and large drops dripped from her arms and breasts as she sat up.

"How do you want me?" she whispered. She could feel her throat tighten, and her fingers, as they always did, trembled with excitement.

"Hurry," she told him. Tom stepped gingerly into the tub, and she reached out for him, gently nipping his penis with her teeth.

"Easy, honey," he said, "that hurts." He couldn't move. She had total contol of his body, holding him by his genitals. "Don't," he demanded. He tried to ease himself down into the water, but she wouldn't release her hold on him. "Jenny!" He was becoming angry.

She kept at him, ignoring his protests. Whenever they made love, he was the one who dictated the terms, and now she wouldn't give up her advantage. A part of her wanted only to relax, to let him have his way, but right now she couldn't stop herself from playing with him, from making him do what she wanted.

She grabbed his waist and tugged him down, her teeth still clenched around his penis. As his erection began to fade, Jennifer gently caressed the inside of his thigh with her warm hand and then abruptly shoved her index finger into his rectum.

He came in her mouth.

She gulped, trying to swallow the flood, then choked and pulled away as he showered her face and hair with jetting semen.

When she could breathe again, she laughed at her own foolishness.

"What are you trying to do, kill me?" Tom said, lifting her into his arms. "Trying to bite off my cock, are you?" He grinned. "Well, I know how to shoot back."

"It feels like sticky molasses in my hair," Jennifer complained, and immediately turned on the shower, drenching them both in hot water.

"More S and M," Tom shouted over the water, but his voice was happy and excited. Both of his arms were wrapped about her body, with his fingers grabbing her taut bottom.

Jennifer spread her legs and, hooking her arms around his neck, she clung to him as he slipped inside her, and rode him a moment with her face turned into the hot spray. Then she concentrated on coming, moving against him as he drove up against her. She jabbed her nails into the flesh of his shoulders, wanting to draw blood, and her breath came in a quick series of gasps. They were splashing water all over, soaking the towels, but she didn't care. All she wanted was to sustain the driving, escalating force which gained and gained, until she was breathless and in wonderful, excruciating pain. She was gasping, trying to consume his life, trying to suck the breath from Tom as she drove her tongue into his mouth, reaching for the very soul of him, and then the orgasm slammed through her, leaving her limp, out of breath, and clinging to him for safety. She ached with pleasure.

"Oh God," she whispered, and licked the damp hairy mat of his chest.

Tom was not done with her. He seized her buttocks again in both his hands and hoisted her up. She still was impaled, and he turned her to the wall, centering them both under the driving shower. He had her pinned to the wall, and braced his feet against the corner of the tub as he drove into her.

He hit her bottom once, slapped it hard, and she gasped with delight. He slapped her again, and she grabbed his head, slipped her long fingers into his thick black hair, then stuck her tongue in his ear, licked him, and snapped at his right earlobe. He slapped her again, harder and harder.

He had spanked her before when they made love, and she had liked the tingling sensation as she came, the naughty notion of being beaten. He had never hurt her, and always he had been gentle with her later, kissing her flesh, soothing her bottom.

Now he did not stop and she did not want him to stop,

and he slapped her harder and she fought back, growling at him, digging her fingers into his shoulders. He swore at her and pumped harder, kept her jammed back into the corner of the tub.

She lashed out at him, hitting him ineffectually on the neck and shoulders with her fists, but her fingers were slippery, wet with water and the blood that she now saw was discoloring the water. She did not want to hurt him, but she did want to resist; she wanted him to ravish her, and she did not know why.

He came. He stopped fighting her. He squeezed her body and shuddered. His face was turned against her; her ear was in his mouth, and her head was pinned to the corner of the shower stall. She was momentarily thrilled at her success, at having made him come with such violence.

When he stopped gasping for breath and kissed her gently on her neck, they slid down together into the deep water and forced another tide of it onto the bathroom floor. Tom reached to shut off the shower, and Jennifer was briefly stunned by the silence. She shook her head to clear the water from her ears, then she lay resting against Tom's wet chest.

"Well," he said, laughing, "that's one for the record books."

"Are you still bleeding?"

"I don't think so." He strained his head to look at his shoulders. "I hope I don't have to explain this to some doctor."

"I'm sorry," she whispered and sat up. "I don't know why I tried to hurt you."

"You didn't hurt me, darling." Tom pulled her again into his arms. "That was fun. You surprised me, that's all. Where are you learning all these new tricks?"

"I don't know any new tricks! What do you mean?" She turned to him. She was wedged between his raised legs in the tub, which now seemed too small for both of them.

"Honey, you came on to me like some goddamn animal."

"Don't say that!"

"Well, it's true!"

"Don't say that! Don't ever say that!" She pulled herself

out of the tub, wrapped her terry-cloth robe around her, and went at once to the sink, where she wiped the palm of her hand across the foggy mirror. Seeing herself reflected there made her feel immediately better. She had begun to have a terrifying premonition that she'd look into a mirror one morning and see some sort of she-ape grinning back.

Behind her, Tom splashed out of the water and grabbed a towel to dry off his hair.

"I'm sorry I upset you," he said, his voice muffled by the thick blue bath towel. "What's the matter?"

She watched his face in the bathroom mirror.

"You make me feel like I'm weird, the way I make love."

"I love the way you make love." He kissed her earlobes.

"I don't do tricks."

"Okay, I'm sorry. What's the matter? Why are you so edgy?" His face darkened, as it always did when he was upset.

"Oh, great. You insult me, then call me 'edgy' because I don't just sit back and take it."

"You've been edgy for weeks, since Washington, really." He stepped up behind her and began to dry her wet hair. "I think that thirteen-mile run drove too much blood into your brain."

"Damnit, Tom, stop making comments like that." Jennifer took the towel from him, threw it on the floor and walked out of the bathroom, making large wet footprints on the hall rug.

He caught up with her in the kitchen. She had taken out a carton of milk and a packet of gingersnaps and was dipping each cookie into the milk before she took a bite.

"What do you want me to do, Jennifer?" he asked, standing in the doorway and tucking the large blue bath towel around his waist. "Tell me, what in the world do you want?"

"I want you to take my kitchen knife and plunge it into your heart," she answered back, biting a gingersnap cookie in half.

"Jenny, please." He stepped into the narrow kitchen.

"Don't touch me!"

"I'm not going to touch you. I just want a gingersnap

before you devour them all." He grabbed one and stepped away, then chanted plaintively, "I'm sorry. I'm sorry. I'm sorry."

"No, you're not." Jennifer reached up into the overhead cabinet and took down another large tumbler. "Would you like a glass of milk?"

"Yes, please." He grinned and stepped closer.

"Don't touch me," she ordered again.

"I'm not!" His hands shot into the air. "I'm just trying to get along here, you know. Get through the next few minutes, that's all."

"It's not something to joke about. I don't want to be jollied out of my mood. Okay?" She turned around and looked at him. "I want you to take me seriously, that's all."

"I do."

"This morning over coffee you told me I needed to see a shrink—but wasn't I right about David?"

Tom nodded, munching on the cookie.

"Look, I don't understand what's going on with me any more than you, but I need your help. I need you to support me. Is that too much to ask?" She looked up at him, tears beginning to form in her eyes.

"Of course not, darling. Of course not," he whispered, and wrapped his arms around her.

Jennifer let herself be held by Tom, taking comfort in being held and cuddled. For the moment neither one of them spoke. She wrapped her arms around him and squeezed, then used his hairy chest to wipe away her tears.

"Stop it! No!" Tom laughed, edging away. "That tickles."

"Good!" She nibbled his right nipple, then licked his breast.

"See!" he said at once, "you're doing it again. I mean, don't get me wrong, I think it's wonderful, but you're much more—"

"Careful, Tom," she said, stepping away and opening the refrigerator door to put away the milk.

"I'm just telling you how much I like it, that's all." He tried to recapture her in his arms, but she moved his hands

away and walked back to the bedroom, where she stripped
out of the bathrobe and stood naked for a moment in the
shadowy light of the room.

Tom came to the bedroom door and watched her while he
finished his glass of milk. Jennifer crossed to her bed and
pulled back the quilt.

"God, you're beautiful," he said from the doorway.

"Thank you." She knew she was. She felt beautiful. Having sex always made her feel beautiful, and she was aware,
too, that the shadowy light on her body aroused Tom. She
turned toward him, and beckoned him toward her. He was
right; she was behaving out of character. She felt as if she
were watching herself on film.

"Jenny?" Tom whispered, approaching her. He sounded
slightly nervous.

She smiled, inviting him closer with the coy downward
slant of her lips, enjoying her control over the pace of their
lovemaking.

"It's all right," she whispered, and she reached for him,
slipped her arms around his shoulders and brought his face
close to her breasts. "Here," she told him, "they want you,"
and then she slowly, softly tumbled him over onto the bed
and made love to Tom again.

O boy with the slim limbs,
I seek you but you do not listen,
for you see not me, nor know
you are the charioteer of my soul.

Anakreon set down his split-reed pen and his papyrus,
then leaned back against the cool wall of the palestra.
The boys had come into the center of the gymnasium
and were stripping off their clothes and lathering their
young bodies with olive oil, and his eromenos was
among them. His heart tugged at his throat, spotting the
lean youth. He could not take his eyes off Phidias, who
now, among the other boys, was laughing at some remark, enjoying himself. Anakreon smiled with pleasure,
simply enjoying the sight of him. He had waited there in
the shade of the colonnade for just the chance of seeing
him.

"Ah, there you are, Anakreon," a voice said from down
the hallway.

Anakreon reached out and rolled up his piece of papyrus, hiding his poem from his friend Xenophanes, another of Athens' aristocrats.

"Writing to the Gods, huh, Anakreon?" the man
asked, folding his cloak beneath him and sitting down
next to Anakreon on the bench. He was a large, fleshy
man who was already sweating beneath his white cloak
in the hot Athenian morning. "And which of these lads
has your fancy this season, my friend?" He watched
the pupils as he spoke, squinting his eyes against the
bright sun.

146

"The finest of fair," mumbled Anakreon, pulling himself up on the bench.

"They're all fair at the age of puberty," whispered Xenophanes, still keeping his eyes on the courtyard.

"True, Xenophanes, but my soul sings for young Phidias, the son of Ptolemy, there!" He nodded toward the courtyard where a red-cloaked instructor had divided the boys into wrestling teams, setting an older pupil to instruct the younger ones.

"Do you remember our days here, Anakreon?" Xenophanes asked, glancing at his friend, who still watched the courtyard and his young eromenos. When Anakreon did not respond, Xenophanes asked, "Have you coupled with the boy?"

Anakreon shook his head and sighed. "I have showered him with gifts, told him of my love. His family knows, of course." He redraped his blue cloak and glanced at Xenophanes, adding, "Life was simpler, my friend, when we were the loved objects, not the lovers. The boy drives me mad with his cleverness."

"His coyness, you mean," Xenophanes answered, laughing.

"True. True. I would not have him be a prostitute, but by Zeus, his passivity drives me mad. He'd rather be with his friends, at his games, instead of walking about the city with me. There is much I could teach the boy."

"I'm sure there is, Anakreon," Xenophanes commented, glancing at his friend, "but your time will come. It always does, doesn't it?" Xenophanes whispered, leaning closer. "You have had your way with many of these palestra boys."

"It is my poetry, I confess, Xenophanes, and not my gross flesh that keeps their interest. And yes, I have had my way with some. I know. Yet the wait is always maddening." Anakreon sighed. "And my loins ache."

"So meanwhile, you have your poems to keep you company, to sing your song: 'For my words the boys will all love me: I sing of grace, I know how to talk with grace.' "

Anakreon smiled, pleased by his friend's acclaim, then said in verse, " 'Again I am in love and not in love, I am mad and not mad.' " He nodded toward the boys. "So goes my life. I'd rather have one moment with his flesh than a room full of papyrus poems or an olive wreath at the Olympic games."

"The games! Come, come, your days of sports are over."

"I am not yet thirty, my dear Xenophanes."

"And they are not yet fifteen," Xenophanes commented, with a gesture toward the young sportsmen.

Flute music began and at once the athletes threw themselves into their wrestling matches. A chorus of shouts came from the courtyard, and the dust from their trampling feet rose in clouds, obscuring the men's view.

"We'd do better in the Agora, buying hares from Boeotia, than standing in this dust storm. Let us go to the baths. My skin is filthy. I spent the morning with a Sophist at the foot of the Acropolis, and even there, the dirt and dust from the Agora were awful."

"My loins sing for the boy," Anakreon answered, "that boy is my muse."

He glanced back at the courtyard. The instructor had called a halt to the wrestling matches and the dust had settled. Anakreon could see his young eromenos, wet with sweat and oil. He stood with his hands on his bare hips, panting in the bright sun. The fine gray dust of the courtyard clung to his lean frame, glistened in the daylight. Then the boy looked up, saw Anakreon standing there beyond the colonnade, and smiled. His white teeth flashed in his face, his bright blue eyes gleamed.

Anakreon's heart soared. Tentatively he waved back and then went gladly with Xenophanes, swelling now with joy, for he had been noticed. In time he would plan to visit the family again, shower the lad with gifts, and someday soon, soon ... His heart ached with anticipation and he said to Xenophanes, buoyant with his good fortune, "Come, my friend, let us go drink some wine at the baths, and I'll write a poem about you, sing of your long-gone days of glory at the games."

"It was only for you, Anakreon, that I wanted to win," Xenophanes said, pausing to look at the poet.

Anakreon stopped walking. The two men were in the narrow street outside of the gymnasium. Below them lay the wide expanse of the Agora, the Athenian market square, above them was the Scambonidai, where all the wealthy of Athens lived in two-story stone houses with wide porticos and courtyards, and gynaecea, rooms for the women.

"I never knew," he said seriously.

Xenophanes nodded. "Ah, my dear friend, we, too, suffer who do not have Apollo's gift for poetry." He tightened his cloak on his shoulder, smiling sadly at Anakreon. His round, fat face was losing its shiny glow. He seemed suddenly older in the fierce Aegean sun.

His abrupt confession had stunned and silenced Anakreon, and the poet reached out and touched Xenophanes's arm, whispering, "I will go to Delphi and sacrifice a goat to Apollo, so that he will send me the muse to write a poem in your honor, Xenophanes. Soon, you will be known throughout the world, the great Xenophanes. Schoolboys and students at the academy will recite my poem of your heroic deeds."

"I have no heroic deeds, Anakreon, except for the number of kraters I can consume at a banquet." He was smiling, trying to shake the moment of melancholy, and the two men turned again to walk to the baths.

Together on the narrow street, jockeyed as they were by the press of people and animals going also toward the center of the city, Anakreon reached over and gently touched his old friend, saying, "We have had more than one moment of bliss, my dear Xenophanes. We have had a lifetime of shared brotherly pleasures. We heard Aeschylus together at the theater and saw Alkaios win the stadion at the Olympics."

"I'd give it all up to have had you once look at me the way you gazed on young Phidias."

"I didn't know, Xenophanes. I did not know."

"Ah, the pity of it, as you poets would say."

Anakreon looked up, and in the distance he could see the sea, blue and calm to the edge of the horizon. He thought of his current quest, the young Phidias, and recalled the look of his lean limbs, his bright eyes, that wonderful innocent smile, and Anakreon's heart tugged in his chest. Then the lumbering Xenophanes brushed against him on the rocky street, and Anakreon felt the weight of the big man, felt his sweat and gross flesh, and he, too, whispered, "Ah, the pity of it." Then he fell silent and the two aristocrats walked in silence down the steep Athens hill to their drinking club.

16

"I THINK IT'S TIME for us to try to discover who you really are," Phoebe Fisher said, after she had listened to Jennifer's account of her recent behavior. It was the first time that Jennifer had seen the channeler since she killed her attackers. It was early in the afternoon and the midwinter sun filled the rooms and reflected off the waxed hardwood floor. Again Jennifer thought how lovely and charming the apartment looked. She wished that she could bring this kind of warmth to her own Brooklyn Heights place. It was all the wall hangings, the fabrics and the exotic plants, she decided, that gave the living room its special quality.

Jennifer had not told Phoebe about the killings but did allude to the change in her behavior with Tom, how she was becoming increasingly more aggressive in her lovemaking.

"And was he upset?"

"No, I guess not," Jennifer answered, laughing. "But I was! I mean, it makes me nervous to be that . . . way."

"There's no need not to enjoy your new intenseness. You are just experiencing what is truly you. Your essence."

"I'm afraid I'm going to frighten him away," she told Phoebe, as if to make a joke of her fierceness in bed.

"Do you want to talk to Dance?" Phoebe asked next.

"Oh God, I don't know. That's scary." She sat back in the oversized mission rocker.

"Good!" Phoebe said, smiling. "Being frightened is good. It clears out the pores, makes us more aware of our surroundings." She lifted up her teacup and took a sip.

Jennifer looked again toward the flames of the fire. Phoebe was giving her time to decide. She wasn't rushing her, but that only made her more nervous.

"How do I talk to him? I've never done anything like this."

"Well, when I go into a trance," Phoebe explained, "and he comes through, he usually says something that shows he understands your problem, and then he'll say something like, 'How may I help you?' That's his signal. Then you may ask anything, talk about anything, whatever. There is no such thing as a stupid question. Out of the most mundane questions have come answers and information for all of us. To him nothing is boring, everything is for the first time. This is what he has been sent to do for our society. If he feels a reluctance on your part to talk about something, he will not volunteer information. If he feels you want to get the ball rolling, he will go as far and as fast as you want to take it. He reflects whatever energy you put out."

"But can he help me understand what is happening?"

"Jennifer, I don't know. I think he might be able to point you in the right direction. He might even have some specific answers. He might be able to look into your spirit life and see where you have been, in what ways you have been reincarnated."

"How will I know that Dance is here? Do you tell me or what?"

"Well, when the connection is made you'll see my body go through a few little reactions. Nothing about this is painful to me, you should know. The experience is very energizing and very valuable. For me it is like a very deep dream. I really don't hear the words because consciousness is not focused in that way. I am aware that there is an interaction going on, and I feel the emotions, I feel the energy, but that's all. I don't listen to your conversation. Dance and I are having our own conversation.''

''Does he speak English?''

''They don't use language at all in his world. His mind sends thought, and because my consciousness is diffused, it allows his mind to sort of imprint its vibration on mine. So basically my energy is being used as a translator box for him. Whatever language I'm programmed in, that is the language in which his thoughts will emerge from my mouth. That's what you hear. He is not actually speaking at all.''

She paused a moment. ''Are you ready?'' she asked.

''I don't know. I guess.'' Jennifer laughed nervously.

''All right, then, help me prepare myself to be receptive. Let's meditate for a few minutes.'' Phoebe drew herself up and crossed her legs. ''Let's close our eyes. After the meditation, when I'm in my trance, you can drink tea, whatever, but at the beginning let us be quiet and keep our eyes closed. Get comfortable yourself and try to breathe as fluidly as you can.''

Jennifer did not close her eyes. She was afraid of the darkness, afraid of not knowing what Phoebe Fisher was doing.

The small woman linked her legs together and laid her arms loosely in her lap. Her eyes were closed and her head was bent forward as she softly spoke.

''I ask the salamanders to put a ring of fire around us tonight, to protect us during this session, and Dance, I ask you that you only bring the spirits for our highest good to us.''

For a moment Phoebe was silent, meditating. She had lit small candles in the room, and in the gathering darkness and the dying fire, they glowed like distant vigil lights.

''I want you to see yourself surrounded by a big ball of blue,'' Phoebe said, whispering now. ''A very bright, vibrant blue color. All around you. It covers you from head to foot like a big cocoon. It goes through you, permeating you. This beautiful blue brings peace and serenity and spiritual awareness. In front of you, behind you, over your head, through you. Now clothe and purify us. I want to bring down one white light through both of us. See it entering through the top of your head, gently coming into every part of your body. Don't block it, Jennifer. Let it gently wash through you from head to foot. See it entering every cell and every pore. This beautiful beam of white light.''

Jennifer closed her eyes and tried to concentrate on the beam of light.

''Now, Jennifer, I am going to say a few words. Let your mind freely associate with these words in a positive way. This is an exercise in raising your vibrations so we invoke only the higher entities.

''Love.''

Jennifer thought of Tom, of the first time she had seen him striding into a courtroom, and how he seemed to overwhelm everyone else with his presence and authority.

''Joy,'' Phoebe whispered.

She thought of running across the meadows of the nature center at Planting Fields. She had been with Kathy Handley and Eileen. It was a wonderful warm spring day, and they were all skipping school.

''Peace.''

She had made love to Tom and was lying in his sleeping arms. It was a quiet afternoon in the city, and she did not want to be anywhere else in the world, ever. And she had thought then that that was real peace.

''O Master of Creation,'' Phoebe went on, ''Thou art the sky full of happiness that displays all the stars of the universe. I humbly ask to be a channel today to Jennifer, that I be out of the way, that I give up control of my body to the spirits so that they may come and speak to her. We want to thank all of you who are with us today for coming and giving us your time and your energies. God bless you all.

''Let us now return to the silence. Be very still and quiet in guiding the spirits to come and to speak.''

Jennifer opened her eyes again. They had adjusted to the darkness, and she could see clearly. Phoebe was before her, still sitting in her yoga position. Her head was still bowed, but her body moved, as if she were unsettled and disturbed by a nightmare. Her small shoulders drew tight, and like a reflex, her arms jerked, then settled down again into her lap. She took several quick, deep breaths.

Jennifer's eyes widened. But then Phoebe settled down again, and from deep within her came a man's voice.

"I come in love and fellowship, to clear the blocks that are in your way so that you will become more enlightened about where you are going and how to get there. Now how may I help you?"

Jennifer, mesmerized, could see Phoebe's small body react, see her shake and jerk, as if the voice were tearing her apart with the force of its power.

"I see that you do not consider your feelings valid. When you were a child, your parents did not treat your feelings with respect."

"Yes," Jennifer whispered. She had never put the feeling into words for herself before, but she knew he spoke the truth.

"Your feelings, your emotions, were discarded, and now in your adulthood it is difficult for you to feel valued. You are questioning something. There is doubt. There is mistrust of yourself, and this reflects directly onto others. There is anger."

"I'm not angry," Jennifer whispered.

"Support yourself," Dance continued, not responding to Jennifer. "Begin to know yourself and your reactions. You are human just like everyone else, and your feelings are natural."

Dance stopped speaking, and Phoebe took several deep breaths. Her eyes were still closed, and her face was calm, showing no emotion.

Jennifer leaned forward in the dying light of the fireplace and peered closer, trying to see if Phoebe were truly in a trance. Then Dance spoke up again, his voice loud and hard in the silence of the room.

"You have come with questions?" he asked. Phoebe lifted her head and her eyelids fluttered.

"Yes, I have some," Jennifer responded, surprised by her own courage. "I am told my body is carried forward. What part is carried forward?"

"Just your spirit, that is all."

Jennifer thought a moment. "Like if I see someone I think I know from before, but there is no way I could know him or her?. . ."

"That is an energy recognition. Everyone vibrates a certain way. Other spirits will recognize your energy. That is what soul mates are all about. The flesh body is just what you have chosen. Some people choose to be crippled in this lifetime to balance a karma from a previous lifetime, perhaps one in which they were abusing their flesh."

"How far back do I go? I mean, how far back do my lives go?"

"To the very beginning, where everyone was created equal. All souls are the same age. Now, some people are called 'old souls' because they have been through many reincarnations. Other souls have chosen to return only once or twice. Some have never been reincarnated."

"We ourselves choose to be reincarnated?"

"Yes, but only a part of you is reincarnated each time. There is a highly evolved part of yourself—part of your total soul group—that is called the higher self. Only the parts of your soul that needed to experience this incarnation are here today. Part of you has already gone through a more highly evolved development and is now above you, guiding you."

"What about my other incarnations?" Jennifer asked. "What was I in past lives?"

Dance stopped speaking for a moment, and Phoebe's head jerked back.

"I see one lifetime. You were a nun in Italy, and a sinner."

"Was I evil?" Jennifer thought of her murders. Maybe she had always been evil; maybe that was her destiny.

"All souls—or spirits, as you call them—are given the opportunity to be the creator as well as the created. Some spirits create bad in their lifetimes, and some, good. There was an upheaval at the source of the universe—all our universes—and that was the beginning of karma."

"When did that happen, in time?"

"Time is not relevant. There is no real time; we don't measure. There are none of your words to explain it. Some of the karma lessons are painful, but they are always for the good of the soul. I wish you could see—with my mind—how far you have come."

"What will happen to me in this life?"

Phoebe Fisher shook her head. "I know, but I wish not to tell you, Jennifer," Dance replied. "This life you must live. Yet do not fear. You are not alone. You have spirits around you, parts of your soul group, your teachers and mentors, and they will guide you, as they always have. Listen to them."

"Are they always with me?"

"Yes and no. Spirits come and go. We don't own each other. If you seek them, if you enlighten yourself, they will come to you and aid you."

Jennifer watched Phoebe Fisher, wondering if it all was a game, playacting. And as soon as she had the thought, she dismissed it. The happiness she felt in Phoebe's presence was not something that could be faked.

"Do you have any more questions?" Dance asked.

"Yes, I do. Do you know what has been happening to me, what I've been doing to other people?"

"Tell me," Dance said, and Phoebe's body leaned forward to listen.

Jennifer told her story, told of the incidents and her violent reactions, and when she finished, she asked only, "How do I keep myself from doing this again? From hurting people?"

"I cannot help you," said Dance, as Phoebe rocked back and forth. "Someone from your past life—not your future lives—is trying to gain hold of your spirit. In the past, in the deep and hidden past of your soul, lies a secret and a tragedy. You must discover yourself what this secret is. And to discover this truth, you must return to your first breath of life. And there lies the mystery of your life.

"And now I must leave you. My dear Phoebe is tiring. I leave you with one warning. Do not fight this spirit who wishes to speak."

Jennifer nodded, then realized that Dance was slipping away, but before she could speak, Phoebe's shoulders shook. Her head rocked back, and her small body trembled. Then she looked up and smiled at Jennifer. "Well, he came, didn't he?" she asked in her own voice.

"Yes," Jennifer said. She had become so accustomed to Dance, she was shocked that Phoebe was herself again.

"And was he helpful?"

"You didn't hear?"

Phoebe shook her head, smiling apologetically. "Dance was helping me with some of my own questions."

"He told me I was once an Italian nun."

"Oh, how lovely! I was once a maid in the royal household of King James, as well as—briefly—his mistress. It's exciting, isn't it?" She smiled at Jennifer, looking more alert than she had seemed earlier.

"I don't know. I don't know what to believe," Jennifer said, sighing. "But at least he told me what I had to do. Learn to meditate." Jennifer smiled and stood up. "I must go. I'm exhausted." She began to collect her belongings.

"What else? Do you want to share with me what else he said?" Phoebe asked.

"You don't know, do you?" Jennifer said, staring at the smaller woman.

Phoebe shook her head. "No, really, I don't. I mean, it must seem silly, my talking to you, but I wasn't consciously there. I had turned over my body to Dance."

"Well, it seems there's someone struggling to get into my body. One of my past lives."

"Yes," said Phoebe, nodding. "As I said when we first met, I had this feeling, this emotion, that there was someone else—a trapped soul—who wanted to speak."

"Well, he's not speaking," Jennifer replied, then kept herself from saying more.

"Perhaps it is a she," Phoebe answered. "Gender isn't an issue in the spirit world." She hugged Jennifer as they said good night. "Good luck to you," she whispered. "And remember, I'm always here for you."

"Thank you," Jennifer said, with tears in her eyes. It

had been a long time since she had felt this close to another woman. "Thank you for everything. For your understanding most of all."

"Yeah, that's my job." Phoebe laughed, then looked up into Jennifer's eyes. The smile was gone from her face.

"What's the matter?" Jennifer asked.

Phoebe shook her head. "I'm not sure. I felt something, that's all. I felt danger, I think. I mean, it was a new emotion for me. Be careful."

"I'm going right home."

"Good! I want you to promise you'll call if you want to have me channel Dance again."

"Thank you."

"And I think you need a crystal."

"Oh, I have one!" Jennifer answered. She produced the small piece of quartz from the pocket of her coat.

Phoebe frowned at it a moment. "Did you buy it for yourself?" she asked.

"No. A good friend who knows Kathy Dart gave it to me."

Phoebe shook her head and plucked the small crystal from Jennifer's palm.

"I think it is best," she said carefully, "if you have your own crystal." She slipped Jennifer's quartz into the deep pocket of her own wool skirt, then drew a pencil and pad from the same pocket. "Here is a name of a crystal store downtown," she said. "I know the owner. Please go see him as soon as you can. This afternoon if possible." She handed the slip of paper to Jennifer, and patted the pocket where she had hidden the quartz. "I'll see about 'deprogramming' this one. For the moment, I think you're safer without a charged-up crystal that doesn't have your best interest in mind."

"What?" Jennifer stared at Phoebe, completely baffled.

"I'll explain everything in time." She gently pushed Jennifer out the door.

Jennifer nodded, too confused to respond. "Oh, I almost forgot," she said, reaching for her purse. "You have been so helpful to me. What is your fee?"

"Well, I usually charge fifty dollars for a thirty-minute session, but . . ." She was looking away, as if embarrassed to be talking about money, "But yours is such an unusual case, and you are clearly a sympathetic soul. Let's say twenty-five dollars, shall we?" She looked up at Jennifer with a smile.

Jennifer pressed the twenty-five dollars into Phoebe's hand and pushed open the heavy iron gate. It had started to snow again, and she realized she wasn't going home to Brooklyn Heights until she had a crystal to protect her.

"I'll call you," she said, turning to Phoebe.

"Yes," Phoebe replied, "I know you will." Smiling still, the channeler closed the iron gate of her basement apartment and stepped back into the dark interior of her home.

17

JENNIFER TOOK THE SUBWAY to the Village. It was not rush hour, so the train was half deserted. Instead of burying her head in a book as she usually did on the subway, she glanced around, checking for transit police. When she saw one, she slipped down into her fur coat and hid her face.

The store was located off Fourteenth Street. It was a tiny sliver of a place, with steel bars drawn across the showcase window. Not open, she thought, disappointed that she wouldn't be able to buy a crystal. But then, behind the counter, she saw a man, and she stepped up the snowy front steps and opened the door.

"I thought you were closed," she said.

The man smiled. "We keep the bars around the windows all the time because of the location. You never know what people will do."

"I'd like to buy a crystal," Jennifer said, embarrassed to be saying it out loud.

"Well, let's hope so!" The man smiled. He held a quartz crystal in his hands and wiped it lovingly with a piece of soft cloth. "Is it for you, or are you buying someone a gift?"

"Does it matter?"

"Oh, yes." The man slipped the crystal back into the case, then gave Jennifer his full attention. "If you're buying one for yourself, then I'd want you to hold it in your hands. To see if you feel anything." He gestured at the hundreds of crystals on display. "One of these is right for you. You'll see. The crystal will choose you, not the other way around."

Jennifer liked the man, liked his soft blue eyes. "Well," she confessed, "I want to buy a crystal for myself."

"Fine. Take your time, look around."

"I want a small one," Jennifer said quickly. "One I can carry around with me. In my pocket." Jennifer stepped closer to the small glass case. Dozens of clear quartz crystals were displayed on blue velvet trays.

"This is your first crystal?"

"Yes, I guess. I mean, a friend did give me one, but . . ."

"Do you know why you want a crystal?" he asked next, reaching into the case and pulling out two trays.

"Do I have to have a reason?" Jennifer realized she sounded defensive. "I mean, a friend suggested it. And I thought it might be fun." Her voice had risen.

The salesman looked over at her questioningly. His blue eyes were even softer and kinder up close. Jennifer felt foolish for having raised her voice.

"Well, what I meant is that people buy crystals for different reasons. Besides, the crystals are themselves different. Now this is a lovely single-terminal quartz crystal. As you see, it has just this single point. And this smokey quartz here is helpful if you're seeking to calm yourself down, gain control of your feelings. Or this amethyst. Amethysts are very protective crystals; they're used by many people to raise spiritual powers." He paused to look at Jennifer for a moment. "You don't know much about crystals, do you?" he asked. "I mean, the power of crystals and why we use them?"

Jennifer shook her head, feeling foolish.

The salesman lifted a small crystal off the tray and held it out to her. "Hold this in your hand, why don't you, while we talk. My name, by the way, is Jeff."

Jennifer nodded. "Hello. I'm Jennifer."

"Okay, Jennifer, here comes Crystals 101." He, too, was

holding a crystal in his fingers as he talked. "Crystals hold the four elements of our world within their very being. Earth, fire, water, and air. They are also beautiful, as you can see, in their pure, clear symmetry. So when you hold your crystal, you are holding the world within your fingers. You are holding creation itself.

"Some crystals are meant for you, others are not, which is why I wanted to know if you were buying the crystal for yourself. It's important to be in tune with the crystal from the first. Here, why don't you hold another." He gave her a second crystal, and as soon as Jennifer slipped her right hand around it, she felt a charge of warmth through her fingers.

"This one feels better," she said.

"Good! We're getting closer. Now you have to program your little friend."

"Program?"

Jeff smiled. "Yes, you need to tell a crystal what you want. Crystals contain energy; you have to direct it."

"How?"

"Hold it in your hands. Think of what you want to have happen or what you wish to do. Visualize. Say it's a health problem. Someone you love is suffering from cancer. You visualize that person active again and place the image of this healthy person in the crystal." He leaned back from the counter. "You don't believe in the power of crystals?" he asked.

"I'm not sure," Jennifer said slowly. "I'm afraid that, you know, it's all so faddish. It's so much the yuppie thing to believe in."

"It's not really, you know," Jeff said. He returned one tray of crystals to the display case and took out two large pieces of smokey quartz. "Some people, I guess, think that crystals are just part of the New Age movement, but primitive societies all over the world have used them throughout time to heal, and to predict the future. There's nothing new about crystals or crystal lore."

"Well, yes, I know," Jennifer said quickly. "It's just that I know it's all tied up with channeling and everything."

The salesman seemed at the moment not to be listening to

her. He had picked up the smoky quartz and was turning it
in his hands, and then she noticed that he had focused the
point at her. "What are you doing?" she asked.

"Smoky quartz has the power to calm. To soothe nerves."

"Please," Jennifer said, "don't point it at me." She
backed away from the display case.

"You have nothing to fear," Jeff said, watching her.
"Crystals are harmless. You bring to them your own energy,
and they expand it, energize it, that's all."

"That's what I'm afraid of," Jennifer answered, trying to
make a joke of her concern, but she was thinking, too, of
what she had already done.

The man carefully returned the quartz to the blue pad.

"Why are you here?" he asked, frowning. "Why do you
want to purchase a crystal? I'm not sure you're ready for
one."

"Please," she said, stepping toward the counter. "I was
told . . . that a crystal would help."

"It will help," he answered, "but you have to be ready
to accept that help. I'd be more comfortable with myself if
I didn't sell you one at this time. You can try elsewhere, of
course."

"Oh, come on. Are you in business or not? What's the
owner going to say?"

"I am the owner," he replied softly. He walked around
to the other counter, as if he had already dismissed her from
his store.

"I was told to come here. To buy a crystal from you."

"By whom?" He looked directly at Jennifer.

"By a channeler," Jennifer said carefully, not sure if she
should give out the name.

"Who?"

"Kathy Dart," she lied.

The store owner flinched at the mention of Dart's name.
"I must ask you to leave," he said.

"Why?"

"I don't want anything to do with that woman."

"She's a nationally known channeler. She has made video
tapes and records."

"Please leave." The owner came out from behind his counter.

Jennifer began to back away from him. "Please," she said quickly, "I really need my own crystal."

"Out!" He was angry. "Kathy Dart is a charlatan, not a shaman."

"You may be right," Jennifer answered, noting the antique words he used.

"I am right."

He opened the front door. Snow was blowing into the store, but he stood there, grimly, waiting for her to leave. What has Kathy Dart done to this man? Jennifer wondered.

She stepped outside, thankful at least that she hadn't turned her rage on him.

"Would you tell me something else?" Jennifer asked, standing on the snowy sidewalk. "Do you know Phoebe Fisher?" He nodded. "Is she who she says she is?"

The question seemed to surprise him. He stared at her for a moment, as if deciding how to respond, and then he said simply, "Yes," and closed the door.

Jennifer turned and walked toward the subway. She had gone nearly a whole block before she realized her right hand was still clutched around the small, clear, single-terminated quartz crystal. It was small and warm in her hand, as if it were a tiny bird, lovely and alive. With her fingers nestled around it gently, she tucked it into the safety of her deep coat pocket. She should return it, she knew. She should walk back and give the man money for it, but she didn't. She continued on her way toward the subway. Later, she would send a check to the Crystal Connection. Now the crystal belonged to her. It felt warm and snug in her pocket, and for the first time in days, she felt secure.

As she walked the several snowy blocks to the station, lost in her own thoughts, she never saw the solitary hunter limping along behind her, never heard the steel-tipped cane digging deep into the snow as she was followed from the Crystal Connection.

This hunter had spotted her first in front of the Ice Age hut built of mammoth bones and tusks twenty thousand years ago.

The hunter rode the subway out to Brooklyn Heights, got off with Jennifer, and moving ahead when she stopped to buy a small bouquet of flowers, limped off into the gathering darkness of early evening to await her arrival home.

Jennifer never bought flowers at the small subway shop, but seeing the cluster of fresh bright bouquets near the newspaper stand, she had acted on impulse and paid an exorbitant five dollars and forty cents for a half-dozen carnations. It was something, she thought, to brighten up her spirits on a dreary day.

Out on the street, she thought briefly about buying some groceries before going home, but she was suddenly afraid again of being spotted, of somehow being recognized as the "ape killer," so instead, she buried her head in the deep collar of her fur coat and hurried home.

Also, Tom was coming over later, and she had so much to think about. He had come to accept her knowledge of David Engle's guilt as an instinct on her part; while he still didn't buy her story of seeing Margit, he was willing to believe that in some vaguely spiritual way, her close friendship with Margit had given her some special insight. But Jennifer wondered what he would do if she told him about Dance.

She was too tired to think about it. The fresh air was making her feel better, though. She was glad to be back in Brooklyn, and the thought of being safely inside her apartment made her smile in anticipation. She was away from the busy streets, going downhill toward the water, where the streets were darker and less congested.

She stepped between two parked cars and dug deep into her pockets, hunting with her fingers for her apartment keys, and then she stopped and stared ahead at the empty sidewalk. There was no one approaching. The dark sidewalk was shadowy but deserted. She heard nothing but the cold wind. A car passed, its tires crunching in the new snow.

Something was wrong, but she did not know what. The feeling she had was vague and unfocused, like a tiny nag at her subconscious. She was being paranoid, she told herself.

She stepped ahead, forced herself to continue down the street, still wary from her premonitions.

She walked slowly, edging away from the buildings, keeping some distance between herself and the dark front steps of the brownstones, with their small gated stoops. She kept away from the garbage cans, glanced to see that no one was crouched behind them, hiding until she got within reach.

She felt her fear. It pumped through her body, making her sweat under her layers of clothes. She loosened her fur collar and took a deep breath. She was damp under her arms, between her legs.

Then she smelled the hunter. She caught a scent in the swirling wind, and she raised her head and sniffed the air. Someone was here, somewhere in the darkness, behind a car perhaps, hidden in the shadows next to a building.

She spun around. Her primal rage swept through her, pumped rage and fear into her veins. In the gathering darkness, she dropped her fresh flowers and crouched down, growling and baring her teeth. She backed away from where she sensed the hunter was, hiding behind a cluster of metal garbage cans. She would not attack unless she was attacked. She kept moving backward, watching the dark corners of the buildings, the hidden doorways of basement apartments, the shadowy hedges. There were now, she knew by instinct, dozens of places where a person might hide from sight until ready to strike.

Snow blew against her face and blurred her vision, but she could see better now in the darkness, and she cocked her head, listening for sounds, the deep steady breathing of some animal waiting to pounce, the sudden motion of a hunter as he got her within range.

She heard the cane before it struck. She heard the thin walnut stick slice the winter air, caught a glimpse of the silver knob, and she tried to duck, but the hunter had surprised her, leaped down from the low branches of a sidewalk sycamore, and struck her in the back of the head. Jennifer was dead before her knees buckled and hit the ground.

When Amenhotep returned from Abu Simbel, Roudidit had already crossed to the other side. Amenhotep went immediately into mourning for his wife, spending the long days as custom required, in idleness, waiting for her body to be prepared for the tomb. He kept himself from thinking what the embalmers were doing to her beautiful body, how they were cutting out her brains and organs, wrapping them up in jars for burial, then filling the body with spices. It took all of three months before Roudidit was properly wrapped in bandages for burial and the funerary furniture was ready.

Amenhotep insisted on adorning her, though the first sight of her terrified him as nothing had ever frightened him in battle. Her beautiful face had shriveled and sunk, and her lips were wizened.

He stood looking down at his dear wife, wrapped in linen, with beeswax covering her eyes and ears, and whispered his farewell.

"I was a young man when I married you, and I spent my life with you. I rose to the highest rank but I never deserted you. I never caused you unhappiness. I never deserted you, from my youth to the time when I was holding all manner of important posts for Pharaoh. Nay, rather, I always said to myself, 'She has always been my companion.' Tell me now, what do I do?"

Amenhotep stood a moment longer, and then slowly, gently, he adorned the mummy. He covered the incision where they had removed her organs with a thick gold sheet inlaid with the oudja, the sacred eye with the power to heal wounds. Then he placed a copy of the Book of the Dead, the guide to the underworld, between her legs, and dressed her with necklaces and amulets, as well as finger stalls for each finger and toe, rings and sandals, all for her long journey to the other bank of life. All of this was new jewelry that he had had made after her death. He had a winged scarab with the goddesses Isis and Nephthys carved as the supporters, and then engraved the back with the words, "O my heart, heart of my mother, heart of my forms, set not thyself up to bear witness against me, speak not against me in the presence of the judges, cast not thy weight against me before the Lord of the Scales. Thou are my ka in my breast, the Khnoum which gives wholeness to my limb. Speak no falsehood against me in the presence of the god!" He added other engraved scarabs, not mounted, but with hearts of lapis lazuli, and all carrying his dead wife's name.

He had amulets and statuettes of the gods Anubis and Thoth, which he hung around her neck and attached to the pectoral. Besides the ornaments, he placed tiny reproductions of walking sticks, scepters, weapons, for he left nothing to chance in his wife's house of eternity. The next world, he knew, was no place of peace and quiet. It was full of hidden traps and dangers, and Roudidit must be prepared for her journey.

When he was done, he stepped back and let the embalmers wrap her again in linen bands and place a gold mask over her face. Then, turning to him, they nodded. She was ready for the cortège.

His servants went first, carrying cakes and flowers, pottery and stone vases. Behind them came the furniture: beds and chests, cupboards, and the chariot, everything that Roudidit would need in the other world. Behind them came his wife's jewelry, all Roudidit's necklaces and jewels, carved human-headed birds and other valuables, displayed on dishes so the crowds would see her wealth, the wealth he had given Roudidit and which would travel now with her to the other side.

The idlers watching the procession could not see

Roudidit herself. The stone sarcophagus containing her body was hidden beneath a catafalque drawn by cows and men, all of it mounted on a boat and flanked by statues of Isis and Nephthys.

The women followed, his sisters and relatives, and all the hired mourners, who had smeared their faces with mud and bared their breasts as they wailed and rent their garments, lamenting Roudidit's departure.

At the Nile they were met by a priest with a panther's skin draped over his shoulders. He carried with him burning incense, and the bare-breasted mourners bowed and stood back, letting the boat bearing the catafalque be lowered into the water.

Amenhotep, too, stood aside, and watched in silence as the catafalque was launched into the Nile River. He stood thinking of his wife, of when they were young and first in love. She had been promised to an Ethiopian monarch, and he to Tamit, the daughter of Nenoferkaptak. He had beseeched Pharaoh, and the gods had said he could marry Roudidit if he won her in battle, if he defeated the Ethiopian and brought the kingdom of Kush as ransom. He had gone off to do battle with an army of Nubians fully armed with coats of mail, swords, and chariots. And when he reached Egypt again, he drafted the Nubians into his army, gave them command of the archers and leaders of their people, and branded them all slaves under the seal of his name. And Pharaoh, seeing the wealth he had gathered, gave him Roudidit to wed.

He had never loved another woman in his life, and he knew now he would never love another, though already he had been offered the young sister of his brother's wife. He was too old, Amenhotep knew, to let another come into his heart.

As the boat bearing the catafalque slipped away from shore, he and the mourners stepped into a second vessel to follow close behind, accompanied by two boats full of Roudidit's possessions. The women went at once to the roof of the cabin and continued to cry, sobbing in the direction of the catafalque. Their dirge carried across the wide river:

> Let Roudidit go swiftly to the west, to the land of
>   truth.
> The women of the Byblite boat weep sorely, sorely.
> In peace, in peace, O praised one, fare westward in
>   peace.
> If it please the god, when the day changes to
>   eternity,
> we shall see thee that goest now to the land where
>   all men are one.

From the eastern shore came the reply from others, wishing their farewells, their voices carrying clearly over the calm Nile:

> To the west, to the west, the land of the just.
> The place thou didst love groans and laments.

Amenhotep stepped to the bow of the boat, into the hot Nile sun, and shouted in the direction of the cata-falque, to where his lost wife lay wrapped in her scented linens:

> O my sister, o my wife, o my friend!
> Stay, rest in thy place,
> leave not the place where thou dost abide.
> Alas, thou goest hence to cross the Nile.
> O you sailors, hasten not, let her be:
> Ye shall return to your houses,
> but Roudidit is going to the land of eternity.

When he had sung the dirge, he moved again into the shade of the cabin and out of the blazing sun. The cries and laments of the female mourners rose up, fill-ing the air, but he turned toward the western shore and saw that a group had already gathered on the sandy bank. A number of little stalls had been set up to sell goods, food, and devotional objects.

Everyone profits from the crossing over, Amenhotep thought, everyone but myself. I am the one who has lost his world.

She had almost died once, in childbearing when they were first married, and he had prayed to the goddess Hathor, the Lady of Imaou and of the Sycamore, to save Roudidit's life and that of his newborn son. And then the baby had cried "Mbi" and turned his face to the earth, and Amenhotep knew then that nothing but evil would prevail. And he had taken his son out then, and without naming the boy, without entering it in the House of Life, killed the infant, before more harm could come to his family.

She had never given birth to another child.

The four boats were docked and unloaded, and the procession was gradually reformed. They moved up the bank and away from the booths, following behind the catafalque, which, across the flat, cultivated land, was being hauled on a sledge by two cows. Ahead of them all was the priest, sprinkling water from a ewer.

There was only the funeral procession now, all the elders had fallen away, left behind at the bank. Amenhotep moved ahead to greet the goddess Hathor, who, in the shape of a cow, emerged from a clump of papyrus at the entrance of the tomb.

The catafalque was brought to the entrance and the sarcophagus removed. He stepped to the sarcophagus and placed a scented cone on its head, as if greeting a guest in his own home. Behind him, the female mourners began again to weep and beat their heads in anguish. There were more priests now, coming forward with bread and jugs of beer, as well as an adze, the curved knife shaped like an ostrich feather, and a palette ending in two scrolls.

All these, he knew, were objects to empower the priests to counteract the effects of the embalming, to restore his dead wife on the other side so she could use her limbs and her missing organs, so she could see, could open her mouth and speak, could eat and move once again.

The long months of mourning, of suffering his losses, were over.

Amenhotep cried out, "O my sister, it is thy husband, Amenhotep, that speaks. Leave me not! Dost thou wish that I should be parted from thee? If I depart thou wilt be alone, and none will be left to follow thee. Though thou wast wont to be merry with me, now thou art silent and speakest not."

He turned away from the women and stepped down into the tomb, down to the square stone receptacle that had been carved out, and watched as his servants carried his wife and lowered her into place. He placed Roudidit's amulets beside her, then moved away so that the heavy stone lid could be set in place. The jars containing her organs had been put in a chest, and this chest was set down in the tomb by the priests; the funeral furniture had been arranged, and then boxes of oushebtiou, the small statuettes of all her loved ones, were placed in the vault.

He moved out of the tomb, back into the brilliant sunlight of midday. The priests came out, still sprinkling water, and the masons moved to wall up the entrance of the tomb.

Before him, in the sunlight, Amenhotep could see that food for the mourners had been placed out in the courtyard of the building that he had constructed, years before, above the tomb.

He walked through a small garden of sycamores and palm trees and sat in one of the newly decorated rooms of the building. He had always thought that Roudidit would be the one to sit there when he crossed over to the other world. He had never thought that he would be the one left behind on earth.

A harpist came forward from the entrance and thanked

all of the mourners for coming, singing that Roudidit was
happy in the world beyond. Another harpist picked up
the melancholy strain, and sang:

Men's bodies have gone to the grave since the
    beginning of time and a new generation taketh
    their place.
As long as Re shall rise in the morning and Atum
    shall set in the west, man shall beget and woman
    conceive and breath shall be in men's nostrils.
Yet each that is born returns at the last to his
    appointed place.

The song was not meant for Roudidit, Amenhotep
knew, but for him. The gods were telling him that he
must go on with his life, that his lovely wife was safe and
happy in the land of the west, and that he must turn to
human concerns.

He smiled and motioned his servant to pour him wine,
to bring him food, and he noticed that his sisters smiled
at his sudden enthusiasm. Then he stood and raised his
cup to his lips, and over the cool rim, he studied one
woman, a maidservant, who had come to beat her
breast, rend her garments, and mourn the passing over
of his wife to the other side.

18

JENNIFER SAW HERSELF FLOATING above her body. She was dead, she realized, but the thought caused her no pain or fear. She felt only free and oddly happy. All her guilt was gone. She regretted nothing. She missed no one. Not Tom. She would have liked to have said good-bye, but that was all.

How wonderful death was. Why did people fear it? She watched the team of doctors hovering over her body, inserting tubes and needles. She felt nothing. She had always been so afraid of injections, but now she smiled, and her smile bubbled up into a laugh. It was as if she had drunk too much and was losing control. But now there was no control to lose.

The doctors were blocking the view of her face, and she moved into a different position. It seemed as if she were hang gliding, surrounded by the silence of the wind. Doctors and nurses were shouting to each other. She was aware of their urgency, but she didn't listen. The details they were discussing no longer mattered to her. It was so much easier to have died this way, without any pain, without any long illness, without having to see her life slip away year after year as she grew older. She had died young, that's all. It was no big deal.

And then she felt pain. A wedge of excruciating pain took her breath away. She saw her face on the table reflect it.

"It's not time, Jennifer," a voice said, a voice that she recognized although it had been years since she heard it.

"Danny! Danny! Where are you?" She looked around, but the world she floated in was gray with clouds.

"I'm here. I'm here."

She understood him, but there was no one speaking to her. Somehow, she just knew what he wanted to tell her.

"Let me see you, Danny," she begged, still scanning the grayness for a sign of life.

"You would not know me, Jennifer. I'm not as you knew me. That was another life, another time for me."

"Oh, Danny, I don't understand. I don't know what's happening to me. Please . . ." She sounded like a little girl, as desolate as the day Danny had disappeared from her life, gone off to die in Vietnam.

"You will, honey. You will. And I'll be there to help you."

"I love you, Danny. I love you, and I'm sorry you were killed."

"It had to happen, sweetie, and it's all right. You know that now. You know it means nothing to die."

"I don't want to live, not anymore. Let me stay with you."

"You can't, Jennifer. It's not your time. But we'll be together again in another time. Go and fulfill your destiny, what your soul chose for you."

"I thought I understood. . . ." Jennifer was weeping again. She had a piercing headache centered between her eyes.

"You will in time."

"I'm sorry you were killed. I didn't want you to die. I loved you, Danny. You're the only one I've really loved." She reached out for him, although she couldn't see him, then realized she was moving, falling, slipping away from the safe place of her death, down and down into her very own body.

She struggled, she fought it, but the battle was over; she was slipping back again, into life.

"Okay, we've got her," one of the doctors shouted, eyeing the gauges of the life-support system, seeing that the flickering needle was responding. "We've got life here."

"Thank God," one of the nurses was whispering. "She was really gone."

"I know. I know," the doctor said, unsnapping a rubber cord from around Jennifer's right arm, "but we got lucky this time. Clean her up and take her upstairs." As he turned away, Jennifer fell asleep, feeling no more exhausted than if she had had a tough day at work; but she had been on the emergency-room table for over an hour.

When she woke, Tom was with her, dozing in the chair near the hospital window. She watched him while he slept. The sunlight was on his face, and he had not shaved. He had on his old blue Oxford button-down and gray cords. He had kicked off his Adirondack moccasin shoes and was wearing the pair of thick red wool socks she had bought him for Valentine's Day. She realized she wanted to hold him, but when she tried to sit up, she was too weak to move. Her wrist was taped and she was being fed intravenously.

"Tom," she whispered, and at the soft sound of her voice, he stirred and blinked his eyes open and quickly came to her, lifting her hand to press her soft palm against his cheek. She could feel the stubble of his dark whiskers. "Tom, I'm sorry," she told him.

"It's okay. Hey, you were mugged." He was smiling at her, his gray eyes cloudy with sleep, but soft, too, and tender. "You're going to be fine. Just fine." He kept smiling.

"I'm sorry for everything I've done to you." She began to choke on her tears, and he stood quickly and pressed the buzzer for the nurse.

"I spoke to the cops. I'm having this room guarded."

"Honey, it wasn't your drug dealers."

"Don't try to talk, sweetheart. Don't say anything," Tom said urgently. He glanced at the doorway, then called out "Nurse! Nurse!" in a loud, panicky voice.

"It's okay. I'm okay," she told him. "Come and sit by me." She wanted him close.

"You're fine, darling. Everything is going to be fine now. I love you. I do!" He leaned closer still to kiss her eyelids.

"I want you to listen. Please," she pleaded. "I saw Danny. I mean, I talked to Danny. And he's all right. He's happy."

Tom nodded, but his eyes were clouding over again.

"I'm okay, Tom, I'm not crazy."

"Of course you're not."

"I died. I left my body. I saw the doctors, everything. I wanted to stay dead. It was so wonderful, Tom. Then I saw Danny and he spoke to me, told me that it wasn't time yet, not yet the end of my lifetime."

Tom nodded. "Jennifer, you've got to sleep. Why don't you try to sleep."

Jennifer smiled. He didn't understand what she was talking about. Of course not. He hadn't died and come back to life. She closed her eyes. Yes, she should sleep. She needed to rest and regain her strength. She had so much more to do. It was time.

19

TOM WATCHED JENNIFER PACK. He had made himself
another drink and now stood in the doorway of her bedroom
as she went back and forth from the closet to her suitcase on
the bed.

"Are you going to say anything at all, Thomas? Or are
you just going to stare at me all evening?" Jennifer asked.
She was holding up a white cotton blouse by the shoulders
and deciding whether she should pack it for Minnesota.

"You know what I think," he answered back. The two
double scotches he'd downed had put an edge on his voice.
"You've just got out of the hospital. You need to rest, not
take a goddamn trip out to the middle of nowhere!"

"I have to do this my way," she said.

Tom nodded and sipped the scotch. "It's going to be fucking cold out there," he said softly, as if to make amends.
"Why does she live in Minnesota, anyway?"

"It's where she is from."

"She knows you're coming?"

"Yes, of course." Jennifer decided against the blouse.
"Eileen telephoned her at the farm—that's what the center
is called." She hung up the blouse and reached to the top

shelf to pull down her heavy wool sweater, while she waited
for his next question. It was as if they were playing tennis,
lobbing responses at each other. Then she stepped away from
the closet, turned, and faced him.

"Tom, I told you. I'm being driven nuts by this, too. I
don't want to have 'out-of-body' experiences. I don't want
to know that I can suddenly turn into some sort of caveman
who can kill people with a blow of his fist. I don't want to
think that every time I'm threatened, I'm going to turn into
a freak."

"Jenny, you don't—"

"Yes, I do. Let's not gloss over it, okay? Maybe those
people deserved to be killed. Maybe they were scum, or
whatever you called them, but then so am I. I killed them.
Maybe not me, but some part of me. A past-life person."

"Oh, for chrissake!"

"Give me a chance, Tom." She stared up at him. "Let
me go find out what's wrong with me, okay?" Her eyes had
swelled up with tears, and to keep herself from crying, she
turned to the bed and continued to pack.

"I talked to a couple of shrinks," Tom said slowly, coming
into the room.

"Of course," Jennifer replied.

"Of course, what?"

"Of course you would talk to someone. That's you." She
glanced up to show she wasn't upset with him. "What did
they say?" she asked, softening her voice.

"I spoke to Dr. Senese, the one I saw for a while after I
broke up with Helen. I told him about this woman, Phoebe
Fisher."

"And Kathy Dart."

"Yeah, about all this goddamn channeling shit."

"Tom, please!" She felt a wave of anger and immediately
tried the exercise Phoebe had taught her, focusing her attention on the word *love*. Gradually she felt her body ease and
the tension diminish. She glanced at Tom. He was sitting on
the edge of the bed now, his drink still in his hand. She
noticed that he had put on weight, that there was a new roll
of fat around his middle, and that his shirt had grown tight

at the neck. He was like an animal, she thought, who stored up fat for winter. Perhaps he had stopped jogging. She had not run since her Washington trip. She was afraid to run, afraid of what might happen to her body.

"Senese says that these channelers are suffering from personality dysfunctions. According to him, a fractionalized piece of their personality gains control. You've read about these multiple personality cases."

"Multiple personalities, Tom, happen within the same person. Habasha was a living person from another time period. Dance is from another galaxy. It's not the same thing."

"Oh, for chrissake."

"Tom, I'm not asking you to understand any of this, either. I just want you to have some faith in me, that's all. I want you to be at least as supportive as Eileen Gorman."

"That loony! I talked to her at the hospital when she came to see you. She's out of her fucking mind!"

"Tom! How dare you!" Jennifer threw down one of the sweaters and turned on him. "Eileen has been absolutely wonderful, coming to me when I need her, listening, understanding. How can you sit there and . . . and . . ." Jennifer felt a surge of rage sweep through her body. There was a pattern to her primitive urges. They sprang from the base of her neck, shot down across her chest, and poured strength through her body; the result was an overwhelming urge to attack. It was becoming worse, she knew. Each time the rage returned, it came in stronger waves, and sometimes she realized she wanted to sink her teeth into someone. She could feel the desire to satisfy that pleasure. It was like having sex—once she spun off into an orgasm, she never wanted it to stop. She wanted only to ride the waves. She took several deep breaths and brought herself under control.

"If you hadn't met her in Washington, then none of this nonsense would have started in the first place," Tom shouted back.

He was drunk, Jennifer realized, drunk and angry and threatened.

"It would have happened anyway, Tom," she answered. "It was meant to. These events aren't coincidences or happenstance.'' She looked across the bed at her lover. ''Let me work this out my way,'' she told him.

Tom stood staring at her in the dumb way drunks do when trying to comprehend. She went back to packing but watched him out of the corner of her eye. She was leaving first thing in the morning; Eileen was coming in from Long Island to pick her up, and they were going to drive together to Minnesota.

She could send him home in a taxi, Jennifer thought, or let him sleep there tonight. He'd be sick in the morning.

''Tom, why don't you go into the living room and lie down on the sofa?'' She encouraged him with a smile, but his eyes had glassed over, and he kept swaying against the bed. She went to him and took away his drink. ''Come on into the living room, honey,'' she whispered.

''You're leaving me, I know,'' he mumbled, but let himself be led away. ''You're leaving me because I didn't do anything about Helen.''

''Darling, I'm not leaving you. I'm going to see Kathy Dart and talk to her about what is happening to me. I'll be coming home to you soon. And I'll be okay again.'' She spoke brightly as she eased him from her bedroom. Now his full weight was against her, and she had to struggle to keep him from toppling them both over. Where was her strength when she needed it, she thought, gasping for breath as she slid him down onto the sofa. When Tom dropped onto the cushions, Jennifer sank to her knees.

At least he would sleep until early morning. And he wouldn't hurt himself. She slipped off his shoes and pushed his legs up onto the sofa, then loosened his shirt and his belt. She peeled off his black socks and dropped them into his shoes, then went back into her room, took the extra quilt from the cedar closet, and tucked it around him.

He was already sleeping soundly. Jennifer knelt beside him and gently caressed his face. The deep sleep had swept away all the tension; he looked like a teenager, with nothing more on his mind than the pleasure of a wet dream. She leaned forward, kissed his cheek, and whispered, ''I love you.''

* * *

It was after midnight when she woke and sat up in bed. She was suddenly wide awake and quite clearly she heard the front door of the apartment being unlocked, heard the two tumblers turn. She jumped from the bed and rushed to the bedroom door. Tom was up and off the sofa. He had grabbed his pistol from his briefcase, and when he spotted her, he put his finger to his lips, motioned for her to be silent.

She watched as he carefully stepped around the sofa, moving silently in his bare feet. Then she heard the dog, heard his paws on the bare hardwood floors of the front entrance.

She started to move out of the bedroom, and frantically Tom signaled, waved her back into the room, motioning that she should close the door.

"What is it?" she whispered, and then she caught a glimpse of the dog in the dim light of the living room. It had run in from the front hall, and spotting Tom, it immediately growled and bared its teeth. It was a pit bull, Jennifer saw, watching the small blunt-faced beast.

"Get away, Jenny!" Tom ordered, raising his pistol. He fired as the dog leaped at him. The bullet missed the animal and shattered the glass in her breakfront beside the bedroom door.

Jennifer screamed.

The pit bull landed on the back of the sofa and then jumped at Tom. Backing off, Tom tripped over the coffee table and shot again. This time the bullet dug into the high ceiling.

The dog was on top of him now, had seized his forearm in his teeth. Tom swung the pistol around and shoved it against the pit bull's face and pulled the trigger. The automatic pistol jammed, and before he could get off the next shot, the dog ripped the flesh off his forearm. Now Tom screamed.

Jennifer went for the beast. She dove at the animal, grabbed his white slavering muzzle with her own bare hands and wrenched open his jaw with one smooth strong motion, as if she had been killing animals in the wild all of her life.

Then with her arms outstretched, she let the heavy beast twist and turn under her strong grip, let him struggle to get loose. She saw the anguish in the dog's yellow eyes as he gasped for breath, and then with a sudden jerk, she ripped open the beast's mouth and broke his jaw. The fresh blood from the soft white insides of his mouth sprayed her face and splattered the pale yellow rug of her living room. She dropped the prey.

Tom crawled away from the pit bull. Crawled away in pain. His arm was bleeding and his flesh hung loose from the muscle.

"Jenny!" he gasped, seeing what she had done to the dog.

He was frightened, she saw. Frightened now of her. But Tom wasn't her enemy. He did not want to harm her.

Jennifer smiled at her lover, and slowly, carefully, as any animal would, she wiped her lips clean with the tip of her tongue.

BOOK THREE

If we open to these sources of inspiration and creativity, we open a window to a universe that is going to be becoming better. Someone once asked me about which model of the universe I favored. I said, "To hell with the model, let's just channel the universe. Let's become one with it. That way we don't have to play little games."

—*Channel Alan Vaughan*

He [my guru] asked me to pray, but I could not pray. He replied that it did not matter, he and some others would pray and I had simply to go to the meeting . . . and wit and speech would come to me from some other source than the mind. [I did as I was told.]

The speech came as though it was dictated, and ever since, all speech, writing, thought and outward activity have so come to me from the same source.

—*Sri Aurobindo*

20

JENNIFER SLEPT AS THE car swept across New Jersey. When she woke, stretched out in a sleeping bag in the back of Eileen's station wagon, she saw they were on an interstate, passing through bleak farmland. The trees were bare, and icy snow covered the low, rolling hills. The sun, reflecting off the snow, blinded her for a moment, and she thought at once of how she had killed the pit bull, and to keep her mind off the frightening memory, she asked, "Where are we, Eileen?"

"Well, good morning, sleepyhead. According to the last signpost, we're just beyond Lock Haven, Pennsylvania, heading west on 80. Do you want coffee?"

"Oh, no, just keep driving." Jennifer did not want to stop. She liked feeling that she was escaping from New York, driving away from danger.

"I have some with me. Here." Without taking her eyes off the road, Eileen handed back a thermos. "There are sandwiches packed, too, and sodas. Would you like to drive?"

Jennifer shook her head. "Not unless you want me to," she said. "I'm exhausted." When Eileen had picked her up that morning at the apartment, she was still trembling from the dog's attack. She was afraid that Tom wouldn't let her go, but he had wanted her to go then, thinking that she would be safer in Minnesota, far away from the drug dealers. But it wasn't drug dealers, Jennifer knew, who had sent the pit bull into her apartment.

"Well, you're okay now," Eileen told her, smiling into the rearview mirror.

"I don't know. I don't think I'll ever be all right again."

"Yes, you will. Kathy's going to help you."

Jennifer smiled, then reached over and tenderly squeezed Eileen's shoulder. She closed her eyes again but immediately conjured up the nightmare vision of the dog attacking. She saw the animal's slobbering mouth, its bare white teeth. Jennifer opened her eyes and blinked again at the brilliant winter sun.

"Tom thinks the dog was sent after him," she said. "By drug dealers he's prosecuting."

"You don't believe that." It was a statement, not a question. Eileen's eyes found Jennifer in the mirror.

"The dog was after me, Eileen," she said. "I just have this feeling that whoever attacked me outside of my apartment is still after me." Her own words frightened her. "I guess I'm trying to warn you, Eileen, even if it's too late. I mean, here we are all alone on the interstate in the middle of nowhere."

"We'll be careful," Eileen said reassuringly.

"I'm just sorry that you have to be involved."

"I want to be involved. Kathy Dart practically told me to hand-deliver you to Minnesota."

"Oh?" Jennifer looked over at Eileen. From where she was sitting, she could see her right profile.

"You know Kathy is concerned about you," Eileen said.

"Yes, I know. Is she this concerned about your well-being, too?" Jennifer shifted around and rested her chin on the back of the driver's seat.

"Yes, I think so. Habasha says that I was once in King Louis the Fourteenth's cavalry. That must explain my love for horses. Anyway, Kathy was my commanding officer and I saved her life. That explains why she is linked to me. And look at us, you and I. Why were we so close in high school?

Why did we just—you know—pick up afterwards? There's a reason. It's not coincidence. We're totally different people. My parents weren't wealthy; yours were. I was raised a Unitarian. You were what, nothing?''

"I wasn't nothing!" Jennifer answered back, laughing. "I was raised a Lutheran. And Lutherans believe in God. I do!" she added defensively. "So there!"

"So there yourself!" Eileen answered back.

They rode in silence for a moment, watching the highway ahead of them. There was very little traffic, and Eileen was speeding in the left lane, passing an occasional car. At that moment, Jennifer felt happy and secure. She had turned her life over to Eileen and Kathy Dart. They had answers about what was happening to her, and that was more than she had herself.

"It's scary sometimes, I know," Eileen said softly. "I remember one of the first sessions I went to with Kathy. A man there was having trouble with his wife and teenage daughter. There was a great deal of bickering, he said, and he couldn't understand why. None of them could, really. Well, Kathy used acupuncture on the man to release his past. It was scary. I had never seen anyone being pierced with needles, but it didn't seem to hurt him, and then when Kathy began to lead the man back through time, he reached this point where he was an Indian living on the plains. In that lifetime the soul who's now his daughter was his wife. *That* was the problem. His wife today was jealous of their daughter because she was her husband's lover in America before Columbus landed here.''

"It all seems so crazy," Jennifer whispered, doubting for a moment why she was going to see Kathy Dart, why she needed to see the channeler.

"It's not so crazy. Reincarnation is a part of every religious tradition.''

"I'm just having such a hard time rationalizing it.''

"That's the trouble. You shouldn't try to rationalize reincarnation. You'll see, once you speak with Habasha. Then you'll understand why you are on earth. And what the purpose is for all your heartaches and joys.'' Eileen was speaking urgently now, with conviction. "If you believe in reincarnation, all the coincidences have meaning."

"That's what I don't like," Jennifer spoke up. "I don't like thinking that all those coincidences are linked together. It seems too planned, too neatly worked out to be real."

"But it makes sense, Jenny. Your spirit is created by God, or whoever, and it passes through lifetime after lifetime. The spirit never dies, but it keeps changing. You're born a man. You're reborn as the same man's great granddaughter. It's wonderful when you step back, when you think of all the possibilities, and the wonderful art of it, really."

"Maybe it's not so wonderful," said Jennifer. "Maybe someboy's 'soul' has come back from another life to kill me."

"Easy, Jenny. We don't know that." Eileen shifted again into the left lane and passed a long distance trucker. As they sped by, the driver blasted his horn. The noise startled Jennifer, and she spun around and gave the finger to the truck driver.

"That wasn't such a great idea," Eileen said coolly.

"Why? I hate it when jerks like that think it's cute to harass women drivers."

"Yes, I know, but now every trucker on Route 80 is going to be watching for two women in a gold '87 Buick."

"How? What do you mean?"

"CBs, honey. They're all linked together."

"Damnit! You're right."

"It's a long trip, and these guys have nothing else to do but amuse themselves. Don't worry. We'll avoid their hangouts. It's okay."

"Thanks. I guess I'm like someone's obnoxious teenage daughter."

"Well, you might have been mine. . . ."

"Yes, I know. In another life."

They both laughed and then fell silent, watching the white lines flash beneath the car as they sped west, and listening to the hum of the tires and the wind whipping against the windows. It was cozy in the station wagon, and Jennifer slipped down into the sleeping bag and curled up in its warmth.

"Do you mind if I go back to sleep?"

"Please do. I'd like you to drive later, if you don't mind."

"Sure," mumbled Jennifer, already half asleep.

"Sweet dreams," Eileen said, glancing back. Jennifer had closed her eyes. She couldn't see that the smile was gone from Eileen's face. Her high-school friend's bright green eyes had glazed over and were as cold as crystal.

21

"WHAT DO YOU THINK, Jenny, are we ready to stop?"

Jennifer glanced at the dashboard clock. It was six o'clock, and Eileen had been driving in the dark for over an hour.

"Yes, I guess. I need a drink and an early evening. Have we covered enough territory?"

"Yes, you made good time on the second leg. We'll catch the turnpike first thing in the morning and be just south of Chicago by tomorrow evening." Eileen moved the station wagon to the right lane. "I've stayed at the Howard Johnson at this exit before," she explained as she exited Route 80.

Jennifer, now sitting in the front seat, watched Eileen's profile reflected in the windshield. They took the brightly lit exit, then turned right at the intersection and drove into the Howard Johnson parking lot. "What are you looking at, Jenny?" Eileen flushed under Jennifer's steady gaze.

"I was just thinking that you've been incredibly nice to me, that's all." Jennifer usually found it difficult to tell people how she felt, but she had always been able to talk to Eileen, ever since they first sat next to each other in their freshman home-room class.

"Oh, you'd do the same, if I needed help," Eileen said quickly.

Jennifer saw that her eyes were glimmering with tears. She reached out and squeezed her friend's arm as they pulled into a parking space. Then, as she reached to open the car door, she said, "Let's check in and then hit the bar." She stopped and turned back to Eileen. "Do you mind if we share a room? I mean . . ." Jennifer looked away, suddenly embarrassed. She saw several men opening the trunks of their cars and taking out luggage. "I mean, I'm still a little nervous. I'd feel safer with you sleeping in the same room."

"Sure, of course. I hate traveling alone, myself," Eileen answered quickly. "It's scary, all the weirdos out here. You never know."

"Listen!" Jennifer said, laughing. "The weirdos I can handle. I'm worried about Mr. Nice Guy." She lowered her voice as they entered the hotel lobby. "I'm afraid I might cut off his balls if he steps out of line."

"It would serve him right, cheating on his wife," Eileen replied.

The vodka on the rocks made Jennifer giddy. She was telling Eileen about Bobby Scott, a boy they had gone to school with, and how he had tried to kiss her underneath the stadium stands when they played Westbury for the division championship. "Here I was trying to go and take a pee. It was cold, remember? And he just wouldn't let go. I started to cry from pain."

"He was not too smart, Bobby."

"Whatever happened to him, anyway?" Jennifer stared down at her menu and tried to concentrate. Now that they were out of the car and in the warm hotel, she suddenly felt very hungry.

"Oh, he married Debby O'Brian. Do you remember her?"

"He married Debby? She was such a sweet girl, with that beautiful long red hair."

Eileen nodded. "He went to Queens College, then married her, and they had four kids quick as rabbits. She was a big

Catholic. Anyway, now he works for Goldman Sachs. I hear
he owns a brownstone and is worth millions.''

"Well, good for Debby.''

Eileen shook her head. "Oh, he dumped her for someone
else, a real hotshot investor herself. I met them both a few
years ago at a benefit. He was with his new wife, who bought
junk bonds, or sold them, or something, and she and I talked.
The men were working the room, you know, and here was
this woman—Rita, that was her name. She was so unhappy
she started to cry, right there in the Grand Ballroom of the
Waldorf.''

"With millions of dollars and a brownstone! Why?''

"Bobby beat her. She told me it was the only way he could
get it up. Here we were two strangers, and she unloads this
gruesome story on me.'' Eileen shrugged, then sipped her
drink. "She had to tell someone. She was so pitiful and
desperate, and I, at least, had known Scotty when he was a
kid.''

Jennifer sat back in her chair. She remembered Bobby Scott
and how he hadn't known how to kiss her, or any girl. She
remembered again the beer on his breath on that cold Friday
night. She had kissed him back just to get rid of him. "Maybe
it was my fault,'' she joked. "Maybe I shouldn't have played
so hard to get.''

"People choose what they want out of life, Jenny. That's
one of the first things you learn from Habasha. People choose
their parents. They choose their lovers and their friends. They
choose because they need to fulfill whatever is unresolved
from a past life.'' Eileen set down her menu. "I think I'm
going to have chicken,'' she announced. "I never get anything too fancy when I'm eating on the road.''

"Choice, and deciding for others, is all based on experiences from previous lives,'' Eileen continued after they had
ordered.

"I don't get that. What do you mean?''

"Well, take us. Who was class president?''

"I was!''

"And I decided you should be.''

"Eileen, don't be silly!'' Jennifer leaned forward. She had

had too much to drink and was trying to keep her voice down.
"It was my clique, you know that."

"You're wrong."

"I don't believe this." Jennifer sighed, baffled. "I remember everything about high school. Everything! It was
one of the happiest times in my life. I mean, why would I
screw up something like that? I remember when I decided to
run for class president. You were the newspaper editor; Karen
was in charge of the yearbook. And if I could be president,
then our clique—my clique!—would control the senior class
and practically all of Shreiber High." Her voice had risen,
and she saw out of the corner of her eye that she was attracting
attention. Several diners looked up from their meals, and two
men at the bar swung around to stare at them. Jennifer realized
suddenly that she and Eileen were the only single women in
the restaurant. She lowered her voice.

"Jenny," Eileen said slowly, "let me tell you a story and
see if you recall it. Okay?"

Jennifer nodded. The two drinks had given her a slight
headache. She reached over and took a sip of water and saw
that her hand was trembling.

"Do you remember our junior year?" Eileen asked.

"Of course."

"Do you remember Sam Sam and when we went to Jones
Beach?"

"Yes! Sam Sam!" Jennifer smiled. It was a name she had
forgotten, the girl from Thailand who had been an exchange
student at their school.

"Do you remember what happened to Sam Sam, Jenny?"
Eileen asked. The waitress had returned with their food, and
Eileen was calmly unfolding her napkin, watching Jennifer
carefully.

Jennifer shook her head. She could picture Sam Sam, a
small girl with beautiful long black hair, pretty brown eyes,
and a wonderful smile.

"You don't remember those jerks from Bay Shore? Those
three bikers on the dunes? You and I and Sam Sam were on
the beach that Saturday, sunning?"

"Yes, I do!" Jennifer said, suddenly recalling. She re-

membered then the young hoods swaggering along the beach.
They looked so weird coming through the sand in their tight
jackets and their long hair. They had wandered down to the
patch of sand where she and Eileen and Sam Sam were
stretched out on blankets.

"And one of them called Sam Sam a nigger?"

"Yes," Jennifer whispered.

"See, Jennifer, you do block events, don't you? We all
do."

"I was so afraid," Jennifer confessed.

"But do you remember what you did?"

Jennifer shook her head.

"You stood up to all of them, told them off, and told them
you'd have them all arrested."

Jennifer nodded, smiling, pleased to recall the long ago
incident. "I guess I did. I was so scared."

"And I was so proud of you. I remember Sam Sam thank-
ing you. I decided then you should be class president. I told
everyone what you had done."

There were tears in Jennifer's eyes. "She was really lovely.
I wonder what happened to her."

"She was killed in an auto accident in Thailand when she
was nineteen."

"Oh God! No! How do you . . . ?"

"We wrote once a year or so, and then her brother wrote
saying she had been killed."

"I can't believe it. Little Sam Sam . . ."

"It's all right," Eileen said quickly. "She was reincarnated
as a member of a royal family in Asia somewhere. Habasha
told me. Within our lifetime she'll be a great leader of her
people. We didn't lose Sam Sam. She simply went on to a
better life, a more important and perfect life. It was her
destiny. You must learn to accept this, Jenny. Let life happen
to you. Know in your heart that all these events—good and
bad—will pass, and that you, too, will pass into other ex-
istences, other worlds."

Jennifer sat back in her chair, shaking her head. "It's all
so strange." She looked away from Eileen, glanced around

the room, and saw that the men at the bar were watching them, whispering to each other.

"You're just not ready, that's all." Eileen reached over and seized Jennifer's wrist. "But you have great ability, Jennifer. Your electromagnetic frequency is much better than mine, more powerful, perhaps, than Kathy Dart's. She has said as much to me."

"I can't do anything," Jennifer whispered back across the table, "except kill people."

"You have only destroyed what needed to be destroyed. You have only rid this world of individuals who needed to be reincarnated as better, purer spirits."

"I can't channel. I don't know—"

"I understand." Eileen broke in. "You can't summon guiding spirits the way Kathy does. But you're gifted in a way that she isn't. You can 'see,' Jennifer."

"Then why didn't I see that guy with the club? The one that hit me?" Jennifer had raised her voice again, disturbed by Eileen's certitude.

"As I said, you weren't ready," Eileen answered calmly. "I have a feeling that soon we'll know why you've been singled out. There's a connection somewhere." Eileen, excited, was waving her hands and inadvertently summoned a busboy carrying a coffee pot. "I'm sorry." Eileen laughed. Both she and Jennifer began to giggle, exhausted by their long drive, their drinks, and the intensity of the conversation.

"Excuse us," Jennifer said, recovering, "would you please have the waitress bring us the check?" She smiled warmly at the young man, who stared blankly at both of them and then wordlessly walked away.

The waitress approached then with a tray of drinks. Jennifer looked up and shook her head. "We didn't order another round," she explained.

"The gentlemen at the bar asked if they might buy you all a drink," the waitress said, leaning over to set down the glasses.

Jennifer stopped her, saying quietly, "Please thank the gentlemen, but we don't accept drinks from strangers." Although she did not glance over at the men, she knew they were watching, and at once she felt her pulse quicken and her blood surge.

"Jenny, easy," Eileen whispered, "let's not—"

"It's okay, Eileen," she said calmly.

"Jennifer," Eileen whispered urgently. "Let's not have an incident with these jerks." She reached over to grab Jennifer's hand and immediately pulled away, her eyes widening, as she caught the look on Jennifer's face.

"Get me out of here," she told Eileen.

Eileen had her purse open and was dropping money onto the table. Jennifer stepped around the table and rushed for the door. She would be all right, she kept telling herself, if she could get outside, away from the two men at the bar. It was only a question of control. She had to control herself. Nervously she licked her lips.

"Hey, honey, what's the rush?" One of the men had come off his bar stool. He was a big man, the kind who had played football in school, and whose muscles had since turned to fat. He had no neck and a brick-shaped head.

Jennifer made it out of the restaurant and turned down the long, red-carpeted hallway that led to their room. But if he followed her, she realized, he'd know where to find them. She stepped abruptly out of the hallway and into the small alcove that had the ice and Coke machines.

"Hey, I've got some rum to go with that Coke of yours," the man said, turning the corner. He wore steel-rimmed glasses that pinched his face. He was grinning.

"Please, go away," she asked, refusing to look at him.

"Hey, honey, Pete and me, we just wanted to buy you and your girlfriend a drink. Jesus Christ, you could be a little sociable. I mean, we aren't out to rape you. Hey, here's my card." He flashed a small white card from his vest pocket. "The name's Buddy Rich. No relation, right? I'm the district salesman for Connect Computer." He seemed to swell before her. "We're the largest computer firm east of Illinois, servicing hospitals, universities, major companies." He had blocked her from the exit as he waved the card in her face. "Take it!" he ordered.

Jennifer took it from him.

"There! That's not so bad, right?"

She could smell the liquor on his breath, smell his sweat, and she was knew what was coming. She knew she could not stop herself, not without help.

"Please," she whispered.

"I think a couple of granddaddies and you'll be just fine. Whatcha say?" He was leaning close.

"Please?" she asked. By now she was backed up against the wall of the alcove. She concentrated on sounds—the humming of the giant Coke machine, the rumbling of the ice maker. Then he touched her.

Jennifer grabbed him by the throat before he took his hand off her shoulder. She looked up and saw his pale blue eyes bulge in his face. She smiled at him so he knew she was enjoying this.

She was holding him several inches above the cement floor with one outstretched arm, marveling at her own strength. Then she turned slowly around, spinning until she realized he had lost control of his bowels. Without pausing, she slammed his face against the ice machine. The blow broke his glasses and bloodied his face, and a bucket of small cubes tumbled from the machine and cracked against the concrete floor. Still holding him with one hand, she shoved his square head into the opening of the ice maker. His head was too big for the slot and she had to press harder, tearing the flesh off his forehead and the tips of his ears before she had successfully wedged him into place.

She left him there with his head jammed in the ice maker, kneeling in his own urine and excrement, and stepped into the dark hallway where Eileen stood, trembling and terrified.

"I think we had better check out," Jennifer said, and walked down the long hallway to their room.

22

"STOP LOOKING BACK, JENNY! He's not following us."

"How can you be so sure?" Jennifer glanced again out the rear window of the station wagon but saw no cars or flashing police lights gaining on them. The road was blank. They were alone on the dark interstate, traveling west through Ohio. It had begun to snow slightly, and the high beams picked up the flakes blowing against the windows. Jennifer felt the car shake as it was buffeted by bursts of wind.

"He's not about to go to the police and tell them some woman shoved his fat face into an ice machine." Eileen started to giggle, remembering. "I don't think I've ever been so impressed in my life. Jenny, you beat the shit out of that guy! Like you were Rambo or someone!"

"More like Hulk Hogan," Jennifer answered. She was sitting in the backseat with a car blanket wrapped around her, shivering. The cold was something that came with her power. When she calmed down, she knew, she'd feel better, and her hands would stop trembling. She wondered if it was her fear that provoked the trembling, or simply the aftermath of her rage.

"We're okay, Jenny. I tell you, stop worrying."

"I wish I could." Jennifer buried her face in the thick blanket to smother her tears. She was so tired of crying. Her emotional swings, she thought, were as disturbing as her extraordinary strength. "Eileen, I don't think I can do this. I can't sit in this car all the way to Minnesota."

"We're not going to drive all the way. Right now, we're an hour from Akron. We can leave the car there and fly to St. Paul. I'll telephone Kathy, and she'll have someone meet us at the airport. If we make good connections, we'll be on the farm by tomorrow afternoon."

"Where is it, exactly?"

"About an hour north of St. Paul. It's beautiful country. You'll love it!"

"Who's there? Besides Kathy?" Jennifer pulled herself up in the backseat, realizing how little she knew about Kathy Dart. She would never have taken such a spontaneous trip if it weren't for Eileen. It was really Eileen Gorman whom she trusted.

"There's Aurora, Kathy's daughter. She's a beautiful child, so gifted, just like her mother."

"What about her father? Kathy's husband?" Jennifer asked. She had been so wrapped up in her own problems that she had never even considered the personal life of Kathy Dart.

In the car's dark interior Jennifer could see Eileen shaking her head.

"I really don't know that much. No one does. I mean, you heard what Kathy said in Washington, how she was living in California and unhappily married." Eileen shrugged. "That's about all any of us know. The outsiders, I mean."

"But there must be more. There's always more," Jennifer said. They drove in silence for a moment. Jennifer found she did not want to look out the window. She was afraid of the dark, afraid of everything that was new to her. And that fear made her angry. It was as if part of her life had been taken away from her.

"So besides Aurora, who's on the farm?" she asked next, breaking the silence.

"Let's see, I'm not really sure. People come and go. When

Kathy isn't traveling, she holds sessions in the tukul. That's the main building, where they all have their meals and hang out. And it's the place for community meetings."

"Is it like that place out in Oregon—that Indian cult with free love?" Maybe she had taken too much on faith.

"No! It's nothing like that, Jennifer," Eileen soothed. "You're getting yourself all bent out of shape over nothing. I wouldn't do that to you. I wouldn't do that to myself!"

"I don't know what to think. But I do know I don't want to get mixed up in any sort of weird movement, with chanting and wearing red and having sex with guys who shave their heads. I just want to talk to Kathy Dart."

"And you will," Eileen answered, encouragingly. "People consult her all the time. When I was out in September, a group of corporate types—you know, chief executives, vice presidents—were taking this human-potential training that Kathy offers. She has a one-week session called Desta, which is Ethiopian for 'happy,' and during the week she channels Habasha.

"But there's other stuff, too: role-playing, confessions, meditation. Kathy says that it's helpful for people—especially managers—to discover their own self-defeating attitudes. And I tell you, Jenny, after a week out there, these guys were just flying! They were so excited. I remember thinking that if all Kathy Dart and Habasha ever do is bring such joy to a bunch of businessmen, well, then, channeling is worth it."

Jennifer smiled as she listened. She had forgotten how enthusiastically Eileen embraced the world.

"Okay, business guys, who else?" she asked, trying to envision what the farm was like.

Eileen shrugged. "People like you and me."

"That bad?"

"And worse, can you believe? Everyone has heard about Kathy, seen her on television."

Jennifer nodded. She remembered how she had seen Kathy Dart at five o'clock in the morning. "Where do we sleep?" she asked. "They don't have dorms, do they?"

"Oh, no. Everyone has his own room, with a single bed. Kathy believes that people need to be isolated, especially if they're meditating. Also, she believes that everyone needs their own personal space. Especially twin-souls."

"Twin-souls?"

"Yes. A twin-soul is someone with whom we may once have shared a lifetime. There is a tremendous attraction between twin-souls, but also great resentment. Elizabeth Taylor and Richard Burton were twin-souls. And Madonna and Sean Penn. Real twins often function like that in life. They love and hate each other simultaneously. Your problem might be because of some conflict with a twin-soul."

"What has happened to me—is still happening to me!—is more than just a love-hate relationship."

Eileen nodded. "I realize that, and I don't know the reason for these outbursts, but you seem to be suddenly attracting other souls who once shared a lifetime with you. Your past lives are coming together in this one."

"Why now?" Jennifer sat back, and for a moment they rode in silence. "I didn't ask for any of this," she finally said.

"I know," Eileen admitted. "Maybe I'm the cause. I exposed you to Kathy." She kept her eyes fixed on the road. "But Kathy can save you, too. And if not Kathy, then Habasha."

Jennifer closed her eyes and was comforted with the thought that help was waiting for her in Minnesota. When she opened them again, she saw bright lights on the dark horizon. The sudden sweep of lights made her think of the movie *Close Encounters of the Third Kind*, when the sky lit up with the arrival of the spaceship.

"What's that?" she asked.

"I believe," said Eileen, easing her foot off the gas pedal, "that it's downtown Akron."

"What if there is no such thing as reincarnation?" Jennifer asked next, as Eileen pulled off the highway. "What if there are no twin-souls or collective lives or multiple personalities!"

Eileen did not take her eyes from the interstate as she answered. "Then I think you are in real trouble," she said quietly.

"Why?" Jennifer asked.

"Because it means you are a killer. A cold-blooded killer."

It was colder now during the day and the light of the sun disappeared before Bura and the others had time to gather wood from the valley.

Because Bura was older, having lived through thirteen winters, and strong, strong as any of the males, except for Nira, she carried a full load back along the length of the valley.

She paused on the grassy slope where they had lived as long as she could remember. As she looked into the deep caves that had been cut with flint axes into each ledge, she thought of what her mother's mother had told her. When her mother's mother was a girl, they had come to live in these limestone caves, spending the cold months huddled by the charcoal fires, wrapped in the skins of wolves. Only the men would go out during the few hours of sunlight to hunt, and when they returned with a beast, there would be a great feast for all their people.

Bura thought how wonderful it must have been to live in the cave. Her mother's mother had shown her where she slept on the cold ledge, hidden from the north winds, while the old men talked, and told Bura how she used to lie awake watching the flame dance against the rock walls, huddled there beside her sisters.

But now they lived in a round hut made of bones and bear skin, and now only children played in the caves during the warm months. Bura had bled from her womb, and her mother and her mother's mother had taken her to the cave of drawings, and there she had drunk of her own blood, and her face and breasts had been marked with thick dark smears, and the women had prayed to all the spirits that her womb would flower with offspring. Her mother had said that Bura would go to live with Nira's people, and she had gone that night to sleep in the thick warm skins with his sisters, and now it had been three days and three nights, and he had not come for her.

Bura knew that he would come that night. She had been told that the men never came to take their women on the first night, and that the longer they waited, the more powerful was their coupling. She was not afraid. She had seen her brothers coupling with their new women, heard the moans of pleasure and pain.

Bura was climbing up the cave path at dusk, bent forward to balance the driftwood on her back and shoulders, when they seized her. They had hidden themselves in the shadows of the ledge, kneeling out of sight and waiting for the women to climb up and out of the riverbed. One covered her mouth with his hand, slipped his arm around her naked waist. The second one pulled her legs out from under her, tumbling her over as if she were a thin-legged deer. They dragged her back into the forgotten caves, littered now with the bones of animals.

Bura bit the thick hand that covered her mouth and kicked out with her legs, but the two men had her between them. They had seized her skin covering and ripped it from her waist. She was naked now except for the shells she had strung around her neck, and one of the men seized them, twisting the thin cord of leather tight around her throat until she could not breathe.

They were trying to mate with her. Already she could feel the one who had her from behind, his arms wrapped around her stomach, shoving his organ into her. She twisted in his grasp until the leather cord grew even tighter around her neck. She broke one hand free and scraped her fingernails down the face of the man in front.

As the strip of leather around her neck loosened, Bura tumbled into the dirt, gasping for breath. She knelt on the ground, and when she had swallowed one long

breath of air, she bolted from them, darting off like a
rabbit caught in an open meadow.

They ran to catch her as she climbed up the steep
limestone path. She was taller than both of them, and
faster, and even in the dark, she knew the caves and
ledges. If she reached the ridge, she would be all right.

Her breath was on fire in her throat, and there was a
pain in her side. But if they caught her now, they would
kill her. She could not see them behind her on the path,
but she heard them, knew they were still after her.

She reached the top of the path, ran into the open
meadow, and sighed with exhaustion and relief. She was
safe. She saw the sparkling flames of the fires, twinkling
like stars, and pushed forward for the safety of her mother's hut. She could even smell the meat burning on the
flame as she lengthened her stride and ran into Nira's
arms.

"Where were you?" he asked.

She tried to speak, to explain, but managed only to
raise her arm, a signal that she was being followed.

He saw them at once, stumbling into the open
meadow, and he leaped at them, hitting one of them at
the base of the neck with his club. Bura heard the bones
break, like a tree struck by sky light. She ran after Nira,
jumping over the dead body of the fallen male, and followed him down the limestone path as he went after the
other.

Swinging the short club with all his strength, Nira
struck the other male once on the side of his face, killing
him as the men of the plains killed the lynx that came
down from the hills, and pushed him over the edge.

Bura ran to Nira and wrapped her arms tightly around
his waist. She leaned forward to stare into the deep black
pit. There was no sound, no echo that came back to
them as it did when they tossed rocks off the high ridge.

She looked up at Nira and saw his black eyes studying
her. She wanted him to take her into the private, forgotten
caves and mate with her, but he didn't seem to hear her

silent longing, so she took his hand and brought it up to touch her naked breast.

As she brushed her bare bottom against him and felt his organ swell, she heard his breathing grow rapid and hard.

"You!" Nira said. "You bred with the Yellow Eyes."

Bura shook her head. "No!" she said.

"Your opening is wet from them," he told Bura, pushing her away.

"Nira, they caught me, but I got away. I ran." She was frightened now. "I have mated with no one," she begged, dropping to her knees.

Nira swore at her and tried to kick her away, but she clung to him, knowing that if he left her, she would be banished by his family. No one was allowed to mate with outsiders and come back to the tribe.

"No, Nira! No!" she cried, grabbing his waist and pulling herself up. Her fear gave her surprising strength, and when he wrestled her, she fought back. Her naked body, slippery with sweat, made it harder for him to push her away, but then he seized her by the hair and drew the sharp edge of his quartz stone across her breasts, marking her body, branding her as one who had mated with Yellow Eyes.

Enraged, she kicked out, aiming for his organ. He moaned and doubled over. Unable to stop her rage, Bura hit him again, and this time she seized his thick black hair in her fingers and pulled him forward toward the sheer edge of the limestone cliff. He tried to stop her, but she ducked away, and with the strength gained from long days of gathering wood, she pushed him off the edge. Nira screamed as he tried to seize the thin air, and then he dropped into the dark gorge.

Bura fell onto the hard path and cried, reaching out over the edge as if to pull him from the abyss. Now she had no man, and she knew the elders of the tribe would learn what she had done and would take her life.

All was lost. Her life was over. Standing at the rim of the deep gully, she thought briefly of her mother, of how she had disappointed her own, and then she leaped soundlessly into the void, falling endlessly into black space.

In the morning, word reached the highland huts, and the bodies of Nira and Bura were carried up to the high ground. As the people of the highlands moved away from the limestone cliffs, to better hunting lands farther south, new tribes came into the great meadowland and cut up the earth for planting. The old people remembered the time they left the cliffs, and some talked of the death of the young people. No one remembered their names.

23

"YOU'RE SAFE NOW," KATHY DART said, pulling Jennifer into a gentle embrace. She was smiling, but it seemed to Jennifer that she was also close to tears. "You've had a long journey," she said softly, "but now you're home."

Kathy led her away from the front door and into the center of the living room. The house had once been a barn, and Kathy had stripped it back to its original log beams. The interior was quite grand, with stark, bare-wood walls that swept up to a cathedral ceiling.

The south end of the long room was filled with windows, and Jennifer glimpsed a lake below the house, and more buildings clustered together by a nearby evergreen grove. But her attention was quickly drawn back to the massive stone fireplace that dominated the room. Soft leather chairs and sofas were grouped around the open fireplace.

"This hour is scheduled as personal time. Everyone is off in meditation or sleeping or skating down on the lake. I'm channeling Habasha after dinner. Oh, I'm so glad you're here!" Kathy beamed as she took Jennifer's hands in hers.

She was much more beautiful than Jennifer had remembered, with a clear, perfect complexion. Kathy Dart must be a very happy woman, Jennifer thought.

"We'll have lots of time later to talk, Jennifer." She glanced at Eileen. "I've told Simon I wanted you both in the big house with me. That way we can get together easily to talk. So let's get you settled. You both must be exhausted." Kathy turned and led them across the room.

"Oh, is there somewhere I can make a call to New York?" Jennifer asked. "I should check in with my office." When they arrived in St. Paul, she had called and left a message for Tom that she had arrived safely.

Kathy paused at the entrance to the hallway. "Of course, Jennifer. But I should mention that one of our objectives here on the farm is to separate you from all worldly, everyday concerns. I've found—Habasha has found—that the channeling sessions go much more smoothly if you can concentrate on what is happening here, rather than thinking about outside problems. I'm sure you understand."

"Yes, of course," Jennifer said quickly, embarrassed.

Kathy kept smiling, and added, "When Simon comes in with the luggage, I'll have him show you to my office."

"Simon?" Jennifer asked. "Does he work for you?" She felt Eileen nudge her in the small of her back.

Kathy laughed. "Oh, I don't know if any of us work for each other. Although there are days, as I tell Habasha, when I think I spend my whole life in slave labor for him. No, Simon doesn't work for me." She opened the door leading to the east wing of the barn, where their rooms were located. "We're twin-souls and have been together in previous lifetimes. Now, I guess you'd say we're lovers."

Jennifer's room had a view of the shallow valley that stretched away from the farm. The sun was setting, and its northern light softened the harsh landscape with an orange glow. She stood very still, concentrating on the lovely winter scene.

And then she heard a soft knock on her bedroom door. Without turning her eyes from the scene, she said, "Come in."

"Your luggage," a man's voice replied. Jennifer turned. The man standing in the doorway was silhouetted by the hallway light. She could not see his face, but she knew that he must be Simon.

"Thank you."

He set the bags aside and came to her, pulling off his leather gloves as he approached. His presence filled the room, and she found herself unaccountably giving way to him.

"I'm Simon," he said, "Simon McCloud."

"Yes, I know," she said. "Kathy's friend."

He smiled.

"Don't I know you?" Jennifer asked, staring up at him.

"I don't know. Do you?" He was still smiling.

"I mean, your face is so familiar." He looked like a lumberjack, with a full beard, dark brows, and thick hair that curled out from under a wool cap.

"That's what they all say," he teased, slowly stuffing his gloves into the pockets of his jacket. "And you're . . . who?" he asked politely.

"Jennifer. Jennifer Winters." She could feel her face flush with embarrassment, but still she couldn't take her eyes from him. "I'm sorry I'm staring," she apologized, "but I keep thinking I'm going to remember. Did you go to school in Chicago?" She tried to imagine him on campus.

He laughed then, and his blue eyes sparkled. Jennifer laughed, too. He was so unlike a New Yorker, she thought, immediately friendly and open. So this was the Midwest. No one had a hostile edge.

"I've never been to Chicago. I've never been anywhere, really, except Duluth and St. Paul." He shrugged good-naturedly.

"Well, you just look so familiar," Jennifer replied. Finally able to break her gaze, she glanced out the window. "I was just enjoying the sunset," she explained.

The orange glow had disappeared from the hillside, and now in the fading light, Minnesota's winter landscape looked threatening. Simon came over and stood beside her, staring out at the disappearing day. She was acutely conscious of him near her, of his warmth, and as she watched his breath fog the windowpane, she realized how much he was affecting her.

He broke the stillness. "It does look bleak, doesn't it? Not a night to be outside. But later, after dinner, the moon will come up and the whole valley will be lit. We usually go skating by the lake, build a fire there on the bank, and make hot chocolate and hot buttered rum. Do you skate?" he asked.

"Well, I try."

"Good! I'll help. All of us Minnesotans are born with either skates or skis on our feet." He tapped the glass with his fingernails, making a sharp click. "It's going to be a cold one." Then he grinned and moved away. "I better deliver Eileen's luggage. Kathy said you had a long trip and you need to rest." At the doorway he paused and turned to her. Jennifer had not left the window. "Welcome to the farm, Jennifer. It's your first visit?"

Jennifer nodded. She was searching frantically for something to say that would keep Simon with her.

"It changed my life, coming here," he said. He paused. "I owe my life to Kathy." He looked over at Jennifer and smiled that warm, honest smile. "She'll save you, too. I know." And then he closed the bedroom door and disappeared.

Jennifer did not move. She held her breath in an effort to hold on to his presence, to hold the intimacy of their shared moment. Gradually, she returned to the present, heard distant sounds from the huge old building, heard footsteps and muffled sounds, and took a deep breath, all at once exhausted from the long trip and from the week of tensions. She sat down on the edge of the single bed and pulled off her boots. Then, standing again, she slid off her wool skirt, unhooked her bra, and still in sweater and panties, slid under the heavy blankets and surrendered herself to sleep.

Jennifer felt a hand on her shoulder. Not yet fully awake, she reached out and grabbed the intruder's wrist.

"Jenny, it's me!" Eileen cried. "Ouch!" She fell against the bed. "Wake up, Jenny. Wake up. You're okay. Everything is fine."

Jennifer let go and pulled herself up. "I'm sorry. I was so
. . ."

"I know. I knocked, but you didn't answer. I'm sorry I
had to disturb you."

"What time is it?" Jennifer asked, rubbing her eyes.

"Around six. You've been asleep for two hours."

"Oh God, I could sleep for a week." Jennifer fell back
on her pillow. "It's pitch black out!" she said, staring out
of the window.

"It's the country, Jenny. That's what it's like." Eileen
moved from her perch on the bed and turned on the desk
lamp. "Better?"

"Yes," Jennifer agreed. She sat up. "I guess I'll get
dressed. After a shower, I'm sure I'll be okay. Where are
the showers, anyway?"

"Down the hall. They're communal."

"Oh, great!" Jennifer yawned. "I won't take a shower at
my health club, let alone here."

Eileen shrugged. "Oh, it's not that bad. There are private
stalls, if you need them, but Kathy believes we're too cul-
turally bound. This is one way to break down our inhibi-
tions."

"Taking showers with strangers should do it."

"I'm sure you wouldn't mind taking a shower with Simon
McCloud." Eileen smiled.

"Why? What do you mean?"

"Oh, I saw that he took his time to 'drop off' your bags."

"Eileen, come on." Jennifer tossed back the blankets and
stood. She picked her wool skirt off the back of the chair
and stepped into it.

"Well, what were you doing in here?"

"We were watching the sunset," Jennifer replied curtly.

"He's incredible, isn't he?"

"Incredible, how?" Jennifer waited, curious to know what
Eileen thought of Simon.

Eileen shrugged. "I don't know. Incredibly 'country,'
don't you think? I find it odd that Kathy, who's so sophis-
ticated, would be involved with him. Don't you?"

Jennifer concentrated on unpacking. She pulled a terry-cloth robe from her suitcase.

"Don't you?" Eileen persisted.

"Getting involved with anyone that gorgeous can't be considered too odd," said Jennifer decisively, folding the robe over her arm. She knew she couldn't lie to Eileen about feeling an attraction. Better just to acknowledge it and forget it. "But I also know that he's involved with Kathy Dart, just like I'm involved with Tom. I'm not going to jump the poor guy in some dark corner. Or the shower." Eileen laughed as she walked out, heading for the bathroom.

The showers were empty. Jennifer sighed, thankful for small favors. She remembered how she and Tom had made love in the steamy bathroom back in Brooklyn, and the memory aroused her. To cool down, she turned on the faucet and doused herself with water.

When she came out of the shower room ten minutes later, she was wrapped in towels. She stood in the doorway of the bathroom and glanced down toward the living room to see if the coast was clear.

The door was open at the end of the hall and a shaft of light from the living room filled the entrance. She could hear voices from farther away in the house. There were several people talking and laughing among themselves. Perhaps it was the skaters having a drink before dinner.

Jennifer turned toward her room and saw a figure step into the hallway, coming from the living room. She stopped at once, startled by the sudden sight of the man, and took a deep breath. She wasn't driving herself crazy, she thought, and started to say hello when she realized it wasn't another guest.

The man's size alarmed her. He was immense, larger, it seemed, than the doorway itself, and he was moving slowly toward her, coming at her from the only exit. She backed off, terrified. She was immediately assailed by the odor of sweat and urine.

"Hello," she said, needing to hear her voice, and peered into the dark hallway, hoping to see his face. But his features were hidden in the rags he used to keep out the cold. Then she realized who it was. This was the man she had killed outside of the museum.

He was not dead. He had come to get her, and now he had her cornered in the hallway. She backed away from him and the lighted living room, but he kept coming toward her. His body filled the narrow hallway, squeezed out the light from the living room, plugged up the exit as if he were a stopper. She was trapped.

"No," she whispered, clutching a towel to her breast. She tried to scream, but no sound escaped her throat. She waited for the inhuman rage to take over her body and turn her into a beast, but this time there was no transformation. She felt no cold draft of air, no pumping of her muscles. No rage.

Jennifer stumbled against the wall. She reached the end of the hallway, glanced around for a door, but there was just a window, sealed against the cold, and beyond it, the darkness of the rural night. She slid sobbing to the carpet and waited for him to kill her.

"Jennifer, are you all right?" Kathy Dart's voice broke into her consciousness. She was curled up, shrivering in the corner, and barely felt Kathy Dart's comforting hands stroke her hair. "It's all right, Jenny," Kathy whispered. "I am with you. Something frightened you, that's all. You're safe."

"I thought I saw something," she tried to explain, not looking at Kathy Dart. Jennifer realized then that she had wet herself, and humiliated, she struggled to a sitting position. She felt like a child.

"Yes?" Kathy waited patiently for an explanation. She knelt beside Jennifer on the carpet. "Tell me. You saw someone from your past? Was it Margit?"

Jennifer shook her head. "It was no one I knew. I mean, it looked like a homeless man. Someone I . . ." She tried to concentrate. "It was weird. I thought it was the man . . ." Jennifer shook her head, then began to sob. Kathy Dart pulled Jennifer into a gentle embrace.

"I'm going crazy," Jennifer whispered. "I kill people. I

have conversations with dead people in my apartment. I hallucinate. Oh, dear God, help me.''

Jennifer pulled her head from Kathy's embrace, leaned back against the wall, and closed her eyes. She felt Kathy reach out and wipe away her tears. For a moment Jennifer let herself be comforted.

''In the next few days, Jennifer,'' Kathy said softly, ''we will answer these questions and straighten out all the mystery. You are at the edge of great possibilities.''

''I'm at the edge of an abyss.''

''It is when we look into that abyss that we discover the truth. You are so close, Jennifer.''

Jennifer looked up at Kathy Dart. Her eyes gleamed. Her smile emanated confidence and enthusiasm. Jennifer nodded. She would try. ''Thank you,'' she whispered.

''Give yourself a chance,'' Kathy continued, ''to become the great person that is your destiny. I believe there is someone seeking to use your body as a medium into this world. Someone wants to channel through you. Someone wants to 'get out,' and I find that terribly exciting.''

''It has only been terrifying for me,'' Jennifer answered, pulling herself off the hallway floor. She needed another shower.

''I went through this myself, Jennifer,'' Kathy said calmly. ''Habasha wasn't just someone I met by chance in an aisle at the A and P.''

''I was happy the way I was,'' Jennifer answered.

''You only thought you were,'' Kathy Dart answered back.

''I would rather have been left alone.''

''But don't you understand,'' Kathy said quietly, ''this person who wishes to be channeled won't let you be your old self.'' And then, smiling, she leaned forward and kissed Jennifer softly on her cheek.

''When you're dressed, come into the living room, and we'll talk. There's so much to tell you.'' Then Kathy Dart nodded good-bye and walked back to the living room, blocking out the light at the end of the hallway as she disappeared from sight.

24

"HI, HOW'YA DOING?" Simon McCloud was suddenly at her side in the living room. "How 'bout a cup of tea?" he asked solicitously.

"Fine. I'm just fine," Jennifer answered, accepting the warm cup. Kathy Dart must have told him what happened in the hallway. "I think I'm finally adjusting to the frozen north," she added. She nodded toward the blazing fire. "That helps a lot. It looks so warm and inviting."

"It's actually a waste of energy." Simon shrugged. "We'd do better closing it down and putting in a wood stove, but Kathy's a great believer in the illusion of the fireplace . . . everyone sitting cozily around it." He smiled, as if amused by the deception.

"Well, I think it's lovely, illusion or not," Jennifer answered back. "Isn't there room for illusions in your life, Simon?" As she sipped her tea, she scanned the room for Eileen.

"Do you want to meet any of these people?" Simon asked, ignoring her question.

"No," Jennifer said truthfully, glancing around at the dozen other guests who were milling around the room. Many of them looked flushed, as if they had just come in from the cold. "Who are they?"

"International consultants. They work with Third World countries, telling their citizens how to act, teaching them to eat with knives and forks, and how to get along with Americans." He shrugged dismissively, then added coolly, "To tell you the truth, I don't pay that much attention to most of the people who come through here. There's a different group nearly every week. This place is like a bus station sometimes. I just stand at the front door, punch tickets, and take money." He reached over and set his cup of tea on an end table.

Jennifer was startled by his candor. "Is that how you consider me . . . and Eileen?"

"No, of course not," he replied. "You're not like these people. You're one of us."

"Us? What do you mean?"

"Us . . . you know." He shrugged. "You and Eileen, and Kathy, of course, and me. I mean, the four of us are linked. Hasn't Kathy told you about all of this?" Suddenly Simon looked worried, as if he had said too much.

Jennifer shook her head and kept her eyes on him.

"Kathy explained what happened to you," he went on. "She told me before you came that we . . . you and I . . . had this . . . connection. She said I'd have an emotional pull toward you." He was staring down at her, and Jennifer returned his gaze. She felt as if she could lose herself in his deep blue eyes.

"What exactly are you saying, Simon?" she found herself asking calmly, though she knew exactly.

They were both sitting now on the window seat at the far end of the room. Jennifer felt as if she and Simon were completely alone. Her heart was pounding.

"Kathy told me how you and I, and she, too, were all once—maybe more than once—connected in another life." He suddenly seemed embarrassed and he looked away.

"Why are you saying this, Simon? What are you suggesting?"

"I'm saying that the moment I saw you I knew I wanted you."

"I don't think Kathy would appreciate hearing that," Jennifer said.

"But she knows," Simon explained. "And she understands. Habasha told her. In a previous life, you and I were living in an Idaho mining town. You were Chinese and married to an old man. I was killed—"

Jennifer stood up. "I don't know anything about that," she said. She knew that she had to get away from Simon. Her desire for him was dizzying. She made an effort to move, but he seized her by the wrist. Jennifer felt faint.

Just then, she spotted Eileen approaching from the other end of the room. "Stop, Simon," she whispered. "Please."

He let go of her wrist.

"There you are! You didn't come and get me after your shower. Hello, Simon." Eileen's eyes took in Jennifer's guilty look, and she smiled.

"I'm sorry, Eileen. I forgot. After my shower, I ran into Kathy."

"It's my fault, Eileen," Simon interrupted. "We got to talking about our shared past lives."

Jennifer took a deep breath and stared into the blazing fire. Simon was smiling at Eileen, enveloping her with his charm. As he explained that he and Jennifer once lived together in an Idaho mining town, he slipped his arm around her in a brief embrace.

Jennifer felt her knees weaken, but she forced herself to recover, to pull away from Simon's embrace. This was crazy. Her emotions were totally out of control.

"And what about me?" Eileen made a face at Simon, fretting about her exclusion.

"Yes, you were with us. Kathy has told you that, hasn't she?" Simon cocked his head.

"Of course she has. I was just teasing." Eileen reached to touch Simon's arm.

But she wasn't teasing, Jennifer realized. Something was wrong. Eileen was upset. But before Jennifer could question her, Simon interrupted, nodding toward the center of the room.

"I think we're ready."

Jennifer turned to see Kathy Dart standing in front of the blazing fire. Many of the other guests had already settled into the leather chairs. Kathy looked up and smiled over to where they stood, and immediately Jennifer stepped away from Eileen and Simon and walked into the circle of chairs. Now she needed distance from everyone.

She squeezed herself between the others on the brown leather couch and turned her full attention to Kathy Dart.

"We have several new people with us this evening," Kathy began, as she introduced Jennifer and Eileen. "As some of you know," she went on, "I like to spend a few minutes each evening before dinner talking about various aspects of parapsychology. To remind everyone again, this is a relatively new discipline that studies extrasensory perception, or ESP; psychokinesis, or PK; and survival phenomena, which include channeling, reincarnation, afterlife evidence—you name it, the list goes on." She paused to smile at the group. "I know that many of you have questions about us and what we are all doing here at the farm. So, let's take a few minutes to answer some of your questions."

Kathy paced slowly back and forth before the small gathering. She was wearing stone-washed jeans and a white cashmere sweater. But despite the casual clothes, Jennifer noted, she was perfectly turned out with pearl earrings and makeup. Her long, glossy black hair was loose and tossed over her shoulder.

"Channeling, to give a definition developed by Jon Klimo in his wonderful book, is that 'process of receiving information from some level of reality other than the ordinary physical one. And this includes messages from any mental source that falls outside of one's own.' "

She paused and grinned down at the group. "Got it?" she asked with a laugh.

Jennifer found herself smiling. She had promised herself that she would be skeptical of everything she heard and saw. But she had to admit that Kathy's warmth and humor made her sound especially convincing.

"But who are the channelers of today?" Kathy went on. "And where are our oracles? Do you think I fit the mold?" She was laughing again.

"Actually, I think I'm a channeler because I'm such a lazy person. It's true, really. My spiritual guides say that lazy people make the best mediums because they don't have an agenda. They're not trying to hit home runs for God." She paced across the hearth and then nodded to one of the guests who had raised a hand.

"But, Kathy," the woman asked, "how did you know that you could channel? How does it actually happen?"

"It really began before I first saw Habasha, but I didn't understand what I was experiencing. I think I was always a channel. For example, I've never been afraid of ghosts or graveyards or horror movies. When I was a child, I wanted to have a ghost as a friend. Even back then, I began to have a sense that I could talk to the dead, and I was drawn to certain people because they seemed somehow to be connected to me.

"I began with automatic writing, which, by the way, is nothing more than doodling. I'd hold a pencil in my hand, usually during a boring college class, and without warning my hand would start moving.

"And I used the Ouija board, even though my priest denounced it as the devil's tool. And in a way he was right to warn people. Ouija boards are not toys. They have great power.

"Once you enter the world of the spiritual, you must tread carefully. I know this sounds a little medieval, but one has to use caution."

"Are all channels alike?" someone asked.

"No, they're not. Think of musical instruments. You can't play keyboard music on a flute, which plays only one note at a time. But you can play Bach on the flute; you can play Bach on the pipe organ. It's just that it sounds different on each instrument.

"Different mediums are like different instruments. Each one has an inherent limitation, but also a unique quality. The sound of a pipe organ, for example, is different than the

sound of a piano or a harpsichord. Not better or worse, but
different. It's like that with channels. Not all spirits can communicate or even want to communicate through all channels.

"Besides, not all mediums are verbal. Some channels have
healing energy. Some sing. Some dance. Isadora Duncan, I
believe, was a great channeler."

Jennifer glanced across the room and saw another raised
hand. "What about these spirits that I hear talked about?"
the woman asked. "Are they around us now? Do we need
to worry about them or what?" She laughed nervously.

"No, you don't have to worry," Kathy reassured her.
"They are very much like the rest of us. Some are between
incarnations. Others will be spirits forever. They may be
positive or negative. But they are all angelic forces. Manifestations of higher consciousness.

"And, of course, we have their polar opposites, the demonic forces—spirits consumed by unevolved energy that
pulls everyone down. The Greeks summed it up when they
talked about the harpies and the sirens. The sirens are the
seductors who lure you into actions that are not in your best
interest. The harpies shriek guilt and self-hatred into your
ear. Both are very real."

"Are these spirits our personal angels?" someone asked.

"No, they're universal. No one owns a spirit. But spirits
do befriend and work with certain people, and some of them
may represent our spiritual brothers and sisters, or perhaps
even higher aspects of ourselves."

"What about all this out-of-body stuff I keep reading
about?" another guest asked.

"Very simple. You leave your body and go somewhere
else. Where, precisely, we don't know. Remember that the
mind is not a physical entity. When we lose consciousness,
it is because our mind, or consciousness, is somewhere else."

"But where exactly?" Jennifer heard herself ask.

"We don't know, Jennifer," Kathy said, softening her
voice. "The Russians have been studying this phenomenon.
I guess they'd like to spy on us by sending people out of
their bodies, to go through walls.

"But let's look at it from another angle," she went on.

"Let's talk about dreams. Basically, dreams are out-of-body experiences. If you didn't sleep at night, you'd go crazy! The stress of being 'in body' is too great to maintain."

"And reincarnation?" a woman asked. Jennifer found herself nodding. Yes, what about it? she thought.

"Well, technically speaking, you're either in the body— 'in carna'—or out of the body—'discarna.' Carna is, literally, the flesh. And death is the ultimate out-of-body experience. But, in fact, we leave our bodies all the time! Sometimes a person's mind is half in one place, half in another. The truth is, it can be in both locations at the same time. You see, the mind is not physical, and so doesn't need to follow the physical limitations of the body. When we talk about being out of body, we're talking about energy that travels.

"So the idea is this: the mind goes out of the body. The body dies, but the mind continues to exist. It is free to form a new relationship with physical matter. A relationship that is not necessarily confined to human form."

As Jennifer sat listening to Kathy Dart, she suddenly felt a curious spasm and saw a clear image of Phoebe Fisher, sitting by the fireplace in her apartment in New York. Phoebe was speaking to her, but Jennifer couldn't hear the words: she saw only that Phoebe was frowning, beckoning her away from the living room of Kathy Dart, telling Jennifer to flee. Jennifer raised her hand to reach for Phoebe's image, and then she felt the warmth of a soft palm, and she looked up to see Kathy Dart lean forward and smile down at her.

"Dinner, Jenny?" she asked.

"Oh, yes, sorry."

"There's no reason to be sorry. Were you trance-channeling?" Kathy teased, smiling.

"I don't know what I was doing," Jennifer admitted, chagrined by her behavior, and by what she thought she had just seen: Phoebe Fisher sitting next to Kathy and warning Jennifer to get away from her.

"Jennifer, I know you have been approached by Simon. I know you two were once lovers."

Jennifer glanced to the channeler, waved her hand and said, "It was a simple misunderstanding."

"It's all right, Jenny. Please, you're getting yourself upset. Of course you are attracted to Simon. He must have told you that we were all once together in a previous life. The physical attraction we have for each other is extremely powerful." Kathy flashed one of her bright, wide smiles and linked her arm into Jennifer's. "And if you two decide you want to make love, please follow your instincts. I don't own him, Jennifer. We're all free to act on our impulses and desires, especially here at the farm. I can't keep you two apart. I wouldn't if I could."

And then she grinned like a schoolgirl.

25

WHEN THEY RETURNED TO the living room after dinner, the furniture had been moved away from the fireplace. Kathy Dart was already sitting in an overstuffed chair in front of the windows on the other side of the room. She was wearing a long white gown and had combed out her black hair so that it fanned over her shoulders. Her only piece of jewelry was a gold chain and the crystal that rested between her breasts. It was the same crystal she had worn when Jennifer first saw her in Washington.

Jennifer slipped into a straight-backed chair away from the others, craning her neck to make sure she had a clear view of Kathy. She wanted to be able to see her when she went into her trance. Eileen had produced a small tape recorder from her purse; unable to find a chair close enough, she slipped to the floor at Kathy's feet.

From her angle against the side wall, Jennifer saw the whole room, and she watched the others as they found seats. Some of the young students who were on work/study programs at the farm came out of the kitchen still wearing aprons over their jeans and slid down as a group against the length of one wall.

Jennifer spotted one young man who looked familiar, and she studied him for a moment, trying to place where she had seen him. He looked like the other students, but with short hair, and the build of an athlete. He looked up at Eileen then and smiled, and Jennifer remembered where she had seen him. He had been the young reporter writing the article about Kathy Dart. They had met briefly outside the meeting room, and he had reminded her of her brother.

Simon stepped into the room, and Jennifer kept herself from looking at him. She was afraid he might walk over and sit beside her, and she did not want him near her, not when Kathy Dart was in her trance and Habasha was speaking.

Simon, however, was busy. He had brought a large pitcher of water and a glass from the kitchen, and he set them down on a small table beside Kathy, who glanced up and smiled briefly at him. When he leaned over and whispered something, she laughed, then he stepped away and took a seat by the fireplace. Kathy turned to the group and asked cheerfully, "Are we all here?"

She glanced around the room, smiling at everyone, and went on. "I'd like to explain to our new people a little of what happens when I do this trance-channel. So everyone who has been with me before please indulge us." She directed attention initially to the row of young students and then went on.

"I begin with a short prayer, and I ask that you join in with me. This enables us to come together as a group, as one being, so to speak. I'll lead the group in an African chant— one of Habasha's chants—that I find pulls Habasha closer to me and, of course, to you as well.

"After the chant, there will be a moment of meditation as I slip into the trance and allow Habasha to come forward. As many of you know, I am elsewhere during the trance; if it were not for these tape recordings, I wouldn't know what was actually said by Habasha."

"Where are you exactly?" someone asked.

"Sleeping, actually," Kathy responded, and they laughed. "I get a good nap while Habasha does all the work." Kathy glanced around the room again, caught Jennifer's eye, and smiled. Then she spoke again to the group. "Usually Habasha has something to say, perhaps a story from his own life, and he'll be prepared for questions. I know that many of you have things you'd like to ask, so please, don't be shy." She looked pointedly at Jennifer. "Oh, you should be aware that Habasha will often use African terms when he speaks," she added. "Later, if you wish, I will explain to you what he has said."

Jennifer felt as if her heart were freezing up inside her. She slipped down farther in the chair but did not take her eyes off Kathy.

"Also, I'd like to request that none of you cross your arms. We don't want to close ourselves off from each other, from the flow of energy in the room."

She smiled, then turned to Simon, who reached over and dimmed the overhead lights. A dozen blue candles had been lit throughout the room, and their small flames flickered in the darkness. "All right," Kathy said softly, "let us begin."

She moved forward to sit on the edge of her chair, lifted her arms, turned the palms of her hands up, and said clearly, "Spirit of light and truth unite us. Inspire our minds and fill our hearts with love. Heal and energize our bodies. Receive our thanks for the many gifts that have come to us. Guide us on the path that we may please and serve thee.

"Holy art Thou, Lord of the Universe. Holy art Thou, the Vast and the Mighty. Lord of the light and of the dark. O Jehovah! O Yahweh! O Abba! O Jesus! O Allah! O Brahma! Be with us today in our work."

Kathy bowed her head for a moment, and when she looked up again her eyes were closed and she chanted:

Ommmmmmmmmmmmmmmmmmmmmmmmmmmmmmmmmmm.
Ommmmmmmmmmmmmmmmmmmmmmmmmmmmmmmmmmm.
Ommmmmmmmmmmmmmmmmmmmmmmmmmmmmmmmmmm.

She fell silent, rocking gently back and forth on the edge of the chair.

Then her own sweet voice was given over to the voice of

Habasha, the ancient African, a strong, full voice that roared into the silent gathering.

"I am Habasha, the great one! How are my dear friends of America? *Tenayistilligan.*"

"*Tenayistilligan,*" a few replied. "*Tiru no.*"

"*Ameseghinallehu,*" Habasha answered.

Kathy turned her head slowly from left to right. Her eyes were open, and they seemed even larger than usual. So she was not going to channel with her eyes closed, as Phoebe Fisher had done.

"We are very well, Habasha. *Ameseghinallehu,*" Simon said quickly, and there were a few other soft, mumbled greetings from the students and from Eileen. But most of the audience sat silent, staring up at Kathy Dart.

"I am happy to be with you today," Habasha went on in his strong bass voice.

"I take pleasure to say that there is amongst you this evening one who has singular spiritual gifts, which, in due time, will manifest themselves to the benefit of your society. We are certain that all of you who have committed yourselves to the path of enlightenment shall know more and more with each day that comes, and you shall soon be in positions to shed much light, from the light which you possess, on where there is great darkness in this world.

"And, therefore, let us say that by taking care of your own need to know, you sooner will take care of others who need to know, for this light which you acquire for yourself will be the light that shines for others.

"For when you are illuminated you are like a light that shines. Wherever you go, if there is darkness, your own light will shine.

"You have come to the light, my dear friends, and you will go to another place. And we congratulate you for doing this goodness in our world.

"Let the truth be your essence. Let the truth lead you to your higher self. Know yourself and let that truth flow through your consciousness.

"As for those who will not understand, some prefer the

darkness. Remember, my dear friends, that all those who walk in the shadows do so by their own choosing. We ask that you will not be followers. Neither let yourselves be leaders. For if you are a follower you are standing in someone else's shadow; if you are a leader, you are casting a shadow upon others.

"We commend to you this work and say: Do not hope for perfection. Do not seek a perfect heaven where all things will lead forever, without fault and without flaw, without need of further thought, or further exercise.

"All life, my dear friends, is an adventure. It is an adventure! Indeed, to know everything that was ever going to be, to have absolute and total knowledge—if you could have that knowledge, would it not deprive you of a great sense of adventure?

"If one knows everything, what more can one know? If one has done everything, what more can one do? We cannot know the end of knowledge, and that is the mystery of existence. How much power is in the universe? How much gold is in the mountain? How much love is in your soul? It is all there. The great adventure of life is to find out how much there is, and the only way you can find out is to start to use it, start to spend it. Truth is. It is all here, waiting for your adventure and your discovery."

Habasha suddenly fell silent and Kathy Dart rocked in the soft chair, then sat back, as if exhausted by the long discourse. She placed her arms on the chair's arms, raised her head and again in that strong voice asked, "If any of you have questions, I will try to answer them. Speak up!" Her eyes were now closed.

"What is the purpose of life, then?" came a voice from one of the front rows of chairs.

"*Woizerit*," Habasha answered, "the process of living is living."

"What about past lives?" Jennifer spoke up. "My past lives."

"You may have past lives, or not, *Woizerit*. You may still be living your past lives. People live different lives simultaneously."

"What about our spirit, then? I mean, how can our spirit, or our soul, whatever we call it, be everywhere at once?"

"Each of your lives is lived with but a part of your total soul," Habasha replied.

"But then how can we have good lives and bad lives?" Jennifer asked immediately.

"If those lives are beautiful and benign and contribute something to the lives they are living now, on this plane, then I think the answer is that you consider them gifted. If the lives they are living on other planes create conflict with what they are trying to do here, then we consider them to be mentally and emotionally disturbed. And they all are the result of lives you have lived before, in other lifetimes."

"What do you mean," one of the men asked. "Other planes?"

Kathy Dart slowly turned her face in the direction of the speaker and Habasha said, "Other planes are dimensions beyond our existence here. These planes, or dimensions, are not necessarily stacked upon each other. Different planes may exist in the same place. Heaven and hell exist in exactly the same place. People used to think that heaven was up, and hell was down. But two people can be sitting together on a sofa, and one can be in hell, the other in heaven."

"Who or what are extraterrestrials?" Jennifer asked, thinking of Phoebe Fisher's Dance.

"Extraterrestrials are bound by the specifics of a time and the physical laws that govern their particular planes, wherever they are, but once they transcend those planes, they may be bounded by other considerations, such as weightlessness.

"We are all bound by laws. In terms of time travel, you have to know that time stands still and matter moves through it. Time does not move. Time simply is. Because all things exist now, there is no other time but now in any direction or plane. Therefore, the phenomenon of time is better understood as the distance between nows."

"But if you have a past life," Jennifer asked, pushing the point, "how would that be? Would you have a past life now?"

"Where did you put your past life?" Habasha challenged.

"Did you hide it under your bed? Where did it go? Does the past just dissolve? Does it disappear? Where is yesterday?"

"It's used up," Jennifer responded, anxious to hear where the argument might lead.

"You cannot destroy anything, only change it. Can you say that the whole of yesterday is just banished from the face of existence? And for that matter, what about tomorrow? Is it all being re-created for you to experience anew?"

Kathy Dart sat back again in the chair. She was nodding her head, as if Habasha had summed up the question.

"Is it tomorrow already?" the young reporter asked from the floor.

"Yes."

"I'm still confused," Jennifer interrupted. "If in a previous experience you lived completely in the past—as we usually understand the past—then are you simultaneously living that past life as you are living this present life?"

"Perhaps. Let's talk about the nature of existence. Is it physical or mental?"

"Both," Jennifer answered.

"How much of life does your physical body encounter?"

"Very little, I guess. I mean, just where I am. Who I am."

"And your mind embrace?"

"More."

"More! Indeed it does. Your body experiences only the physical now. So everything about the nature of your existence is a reality of the mind. It is a reality of the spirit."

Kathy Dart suddenly sat forward again and gestured with both arms, then Habasha said loudly to Jennifer, "Do you love anyone?" he asked abruptly. Kathy's head was tilted up, and her eyes were now closed, but still Jennifer tensed.

"Yes," she whispered, thinking immediately of Tom.

"But you don't at this moment have a physical relationship with that person, do you?"

Jennifer shook her head.

"No, you only have that physical relationship when your bodies touch. The real nature of this love is spiritual. If you did not exist as a spirit, then that love would cease to exist the moment your bodies ceased to touch. If you have knowl-

F U R Y   235

edge of the world, if you have a sense of the past or the future, if you have a sense of the meaning of things, the purpose of life, it is only because of spiritual awareness. That is the nature of existence.

"And what about that?" Habasha asked next. "If you remember your life, do you remember it chronologically?"

Jennifer shook her head.

"No! You remember the most important things first. The most important thing that ever happened to you might have occurred many years ago. It might be easier for you to remember something that happened when you were twenty than something that happened two weeks ago. Or yesterday.

"Indeed, something that happened to you as a child might be much more important than what you do now. And something that happened to you in ancient Egypt or Atlantis or Greece might be stronger in your consciousness now than what you do today, here on the farm."

"That's what I mean," Jennifer said quickly. "If I had another life in ancient Egypt, or whatever, and that feeling is very strong in me, does that mean it is taking place right now, while I am also living this life?"

"It couldn't be very ancient if you're still thinking about it," Habasha said, and around them everyone laughed.

"No, it couldn't," Jennifer admitted, smiling.

"It's obviously contemporary, then."

"How do you explain history books," Jennifer went on, sensing that she had trapped Habasha in her argument.

"History deals with linear time."

"Chronological?"

"Yes. You must understand that what is called 'ancient Egypt' is only ancient because it is measured relative to this date in history. It seems ancient, but it did not end; it continues to exist in another time dimension, another part of the now, a part other than the physical plane you occupy at this moment."

"Habasha, why are you here?" one of the women students asked. "Why did you come to earth again?"

Jennifer glanced from the student back to Kathy Dart, who was slowly nodding before Habasha replied.

"Many have asked me that, *Woizerit*. Some say, 'Habasha, do you not have a better place to go than here on this planet, at this time? Is there no paradise that awaits you? Is there no heaven in which you would rather be? Why would you come here? Why?'

"Because," Habasha answered himself, "sometimes we see wonderful things happening. We cannot help the whole planet, but we can help some of the planet, and you seem more than willing to let us be a part of your lives. I am pleased. Pleased with what I hear, pleased with what I see.

"My message to you is go where you are wanted. My message to you is that there are some people on this planet who really want what you have to offer, and they will love you and thank you and work with you if you will look for them. We spirits look for those who are willing to work with us and to receive us, and that brings us pleasure because then what we have to share is meaningful.

"And I say, too, there are people on this planet, among your friends and acquaintances, who do not wish you well, who plot against you, and will cause you pain." Kathy Dart raised one hand, and Habasha whispered, "I warn you. I have come now to warn you."

"Who?" Jennifer asked at once.

"I believe, *Woizerit*, that you do know."

"Who is trying to harm me? I don't know!" she said, raising her voice.

"You are an unusual one, *Woizerit*," Habasha said. His voice had slowed its cadence. "I see spirits, good and evil, who surround your aura and fight to dominate your soul. Do not be afraid. You are in good hands. Here at the farm, the healing graces will conquer the evil that confronts your mind. Much is being asked of you, *Woizerit*. You have suffered. You must be careful." Kathy Dart raised her hand, cautioning her. Her head was cocked, as if still listening to a faraway voice.

"How do I protect myself, Habasha?" Jennifer asked, pulling his attention again in her direction. "From these evil spirits?"

"You want answers always, *Woizerit*. Answers are only

part of the solution. What is more important are the questions." His voice had shifted. There was an edge of anger in his tone.

Jennifer felt it but kept pushing. "I need the answers," she insisted. "My life, this life, you say, is in danger." She caught herself from saying more. She glanced at Eileen and saw her friend furiously shaking her head.

"He who seeks danger receives it. He who looks for happiness finds it. Your unconscious has been responsible for getting you where you are. So you say that the unconscious part of you is somehow manipulating your affairs. Perhaps you are more responsible for your actions than you know. But how can you come to a place in life where you are able to take conscious control of your life and not be the victim?"

Habasha stopped speaking. Kathy Dart's eyes were open again, and they were blazing, as if blue candles were shining from the irises.

Habasha stopped speaking, and Kathy Dart suddenly stood and stepped away from the chair. Eileen and several of the young students pulled back to give her room, but Kathy moved with the assurance of a sleepwalker through the crowded room.

She had turned away from the sofa, turned toward the wall of students, and Jennifer knew at once that she was coming for her. She should have left when she had the chance, she told herself. Now she couldn't move. It seemed as if she were frozen to her chair.

Kathy Dart stepped to where Jennifer was seated and, clasping her hands together, raised them to her neck and carefully took off her crystal. Grasping the stone, she placed her hands gently on top of Jennifer's head. Jennifer closed her eyes, afraid of what was coming, afraid of all the faces watching her.

"O spirits of the past, spirits of our lives, leave this woman, my *Woizerit*. I implore you in the names of all our gods to seek peace with her. Rise up now and flee us. Rise up and flee us, I, Habasha, ancient of ancient, Dryopithecine, Cro-Magnon, warrior of Atlantis, poet of Greece, priest and lover, knight of the Round Table, Crusader for Christ, pioneer, and

profiteer, command the evil spirits that possess this woman
to flee this plane, these dimensions, this human body.''

Habasha's voice had risen. It filled her mind and rang in
her ears. She felt the pressure of Kathy's hands on her head,
felt the weight of the crystal, and then she felt the fire. It
started in the tips of her toes, seared the soles of her feet,
then snaked up through her legs and thighs. It tore her flesh
from her bones, flowing to the center of her body in a ball
of flame.

She heard her own cries of pain as the fire consumed her
body. Flames licked her breasts, rose up around her throat,
and set her hair on fire.

Kathy Dart grabbed her then, before she fell, before she
disappeared into the shock and pain.

Nada waited for the sun. She had made her paint from the reddish-brown clay by the river's edge and carried it back to the cave. Now, stacking the clay onto thick green palm leaves, she carried the paints to the wide back wall that faced south. Soon the sun would reach the entrance of the cave, and she would have only a few hours of sunlight in which to paint clearly the pictures that exploded like stars in her mind and filled her up. She could almost taste her desire to depict the scenes of battle that she'd heard as a child, the great battles between her people and the hunters from the north.

Ubba had called her to his side when he saw the pictures she had carved on the cave walls and told her to use her magic hands to paint the battle so that his sons, and the sons of his sons, would see what a warrior he was.

"No man among us will forget the day we battled and killed the Saavas," he whispered, "and they will remember me when my spirit leaves the earth and goes to sing with the birds."

Her mother's heart had swelled with pride, and she, too, had felt her heart fill. She knew she would never be hungry again or want for a warm bed, for Ubba would take her into his own cave and give her to his son, Ma-Ma.

But with the excitement was fear. If Ubba did not like the sketches on the wall, if something displeased him, then he would banish her from the clan. She knew of others who hid in the woods, who slept without fire, and stayed in trees to save themselves from the wild beasts.

Sometimes she caught glimpses of their shadows, following the clan as it migrated with the sun, trekking north after the bears came out of the trees and the frozen north to slap at the fish in the swift waters of the Twin Rivers.

Stories were told in the depth of the caves, stories of Ma-Ta and her brother Ta-Ma. Stories told, too, of Zuua and Chaa and the sons of the old woman Arrr, who was killed by the Spirits, struck down with the fiery flash of lightning. Ubba had banished her male offspring to the forest, fearful that the Spirits would strike again with flaming sky-bolts.

As Nada got ready to begin, others of the clan left their fishing and came up from the river to sit hunched at the entrance of the cave. They sat and watched her with their large brown eyes, waiting for her magic on the wall. Nada paid them no mind, though she was aware of their silent looks. She felt proud, though she did not know the word for her feeling, and busied herself with her drawing tools, slivers of rock that she sharpened herself.

Ubba approached the hillside with the aid of a bone, helped, too, by the sons of his sons, who huddled around him and bayed for favors. One carried a stool cut from the trunk of a tree. A dozen men had labored with the tree stump and fashioned for him a round chair, smoothed with river water and the oil of pigs.

Now it took three of the sons of the sons to carry the chair up the hillside to the flat entrance of the new cave. Nada waited there, hunched beside the gray cave wall. She waited for Ubba to begin his tale of fighting the Saavas. As he remembered his battles, he told of how he fought with blood dripping into his mouth. It was a tale Nada knew, a long story that she had first heard when she still sucked her mother's teat. Still, she listened, tried to find the pictures in her mind. She tried to summon up the images of Ubba's past, the evil dreams that had come to him, and followed him even now, many winters after the spear had sailed through the jungle trees and struck his throat, leaving him to whisper for the rest of his life. She listened with her eyes closed, still sitting on her haunches, thinking of him as a young man, fleet as the deer of the north.

Ubba stopped. The tale was told, and now the brown eyes of the clan all turned to her. She waited, pleased that she possessed the truth of his tale in her mind, held as she might hold a bird from a net in her fingers.

She lifted the slivers of rock crystal and went swiftly to work, dipping their sharp edges into the red clay. She drew and drew, dancing before the crowd of clansmen, as excited as she was by the painting. When she had filled the back wall with the story of battle, she stepped away from the pictures, exhausted and afraid of Ubba's judgment.

She sat again on the heels of her bare feet and rocked back, not daring to look up at the great man as he was lifted from his stool to peer up at the red clay drawings.

He paused at each figure, touching none, as he carefully walked the length of the south wall, seeing the story of his battle there in the pictures she had made of red clay. Then the old man stepped close to her and lifted her chin with his crippled hand.

"Nada, you tell the truth," he whispered. And he motioned to his eldest grandchild, the son of his daughter Noo, and said, "She is yours."

Nada fell to her knees in front of the warrior king and kissed his feet, as she had seen other females do when receiving a great honor from their leader. She was saved. Her mother and sister were saved. She let herself be lifted up by Ubba's grandson, and she glanced quickly at her mother as she was led away to his bed of skins. Nada's eyes sparkled with joy, for she had been saved by her magic fingers, and now the children she bore would someday be leaders of the people who lived beside the Twin Rivers.

26

KATHY WAS WAITING FOR Jennifer when she came into the dining room for breakfast the next morning. Several of the other guests were already serving themselves from the buffet table, but the house was still quiet. It was not yet seven o'clock.

"Why don't we have some quiet time for ourselves," Kathy whispered, coming up to Jennifer and kissing her lightly on the cheek. "How do you feel?"

Jennifer nodded, too distraught even to speak. She let Kathy direct her into a small area off the dining room.

"This used to be the hothouse when the farm was working," Kathy explained, "but I use it a lot during the cold months. It gets most of the winter sun."

The bright, sunny room had a vaulted ceiling, large windows, a tiled floor that Jennifer realized was also heated, thick Indian throw rugs, and oversized chairs.

"Sit here, please," she went on, motioning Jennifer to a deep chair next to a glass table. "Nanci will serve us."

Jennifer looked up to see a young woman who had been in the audience during the last channeling session.

"Jennifer, this is Nanci Stern. Nanci is teaching our New Age dance classes. That's something I wish you would try. She also is taking my course on the secrets of the shamans, learning how to bridge the communication gap between humans and other life forms. Aren't you, Nanci?"

The young woman nodded shyly as she placed a teapot on the glass-topped table.

"The shamans? Who are they?" Jennifer asked, unfolding a damask napkin on her lap.

"You've heard the term?"

"Yes, I guess I have," Jennifer admitted, shrugging. "I mean, somewhere in the recesses of my mind. I must have heard it in an anthropology class I took once." Again, she felt like a child in a room full of adults.

"Well, primitive cultures had a person whose role was to act as the intermediary between the spirit realm and the society. The shaman altered his or her condition by chanting, singing, or eating psychoactive plants. There have been shamanlike figures in cultures as diverse as Siberia and the West Indies. Voodoo is a good example that's close to home."

"And you," said Jennifer.

"Yes, of course. And other channelers like me. In a way, we're modern-day shamans. We interpret the other realm, the spirit world, for people." She nodded toward Nanci, who had gone into the other room. "She has a real gift," Kathy continued, her eyes shining. "I'm very proud of her. And she has a wonderful relationship with Simon."

Jennifer kept her eyes down as Kathy poured tea for both of them.

"They've been lovers now for about three weeks. It's wonderful to watch, to see their affection for each other grow and develop. Both of them have so much to give."

"I thought you said that you and Simon were . . ."

"Lovers?" Kathy glanced over at Jennifer as she set down the teapot.

"Yes." Jennifer tried to return Kathy's gaze, but the woman's steady, unblinking blue eyes unnerved her and she looked out the windows instead. Through the foggy glass she could see an edge of the frozen lake, and in the distance, farm fields, all bare and snow covered on the bright winter morning.

"We are, Jennifer, and so are Nanci and Simon. It isn't a secret, you know." Nanci returned with glasses of orange juice and plates of scrambled eggs, then retreated quickly.

"I'm sorry," Jennifer began. "I didn't mean to imply—"

"Nor are we promiscuous here on the farm."

Now Jennifer looked across at Kathy Dart and simply raised her eyebrows. "What about AIDS?"

"What about it?"

Jennifer shrugged. "I'm sorry," she said simply. "This is none of my business."

"But it is!" Kathy insisted, leaning across the table. She sat poised, holding her knife and fork above the heavy brown ceramic plate. "All of you, us, are connected. Nanci, Simon, you, me, and Eileen. We are all part of the oversoul, and therefore, there's a natural attraction—a physical attraction —among us."

"Has Eileen slept with Simon?" Jennifer asked without thinking, then quickly added, "I'm sorry. That, too, isn't my concern." She stared down at her food.

"I don't know. I haven't asked her. It doesn't matter, does it?"

"Of course not." Jennifer lifted her fork and tried to eat. She wanted only to get through breakfast, but she realized she had suddenly lost her appetite.

"It is your business, Jennifer, and that is what I am trying to tell you. I know you're attracted to Simon. I know that he is attracted to you. I am simply saying that there is nothing wrong with that. It is normal! It is healthy! It is right!"

"I'm sorry, that's not the way I conduct my life." Jennifer poked at her eggs with her fork, feeling better now that she had answered back.

"Simon approached you last night, didn't he?"

"Yes. You know that."

"But I don't know what happened between you."

"Nothing."

"Perhaps not."

Jennifer glanced over at Kathy, furious now. "Nothing happened, Kathy," she insisted.

"It is not necessary for Simon to physically sleep with you, Jennifer, for something to happen."

Jennifer dropped her knife and fork and pushed back her chair.

"Don't run away from yourself, Jenny."

"I'm sorry. I'm sorry I came here. I will not be . . . I do not have to put up with this." She would pack and leave, she decided. If she had to, she'd walk to the airport, anything to get away from these people.

But Kathy seized her wrist and forced Jennifer back down into her chair.

"I'm sorry," she said firmly. "But I want you to carefully think about what you are planning to do."

"And what am I planning?" Jennifer shouted.

"You want to leave. You want to run away," Kathy calmly told her. "But you cannot escape. It doesn't do you any good to flee from here. You aren't going to escape your past—all those lives you have already lived, in other generations, at other times."

"I'm afraid of you," Jennifer told her.

Kathy nodded. "Of course you are. I would be afraid, too, if I were you. But it is only through fear and adversity that the soul is enriched. When we are totally happy, wrapped up in our own affairs, we float through life and nothing is impressed upon our souls. We do not gain in wisdom."

Fear swept through Jennifer's body. "You are going to hurt me," she said. "I know you are. I can feel it." Yet she continued to sit there, unmoving. She had the sudden revelation that no one could hurt her, that she had conquered this woman before, in her past.

"We have been connected, Jenny, I keep telling you this," Kathy Dart said patiently, but there was an edge now in her voice. "And the only way we are going to understand the connection, see what the problem is, is to go back in time and look at who you were and how we are all linked.

What is the cosmic connection?'' She smiled softly. ''In a
way, we have already begun. Habasha has cast out the
negative spirits in your body. The pain and consuming fire
you felt last night when Habasha touched you through my
fingers was his way of expelling the evil spirits from your
body.''

''You admit that you're going to hurt me,'' Jennifer insisted again, staring at Kathy.

''The truth hurts, yes,'' Kathy agreed, nodding. ''But it's
also the only way that you can overcome this rage that is
within you.''

''Are you talking about acupuncture?'' Jennifer asked.
''Maybe that's how you're going to hurt me.''

''It does hurt a little,'' Kathy said, nodding, ''I won't
lie to you. But the pain dissolves quickly once the needles
are absorbed by the body. It's like a pin prick, nothing
more.''

''Then what happens?''

''I use what is called periosteal acupuncture, placing the
needle deeper into the body. It is hardly more painful than
the simple tip contact, and it goes only an inch into the skin.
I use a collection of needles, either silver or gold, but I do
not use as many needles as, say, a normal acupuncturist. I
am seeking other answers.

''The body remembers, Jenny. You've been told this, I
know. But it's true. Your spirit carries forward, from one
generation to the next, the history of your lives on earth.''

''You just put these needles into me and I start sputtering
out past lives?''

Kathy Dart shook her head. ''No, it's done much more
subtly. I twist the needles as my spirit guides instruct me,
and this in turn stimulates your recall. You'll 'see' what lives
you have lived, as if you were watching a movie.''

''Will you be watching the movie, too?''

''Well, I won't see your lives, but we can discuss the
images, if you like. We are set up to record what is said in
the sessions—you'll want to listen to yourself again afterward.''

''It doesn't seem possible,'' Jennifer said.

"Yes, I know." Kathy Dart sank back in the chair and looked across the frozen landscape of Minnesota. Her customary confidence and poise had slipped away, and Jennifer thought she saw a flash of fear in those brilliant blue eyes. "The truth is," Kathy admitted, "that I don't understand my own ability, but I fear it. I never wanted it."

At that moment Kathy Dart looked lost, a slender, delicate young woman overwhelmed by her life. She was very beautiful, Jennifer noticed again, in a way that had nothing to do with style or fashion. She was blessed with pure white skin and fine small features, and ironically, her clarity of expression hid her very heart and soul. Jennifer knew she could never fathom what Kathy was really thinking.

"Once Habasha walked into my life," Kathy went on, "nothing stayed the same. I left my husband. I left my friends and my teaching career. When I moved back here with my daughter, who was just seven, I had no money, no plans of any kind, but Habasha told me to go home to Minnesota. I was to build a new life, here on the banks of the St. Croix River."

Kathy glanced over at Jennifer. "This is where I was born, you know," she explained. "My grandparents and parents farmed this land. Then my brother, Eric, took over and mortgaged all the five hundred acres and lost the place. I was able to buy just this old barn and the outbuildings at a public auction four years ago. I used all the money I had from my divorce settlement to buy back my home. I had to do it. Habasha told me I would only find real happiness by being close to my roots. In the spring I love to go outside when the fields are being plowed and smell the fresh earth as it turns. It's all so wonderful and right."

Kathy Dart stopped talking and Jennifer reached over and took hold of her hand.

"None of this is very easy, Jenny, I know. But we have to go where our hearts tell us. We have to listen to our own spirits and respond to their directions. We are not alone. That's what you, what I, what we all have to remember. We have each other. You must know that. You came here to the farm in search of the truth."

"The truth can be very frightening. Sometimes, I guess, I'd rather turn my back on it, walk away."

"But you don't feel that way now, do you?" Kathy asked, searching Jennifer's face with her eyes.

Jennifer nodded. "I don't think I fully realized I couldn't hide from the truth until last night, until Habasha touched me. When I felt the burning—"

"His energy hurt you. He was casting off the evil guides that had surrounded your aura. Jennifer." Kathy squeezed Jennifer's hand. "He has set you free, Jenny!"

Jennifer stared back into Kathy's eyes and said firmly, resolve in her decision, "I'm ready, Kathy. I want to know who is trying to reach me. I want to end my misery. I want to know the truth, whatever it means for my life."

27

IN A SMALL, ENCLOSED room off the living room, Jennifer slipped behind a screen and took off her clothes, then draped herself in a warm flannel sheet.

"This used to be the birthing room on the farm," Kathy said. "When a mare or cow went into labor, she was brought into this section of the barn. It was always the warmest, because it was in the center."

She was carrying a small tray on which a dozen silver and gold needles floated in alcohol, next to a package of gauze. She set it down near the wide, padded massage table in the middle of the room.

"Would you prefer it if someone else were here?" she asked, as Jennifer emerged. "Eileen, for example?"

"Oh, no. I'd be too frightened."

Kathy laughed. "Well, some people are frightened to be alone when they go through the treatment."

"What's it going to be like?" Jennifer asked as she approached the table. There was very little furniture in the clinic: a few white steel cabinets, a wash basin, and open shelves filled with flannel and cotton sheets and stacks of white towels.

"It's a different experience for everyone. For me, it went very slowly. Each vision, each lifetime took several hours to view; it took me a month of past-life treatment to complete my history. For others—Eileen, for example—we went through centuries in a matter of minutes. She could only get a glimpse of herself, she said. Often, it was just a suggestion that she had been there somewhere—among the Romans, or the Irish." Kathy shrugged. "It depends. A man named Howard, who is doing research on the right side of the brain, has a thesis that the more creative you are, the more vivid your recollections will be.

"Also, you might not recall anything during this first session. Your defenses may try to protect you, keep you from knowing. It might take several sessions before we break through the median points and reach what I call the Core Existence, the center of a past-life experience. Think of it this way, Jenny. Your past lives are like blisters. Once I prick a blister with my golden needle, you'll be able to 'see' the lifetime that you have already lived."

"How can you find the right blisters?"

"Oh, that's easy. My spirit guides will tell me where to place the needles. They know where your past lives are recorded in your body. Ready?" She smiled reassuringly at Jennifer. "I want to meditate before we begin."

"What will I feel?" Jennifer asked, delaying.

"It depends. If you feel, for example, a sudden rush of warmth, you're getting a negative reaction from hostile spirits. I call them the little devils." Kathy Dart smiled down at Jennifer. She had moved a tall stool closer to the massage table and was perched on its edge.

"What if we don't find anything?"

"Is that what's worrying you?" Kathy asked. "That you won't recall?"

Jennifer shrugged. "That there won't be anything, period! No past lives."

Kathy Dart nodded, then said thoughtfully. "It's never happened. I have never had a patient who didn't recall a previous existence. Some, of course, are much more vivid than others. Some are lives of great importance, but the majority, I'd say, are ordinary lives: farmers, serfs, one or two adventurous types, a bandit in one generation, a thief in another.''

''Have you had any patients who share my experience?'' Jennifer asked. ''That strange rage and physical power?''

Kathy Dart picked up a silver needle from the white towel and replaced it carefully. ''That's what frightens you, isn't it? That somehow I'll tap a certan cell in your body and you'll become—''

''A raging primitive, yes.'' She looked directly at Kathy Dart.

''That won't happen.''

''How do you know?'' Jennifer challenged.

''Because nothing like that has ever happened to me, or to anyone I have treated. You will 'see' your past, but you won't become it. No one ever has.''

''No one else is me. I'm the one who has the out-of-the-blue surges.''

''But they are not out of the blue. They only occur when you're threatened. Do you feel threatened now?''

Jennifer shook her head, remembering how she had even tried to summon up her rage in the dark hallway the previous evening.

''Perhaps what has happened is that you feel safe on the farm. You're not in a hostile environment, and your senses intuitively know that.'' Kathy shrugged. ''It's really as simple as that.''

Jennifer nodded. Perhaps that was it. She remembered the computer salesman at the motel. She would never have touched him if he hadn't threatened her.

''Look, you'll be fully conscious,'' Kathy explained. ''If you begin to feel that you're losing control in any way, I'll stop.'' She hesitated. ''Are you sure you wouldn't like Eileen to be with you?''

Jennifer shook her head. ''No, thank you. I better go at this alone. Aren't you afraid my monster self will attack you?''

Kathy Dart laughed. "Not me! I've got Habasha, and he's king of the jungle. He told me so." She swung Jennifer's legs up onto the wide table. "Now, relax," she instructed.

"Are you kidding?"

"Try," Kathy Dart insisted. "I'll spend a moment in meditation and channel my spirits." She moved around to the end of the table and out of Jennifer's line of sight.

Jennifer closed her eyes and took long breaths. She would try, she told herself. She would try to surrender herself; maybe Kathy Dart could find out what was happening to her body.

"Try not to think," Kathy whispered. "Just let your mind flow. Be at peace."

Jennifer took another deep breath. She felt a wave of cold air cross her body, then a hot flash. She listened to Kathy sitting behind her at the head of the table and tried to match her steady breathing. Then her thoughts shifted, and Jennifer let herself go with them. She was listening to the house, but only occasionally did a muffled noise filter into the room. The acoustic tile on the walls told her the barn was soundproofed. She felt far away from the world, far away from time. And happy. So safe.

Kathy had moved around the table to her side.

"I am ready," she whispered to Jennifer, but her voice had changed, become more confident. "My guides have told me where to seek your lives." She reached up for the edge of the flannel sheet and pulled it off Jennifer's shoulder, then tucked it in at her waist. Jennifer did not open her eyes.

"I will place the first needles at pressure points on your shoulders and chest," Kathy said calmly, "and later in your third eye, which is the center of your forehead. You will experience some pain, as I mentioned, but it will pass. Also, you will feel that the needles are warm. That is because I am taking a ball of dried wormwood—it's an herb—and I'm placing it on top of the needle's handle. Then I light it when the needle is inserted. The warmth will aid in the stimulation of your memory cells."

"Tell me when you're about to begin," Jennifer asked.

"I've already begun."

Jennifer opened her eyes and saw two long needles pro-
truding from her chest.

"Jesus," she whispered.

Kathy smiled sweetly and asked, "Do you want to watch?"

"I don't know. Do I?" She felt better now that she had
actually seen the needles in her body. "Ouch! What happened?" Jennifer blinked back tears.

"Nothing. I stimulated your cells by twisting the needles,
that's all." She reached across to select another needle, slipping it behind Jennifer's right ear.

"I don't feel a thing," Jennifer whispered. At that moment
she felt wonderful, warm and comfortable.

"Of course not. You're doing just fine." She smiled down
at Jennifer. "Soon you'll begin to see your lives unfold. Take
another deep breath."

She did.

"This will help stimulate your memory."

"I'm getting excited," Jennifer said, smiling.

"I've turned on the tape recorder, so speak up when you
notice anything. Sometimes it's only an odor or taste that
comes back to us from another time. Anyway, speak up, talk
to me, and we'll have all the memories recorded for you."

Jennifer waited, her eyes closed again. She felt Kathy's
soft hands on her body, felt another fine needle pinch the
skin between her breasts, but there was no pain. Then Kathy
drew the sheet up over the tops of the half dozen needles,
and when Jennifer opened her eyes, it looked as if she were
enclosed inside a tent.

"Your spirits are arranging themselves, battling for position, so to speak," Kathy explained as Jennifer felt another
wave of cold air. "Do you see anything?"

Jennifer shook her head. "No," she giggled. "I feel as if
I'm waiting for my life to begin or something."

"Well, you are. But don't be afraid. You won't see anything that you don't want to see. Our bodies protect us in
that way." She fell silent.

Jennifer felt herself drifting off, as if she were taking a
morning nap. She started to resist the urge to lose conscious-

ness but remembered that Kathy had told her to let her mind wander, to let it find its own place in the depths of her subconscious. She stopped thinking. She forgot about her body and focused her attention on trying not to think. Everything slipped away. She felt as if she were falling gently through the space of her memories, dropping and dropping without fear. Then she was floating free of her body, like the night she was attacked and was looking down at herself on the operating table.

"You're beginning to recall," Kathy said, speaking, it seemed, from across the room. "I see flashes of your life. I'm picking them up."

"What?" Jennifer stirred but did not open her eyes. She smelled eucalyptus.

"Are you getting any reactions? Any sensations?"

Jennifer nodded. "Yes," she whispered. "It seems I'm in a tropical jungle or something. I can smell fruit, figs particularly. I am high up, sitting in a tree, I think." She shook her head as the image faded, then quickly was replaced with a stronger, more vivid picture. "I'm seeing primitive people. Very primitive people. They are running, throwing spears at each other. It's so weird. I mean, I don't know." Jennifer smiled, amused by the images that floated to the surface of her memory.

"Keep talking," Kathy instructed. "What else do you see?"

"I don't know. I mean, I'm seeing lots of things. I see a little girl. I know it's me, somehow. I am pounding on an animal's skull. Someone is going for me. A woman. She's running fast. My father is there, I think. It's all whirling past me, out of control." Jennifer felt her body tense, opened her eyes. She saw that Kathy had pulled away the flannel sheet and was gently twisting a few of the gold needles.

"Don't open your eyes. Don't stir. Everything is fine, just as it should be. Talk to me, Jenny, and tell me whatever you can about these images."

"I see myself. I mean, I know it's me. I'm somewhere else, I think. I'm standing at the entrance of a cave. I'm bare breasted, and I'm wearing just a piece of leather around my waist. I am happy, very happy. And I am beautiful. An African, maybe. My skin is chocolate colored. I am carrying this bowl in my hands. I am a painter, I know. I hear something. I'm looking around, looking at this dense jungle, and I think I am hearing something. Then I see a crowd of people—cavemen!—they are coming towards me. I am frightened, but I don't know why."

Jennifer stopped speaking.

"Yes," Kathy whispered, leaning closer. She had taken out a pad and begun to scribble down notes.

"It's gone. Nothing."

"That's all right," Kathy instructed, "let the image go and wait for the next one. There's more. Your body is in tune. Your meridian points have been reached."

"I see Rome or somewhere like that. Greece!" Jennifer interrupted. "It's a building with an open courtyard. I see two men talking. They're talking about me. I'm a student here, at the palestra, a young boy. One of the men, the man on the left, will be my lover. I know that, looking at him. He's a poet."

Jennifer fell silent. The recollection stunned her.

"Don't try to evaluate anything," Kathy urged. "Just describe. We'll talk later."

"I see something else," Jennifer whispered, concentrating on the visions. Her eyes were closed, but the images that filled her mind were fully realized and brilliantly rendered.

"I see a ship. On the Nile, I believe—and it's extremely warm. Blistering hot, really. I am wishing for a breeze, any sort of breeze. The boat is moving with the tide, toward the sea. I'm a maid, a lady-in-waiting or something." Jennifer saw a man turn to her and ask a question. She did not hear the question, and the handsome Egyptian was someone she had seen before. It was the young reporter from the magazine. But before she could even describe the scene, explain it to Kathy, the scene faded, and dissolved. Then her mind was filled with another world.

"I'm walking down a cobblestone street. I'm wearing nun's clothes. A long black habit. There's a crowd of people. I'm being led to a square. I'm being punished for something, I think." Her body began to perspire on the massage table.

The flannel sheet suddenly was too warm. "Take it off," she begged, and Kathy Dart reached over and pulled off the long sheet. Jennifer felt a cool breeze, but her body was clammy with sweat.

"Go on," said Kathy.

"I'm to be burned to death for my sins." She felt herself being pulled forward by black-hooded monks, saw herself going up onto the great stage where the Grand Inquisitor stood. She glanced around at the open square, crowded with peasants, then at the high bleachers, filled with the aristocracy of the Italian town. She saw Margit there, staring down at her. She kept turning and saw another woman, dressed, as she was, in the habit of a nun. Then the Grand Inquisitor stepped into her line of vision and began to read the charges against her. He turned to the crowd as he recited the list of her sins against God, and Jennifer realized it was Simon McCloud, condemning her to death.

"Are you okay?" Kathy asked.

"I don't know." Jennifer realized she was crying.

"Perhaps we should stop." Kathy stood to remove the half dozen acupuncture needles.

"No, please, let's continue." Jennifer wanted now to know the secrets of her past. The Italian scene had slipped away to be replaced by another image. Men were riding horses across open fields. She could see snow-covered mountains in the far distance, saw, too, that the men were being chased by Indians. Hundreds of warriors were swooping down off the hillside, billowing dust across the landscape as they galloped after the fleeing white men.

Behind them, in the distance, an overturned covered wagon tipped into a rushing riverbed. She saw a child running from the prairie schooner and realized that it was she. She saw the fright on the little girl's face, the terror in her eyes, as she came running. One of the Indian braves swept down on the fleeing child and lifted her effortlessly into his arms. The child screamed in Jennifer's ears as she was carried off into a cloud of dust, and she saw that the Indian was Tom. Tom, as an Apache, was stealing the white child.

On the table, her legs jerked.

"I think we've had enough," Kathy whispered.

"No, no," Jennifer shook her head. She was naked and wet with perspiration, but she was not cold. Her body felt aflame. "Please, I want to know."

"All right," Kathy whispered, "but remember that you have already lived these lives. Nothing can hurt you now. Lie quietly," she instructed. "We'll go on in a moment. Now, just calm yourself. Do you want me to explain anything of what you have seen?"

"Yes," Jennifer said at once. "Am I seeing a lot more than other people? Or less?"

"You are a very good subject, attuned to your previous lives. We say that such a person has 'clear antennae.' It isn't often that we receive such rich material on our first attempt. People often can only locate one or two such images from their past lives. I have to credit my spirits, too; they've guided my needles well."

"I was seeing people that I know today. What does that mean?"

"It's not surprising. We're all connected; what's important is the relationship. Who did you see?"

"Tom. Simon. And that young journalist who is doing that story about you."

"I wouldn't be surprised if we find out that Simon was once your husband. Or even that you were Tom's slave in a former life."

"And Margit was with me in one lifetime."

"The connection between you two is very strong. Perhaps she was your mother in another lifetime. What we have here is the intense bonding that is only possible in such maternal relationships. That is why Margit came to you after she was murdered. Are you ready to go on?"

"Yes."

Kathy Dart stood again and twisted the long gold needle that she had planted in Jennifer's third eye. "I'm going to stimulate your recollections." She pulled the flannel sheet up again over Jennifer's body.

"Have we been doing this long? I feel like I've been on this table for hours."

"Linear time means nothing to us, Jenny. Let your mind flow."

Jennifer kept her eyes closed and concentrated on relaxing, on keeping her mind free. She tried to keep herself from dwelling on what Kathy Dart had said about Tom, that he was such a dominant force in her life, her master.

Suddenly her mind was crowded with vivid pictures. They came swirling at her, and for an instant she panicked, worried that she would lose all this valuable information.

"I see a young girl, I think. I am a Chinese girl. I am being held, captured. People are after me. Chinese miners or something. They're going to kill me, kill the person who is holding me. I can't see his face."

"Relax, Jenny," Kathy instructed, touching her shoulder. "Let the images pass. They can not harm you. Don't concentrate too much. The images will find their way to the surface of your memory. Wait."

"I see a bedroom. An old-fashioned bedroom, you know, from the forties," Jennifer began again. "It's a little girl's room." She tried to scan the dark room. Though it was daylight, the blinds had been pulled, and the room was in shadow. A dozen dolls were stacked neatly on shelves, and there was a large dollhouse in the corner. "It's my bedroom, I just know!" she exclaimed.

"Is anyone there?" Kathy asked.

Jennifer shook her head. She was frowning, straining to see deep into her history. "There's a woman coming in," she said. And then, in her mind, the door opened and a shaft of light filled the dark bedroom.

"It's Margit!" Jennifer told Kathy. "She's my mother and she's come looking for me. I'm there, I know, somewhere in the room." Jennifer turned her head from side to side, trying to force the recollection, to pull the hidden memories to mind.

She saw herself then. She was just a teenager, not yet fifteen. She sat up in bed, just wakening, it seemed. She was naked. Then Jennifer saw the man, the young man beside the

girl, saw him roll over in the bed. She knew even before she
saw his face that it was Simon. And she knew, too, that these
two were brother and sister. Her mother, Margit, screamed
and brought her fists down on her daughter and son, striking
them in blind rage.

Jennifer was shaking. She could not control her own body.
She let Kathy tuck the warm flannel sheet more closely around
her, then gently, expertly, Kathy began to massage Jennifer's
temples. It took Jennifer several minutes to focus on what
Kathy Dart was saying.

"You had an episode, Jenny, that's all. It happens sometimes. You pull up a past life that fills you with enormous
guilt or remorse, and the realization has too much pain for
you to handle now. But once it is uncovered, then the trauma
is released. It won't haunt you. You have lived through the
experience."

Jennifer was weeping quietly, and she kept crying, but her
tears made her feel better. She was purging her body of the
memory.

"I didn't know it would be this therapeutic," Jennifer
whispered to Kathy, who was still ministering to her, arranging a small pillow beneath her head, wiping away her
tears.

Kathy nodded. "At times, it is. We made tremendous
progress this morning, but I think it's time for you to let your
body rest." She smiled down at Jennifer. "I'll turn down the
lights and leave you for a while. You'll be able to sleep.
Often such past life experiences completely knock you out."

"I'm just haunted by the thought of me and Simon. I mean,
in another life . . . brother and sister . . ."

"That's why you found him so attractive in this life,"
Kathy said. "Brother or not, he's quite handsome."

"I have a lover."

"We all have many lovers, Jenny."

"Not me."

"Why?" Kathy asked. She waited patiently for Jennifer
to respond.

Jennifer shrugged. She was suddenly uncomfortable talking about her life in such detail.

"I think you would feel less stressful if you allowed your true emotions to emerge."

"I don't think that the way to establish a permanent relationship with Tom is to become involved with another man, with Simon," Jennifer replied. "You know we're living in the age of AIDS! Women don't sleep around. Why do you want me to sleep with Simon, anyway?"

Kathy nodded toward the stack of silver and gold acupuncture needles.

"I can only do so much with my treatment. I think that a loving encounter with Simon, where you share the pleasure of each other, will enrich you. It will help break down the tensions you feel, the rage you have against men."

"I don't have any rage against men," Jennifer said quietly.

"Eileen told me what happened in the motel."

"Okay, I was angry, but you would have been, too, if you had seen him. Look, I'm not going to sleep with every man who hits on me just to show that I don't have hidden hostility toward men. What are you trying to say, anyway?"

"Look what happened to you when you saw Simon in that recall from the forties," Kathy said patiently.

"Kathy, he was my brother! I was sleeping with my brother!" Jennifer began to cry. Lying back on the massage table, she choked on her own tears and had to lean up on one elbow, coughing and sobbing.

Kathy waited until Jennifer had gained control of herself. She used the corner of the flannel sheet to wipe the tears away, then said softly, "I am not judging you, Jennifer, or prescribing a course of action. I am merely an instrument. The anger that you've been expressing, the conflict you have with your lover, Tom, are simply manifestations of a deeper and more profound unrest that is lodged within the cells of your body. Your spirit holds these memories and carries them forward, from one incarnation to the next. The body remembers everything, Jennifer. Everything! You have reached a critical moment in your life." She leaned back. "I don't know, Jenny, what is suddenly haunting you, driving you to such primitive rage. But I do want to help you discover its cause. Only by 'seeing' your past lives, by conversing with

Habasha, by accepting who you were in other lifetimes will you find out who you are today. Jenny, you must accept your past.''

"Am I to achieve this by fucking Simon McCloud?''

Kathy shrugged. "I only know that you two have a strong attraction to each other and that perhaps by sharing such an intimate moment, you'll learn something about yourself." For a moment she was silent. Then, slowly, she began to speak. "Our most intense experiences in life, Jenny, are with our family. Our lives are shaped from childhood. We're drawn to the kind of people we grew up with. I don't know yet what your parents are like, but I can guess."

Jennifer glanced over at Kathy Dart and waited for her explanation.

"You were born late in their lives, and I sense that you were an only child."

"I had a brother," Jennifer corrected.

"Yes, but he was much older, wasn't he?"

Jennifer nodded. "Eileen would have told you this much."

"I haven't discussed your family with Eileen."

"But she knew them. Eileen and I went to high school together. My parents are retired. They live in Florida."

"Yes, but you were never close to them. They were older. They were not pleased that you came along so late in their lives. From childhood, from infancy, really, you felt that you were unwanted. They did not give you the nurturing you needed. It was your brother—''

"Danny," Jennifer whispered.

"You lost Danny, didn't you?"

"Yes, in Vietnam. He never came home. They said he was killed in a bombing raid. They never found his body. I was only twelve when he died." She began to cry.

"You know, Jennifer, what you have to realize is that we choose our parents, choose our siblings. And we do this to resolve our experiences from previous lives."

"Why did Danny die and leave me?" Jennifer blurted out. "Was his death caused by something I did in another lifetime?"

Kathy shook her head. "I really don't know. Perhaps he

had to fulfill another destiny. His destiny. But you were not really left, Jenny. You have seen him in your dreams, haven't you?''

''He's always with me,'' Jennifer acknowledged. ''I feel him with me. He came to me when I almost died on the emergency-room table.''

Kathy Dart reached out to touch Jennifer's arm. ''Danny is with you, Jenny. Always. He is one of your spirits. And Margit Engle is another. They—and others from your oversoul—are here to guide and protect you. Just like myself, Habasha, Eileen, Simon. We're all part of your oversoul, members of your support system.'' Her pretty face was full of assurance.

''But I still don't know what is troubling me, or which life is the source of these rages.''

Kathy Dart nodded sympathetically.

''Soon,'' she whispered, ''soon.'' She nodded toward the row of needles. ''I think with another session, we'll have the truth.''

Now she stood and patted Jennifer on the shoulder. ''Why don't you rest here for a while,'' she said. ''I'll shut off the light and you can take a nap.''

Jennifer smiled. ''Thanks. I think I will. I do feel sleepy.''

''Regressions are exhausting.'' Kathy went to the door and dimmed the lights. ''I'll come back later to see if you're all right. You've had an exhausting morning, Jennifer, but I think we're very close to getting some answers.''

''Yes,'' Jennifer whispered, closing her eyes. ''I think we are, Kathy. Thank you.''

''Thank Habasha, Jenny. He holds the eternal truths. I'm simply the messenger.''

Kathy Dart closed the door, leaving Jennifer in the dark.

28

JENNIFER OPENED HER EYES in the dark clinic and saw that Simon had come into the room. Her heart beat against her chest. He must hear the wild pounding, she thought, and she took a deep breath in an effort to silence her body.

"Yes?" she asked, not moving.

"I spoke to Kathy. She said you were resting."

"Yes."

"Well, I came to see if you were okay." He was beside her. His face, inches away from hers, was silhouetted in the dark room.

"Yes, I'm okay. Thank you."

They were almost like lovers, Jennifer thought, whispering in the dark.

"Would you like me to give you a massage?" he asked. "I know that past-life recall is very tiring. You go through so many time frames."

"I've never had a massage," Jennifer admitted, "except when—" She stopped midsentence, remembering how in college her boyfriend had given her massages before they had made love. "What do you do? What types of massage, I mean."

"I know a lot of different methods, actually. There are the shiatsu and acupressure systems. They use finger and hand pressure on the body's energy meridians—the same principle as acupuncture, except without the needles. Or Swedish, which is body manipulation. I was taught that as a kid by my uncle. Then there's reflexology, you know, the kind that focuses on your feet and hands."

"They're all different?"

"Yes, and all are for different purposes. Hydrotherapy, for example, uses water and develops muscle tone, helps reduce swelling. Esthetic massage is a way to improve your looks."

"Good, I could use that one."

"No, you're already very beautiful," he said.

Jennifer smiled, afraid to say anything.

"And then there's myotherapy for the treatment of muscular pain." Simon went on. "And sports massage for runners, you know." He shrugged. "Whatever you want."

"And you know them all?"

"Kathy sent me to school."

"Of course." Jennifer pulled herself up on her right elbow and turned toward Simon. "What massage does Kathy have?" she asked.

"I always give her a Swedish massage."

"Then that's what I want."

"Good!" Simon smiled. He stood up and stepped across the small room, moving carefully in the darkness.

He was out of the wash of light, but still Jennifer could see him open the closet and take out a low, padded bench. He placed it on the floor, then returned to the table and handed her a folded white sheet.

"You'll need to put this on," he told her, and turned away.

She swung her legs over the side of the table and put on the sheet. "Oh, it's cold," she said.

"That's okay. I'll warm you up." Simon had knelt beside the table and was pulling several thick towels from the bottom drawer of the built-in wall cabinet.

"I'll be using oil on your body," he told her. "It's warm and it will keep your skin smooth." He was all business.

Now that the early intimacy between them had passed, she felt curiously let down. He glanced around and saw that Jennifer had tucked the long sheet around her body. "Ready?"

"I guess." She felt foolish now and vulnerable.

"Here," he whispered, taking her hand and gently maneuvering her into position on the table. He slipped a thick, rolled-up towel beneath her ankles, and another under her head, then turned her head so she faced the corner of the room. Jennifer closed her eyes, aware only of his strong hands on her back.

"I want you to relax and keep your eyes closed," he whispered. "I'm not going to talk at all, and I want you to focus on your body. Your neck muscles are very tight. Let me begin there." Leaning forward, Simon placed his hands, wet with oil, on her back. She shivered at his touch, and he whispered, "Relax, Jenny, relax and enjoy."

He began slowly and steadily to stroke her neck and back muscles with his strong hands, sliding them evenly down her back and up again. Jennifer felt herself grow sleepy, and gradually she let go of her defenses and surrendered herself to the pleasure of the massage.

Simon moved to her legs, kneading the calf muscles. She moaned when his fingers tightened on her legs, and he whispered an apology.

"It's okay," she answered, tucking her arms around the thick towel. She could lie there forever, she thought. She loved the feel of his hands on her body. "You have wonderful fingers," she told him.

"Shhh," he whispered. Moving to the bottom of the table, Simon began to gently stroke one foot, then the other. He began at the ankle and stroked toward the toes. She felt the tension disappear from her leg.

"I want you to do this to me every day," she mumbled.

"My pleasure," Simon answered, smiling in the dark. Slowly, he stroked up her leg, across her calf, up her thigh to her buttocks.

The loose sheet had slipped off her back, but she didn't care. It was dark in the room; she could not see him and was aware only of his hands and what they were doing to her body.

"Do you do this with Kathy?" Jennifer asked.

"Yes," Simon whispered. He was close beside her now, and she could smell the warm, fragrant oil on his fingers. "And now I'm doing it to you."

Simon turned her body with his hands, exposing her breasts. She reached down and draped the end of the long sheet across her waist. Slowly, carefully, he used his fingers and the palms of both hands to stroke her shoulder muscles, to pinch away the tightness and pain. Then he moved down the length of her body, using his hands carefully on her abdomen, kneading her thighs and calves, returning to her feet and stroking her to the tips of her toes.

He was working steadily, breathing harder from his steady effort, but he did not stop, and Jennifer fell silent, following obediently his hand signals, turning her body the way he directed. By now she was naked on the low table, and in the dim light, she saw the crumpled shapes of the discarded sheets.

Then she felt his hands on her thighs, rapidly striking her with the palms of his hands. He stopped and kneaded her legs with his strong fingers, then slipped his hands between her legs. She gasped.

With her eyes closed, Jennifer could not see him. She felt only his breath as he leaned across her body, using his full weight to bring pressure to his strokes. His fingers were warm and oily and lovely. When he touched her breasts, she felt her breath catch in her throat. Then he moved his hands up to her neck and, with his fingertips, massaged the tender skin at the base of her throat.

"Am I hurting you?" he asked.

"No," she whispered, her eyes still closed.

Again, he moved down the length of her body, silently stroking her flesh, as if her body were nothing more than an instrument for his use. This was what true submission was, she realized as she lay there. This was what real emotional slavery meant.

Jennifer knew now that she would give her body to him.

She would surrender simply and gladly. She wanted to be his lover, if only once. This had nothing to do with Tom, with her life in New York. This moment in the dark room had meaning only to the two of them. It did not matter that Simon was Kathy's lover. They were all of the same soul; Habasha had told them. They were all connected in another life.

She opened her eyes and lifted her arms to take him into her embrace, and he smiled and whispered, "No. Not yet." Then he leaned over and slowly, lovingly kissed her breasts, then gently pulled a warm blanket over her. "Lie here a moment," he whispered, and then he was gone.

She lay still, as he had instructed, stunned by his unexpected refusal. He wanted her to wait. Wait. She was alone in the small room, warm and close under the heavy blanket, with voices coming to her from deep in the house, and the sharp Minnesota wind whipping against the walls. She thought of his lips touching her breasts, his warm cheek brushing against her aroused nipples, then she came.

29

JENNIFER OPENED HER EYES. It was already evening, and she heard voices in the other rooms, laughing and talking. It must be time for predinner drinks in the living room. Later, Jennifer knew, Kathy Dart would be channeling Habasha.

Naked, Jennifer slipped off the table and quickly put her clothes on, pulling her thick navy blue turtleneck over her head and sliding into her leather pants. Her fear had made her jumpy, and as she left the small clinic, she glanced through the curtains of the windows, half expecting to see Simon's face there, watching her from the darkness. But there was only a vast expanse of frozen snow, glistening from the outside floodlights. She saw a car swing into the small lot. Its lights swept across the fields before it pulled in.

She was afraid of Simon now, afraid of his power over her. She remembered vividly the past-life regression, how he had condemned her to death as the Grand Inquisitor. She had to get away from him, from this farm, before something else happened to her, before Simon tried to make love to her.

In her bedroom, Jennifer grabbed her parka from the back of the chair, then quickly threw her clothes into her bag and hurried out of her room and down the hall and into the night. Only when she reached the cold did she realize she didn't know how she would escape the isolated farm.

She glanced around. No one had followed her from the house, and the yard was silent and dark. She ran at once onto the road and waved at a passing car, which slowed for a moment, then sped away. Just as well, Jennifer thought. The driver had been a man, and she didn't want to tempt fate.

Another car swung out of the farm's driveway, and for a moment she was pinned in the bright headlights. The car came straight at her, and she backed away from the highway, looked to see where she might run, but there was no shelter, no woods, only miles of farmland and open fields. The car slowed, and she saw the driver lean over and open the passenger door. When the interior light came on, she saw it was the reporter who was doing the article on Kathy Dart.

"Hi!" he said, grinning. "Car break down?"

"Yes, I'm afraid so." She smiled back. "A rental car. I need to get to the airport in St. Paul. Could you give me a lift in that direction?" She stared at him. Her heart was pounding, and she was suddenly afraid that he was lying, that he knew she was trying to get away and had been sent to get her. He was one of them, not a reporter at all.

"Sure, hop in." He reached over and moved a stack of audio tapes from the seat. "Where's your friend . . . ?"

"Eileen?"

"Yeah, that's the one. I met you in Washington, D.C., right?" He was watching her, still smiling.

Jennifer nodded as she tossed her bag in the back and slid in beside him.

"She's staying longer?" he asked, starting up the car.

"Yes. Yes, she is." Jennifer took a deep breath and glanced around. No one else had come out of the farm's parking lot. "I saw you at the Habasha channeling session the other night. Is the article done?"

"Yeah, just about. I've got all of my research done on Kathy Dart. You had some reaction to old Habasha last night, didn't you?" the reporter commented.

Jennifer glanced at him again. He wasn't quite as young as she had first thought. And she hadn't realized how good-looking he really was.

"Are you going as far as the airport?" she asked, avoiding the question.

"Yes, I'm going back to Chicago. My name, by the way, is Kirk Callahan."

"Yes, I remember."

"And I remember you didn't want to be interviewed." He kept smiling.

"I didn't have anything to say. I'm not into channeling."

"But you're here now." He gestured toward the farm.

"Well, I was." She kept staring ahead at the dark highway. Each mile, she realized, was taking her away from the farm. What would Kathy do when she discovered that she had left? She glanced again at the dashboard, thankful that Kirk was driving so fast.

"Where are you going?" Kirk asked, and she jumped, startled by his voice.

"Hey, I'm sorry." He slowed the car.

"Oh, New York. I'm going to New York City." She glanced out the rear window.

"I've never been to New York," Kirk said. "I'd like to visit sometime, to see a Broadway show or something."

Jennifer had forgotten what clean-cut, Midwestern kids were like. It was as if he were from another planet.

"You live in Manhattan?" he asked.

"No, Brooklyn. Brooklyn Heights, actually. It's right across the river." Still no headlights behind her.

"No one is following," he said, frowning.

"I'm sorry. I just keep thinking . . . you know, you're driving so fast. I'm worried about cops."

"It's okay. I'm keeping an eye out. We have nothing to worry about."

Jennifer nodded. "That's a nice notion, saying we have nothing to worry about. I wish it were true." She forced a smile.

"You like some music or something?" Kirk asked.

"Sure."

"Here." He handed her a box of tapes.

"No, you pick something you like. Anything." Jennifer noted with satisfaction how her smile flustered him.

"Okay, how 'bout a little John Cougar Mellencamp?" He slipped in the tape and hit the play button.

"Great!" Jennifer said. She had no idea whom he meant.

They drove without speaking as they both listened to the music, and Jennifer began to relax. The music helped to distract her, but it was really the car, speeding through the dark night, that did it. She was driving away from the farm with this attractive young man, and she took a perverse pleasure in the knowledge that no one—not Eileen, not Kathy Dart, not Simon, no one—knew where in the world she was.

She slipped down farther in the soft bucket seat. "This is a nice car," she said. "What is it?"

He grinned proudly. "It's brand new," he said. "An Audi 80. Five cylinders, a two-point-three–liter engine. And this is all leather!" He reached over and ran his hand lovingly across the upholstery.

"A present?"

"Yeah. I bought it for myself. I made some money in the market."

"Congratulations."

"Thanks. But I was just lucky. I got out when the market heated up. It's due for a crash."

"You play the market?"

"I did. Now I'm into CDs and cash."

Jennifer nodded but said nothing. When she was his age, she had only college loans and debt. She didn't know anything about stocks. She slid further down into the seat, curling up as best she could in the tight space. She saw Kirk reach over and lower the music, and she smiled at him. Then she closed her eyes and thought how nice he was to leave her alone. She fell asleep in the bucket seat of his new Audi, grateful that he was such a nice guy.

In the last moments of her troubled dreams, in the silent drifting fog before consciousness, Jennifer saw the hand coming at her throat, and she tossed and turned trying to escape.

Then she was startled awake. Kirk Callahan's hand rested gently on her shoulder, and he was whispering to her.

"Hey, Jennifer? Hey, I'm sorry. We're getting close to St. Paul; it's time to wake up." He withdrew his hand as he slowed the car.

Jennifer saw overhead expressway signs slip past. They were in traffic, and she was aware of buildings, flashing billboards, the roar of trucks. She felt a wave of panic. The car's dashboard clock read 7:32.

Kirk looked older now. His face was more sharply defined, with a blunt chin, a large, generous mouth, and a straight nose. It was a strong, masculine face, and it was made more masculine by his forthright manner. Jennifer mused as she watched him. A farmer's son. A Minnesota lumberjack, perhaps. She remembered then that he had been in her Egyptian past life, and to keep herself from recalling anything more, she said, "Okay, Kirk, tell me about yourself?"

He blushed, as she knew he would, and shyly, hesitantly talked about growing up on a farm in the Midwest, about high school football and girlfriends, and going to college on a track scholarship. Jennifer listened attentively for a while, and then she realized she wasn't listening to him, but was watching the way his lips moved, and how he cocked his head to the side when he started a new story, and how his eyes brightened just before he came to the punch line of a joke.

"What about it?" he asked.

"Pardon me?" Jennifer sat up, taken aback.

"What about riding with me into Chicago?"

"Are you going to Chicago?" she asked.

"Well, yeah, I've got an interview tomorrow afternoon downtown in the Loop, then I'm headed home."

"But where do you live?"

"St. Louis. But I can drop you at O'Hare, that's no big deal." He kept glancing at her.

"I don't know. That's a long drive. We'll have to spend the night somewhere, right?" She thought of the guy she'd shoved into the ice machine on the drive out from the East. She wondered if there was a warrant out for her arrest.

"They're not going to get you, not if you're with me," he said softly, watching her.

"What do you mean?" Jennifer realized her hands were trembling. "Who's out to get me?"

Kirk shrugged. "Those people at the farm." Kirk held her gaze evenly. He was waiting her out.

She did not want to lie to him. She wanted to tell him what had happened to her, how she had gotten to the farm, and why she was now running for her life. It was true, she realized, how one would tell strangers the most intimate of secrets and hide the truth from friends. And so, there in the small car as they raced toward St. Paul, she told Kirk Callahan how she had met Kathy Dart and why she had come to the farm in the first place. All she withheld was her crimes.

What startled her most was that he didn't seem surprised by anything she said. As she talked, he kept glancing at her with his sober gray eyes, never once registering surprise or astonishment at her story.

When she was finished, she finally asked, "Are you a follower of Kathy Dart? Do you believe in this New Age stuff? Are you going to turn me in or what?"

He shook his head as he looked ahead and watched the road. "All this New Age stuff is just a mind fuck. You do it to yourself. I took this course—abnormal psych—last fall, and you know, you start reading these cases, and suddenly you begin to think, Hey, I'm like that. That's me! Or you know someone who's slightly off and you think, He must be a paranoid schizophrenic, or whatever."

"But you're writing an article about it?"

"That doesn't mean I believe in any of that shit."

"Maybe you're right," Jennifer said vaguely, now not knowing who or what to believe. She thought again of the session with Kathy Dart and the vividness of her past lives. Those were true, she told herself. Whatever else had happened to her, she had seen into her past, she thought, sighing, and she had killed people with her primitive strength.

They drove in silence, out of St. Paul on Route 94, and into Wisconsin, then south through more flat farmland. For a while, Kirk fed cassettes into the tape deck. He played tapes of George Harrison, Billy Idol, and more John Cougar Mellencamp. She wished he wouldn't play anything at all. She would have liked the silence, but it was his car, his drive, and she wouldn't be demanding. She wanted only to get back to New York.

30

"DO YOU MIND SHARING a room with me?" Jennifer asked when Kirk decided to stop driving for the night. She had made up her mind when they had started across Wisconsin that she couldn't spend a night alone in a motel room.

"Hey, sure." Kirk grinned.

"I don't mean anything by that," she said firmly.

"Yeah, you can trust me!" he said, grinning.

"I know that." She opened the car door.

"Wait!" he told her.

"What? Did you see someone?" She slipped down into the car seat.

"No, of course not. Hey, Winters, no one is going to find you out here in the middle of this farmland. The farm doesn't employ the KGB. Just wait here until I get the room, that's all."

"Oh! How are you going to sign us in?"

"Well, I thought I'd put down Mr. and Mrs. Kirk Callahan. Or is that being too pushy?"

She allowed herself to smile back. "Fine! But don't use my first name, okay?" She knew she was being paranoid, but still. . . . "Here!" She reached for her purse. "Let me give you some money."

He waved her off. "Buy me dinner." He opened the car door.

"Okay, but we're eating in our room. And make it the second floor, okay?"

He sighed. "Any other motel obsessions?"

"No." She smiled after him, thankful that he was handling all the details. Then she reached over and locked the car door.

"How's this, Mrs. Callahan?" Kirk asked, opening the door and letting Jennifer lead the way into the motel room.

"Good!" she said, taking in the dimly lit room. "There are two beds."

"Hey, I asked for them!" He sounded hurt.

Jennifer watched him for a moment, holding her small plastic bag of toilet articles. She knew he hadn't been told enough to know why she was so on edge, but at least he was willing to take a chance with her, to go along with her erratic behavior. How did he know that she wasn't some wacko from a mental hospital?

She stepped over to sit down on his bed and said softly, "Kirk, I'm not trying to order you around or treat you like a kid."

"Then stop doing it, okay?"

"We're in an awkward position, thrown together, and I'm grateful for what you've done for me. You've saved my life. I just don't want you to misunderstand, that's all."

"I'm not misunderstanding anything."

Jennifer stood up. A single room had been a big mistake, she realized now.

"I'm sorry," he said.

"It's all right."

"Jen, I just"—he looked off when he spoke—"I'm sorry, I . . ."

"Kirk, it's okay," she soothed. She kept herself from reaching out and touching his cheek. "I'd better take a shower," she finally said.

In the small bathroom, she turned on the shower, buried

her head in a thick bath towel, and let herself cry, knowing that it would calm her down. She didn't bother to lock the door. She wasn't afraid of Kirk. Of all people, she knew she could trust him.

She took a long shower, washed her hair, then went ahead and washed her panties and bra and hung them on the curtain rod. When she returned to the bedroom, she had wrapped up her hair in a bath towel and was wearing her red flannel nightgown. She'd thought about putting on her shirt and jeans again but decided against it. There wouldn't be a problem. Besides, after dinner, she wanted to get into bed and go right to sleep.

"Dinner is being served," he told her, pointing to the tray.

"Thank you," she said. "Where did this come from?"

"I told the desk we were on our honeymoon and I wanted to serve you dinner in bed. And they sent up the tray." He lifted a bottle of champagne from a plastic ice bucket and held it up with a flourish. "And this," he added.

"Kirk, you've got class," she said, impressed.

"You think so?"

"I know so. You're an all-right guy."

"An all-right kid, you mean."

"We're friends, remember?"

"Right!" He sat down on the edge of his bed.

"Hey," she cocked her head, smiling out from under the towel turban, "come sit with me. Let's talk. I've told you about Tom. Now it's your turn. Tell me about your girlfriends."

"Which one?"

"Well, let's start with the most recent." She bit into her hamburger, then took a sip of the champagne while Kirk told her about Peggy. They had gone to school together, but that Christmas she had announced her engagement to someone in law school, a guy she had met the summer before.

"She was your great love?"

"Yeah, I guess. I didn't date much in high school. We lived outside of town; there were always too many chores to do. Then when I got to college, Peggy and I hit it off right away and went together pretty much all the time until last summer. When she came back after Labor Day, it was all over between us.'' He shrugged his shoulders and went back to his hamburger.

"Well, don't worry. You're a good-looking guy, and there'll be plenty of others."

"You think so?" he asked.

"Of course there will be."

"No, I mean, do you really think that I'm good-looking?"

Jennifer glanced at him as she drained her glass. The champagne had had an effect. She felt relaxed for the first time that day, warm, and even safe. Impulsively, she reached over and touched his cheek with her hand, drawing her fingers down the length of his jaw. Fleetingly, she imagined what it would be like to make love to him, and then she pulled her thoughts under control and simply said, "Yes, you are a good-looking man." She paused. "But I think you should let your hair grow out a little. And now I'm going to sleep."

Kirk picked up the tray, and Jennifer crawled under the blankets and put her head down on the pillow. Her hair was still wrapped up in the towel and she knew she should comb it out, but she was too tired to even move.

Kirk leaned over, tucked the blankets up to her neck, then reached out and shut off the bedside lamp. Before he stepped away, he leaned down and kissed her softly on her cheek.

Jennifer smiled and mumbled thank you, and then she was asleep.

Much later, she woke up and saw Kirk standing by the windows in his white boxer shorts. She thought what a great body he had and then fell asleep again.

When Jennifer woke next, it was daylight. She turned over and saw that Kirk's bed was empty and she was alone in the room. She jumped out of bed at once and went to the windows, peeking out from behind the heavy curtains. Kirk's Audi was still parked where they had left it.

Jennifer sighed. What had she thought? That he would leave her there in the middle of nowhere?

She spotted Kirk then, jogging across the lot. He had been out running, that was all. She sighed and watched him slow down and walk by a station wagon that had just pulled into the motel. It was only when the driver lowered the front window to speak to Kirk that Jennifer realized who it was. Kirk was telling him something, pointing across the parking lot, but Jennifer had fallen away from the second-floor windows, fully comprehending what had happened. Kirk Callahan, the young man she had allowed herself to trust, had led Simon McCord to her.

He ran. Clutching the fist-sized piece of quartzite in his hand, he scampered down the bank and headed for the muddy river. The others were close behind. They had found the body of the female, and now they were after him, following his scent through the underbrush, following his footsteps in the soft soil.

He ran for his life. They would kill him, just as he had killed the female. He did not know why he had killed her. She would not come with him. But other women in tribes near the river had not come with him, and he had not hurt them.

Yet her refusal had enraged him, and without thinking, he had swung the quartzite at her, its sharp point piercing her neck, spraying blood in his face. He could taste her blood on his lips, in his mouth.

He reached the river and dove into the deep water, letting the swift tide carry him farther downstream. There were rhinos in the water, and crocodiles, too, sleeping up on the banks and in the shade of acacia trees. The sleeping crocs frightened him, but he feared more the band of men running along the muddy riverbank.

If he didn't bother the animals, he was safe. The river widened at the next bend, then swept away to the horizon. He did not know where the river flowed, but once, when he was younger, his grandfather had stood on the high cliffs behind their campsite and told him of lands beyond the grassland where elephants were as plentiful as raindrops and where berry bushes and yarrow plants grew beyond one's dreams.

He would have to leave this valley, he thought, catching hold of a bamboo limb and swinging up to perch on it. There were too many others living together in the valley of the honeycombs. He would be killed if he re-turned; the males of the woman's clan knew him. They would kill another member of his family, sweep down into their camp that night and slaughter one of the women for what he had done to the clan.

He knew that her people thought of him and his kind as nothing more than monkeys to be killed, their heads smashed with rocks so the sweet-smelling meat of their skulls could be scooped out with fingers, their eyes sucked like shellfish; and then, later, her men would heat the thighs and arms of their enemies' dead bodies over the campsite fire and linger in the shade with no pain from hunger.

Her people kept his kind away from the grasslands, away from the berry bushes on the far side of the river. Still, he and his cousins crept across the river after sun-set, slipping by the sleeping crocodiles to steal the honey or to find the patches of yarrow and take away the white flowers in the dead of night. Her people said these fruits and berries belonged to them, to all the cave people who lived high up on the steep cliffs, and they drove off his people, kept him and his cousins from the lush vege-tables. They fought his people off from the water holes where the bushbucks lingered, where they could trap and snare a zebra or giraffe, kill it with blows from their axes.

He slipped his knife into his buckskin pouch as the swift river bore him away. It had taken him weeks to find the stone, then to shape it as he wanted, chipping away the slivers of quartz as his father had taught him. With it, he could kill. With it, he could defend himself against the cave people.

He thought of the woman he had killed. He had seen her first by the river's edge, then followed her to the crest of the hills. He had called to her then, but she had mocked him, jutting her chin out, pushing her breasts at him, slapping her thick upper lip with her tongue, and saying, "Maa-naa, Maa-naa," as she turned to show him her behind.

He had wanted to lure her from the track, to entice her into the deep gully beside the huge banana trees where the ground was soft and mossy, but she wouldn't budge from the clearing. He watched her prance in the bright sunlight, flicking out her pelvis as if to entice him. He rushed out from the safe patch of underbrush, and she scooted away, giggling. Enraged, he had grabbed his new quartzite ax and struck her.

He would stay with the river, clinging to the thick log of bamboo. His grandfather had told him tales, stories told to him by his grandfather, of hills beyond hills, of other people, tall and slim like running giraffes, who wore the skin of animals, and told tales of giant mountains where the rain was white and cold.

These were only tales, he knew, shared around warm fires on cold nights, when the old people huddled and sang stories of lands beyond the river, stories they said that came to them in dreams, when the body sleeps, and the spirits sail with the moon, and they painted such songs on their cave walls.

He did not believe the old men's stories. He knew only what he saw, only what he tasted in his mouth, only what had happened to him.

He had killed the woman, and the cave people would kill him. He did not want to leave his own woman, his children, or his mother and father, but he did not want to die from a flying spear and have his eyes sucked from his head.

He clung to the bamboo stump and was happy to be alive, happy, too, that he had killed her. She had laughed at him with her eyes and jutted out her sex as if it were the lush fruit of a berry bush, but would not mate with him. Yes, he was glad that he had killed her, and he kept sailing away on the tide of the wide river, heading toward the rising sun and the land of white cold rain and tall slim men.

31

JENNIFER BOLTED THE BATHROOM door and spun around to face herself in the mirror. Under the bright lights, she was amazed at how frightful she looked. It was as if she had stuck her finger in an electrical outlet.

She thought of Kirk, of how he had come out of the night and helped her get away from the farm, of how he had been so nice to her. Her mind whirled as she linked together all the strange coincidences that had brought this man into her life. She had been trapped and double-crossed by this innocent-looking guy.

"Oh God!" Jennifer exclaimed. The familiar rush of fear crippled her, and she slid to the bathroom floor, trembling.

It was so obvious. He had been sent out onto the lonely Minnesota road to pick her up when she ran away from the farm. He had been sent by Kathy Dart to keep an eye on her. No wonder he was so willing to indulge her whims, to go along with her scatterbrained theories about the farm and Habasha. He was one of them.

She curled herself into a tight fetal position, sobbing, but part of her mind had already begun to sort out what she must do to save herself.

Why did they want her? she kept asking herself. Who was she that they kept coming after her?

She forced herself to stop guessing and concentrated on how she was going to escape. Kirk would be returning soon, perhaps with Simon in tow.

She would call the police, tell them she was being kidnapped. She remembered reading stories about cult groups and how they always fled once the police became involved.

Jennifer pulled herself up from the floor and glanced around for a telephone. When she saw there wasn't one in the bathroom, she leaned against the door and listened for sounds of Kirk moving in the room.

Slowly, quietly, she pulled open the bathroom door and peeked into the bedroom. Kirk was standing in the door, filling the frame with his body. He was grinning at her, still sweating from his early-morning jog.

Jennifer jumped him.

"Jesus Christ, what's going on?" He ducked her swinging fists.

Jennifer tried to grab him by the hair, but it was too short. Frantically, she flailed out with her arms. Swearing, Kirk caught her arms in his hands and pinned them to her sides. She kept struggling, and he picked her up and dropped her on the bed. Then, with some effort, he turned her face toward him and forced her to look at him.

"Hey," he said softly, as Jennifer kept kicking. "Hey, what the hell is going on?"

Her nightgown had torn open and exposed one pale, milky breast.

"Christ," Kirk murmured, keeping her arms pinned to the pillow above her head.

"You! You're one of them!" She tried to keep fighting, but then, exhausted, she broke down into tears.

"What are you talking about?" he asked, holding her gently now.

"Simon . . . in the car . . ." She kept sobbing and explained how she had seen him talking to McCloud in the parking lot.

"Yeah, I know who he is. He wanted to know where the restaurant was, for chrissake!" He let go of her and stood up. "What are you talking, anyway?" He grabbed his sweatshirt and pulled it over his head.

"He's after me!" Jennifer said, sitting up. "Kathy Dart sent him after me."

"Jesus, you are paranoid." He glanced over at her, shaking his head.

"Why is he following me?" she shouted.

"He asked me where the restaurant was. He told me he was driving to Madison. He's giving a lecture or something," Kirk explained, returning to the bed. "And what else, he doesn't know you're even in this motel." He stared down at her.

"He'll ask at the desk!"

"And no Jennifer Winters is registered." Now he allowed himself to smile.

"I'm so scared," Jennifer whispered and, reaching over, touched Kirk. Her eyes were puffy from crying.

"It's okay," he answered softly. "It's okay." He pulled her into his arms.

"Let's get out of here," Jennifer pleaded.

He was shaking his head. "We've got time. He's having breakfast. Let him finish and get back on the highway."

"We can't stay on that road."

"Okay, we won't. We'll take another route. Don't worry, he won't find you. I won't let him. Okay?" He smiled at her.

Jennifer nodded, unable to speak, overwhelmed by his closeness and his strength. She realized that all she wanted at that moment was for Kirk to hold and comfort her.

He moved her then, gently eased her down onto the pillows. His eyes never left her, but his gaze moved from her face down to her breasts, then to her slender hips and thighs. He swallowed hard, and his gray eyes darkened. There was a long silence as they stared at each other.

"I'm sorry," she finally said. "I saw you, and . . . I started to get paranoid again."

"Hey, I said I'd get you to O'Hare."

"I can't go to O'Hare."

"Okay, come with me."

"And what?"

"I don't know! We'll figure something out."

Jennifer kept looking into his eyes. "You mean that, don't you?"

He nodded, and she saw him swallow hard again. He didn't take his eyes off her. She saw the blind, moonstruck look in his eyes. With a mixture of fear and desire, she waited for him to touch her.

"Is it okay if I kiss you?" he asked, sounding very young.

"I want you to kiss me," she told him.

He brushed her lips gently.

"Ouch," he said, backing off.

"What?" She looked up, concerned.

"My nose. Where you bashed me."

"Oh, I'm sorry, Kirk." She took his face in her hands and tenderly pulled him closer to kiss the tip of his nose. "I'm sorry," she whispered again. This time their kiss was more insistent.

Jennifer gasped as Kirk moved to stroke her breast. With his head still between her hands, she moved his face to her breast. Sighing, she relaxed and let her young man make love to her in his own way.

He came quickly, and she was surprised that she was ready for him. She was sometimes slow to be aroused, but their battle had excited her. When he slipped inside her and came again, she had an orgasm of such power that for a moment she thought she might burst.

His body, too, was aflame as he lay by her side, his eyes wide. She turned and curled in against him like a matching spoon, and reaching back, took hold of his penis and smiled as it swelled to her gentle caress. This time, at her encouragement, he came at her from behind, kneeling on the soft mattress, and rode her until they were both panting with pain and pleasure. She pressed her palm flat against her abdomen, felt the length of his erection filling her, and then the sudden shudder of his orgasm.

* * *

Jennifer's body ached both from their fight and their sex, yet she could not sleep. She got out of bed and slipped into the bathroom for a quick shower, then dressed in jeans and a sweater.

When she reentered the dark room, he was still sleeping. She resisted the temptation to kiss him, though she did pull up the top sheet and blanket and tuck them around him. Then she carefully unlocked the door and slipped out into the hallway.

It was still early morning. She walked toward the front desk, thinking that she would pay their bill and check out.

The motel hallway was long, and when she reached the end, she stepped into a glassed-in stairwell. She took the stairs to the first floor and saw the parking lot was to one side and the empty swimming pool to the other. And then she spotted Simon.

He was standing behind the full-length glass doors in the lobby of the motel. Jennifer saw his foggy breath on the glass, saw him turn his head and speak to someone hidden by the curtains.

Simon spotted her. He waved, then pulled open the glass doors and ran across the snowy yard, circled the pool, and tried to catch her before she got away.

Jennifer took the steps two at a time, ran up to the second floor hallway and through the swinging doors. She stopped then and concentrated. Deliberately, she thought of Simon and how he was coming after her, coming to kidnap her. And as she had hoped, she felt the familiar surge of strength, felt her muscles bulge. Stepping into a supply closet, she stood there under the bright light, surrounded by rolls of paper towels and tiny pink bars of soap and an empty cleaning cart. She waited for Simon to burst through the door and see her.

Moments later the door swung wide, and Simon filled the frame, a smile spreading across his face when he saw her.

"Hi," she said. She stood with her fingers laced together, like a girl at a high school gym waiting to be asked to dance.

"Jenny, Jenny," he said with a sigh. "What happened to

you? Why did you run away? Kathy was so worried. What
are you doing in here?''

"Waiting for you," Jennifer said calmly, holding back the
surge of adrenaline that swelled her strength. She wanted to
wait until she was strong enough to kill with one swift blow.
She wanted to wait until he was close enough for her to grab
his throat.

"How did you get here, anyway?" he asked, frowning.
He stepped inside the door. "Why are you so afraid?" he
asked.

She grabbed him easily, with one sudden move. Her hands
were around his neck before he could react, the scream in
his throat sliced off by the pressure of her grasp. She felt the
words die as she tightened her grip. She watched his face,
saw his ice blue eyes pop out in his head, saw a bubble of
blood squeeze from his mouth and drip down his lower lip.
She lifted him up and flipped him over easily, dumping him
headfirst into the empty cleaning cart.

Then she grabbed a clean bathroom towel and wiped his
blood off her fingers. She threw the towel into the cart, turned
off the light, and went back into the hall. It would be another
hour before the maids finished the rooms on that floor and
came back to the supply room and found him there, stuffed
upside down in the cleaning cart.

"You killed him?" Kirk asked again. They were back in
his Audi, speeding east on Route 80.

"No, I don't think so. He was alive when I left him."

"Jesus H. Christ."

"Kirk, I know this is more than you bargained for." Jennifer nodded toward the next exit sign. "Pull off there. You
can drop me at the nearest car rental place." As she spoke,
she rested her arm across his thigh. She could not keep herself
from touching him. She needed the physical contact. If he
did stop and put her out, she would truly be lost. She didn't
think she had the strength or the courage to drive a car.

"I'm not going to ditch you," he told her.

She sighed, then leaned forward and briefly rested her head
on his shoulder.

"I don't think anyone will be looking for us," he said next, taking charge.

Jennifer shrugged. "I don't know. I mean, he might call the police and tell them he was attacked."

"By a woman? Come on, no way." Kirk was shaking his head as he speeded.

In New York, Jennifer knew, she could get away with hurting, even killing, a person. It was done every day. But not in the heartland.

He reached across her and took several maps from the glove compartment. "But just in case," he said, handing them over to her as he kept his eyes on the road, "look at these and find some secondary roads that will get us across the state. Look south."

Jennifer stared down at the open maps, unable to focus. She couldn't go to St. Louis with him. Besides, he had a meeting in Chicago. No, running away with Kirk Callahan wasn't the answer. How long could she hide away there? Kathy Dart would find her; when she learned Simon had failed, she'd send others. She wanted Jennifer, and she would find her wherever she went.

"I can't go with you," she said, looking up from the maps. "I have to go to New York."

"I'll come with you."

"No, you have your work, that interview in Chicago."

"I'll do the interview, then catch a flight to New York." He glanced over and smiled. "Come on, you can show me Broadway."

"I would love it if you came to New York." She took hold of his hand again.

"But what about this boyfriend of yours?"

Jennifer shook her head. "I have to speak to Tom, tell him what has happened. The only one good thing out of this trip is I know now that it's all wrong, Tom and me."

"But what about me?" Kirk asked. "You met me on this trip!" He kept grinning.

Jennifer stared at him and studied his face, then she asked, "You do want to come see me in New York?"

"You're damn right!" And then, as if to prove himself,

he pressed down on the accelerator and speeded up the car.
"But I think you should stay with me in Chicago. Then we'll
fly together."

"It will be all right, Kirk. In New York, I have help."

He glanced over at Jennifer. "You mean Tom?"

Jennifer shook her head. She was staring ahead at the long
straight highway. "No. A woman. Another channeler." Jennifer could see Phoebe Fisher now, see her in the lovely
basement apartment on Eighty-second Street, see her walking
slowly with her silver cane, see the way the soft, orange sun
warmed the brick walls of her living room. She saw Phoebe
waiting, smiling, encouraging her. It would be all right, Jennifer told herself. She had Phoebe. She had someone to turn
to for help.

BOOK FOUR

Know that if you become worse you will go to the worse souls, and if better, to the better souls; and in every succession of life and death you will do and suffer what like must fitly suffer at the hands of like.

—Plato
The Republic

And as Jesus passed by, he saw a man which was blind from his birth. And His disciples asked Him, saying, Master, who did sin, this man or his parents, that he was born blind?

—John 9:1–2

32

"YOU'RE SAFE NOW," PHOEBE told her, welcoming her into her basement apartment. "And where's this young lover of yours?" she asked next, smiling.

"But how could you know?" Jennifer stood back, startled by the channeler's question.

"Dance told me." She kept smiling, looking up at Jennifer. "I think it's wonderful!"

"Kirk saved my life, really. He came racing by in his little car and picked me up. God knows what would have happened to me if he hadn't stopped."

"He didn't just happen by, Jennifer, as you must realize by now. People don't meet by chance. It's all planned and ordained. It's your karma. Both of your karmas."

She had her thin arm linked into Jennifer's and was using Jennifer to support her as they walked into the living room, which on this cloudy afternoon was lit by a dozen small candles casting shadowy light.

"Where is your young friend now?" Phoebe asked offhandedly as she eased herself onto the small sofa.

"He's flying in later this afternoon. He had an appointment in Chicago."

"Good! Then you'll be together in a few hours." She seemed pleased.

"Why?" Jennifer asked, watching the small woman, wondering about the odd collection of questions.

Phoebe shrugged. "It's always better if you are with someone who understands you, especially now while you are having such intense past-life regressions."

"I have you," Jennifer whispered, wanting to show the woman how much she depended on her.

"Thank you." Phoebe smiled, nodding her thanks. "It is my privilege, really, to be so close to such a powerful source as yourself."

"Except no one knows who I am! Or who I really once was, I should say."

"I think it's time we did force this spirit into the open, Jenny. We need to identify it." She was not looking at Jennifer, but reaching down beside the sofa and pulling out a large box.

"Can Dance tell us?"

Phoebe shook her head. "Dance can't help us. He operates on another level of consciousness. He isn't a reincarnated spirit like Habasha. What I must do is contact directly the spirit that is using your body, trying to work through your consciousness."

The channeler leaned forward and lowered her voice. She held Jennifer's attention steady with the intenseness of her gaze, the look in her brown eyes. "The entity that wants to be channeled by you, Jenny, is also protecting you. He or she is waiting for the right moment, waiting for you to come into your full powers, so that you'll accept him. So far, however, this spirit has only been protecting you from physical attacks. It is also clear that there is another reincarnated spirit, Jennifer, that is trying to kill you before you realize your full spiritual power."

"But who is that person, or whatever. Is it Kathy Dart?" Jennifer had raised her voice. She was frightened again.

"I don't know," Phoebe said softly. "But this may help us." She held up a game box.

"A Ouija board! That's a children's game."

"Yes, unfortunately it is treated as a child's game, but it is a dangerous toy and should not be used by adults, either, without training and experience."

Phoebe set the board on the coffee table and opened it, continuing to talk as she took the board from the box.

"A Ouija board, or talking board, as it is sometimes called, is very old. In 540 B.C. Pythagoras used them in his seances. This board was reinvented in 1892 by a man named Fuld. It's very simple, really, just a semicircle of the letters of the alphabet, and the words 'YES,' 'NO,' and 'GOOD-BYE.' " She looked over at Jennifer. "Have you ever used one?"

Jennifer shook her head. "No, not even as a child. I seem to remember it was banned from our house—something to do with the devil."

Phoebe smiled. "Yes, that's the cultural superstition. And today among parapsychologists it is accepted that Ouija boards attract channel entities of the lower classes, unless handled by a channeler."

Phoebe picked up a small platform supported by three inch-long legs. "This is a planchette. See how it's shaped like a pointer? As I ask questions, the pointer will indicate letters to spell out a message." She handed Jennifer paper and a pencil. "I'll ask the questions, Jennifer, and would you please take notes."

Phoebe lifted the board off the coffee table and set it on her lap. "I need to have physical contact," she explained, placing her fingers lightly on the planchette.

"We'll begin slowly," Phoebe went on. "I'll ask the questions and summon up the spirit. It may take several minutes after I ask a question for the spirit to announce itself," she added. "You'll see the planchette move. When the planchette indicates a letter, just jot it down."

Jennifer nodded, but she was already tense.

"Relax, Jennifer," Phoebe advised, and then she placed her fingers lightly on the planchette and, closing her eyes, asked the Ouija board, "Do you wish to communicate with us?"

Jennifer glanced from Phoebe's hands to her soft, pale face, and then steadied her gaze again on the channeler's fingers.

For several minutes nothing happened, and Jennifer realized she was holding her breath. She took a deep breath to calm herself and was about to speak, to tell Phoebe that she was too frightened and tense to go on with this, when the planchette suddenly moved and the pointed end of the plastic platform turned in the direction of the word "Yes."

"What are you called?" Phoebe asked.

Jennifer kept staring at Phoebe's hand as the instrument moved again and in rapid jerks pointed to more than a dozen letters.

Quickly, Jennifer scribbled down the letters as the planchette tracked across the smooth board, then read the words out loud: "I am one of many names."

"You say you are one of many names," Phoebe said, still with her eyes closed. "But what do you wish us to call you?"

PHARAOH

Next to the name "PHARAOH," Jennifer wrote "Egypt."

"Do you know Habasha?" Phoebe asked the board.

ETHIOP

"Yes, an Ethiopian. Have you and Habasha been reincarnated many times?" Phoebe questioned the spirit.

Again the planchette moved.

YES

"And our Jennifer?"

YES

"Is our friend Jennifer in danger?" Phoebe asked, softening her voice.

The planchette moved quickly under Phoebe's fingers. The heart-shaped instrument crossed the flat smooth surface on its own accord. It pulled back to the middle of the board, then sped again to the word "YES" and the symbol of the

bright sun. Jennifer stared at Phoebe. The channeler's brown
eyes had opened and widened.

Phoebe continued with her questioning. "Tell us, spirit,"
she asked calmly, "who wishes to harm our soulmate Jennifer?"

The planchette hesitated, spun freely under Phoebe's fingers with a life of its own and quickly spelled out a message.
Jennifer read the letters aloud as the planchette rapidly moved
across the board: "T-A-M-I-T."

Phoebe, her eyes closed again, paused a moment to frame
her next question.

Her hands stopped moving. The heart-shaped planchette
froze. Jennifer held her breath and watched Phoebe.

"Tell me, Pharaoh," Phoebe said to the Ouija board, "who
in this lifetime is Tamit?"

KATHY

"No!" Jennifer whispered, and the breath went out of her.

Jennifer looked down at the board as the planchette, moving under Phoebe's touch, spelled out the story from the days
of Ramses the Great, of how Amenhotep had fought a battle
and killed the Ethiopian monarch to marry Roudidit. Then
Tamit, the jealous daughter of Nenoferkaptak, had Roudidit
murdered when Amenhotep was away at Memphis.

"And who is Amenhotep?" Phoebe asked.

KIRK

Phoebe Fisher pushed the Ouija board away and looked
over at Jennifer. She looked worried now. The warm softness
had slipped off her face. She seemed older in the winter light
of the afternoon. "It is clear from what this 'Pharaoh' spirit
is telling me," she said carefully to Jennifer, "that an ancient
drama is being played out today."

"I just don't understand why *now*." Jennifer kept shaking
her head. "It's an endless puzzle. We keep going around in
circles. Everyone used to be someone else; no one is who

they are. I'm not me!'' She looked at Phoebe, her eyes show-ing her feeling of helplessness.

Phoebe reached over to hold Jennifer's hand, telling her, ''You are frightened, I know, Jennifer, and with good cause. Your spirit has been in revolt against your rational conscious-ness. Your friends appear to be your enemies. Your whole world has changed beyond recognition. But you cannot let your fear become your prison. You must not lose hope, or you will not transform your life.''

Jennifer shook her head, still bewildered.

''To reach the light, you must endure the burning,'' Phoebe summed up.

''I've had the burning,'' Jennifer replied soberly. ''And there is going to be more.''

''Yes, you must face your enemy.''

Jennifer nodded, then asked, ''Will you help me?''

''I'll try,'' she whispered, her eyes not leaving Jennifer's face. Then she said, ''You could be killed, Jennifer.''

''Or I could kill again.''

Phoebe nodded. ''You have no choice.'' Then she stood up, saying, ''I'll get your coat.'' The channeler stepped around the coffee table and limped into her bedroom, to where she had left Jennifer's fur coat and luggage.

Jennifer pulled a tissue from the pocket of her jeans and wiped her nose. She was staring down at the Ouija board that Phoebe had left on the coffee table. It looked so innocent, she thought, nothing more than a silly children's game.

She reached out and touched the smooth heart-shaped plan-chette, let her fingertips rest lightly for a moment on the plastic surface. Her hands trembled, and she felt a sudden bolt of energy rush into her fingers, up her arms. It took her breath away. She jerked her hand away from the planchette and sat back.

What are you? she thought, staring at the Ouija board.

The heart-shaped planchette moved then without the touch of her fingers. It traced across the smooth surface of the board spelling out an answer. But this time it was not ''Pharaoh'' who replied to Jennifer:

I AM YOUR SOUL

Jennifer sat very still as she watched the planchette spell out the answer. She was frightened again, holding her breath, but she was also thrilled, as if she were lifting up the edge of a forbidden universe.

Who am I? Jennifer thought next, concentrating on the board. Her eyes did not waver from the plastic planchette. Again it moved, responding to her silent thought, spelling out the words:

YOU ARE THE FIRST

Jennifer sat staring at the Ouija board, puzzled by the replies and not sure what to say. She heard Phoebe in the next room, heard her say something about the weather, the terrible winter New York was having, and Jennifer quickly directed her concentration to the board and asked: I am the first what?

The smooth marker slid across the flat board, spelling out one word:

HUMAN

Then Phoebe reached the living room, carrying Jennifer's heavy fur coat, and saw that the heart-shaped planchette was moving effortlessly under the power of Jennifer's spirit.

"What are you doing?" the channeler shouted, dropping the coat and stumbling forward, tripping on her deformed leg.

"Nothing! I'm not doing anything!" Jennifer exclaimed, jumping up and tipping over the Ouija board, terrified by the violence of Phoebe's reaction. "I'm sorry. I'm sorry. I didn't mean to do anything."

"What did it tell you? Didn't I tell you the board was dangerous?" The small woman had regained her balance and had pulled herself onto the arm of the sofa. She kept glaring at Jennifer, her eyes white with fright.

"I'm sorry, Phoebe. I didn't mean—"

"What did it tell you?"

"Nothing. I mean . . ." Jennifer kept shaking her head, still terrified and upset by the channeler's violent reaction. "I'm terribly sorry, but I didn't understand. I mean—" Jennifer took a deep breath and, recovering her composure, said forcefully, "Phoebe, I'm sorry I upset you, but you shouldn't have shouted at me! I'm a case of nerves as it is." Jennifer glanced down and was surprised to see her hands were not trembling.

"What did you learn?" Phoebe demanded.

"Nothing! I was just asking a question."

"You're not trained to use a talking board," Phoebe said again, watching Jennifer. Her face had lost all of its soft, smooth glow.

"I'm sorry," Jennifer said slowly, not looking at Phoebe. She was afraid to trade glances with the channeler.

Phoebe stood again, fully recovered. The softness returned to her voice and she said, "I'm sorry, Jennifer. I just don't want you to be misled. Ouija boards, as I mentioned, are often controlled by spirits of a lower order." She bent then to pick up Jennifer's coat, and Jennifer glanced at the board, directing her thoughts at the heart-shaped planchette, asking one last question of her hidden spirit: Who wants to kill me?

The plastic planchette began to move on the smooth surface when Phoebe jumped forward and swept the instrument off the board, knocking it across the room, where it skipped off the stone hearth of the fireplace and flew into the fire, sizzling at once in the heat of the flame.

"You must never—!" The channeler regained her stance and focused on Jennifer.

Phoebe was trembling, Jennifer realized. The channeler was the one who was truly frightened.

"I am trying to save your life, don't you see?" Phoebe shouted at her.

Jennifer nodded, reaching for her coat. "I'm sorry," she said again.

Phoebe reached out and touched Jennifer's hands.

"Jennifer, I'm sorry I shouted at you. It's just that you

must be careful when you involve yourself in the spirit world.'' She had both her hands on Jennifer's arms and was looking up lovingly at her. ''You will be careful, won't you?''

''Yes, I'll try.''

''Good!'' And she reached up and quickly kissed Jennifer good-bye. ''Remember, I love you. I'll see that you are protected from your ancient lives,'' she said, speaking softly to Jennifer, but the channeler's lips were cold on her cheek.

33

JENNIFER GRABBED A TAXI on Columbus Avenue and
told the driver she wanted to go to LaGuardia. Kirk's flight
was not due until after seven, and though she had time to go
home to her place first and unpack, she was now afraid to
go there by herself, especially after witnessing what the Ouija
board had done, how the planchette had moved, spelling out
her fate. What would it have told her if Phoebe hadn't knocked
the instrument off the board? Jennifer shuddered, recalling
Phoebe's act of violence, her sudden strange reaction to what
the Ouija board was telling her. Phoebe's behavior had upset
her, Jennifer realized, as much as what had happened to her
on the farm.

The taxi crossed Central Park at Eighty-sixth and paused
at the stoplight on Fifth Avenue. Jennifer glanced out the
window at the Metropolitan Museum of Art. The lights were
on in the Sackler Wing, and she could see part of the Temple
of Dendur. The ancient Egyptian temple glowed in the soft
yellow light, casting shadows the length of the immense wing.

Jennifer remembered how she had gone once to the museum when she was a teenager. It had been a junior-high

class trip and she had got upset, wanted only to get out of
the museum. Jennifer tried to remember what it was about,
why she had been so upset by the Egyptian wing. It had been
new then, built to house the Temple of Dendur, the small
temple that had been saved in Egypt when the Aswan Dam
was built. The temple had been removed from lower Nubia
in Egypt, stone by stone, and rebuilt in the Metropolitan
Museum. There was a pool of water in front of the temple,
and a wall of windows overlooking Central Park.

It was a beautiful setting, Jennifer recalled, but when she
had first come into the wing it had frightened her, upsetting
her for some unknown reason.

Of course, Jennifer thought. Of course!

She leaned forward at once and tapped the glass partition
of the taxi, telling the driver that she had changed her mind.
She wasn't going to the airport. She was stopping first at the
Metropolitan Museum. She was going back into the Temple
of Dendur to learn what secret of her past was locked away
in her memory. She was going to let the ancient stone tell
her what had happened to her on the banks of the Nile.

The new wing was at the rear of the huge Metropolitan,
behind long galleries of Egyptian art and artifacts. Jennifer
didn't rush herself through the exhibition. She moved slowly,
waiting for her memory to be triggered by the objects, waiting
for some connection to her life in Egypt, to the earliest time
of her existence. The Ouija board had told her she was the
first human. Was this what it meant? Did all of her troubles
begin here, in one of the great dynasties?

Jennifer kept moving slowly through the rooms, from the
time of the New Kingdoms, back into the Middle Kingdoms
and the Archaic Period. She glanced from object to object,
scanned the artifacts that the Metropolitan had in its vast
collection. She waited for some memory. It had happened to
her at the Museum of Natural History. When she had seen
the primitive hut, she knew that she had once lived in that
prehistoric hut, slept under those mammoth bones and animal
skins.

Jennifer pushed the door and went into a room of glass cases and burial objects. There were mummies sealed behind the cases, shelves of ancient linens and small Canopic jars.

She reached out and pressed her fingers against the cases holding the mummies. No sensation touched her. She felt only the cool glass. There were no memories of her past life here, she understood.

She kept moving through the deserted rooms. It was late, she realized. The museum would be closing soon. She glanced at her watch to see how much time she had left, then opened another door and stepped into the vast Sackler Wing with the reconstructed Temple of Dendur.

Now she felt something. Her attention was alerted. It was as if some memory was trying to reach her from her early lifetime on earth. She was suddenly not frightened. The recollection was comforting, as if she had finally solved her problem, found the missing piece in the puzzle of her life.

She moved forward, closer to the temple itself, keeping her eyes now on the huge stone structure.

There were few other people in the wing. A tour guide was speaking to a group of women sitting on a stone bench. She was aware, too, of two guides standing together by the windows, but she concentrated on the temple, focusing her attention and waiting for more memories to flood her mind.

She stepped up onto the level of the temple, walked around the small pool of water, and approached the front of the reconstructed temple. In the foreground was an archway, and behind that, the temple walls. The spirit called Pharaoh had told Phoebe that Kathy Dart, as Tamit, had killed her when she was Roudidit and married to Amenhotep. It was the days of Ramses, and Kirk had been Amenhotep, her husband.

Jennifer paused on her approach to the temple. If this was the first incarnation and she had been murdered, she thought, then why now, after all the other lives she had lived, would Kathy Dart still be seeking revenge? It was her spirit, not Kathy Dart's, that had been violated!

It couldn't be her first life on earth, Jennifer thought next. She remembered the images she had seen of herself when Kathy Dart had pierced her third eye. She had been a wild

creature then, living in a jungle world. But what had the
Ouija board planchette spelled out? That she was the first
human.

Jennifer shook her head. No, Phoebe was wrong. Phoebe
was hiding information. She had swept the planchette off the
board. She hadn't wanted Jennifer to know. But to know
what?

Jennifer stepped closer to the interior of the temple and
closed her eyes, concentrating on the temple, on her stone
surroundings. When she opened her eyes again, she saw the
temple women who sang and shook the sistra and crotals
during services. They lived in the innermost sanctuaries of
the temple and were called God's handmaids. All of these
virgins were daughters of the wealthy families, of kings and
queens, and she was among the selected few.

Jennifer stood perfectly still watching herself, the other
young women of the temple. They wore shifts under trans-
parent white pleated robes that were gathered over their left
breasts. Their right shoulder was uncovered. She watched
herself as she moved in procession. She was wearing rings
of solid gold and strings of gold beads. A black curled wig
fell over her back and onto her shoulders. She had a tiara of
turquoise and gold tied at the back with two tassel cords, and
her head was crowned with a scented pomade.

She was a beautiful young woman in this lifetime, Jennifer
saw, and she wondered how she knew it was even her. Yet
she knew. And she saw, too, as she searched the faces of the
other virgins that Phoebe Fisher was with her, another of the
young women. She scanned the corps of singers. Kathy Dart's
spirit was not part of this divine harem.

The scene faded from her sight. She reached out, as if to
pull back the ancient memory, but saw only her hand reaching
into the vast wing of the museum. Behind her she heard the
museum guard make a point to the tourists, heard a child's
happy voice echo off the high ceiling. She glanced around
and saw that she was being watched by a museum guard. To
mask her confusion and hide her bewilderment at what she
had seen, she walked to the edge of the wall and sat down.

Her legs were weak and she was out of breath. She leaned

over and dropped her head between her legs. She would faint, Jennifer realized, if she wasn't careful.

"Are you okay, lady?" the guard asked, stepping over to her.

Jennifer sat up and tossed her hair back off her shoulder. She forced a smile. "Yes, thank you. I just felt a little funny." The man's face was swimming in her eyesight.

The man nodded and moved away, saying as he did, "Well, you looked a little odd there."

"I'm fine now, thank you." Jennifer took a tissue from her purse and wiped her eyes. She waited until the man had gone back to his post before she looked again at the temple. The gray stones of the small building looked the same. There were no young virgins, no divine harem. She had imagined it all, she thought. It was nothing more than a psychic episode.

She kept staring at the Temple of Dendur, the silent gray building, nothing more than a few ancient walls dug from the muddy banks of the Nile River.

She calmed down, pulled herself under control. She was all right, she realized. She didn't have a psychic episode, she realized. She had seen herself as she had been as a young woman in Egypt. She had married Amenhotep—Kirk, in this reincarnation. She had seen Phoebe Fisher but not Kathy Dart. Why was Phoebe in her Egyptian days and not Kathy? The spirit of the Pharaoh said Tamit had killed her when she was Roudidit and married to the warrior Amenhotep.

The guard moved toward her again and signaled that the museum was closing. Jennifer nodded and stood up, collected her bag. She glanced over at the temple, half expecting to see more shadowy shades from her reincarnated life drifting through the vaulted arch, appearing like a whiff of memory. Nothing now surprised her. But there was no image, nothing but the empty gallery, the silent walls of the temple. Jennifer stood and followed the last of the tourists from the Sackler Wing, taking the exit doors and going through more long, low-ceilinged hallways and galleries filled with the artifacts from the Old Kingdom of Egypt, at the time of the First Dynasty, over twenty-five hundred years before Christ.

In the last gallery, Jennifer stopped momentarily to look
at a huge map of Egypt. She wanted to see where the Temple
of Dendur had been located on the Nile River, but what caught
her attention immediately was the vast expanse of Lower
Egypt and the names Kush and Ethiopia.

There had been great civilizations on the Nile River before
the ancient Egyptians, and before those, man had traveled
north out of the primitive jungles of Africa. She remembered
what Kathy Dart had said in Washington, how her connection
with Habasha had come from a piece of crystal found in
Ethiopia. Habasha had been alive then, 4 million years ago,
and his spirit was on earth even before that, over 23 million
years ago.

Jennifer kept staring at the old map of Lower Egypt, at the
vast expanse of the Sudan desert and the high plateaus of
Ethiopia. It was here, deep in the the gorges of southern
Ethiopia, where Habasha had lived, that man first stood upright and changed from a beast of the jungle to a creature
possessing a spirit, having a soul, a reincarnated soul that he
carried with him throughout time and filled with all the memories of all his lifetimes.

Phoebe Fisher had not told her the truth, Jennifer realized.
The spirit of the Pharaoh was not her first moment in time.
Her spirit, her oversoul, which had moved the heart-shaped
planchette, had existed before the great civilizations of Egypt.
It had said she was the first human!

She was like Habasha—that was the connection! She, too,
like Kathy Dart, went back to the dawn of mankind, to the
first moments of the human spirits, millions of years before
the Temple of Dendur. She had been reincarnated as a member of the divine harem in the temple, had married Amenhotep, and died in Egypt. Her body, she was sure, had been
mummified and ferried across the Nile to be entombed. But
she now knew she had lived even before this great civilization
of pharaonic Egypt. She had lived with Habasha. She had
lived at the same time as Kathy Dart's first incarnation. And
now, she realized, Phoebe Fisher had been there, too. That
was why the channeler had kept her from learning more from

the Ouija board. They had all been alive together in their first incarnations on earth. And something had happened to them, there at the dawn of time.

Jennifer glanced around, suddenly afraid, fearing that Phoebe had followed her to the museum. But the Egyptian gallery was empty. The Metropolitan was closing.

The answer, she realized, would not be found here in the great dynasties of Egypt and in the days of Ramses the Great. Yes, she had suffered and died, murdered by Tamit, but this was not her first life nor her first death. She had to return to the prehistoric exhibition at the Museum of Natural History, where she first realized she had lived in the primitive hut from the Ice Age.

She walked out through the front doors of the museum and stood at the top of the stone steps, looking down at Fifth Avenue, crowded now with rush hour traffic. The city skyline was already aglow with lights and bright flashing signs. She needed to hurry. Kirk's flight was due from Chicago, and she needed to be with him. But first she had to telephone Kathy Dart and Phoebe Fisher. She wanted both channels to meet her at the Museum of Natural History. She wanted them to walk with her through the Ice Age exhibition. It would be there, Jennifer knew now, in that prehistoric graveyard, that she'd remember what had happened to her spirit when they had evolved as humans and come down out of the trees to walk upright as man.

Jennifer smiled. For the first time in weeks, she knew exactly what to do. She knew how to solve the mystery of her past, of all her reincarnated lives, and she hurried down the stone steps, rushing to meet her lover, her great love, she realized, of all her lifetimes, and she smiled with anticipation, her face suddenly bright and shiny with hope.

34

THE FRONT DOOR OF her apartment had been replaced and the locks changed. Jennifer took the set of keys given to her by the superintendent and unlocked the door, but she didn't step across the threshold. The apartment was dark.

"What's next?" Kirk asked. He was standing beside her, still holding their luggage.

"I'm not sure. I thought perhaps Tom would be here. I called his apartment while I was waiting for your plane and just got his machine."

"Is he at work?"

Jennifer shook her head. "No, I called his office, too." She stepped into the room then and realized at once that something was wrong. She flipped on the entrance light and peered into the living room. Her furniture was in order, and what she could see of her small kitchen looked untouched. In the three days that she had been gone, the super had cleaned the entrance and the living room. There was no trace of the dog's blood.

"Do you want me to look around?" Kirk asked, edging past her to set down their bags.

"No," she said. She moved a few steps farther into the

apartment and glanced to her right. "Do you smell any-thing?" she asked Kirk.

He sniffed the air and shook his head. "The place could use a little fresh air, though. Shall I open a window?" He stood with his legs apart and his hands deep in the pockets of his red jacket.

"No, don't do anything. Please." Jennifer was apprehensive, but she tried to keep her voice steady. She slipped off her coat and dropped it on the living room sofa, then turned toward her bedroom.

"Hey, Jen . . ."

"It's okay, Kirk. Everything is all right." She didn't look at him.

The bedroom door was slightly ajar. Jennifer stepped over and pushed it with one finger. Light from the street filtered through the closed blinds and left dim streaks on the opposite wall. She could see the clutter on top of her dresser. Everything was just as she had left it. She moved farther into the room and looked at the bed. It hadn't been touched.

"Hey, Jen, what's going on?" Kirk's voice trembled slightly.

Jennifer didn't answer him, just held her hand up in a gesture for silence. There was someone here, she knew. She felt someone's presence. But who? And where?

All at once, a breeze blew the heavy window curtains out, scattering the loose papers on her desk. Tom was here, Jennifer realized. She could feel his presence. But why would he hide from her? Was he waiting for her? Did he want to kill her?

"Tom?" she asked, turning and scanning the room.

Kirk remained standing in the bedroom doorway. He was afraid to enter, she guessed.

Jennifer opened the door to the bathroom. It was empty. Her towels were as she had left them the morning after the pit bull attack, crumpled on the floor.

"Is he there?" Kirk asked.

Jennifer shook her head, then reached over and turned on the lamp beside the bed.

"Are you okay, Jen?" Kirk asked, stepping into the room.

She nodded. "I think so. I feel him, that's all."

"Tom?"

"Yes." She sat down in a chair and pulled off her boots. "It was so strong, I thought he was here."

"Maybe he's under the bed or something," Kirk joked, pulling off his jacket.

Jennifer sat back in the wing chair. "Would you look?" she asked.

"Under the bed?"

"Yes."

"Hey, Jen, quit kidding."

"I'm serious." She was smiling in spite of herself. "I get myself scared sometimes. . . . Please, I know he isn't, but I can't look."

Kirk grinned. "Sure!" He dropped to his knees and lifted the bed skirt, peeping underneath. "He'd have to be a goddamn midget."

"Kirk . . ."

"Okay! Okay! No, he's not there." He stood up.

"I'm going to call his apartment again." She reached over to her bedside phone and quickly dialed his number.

"How about a drink?"

"Good!" Jennifer said, smiling up at him as she listened to Tom's phone ring. At the third ring, his machine clicked on, and she heard his message. He wasn't home, but he'd call back as soon as possible. She waited for the beep, then left another message, asking him to telephone her. "It doesn't matter when," she said, "just call."

Jennifer hung up and went back to the kitchen, where Kirk had found the liquor.

"Hold me," she told him, and wrapped her arms around his waist, snuggling her face into his shoulder.

Kirk turned around and lifted her up, grabbed her bottom with both of his hands, and pressed her against him. She felt his erection at once.

"Let's go to bed," she said.

"No drink?"

"I want you, not a drink."

He kissed her and began to unbutton her blouse.

"We'd better lock the door," she told him, a little breath-lessly.

When Kirk left her, Jennifer unzipped her jeans, pulled them off, and tossed them onto the back of a living room chair as she walked back into her bedroom. There she dipped her head to one side and took off first one earring, then the other, and set them both in a tray on her dresser. As she pulled her blouse up over her head, she thought she saw something move in the far corner of the room. With her blouse still tangled in her arms, Jennifer stepped to the wall and flipped on the light switch. There was nothing in the corner but a bookshelf, filled with her familiar night-time reading and a few framed photographs.

She could hear Kirk's sneakers squeaking on the hall floor as he returned to the bedroom. Jennifer turned off the light, unsnapped her bra, and slipped into the bed.

"The barn door is bolted," he announced, and paused at the doorway, surprised that Jennifer was already in bed.

"Come here," she told him. She longed for the warmth of his body, ached to make love with him, and when he smiled lazily at her and unbuttoned his jeans, the sweetness of anticipation excited her more. She lifted her arms toward him, and he slipped into bed, under the down coverlet, and pulled her into his strong arms.

Jennifer felt safe, protected by his broad shoulders, and dizzy with longing as he moved to touch her. His mouth and hands were everywhere, and his eagerness made her more excited. She had never been with such an ardent lover.

In the darkened bedroom, Kirk's face glowed with plea-sure. Jennifer held his face close to hers and worked her tongue into his mouth. She wanted to consume him. She wanted him inside her. She wanted their flesh to be glued together. For a moment she was afraid that her passion would frighten him off.

With trembling hands, she reached down to guide him into her body. She liked leading the way, making her lover re-spond to her needs. Jennifer pushed Kirk back onto the pil-lows as she straddled him. He rose high and tight up inside of her, and she twisted her hips to create more friction.

She leaned down and licked his chest, then tossed her loose mane of blond hair across his face like a wide, soft brush.

"Do you like this?" she whispered, smiling down at him.

Kirk nodded, then reached up and pulled her down on top of him, probing her mouth with his tongue. Jennifer felt his erection swell as he came inside her. She let herself ride with him, waiting for her own orgasm, shifting slightly so that her right nipple was exposed, and she arched her back so that he could reach her swollen breast with his tongue. With a sudden shudder, she came, driving her body onto his. Her heart pumped wildly, driving her blood to the center of her body, where her muscles exploded in passion. She found that she had detached a part of her mind and was watching her body rock in its own selfish ecstasy.

Suddenly Jennifer grew teary. She turned her face into the pillows, then kissed Kirk tenderly in the hazy afterglow of her orgasm. She nestled closer to him, longing to stay this way forever, to hold him captive for her delight, and she shifted her legs so that his erection was pinned inside her.

Kirk was kissing her gently, nuzzling her ears, her closed eyes, the dampness on her throat. He was coming again; she marveled as his orgasm pulsed within her.

Jennifer wrapped her arms around him and kissed his hair. The only light in the room came from the street, filtered through the drawn curtains, but her eyes had adjusted to the dark and she could clearly see the shadowy figure emerge from the dark corner of the bedroom. It watched them, watched her, and then stepped over to the doorway and paused there. There was no hatred in the figure's eyes, nor anger, only an immense sorrow, as if he had lost everything, lost her, lost his whole world.

"Jenny, what's the matter?" Kirk asked, pulling back from her breasts. Her body had turned cold in his arms. "What's the matter?" he asked again, frightened by the look on her face. He turned to see what she was staring at. But there was only the open doorway, a dim slanting light beyond.

"What is it?" he demanded, grasping her by the shoulders.

"He's here," she whispered, keeping her eyes on the doorway.

"Who? What are you talking about?"

"Tom is here."

"Jesus Christ, Jenny, what are you saying?" Kirk sat up on his knees.

"I just saw him. He's dead. He was here, watching us make love."

"Hey," Kirk said gently. "No one is here, Jenny; you're driving yourself crazy." He moved to the doorway and turned on the overhead light. "No one is here, I promise." When he looked at his hands, he realized he was trembling. "Christ, Jenny, you frightened the hell out of me."

"He was here. I saw him. His spirit was here," Jennifer said calmly. She was no longer afraid.

"Look for yourself! We're all alone," Kirk insisted.

"You don't understand," Jennifer whispered, slipping out of bed. She knew he was frightened, but she had lost all of her fear.

"Jenny, come on! Where are you going?" He watched her as she got out of bed and moved toward her closet. He swallowed hard, watching her tall, slender body. "Let's go back to bed," he cajoled.

Jennifer pulled open the door to her walk-in closet and reached in to where she always hung her flannel nightgown. Before her mind could react, before she could scream out in horror, the tips of her fingers touched the soft film of his still-open eyes. She saw him fully then, saw that her kitchen knife had been plunged into his heart, saw his bloated, grayish tongue and his swollen white face, and saw that her dresses and blouses had been shoved aside. Tom was hanging from the metal bar by his own black belt, the one she had bought at Brooks Brothers and given to him for his thirty-sixth birthday. He had been dead for several days and he smelled of death.

And then she screamed.

35

JENNIFER LEFT KIRK ON the street, telling him only to wait for her, and entered the museum from West Eighty-first Street. It was after ten o'clock. They had spent most of the night and early morning with the police, at her apartment, and downtown at the office of the Justice Department, giving statements, explaining where she had been for three days.

They were due back at the Justice Department later that day for more questions, but Jennifer had told the police she had to meet someone at the museum, that it was important for her job. She didn't tell Kirk that she had arranged for Phoebe Fisher and Kathy Dart to meet her when the museum opened.

She took the elevator to the third floor and followed the signs to the prehistoric exhibits. It was early, and the museum was virtually empty as she walked quickly through galleries, heading for the one where the prehistoric fossils were displayed. It wasn't until she approached the special exhibit that she grew frightened. Stopping between two life-size models of reptiles, she tried to decide what to do next. She realized then that she had no plan for the confrontation. Phoebe Fisher had told her that she couldn't trust her rational mind, but that was wrong. She had listened to Phoebe and to Kathy Dart; she had let her emotions dictate her response, and she hadn't used her common sense. Well, she would figure it out as she went along.

Reminding herself to keep calm, she pushed open the glass doors and resolutely stepped into the darkened room, filled with artifacts of prehistoric man. She moved slowly past the glass displays of mammoth bones, the enlarged photographs of cave drawings and primitive sculptures. She kept herself from glancing to either side, afraid that seeing some ancient engraving would trigger a past life. She had to be alert. She had to be ready. She had to keep her attention focused.

She watched the few other museum visitors—couples, mothers with babies in strollers, school kids scribbling notes for a class assignment. She kept away from the center aisle and moved toward the rebuilt hut that dominated the exhibit.

It was here that she had first experienced the strange vibrations, here that she had told Tom the Ukraine model was built wrong. He had looked at her as if she was crazy. Well, she thought wryly, she wasn't crazy. She was worse than crazy. She felt herself tense up, become more alert to her surroundings, to the other people in the gallery. She was an animal on the prowl. She kept walking, moving slowly toward the next gallery, the one built with the remains of man's first family, the fossils of "Lucy" and the other early *Australopithecus* found on the banks of the Hadar River in the Afar Triangle of Ethiopia.

In the dark passageway between the two rooms, she caught a scent. She paused and sniffed the stale air of the closed rooms. Yes, she realized, someone was ahead of her, hiding perhaps in the next gallery, the large diorama that had been been built to resemble an African water hole. Through the thick leafy underbrush, she spotted several giraffes and the hunchback of a black rhinoceros, wallowing in the muddy African waters. And beyond them, reaching into the fig bushes, was a cluster of male and female hominid models, constructed by the museum to show how the first family of *Australopithecus* lived with the beasts of the African jungle.

Jennifer raised her head and snorted, then kept moving

loser, keeping to the wall and out of sight as she approached
ne water hole. She was ready. Her blood was pumping
hrough her body. Her neck muscles swelled; her nipples
ardened. She kept moving.

Jennifer caught Kathy Dart's distinct scent, then spotted
er on the other side of the diorama, near a grassy plain that
ad been built into the horizon, as if one could step into the
nuseum diorama and travel to the horizon. Kathy was looking
way from her, searching the room. She was looking for her,
ennifer realized. She sniffed the air. She was downwind,
nd Kathy hadn't caught her scent, hadn't realized she had
ome into the exhibition from the rear exit.

Jennifer flattened herself against the wall. She watched
Kathy Dart, waited for Habasha to stir, waited for Kathy to
ealize what she had finally understood at the Temple of
Dendur, that all of them had lived together at the dawn of
ime.

Jennifer moved from the pocket of shadows and stepped
loser. She was less than twenty yards from the jungle water
ole when she spotted Phoebe. She was standing away from
Kathy and also watching the main entrance of the gallery.
They had expected her to come that way, she realized, and
miled, pleased that she had outsmarted them.

She knew she wanted to battle now, and this realization
urprised her. She had been terrified before by her primitive
strength; now, as she gazed around the strangely familiar
diorama, she felt stirrings of recognition deep in the lymphatic
system of her brain that stored and carried through time all
of her emotional memories. Yes, she had been here before.
Jennifer knew that now for certain. She had felt this earth
beneath her webbed feet, she had once climbed down from
those thick branches and reached with short and hairy fingers
to pluck sweet figs from the low bushes. She snorted again
and crouched low, creeping closer to her enemy, this tribe
that shared with her family the muddy water hole, here by
the edge of the great lake and in sight of the smoldering
volcano.

She spotted a mother with a child in a stroller glance at
her and scurry away, as the deer did in the forest, frightened

by the mere sight of her and the others who slept together in trees and lived off the fresh sweet fruit of the forest.

Jennifer took a deep breath, thinking: I will draw Kathy Dart away from Phoebe. She will attack if it is me that she has been stalking.

Jennifer left the hidden protection of the museum wall stepped into the center of the gallery and closer to the African diorama. Then she shouted and waved her arms to attract Kathy Dart's attention.

Kathy saw her, smiled, and mouthed a hello across the wide water-hole diorama. Kathy did not rush her. Jennifer stared back at Kathy; she waited, breathing harder now, her body coiled and ready to defend herself.

"Are you all right?" Kathy asked, mouthing the words across the silent gallery.

Jennifer cocked her head. She heard Kathy and understood what she had said, but Jennifer was remembering another morning in a distant time, when she had come out of the trees to find a mate among the males who had gathered to forage for fresh sweet fruit. She remembered now how she had been killed. And she screeched, recalling her anguish.

From the corner of her eye she saw the black museum guard looked alarmed and was coming at her. Jennifer knew that man. She had seen him once before on a paddleboat in the James River. Jennifer moved at once, she jumped over the low railing surrounding the water hole diorama.

"Be careful!" Kathy shouted at her.

Jennifer stood up straight. She saw that the guard was talking on a portable phone. More guards were running toward the gallery, coming at her from the other exhibits. But Jennifer was in the middle of the African jungle now, standing in the underbrush, surrounded by thick, hanging vines, enormous mahogany tree trunks, and the posed figures of short hairy hominids, dull eyed and dumb, who stared at her.

She hooted for their attention, to get them away from Kathy Dart, to let her fight this woman who also had stepped forward and come into the re-created ancient water hole.

"Jenny! Jenny, you don't understand!" Kathy was saying. She spoke softly, as if to reason with her voice.

The museum guard glanced back and forth between the
two women.

"What the fuck," he swore, standing at the edge of the
exhibit. "What in hell's going on here?"

Jennifer squatted in the green underbrush. She felt the heat
of the day, the wet air, and smelled the pungent odors of
tropical evergreens rotting in the steamy heat of the equatorial
jungle, mixed with the sweet smells of fruit and flowers. She
could hear the jungle, too, the incessant noise of birds, flying
squirrels, and monkeys swinging through the heavy overhang
of vines. She saw the hippos wallow in the deep water and
a dozen crocodiles slip off the muddy bank and slap the mucky
water as they disappeared from sight.

Jennifer was not frightened by the crocodiles or a small
herd of woolly mammoths thrashing through the trees and
down to the water. She sprang out of the dense wood
and, running forward, screeched again at Kathy Dart, starting her.

"Jenny! Jenny!" Kathy screamed, holding out her hands
with her palms down, gesturing, whispering, and trying to
placate Jennifer. "It's not me. It's not me that you want."

Jennifer bared her teeth, hissed again.

"Jesus H. Christ!" The guard stepped over the low railing
and reached for Jennifer.

"Get back!" Kathy Dart told him. "She's out of control.
She doesn't know where she is."

"But I know where the fuck she's going," the big man
mumbled, approaching.

Jennifer hit the guard with her right forearm, knocking the
man off his legs and sending him tumbling. He fell backward,
hitting one of the poised figures of an early *Australopithecus
afarensis*, knocking the plaster-of-paris hominid into the plastic lake.

In that moment, as she hit him, Jennifer saw Phoebe coming at her from the early morning mist. She had been hurt in
a fall from the cliffs and was using now the short branch of
a tree to support herself as she dragged her lame leg across
the ground. Jennifer spun around to face the other channeler.

"Jennifer, come with us," Kathy ordered. "We know

about Phoebe. We've been trying to save you from her. Ha
basha was there. He knows.''

"Her!" Jennifer thought to herself. "Her!" She did no
at that moment remember how to talk, and her anger and
anguish came screeching out in the terrified sound of an
animal of the jungle. She leaped forward, to the edge of the
diorama, and turned on Phoebe Fisher, hooting and screech
ing, frightened and enraged. Inside the prehistoric diorama
in the midst of the jungle heat, Jennifer recalled those mo
ments of her very first life. She knew who she once was
realized, too, what had happened millions of years ago at the
dawn of time.

Phoebe raised her steel-tipped cane above her head and
rushed Jennifer.

"No!" Kathy Dart shouted, pushing forward and trying to
stop Phoebe. The raised cane, like a primitive club, whistled
as it cut through the air and struck Kathy Dart. The cane'
sharp point sliced across Kathy's right cheek and dug itself
deep into the thick muscles of her throat. The channeler
gasping for breath, grabbed her own neck in a stranglehold
The blood from her jugular squeezed through her fingers.

A woman screamed. Her screams kept coming and coming
They filled the gallery, echoing, gathering strength, as she
ran in hysterical, blind bursts of speed, trying to escape, to
flee the gallery like any frightened animal would.

Jennifer remembered. She had come scrambling out of her
rubber tree, out of her high nest in the jungle, stirred by the
needs of her swollen sex. She had come to mate on the fores
floor, followed by the other females of her family, including
the mother who had once nursed her from breastless teats
and her own child. She danced off from the first male who
came after her, but watched over her shoulder while scram
bling quickly on all fours. He kept advancing, screeching
and waving his long arms. It was Habasha, Jennifer realized
It was Habasha in his first incarnation, and then, with a speed
that she had not anticipated, Habasha mounted her from be
hind, entered, and ejaculated.

The other males were on her next, fighting with each other
to be first. They were screaming, hooting, and dancing in a

circle, sniffing her sex. The fig fruit was forgotten as the males kept after her. Pushing and shoving each other, they mounted her again and again, until, exhausted from their efforts, they slipped away into the heavy shade of the trees and slept. They had no fear. They were with their own kind.

None expected that one of their own would attack.

The old female had been chased away from their band for fighting with the others, and now suddenly she had returned. Screeching, she leapt from the tree and landed on all fours. Then, glancing around, she grabbed a mammoth bone and swung it, Jennifer saw again, at her. The bone glanced off her shoulder and hit her face. She howled in pain, and the other females, too, hooted and danced away.

The old female was white haired and smaller than her, less than two and a half feet tall, with a flat, hairy face, and a mouth misshapen by the swat of a saber-toothed tiger's paw. She kept after her, thumping the long bone on the earth, then raising it up with both arms and swinging wildly. Then without warning, the female turned aside, struck her mother, then killed her child.

She screeched when her child was struck down, and baring her teeth, she charged the cast-off female, knowing in the dimness of her brain that this predator was more dangerous than warthogs or two-tusked deer.

Phoebe Fisher raised her cane to strike. Jennifer screamed, leapt aside, and attacked with her ancient rage. She raked her nails across Phoebe's face, seized her hair, and jerked the head of the small woman back, exposing her pale white neck.

Her lost spirit possessed her now. She was living out her prehistoric revenge. She screeched and bared her teeth. She would rip out Phoebe's throat and kill this beast.

"Jenny, no!" Kirk screamed.

He came running through the gallery and lunged at Jennifer, knocking her to the floor. Phoebe Fisher scrambled to her feet, swinging her cane. She caught the black museum guard in the neck. The cane's sharp tip sliced him like a razor. Without a pause Phoebe stepped over Kathy Dart and lunged again at Jennifer, who was on the floor now and beyond the edge of the water hole diorama.

Kathy Dart stumbled to her feet. She was holding both hands to her cut throat, but the blood kept spreading between her fingers. She reached toward Phoebe, tried to keep her from killing Jennifer.

"Jenny!" she whispered, and her mouth bubbled up a mouthful of blood.

Phoebe struck again, swinging her cane down at both Jennifer and Kirk, who was down on the carpeted floor trying to shield Jennifer. The metal tip of Phoebe's cane jabbed Kirk's shoulder. He cried out and rolled away from Jennifer, leaving her momentarily helpless on the gallery floor.

Phoebe, raging, screeching, attacked again, aiming for Jennifer's face, trying to drive the ice-pick tip deep into her eyes.

Jennifer's ancient memory summoned their long-ago battle. It was at the African water hole that the first incarnated spirit of Phoebe had struck Jennifer with the mammoth bone, knocking her back into the deep water. She had tumbled and splashed, unable to swim, and then the crocodile had struck, seizing Jennifer's arm and pulling her deep into the jungle pool.

Jennifer smiled. She knew finally who it was that had been trying to kill her now, before she could remember, before she could gain all of her channeling powers. Jennifer jumped to her feet, avoided a wild swat by the small woman, and seized the cane from Phoebe Fisher, then raised it herself as a weapon. She saw the sudden terror in Phoebe Fisher's eyes. Jennifer knew that in one swift stroke she could kill her ancient enemy.

Jennifer stood poised, aiming for her mark. The old female had attacked her because she had mated with Habasha, attacked her because the other males had cast her aside. Now Jennifer would avenge the killing of her mother and first offspring.

"No, Jenny," Kirk pleaded from where he lay, clutching his wounded shoulder.

Jennifer swung the light cane at the channeler, aiming the steel point at the small woman's face, and as she did, Phoebe Fisher's face changed before her. The beautiful, bisque white skin exploded in blood, and Phoebe's small body jumped back, away from her. Jennifer missed her mark, and then she heard the sound of the museum guard's pistol shot.

Phoebe Fisher bounced off a plaster-of-paris model and slid over the top of the plastic lake and disappeared into the grove of fig trees. She died in the mists of prehistoric time.

Deep in the heart of Africa, at the dawn of life, she had been the first hominid to kill another. She had come down out of the trees to kill the incarnated spirit of Jennifer Winters.

The death of the first human was murder.

Epilogue

JENNIFER DROVE SOUTH ON the New Jersey Turnpike. It was a month since the museum, and Kirk was still in pain, but she knew how desperately he wanted to get out of New York, at least for a while. She would never get him to live in New York, she thought, but so what? She wasn't sure she wanted to, either. Not in this lifetime anyway.

It was over. Phoebe was dead. Kathy Dart was in the hospital, as was Simon. She had not killed him, after all. She was thankful for that. But poor Tom. He had been just an innocent victim, killed by Phoebe in her lust for revenge. But there was no innocent victim, Jennifer knew now. Whatever happened in life was simply the playing out of one's destiny.

At the dawn of time Phoebe had killed her, and in another life she had avenged that act. She had once been a poor black girl in the south who had jumped to her suicide, and Phoebe had been the white man. At every incarnation their spirits had returned to seek revenge on the other.

Spontaneously, she reached out and touched Kirk, let her right hand linger on the inside of his thigh.

"Happy?" she asked.

He nodded. "I'm happy you're with me, and I'm happy to be getting away from that place." Without turning around, he jerked his head back toward the city.

Jennifer glanced in the rearview mirror. She could see across the marshy industrial flatlands of New Jersey and the lower west side of the city. She saw the twin towers of the World Trade Center, and Battery Park City, both cast in the deep orange glow of the setting sun. It would be dark in another hour, but by then they'd be far from New York. Safe.

She touched him again to reassure herself. "Thank you," she said softly.

"Why?" he asked.

"You know why." She longed to kiss him, to be in his arms, and she almost suggested that they stop, that they find a motel right off the highway, but she knew he wanted more distance between them and the city.

Jennifer took a deep breath and kept her eyes trained on the expressway, at the rush of cars and trucks on the turnpike. Newark Airport was to their right and planes were landing and taking off, gliding onto distant runways, their colored landing lights flickering in the sunset. The air was warmer than it had been, and they were headed south, away from all her tragedies. Everything would be all right again.

She glanced again into the rearview mirror of the small rental car and saw Margit sitting quietly in the backseat, enjoying the drive. She caught Jennifer's eyes in the mirror and smiled.

"What?" Kirk asked again.

Jennifer shook her head. "Nothing. You wouldn't understand."

"Hey, come on, don't give me that!"

"I love you," she said instead, then weaved the car smoothly through the traffic.

"You don't really believe any of that stuff, do you?" he asked her.

"Of course not, darling, it's just a silly game, like reading your horoscope in the newspaper."

Kirk smiled and seemed to relax.

Jennifer reached over again and gently stroked the inside

of his thigh, letting her fingers enjoy the touch of him. She could not see his eyes, but she knew they were the same beautiful sweet eyes of her Egyptian prince, the same eyes as her brother Danny. It was not necessary, she realized, for her to share her new knowledge with him. She would take care of him, now that he had come back into her life.

Someday, perhaps, when they were older, she might tell him how they had been together once in Egypt, and before that in other lifetimes. In some they had been lovers, and at other times a sister and brother.

It wasn't necessary to tell him everything now. They were together again, and soon, she knew, they would be husband and wife. Jennifer glanced around. Margit was gone from the backseat, but Jennifer knew the other woman's spirit would never leave her. Just as Kirk had returned, Margit, her lost mother, had returned in this life and would come again in future lifetimes.

Jennifer watched the traffic and the approaching darkness and let her thoughts wander. In the close warmth of the front seat, she smiled, happy and at peace. She wondered about the other lives she might have lived. So far she had remembered lives of retaliation and revenge, yet there must have been happy lives as well. She sat up and regripped the steering wheel of the car.

Perhaps in other incarnations she had been a woman of importance, a high priestess, even a princess or queen. Someday she would remember those lives, all those glorious lifetimes when she wasn't doing battle with the spirit of Phoebe Fisher.

At that thought, Jennifer's heart soared with anticipation. Her life was not over, but her days of anguish were.

"Why are you smiling?" Kirk asked, watching her.

Jennifer kept watching the expressway. She shook her head and said, "I'm just happy, that's all, and in love." The nightmares of her primitive past were over. Phoebe's spirit was gone from her life. Because the channeler's death had not come at her hands, she had finally escaped Phoebe's vengeful spirit.

Yes, Jennifer thought, she would ask Kathy Dart to help